Also by Vanora Bennett

Portrait of an Unknown Woman
Figures in Silk

THE QUEEN'S LOVER

VANORA BENNETT

THE QUEEN'S LOVER

wm

WILLIAM MORROW
An Imprint of HarperCollins*Publishers*

FIRST EDITION

Library of Congress Cataloging-in-Publication Data has been applied for.

ISBN 978-0-06-168986-4

10 11 12 13 14 WBC/RRD 10 9 8 7 6 5 4 3 2 1

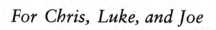

For Chris, Luke, and Joe

CONTENTS

ACKNOWLEDGMENTS   ix

PART ONE
The Book of Peace   1

PART TWO
The Book of Deeds of Arms and Chivalry   107

PART THREE
Lamentations on the Troubles of France   187

PART FOUR
The Vision of Christine   247

PART FIVE
The Prison of Human Life   275

PART SIX
The Book of the Body Politic   357

PART SEVEN
The Song of Jehanne of Arc   425

PART EIGHT
The Mutability of Fortune   463

PART NINE
The Treasure of the City of Ladies   523

HISTORICAL POSTSCRIPT   577

ACKNOWLEDGMENTS

With thanks to Laurie Chittenden and her colleagues at William Morrow, to Tif Loehnis and her team at Janklow & Nesbit, to Eric Simonoff, and, of course, to my endlessly patient family.

PART ONE
The Book of Peace

ONE

The page made himself as inconspicuous as possible at the back of the English delegation, looking at the vast tapestries on the walls of this dusty, splendid Parisian hall, clutching his box to his chest, waiting for his cue.

His latest master, the Duke of Clarence, had turned away from the repulsively fat French Queen, his hostess, whose eyes were glittering as wickedly as the jewels half buried in the flesh of her slug fingers. Clarence fixed his eyes on the fourteen-year-old Princess at her side. The Princess was Owain's age, and quite a pretty girl, Owain judged, with light brown hair and freckles and gentle eyes over a long nose; it would be sad if time turned her into a swollen monster like her mother. Owain also noticed that the Princess's cheeks were very pink, which perhaps wasn't surprising since her top garment was an enormous green velvet houppelande, magnificently trimmed with miniver fur—very stately, but far too hot for this bright May afternoon. Perhaps they felt the cold more in Paris, he thought. Or perhaps she was just blushing because she knew what was coming.

Thomas of Clarence opened his pop eyes wide, broadened his mouth into something like a smile, and bowed slightly to the girl—the closest an English soldier-duke would ever come to the elaborate manners of the French court. The Duke had been a little thrown, when he and his men had reached Paris at noon, by the news that the King of France was indisposed today and couldn't meet him, and that the French side in these negotiations would be led by Queen Isabeau instead. After a whispered conference before the French delegation walked in, he'd decided to proceed regardless. But he wasn't a ladies' man. He didn't know how to talk to women. He was far too abrupt.

"Your Highness," he said to the Princess, "I am bidden by my master to seek you out and raise with you the question that is uppermost in his mind."

He paused. She paused. There was an expectant silence from the two dozen other people in the hall.

"If it please God, and your father and mother, he hopes you will marry him, and become our mistress and Queen of England," Thomas of Clarence barked, without the slightest attempt at diplomatic finesse.

There was a collective indrawn breath from the French side of the room. Owain knew the French were supposed to be grateful for this offer, because the French, though grand, were weak. Their King was ill. They said he went mad every time the moon was full. And while he was mad the French quarreled among themselves. So they hadn't managed to put up much resistance to the English army's rampagings through Normandy. Now they were meant to think that this promise of a marriage between this Princess and the King of England must mean the King of England planned to stop his brother from attacking Normandy and pursue an alliance with France and England instead. And, if the French nobility didn't have to fight the English, they could go on plotting against each other to their hearts' content. Still, Owain's impression was that the French side of the room was not exactly grateful. Looking from one polite, squeamish, uncomfortable expression to another, he guessed: they want the marriage; they'd just rather have heard this another way. They can't believe he's made the proposal without days of entertainments and compliments, hints and maneuverings beforehand. They're shocked.

One of the English dug Owain in the back. It jolted him back to what he was supposed to be doing. This was his moment. He took a dozen steps forward, with his heart thumping, his palms damp, terrifyingly aware of every eye in the room being on him. When he reached the middle of the hall, beside the Duke, he sank down on one knee, with the flamboyant arm and head movement he'd been practicing (perhaps he could be courtly enough to make up for the Duke's gruffness). Making sure he was perfectly steady on his knees, he opened the clasp on the little casket and threw it open so the jewel inside glittered.

Thomas of Clarence nodded and half winked thanks at him, aware of the youth's embarrassment. He was a kind man in his way. Then he stepped up to the casket to take out the huge ruby on its gold necklet and offer it to the Princess. Obligingly, she moved closer, looking down at Owain, her cheeks pinker than ever, her eyes opening very wide and the beginning of a smile on her lips. She wasn't really seeing him, Owain thought; he was just something to fix her eyes on so she could look composed. She was embarrassed too. But he could see she had green eyes; beautiful eyes, he thought gratefully, gazing back at her, feeling his leg muscles strain in their precarious one-knee position, hoping he wouldn't wobble. This part of the procedure, at least, was going well.

No one expected an interruption. So everyone was startled when a thin, reedy male voice suddenly said, with a note of challenge in it: "My family has a history of English marriages, after all."

The Duke turned.

A young man, a few years older than Owain and the Princess, had appeared in the doorway. He was lounging there insolently, with a nasty little sneer on his handsome face. Owain's leg suddenly started shaking so badly he thought he might fall. He shifted, put a hand quietly on the floor, and lowered himself to a more stable two-knee position. He didn't need to worry about looking a fool before the entire room, at least; all the eyes had shifted to the young French nobleman in blue silk. As Owain looked furtively round to make sure no one had noticed his lapse of dignity, he saw just one pair of eyes still on him. To his horror, he realized it was the Princess staring down at him. But even that was all right. When she saw the panic in his eyes, it was as if she'd suddenly focused and realized there was a real person down there on his knees. She was looking straight at Owain, and reassuringly; she briefly screwed up her face and nodded at him.

Then she turned, like everyone else, to stare at the young man in the doorway. Still hot and cold with his own embarrassment, left stranded, kneeling in the middle of the room, Owain stared too.

"You will recall that our sister Isabelle, now called to God," the young man was saying, eyeing the Duke of Clarence, "was also married to a King of England. The late lamented Richard II."

Watching the French faces cringe, Owain realized that this unpleasant young man must be one of the Princess's older brothers, a Prince of France, and that he'd come to this room deliberately to pick a fight with the English delegation. The shame and embarrassment that swept over Owain now, on behalf of his master and of England, was of an altogether different magnitude to what he'd felt on his own account a moment before. He could hardly breathe.

Thomas of Clarence crossed himself briskly. "Late lamented," he agreed in a peaceable mutter, without letting his eyes meet those of his challenger. Owain could see he wasn't going to get himself embroiled in that discussion. The Duke was a man who picked his fights carefully and this wasn't a good fight for any English ambassador. Richard II had been deposed by a cousin after his French marriage nearly twenty years before; and Richard's wife Isabelle, this Princess's eldest sister, sent weeping and humiliated back to France. The new King, Henry of Lancaster, had tried to keep her in England: he'd wanted to remarry Isabelle to his own eldest son, the man who now reigned as King Henry V of England. But Isabelle had been proud enough to refuse. So Henry IV had let her go, but kept her dowry and jewels. They'd probably been spent on funding the English armies now skirmishing around Normandy. The French still thought of the new Lancastrian kings of England as usurpers. And they'd never forgiven the insult to their Princess.

The young Frenchman in blue stared at the English Duke, as if willing him to rise to the bait. Then, when he got no response, he went on, very deliberately and insultingly, "The late lamented King Richard II of England, who died by God knows whose orders."

The silence deepened. No one did know how the deposed English King had died. The Duke of Clarence let his eyes rise to those of the French Prince. The Frenchman let a taunting half-smile flicker on his thin face. Everyone in the room seemed to stop breathing. The Duke's face went red. He'd clearly forgotten all about being diplomatic with the French. He just wanted to hit the sneering Frenchman. With muscles tightening everywhere, he took a threatening step forward.

Owain flinched and looked down.

But, even while staring fixedly at his knees and the forgotten casket he was hugging, he was aware of the Princess just next to him. Now, unexpectedly, he felt her move into the middle of the fray.

Hardly seeming to know what she was doing, the Princess grabbed the Duke's swinging arm, then swiftly turned that movement into a trusting gesture, putting his muscly limb with its clenched fist through her thin green-covered arm, and turning him gently but firmly away from the doorway and back toward the French Queen.

The Duke looked at her in dull surprise, but he let himself be turned. The Princess said, very quickly, in a voice so tense with suppressed panic that it somehow came out gay and flirtatious, "Sir, if it please God and my lord father and my lady mother, I will very willingly be your mistress and the Queen of England."

Owain looked up, impressed by the Princess's bravery. She'd brought the Duke right back to the French Queen's feet. Looking to her mother for approval, and getting a brief nod, she went on, in a less formal way, with the beginning of laughter that might have been caused by relief in her throat, "After all, I've always been told I'd be a great lady one day."

The Duke seemed to be adjusting only slowly to the change in tempo. He looked from the Princess to her mother. He glanced over to the doorway, where the Princess's older brother, if that was who the insulting Frenchman was, was also staring openmouthed at the girl. Then, very slowly, his head began to nod. Up, down, up, down. He was still thinking. It seemed hours before his mouth opened and a great choking guffaw of a laugh came out.

He didn't laugh alone for more than a second. The whole hall filled with a wolf pack's howling; mirth and the release of fear mixed. The French Queen was cackling so hard her whole body was wobbling with it. She was so pleased with the way things were turning out that she didn't even notice her pet squirrel grab the sweetmeat on her golden saucer and start chewing at it, sitting on its hind legs, watching the spectacle with bright round eyes. And all the French officials were giving their Princess soft, thankful looks as they snuffled into their hands.

It was the first time she had really understood what it meant to be Princess Catherine de Valois: that people would listen. It was the first time she had ever exercised any sort of power. It was the most exciting thing she'd ever done. Her heart was racing. There was blood drumming a tattoo in her ears.

Ignoring the baleful look her eldest brother Louis was giving her from the doorway, and the baleful look her mother was giving Louis from her carved chair—there'd be trouble between the two of them soon enough—Catherine breathed in deeply and let herself enjoy the laughter that meant her words had saved the day.

Then she looked down. The poor English page was still kneeling there, holding that casket. The English Duke had forgotten all about him. The handsome boy with blue eyes and floppy dark hair was gazing at her with the same soft, adoring look everyone was giving her now, but he was obviously also longing to get up off his knees and rush back off to the shadows. But she could do anything today. She could cut his agony short; she could save him too.

"Is this for me?" she said, touching the Duke's arm and indicating the casket with a nod. "How beautiful . . ." and she bent her neck for the Duke to lower the jewel over her head. Startled, but still chuckling, the Duke reached out for the necklet, murmured, "Thank you, Owain," and leaned over her to

8

do his courtly duty. She was aware of the English page with the name that wasn't English at all scrambling to his feet and moving quickly away, free at last now his master had dismissed him. She could imagine the ache in his knees; she hoped he was grateful.

Then she concentrated on the English Duke's thick, corded neck and the giant fingers fumbling over the chased gold at her throat. Thomas of Clarence was rather like a bull with a ring through his nose, she thought, a little smugly: dangerously strong, but quite easy to steer once you had a hold of the ring. Would his brother, the King of England—now, just possibly, her future husband—be as amenable? She hoped so. But she also found herself hoping Henry of England wouldn't have that thick neck and pop eyes and grizzling temple, and that he wouldn't wear the muddy, dull greens and browns that these Englishmen were all covered in. Letting her mind flit off to a future in which an archbishop put the crown of England on her head, in a blaze of candlelight and jewels, the husband her imagination sketched in was as young as she was. He was tall and slender and lithe; with dark blue eyes and floppy black hair and a shy, adoring smile.

The ducal fumbling seemed to take a very long time.

The first time she glanced up, she saw her little brother Charles, looking very pale and much younger than his twelve years, stumbling out of the hall past Louis and into the corridor, where she could just see Christine de Pizan beckoning to him from the shadows. She hoped that meant Charles was going to be fed. Neither of the royal children had been fed all day. She was suddenly achingly hungry herself now she remembered how long it was since she'd last eaten. But Christine was as loyal and busy as a terrier, and good at gingering up the sullen, scary servants into making them meals. And perhaps Charles would save some of the food for her for later.

The second time she glanced up, as the Duke muttered "There!" in a kind of thick-fingered triumph, she was relieved to see Louis had vanished too. There was no one in the doorway but men-at-arms.

TWO

It was sundown before Christine de Pizan got out to the palace gatehouse. She'd managed to persuade the Queen's cook to part with some bits of meat and bread for the two youngest royal children, since their own cook was nowhere to be seen (which was unsurprising, perhaps; the children's servants hadn't been paid for two months, since the King's latest bout of illness began, and you couldn't rely on the Queen for anything). Suppressing the rage she habitually felt when she saw how that idle, self-indulgent Bavarian schemer let her own youngest son and daughter be neglected, Christine had tucked an unusually quiet Charles into bed. Catherine, she supposed, was still in the audience hall. She'd made Charles promise to save his sister some meat. Neither Christine nor the boy had had the heart to mention the proposed abomination of an English marriage that the Queen had just so shamefully accepted.

Christine was really only supposed to read with the Prince and Princess—to guide their minds. That was a natural appointment for someone who'd written as much as she had, to the acclaim of all Europe, about how princes should be educated. But, whenever their father was in the grip of his demons, Christine also found herself going every day to the Hôtel Saint-Paul, the garden palace their grandfather had built just inside his new city walls, to the cobwebby children's annex and their mother's overheated, parrot-filled, sweetmeat-loaded quarters, where Christine's only role was to play nursemaid-cum-mother:

making sure they had enough to eat, and clothes to wear. It wrought havoc on her concentration and disrupted her writing and the direction of her manuscript-copying workshop. But how could she do anything less? She was grateful to poor, kindly, afflicted King Charles for letting her live out her life in France—she'd had no desire, when she was widowed, to go back to Venice—and for showing her such favor over the years. And she felt sorry for him, in his troubles, and sorry for the children too. So quiet, the pair of them, as if neglect had withered their tongues (though Christine had noticed that Catherine, at least, was now becoming resourceful enough to marshal what she needed in the way of food and friends even without words; using the wistful looks and ways of a girl coming to her adult beauty to charm the people she needed. And she'd risen to the occasion today, all right, with a quip that had pleased everyone).

But this wasn't the time to worry about little Charles and Catherine. All Christine had time to feel now was anxiety on her own account. She whisked her wiry body briskly toward the head guard. How had it got so late? Outside the Hôtel Saint-Paul, she could already see a glitter of red on the river, up past the Island and the old royal palace and Notre Dame Cathedral. Night was dangerous. The men were ready to close the gatehouse, locking the inhabitants inside for safety.

"You're late," one of them said roughly to her.

"It's only ten minutes' walk to my house," she said firmly back. "You know I live just nearby."

The man shook his head doubtfully. They all knew the figures: ten bodies a night delivered to the morgue at the Louvre. Ten throats cut on the streets after honest folk were supposed to be inside and asleep. Paris was a frightening place these days, even now, when things were relatively quiet.

"I have to get home," she said. "I have children. Grandchildren. Work." She gestured down at her simple blue gown and laughed reassuringly, giving them her most flirtatious smile. It was always best to use charm first, before letting the man know she meant business. Her smile had always melted hearts. "I don't look worth robbing. You can see that. I'll be all right."

She wished the man would hurry and make his mind up to let her go. She didn't want to be out at night either.

Suddenly the guard nodded, as if he'd just seen a way of killing two birds with one stone. "We've got an Englishman here who needs a bed for the night," he said. "I'll let you out if you put him up. He'll keep you safe."

It would be crowded, but if they'd let her out she'd find a corner for a guest. Even an Englishman. She nodded. Brisk with relief, the guard whistled out a mule and handed her onto it. Christine recognized the young man holding the harness. He was tall but still hardly more than a boy—the black-haired page, or aide, or whatever he was, who'd held open the casket while the Duke of Clarence gave Princess Catherine her jewel. He had a big pack on his back and was wrapped, ready to go, in a cloak too heavy for the mild evening weather. He gave her a small, shy smile. He wouldn't save her from any footpads, she saw. But at least he'd be no trouble.

She noticed the boy moving his head to stare at everything they passed. He stared at the great paved sweep of Saint Anthony Street, where fruit blossoms peeked over the walls of the Duke of Orléans' home and the convent of Saint Catherine of the Schoolboys. Once inside the Saint Anthony gate, when they turned away from the river into narrower streets, where the paving stones stopped and the sound of the mule's hooves was muffled by ankle-deep filth, he gazed at the pink blossoms waving over the King of Sicily's home on one side and Little Saint Anthony convent on the other.

At first she thought he was scared, and listening for footsteps. She was, though she'd have died before admitting it. They passed the crowded space of the Jews' road on one side, and more walls swaying with pink and white clouds, with more slender towers and spires rising behind the wafts of flowers, then came up to the Bishops of Beauvais' hotel. As they reached the crossroads, she looked straight at him to show him he had to turn the mule's head to the left here, and she realized, from the alert, curious, joyful look on his face, that he wasn't scared at all. He was just drinking in every detail of their surroundings. From the slightly raised ground here, you could see down to the Grève port. You could see the top of the crane that was used for unloading hay bales and the last speckles of glitter on the river. You could see the double towers of the cathedral, the turrets of the palace, and the dark green of the bare vineyards on the slopes of the Left Bank, with the University and church buildings scattered behind them up the hillsides, silhouettes in the dusk.

Because she was suddenly seeing it through his newcomer's eyes, the sight humbled and amazed her as it hadn't for years. She hardly ever remembered anymore even what had made her write, in one of her most famous books, about the experience of coming here from Venice as a child, and about the extraordinary impression that her first months in Paris had made. She'd forgotten the beauty she lived amidst. These days, all she thought about in these streets was the troubles they all lived with. But look at this boy, staring. Paris must still be a dream, a miracle, to anyone who'd never seen or imagined two hundred thousand people living, working, singing, praying, and thinking together.

"I had no idea," the boy said, turning frank eyes to her, "no idea it would be like this." His French was accented but fluent. Taken aback by his warmth and openness, she almost smiled.

A dog barked somewhere near; something creaked. She jumped. There was no point in getting your throat cut just for the joy of exchanging pleasantries with an Englishman, she told herself. "Come on," she said gruffly. "Let's get you inside."

It was so dark by the time they stopped in Old Temple Street that they had to bang at the locked courtyard gate, and when Jean came out to let them in, he was carrying a lantern.

"We were worried," he said, not noticing the visitor at the head of the mule, coming straight to her and slipping her off its back. His voice was quiet but she could feel the tension vibrating in it.

"I'm sorry," she said, tilting her head up, feeling the usual rush of wonder at his olive skin and black hair, the elegant slant of jaw and nose, the clean smell. Her son: the man her love with Étienne had made. The way he reminded her of Étienne, who'd been dead these twenty years now, brought a tragic undertone into her husky voice. "There was nothing I could do. Everything got late. There were visitors from England."

Jean screwed up his face. He was no fonder of the present-day rulers of England than she was. Once, long ago, when Jean was just a boy, she'd sent him to England as pageboy to the old Earl of Salisbury. That had been a good placement for a boy who needed to make his way in the world. But the Earl had been killed soon after old King Richard was deposed. The new King of England—*so-called* King of England, she added fiercely to herself—who'd replaced Richard had wanted to keep young Jean de Castel, and even to get Christine to move to England to be with her son and light up his court with her writing. But she wasn't having any truck with usurpers, and she'd had no intention of moving from civilization to that damp wilderness over the water. So she'd sweet-talked that first Henry of Lancaster into sending her son back to France while she pretended to be making up her mind, and, eventually, she'd found Jean his place here in Paris. It was better the way things had worked out. They were together. Still, Christine and her son knew too much about the betrayals and bloodshed Henry of Lancaster had provoked to enjoy thinking of England. And they liked the idea of England even less now it was ruled by that Henry's son—now Henry V—who, no sooner than he'd become King, had sent his brother over to France with an army to fight the French in Normandy, and who seemed to want to revive the old claim of the English kings to lands in France—which had been wrongful even when the kings were still rightful—to be the God-given rulers of France. The English were dangerous: king-killers, scavengers, wolves. This Henry was no kind of husband for Catherine. Anyone could see that.

"What English visitors?" Jean was asking, with the lantern flame reflected in his eyes.

"The brother. The Duke of Clarence. With a proposal for our Princess Catherine to marry King Henry," Christine replied quickly, keeping her voice neutral.

Jean rolled his eyes. "I see," he said drily, raising his eyebrows, obviously not believing anyone could have taken such a proposal seriously, taking it as a cue for wry laughter. "And who did he talk to, if the King's . . ." Then he looked round, as if noticing the boy holding the mule's head for the first time, and raised his eyebrows in a different, mute, cautious question.

"This is a member of the Duke of Clarence's entourage," Christine explained, still in her watchful public voice. Jean inclined his head at the newcomer—not quite a bow. The boy, grateful to be noticed at last, was already bowing eagerly and murmuring thanks for his bed in his fluent but guttural Anglo-Norman French. He was surprisingly tall. He towered over well-knit Jean.

"They asked me to put him up here," she went on. "An Englishman . . ." She turned to the boy with a question in her voice. "Owain Tudor," he said, and bowed again. But there was something unboyish in his eyes—a flicker of pain? Embarrassment? Grief? Pride?—as he added, with a slight twist of the lips: "Not English. I'm Welsh."

They'd heard of the Welsh rebellion against King Henry, in the remote western Marches of England. Of course they had; France had supported the Welsh rebel, Owain Glyndŵr, against the English usurper. A French army under the then Chancellor, the Breton lord Jean de Rieux, had even spent a couple of years in Wales, once the Welsh leader had been crowned King Owain IV, leading three thousand Breton horsemen under the Welsh dragon flag. French and Welsh alike had been for old King Richard of England, already dead by then, rather than the king-killer Henry; it had all started from that. So Christine and her son knew that the uprising, which for a while had spread through the English aristocracy and turned even some of England's greatest lords into mutineers, had nearly destroyed that Henry of England. The rebels had carved up England in their minds, before they'd even won it: the Midlands to the Welsh, the south and west to the Mortimer lords of March; the north to the Percy clan. But the uprising had finally been defeated, even if its Welsh leader was still hiding out in the misty hills, raiding; even if he still called himself the

King of Wales. So they looked at this youth in puzzlement as he told them that Owain Glyndŵr, the rebel leader, was his cousin—King of the old Welsh royal house of Powys Magog, as the boy put it, not without pride, in his excellent French. If this boy was that rebel's kinsman, what was he doing here, nicely dressed, in Paris, in the service of an English duke?

The boy only shook his head at the confusion he saw on their faces. He looked older than his years again; as if he was used to people being puzzled about who he was and what his status might be.

"My family's been punished," he said, with the light shrug of someone affecting indifference. "One of my uncles was executed. Our lands are confiscated. But I was only a child. Prince Henry took me in; not as a hostage . . . out of kindness . . . and made me a page in his household," he said, retreating fully from his moment of touchy self-assertion; putting the others at their ease. "King Henry now. So I suppose I'm nearly English, after all." He met their eyes boldly. "I was lucky," he added with another of those deliberate light smiles, as if daring them to disagree.

Saying that so confidently gave Owain the usual dizzy feeling of being in two places at once. As he smiled for his hosts, he couldn't help also thinking, privately, for a flash, of what might have become of him if he hadn't become English. He thought of the cousins he'd played and ridden and hidden with, who'd been kept by their father to stand or fight with the Welsh armies, who were all now prisoners in the Tower of London: Glyndŵr's oldest son Gruffydd, twenty or so, with his father's light eyes and quick wit, who could cut a raindrop in two with his sword, the fastest runner Owain had ever seen, the fastest rider too. Owain's childhood hero. The three little blond Mortimer girls, lisping and giggling, none of them older than eight or nine, with their tired-eyed mother, Catrin, Glyndŵr's daughter and Owain's aunt. The women had all been taken captive when Catrin's husband, the powerful Englishman Edmund Mortimer, had been killed at the siege of Harlech, when the English King's men had finally broken down the walls. Not everyone he'd grown up with was a prisoner now; not quite. Owain thought of Glyndŵr's younger son, Maredudd ap Owain Glyndŵr, hiding with his fugitive father in Herefordshire—laughing quietly over their place of refuge— with one of Glyndŵr's English sons-in-law, paradoxically the English Sheriff of the County, still very much on the run. He thought of his own immediate family: his mother long dead, they said of shock and fear after hiding from Prince Harry's raiding party come to burn down Sycharth Castle. He couldn't remember her. His father, a joyous smile or a giant puff of rage, depending on his mood; riding out with the French and taking Owain with them; teaching Owain a first few words of the incomers' ways and language when he was only five or six and prouder than any boy had ever been to be taken on the army's marches. Even if Owain no longer respected that reckless father—who'd handed him over to the enemy when it suited him—or the uncles who'd saved their skins by handing over their own men to be tortured and killed, he couldn't help but feel sorry for them all. His father, Maredudd ap Tudur, like all the other surviving brothers, was living on nothing now: on the run, lodging in attics and churches, surviving on pity. The houses had gone. Owain remembered two of the moated manors burning; a confused child's recollection of peering out between fingers clamped over eyes, choking on smoke; being hushed into tickly, terrified silence. They'd been somewhere among the smooth stretches of gray-green turf and tree and sea on the island some knew as the Dark Island, or Honey Island, or the Island of the Brave, which had once been his family's home: Môn, beyond the great snowy mountains of Gwynedd, which the English called Anglesey, and which he would never see again. Uncle Rhys' head was on a pole at Chester. Uncle Rhys' boys were not allowed back to Erddreiniog. Uncle Gwilym had lost Clorach; Uncle Ednyfed's children had lost Trecastell. Only Morfydd, his bravest cousin, Uncle Goronwy's daughter, who had charm and more determination than every other member of his family put together, and, what was more, was blessed with a husband not quite so out of favor as the rest of Owain's family, still dared to petition the

King of England to get the family lordship of Penmynydd back.

In his mind's eye, Owain saw the thousand children taken as servants when the English King had stabled his horses in the church of Strata Florida Abbey, letting them foul God's altar. That older Henry had been a cruel man. He'd enjoyed demonstrating that he feared no one, not even God. If it hadn't been for young King Henry, with his pardons and his peace . . . Owain heard the anguished howling of the mothers that night; the fearful quiet of the children, their lost stares, driven off like sheep into the abbey and on into the unknown. That had been the beginning. Owain saw the end too: grass in the streets; roofless houses; burned-out villages; a land without men.

"I was lucky," he repeated lightly. "My King Henry is a good master."

Christine and Jean exchanged glances. Then, putting an arm on the boy's shoulder, Jean led him inside.

They gave the boy a drink and a bite to eat. He said politely that he couldn't take a thing, but of course in the event he wolfed down slice after slice of meat and bread, and washed it all down with a big cup of wine. He was young, after all, whatever he'd seen in that remote war; fifteen, maybe; and he had a healthy appetite.

Seeing them all standing around the circle of light, watching him—not just Christine and Jean, but Jean's wife Jehanette and little Jacquot and Perrette—he watered his wine liberally, and explained, through a cheerful mouthful, "We're under orders not to drink French wine without water, because it's so good and strong; we're not allowed to get drunk." He hesitated; they could all see him wondering whether to tell them the reasoning behind the order too—too obviously "Don't get drunk in case a Frenchman ambushes you"—then realizing that would be tactless, and blushing. Instead, he ran an appreciative tongue round his mouth, which was stained dark red. "I don't know yet if it's strong, but it certainly is good," he finished, giving them all a beaming smile. Christine saw Perrette's snub nose wrinkle in the beginning of a return laugh; warningly, she caught Perrette's eye. There was no point in being too easily charmed.

As soon as he'd satisfied his appetite for food, the boy sighed, pushed his stool back from the table, and, in the biddable fashion of a well-bred child, set to trying to entertain his silent hosts with stories from his day and his life. Eagerly, he started talking—gabbling, Christine thought severely—about the audience his Duke had had with the Queen of France—well, not *his* Duke, exactly; Owain had just been seconded to Clarence for the trip to Paris. He fixed his eyes rather pleadingly on dimpling, curly-haired Jehanette, who looked the readiest to smile. "My master sent your Princess a jewel with the marriage proposal. It was my duty and pleasure to hand it to her today . . . I think your Princess liked it. She's a very beautiful princess. A jewel herself. The marriage will be a blessing for both our lands . . . don't you think?" he finished, and even he could hear the imploring note in his own voice.

He had no idea why they were looking so cheerless. Even the pretty wife. He sensed he must have said the wrong thing—but what? Did he smell? He restrained the impulse to sniff at his armpits.

But he watched in dawning alarm as the elderly woman who'd brought him home pursed her lips and drew her back up very straight. She'd been beautiful once, this Christine de Pizan, you could see that; there was still the ghost of beauty in her ravaged face and in the pride with which she carried her small, tough body, prodding out her barrel chest, half pugnacious, half flirtatious. But there was something frightening about her too; he certainly didn't want to get on the wrong side of her.

Christine glared at him. She said severely: "I'm not so sure about that, young man. And I wouldn't get your hopes up too much, if I were you. I doubt very much whether this marriage will happen."

She dropped her chin and went on gazing implacably at him.

Owain shrank into himself, wishing himself invisible, wondering how he could have given such offense.

He noticed the younger Frenchman quietly putting a restraining hand on his mother's arm. He also saw Madame de Pizan didn't seem to care. The gesture almost seemed to goad her into going on.

"No doubt your English . . . *King* . . . wants a marriage with the oldest and greatest royal line in Europe," she said, and her husky voice vibrated deeper with contempt. "But one of our royal princesses has already turned down a proposal of marriage by your King, don't forget. As I recall, there was a question of the validity of his claim to the throne, at the time . . . and I'm not aware of anything having changed in that regard since then." She pushed her head a little closer to his. "Are you?"

Owain felt like a rabbit being hypnotized by a snake. "Ye— no . . ." he stammered, desperate to please but sensing he was being lured into danger too; and, mostly, simply not knowing what answer was expected.

"In any event, it's our *King* who will decide, when he recovers from his . . . his illness," Christine was sweeping superbly on, overemphasizing her words and raising her eyebrows to add yet more insistence to her speech. (Owain noticed she didn't say, the King's "madness"; in fact, he realized, no one he'd met in Paris seemed to talk of the madness that everyone in England knew the King of France was afflicted with.) "Not our *Queen*. And as for our Queen . . . she might have seemed to you to be enthusiastic about marrying Catherine to your King, but don't forget you're an outsider here, and a very young one at that. If you were a Parisian, you'd know without needing to be told that her main pleasure in life these days is goading her son into behaving badly. It amuses her. She's of a mischievous turn of mind, and the two of them don't get on. You saw how he reacted. That was him—Louis, our Crown Prince, the Dauphin—making a scene back there. He was right, of course. He should never have risen to her bait; but that's Louis for you. Always been a fool. He didn't see she was only considering the idea to provoke him into making the scene he made."

"Maman," Jean de Castel murmured.

She shrugged off her son's hand with an irritated little puff of breath: "Pah." But then she paused. "Well, perhaps you're right," she said a moment later, sounding less angry. "I'm speaking out of turn. Still, I wouldn't trust the Queen's enthusiasm. It's liable to wane. There'll be no marriage."

Owain nodded, less worried about trying to defend his King than about just trying to keep quiet so the alarming Madame de Pizan wouldn't go on the attack again. He was mystified by her air of imperious assurance. He was even more mystified by the familiarity—if she'd been a less frightening person, he'd have called it impertinence—with which she described the French royal family. He looked furtively around the quiet and modest room in the quiet and modest townhouse in which he was sitting. He stole another glance at Madame de Pizan's quiet and modest blue and white clothing. There were no signs that she was a great lady. He'd have said the son was a government official of some sort; not privy to the counsels of the highest in the land, by any means. Was it normal here to discuss the failings of the rulers of the land at every table?

Changing the subject, Owain hastily asked Jean what his calling in life was. Everyone breathed a little easier, but it wasn't a subject that brought joy to anyone's face either. There was a shadow on Jean's fine dark face as he replied, very carefully and neutrally, that he was an administrator; that he'd had some small experience under the Duke of Burgundy; but that, as Owain might know, the Duke was no longer in Paris, so Jean was now doing some work for the Chancellor of France and seeking a new permanent position and patron.

Owain nodded, feeling he was beginning to understand. He'd heard about the troubles in France. He knew what Englishmen knew: that since the King of France was too mad, most of the time, to make decisions, the royal uncles and cousins were all wrangling for the chance to power as regent in his "absences," and France had fallen into something like civil war as a result. The Queen and the various quarrelsome princes were almost all on one side, more or less, with their armies, usually led by the Count of Armagnac—and they were all against the Duke of Burgundy. Burgundy was the most powerful nobleman in

21

France—rich, with lands all over northeastern France and across the Low Countries, and expanding his territory still further in every direction as fast as he could. He was the only prince whom the people of Paris loved, because they found him reliable. He might be too fond of plotting, but at least he paid his tradesmen's bills. But he'd overstretched himself last year. He'd been blamed for stirring up riots in Paris against the King's government, and had taken himself prudently off to his lands when the rioting had petered out. No wonder this family was so gloomy, if their breadwinner had been employed by Burgundy; if, now Jean had lost his patron, they were consumed with money worries . . .

Owain turned sympathetically to Christine, seeing lines round her eyes and mouth etched by hardship. Riots, civil war, fear, money problems, a son needing a patron; this was a story he suddenly felt he understood. It must be a constant worry for a widow in her sunset years, he thought. "It must be very frightening for you, sitting at home with the grandchildren . . . with nothing to do but wonder how your son's faring . . ." he ventured kindly.

He sensed, rather than heard, the indrawn breaths; felt the silence. He'd said something wrong again.

He didn't dare look at Madame de Pizan's face. He could hardly bear the outrage in her voice as she replied, in freezing tones, "*Well!* I do my best to keep busy. *In my humble way. I, Christine de Pizan.*"

He fixed his eyes on Jean instead. He saw Jean glance at his mother; he saw the expression of wry amusement on the older man's face, and realized, feeling mortified, though less full of dread than he'd been a second ago, that Jean was enjoying what must be a look of the purest fury from Madame de Pizan.

"Young man, there's something you should know . . ." Jean said, quite kindly. "I could see you didn't recognize her name when we introduced ourselves out there, but my mother is a very famous woman. She's written dozens of books, on everything from love to military history. Kings come to her for guidance; dukes seek her advice. Even your King—well, his father—once tried to tempt her to live at the English court. She brought me and my sister up, after our father died, on the money she earned from writing poems; she's taken on the greatest minds in Europe to teach them the dignity of women. She's unique; known all over Christendom; an ornament to the civilized world. Also, she has a very short temper. You should know all that before you go on."

He paused. He gave Owain a quizzical look, as if waiting to see how he'd react. Owain could see Jehanette was trying not to laugh.

"But," Owain faltered, hardly daring to speak for fear of falling into yet another trap he hadn't suspected. He'd never heard of such a thing. "A woman . . . ? Educated . . . ? Writing . . . ? What . . . ?"

Christine snapped: "A woman can educate herself, if she has the wit and application to. I did; why not?" Then, less angrily, "In any case, if this was a just world, all girls would automatically be properly educated, without having to teach themselves—just as boys are. So, no, I don't just sit at home worrying. You have to help yourself in this life; there's no guarantee anyone else will help you if you don't. I go to court. I get commissions. I write: *I, Christine*. What's more, I run a manuscript workshop out at the back here, to have my work copied and presented to clients. I don't have time to sit around being frightened. And let me tell you one last thing, young man," she added, with her eyes still full of flash and injured pride, but also, Owain suddenly realized, just the faintest glimmer of dawning humor. "My most talented employee, by a long chalk—the best illuminator of manuscripts in Paris, and probably in the world—is a woman too."

Owain opened his eyes very wide—even wider than the astonishment he genuinely felt was merited. It had taken a while, but now instinct told him he might have the measure of her at last. To be impressed would appease her. If he could only appeal to the humor he sensed in her eyes; to the good heart that he sensed lay behind her fierce exterior . . .

He opened his hands wide, too, in an imitation of the French shrug he'd seen so often today.

"They told me," he said, with all the worldly charm he

could muster, staring back at her as boldly as he dared, "that Paris was a city of miracles. And now I know they were right."

He bowed. "Bravo!" he heard Jehanette whisper.

"Madame de Pizan," he went on, in the same light, unfrightened tone—the words coming glibly to his tongue now he was finding his way; knowing he was on safer ground—"I'm honored to know you. And I beg your pardon for my ignorance. Truly. I didn't mean to give offense . . . but I wasn't to know . . . there are no women with your genius in my country . . . and I'm not a man of letters myself . . . I've never read . . . well, not properly . . . only the Bible, and my Book of Hours . . ."

He could see, from the little nods of Jean's head, that he was doing all right now. And, as his panic receded, he remembered that he had always wanted to know more about the world of letters. He'd always been intrigued by the priestly scholars in the castles he'd moved between since he came to England; by their austere, dusty calling; but repelled, too, by their elderly, glum faces. He'd always wished they had some of the life and lightness of Red Iolo, Owain Glyndŵr's bard, who in spite of being unimaginably ancient—more than eighty, people said—with a white beard and a bowed back and a stick, and white-blue cloudy eyes, still had an amused smile and a joyful wit and a poem always on his tongue. Not that it mattered, back in England. As a Welshman, one of the Plant Owain—the Children of Owain—he was banned from university anyway. He didn't care. But here, in this great city, home of the greatest university in Christendom, every young man was reputed to know his astronomy and even the women were scholars . . . There'd be no sour old faces here; it might all be different.

"I'd like to read more widely," he added eagerly, for Owain was a young man of irrepressible optimism and adaptability, "I'd really like to. If I'm to stay with you while my Duke's embassy is here, will you show me your books?"

When he dared look up into the next silence, he saw everything had changed. Christine de Pizan was smiling at him—a smile so dazzlingly beautiful that, for a moment, he could no longer see the lines etched on her face by time. And she was nodding her head.

They sat up late, after that. They drank another pitcher of wine together (Owain was wise enough not to water his anymore). He didn't know whether he was drunk. He only knew he was overwhelmed with the excitement of this adventure: with being in this extraordinary city, developing a camaraderie with a woman so learned she was the talk of Christendom, and knowing that his refusal to give in to his fear of her had helped make her eyes go soft and her voice gentle as she talked.

Christine was telling him about coming to Paris for the first time herself. Her father had been a Venetian; he'd brought her to Paris when she was four and he had been appointed as the astrologer to the old French King's court. She still remembered her first sight of Paris's four bridges and the hundreds of princely hotels in the town along the Seine's right bank; the glittering pinnacles of palace and cathedral in the city, on the Island in the middle of the river, and the sweeping vineyards, cornfields, churches, and colleges of the university districts on the Left Bank. "And the King's library . . ." she reminisced, with a soft look in her eye, ". . . a thousand books, each more beautiful than the last . . . and the graciousness of the King himself . . . a true philosopher-king . . . So I understood your astonishment when you saw the city spread out before you this evening. I remember that moment myself. Paris is the most beautiful city in the world . . . and always will be."

When Owain asked about the riots last year, and whether they hadn't damaged the city—destroyed buildings, caused fires—she only waved a magnificent hand and made her "pshaw!" noise, as if what Owain guessed must have been a terrifying couple of weeks had been an insignificant triviality. "Butchers!" she said dismissively; "A hangman! What damage could people of that sort do?"

But, before she let Jean show him to the bed that Jehanette had made up for him in the scriptorium, Madame de Pizan drew him across to the window, and said, more somberly, "Look here."

She opened the shutters. They squeaked. She pointed down at the dark street outside. "Forget the butchers. If you want to know where our civil war really began, it was right there."

Owain let his eyes get used to the dark, enjoying the air, fresh with early flowers. Up on the left, he could see the slender turrets of the Hôtel Barbette; she'd shown him that earlier, on the way here. Opposite, he could just about make out a dark space, where a house should have stood. A froth of weeds; jutting timbers. "Yes," Christine said, "that burned-out space. *That* was where it all happened: the first death in the war. When France began to destroy itself."

Christine fell silent for a moment, looking out, forgetting the boy, remembering that moment. She'd watched the aftermath from this window: the torches, the shouting, the panic. Out there, on a cold November night seven years ago, right outside that house, the Duke of Burgundy had sent men to waylay his cousin and rival, the Duke of Orléans, and murder him.

There'd been quarrels between the two men for years before that. Louis of Orléans had a light, teasing temperament; John of Burgundy was quiet and thorough and ruthless. They could never have been close. Louis of Orléans, charming and intelligent and musical though he was—Christine's most glittering patron, back then—had been provoking too: so many mistresses, so many orgies in bathhouses, helping the Queen steal money from the royal coffers for her entertainments.

Burgundy's men had come to this street for vengeance only after Orléans had hinted mischievously to Burgundy that he'd had an affair with Burgundy's own Duchess. But they'd chosen precisely this spot to do their murder because they knew how often Orléans came here. The Queen, the wife of Orléans' royal brother, had a private house on the corner of Old Temple Street—the Hôtel Barbette, with its white turrets, fifty yards away. Queen Isabeau moved there whenever her husband was mad. For years before he was killed, Orléans had spent too many of his days and nights there too, whenever she was in residence. People whispered that he must be Isabeau's lover.

There was no end to the mischief Louis of Orléans had done, it was true. But Burgundy's response—murdering him—

was a crime so horrifying it blotted out all the pranks and tricks Louis had so enjoyed.

Shedding the blood royal was sacrilege.

God anointed a king to be the head of the body politic. A country's fighting noblemen might be the body politic's arms and hands; the priests its conscience; the peasantry its legs and feet. But the King was the head, to be obeyed in all things, since everything and everyone depended utterly on him to convey the will of God from Heaven to Earth. And the blood that ran in his royal veins was as sacred as the sacrament and so were the persons of his closest relatives, the other princes of the blood, whom God might choose to take the throne tomorrow if He called today's King to Heaven. It was the blood royal that brought life to the body politic—the will of God made manifest on Earth—and anyone who shed the blood royal was going against the will of God.

Once Burgundy, a prince of the blood royal, had ignored that divine imperative, and destroyed another royal prince, like a dog, the whole contract between God and man was destroyed too. The darkness had got in.

That was why, ever since the night of that murder, the hand of every prince in France had been turned against the Duke of Burgundy—even if Burgundy's personal magnetism was such that he'd bullied the poor, sickly King into pardoning him; even if he'd bullied Louis of Orléans' young son, Charles, into saying publicly, through gritted teeth, in front of the King, that he forgave him too, and would not seek revenge for the death.

That was why France was cursed.

Even now that Burgundy had slunk away from Paris, it wasn't the end. That there would be more bloodshed Christine had no doubt. Every prince who would have followed Orléans' son Charles, if he had raised his hand against Burgundy, was taking a lead instead from his fiercer father-in-law, Count Bernard of Armagnac, who was bound by no peace promises. But, whatever the princes thought, the people of Paris still loved Burgundy. He paid his bills, unlike the more spendthrift Armagnac princes; as Christine and her son had both found, Burgundy was a better employer. Sooner or later he'd be back, with an army behind him, to trade the love that Parisians bore him for power. And then . . .

She leaned against the window frame.

"Are you all right?" A timid boy's voice came from her side, making her jump. It was Owain Tudor; still there, staring at her with big gentle eyes. She'd forgotten all about him. She sighed. "Just regrets," she said wistfully, "for so many past mistakes."

He murmured; something optimistic, she guessed. He was too young to know there were some wrongs that couldn't be righted; some sins that would follow you to the grave. She shook herself. Smiled a brittle, social, off-to-bed-now-it's-late smile at him, and began locking up. But perhaps his naive young man's hope was catching. As she heard his footsteps, and Jean's, creak on the stairs, she found herself imagining a conversation she might have, one day soon, with someone still full of hope—someone like this young Owain.

"What are you writing now?" he would ask.

She'd answer: "The *Book of Peace*." And she'd smile, because it would be true.

THREE

Owain meant to lie awake in the room where they'd made up a bed for him, and imagine himself walking through the city streets tomorrow. The room was warm, but furnished only with a huge table scattered with parchments and pens and with two long benches. There was a shelf of books on the wall. He'd imagined himself taking a book off the wall and, very carefully, putting it on the table and beginning to read it by candlelight. But sleep overcame him as soon as he threw himself down on the quilt. Instead of reading, he dreamed: fretful, regretful dreams, of woodsmoke, and stinging eyes, and the blurred outlines of rafters high up, and a woman's arms cradling him, and a lullaby in a language he hardly remembered.

A few streets away, in the Hôtel Saint-Paul, Catherine crept to her bed, shedding her sister-in-law Marguerite's borrowed houppelande, which had made her sweat so much, leaving it on the floor with all the other neglected garments no one picked up anymore. Marguerite wouldn't notice, she thought, with childish unconcern; Marguerite spent so much time lying round crying in the Queen's chambers at the mean way Louis treated her that she didn't have time to worry about where her clothes were. Marguerite was always weeping; always running to the Queen for sympathy, and getting it, too. Catherine couldn't understand why her mother was so much sweeter with Marguerite than she was with her own children. They all hated

29

Marguerite's father, the Duke of Burgundy; they all knew that was why Louis was so cruel to his wife. And the Queen hated the Duke of Burgundy at least as much as anyone else. But it didn't seem to make her hate Marguerite. Struggling with the jealousy that thoughts of her mother's public affection for Marguerite always aroused in her, Catherine thought, without really questioning why: perhaps Maman just hates Louis more than she does Marguerite's father.

All Catherine had on below the houppelande was the dirty shift she'd worn for two days. She'd been tucking up its graying sleeves for hours under the green velvet, to keep them out of sight.

She stopped. There was someone already snuffling under the bedclothes. She held the candle close. Charles, damp and muttering, with his thin boy's arms and legs rumpling the sheets into a linen whirlpool. She stood at the side of the bed and, with one hand, reached down to straighten the covers and stroke his hair. Then she saw there was a trace of meat grease still on his face. She raised the candle to look round the room. Sure enough, there was a hunk of bread and a slice of beef waiting on a platter under the window. "Thank you, Christine," she muttered, as she tiptoed toward it.

She put the candle on the table and ate, remembering the anxiety on Charles' pale little face when he'd slipped out of the audience hall. There was no need for him to worry, she thought, rather sadly. Everyone else knew nothing would come of this marriage offer.

Still . . . it would be nice to be a queen . . . to know you'd always be fed and clothed and happy . . . and safe. She sighed, snuffed out the candle, and got into bed beside Charles.

In pitch darkness, Catherine sat bolt upright in her bed, with her hair wild and her eyes wide in terror. That woke little Charles up too. He sat up; started to shake. He clutched her hand.

She pulled open a corner of her curtains, so they could see out. They waited. They listened. But all either of them could hear, through the thump of their heartbeats, was the doubtful creaking of floorboards, and drafts flapping distant cloth. There was no one there.

"Nothing," Charles whispered stoutly. "You must have been dreaming. Go back to sleep."

He snuggled back down into his quilt. He didn't want to remember the butchers with thick bare arms and leather jackets smelling of death, with aprons streaked with blood, who'd broken into the Hôtel Saint-Paul last summer. Screaming. Sweating and waving sticks and yelling and jeering. Smelling.

Catherine lay down again too, but she couldn't stop listening or controlling her breathing to keep it quiet, in case someone else was listening. She could have sworn she'd heard the smash of glass again.

When they'd come last summer, they'd broken right into the ballroom. There was nothing to stop them. The Hôtel Saint-Paul didn't have proper battlements. It was just a collection of houses and gardens, bolted together by long galleries—a made-up palace of pleasure gardens, created inside the city wall by her grandfather in times when there were no rebellions. They stayed here still because her father liked it; it reminded him of his own happy childhood. But Catherine's memories were different.

She'd watched three of the butchers chase one official down the corridor. The official had flung himself at Marguerite and clung to her skirts. She'd thrown her arms round him, but the butchers hardly noticed. They had yanked Marguerite's arms away and torn her sleeve. They had pulled him off her, sobbing, the terror of a hunted animal on his face. The detail Catherine remembered most clearly was that Marguerite's headdress had caught on one of the men's belts. Marguerite had just gone on standing there, with her arms still outstretched and tears streaming down her cheeks and her blond hair streaming behind her; not even trying to grab for the twin horns of the headdress as it bobbed absurdly on a butcher's behind.

They all said it wouldn't happen again. Everyone said the riots had been Marguerite's father's fault. They said the Duke of Burgundy had paid the butchers to attack. And he was gone now.

The memory of him still made Catherine shiver. So tall and

lean and stooped; and when he looked at you with his cold, hooded eyes you went still, as if he were turning you to stone.

She wrapped her arms round herself. She didn't believe he'd gone for good. She knew it wouldn't take long before there was more fighting. They all hated each other too much for anything else.

If only there were stronger walls around the Hôtel Saint-Paul.

The thought came unbidden to her mind as she lay down again. If she went to England, where there was peace, she'd never need to be afraid again.

She put her hand on Charles' shoulder. He was so small, and so thin. She couldn't leave him.

Trying to still her thoughts, Catherine closed her eyes. When Charles burrowed his small, hot hand trustingly into hers and whispered: "Catherine, are you awake? Don't let them send you to England. Please," she squeezed his hand back, and felt guilty for having hoped, for a moment, for escape.

FOUR

Owain sat at the table in the thin morning light. Upstairs he could hear the excited voices of five-year-old Jacquot and three-year-old Perrette, about to burst down if only the serving girl could persuade them to put their clothes on. No one moved to touch the meal. Owain didn't like to ask why, though he was hungry. He just drank them all in, all those thin, dark, clever faces, enjoying being with this family that had grown up together. He didn't remember his own mother. He'd been brought up in packs of boys, being taught by gruff men to hold a sword and a bow. He was unsure how to act in this easy intimacy. He waited, shyly, for enlightenment.

A bang at the courtyard door shocked him, but everyone else relaxed. "Jean," said Jean, and Jehanette rushed out to open up. A tall blond man in his twenties was there, swinging off his mule; very good-looking, dressed more richly than anyone in the de Pizan or de Castel family, in confident blues and greens, with a sash of red and a touch of gold at neck and wrist; twinkling cheerfully down at Jehanette. He strode in, stopped at the sight of Owain; then bowed and clapped the boy on the back as the explanations about the guest flowed around him.

"Delighted," the blond Jean said, with an easy warmth Owain didn't know from his years in drafty castle corridors among Englishmen, but remembered from a time further back; a warmth that made Owain feel this man, too, might soon become a friend. Blond Jean raised an eyebrow at dark Jean de

Castel; jerked a casual shoulder back outside. "Wouldn't you like to eat before we go?" said the dark Jean; though he was clearly ready to take his lead from his friend and miss breakfast if that was required.

But blond Jean shrugged and gave in with a laugh. "Hungry?" he said; a man of few words. "Well, after all, why not? Let's." He put down the big wooden-backed document case he was carrying and lounged back on a stool. Politely, he picked up a piece of meat with his knife and laid it on a chunk of bread, but he only ate a mouthful. Dark Jean didn't eat much either; an atmosphere of strain and haste had come upon the family.

When the two young men had gone, a few minutes later, dark Jean taking the mule Christine had had from the palace last night, Christine said: "Jean's working with the other Jean at the chancellery. It's important for us all that it goes well. Luckily Jean's friend's father is Henri de Marle . . ." She paused and looked at Owain, who only looked bewildered. "The Chancellor of France now," she explained, with none of last night's softness, just haughty astonishment that anyone could fail to know something so vital, "since the Duke of Burgundy left Paris; he was president of the Parliament before. A good connection . . ."

She bustled around, picking things up; preparing for the day; not looking at him. She was putting things in a basket. When Owain plucked up courage to speak again, she took a moment to turn round in the direction of his voice, as if she didn't really want him there. "My Duke is busy with your Queen today," he ventured; "a hunting expedition. I'm not needed." He sensed, from the hard line of her back, that she didn't want to be reminded that he was the servant of an English duke. "So perhaps . . . I could . . . go with you, if you're going into Paris?" he finished, in a breathless hurry. He was longing to see the city; but he was a little scared of venturing out alone.

She said briskly, "I'll be busy here for a while." She didn't meet his eye. Perhaps she was regretting the warmth of their conversation last night, he thought. She didn't like the English, and even if he wasn't really an Englishman, and knew he'd never be considered as one back home, he could see that, in her mind, he might still count as one. For a moment, he felt disconsolate.

But only for a moment.

Then the memory of the books came back to him. Brightly, Owain asked her if he could spend his free day reading one of her books, if she would choose him one; and then she did turn and reward him with a smile of surprising depth and intimacy. "You really want to learn something, then," she murmured, in her magnificent throaty rumble; nodding as if she were surprised and impressed. He glowed. He wanted to impress her; he could sense she knew many things he'd be interested to find out.

She didn't say any more. She just led him back to the scriptorium where he'd slept, looking approvingly at the way he'd tidied his things into a corner so as not to be in the way. She hesitated over the books on the bookshelf for a few moments, picking at first one, then another. Finally her hand pulled one out. She set it up on a lectern and left in silence.

Owain read.

He'd expected it to be hard. He'd expected to be out of his depth. But the story she'd chosen was a very simple one. It was the story of her life. It was like nothing he'd ever read or heard before. Even the poems and stories he remembered from long ago, before England, back *there*—the legends, the tales of ancient kings, the songs of praise—weren't so shockingly personal. Before he knew what had happened, he'd been swept off into another time and place, lost, for the first time, between the covers of a book, experiencing the love that had once been in the newlywed Christine's heart.

> *The first night of our marriage, I could already feel*
> *His great goodness, for he never did to me*
> *Any outrage which would have harmed me,*
> *But, before it was time to get up,*
> *He kissed me, I think, one hundred times,*
> *Without asking for any other base reward:*
> *Indeed the sweet heart loves me well.*

> *Prince, he makes me mad for love,*
> *When he says that he is all mine;*
> *He will make me die of sweetness;*
> *Indeed the sweet heart loves me well.*

Owain turned the page, realizing only now, with a sudden sickness in his heart, that he already knew that Christine had been widowed young. This story wouldn't end well.

"My husband was the head of the household then: he was a young, wise, and sensible gentleman, well-liked by princes and all those who used to work with him as King's Secretary, a profession that enabled him to sustain his family. But already Fortune had consigned me to its wheel, preparing to confront me with adversity and knock me down. It did not want me to enjoy the goodness of my husband and killed him in the prime of his life. It took him from me in his prime youth, when he was thirty-four and I twenty-five. I was left in charge of two small children and a big household. Of course, I was full of bitterness, missing his sweet company and my past happiness, which had lasted no more than ten years. Aware of the tribulations that would face me, wanting to die rather than to live, remembering also that I had promised him my faith and love, I decided I would not remarry. And so I fell into the valley of tribulation."

Owain flicked forward.

"I could not exactly know the situation regarding his income. For the usual conduct of husbands is not to communicate and explain their revenues to their wives, an attitude that often brings troubles, as my experience proves. Such behavior does not make sense when the wives are not stupid but sensible and behaving wisely . . . I had been so used to enjoying an easy life, and now I had to steer the boat that had been left in the storm without a captain. Problems sprang at me from everywhere; lawsuits and trials surrounded me as if this were the natural fate of widows. Those who owed me money attacked me so that I would not dare ask anything about it. Soon I was prevented from receiving my husband's inheritance, which was placed in the King's hands . . . The leech of

Fortune did not stop sucking my blood for fourteen years, so that if one misfortune ceased, another ordeal happened, in so many different ways that it would be too long and too tedious to tell even half of it. It did not stop sucking my blood until I had nothing left."

Owain jumped. It took him a second to remember where he was. He was in the scriptorium. It must be midday. The sun was brilliant through the square of the window. And Christine was somewhere behind, moving very quietly so as not to disturb him.

He turned round to her; ducked his head in the beginnings of a polite bow. There was something strange now about looking at her; she was as fiercely self-possessed as ever, and three times his age, but he knew so many intimate things about her . . . He'd felt her love as if it were his own . . . and he was in pain for her past grief . . . and he thought he understood why, after all those troubles brought on by her widow's weak helplessness, she'd be quick to attack now if she ever felt belittled. It explained even her sharpness, at moments, with him.

Perhaps she saw. She was nodding to herself; she looked warmer than she had in the morning. She didn't acknowledge the traces of tears on his cheeks. But she did nod her head down at the basket on her arm.

"I'm going to run my errands now," she said; and suddenly she smiled that brilliant smile. "Would you like to come into Paris with me?"

Christine hated the Butchery. There was no alternative but to pass Saint-Jacques of the Butchery Church on the Right Bank, on the way to the Island that was still the heart of Paris: they had to walk by that great show-off church building that the rich bully-boys had spared no expense on, making its stained-glass windows glow and its saints glitter with gold. But at least she needn't tell Owain any more about the butchers, and what they'd done last year, she thought, averting her gaze. He knew enough. The streets of the Butchery were strangely quiet these days: the calves and cows, lowing uneasily, still came here to be slaughtered from Cow Island, their flat last pasture in mid-river, and the tanners still hung skins on ropes from side to side of their street to cure them, like great stinking brown sheets, but now that the butchers weren't allowed to sell on their home territory anymore, the district had lost its old swagger and bustle and arrogance. When Owain asked, "Why is that church chained up?" she only pursed her lips and pretended not to hear. He asked again. With all the old rage coming back at the oafs she could suddenly remember, yelling their slogans and thrusting their torches priapically through the smoke and darkness, so her throat was so tight she thought she might choke, she said, shortly and incoherently, "What sense could there ever have been in men of the streets—monkeys like these; animals—trying to imitate things they don't understand."

It wasn't a question; nor was it an explanation he understood. He just looked vaguely hurt, as if it might be a slur on him. She took his arm and led him quickly away from the Butchery. There was no reason to linger. Enough of it was blocked up—another part of the rebels' punishment—to make it as hard to get to the big ostentatious houses of the butcher clans, the Thiberts and Saint Yons, as it had always been to penetrate the stinking back alleys: Disembowelment Lane and Pig's-Trotter Alley and Flaying Yard and Skinners' Court and the Tripery and Calf Square and Hoof Place.

She crossed herself and passed on. It was only once they were safely on the approach to the river; almost underneath the turrets and crenellations of the Châtelet, with the sun glittering peacefully on the water and the cheerful cries of the boatmen ahead—and behind them the Island from which France was governed, and behind that the alluring world of prayers and vineyards and books of the Left Bank and the University—that she felt the pent-up breath ease out of her.

In a gentler voice, she said: " *'The beauty of the world lies in things being in their own element—stars in the sky, birds in the air, fish in water, men on earth.'* " She meant: There is an order in creation; the likes of butchers shouldn't dream of trying to seize power from the King that God has anointed. But she could see Owain stare; she could see him trying to tease meaning out of her words. Whatever did they teach boys at the court of England? she wondered; he was completely unlettered. "William of Conches wrote that," she said, smiling at Owain, enjoying his visible desire for knowledge so much that she repressed her irritation at his masters for leaving him such an ignoramus. "It's a thought I like to remember, when I see the world stretched out before me like this, in the sunlight; when all is well everywhere you look."

She could see him trying the words out in his own mouth, experimenting with them in a mutter. She knew it wouldn't be long before he'd try them out on someone else. Then his eyes slipped sideways again; she knew now where he was looking. Over to the Left Bank. With a little burst of happiness that she'd recognized one of her own sort so easily, she saw he couldn't keep from glancing at the University.

But Owain was astonished enough by the King's new Notre Dame bridge, just completed, with its seventeen wooden pillars and sixty-five narrow new timber houses and the mills rushing and grinding below, between the columns, to be distracted again from his contemplation of the University. The bridge took them at a sedate pace to the Island, where, until this King's father had moved his family to the gentler pleasures of the Hôtel Saint-Paul a few decades ago, kings throughout history had made their homes under the hundreds of pinnacles of the Royal Palace. "That's where Jean's gone with Jean de Marle," Madame de Pizan said proudly, gesturing at the pinnacles on the right before pointing out the enormous mass of the cathedral on their left, with its strange outside ribs of stone. She showed him the market at the Notre Dame approach, too, on the way to the scriptoria of the Island book business. And she let him peep inside the little red door in the side of the cathedral— the one placed just at the spot, on the body of the church, that would remind worshipers of the spear wound in the Flesh of the Divine Martyr—and watched him marvel at the soaring height of the slim spires, made of honey stone so delicate it seemed like lace, and, further up than he'd have thought possible, at the luminous sky erupting through a vast open fretwork of colored glass that glowed ruby and sapphire and emerald. Looking up was like seeing an explosion. Owain craned his neck toward the glorious luminosity of the heavens until it hurt. Time stood still. Somewhere in the candlelit gloom around him he was aware of male voices chanting; one sustained, ever renewed, bass note, with a host of others rising and falling in a complex movement around it: working the same magic on his ears that the colors he was staring at were working on his dazzled eyes. He knew exactly what Madame de Pizan meant when, without breaking the spell, she murmured, " '*I am that living and fiery essence of the divine substance that glows in the beauty of the fields. I shine in the water. I burn in the sun and the moon and the stars.*' " The unfamiliar words thrilled through him with something that felt like recognition; he'd never understood how God could be light until he'd come to stand in this space, staring up, hearing what felt like the music of the spheres. He was beginning to understand how his new acquaintance's mind worked, too, well enough, at least, to know that she'd also murmur straight afterward, "Saint Hildegard wrote that," and put her hand on his arm, before he had a chance to ask who Saint Hildegard had been (but he could ask later). He could tell she'd nudge him quickly back to the street, where the light was just light, and not poetry and prayer and honey and song spun together, but, even if it no longer made him feel he could float into the heavens, it was still beautiful light, and the sun was warm on his back.

"They call Paris the mother of liberal arts and letters," Christine said breathlessly, in her deep, throaty, musical voice with its rolling southern *r*'s. She walked quickly and easily, propelling her lean little body so expertly over the dirt that her feet didn't seem to touch the ground. Owain liked the respect in her voice. "Equal to ancient Athens," he added. He was just repeating a chance remark he'd heard somewhere; but he felt proud when she turned to him in surprise, and rewarded him with a glowing smile.

"The other colors you dilute in water, with gum . . . pine gum or fir gum," Anastaise said, her voice flat and concentrating, watching the thick liquid hover before dropping into the little vessel. "It's only these two—the red and white lead—that you mix with egg white. Minium, the red one's called. The white is ceruse."

They'd found her fumbling with the bolts at the courtyard gate when they got back to Christine's home in Old Temple Street, Owain loaded up with Christine's purchases—parchment scrolls and a cloth-wrapped package they'd stopped to pick up from a tiny, bent-over goldsmith in a workshop filled with slanting sunlight and glittering dust, one of several workshops they'd dropped in at. She'd looked up in relief as they'd walked up. "I can't open it," she'd said, without preliminaries, and nodded down at herself. Owain realized why: she was trying to do the bolts with one hand. The other big raw hand was nursing a bunch of wilting blue cornflowers, wrapped in muslin.

Anastaise was a big, blowsy woman in her middle years, who towered over Christine. She had a bold look in her eye and a ready tongue, and a rude good humor shining on her reddish cheeks; but she and the fine-drawn, high-minded Madame de Pizan were clearly on the best of terms. "They say Paris is the center of the world of illuminations," Christine told Owain proudly, as they walked inside and put their packages down on the scriptorium table, "and you've met some of the finest illuminators and miniaturists in the world today; but, whatever you hear anywhere else, Anastaise is the greatest of them all."

"Ahhh—get along with you," Anastaise replied roughly, but Owain could see her color up, redder than before; and he caught her smiling to herself as she tucked her greasy pepper-and-salt hair back inside her kerchief.

He stayed in the room, hovering, unwilling to go and miss finding out how this queen of illuminators worked, but uncertain what to do with himself as Anastaise got to work and Christine opened the big ledger in the corner to enter her purchases. He whistled under his breath and tried to be inconspicuous, and watched. He was going over in his mind their brief stop at the illuminators' table on the way out of the busy scriptorium in central Paris, where Christine had bought the parchment scrolls. The little man in there, wearing a splotched apron, almost a hunchback, with piercing pale eyes under a bare head, only a few wisps of baby hair still wafting out of its freckles, had caught the newcomer trying to see what he was drawing.

"You want to see, don't you?" asked the little man, whom Owain now knew was Jean Malouel (until last year the head painter to the Duke of Burgundy). And he'd scuttled off, sideways, like a crab, Owain thought, to the shelves and tables at the back of the room, where unattended pieces of parchment were laid out, weighed down with stones and pots—which Owain guessed must be uncompleted work at different stages, drying, waiting for the next coat of color, or just to be bound.

"Here," Malouel said finally, "no one is supposed to see this; but you've got no one here to tell, have you?" He beckoned Owain over. There was a pleased, expectant grin on his face.

The little square was a jewel: so bright and vividly alive that Owain gasped. He'd never seen anything like this. It was almost like reality. No, it was better than reality: more perfect than anything he'd ever have thought it possible to imagine. The world writ small; but with its everyday flaws and dirt and minor uglinesses painted out. He could see at once that it showed the Royal Palace he'd just walked past outside, though from an angle he didn't yet know. He recognized the blond walls, the gatehouse at the western tip of the Island, and the blue-green roofs, with tall round cones topping the towers, mostly in the same almost turquoise blue as the roofs, but a few marked out in a red as rich as rubies. The delicate tracery of the Holy Chapel tower, with its rose window and fingers of stone rising to the heavens, topped by a gleaming golden cross. The river, lapping against the green by the shore, with a boat and a blue-coated boatman approaching the steps of the gatehouse. The glory of daylight and sunshine. His eyes dwelt greedily on the paler greens of the picture's foreground—the Left Bank, showing early summer grass and sprouting vines, with each tiny tendril somehow got down separately, and three bare-legged laborers, one in blue, one in white, one in red, backs bowed with effort, reaping their corn, swinging their scythes and sweating in their field, under their straw hats. But it was the blue of the sky that truly caught Owain's imagination. It deepened, from a pale, delicate near-white behind the rooftops, through a thousand peaceful shades, to the deep, near-night color of the summer heaven at its heights. How had the artist done that, he wondered; bending down; peering closer; not quite daring to touch. How could anyone but God have so effortlessly imitated the Creator's design?

Malouel had met Owain's eye; bashful and welcoming, both at once. Sagely, he'd said: "That's June, that one. My three nephews are doing it—it's good work. You can see that, can't you? . . . But what you don't know yet is that now you've seen it, you'll see the June outside differently from now on. It changes your eye forever, seeing something as good as this. You mark my words."

Owain remembered that now, as he edged closer to where Anastaise was beginning to lay out careful brushstrokes of whitish paint on her own small, empty square drawn on a leaf of parchment covered in neatly sloping writing. There was another blank—a margin—around the edge of the page. She'd already told him the cornflowers she'd harvested that morning, at dewfall, from the garden of the beguine convent by the Hôtel Saint-Paul, where she was a lay sister, were the ingredient that gave the azure blue of the sky that had so mesmerized him while he was looking at the Limbourg brothers' picture of June. And he wanted to see her make that.

Quietly, from the other side of the room, from above her ledgers, Christine watched Owain inch forward as Anastaise pulled the heads off the cornflowers, ground them with mortar and pestle until there was nothing but a slimy blue juice in the bottom, and dipped her paintbrush into it. She let herself enjoy the pleasure that the boy's intent gaze brought her. It was so long since she'd seen innocence this childlike. It made her feel young.

"There, you see," Anastaise said contemplatively. Owain

didn't jump; but he realized she was talking to him, holding out the square to him, and he was grateful. She'd filled the page with wet, gleaming blue the color of the sky. "That's the first layer," she went on. "It's not how it's going to look in the end, though. To get the color the way you want, you need to paint over it—four or five layers, one by one."

"What will you paint on top of the blue?" Owain asked, but she only rumbled with laughter. "Listen to the boy!" she chortled. "We're not there yet. Do you know how long this will take to dry?"

He felt abashed. Malouel had told him. "Ten days," he said. She nodded; gave him a twinkle.

"Learning already," she replied; then, play-reproachfully, "and that's just one coat. So it can take a good couple of months to do the purple of a cloak or the green of a wood properly. But it's important to get it right. The beauty is in the brightness. And it's important to make it as beautiful as you can."

"May I . . . ?" Owain essayed, growing bolder. "May I see something you've already finished?"

She put her big hands on her big hips, gave him her bold stare, and burst out laughing. "You've got the bug, all right," she said. "Madame Christine; you've infected this one, good and proper."

Christine was smiling too, from her corner. "Show him this," she said; and pulled out another book from the shelf. She brought it forward to the table. Owain hardly noticed the text. His eyes were drawn only to the picture under Christine's pale fingers: another little square full of more moving, breathing vitality than seemed possible. It showed a woman in a modest blue dress, whose white kerchief was pulled up in imitation of a proper fashionable two-horned court headdress. The woman was kneeling in the center of a group of women, and handing over a book to a magnificent red and gold lady with a green and gold silk sash and a rich jeweled headdress and ermine sleeves; a lady sitting with two attendants on scarlet and green cushions by a mullioned window, hung with fleur-de-lys cloths in blue and gold, and with the sky outside glowing the azure blue Owain now knew how to prepare. There was so much to look at; so much to take in.

"That's you," he said, turning to Christine. "Giving your book to the Queen."

The painted Christine looked just as she did in real life: alert, watchful, ready both to fight and charm. But the Queen of France had deteriorated since this picture was made: the painted Queen was still a beautiful woman, with traces of kindness lingering on her face; though you could also see in her set eyes that she'd brook no one else's nonsense. The much fatter, older person he'd seen in the flesh yesterday had become a spoiled, glinty-eyed monster. He'd smelled the selfishness, the willfulness, coming off her; he'd known her at once for the kind of woman who'd stop at nothing to get her own way.

"I knew at once," Owain said warmly, "what a picture." But he was wondering as he spoke, and saw Anastaise dimpled with pleasure, whether she'd deliberately made the Queen seem younger and kinder—she didn't seem the type for flattery. Instead, he asked, "How do you get the gold so bright?"

Anastaise was breaking open one of Christine's packages to show him the wafer-thin sheet of beaten gold and beginning to explain that you took beaten egg white, without water, and painted it over the place the gold was to go, then, moisturizing the end of the same brush in your mouth, you touched it onto the corner of the leaf, ready cut, then lifted it very quickly, put it on the prepared place, and spread it out with a separate dry brush. "And whatever you do, don't breathe; or your piece of gold will fly off and you'll have the worst trouble finding it again. And then it's the same as the painting. You let it dry. You put another layer on. You let it dry. You put another layer on. It's all just patience." When the gold was ready, you polished it—with the tooth of a bear or a beaver; or with an agate, or an amethyst stone—first quite gently, then harder, then so hard that the sweat stood out on your forehead.

Christine slipped away. Owain was so enthralled he didn't notice.

Jehanette's maid was in the kitchen, preparing a meal. The children were playing with their grandmother upstairs; while

Jehanette was at the Halles market. "Take some meat and bread and wine out to Anastaise," Christine directed. "But tell the boy to come here and eat with me."

She didn't think why. It was an instinct: like warming yourself at the fire, or opening your shutters when the sun was bright. Usually she liked her quiet meals with Anastaise: everyone else out of the house; hearing the idle talk the beguine brought with her from the convent where the sisters worked in the cloth trade of Temple New Town, or tending the poor. The beguines knew everything; and no one more than Anastaise. But today she wanted some time alone with this boy with hope in his eyes and hunger in his mind. It was a waste of his intelligence to let him go back to soldiery.

He came quickly, eagerly, glowing as if someone had applied gold leaf to him.

He said, with genuine warmth: "I don't know how to thank you," and, taking a piece of bread and a slab of meat and a slice of onion on his knife, without waiting to be asked, as if he felt at home, while munching, "This has been the best day . . ." Then he paused, and she saw the thought he couldn't name begin to take form on his brow: "I only wish—"

She said, a little brusquely, cutting him off: "Eat up. I find I have some time today after all. When we're done, I'll take you over the river if you like. We could look at the University districts. I can see you're interested."

The look on his face was reward enough. It encouraged her to go on.

"Tell me," she said, leaning forward, supporting her little heart-shaped face with both her hands, and caressing the boy with the gentlest look imaginable, "you're a bright boy; I can see you want knowledge; and, as I understand it, your family history means you aren't encumbered by estates that would take up all your time either. So why haven't you thought of giving a bit of time to educating yourself?" She nodded hypnotically at him, willing him on. "You could, you know . . ."

She saw him stop looking happy. His face got a pinched, miserable expression she didn't like at all.

"What, go to the University, you mean?" he said in a small voice. "In England?"

He didn't know how to explain it to her. He didn't know how to summarize all those years of snubs and sneers from beefy English pageboys and knights and even servants—the jokes about being a wild man from Wales, an eternal outsider—in a voice that wouldn't betray his feelings. "I never thought about it, because I don't think I could. You see, I'm foreign . . ." He gave her a desperate look. "Welsh," he added.

She looked bewildered. "So?" she said; "I'm Venetian by birth; and Guillebert de . . . well, no point in making a list. But there's hardly a native-born Parisian at the University here, or in the world of letters at all. We're all some sort of foreigner. What difference would it make to you, being foreign?"

Owain tried to keep the memory of the sneers he was so used to out of his ears, the mocking of his singsong intonation in English. But he couldn't quite stop tears prickling behind his eyelids.

He took a moment to compose himself. He managed a smile. "In England," he explained, striving for a lightness that still somehow eluded him, "since the uprising in Wales, you can't even marry an Englishwoman if you're Welsh, not without a special dispensation allowing you to be considered an Englishman, which is impossible to get. We're a conquered race, you see . . ."

He looked warily at Christine from under his lashes. Once he'd believed there would be two Welsh universities; they'd been ordered into existence by Owain Glyndŵr when he'd been crowned at Machynlleth ten years before. How could he explain all the details of that history? He thought she'd think he was making excuses. He thought she might get angry.

But Christine wasn't angry. To his surprise, he thought she looked strangely sympathetic. She was gently nodding her head. "So you'd have to teach yourself," she said slowly. "Like I did."

Then she laughed; and she was laughing with him, not at him, he could see. "My God," she said, with grim satisfaction, as if she'd been proved right yet again, "I don't know what would become of our University if there were no foreigners! How provincial the English are . . ."

In this respect, at least, Owain found he was guiltily enjoying her contempt for his adopted country—so much he almost nodded.

She put a sympathetic hand on his, and looked deep into his eyes again. "Shall I tell you how things are here?" she went on. "Norman, Picard, English, German, Fleming, Provençal, Spaniard, Venetian, Roman, you name it, they're all here. The colleges have bursaries, too, so good students don't have to pay for their own studies. You just have to enroll at a college that deals with your nation—they count four nations, and the one that's called the English nation takes the English and the Germans and Flemings and Dutch too. Whyever wouldn't they take the Welsh? If you were ever to want to go to university in Paris, there would be no problem. And if they turned you down, it certainly wouldn't be because of your nationality."

There was a deliberately comical look of astonishment in her eyes at that outlandish notion. She was shaking her head.

"Eat up," she said, suddenly purposeful, and he let himself be drawn to his feet. "Let's go."

It was late when they came back from the University. But Owain's eyes were still shining.

She said: "I'll put another book out for you. For when you've finished this one. It's one of my early ones, something I wrote when Jean was going to go away to England. Advice to a young man; on how to learn to learn. I thought it might appeal."

His face lightened even more; then suddenly darkened with memory. He said: "But I'll have to go . . ."

She said: "How long can you stay?"

He fell silent. He scuffed one toe against the other foot. She could see him remembering his pointless existence; waiting in palace corridors; being left out by English pageboys and aides with a proper claim to their lords' time. "My lord of Clarence will be off in a day or two," he said eventually. He eyed her for a moment, as if thinking.

What Owain was fumbling toward articulating was that he wanted to find a way to stay on after Clarence left. These Parisians—fearful as they all seemed, with the memory of their conflict so recent on them that you could practically smell the blood on them, so fresh that they didn't yet have words to talk about it—were, at the same time, full of a joy he didn't know: the pleasure of being here, where they were, doing what they did. They knew something that made it almost irrelevant if the great men of the day destroyed each other over their heads. They might tremble at the profound crisis they were caught up in, and mourn the passing of the established order of the world they knew. But they believed in something universal that couldn't be destroyed. They were putting their hope in beauty. Owain had never had a day when so many enticing futures opened up before him. He didn't know whether he wanted to go and enroll at the University, or just stay in this house with these warm, kindly people and read himself into the life they lived. But he wanted to be here.

"Did Anastaise tell you?" she asked, as if she were changing the subject. "She took a poultice this morning to an old woman with sores under her arms that Anastaise said looked like plague sores."

She saw the flicker on his face; she didn't think it was fear. "I'm wondering," she went on. "Perhaps I should tell my lord of Clarence you've been exposed to the miasma, out here in the town. Perhaps I should suggest you stay on until a doctor gives you the all-clear." She poured him a cup of wine. "You could rejoin them at Calais later," she murmured; the voice of temptation. Then, realizing that the Duke of Clarence might well be heading straight back to Normandy to go on making war, she added, with asperity, "or wherever the Duke prefers." She put the jug down. There was a hint of mischievous laughter in her voice when she said: "After all, it would be a service to him to make sure his men didn't get ill." She could take Owain to meet a friend or two from the University in the next few days; set wheels in motion.

"But," Owain said, hesitating naively, "there wouldn't be a risk of illness. I haven't really been exposed to any miasma, have I?" Hastily, he added: "Though I would love to stay . . ."

She caught his eye—a challenge. She raised her eyebrows. Cheerfully, she said: "Well then—lie! It would be in a good cause. I can't imagine God would mind." And when she saw the disbelieving grin spread over his face, she knew he would.

FIVE

The English hunted for a day with the Queen. The next day, they invited Catherine and her ladies to hunt with them. Queen Isabeau said no. Perhaps she didn't want to goad Louis anymore. Perhaps she just didn't want to be reminded that her daughter had no ladies to speak of—that the two youngest royal children, more or less forgotten on the edge of the court, lived the peculiar, twilight, scrounging existence they did. So the English left by dusk that night, in the purposeful flurry of green and brown that seemed to be their way. And, a day later, everything was back to normal—at least, back to the upside-down normal of the times of the King's illnesses.

Catherine and Charles sat idly in the garden together. It was too hot to be inside. Their mother's door was shut. The servants weren't there. There was no food. As usual, there was nothing to do.

Charles threw a pebble into the fountain, trying to make it skim and bounce. It went straight down. But he was whistling. She could see he was glad the English had gone, with their marriage proposal.

"I tell you what," he said, a few failed skims later. "I heard Mother and Marguerite whispering away together earlier. Planning something. Both looking really excited." He did an imitation of evil busily on the loose: hunching his shoulders forward in a one-man conspiracy, jokily narrowing his eyes into devil slits, darting them furtively from side to side, smacking his lips,

51

and leering. "Of course they shut up when they noticed I was listening. But I bet I know what they're up to. They're going to get their own back on Louis for being rude to the English Duke."

Catherine sighed. They were both scared of their mother's temper; and her plots.

But there was nothing else to look forward to. "I wonder what they'll do to him?" she said, a little apprehensively. Charles didn't reply. After a long moment's silence, she picked up a pebble herself.

They were lying under an apple tree in the orchard, flicking twigs up at the unripe fruit, when Christine appeared an hour later, calling for them.

She had a basket on her arm. She had a young man with her.

They hardly noticed him. They flew at her; two raggedy children, calling in thin, eager voices, "Christine! Christine!" and "What's in your basket?" and "I'm starving!" They dived at the basket and, with tremendous animation, began laying out the food she'd brought. Very ordinary food. Early strawberries. Some cheese in a cloth. Last night's beef leftovers. A couple of eggs. A hunk of bread.

"Can we eat now?" Charles was begging, hanging on Christine's arm. "Please?" A funny little thing, Owain thought: eleven or twelve, but undersized, like a much younger boy, with a white face and a rabbit's red eyes and a big, bulbous nose. His voice was squeaky and babyish. And why was a Prince of France dressed like that? In old rags that Owain would have been ashamed of wearing; dirty, too?

Then he turned to the little Princess, who was sitting on the long grass, unwrapping the cloth from round the cheese with the tender excitement of someone who'd never seen food before. Like her brother, she was also in plain, old, crumpled clothes, with her skirts so much too long for her that they seemed made for someone else. She'd tied a knot in one side, perhaps to let her run or climb trees without tripping up. Her hair was loose; he could see a kerchief lying on the ground not far away. It was pretty hair; long and thick. But it was all tangles with bits of grass in it. She'd looked a young woman in the royal chambers, in her finery; but now she was nothing more than a scruffy child. Owain was wondering, rather disapprovingly, how these children came to look so neglected, when Catherine absentmindedly lifted one hand, twisted her hair into a knot at the nape of her neck, and turned to smile up at him.

And all at once Owain was lost for breath. How slim and long her neck was, how lovely the line of it, rising from her soft shoulders.

The sun was behind him. She was blinking a little, trying to focus her eyes on the tall shape before her; but he didn't think she could really see him. He didn't think she recognized him, or was remembering her own kindness in sparing his blushes at his Duke's audience with her mother. She was only smiling that blind, vulnerable, enchanting smile out of a child's pleasure at the presence of Christine, and the picnic, and something to do to relieve what he could see had been boredom.

But thinking those sensible thoughts didn't stop the soft sense of wonder stealing through him as he stood and stared back, entranced by the sight of her, feeling his heart swell with joy.

It was Charles who broke the spell: Charles, wriggling and giggling around Christine, until she put firm arms on his skinny shoulders and said reprovingly, "Of course you can't eat yet; not till I've introduced my guest. Where are your manners?"

That got the child's attention all right. He turned straight to Owain, staring. Rudely, Owain thought; but then, whatever he was wearing, he was, after all, a prince of the blood, and allowed to stare at anyone he chose. He narrowed his eyes. "I know you!" he cried, almost accusingly. "You're the one who held the casket while the English Duke gave my sister a jewel. Aren't you?"

Owain nodded, and bowed. "The very same," he said easily, doing his best to charm. "Owain Tudor." He'd half turned to face the little boy; but he was blissfully, agonizingly aware, at the same time, of the girl looking up at him from below, muttering, with pink cheeks and a prettily awkward air, "I remember you now, of course, it's just that you look different, out here in the sun."

You must be informal, Christine had said; just call them by their names; no bowing and scraping. In the gardens they're just children; they're very quiet; shy; it's wrong to scare them with formalities; we're old friends. All the same, he wished now he'd put on something better than the simple tunic he was wearing. For reasons he didn't understand, he wanted to cut as elegant a figure as he could.

Christine, also visibly keen to make the introductions go smoothly, said, in a special child-voice whose gentleness surprised Owain, "Owain is from a noble family of Wales—the kings of Powys Magog." She pronounced the Welsh words strangely, but he was surprised and flattered that she'd even tried to reproduce the unfamiliar name; flattered, too, that she was describing his lineage with such respect, when he'd got used, almost, to being all but invisible among Englishmen; to sitting below the salt; to being ignored. "I thought you'd enjoy showing him the gardens, and the lion."

Little Charles didn't look as though he'd enjoy that at all. For someone supposedly so shy, there was a definite aggression in his expression. He was scowling. He said: "But the English party is supposed to have gone. They told us in the kitchens. Why are you still here?"

Owain opened his mouth to make a soft reply. But he wasn't sorry when Christine got there first. The truth was that he wouldn't have been sure what to say about why he was still in Paris, or, indeed, at the Hôtel Saint-Paul. Christine had suggested he come with her so he could see the famous gardens at the King's favorite Paris home, though he'd had a feeling she really just wanted to show off her friendship with the King's children. Not everyone was on such intimate terms with princes; and he'd begun to see that Christine, magnificent though she was, wasn't above vanity.

"Owain was only temporarily attached to the Duke of Clarence," Christine told the pouting little boy reassuringly. Owain could tell from the practiced way she patted at him that this suspicious, feral child must often take a lot of reassuring. "He's not with them anymore. The rest of the English have gone, darling. I doubt they'll be back." She patted again. The little boy's eyes lost their fierce look. "But Owain wanted to stay on in Paris for a while to see if he'd like to study at the University. He's my guest. And he's reading my modest collection of books while he's here. Racing through them. An example to all of us. An example to you!" she finished brightly.

Little Charles wasn't quite satisfied yet. But he put his concerns, whatever they were, to one side; nodded briefly at Owain, and said again to Christine, even more plaintively: "So can we eat now?"

Owain's heart leapt. He saw that Catherine was still watching him from her place on the long grass, catching his eye so he'd be sure to notice her. She was shrugging slightly and casting her eyes upward, in a quiet, friendly apology for her brother's awkward manners.

He smiled back at her, grateful for the thought; wondering why she had her hand clamped, as she did, across her mouth. It looked like a gag. She didn't seem conscious of it. It was an ugly gesture. Then she forgot him. She was hungry too. And she was still a child. As Charles threw himself down beside her, ready to snatch at the food she'd set out, she moved her hand, freed her mouth, turned a teasing grin on her brother, and plucked the bit of bread he was aiming for off its cloth. "Too late," she mumbled with it in her mouth. Charles pouted; then, seeing Christine smile, he started to laugh too.

There was a breadcrumb on the side of her lip. There was a mischievous glint in her eye. There was sun in her hair. Owain, who'd thought he was excited and happy before, seeing the world, caught up in adventure, could hardly believe the trembling intensity of the joy he now felt just watching her, as he and Christine slid down to their knees to join the picnic.

Charles led the way to the lion cage. Food had improved his mood. So had the exchange he'd begun as soon as he had an egg inside him and a slice of beef and most of the strawberries.

"Does the King of England really want to marry Catherine and take her away?" he'd asked Owain, and his eyes had had both fierceness and a kind of mute plea in them.

"Yes," Owain said kindly, understanding what was making the child look so glum—fear of losing his playmate if she married—and feeling sorry for him.

"*No,*" Christine said at the same time, with much more force. "He knows we'll say no—we already said no to him as a husband for Princess Isabelle, because he's a . . ." Looking at Owain, she refrained from saying "usurper," but only just. "In any case, he doesn't want a marriage. He wants war. He's already started harping on about English claims to France. He'll just use any marriage negotiations to pick a quarrel with France. He's looking for a grievance. It would be naive to think anything else."

There was a short pause. Owain, feeling shocked that he hadn't understood how hostile some of the French might feel toward his King and, trying not to resent Christine's sudden brusque rudeness, looked carefully away. But he saw little Charles nodding, clearly believing Christine. "Let's go to the lions," Charles piped up, looking suddenly much more cheerful. He bounded off through the bowers and trellises and artful fountains and sprays of roses.

Owain brought up the rear. The royal gardens were so extraordinary that he quickly forgot the sting of Christine's tongue and was soon turning his head from side to side, admiring statues; views; flowers; nightingale cages; fountains gleaming with silver fishes. Miracles.

Everyone stopped when they got to the great wrought-iron cage. Inside, a matted, maddened lion paced, backward and forward, backward and forward, over its droppings, snarling. It was menace in animal form. It was golden; it was stinking; a king humiliated. It never stopped trying to escape. Even now, in this heat, it was pulling the chain that ran from its collar to the stake in the ground as taut as it could, testing the possibilities, following its instinct, feeling for a way out.

A silence fell on them all as they admired its powerful shoulders and the magnificent lines of its muzzle and its tawny, deadly eyes.

"Has it ever got out?" Owain asked, in a dazed voice.

No one answered.

Charles whispered: "They feed it a whole dog, or a pig, or a sheep, every day." He added, without expression: "The animals always scream before they die."

After a while, Catherine asked, just as quietly: "Does the King of England keep lions?"

As she spoke, she glanced up toward Christine, who was standing well back from the cage. She was looking past the lion into the distance; lost in some private thought of her own, which, to judge from the tragic expression on her face, wasn't a happy one.

Catherine turned her steady gaze back on Owain.

Owain had no idea if there had ever been a lion in England. And his head was too full of lion-stink and heat to be able to think straight. But there was nothing he wanted more than to feel her eyes on him. "There's an elephant at the Tower of London," he said. He'd heard the story, even if he hadn't seen the elephant on his few brief trips to London. And he'd seen a picture of an elephant once. It was the most impressive thing he could think of to say.

"What's an elephant like?" Catherine asked.

"Huge and gray," he said boldly, describing the picture he remembered, beginning to enjoy his story. "Like a giant dog. And instead of a nose it has an extra limb—curving up, in the shape of a horn."

He'd hoped to astonish her with his fabulous beast. But she just nodded, matter-of-factly, as if she saw elephants every day. Perhaps being among miracles at all times took away the edge of shock.

Then, after another furtive glance at Christine, she added in a whisper: "And what's Henry of England like?"

She moved a little closer.

Owain paused, trying desperately to marshal his thoughts. She smelled of roses.

"Honest," he muttered, thinking defiantly that he could at least do something to right the damningly wrong impression Christine had given of his King. "Straightforward. Good-tempered . . . A good planner . . . And an excellent master: everyone who serves him loves him . . ."

He glanced up at Christine himself, hoping she was still staring past the lions, thinking her thoughts and not listening to him.

Catherine was so close now that she couldn't help but catch the movement of his eyes and know what he was thinking. She bit her lip; but the breathless beginning of a giggle escaped anyway. She nodded conspiratorially at him. "It's all right," she whispered, "Christine's not listening."

For a moment they stood too close, exchanging glances, not quite laughing. He was dizzy with the intimacy of it; dizzy with the bees buzzing around him. Then she went back to prompting him: "And the court, the English court? What's that like?"

Owain hardly knew anything of the court, either. He'd served at banquets—three hours of silent eating. He'd ridden behind hunts. But he didn't know if any of that would impress her, any more than the elephant had. He let the smell of roses and warm skin drift delightfully into his nostrils. He hesitated. He wanted to make England attractive. But he wanted to tell her the truth, too.

Hesitantly, he began: "Not as magnificent as this . . . and London isn't a quarter the size of Paris." His head cleared. Suddenly he knew what might appeal to someone brought up in times as uncertain as those Catherine had known here—times, he thought, with sudden understanding, that had perhaps been almost as uncertain as those he'd known, in a different way. He'd tell her what had appealed to him about coming to England—it had been exactly the same thing. He went on, with greater confidence: "But it's very orderly. Dignified. Decorous. Calm. The King and his brothers and his three Beaufort uncles rule together, wisely and in perfect unison . . . and the people love them all."

She was nodding now; looking thoughtful; wistful even. He'd been right. She was impressed by that.

Louder, because it would be foolhardy to expect Christine not to come out of her reverie sooner or later, and seriously, because he wanted the pleasure of watching Catherine's lips move and eyes dance and neck sway as she considered her reply, he asked: "And what about here? The French court . . . what's *that* like?"

She thought. Her forehead wrinkled enchantingly.

But it was Charles who, turning away from the lion at last, broke in with an answer. "Dancing and debauchery!" he shouted, throwing out both arms as if taunting a mob.

Catherine laughed, a little uneasily. "He doesn't know what it means," she told Owain. "It's just something they were shouting in the street . . . last year . . . when there was . . ." Then, as Owain's startled look sank in, she turned crossly to her little brother and reprimanded him: "You mustn't say that! I've told you so many times!"

"I do know what it means. There was a ball here once when four men dressed up as hairy savages," Charles piped up stubbornly. "They were supposed to jump out and scare the ladies. But their costumes caught fire on a torch, and two of them burned to death before everyone's eyes," he added with ghoulish relish. "You can imagine the screaming."

"Did that really happen?" Owain couldn't help asking. You never knew, here. Perhaps it had. "Were you there?"

With something like regret, the little voice replied: "No . . . before I was born." And the pinched, freckled boy's face clouded.

Catherine said: "But I went to the Court of Love once . . . my uncle's idea . . . the Duke of Orléans . . ."

She dimpled at Owain.

He softened: "And what was *that*?" he asked.

"A kind of repeating ball. No, more than that: an idea, a place where people could meet—the officers of the Court of Love—and talk about chivalry, judge cases of unhappy love, and learn how to be true lovers themselves . . ." she said, being careful with her words. He could see she remembered it with affection.

"And everyone wore beautiful clothes, too," she added,

with childlike regret; "we don't have anything like that anymore . . . not since . . ."

Charles said: ". . . my uncle was murdered." There was ghoulish pleasure in his eyes.

There was a rush of air behind them. All three young people froze, as if they'd been caught doing something terribly wrong. Christine had come to herself. With a whisk of bony elbows, she broke into their little circle, clearly annoyed at the way the conversation was going. "You were three at the Court of Love," she said sharply to Catherine. "And he's been dead for seven years. If there's nothing like that now, then there's no reason to talk about it anymore, either. It might well have done us all more good if there'd been less idle talk about chivalry back then, and more sensible thought about real life."

She put a determined arm through Owain's. Looking sideways as he was pulled away from Catherine's side, their eyes met again; another shared look full of quiet laughter and delight.

"It's getting late," Christine said, pointing at the long shadows. She tried to keep her voice strict, but she couldn't help sounding relieved. She'd never brought anyone here with her, except Anastaise and her own Jean, who hardly counted, to meet these children. She'd always been afraid that Catherine and Charles might turn silent; stare; run away like deer into the woods. But this day had gone so easily. They'd loved the Welsh boy. She'd wanted them to. She admired him herself: she liked the way he'd found through adversity—the questions, the bright eyes, the unquenched hope. He was already bringing the younger children out of their quiet little selves; he was getting them to talk. Christine was pleased with her experiment.

Catherine bowed her head. "Will you come back tomorrow?" she asked submissively, going up to Christine to kiss her cheeks, and, perhaps by accident, almost brushing Owain's arm as she passed. "We have so many books—hundreds of them, the most beautiful in the world. You're allowed into the library anyway, Christine, but what about . . ." She dimpled over at Owain, plucking up courage. "*He'd* like to see them too, wouldn't he? . . . Will you bring Owain?"

The air was cool and dusty in the hush of this room. The library walls were lined with treasures in jeweled calf bindings. Owain couldn't bear even to look at his guide, though he was dimly aware, through the thunderous beating of his heart, that beside him Catherine's cheeks were flushed from the heaviness of the grown-up green velvet houppelande she was wearing again, and that there were tiny, wilting flowers scattered through the loose weave of her veil.

"Show him the beautiful *Consolations of Philosophy,*" Christine was whispering excitedly to Catherine. "And your grandfather's Book of Hours . . . this was the old King's library, once, Owain."

Only Charles, reluctantly bringing up the rear, was spoiling the mood. He was scuffing his feet and looking mutinous, and a stream of unending childish complaints were coming from his lips.

"Let's go and see the lions instead," he kept saying, just too loud for anyone else's comfort; ". . . I don't want to sit inside all day . . . it's so hot . . . I don't know why Catherine's suddenly so interested in books; she isn't usually . . . I want to climb a tree . . . Christine?"

"Shh, darling," Christine kept murmuring, in that strangely gentle voice Owain had noticed her using with the little boy before; "let's just stay here for a while more . . ."

But eventually she sighed and gave in. "I'll bring him back in an hour," she said to Catherine, trying to sound firm. "Not a minute more."

Charles wasn't listening. He was pulling her out of the door.

For a moment, Owain thought his overstretched heart would stop altogether. He had no idea at all what he'd say to Catherine; he was appalled and overjoyed at the same time by the possibility that he might spend the next hour this close to her, yet might also disgrace himself with utter, tongue-tied, childish silence. In the event, however, as soon as the footsteps died away in the corridor, leaving him alone with Catherine, but for the scribe copying something in a shaft of sunlight at the other end of the room, Owain's wits came back to him.

He hardly knew what he was doing. He certainly didn't think it out before he spoke. But he found himself catching Catherine's eye and, with a daring grin, breathing the words: "Do you have the *Romance of the Rose* here?"

It was pure mischief to ask. The *Romance,* he knew, was Christine's great hate: she called it the most immoral book in Christendom. Written more than a century earlier, in two parts, by two men, it was also one of the most famous love stories in existence. But it was only since he'd heard Christine fulminating against it that Owain had started to want to see it for himself. His understanding was that the first part was a harmless enough allegory about a Lover in the Garden of Desire, trying to get near the Rose he adores, but failing, when Jealousy raises walls all around to keep him out. It was the second half, written years later by Jean de Meun, that Christine really disliked. There were two reasons for her hate. Not only did de Meun's Lover manage, after all, to seduce the Rose, (while ungallantly making out that women were capricious, stupid, vicious, garrulous, gullible, greedy, and lascivious by nature)—but the author also made abundantly clear, through his story, that he didn't believe in the sanctity of the lifelong bond of marriage, as Christine did. For de Meun, there was only lust.

Owain knew Christine had made her reputation, while still young and little known, by denouncing the book publicly, in an exchange of letters with University men which she copied to the court, and to the Queen. And Owain wanted to show Catherine, here, today, now, that he was the kind of man who knew about such things.

For a split second, Catherine looked terrified. Then, with an answering flash of mischief, she grinned quickly back. Her lips parted slightly; her eyes went wide, as if she were considering the delicious possibilities of this act. Letting the pent-up breath he hadn't realized he was holding gently out, he could see that she could see he knew Christine's feelings about this book. "Christine would be so angry . . ." she whispered, but she was already disappearing into the gloom. When she came out, she had a book in her hand.

It was only the innocent first volume, Owain saw with disappointment when they put it on the bookstand and, standing side by side in front of it, carefully opened it, finding the first jewel-like colors of tiny lovers listening to miniature musicians strumming lutes in a cloud of roses. Still, he reasoned, that meant Christine would have less reason to be angry; perhaps he should be relieved. Perhaps he should admire Catherine's caution.

But then he forgot everything, except that Catherine was standing by him, so close he could feel the warmth of her shoulder against his arm, and the whole side of his body nearest to her was on quiet fire, and he could smell rose oil. Breathing softly and shallowly, Catherine stretched a finger toward the first words, as if she found it hard to make out the narrow upright script, and as she did so her arm brushed so close to his chest that it almost touched his heart. And all at once they were lost in the roses, caressing the vellum as they gently turned the pages, sighing out the words, as if to themselves, or to each other . . .

Catherine turned the page. "Ohh," she murmured, scarcely more than a breath of regret; "there's no more . . ."

Their eyes met. There was no reason for them to go on standing so close. But Owain couldn't turn away; couldn't step back. For a long moment they went on looking quietly into each other's eyes; as if they could have stayed there forever, just watching each other.

Then Owain heard footsteps from far away in the corridor, and the querulous words: ". . . but it's so boring inside! Can't we have another picnic?" and, when he recovered from the shock and looked back down toward Catherine, he realized, feeling bereft and quietly relieved at the same time, that she wasn't by his side anymore, and the book wasn't on the stand, either.

By the time Christine and Charles walked back in, Owain was standing in front of the bookstand, head bowed, eyes following his finger, struggling to read the first words of Boethius'

Consolations of Philosophy, translated into French; and Catherine, standing well back, with her hands clasped demurely in front of her, was listening.

Christine, whose attention was mostly still on the fractious small boy tugging at her arm, longing to be off, looked pleased at the sight of the older ones reading. She didn't seem to notice either the hint of a smile that kept coming to Owain's face, or the excessively bright innocence of the sidelong glances that Catherine was flashing at her from under thick, sweeping lashes.

So much, in the days that followed, made Owain feel as if he'd walked into a magical world of dreams come true. Without his even needing to do anything to change his life, a future he'd never have thought possible was almost settled, almost at once. Christine's friend Jean de Gerson, the elderly chancellor of the University of Paris (and, in the old days, her great ally in the quarrel of the *Romance of the Rose*), offered Owain a place to study as soon as Christine recommended him. Gerson, Owain knew, was a wise man; Gerson had thought at once of the brilliant, devious former Chancellor of free Wales, Owain Glyndŵr's man, Gruffydd Young—who was now in exile in Paris—and suggested Young might be the man to vouch for Owain Tudor's good character. Now all Owain was waiting for was for Gerson to suggest to the other canons of Notre Dame Cathedral that a bursary be found too. "Once you know about *that*," Christine said, leaning forward so her eyes shone in the trembling candle flame, making her voice resonate darkly and persuasively, "you can write to your Duke, or King, and ask to be relieved of your service for a couple of years."

Whenever Owain remembered the confused, dizzy happiness of the next few weeks, what came first to his mind was the heat: a scorching June, with the flagstones burning underfoot as he came out from the royal library. He was usually alone for a couple of hours in those cool rooms. Charles seemed to have been right; Catherine didn't often want to be in the library. Later, with Catherine (and Charles, though Charles he noticed only with the kindly indifference of a grown-up man for a child) he recalled laughing breathlessly and seeking out shade and water for their picnics; and ignoring Christine's remonstrations, and running barefoot to the fountains, dipping their toes in.

"Have you ever seen someone kill someone?" Owain heard, as he stared up at the ribbons of cloud and smelled the crushed grass under his back.

It was Charles' voice: thin and small and careful.

Owain's voice was also small and careful as—trying not to let any actual memories enter his head—he replied: "Yes."

Charles was lying beside him. The boy had quietly put himself there, in Owain's shadow, like a smaller animal looking for protection. Catherine was sitting curled up round her knees, just behind them, plaiting grasses. Christine was picking grasses for her.

"My brother tried to kill a man," Charles said. "A man in a brown leather tunic. He was one of the men who broke in last year. He ran into the ballroom where Louis was holding a ball and started shouting at him that he was a disgrace and that he shouldn't be allowed to be king."

"Just what Maman is always saying . . ." Catherine added, still braiding. They were both talking quietly, as if in a dream.

"And Louis got a look on his face," Charles went on. "A horrible look. And he got out his dagger. He stabbed him three times. But the man kept shouting. He wouldn't die, however often Louis stabbed him. The blade just got stuck in the leather. Then everyone started shouting and running around. And all the other men ran in; they were breaking windows to get at us."

"You saw all that?" Owain said, raising himself on an elbow and looking at the boy.

"I was behind the arras. We often go and watch when there's a ball. There's a tear in the tapestry. Sometimes the servants let us take some food there. Catherine wasn't there that night. They let her dress up and go to the ball. So it was just me. I thought they'd kill everyone. Then find me."

"How did it end?" Owain asked.

"Our cousin of Burgundy came in. He had his own men-at-arms. He had the ones who were shouting sent out. But after he'd gone, with all his men and all the intruders, everyone who was left, the guests, were saying it was all really his fault—that he must have been behind it all—otherwise how could he have known to turn up at that moment with soldiers?"

He shivered. So did Catherine. "Our cousin of Burgundy is always behind everything," she whispered.

"You must have been scared," Owain murmured, keeping compassionate eyes on Charles.

Charles shook his head and colored up. He shrilled: "Princes are never afraid."

Owain said gently: "I grew up in a war. I was often scared. I was just a boy; I was helpless. Sometimes the things I saw came back to me in my dreams."

"You were scared?" Charles said. He looked thoughtful. Then: "I have bad dreams."

Owain shook his head sympathetically. "Mine stayed with me for years," he said. "But give them time. They pass."

Charles nodded. He sat up too, a little closer to Owain. Christine, who'd said nothing during this conversation, smiled to herself and passed Catherine another piece of grass.

There was a silence.

"This is the happiest summer I can remember," Catherine murmured contentedly, lying down on the grass in the shade of a tree full of green apples and stretching herself out. "Even Maman and Louis aren't quarreling as much as usual . . ."

Charles pulled himself up on his elbows, dazed and sated. He had smears of cheese around his mouth and grass in his hair. "Only because Maman agreed to send Marguerite away . . ." he objected, but he sounded cheerful too; as if he were enjoying the argument. "And Papa's still away too . . . ill . . ."

They both looked very serious at that. They nodded solemnly at each other, like much younger children. "Poor Papa," Catherine said piously.

Owain could feel Christine's eyes warningly on him. He had the feeling these two didn't know what was the matter with their father. Christine might be worried that he'd say something tactless. He kept reassuringly still. But Christine changed the subject anyway. She said, tartly: "And, of course, the Duke of Burgundy has called up ten thousand men, and he's sitting in Dijon, just waiting for your mother and Louis to fall out . . . you shouldn't get so carried away by a few days of hot weather that you forget that . . ."

She gave them a chiding look from under the white head-dress that, despite the heat, she wouldn't take off.

But it was too hot and light and safe here in the walled garden to care about ten thousand men in Dijon. Catherine only giggled, just a little nervously, and reached for another strawberry.

"When I get married, it will be a golden day like this," the Princess said, biting into the fruit, looking at it. She was careful not to say whom she planned to marry. She didn't want to annoy Christine. Owain stared at her mouth; at the glistening fruit. She knew he was looking at her. Taking another strawberry, she went on, dreamily, childishly: "And I'll make Maman let me have a dress with cloth of gold, so I'll glitter like the sun. And you'll all be there, watching me, all three of you," and she flashed a beseeching look at Owain, and smiled at the soft glance she got back. "Won't you?" She ate the second strawberry. "And we'll all be as happy as we are today, forever and ever."

"They trust you," Christine said. "Charles has never talked about that before. I'm glad he did."

Modestly, Owain lowered his head. He was leading her mule. They were walking west, along Saint Anthony Street, homeward, into the sunset, dazzled by the thick honey light. It was easy enough to look down. He knew both Charles and Catherine were coming to trust him—just as, he supposed, their father Charles and their uncle Louis of Orléans must have, long ago, as children, come to trust Christine, their own non-royal playmate in the gardens of the Hôtel Saint-Paul. There was a pleasure in the continuity of that tradition started a generation ago by Christine, as well as the personal pleasure Owain felt at his own deepening friendship with this generation of royal children.

Owain spent large parts of his evenings with Christine's books. He was an acolyte; overwhelmed with respect for her writing. He rushed through the books, feverish with words, eager for the next entire imaginary world he knew would be waiting for him inside the next cover. She had written so much: advice to widows, army strategy manuals (how did a woman do that?), an account of the philosopher-king Charles V's life. But what he really wanted to read most, now, were the poems of wistful unrequited love that she'd earned her first money from.

Finding him reading her old poems, Christine gave him someone else's book: the treatise by Andreas Capellanus, *The Art of Honest Love,* in which the rules of the convention of unrequited love known to lovers all over Christendom were set out in three volumes. Owain found it very strange, and not only because it was in Latin, which he struggled to grasp. The delicious sufferings of the knights he understood all too well; the sighs. But, in true courtly love, as depicted in books, it appeared that the lady must always be haughty and superior. Her role was only to educate her lover, whose moral standing must be improved to make him worthy of her. However, he could never hope to improve himself enough to win her. The true aim of their love had nothing to do with achieving the satisfaction of a romantic union. It was a love that could never be satisfied; it was a love that could only exist outside marriage.

When Owain plucked up courage to ask, at Christine's table, why the ladies of the poems must always be so harsh, it was Jean who replied, with a hint of impatience: "Because, if they ever did give in, there'd be nothing to show for all those years of trembling knightly devotion but adultery and moral disaster, would there now?" He shrugged a brusque apology at his mother, but went on. "The idea of courtly love is . . . safer: a lifetime of *spiritual* adultery. Improve and be improved! Pine and be pined for! But never a moment of physical love. Never so much as a kiss."

He laughed at Owain's hot blush. "I've shocked you," he said. "I shouldn't have spoken so plainly." Getting up, he added: "Courtly love poems can make love seem too pretty.

It's not always pretty—love. You're too young to know. You should leave love poetry alone until you've felt it yourself."

"He's working so hard," Christine said after he'd gone, as if excusing her son's tetchiness. It was true. Jean was out of the house long before everyone else was up, making sure there was money coming in, food on the table, but so rushed off his feet with the chancellor's projects that his eyes were drooping before anyone else had finished supper. Christine sighed. There was a tired silence.

A moment later, Owain realized that Christine's sigh signified something quite different from fatigue, or embarrassment that Jean had talked disrespectfully of poetry. She had something on her mind. She wanted to ask him a favor.

Fiddling with a bit of gristle on her platter, and looking down, almost nervously, she cleared her throat and asked if Owain would make a two-day trip out of Paris with her, to visit her daughter Marie, who was a nun at the monastery of Poissy. "Usually Jean takes me; but I can't ask him now; he can't spare the time," she said, and when she looked up he saw her eyes glisten.

Owain had read in one of Christine's books that she had a daughter in a monastery. In her first months of widowhood, he knew, Christine had discovered that the dowry she thought had been put aside by her dead husband for this daughter had been stolen; and, without a bride price, Christine's girl-child could never marry. Marie de Castel's future had been saved by the King of France. When his own daughter, also called Marie, had entered the convent for royal women at Poissy, he'd found Christine's daughter a place at her side, and paid the dowry the nuns demanded out of his own purse. Christine had written about her gratitude for the King's goodness.

But Owain had never heard Marie's name mentioned in her mother's voice. Now, looking at Christine's imploring eyes, which—although he knew she was much too self-possessed to weep—he could swear were soft with unshed tears, he could guess why. It was simple. She missed her daughter.

"I'm allowed to visit her once a year; at the feast of Saint John . . . I don't want to miss it," she was saying, looking down again, and he could hear the pain in her voice now, so clear that he was touched by the bravery with which she'd lived her hard, odd life. When he put a hand on hers, she took comfort from it. She didn't shake it off. Saint John, he calculated: midsummer; in the next few days. "Of course," he said gently. "It will be my pleasure."

She looked up now, blinking; and the smile that came to her face was both relieved and triumphant. She wanted to lighten the atmosphere, he could see; she knew she'd looked vulnerable, and she didn't like to be pitiful. "Thank you," she murmured; then, in more conversational tones: "You'll enjoy it, I think. It's the most beautiful place, Poissy . . . tranquil . . . serene . . ." She laughed, without amusement. "So beautiful that sometimes I think I should go and end my own days there, with my Marie." She blinked again and smiled; Owain saw that, despite her efforts, her eyes were watery again. She'd never have her family all together under one roof again; she'd never be completely happy with her choice, whether it was to be with her son or her daughter; there'd always be regrets.

". . . But not now, of course," Christine went briskly on. She got up from the table. She gestured with her veiny hands at the familiar room, full of the leftovers of dinner and her grandchildren's clutter and the paraphernalia of family life. "There's too much holding me here."

Owain could see her biting her lip as she headed for the door. He sat on at the table, thinking.

He didn't especially want to go to Poissy, not for himself. Owain could think of nothing but staying in Paris; nothing beyond the next few weeks and months here, in this perfect, frenzied, breathless moment, feeling young and full of joy with his confidence growing that every pleasure in life still lay ahead. There was something of the same feeling, he sensed, in Catherine's endless questions about England, which kept coming even though there'd been no further word from the English court about the possible royal marriage. Whenever Christine wasn't listening, Catherine would be whispering another request for information, about the King, jousting, London, the length of royal processions, Parliament, horses, fashions, the royal homes strung along the Thames Valley . . . Owain couldn't permit himself to examine the combination of hope and unease that this day-by-day interrogation aroused in him, but it hovered on the edge of his mind anyway, like a brilliant sunburst, too bright to look at. It was as if each of them were striving toward the place on the map that they sensed was natural for the other.

Still, if Christine wanted him to travel out of Paris with her, he would do her bidding. Of course he would. Even if it meant leaving the city where the sun always seemed to shine and happiness was within such easy reach, it was the least he could do for the woman who'd opened the door to it all.

The storm broke the next day. Over the ruins of a picnic in the gardens, they all heard the sound of hooves in the heat of the afternoon. Half a dozen horses broke the silence; too close; too fast; only reining in a hasty gallop at the gate long enough for a thin, angry male voice to hiss, "Get out of the way, you bloody fool; don't you see who I am?" and for a whip to crack; and then more jingling and neighing as the skittering horses were urged on again, up to the Queen's house, over the flagstones just behind the nearest bushes.

Owain shook himself and raised his head. He didn't know what was habitual here and what was not; he was only responding to the heightening of tension in the others. Charles was sitting straight up. Catherine's head had jerked round to follow the sounds. They were both watching the bushes for any glimpse of the passing horses. Christine was getting to her feet; brushing grass off her skirts.

"Louis," Charles said. His voice was hushed. He sounded scared.

"Trouble," Catherine said, also in a tone of foreboding, following Christine to her feet. Charles scrambled up too.

No one needed to say more. It seemed entirely natural to start off, at a hasty pace somewhere between a walk and a run, in the direction the horses had taken. Breathlessly, Owain followed, heading for trouble too.

The royal Hôtel Saint-Paul was a compound of separate houses set within the gardens. They watched from under a tree in front of the Queen's house. In the heat and softness and grass, it felt unreal to Owain. None of the men on horseback, now reined in and waiting, seemed aware of the four extra sets of footsteps running up, then stopping; of their quick breath. No one turned when Catherine quietly, protectively, put an arm round Charles' trembling shoulder.

"How dare you? How dare you?" Crown Prince Louis was screaming. He'd dismounted. He was waving his whip, but not at the horse, which had its suddenly placid head down in a tub of flowers. His face, whiter than ever, was all huge, black-rimmed, furious eyes. They were locked on the Queen, who, fat and carapaced in green silk, was gleaming like a poison beetle as she looked down at him from the shade of the colonnade. There were some smaller, bright-colored forms behind her; was the whole court watching? Even from here, Owain could see the Queen was smiling.

"Set them free at once. You had no right!" Louis howled, on and on, beside himself, advancing menacingly up the stairs, never shifting his gaze. The Queen ignored his screechings. She stood her ground, and went on smirking and flashing her eyes hypnotically at him as he got closer; as he moved out of the sunlight and into the shadows. It wasn't a nice smile. Owain thought, with a mixture of fascination and repulsion: She's enjoying this.

There was a fast-moving blur in the shadows. Disbelievingly, Owain thought he could distinguish a raised arm; then the crack of leather on flesh.

The Queen stepped forward into the sunlight. Slowly, deliberately, she raised one hand to cup her injured cheek. Louis had struck her with his whip. Even from this distance, Owain could see the red welt on her face. Even from this distance, he could see the triumph in her eye.

There was a strange little whinny of laughter from somewhere very close. He glanced at his three companions. It must have been one of them. But they were straight-faced; concentrating; so somber that he wondered, for an instant, whether it hadn't been he who'd let that terrified laugh escape.

There was a terrible pause before the Queen spoke. Her voice was quiet but carrying; as taut as a whiplash. "You're making a fool of yourself, Louis," she said. Owain could hear the taunt in it. "This isn't how princes of chivalry are supposed to behave to the mothers who raised them, you know."

Louis flinched, and put down the whip.

"But then, what do you care about that? You just do whatever you want, whenever you want; don't let anything get in the way of your satisfaction, whatever it is, however depraved. Don't you?" The female voice was rising now, enough to instill fear, though not quite enough to sound hysterical. "You're still a spoiled child; you think of nothing but 'want, want, want,'" she went on, carefully nursing her welt and her grudge; keeping her rhythm. "And then you're surprised when things don't work out the way you want them to. You're surprised when people start saying someone who can do all the self-willed, degenerate, *dreadful* things you do, without any hesitation, without the least guilt, is going the way your father's gone"—Owain was aware of the hush deepening—"and should be kept from the throne."

She stuck her face out toward him; making sure to stay in the sunlight so all the watchers could see.

"No wonder there are riots and rebellions in Paris," she intoned, gloatingly; "no wonder people say the harsh things about you that I so often hear. You shouldn't be surprised, Louis. You shouldn't be surprised."

She took another step toward him.

"Are you proud of striking your mother?" she asked, as if this taunting, hateful conversation was a ritual they often observed—which, Owain could see from the looks of dread on the two children's faces, it must indeed be. "Are you? Do you think behavior like this is worthy of a future king?"

Louis' head drooped. He shifted ground; stepped back, further into the shadows. "You overstepped the mark. You had no right to do what you did," he muttered, still angry, sounding truculent but also, already, defeated. She'd got behind his defenses.

Owain had no idea what this quarrel was about, or how to find out. But he could see that those more familiar with appalling, frightening spectacles like this had ways of finding out. He watched as Catherine let go of Charles' shoulder and stepped, as lightly and daintily as a ghost, across the grass to the nearest horseman. "What happened?" she whispered up at him; half whisper, half hiss; a command for information.

The man—an esquire of some sort—looked down at her with fear and blankness and resignation mingled in his face. "*She* came to the Louvre this morning while *he* was out hunting. In a litter. With a lady-in-waiting: *his* wife, Marguerite of Burgundy," he muttered, jerking his finger toward the colonnade. Since Louis so loathed the wife the Queen insisted on harboring, the whole court knew that in itself to be an act of hostility. "They brought troops. And they arrested four of *his* counselors. Including my lord Jean de Croy."

Catherine gave him another look through narrow eyes. "Why?" she asked again.

The man looked still more miserable. He just shrugged. It was clear there was no reason, except spite.

"Where did they take them?" Catherine hissed.

The man shook his head and looked as though he wanted the earth to swallow him up. She shook hers too, and, without thanking the man, moved soundlessly back toward Charles and Christine and Owain. Of course they'd all been straining to catch each whispered word. Owain was aware of the raised-eyebrow look that passed between the two royal children: he thought it was a look of helplessness, but also of deep, shared shame.

Then, suddenly, Catherine ran off, alone, back through the bushes, toward peace. And before he realized he was doing it, Owain was running too, past the others, away from the fighting, after her.

Her shoulders were shaking when he caught her up. She was leaning against a tree, with her head cradled in her arms.

He put an arm on her shoulder and pulled her against his

chest. She was smaller and softer than he'd realized; she scarcely came up to his shoulder. She smelled of crushed grass as well as rose oil. Her skin, under the raggedy cloth, was soft. She was trembling. She buried her face in his doublet.

He murmured, as softly as if he were calming a horse, "Don't cry . . . don't cry." He was trembling too. He let his lips brush the top of her head. His blood was racing. There was nothing he wanted more than for her to raise her face to him, so he could look into her eyes . . . so he could . . .

But when she did look up, her eyes, behind their tears, were full of what they'd just seen. She burst out, bitterly: "I wish, I *wish,* I could go to England . . . and get away from them all . . . everyone hating each other . . . and the fights . . . so many fights . . . and us, being scared . . . hiding behind things . . . no one telling us anything . . . we're always so *scared . . .*"

She burrowed back into his chest, holding him very tight—for comfort, he realized uncomfortably; his mind feeling relieved beyond measure that he hadn't followed the overwhelming instinct of a moment before to put his lips to hers, however much his own rebellious body still wanted him to. Now the sobs that came out of her were fierce and angry, racking her whole body. He heard more indistinct words. He thought he heard: ". . . I don't *want* to be!" and ". . . just sitting and waiting all the time . . ." and ". . . *helpless!*"

Full of appalled pity, he thought: I didn't know . . . didn't know at all . . . I just thought we were all happy here . . .

Gently, trying not to betray how hard it felt to separate the length of his body from hers, he removed her arms from around his chest and stepped back.

There was a rustling behind them. Catherine snuffled bravely. It wouldn't do to be crying when Christine stepped out of those bushes. But her wet green eyes were still on his. He held her gaze. "I'm sorry," she whispered, and gave him a heartrending smile; "I shouldn't have . . ." She gulped. "But it's so unbearable; knowing that Louis will take his revenge; and then *she'll* take hers . . . it never ends . . ." She stopped herself. She tried to smile again. She muttered, "Thank you."

By the time Christine pushed through into their clearing,

followed by Charles, Catherine was dabbing at her face with her sleeve, composing herself; and Owain was standing helplessly two paces away, watching, seeing her misery, wondering how he could have believed they were all so happy.

It was Christine who broke the little group's silence. "Come," she said, touching Catherine's arm, "let's go down to the river, all of us."

Charles nodded too. The look on that odd, pinched little face—as desolate as any feeling Owain remembered—brought a lump to the older boy's throat. "Let's show Owain the embankments your wise grandfather built," Christine said in a soothing voice: an invitation to forget. "And I'll tell you about the trip Owain's coming on with me, tomorrow."

It was a frail enough thread to hang a new mood on. But they grasped at it; trying to lift themselves up on it. "Where to?" Charles said, falling into step beside Christine.

She smiled fondly down at his miserable face, rewarding his effort. "Poissy," Christine replied, and, even in the gloom of this moment, the name filled her heart with light. Poissy, a place apart from worldly troubles; Poissy, as close as you could get to Paradise on Earth . . .

"To see your Marie?" Catherine asked, falling into step beside Owain. She was trying to make her voice matter-of-fact, as Christine would want. But she couldn't help sounding left out.

"So it will be just us here," she went on, and Owain could hear wistfulness in her voice, and perhaps fear.

"For a couple of days," Christine replied briskly. However disturbing the scene they'd just witnessed, nothing was going to stop her going to Poissy.

Her answer didn't reassure Catherine. Turning to her younger brother, and jerking her head back in the direction of the voices, the Princess continued her thought as if Christine hadn't spoken. She added, with a grimace: "On our own . . . with them."

SIX

There was a buzz of conversation behind and in front. But in the middle of the line of pilgrims clip-clopping away from Paris—strangers, talking to the people they were traveling with, or those they'd met at the saddling-up point at the Saint-Germain gate at dawn—two were silent. Owain, behind Christine, looking at her straight, thin back without being aware of doing so, was remembering the tears sparkling on Catherine's eyelashes yesterday.

He was reproaching himself for not being able simply to feel concern for Catherine and her unhappiness. But he couldn't help himself. They'd glittered like diamonds, those tears. He would treasure the memory forever. As the Poissy pilgrims passed between tree trunks, under boughs crossing high above, the broken glitters of sun and whispers of green reminded him of snatches of song drifting down from the heights: a living cathedral; the whole natural world giving praise.

She'd touched him. She'd burrowed her face against his chest. She'd let him cradle her in his arms. He'd felt the breath rise and fall in her. She'd confided in him.

All night he'd thought of nothing else but that moment; all evening, through supper, instead of reading; all morning. He'd woken up to the thought of Catherine. She filled his mind now.

Owain had always thought he'd known what unhappiness was. In his mind it had looked like the war he'd known: familiar people disappearing; living, always, with fear and loneliness; knowing things you loved were gone forever, or soon would be. Knowing there was no guarantee of safety or security; that the roof could be burned from over your head, or an arrow lodge in your heart, at any moment. But yesterday, looking into Catherine's eyes, he'd realized how naive that had been. Unhappiness could have a quite different aspect, could exist even in surroundings of the most settled luxury. Could be Catherine, choking on a sob in a palace. He could have guessed she was unhappy; that Charles was, too. The quietness Christine kept talking about—which he hadn't seen as clearly as she had; they'd both wanted to talk to him, after all—their timid air and neglected clothes and street-urchin hunger. There'd always been something wrong, if Owain had only had eyes to see.

Now Owain had started to see, he burned with the desire to talk to her more intimately about what her life was really like. He knew so little. He might be able to help, as he'd found ways to help himself through his own past unhappiness. If only he understood more. Were her mother and brother usually so poisonous and hateful with each other? Did they often fight in public? If so, what did other people at the French court think of the feud? Who supported whom? Why—when there were so many siblings and cousins of the blood royal—did no one take the two youngest royal children under their wing and protect them? And what did Catherine know about her father's illness, which she and Charles were so vague about? He longed for her to tell him; he could imagine her drawing closer, as he laid a hand on hers; looking up at him from under lashes glittering with tears.

He thought. He rode in silence. The sun rose high. They stopped to eat. The horses stamped and snorted into their buckets. The riders, having attended to them, went into the bushes to relieve themselves, or stood around chatting, or sat down and delved into their packages of bread and meat. Owain didn't eat, or talk. He just sat quietly on the fallen tree trunk he'd chosen, beside Christine, not touching the piece of bread she put in his hand, and remembered the glitter of the tears, so close he could have kissed them away.

He didn't even look when one of the other pilgrims came up to him and Christine. It took him a long moment to become aware of Christine's sudden animation at his side: the kerchief falling back, the look of horror, the rush to her feet, the panicky glances from side to side, the miserable subsiding back to her perch on the tree trunk.

He looked up.

Then he blinked, and blinked again. He couldn't believe the evidence of his eyes, but every time he opened them he still saw the same thing.

Standing before them, in a serviceable brown traveling cloak and a kerchief as plain and anonymous as Christine's own, was Catherine.

There was a scared, defiant smile on her face.

Nothing happened for a long moment—just silence.

"I thought you'd have noticed me before now," Catherine said, trying unsuccessfully to sound casual. Her eyes were fixed on Christine; but she'd had time to give Owain a look, too, and he was glowing privately at that new treasure. "I didn't think you'd let me get this far."

Christine was slumped down on the tree trunk as though not trusting her legs to carry her if she tried to get up again.

Her mouth opened, then shut. She stared at Catherine. Owain, keeping very quiet and still beside her, realized that, unusually, even Christine—confronted with a rebellious, runaway princess of the blood, dressed like a shepherdess, wandering unescorted through the wildwood—was lost for words. He felt for her. She'd be right to be angry. It wouldn't help anyone if she realized how indescribably happy the sight of Catherine was making him.

Eventually, Christine muttered: "For the love of God . . ." and then, with her face darkening into the beginning of a muted fury, ". . . *what are you doing here?*"

Catherine just shrugged; almost a wriggle. She wasn't cowed. She said, still defiantly: "I took a horse. Why not? Why should I stay when I know what's going to be happening there?"

Christine stifled a sigh. Owain knew, from their own conversation last night, that Christine and Jean were also afraid of

what might happen next now open conflict seemed to be breaking out again between the Prince and his mother. They'd all
looked so scared—pale and miserable even in the yellow flickers
of night light, seeming smaller than usual with their flinching,
hunching shoulders, making him realize, uncomfortably, that
the Paris they lived in wasn't the sunlit, calm place he'd imagined. They'd talked for hours about it, worrying away at the
possibility that the quarrel might be Louis' pretext to call Burgundy back to Paris with his army, to keep the Queen under
control. And if Queen Isabeau's worst enemy came near Paris
with ten thousand men, how would she respond?

Still. There were so many things Christine could choose to
be angry about, Owain thought. The danger of riding off into
the woods (though she'd known he would be there, with his
sword; she hadn't really put herself at risk). The disobedience,
and the panic she'd cause at the palace—though, he realized,
now he'd spent so much time there himself, it was unlikely
anyone would notice she'd gone; the two children ran wild and
didn't seem to have a single servant to tend to them.

"Because of Charles," Christine said, in her most terrible
voice, with ice-cold eyes, picking the one argument that, Owain
realized, would be certain to make Catherine feel guilty.
"You've left Charles alone in the middle of one of these . . . *upheavals*. A *child*. And a child who has *nightmares*. He'll be
worried about where you are. And he'll be *terrified* to be
facing . . . *all that* . . . on his own."

Catherine looked uncertain, but only for a moment. Then
she stuck out her chin and stared back at Christine. "He'll be
all right," she said, with a brave attempt at carelessness. "I
couldn't tell him because he'd only have wanted to come
too . . . but I told the Saracen to tell him I was with you."

If she thought she'd get praise for that, she was mistaken.
The Saracen was one of the Queen's most outlandish ladies-in-
waiting, a hostage from the Crusades, gifted to the Queen long
ago, so silent and empty-eyed, padding round the palace corridors, that the children hardly knew whether she understood
French, or even knew how to talk. Catherine went on, faltering
a little: "So he'll know I'm not lost."

The battle of eyes went on: Christine's full of accusation. "Well," Catherine finished, finally dropping her gaze, scuffing at her toes, "I don't care. I had to get away."

She glanced at Owain. Perhaps she saw sympathy on his face. She flashed a grateful half-smile his way.

Owain saw Christine catch that flash of warmth. Then he saw a tiny, surprised frown pull at the older woman's forehead, as if the first hint of suspicion was dawning that Owain's presence might have been part of the reason Catherine had wanted . . . Christine looked searchingly at Owain for a moment herself. He kept his face still and surprised. He was relieved when, with a little shake of the head, as if she was putting aside an unworthy thought, she turned her full furious attention back to the girl digging her toes uncomfortably into the carpet of dead leaves underfoot.

"We should all turn around now, and go back to Paris," she said icily. She added, in a different voice, full of a misery even she couldn't quite hide: "I can come back and see my daughter next year."

Owain remembered the softness of her eyes when she'd asked him to come to Poissy with her. The pity of it caught at his heart. He couldn't let her miss this visit.

"We can't do that," he said, putting his hand on his sword hilt, feeling a man. "It wouldn't be safe for just three of us to strike off back through the forest. If Catherine has left word in Paris of where she is, it would be much more sensible to stick with the group; come back tomorrow as we planned."

For different reasons, both pairs of eyes now fixed on him were full of quiet relief. The trip need not be canceled. He'd given a plausible rationale for riding on. He nodded reassuringly at them both, thanking God that neither of them knew how absurdly excited he felt at the adventure opening up before him—the prospect of hours in the woods, on horseback, with Catherine; and a pilgrims' supper at an inn, later; and another long ride back to Paris tomorrow, following his lady.

Christine didn't wait for any more discussion of whether they should cancel their journey. She just moved swiftly on to considering what should be said about the trip once they were back in Paris. She said: "I suppose we should say you just took it into your head to come to Poissy to visit your sister."

There was no anger in Christine's voice anymore. She'd accepted Catherine's presence. She was making the best of it. So there was no reason for Catherine to demur. Yet, at those words, the Princess frowned and fidgeted, and shook her head, and said sulkily: "Why? I've never even met my sister."

Owain stared at her in wild surmise. Catherine clearly hadn't the least wish to meet an unknown sister at the end of this journey. But what *had* she expected to be doing at Poissy, if not going into the women-only confines of the nunnery with Christine? Not . . . He blinked, feeling as blinded by the possibility dawning on him as if he'd stared straight at the sun . . . Not staying outside all day . . . sitting at some travelers' inn . . . with him?

Christine's patience, always limited, was at an end. "Well, you're about to meet her now," she snapped. "Unless you want to tell your mother you just ran off to get away from *her*." And, standing up, she flicked crumbs off her skirts and called, in her most imperious voice: "Owain! Come; put away the food and get the horses untied. And bring Catherine's up. We'll be off in a minute."

The abbey was inside a great wall that stretched for miles in every direction, in a landscape that seemed almost impossibly green and alive with birdsong and happiness.

The light was golden. There were deer between the trees on this side of the wall, and fishponds. Owain could see clusters of houses that must belong to the nuns' male confessors and spiritual advisers, the doctors, the financial counselors, the overseers, the cooks, the bakers, and the servants. Through the gate, he glimpsed more rooftops and the tall towers of a church inside the enclosure. He could hear the buzzing of bees. He knew he'd never see more. Men weren't allowed inside the wall. His journey, and that of the other men who'd ridden with the women, ended here.

One by one, the men pulled up, dismounted, chatted to the gatehouse keepers. A couple of them, who knew the ways of this place, carried on down the lane that must lead to the town and the inn.

The women hardly seemed to notice. Their minds were on their meetings; on beloved faces hidden behind the walls. Their yearning eyes were fixed ahead. Their horses were almost trotting. They processed through the gate without looking back.

Owain stayed where he was, very still, shading his eyes to watch the women's receding backs. He didn't dismount until after one small head, with its cloak hood up, had turned briefly round from the gatehouse to look his way.

The women heard Mass.

Christine had forgotten the anger that had consumed her when she'd caught sight of Catherine. She couldn't imagine feeling angry anymore, not now she was listening to the soaring soprano voices. There was light pouring down from the window. She was happier than she remembered being anywhere else. Her heart was full of Marie's embrace just now, and of the joy in those cornflower-blue eyes. She could still smell the pure innocence of her daughter's skin.

There was a partition in the church, separating the nuns from the laypeople of the town and beyond. But she was burning with the knowledge that her Marie's shining little face, peeping out over the black habit trimmed with white fur that all the nuns wore, was just behind the barrier. Marie was probably letting her eyes rise, like Christine's, to the ceiling, to gaze at the midnight-blue arches with their golden stars.

They were so pretty, all those girls with roses in their cheeks, all dressed alike.

She had to overcome her selfish sadness at only seeing her daughter once a year. Poissy was the closest you could come to Heaven on Earth. Marie was blessed. It had been right to bring her here.

Catherine would have known her sister anywhere. There were fifteen years separating them, but the unlined face bending toward hers, with a benign stranger's curiosity, had the same long nose, green eyes, and high cheekbones Catherine saw in her own mirror every day. They were of the same blood.

All Catherine had really hoped for from this journey was to have some time to talk to Owain. After yesterday, there was nothing else she wanted in the world but to pour out her heart to him. She wanted to tell him about Maman and Louis' quarrels; about how Louis behaved to Marguerite to punish her for being her father's daughter; about the butchers breaking in last year and how frightened she and Charles still were, especially in the night. She'd seen kindness in his eyes. He would listen.

Yet, for a while, on the road, after Christine had ordered her to meet Marie de Valois, Catherine had also let herself start to imagine that this saintly stranger sister might approve of their mother's notion of marrying her to the King of England. The quarrel yesterday had brought the question of escape into her head again, more urgently than ever before. She'd have been grateful for a word of encouragement.

But now she realized that wasn't going to happen. Her sister's face had taken on a fastidious look as soon as Catherine had mentioned the English marriage—as if she'd smelled something bad. And she was still shaking her head.

"Dishonorable," Marie said simply when Catherine finished. "A princess of the blood royal can't marry the son of a usurper. Don't let them bully you. Just say no."

They seemed to do without flowery turns of phrase in the nunnery, Catherine thought resentfully.

"The English have already tried this trick once, with Isabelle," Marie said. "She said no. You can too."

Then, unexpectedly, she grinned. The lively mischief that came into her face made her look younger, and even more like Catherine. Catherine stared. She hadn't expected a nun to look so cheeky.

"Even I've said no to one of Maman's mad marriage plans," Marie said, and she was clearly enjoying the memory. "Did you know?"

That was astonishing enough to make Catherine forget her disappointment. No one stood up to their mother; and if they did, they suffered. She looked at Marie's laughing face with new respect. "Tell me," she demanded.

All she knew was what everyone knew—that Marie had been promised to the Church at birth, in the hope that giving a child to the nuns would please God enough to make Him cure the King of his illness in exchange. God hadn't kept His side of the bargain. But, at four, Marie had entered the nunnery anyway. And, at eight, she'd chosen to stay at Poissy forever, and had taken her vows.

But it seemed that wasn't the end of the story. For when Marie was twelve, the Queen had changed her mind.

Marie said: "She just turned up here, one fine day, with our uncle of Orléans, and told me to leave with her. She'd decided to marry off one of her daughters to the Duke of Bar. And I was the right age, and not married. So she'd taken it into her head that the bride should be me."

She laughed merrily.

Remembering the hard beds and endless prayer that must be Marie's daily lot, Catherine thought: I'd have done it, without a second thought.

Perhaps Marie realized what she was thinking. The deputy prioress stopped laughing and said, more seriously: "When I thought about going back to court, I knew there was nothing I wanted less. Everything I'd known before coming here to Poissy had been so . . . dirty. Once I'd come here and known the peace of God, how could I go back?"

Catherine had always been told that life at court before the civil war had been civilized perfection; their uncle of Orléans a paragon of charm and intellect. She hardly remembered him. He'd been very tall. He'd jumped her on his knee. He sang. He'd had a light laugh and amused eyes, and a weak mouth. She still loved what little she remembered of him. But she could hear the ring of truth in Marie's frank voice, too. It couldn't have been so wonderful before, after all. Even as a small child, Marie had been searching for an escape.

"I told Maman she'd brought me here, and I was dedicated to God, and I should stay. She didn't want to hear. They spent hours trying to bully me into leaving. But I said: 'You've made a gift to God. You can't take it back.' In the end they went away. They hadn't given up, though. They sent Papa, as soon as he got better, to try again. Dear Papa; he was sweeter than they were. He knew it was my right to choose; so he just asked me whether I would consent to leave. But what could I say? I told him, too: 'I've promised to be the bride of Christ. I will hold to my vow unless you find me a better and more powerful husband.'"

She laughed, a little sadly. "I miss Papa, you know. I pray for him. But I couldn't obey him. I knew he'd forgive me in the end; Maman too, she loves us all, really, God forgive her. But my conscience wouldn't let me."

Catherine sat, stunned, letting it all sink in.

"You can say no to Maman too." Marie drove her point home. "Don't let her dishonor you. She won't mind; not really; she's always changing her mind. He is too; it's all whim and fancy with them."

Crushed, Catherine faltered: "But . . . if she does insist?"

Marie's face shone with the simplicity of virtue. She opened her arms. "Then come to God—here."

Here they came, with their heads drooping like cut flowers pulled out of water: the women, returning from their visit with dragging feet, reluctantly rejoining the outside world.

Owain and the two gatemen who were to walk them to the inn, holding torches, got up. The first bats were fluttering in the luminous sky. The air smelled of cut grass. There was a clanking of keys.

Before he could make out which of the women was Catherine, or Christine, another female form came flying over the lawns behind them. A thin figure in black and white, calling softly, urgently, "Mother!"

All the women turned back. Owain could feel the painful hope rekindled in them.

But it was Christine who rushed into the black-and-white girl's arms. The other women turned away.

Owain was outside the gate. But he still heard—everyone

heard—Marie de Castel's voice break as she muttered, "Please come back tomorrow. Just for an hour."

Christine's arms were around her daughter, rhythmically stroking her shoulders; she was kissing the top of her daughter's head. The gateman moved closer, but he stopped when Christine looked up. He didn't dare intervene. "Of course," Christine told her daughter softly. "Of course."

Mother and daughter looked at each other with no more words, as if memorizing each other in the failing light. Then Christine said, more brightly: "Won't you miss dinner if you're late?" and, when her daughter nodded, "Run . . . I'll be back . . . I promise . . . run now!"

But her hand followed Marie's shoulder away. Even when her daughter was just a shadow again, flitting toward the refectory, Christine's arm was still outstretched and her eyes tender as bruises.

She turned to the lanternman, and said, with painful dignity, "I'm sorry to have kept you," and, again without looking at anyone else, stepped forward into the twilight.

Christine walked ahead, overwhelmed by her thoughts.

She didn't even think of Catherine. Didn't see the child's face brighten when Owain appeared beside her. Didn't see them loiter at the back of the group, out of the torchlight, as the shadows deepened. Didn't hear the low-pitched conversation begin. Didn't see the solicitous way he took her arm to help her over a tree root.

Christine recovered her poise as soon as she got inside by the firelight; it had only been unbearable while she was actually in that heartbreakingly lovely landscape, within touching distance of her daughter. Now that the pilgrims and their friends were pouring the nuns' gift of wine and tucking into the hearty inn food and talking, she was perfectly capable of smiling and chatting with them again. She sat between Catherine and Owain at the trestles. Catherine was quiet, with pink in her cheeks. Owain served them both with food and drink; a good, trustworthy boy. Christine let him talk quietly to

Catherine. Christine was thinking: I will see Marie in the morning.

She took Catherine into the abbey with her the next morning. She would have been failing in her duties as a chaperone if she'd left the child outside with Owain and the horses. But she didn't want the Princess underfoot while she was with Marie, either. So, once inside, she sent her into the abbey church to ask for a blessing.

Five minutes later, Catherine came out of the church alone, and out of the abbey grounds, through the gatehouse. Owain was leaning against a fence, in a shady corner, with his back to the abbey, whistling. He was watching the soft wisps of pink-gold cloud creep across the blue of the sky. He didn't notice her come up behind him and put her hands on each side of his lean warm back. "Boo," she said, and felt him startle; but not enough to dislodge her hands.

Still with his back to her, still with her hands on him over the fence, he said: "That was quick." His voice was trembling.

"Meet you round here," he went on; and she flew along the fence to find a way to the other side.

They found a place to stand, side by side, where the fence stopped at a tree. They leaned against the tree, looking up, both gripped with a euphoric feeling of anticipation. They'd talked for so long last night, but there was still everything to find out. Neither of them meant it to happen now, as their arms touched; it just did. "Listen," Owain said; just to keep her there. "That's a skylark."

She shifted, and more of her yielding warmth was touching him. After a long moment, she moved away. He breathed out. But she turned herself round to face him. She was standing so close.

"How long will you stay at the University, do you think?" she asked softly.

Dizzily, daringly, he whispered back—longing to be a prince who could aspire to ride her off into the gray-green hills, knowing he was longing uselessly, now that everything back there in Wales had turned out the way it had, and he was no one, yet not caring about the futility of that longing because of the blood singing in his veins . . . "Until you go to London?"

There were tears in Christine's eyes as she came out through the gatehouse. They made her vision run and stream.

So, for a moment, she couldn't quite believe what she was seeing in the shadows under a tree outside, where the dappling of light and bark and grass and leaves was so confusing anyway.

Then she knew.

She called, in panic, "Catherine! Owain!" and watched the shifting shape that had been both of them disentangle itself and separate into two bodies, two sets of arms and legs; two downturned blushing faces.

There was no point in saying anything. There had been many disappointments in her life. She knew better than to let her anger out at once. She needed time to think. She lowered her own head to unknot the horses' reins.

She mounted.

"Come," she said coolly, not meeting their eyes. "We'll catch the others up if we hurry."

And she spurred her horse on.

Christine rode and, in the rhythm of the horses' hooves, thought. As the miles slipped by, she let go of her first furious thoughts—that her trust had been betrayed; that Owain, whom she'd come to think of almost as a son, or a disciple, had set out deliberately to besmirch the purity of a princess; and that Catherine had inherited her immoral mother's sluttishness if she was willing to ignore her royal blood and the prize of her virginity to satisfy a casual lust.

Still, it took many hundreds of paces through the forest before Christine was able to understand that she was more angry with herself than she was with either of these children. It was she who'd thrown them together, after all, thinking that Owain would show the younger children how to live through unhappiness. She looked now at the two backs swaying ahead of her; the two bowed young heads. So friendless, both of them, and so beautiful: both of them so strangely left out of the life they found themselves living, worlds emptied of like-minded people; forced into silence. They'd started to talk to each other . . . She should have realized what kind of comfort they'd naturally find themselves seeking from each other. They were young . . . She had no one to blame for this but herself. Thank God she'd been able to nip it in the bud. No consequences. No one need know.

In another life—if Catherine had not been a princess of the blood, descended from Charlemagne and the kings of Troy, the purity of her line a sacred pact with God going back to the dawn of time—Christine, like anyone, might have rejoiced at this outcome. A love between these two young people, if there'd been nothing else at stake, might have been thought beautiful.

She sighed, and kicked her horse out of its trance. That was not to be. Best stick to reality.

Owain rode in front so no one could see the savagery on his face.

He ignored the branches slapping at him; he kept his horse nervously trotting and skittering. He didn't care about its frothing mouth today.

Inside his head, he was conducting a furious exchange with Christine. Inside his head, she'd become every dismissive Englishman he'd ever encountered. What about *my* blood? his own interior voice was shouting. I am descended from Ednyfed Fychan, Seneschal of the Kingdom of Gwynedd under Llywelyn the Great. I am descended from Iestyn ap Gwyrgant, the last King of Gwent. My family are the barons of Hendwr and the lords of Penmynydd and Englefield and Iscoed and Gwynioneth, the leaders of Anglesey. My blood is as noble as any. I grew up the cousin of a king! I could have married any princess I liked . . . back then . . . three or four years ago, when everything was still possible . . .

But he knew it was futile to protest.

He could hear the answers, crushing in their finality: A conquered race now. You're no one now. And: Even if you were the Prince of Wales himself—even if the Welsh weren't ruled by the English—you still wouldn't be good enough for a Princess of France.

Catherine knew this was the end of Owain. He'd go . . . Her head drooped lower. And so would hope.

What a fool she'd been. What a fool. She should have . . . She realized that what she should be thinking was that she should have avoided letting herself feel this for a man she couldn't marry. He wasn't royal. She shouldn't have seen him as a man at all; only as a retainer. But all she actually felt was hot-cheeked shame that she'd been stupid enough to let Christine catch them.

She'd been shaking—shaking with happiness. Just for that moment; drowning in honey.

No, for weeks she'd been happy. Being with Owain was like being let out of prison. Other princes and princesses had a life at court—balls, and dresses, and expenses, and flirtations. But that hadn't started for Catherine and Charles; and, even for those admitted to it, court life only seemed to exist, these days, in muted, miniature form, behind closed doors. The children had always seemed to live in great wastelands of silence: with only the warmth of their friendship with each other and with Christine to sustain them. Then, suddenly, Catherine had found a new friend she could talk frankly to. They'd found a way to talk to each other. It wasn't just the kiss. If she didn't see Owain again, they wouldn't be able to talk together anymore.

It took her breath away. Her mind shied away from the thought that she might not see Owain again. She stared at the pommel in front of her and tried not to think. Her blood was racing.

They were almost at Paris when the trees thinned and they came out into fields. Dusk was falling. A ghostly moon was rising in the luminous sky; the evening star nearby.

She spurred her horse on. There'd be a moment, at least, before Christine caught on; caught up.

He turned as she came level with him. His glance was strained and desperate.

91

"Venus . . . your star," he murmured very quietly, and her heart turned over at the knowledge that they were both still playing the game of not disturbing Christine. His face, as he'd turned, had been so pale; so angry. But now, with her here, for one moment more, he was burning with the torturing fire of hope. "I don't know what I can promise," he said. "But I'll always . . ."

He paused, looking for something he could do; something he could say. Into the silence came the sound of Christine, just behind, clicking her tired horse into life.

Owain closed his eyes, put his hand on his temples, and composed his white face into skull-like immobility.

Then, very suddenly, without looking back, he cantered off.

Catherine saw the distant little figure by the Queen's house start running as soon as he saw her horse. But she ignored it, and kicked the horse on into a trot, straight toward the royal stables. There'd be time enough to talk to Charles later. She needed to compose herself first; to stop feeling so crushed by guilt; to try and erase the memory of Christine's wounded eyes, and Owain's bent head, and the silence.

But she heard Charles' pounding footsteps go on racing toward her. He threw himself into her arms as soon as she had her feet on the ground.

He buried himself in her, shaking. His face was hot and red and snotty. His eyes were swollen.

"I told the Saracen to tell you I'd gone!" she cried, lashing out with her tongue. "She knew!"

That startled him. He looked up with wide eyes. "She did tell me," he snuffled, warily.

"Then why are you crying?" she hissed, still full of guilty fury.

His eyes filled with tears again. He hadn't been panicking because she was gone. He hadn't expected her to shout at him when she got back, either. She'd got it all wrong.

She took a deep breath and tried again. She put her arms round his shaking shoulders and rocked him to and fro while he cried himself out. "I'm sorry," she said, over and over again.

"I didn't mean . . ." When his sobs quietened, she said gently: "What happened, darling, tell me?"

He fixed big, scared eyes on her. "I've got to get married!" he cried.

She stared back. "Who?" she said, without expression.

"Marie of Anjou," he whimpered, and his face puckered up again.

Catherine could see why. Their ten-year-old cousin Marie was solemn and very grand; always too worried about spoiling her beautiful and expensive clothes to want to play. "Big-nose!" Charles wailed. "I don't even like her!"

But Catherine could see why her mother would want this marriage. Marie's father was one of the most important of the French princes who opposed the Duke of Burgundy. Known as the King of Sicily, Marie's father was just back from years abroad, fighting over his various Italian land claims, to formally swear his loyalty to the princes allied, under the Count of Armagnac, against the common enemy, Burgundy. They'd need to keep him sweet with a good marriage (and what could be better than a marriage to the King's youngest son?). The situation was more dangerous than ever. She'd heard the pilgrim gossip on the road. Louis had written to her cousin of Burgundy, denouncing the Queen for making wrongful arrests of his men—and inviting Burgundy and his army back to Paris to save him from his mother. There was more trouble brewing, for sure.

Thinking aloud, she told Charles: "It's not so bad . . . you might get to bring your bride here . . . we could be together still . . . and if you have to go to them, it's only over the road to the Anjou hotel . . ."

"No," he squealed, back in his panic, burrowing once more into her arms. "That's the whole point! Mother says I'll have to go away! Right after the betrothal! To her mother's court! To Angers! I've been looking for you all day! But you weren't here! There was no one to tell! There was no one to tell!"

She clung to him, shocked; a child again too, feeling her brother's warmth, committing it to memory. Angers was two days' ride southwest. She'd never see Charles if he was there.

She bitterly regretted leaving him alone here, now she was forced to imagine him gone for good. She didn't want him to go. They were safe together. They were allies. They trusted each other; loved each other. There was no one else left. Owain would be gone too. There would be no one she could talk to. She shut her eyes.

She didn't want to be left behind, on her own.

SEVEN

Christine knew what Owain was going to say as soon as he walked into the scriptorium the next morning.

Anastaise grinned cheerfully at him, about to make one of her jokes about students. Then she stopped. He had his own traveling clothes on, not Jean's castoffs. He had his pack on his arm.

Christine stepped forward. She walked Owain to the window, away from Anastaise. She stared down at the burned-out house opposite. So many things had gone wrong here; it seemed the right place to hear this.

"Thank you for all your kindness," Owain said, very formally. "But I think after all I shouldn't take up that place you found me at the University."

She nodded. She'd known he would go.

She'd sensed his anger all through the silent ride back from Poissy. Never more than when, as she'd determinedly trotted her horse between his and Catherine's to make sure there were no more possibilities for contact, she'd heard him mutter, ". . . building walls around the Rose."

She'd thought: He's quoting. She'd known: he was quoting from the *Romance of the Rose*. He'd read it, despite her hatred of it. He wanted her to know he'd defied her. He was making her out to be Jealousy, building a tower to keep him from his love—blaming her for the cruelty of life, which was none of her doing.

The look that had passed between them then—quiet, intense anger—had meant farewell. The rest had been only a question of time.

She could see why he would go. Owain must have believed, for a while, that if he came to live in Paris he could escape the burden of his own reduced status altogether. She, Christine, had perhaps been too quick to encourage him in that belief. She'd been so taken with his spirited refusal to be cast down by bad luck; by the optimism that warmed everyone around him. Now he'd suddenly seen that he could never get away altogether from what the lost Welsh war had made him. The solace he thought he'd find in Paris had vanished once he'd realized that, even here, he still wasn't good enough for what he wanted most. Which, after all, wasn't learning, or friends, but just the usual goal of young men at the start of their lives: a girl, a love, and the one he wanted was right out of his reach. It was natural for him to be confused and angry. He was doing the right thing. He had to go; had to grapple with his own problems, alone. She just wished her heart didn't feel as empty as the charred shell of a home out there, over the street.

"Where will you go?" she asked.

"Back to my master," he replied, equally shortly.

She was so sorry for him; and so sad for herself. She'd miss him. But there was no more to say.

She followed him out into the courtyard. "Wait," she said.

He stopped, warily.

She ran back to the scriptorium, took up a book from the shelf, and, trying to ignore Anastaise's astonished eyes, ran back to give it to the tall Welshman.

She said, in a shy rush: "You're an intelligent man. Make yourself a learned one too, one day."

And the ghost of a smile came to her face.

Owain softened. "I will," he said quietly; "I promise." Then he added, in a mutter: "And I'm sorry. About. I didn't mean . . . to abuse your trust . . ."

No more words would come. But she was grateful for the few she'd heard.

Her eyes were stinging as she shut the courtyard door behind him. He was a good man; a noble man.

Owain still had the book in his hand when he came to mount his horse.

He looked at it through a blinding fog.

It was one of Christine's odd, personal love poems.

He opened it, right there in the stable, ignoring the restless pawing of the animal's hooves in the straw, and began to read.

. . . the young lover had no name; Christine called him only the Duke of True Lovers. He was still only a child when he suddenly fell deeply in love with a married lady of royal blood, whom he had seen a hundred times without feeling anything. It was love at its purest, he believed, since he was still too young to feel desire. He persuaded his parents to invite the lady to stay, which she did for a whole summer. Blond as amber, the lady sat beside him and his mother at a tournament in a meadow beside a lake, and on the first day the company was dressed all in green, and on the next day all in white and gold. The lover was too timid to tell of his love, so he suffered in silence, relieving his feelings only by writing love poems he was too shy to deliver. At last, the lady's husband sent for her to go home, and the boy fell into despair. It was only when his cousin took pity on him and told the lady of his love that she understood why. She was flattered and touched, and hesitantly wrote to him to tell him she loved him too.

. . . The pair began, secretly and blissfully, to meet and talk . . . but finally, feeling her honor compromised, the lady told the lover to leave her. The lover fainted on getting her letter and was as distraught as she. He was ready to go and die overseas if she wished; but stop loving her he never could. He set off abroad . . . but their love would never change . . .

There was a great tenderness in Owain's heart as he closed the little book. He wound a cloth carefully round it and slipped it into the saddlebag. Perhaps, after all, Christine hadn't condemned him utterly for falling victim to an impossible love. Perhaps she'd understood him better, all along, than he'd realized.

He'd never know. He wouldn't see her again, or know the illusory happiness of these past weeks. The answers he thought he'd found here were too easy.

There was only sorrow ahead. He couldn't bear to think of Catherine. Not yet. Not till he'd got away.

But at least he wanted to believe this gift was a gesture of forgiveness.

The Queen looked at Catherine, standing in the church, trying not to cry as her red-eyed brother was betrothed to Marie of Anjou. "Don't you think it's time you stopped seeing so much of that disagreeable Madame de Pizan," Isabeau whispered, too loudly. It wasn't really a question. When the litters reached the Hôtel Saint-Paul, Catherine saw her possessions were being moved into her mother's house. The days of picnics with Christine were over. She'd stopped being a child.

Catherine knew that moving in with her mother meant there'd be less escape than ever before from the Queen's simmering hostilities with Louis (though, since Isabeau had forced Louis to retract his written request for the Duke of Burgundy to bring an army to liberate Paris from his mother, and in return had let him cut off his allowance to his wife Marguerite, whom he'd sent to live in poverty at Saint-Germain, the heat had gone out of that hatred—at least for now). Still, Catherine wasn't altogether sorry for the change.

She'd been mortified by her last conversation with Christine. She knew Christine had meant to be as subtle and sensitive as one of the clever attendants in her love poems when she'd sidled up to Catherine just before the betrothal ceremony and begun, in roundabout fashion, to give her a little talk about blood and what it meant to be royal. Charles' marriage was good, because a royal union, in spite of all his fears and tears. Catherine, one day soon, could also look forward to a royal union, a marriage of equals. Royal blood was a compact with God. Princes were the finest of the fine. Their blood was not to be diluted; tainted; made impure by contact with lesser mortals, or God would be angered. Catherine had heard it before. She didn't want to hear it now.

So she could think of nothing to say back. She just shook her head and nodded, over and over, until the nods and shakes got muddled and her eyes screwed up with the effort of politeness. When Christine didn't stop, Catherine had eventually just walked away. "I have to go to Charles," she'd muttered.

Whatever had possessed her, to think that any willful action on her part could change her fate? Dashing off into the forest; discussing the possibility of the English marriage with her sister; talking so much with Owain; letting Owain . . . letting herself . . . the heat of that embrace . . .

It was too painful to dwell on. She knew better now; knowledge was branded humiliatingly on her. There was nothing she would ever be able to do to change her circumstances. She wasn't a Christine, or an Owain, whose lives could be altered by determined acts of will or thought. She shouldn't try. She was nothing but a receptacle for her royal blood. Her duty as a princess was decorously to do nothing. It was a bitter lesson. Now she needed time to make her peace with herself. And time on her own was the only thing that being a nearly forgotten part of her mother's eccentric household would guarantee her.

Christine's Jean, who (God willing) had found a permanent professional home with Chancellor Henri de Marle, was put to work on negotiating the English marriage. The stories he came home with, as the summer of 1414 curdled into a miserable winter, horrified his family, especially Christine.

The new King of England's negotiating style was a ruthless mixture of threat and promise. As Christine had feared, he was turning the negotiations into the pretext for full-scale war on France.

Henry of England was claiming as rightfully his all the French lands that last century's English kings had fought for, and which, after capturing old King Jean the Good, had been granted on paper—a third of France. But this Henry wanted even more than the rightful kings of England had: he was also demanding the duchy of Normandy, which once, centuries ago, had belonged to the ancestors of the English kings, and all the lands in the south and west that had ever been controlled from England—he wanted even the lands that English kings had explicitly given up claims to a hundred years ago.

Jean de Castel wrinkled his forehead as he told his mother the list of demands. Henry of England wanted the lordships of Normandy, Anjou, Touraine, Maine. He wanted the homage of Brittany and Flanders. He wanted full sovereignty over the duchy of Aquitaine, not just the little strip of Gascony that the English still actually held, along with Poitou, Quercy, the Limousin, and the Agenais. In the north, he wanted to add to the English territory of Calais and its march the counties of Ponthieu, Guisnes, and Montreuil. He also wanted northern lands between the Somme River and Gravelines; half the county of Provence in the south; and the castles and lordships of Beaufort and Nogent.

On top of that, he wanted eight million crowns in cash—a fantasy figure.

Once he was satisfied on all these counts, he would marry Princess Catherine and make peace.

"Impossible," Christine said flatly.

"Of course it's impossible," Jean agreed. "He must know that. How can he expect anyone to think he's negotiating in good faith? If we said yes, there'd be nothing left of France." He rested his weary head in his hands. "Still," he added bitterly, "we *are* supposed to say yes, somehow. The Queen's in charge. And this is what she says she wants."

During the winter, the King of France recovered from his illness enough to take negotiations with the English into his own hands. The eventual French counteroffer, made the next spring, was more lands in the south, bordering English holdings in Aquitaine, and 800,000 crowns, with dresses, jewels, and furniture for Catherine.

"It's more than he deserves," Christine said, as ambassadors set off in both directions.

"It still won't work," Jean replied.

It didn't. The French ambassadors were sent back from London. The English ambassadors returned from Paris without agreeing to anything.

On April 7, 1415, Henry of England wrote to the King of France to say again that he was so determined to have peace with France, and to marry Princess Catherine, that he was willing to settle for less than what justice demanded. But why, he added, all injured innocence, had the King of France sent ambassadors to London who had told him that they didn't have full powers to agree to all England's demands? Could the French King kindly hurry and send some proper ambassadors?

On April 12, 1415, Henry of England called a council meeting that placed England on a war footing. He set the rates of pay for soldiers in an expedition to an unnamed location in France.

On April 15, 1415, before King Charles of France could have had time to reply to his letter, Henry of England wrote again. He said he was sending a safe conduct for a new French embassy of 360 people. He demanded they come quickly, so that the peace he so desired could swiftly take shape.

Jean de Castel tried to avoid being part of the French delegation. "I don't want to be humiliated," he said. But Christine reasoned with him. She told him he must do all he could to avoid a war. She used the word "hope." She ignored the set look on her son's face. He left with the ambassadors on June 4.

Jean de Castel was bone tired at the back of the horse train, jiggling along from one inn to the next, through dreary English villages, over potholed roads. The French visitors had gone from Dover to London, where they'd been told the King of England had left for Winchester. The Archbishop of Bourges' pink and white face had gone red at the news, but he knew his duty. They'd turned right around and followed the King south.

They'd had to wait an hour at the gate at Winchester, watched by curious, speculative eyes. There was a lot of traffic leaving the city. The gatemen were letting out cart after cart, loaded with arrows and longbows, tents and lances. They wouldn't let the Frenchmen in until the carts were all gone. "Where is all that going?" Jean de Castel had asked a gateman; his English was good enough to talk to townspeople. The man laughed roughly. "To Southampton," he said, with rude good humor; "like the King, once he's done with you lot."

The King of England was staying in the palace of his uncle, Bishop Beaufort. The leading French ambassadors were put up there too, but there was no room for the retinues; the palace was too full of men-at-arms, obviously preparing for war on France.

Jean found a bed at an inn. There was a green outside. He watched the evening archery practice: all those undernourished yeomen deforming their skinny bodies, struggling to pull back the hundred-pound weight of the string, twisting and crunching their backs. They never healed. They lived with the pain of their bows. They had to. Archery practice was the law in England. Then he watched the men who'd been practicing go marching out of town, in the direction of the coast. "Off to Southampton?" he asked. They roared cheerfully back. Of course they were going to Southampton. The innkeeper wouldn't talk to him, but after an hour sitting quietly in the inn, listening to what people were talking about all around him, Jean knew enough to be sure that six thousand men-at-arms and fifty thousand archers would be taking ships from Southampton any day.

When he rejoined his party at the palace, Jean found them as shocked as he was. They had been greeted by Henry of England's uncle, Henry Beaufort, the Bishop of Winchester. Bishop Beaufort's welcoming words had consisted of no more than a brusque warning: "You have to finish your business and leave before the end of the week."

The French delegation was trapped in its futile peacekeeping role. The Archbishop of Bourges' sermon that night was, "Peace to you and your house." But Henry of England—who turned out to be tall and wiry and mouse-colored, with big girlish eyes fringed with long eyelashes set in a hard, bony frame—sat through the speech blank-faced, drumming his fingers against his book of hours.

The gathering in the council chamber the next day was no warmer.

Henry of England didn't come. Bishop Beaufort (who also had big, odd, knobbly Lancaster features in a pinched face) presided. He strode in at the head of a bristling train of guards. He didn't bother overmuch with pleasantries. In a voice as thin and hard as his face, he set out a new list of impossible demands. England wanted its differences with France settled by the end of the summer. That was the cutoff point for France to hand over all the lands England wanted. Princess Catherine, a treasure trove of jewels, and 600,000 crowns were also to be delivered to Calais by Michaelmas.

Bishop Beaufort was a calm negotiator. He sat down and examined his nails when he'd finished. He pretended not to hear the murmurs of dismay from around the table. He only shook his head and let a contemptuous little smile play on his lips when Bourges tried to make the Bishop of Lisieux explain why that would be quite impossible; when Lisieux deflected the question to the Count of Vendôme; when Vendôme turned to the Baron of Ivry; when Ivry muttered, "Braquemont?" and finally, when Gontier Col indicated Jean and wheedled, wringing his hands, "My lord Bishop, my colleague Jean de Castel is best placed to explain some of the technical difficulties . . ."

The eyes all fixed on Jean. I'm no one; why leave it to me? he thought, with a mixture of despair and panic, hating his superiors for their cowardice. Trying to stop his gut churning, he put suddenly damp hands on the table to keep them still and stood up. It was important not to show fear.

He bowed his head, and suddenly, mercifully, was so sick of the lot of them, French and English alike, that it became easy to tell the truth. "My lord Bishop, Michaelmas is less than three months away," he said baldly. "The French government couldn't hope to lay hands on enough gold to mint the coins you want, if you insist on September."

He sat down. There was another anxious little flurry from the rest of his delegation. Hands fluttered; faces cringed. He kept his eyes fixed on his white fingers. "My lord Bishop," he heard Bourges murmur, "my young colleague overstates the position, I fear. Naturally we would be able . . . but, of course, *difficulties* . . . undeniable. Yes indeed. *Difficulties.*"

Bishop Beaufort bared his teeth. He got up. So did his men-at-arms. "My master has heard a lot about difficulties," he said. "All our talks seem to end with this word, *difficulties*. You can talk to him about your *difficulties* at council this evening, if you like. But it's time you realized that making peace requires you to find ways to overcome your difficulties." He swept out.

"You said the wrong thing," the Archbishop told Jean, with the glaring-eyed anger that the weak reserve for those they know to be weaker. Jean pursed his lips. So it was to be his fault now?

At six in the evening, they were called back into the crowded hall. The King was there this time. Henry of England still didn't speak. He just kept drumming his fingers and staring at the French.

Archbishop Chichele of Canterbury read out a memorandum in Latin. It described Henry of England's many attempts to negotiate. It said he'd been kept from his French heritage for too long. It accused the King of France of being unwilling to search for fair peace. It said Henry of England, "injured by French duplicity," would now be "obliged" to search for his rights in another way.

As soon as Chichele had finished reading, Henry of England got up and left the room, followed by his senior advisers, followed by the small fry. There were no more speculative, knowing glances between English and French. All the English were looking away. With dread, Jean de Castel realized that those averted English eyes marked the end of diplomacy and the beginning of war.

Henry of England wrote one more reproachful letter to the King of France. From Southampton, he offered King Charles 50,000 crowns off Catherine's bride price, if the French King would only give up his unreasonable resistance to peace. Then Henry of England set sail for France, to make war.

The embassy to England was back in Paris by the time the King of France received the letter. The besieged port of Harfleur was already almost in English hands, and when it fell it would lay open a great chunk of northern France to the invader: Normandy, Rouen, and the Seine River supply route all the way to Paris. The Archbishop of Bourges was shaking his venerable head at the letter.

"Well, what am I to reply?" King Charles said helplessly, and the ambassadors shook their heads and murmured. The King's hands were shaking; the letter was fluttering, ready to drop from them.

Jean de Castel spoke up from the back. His heart was racing.

"Don't trust a word he says, my lord," he said, and the King's eyes fixed beseechingly on him. "He doesn't want to marry your daughter. He wants to conquer your country. He is not a man of peace."

The King of France's reply to Henry of England was as gentle as ever, agreeing on the need for peace. But Jean de Castel was pleased to see that the final draft of the letter, sent only after the distressed King had briefly fallen ill again, still contained one drop of acid he hoped his words had inspired. Where the King had addressed Henry of England's demand for the Princess, he had written: "It does not appear that the means you have adopted are proper, honorable, or usual in such a case."

Catherine's mother organized a ball to celebrate the return to court of the noblemen united under the Count of Armagnac—the Orléans faction—after their summer campaigning to contain the Duke of Burgundy. There would be no more festivities: after this one ball, the princes would be off to defend France against the English invader. So Isabeau threw herself into the evening with gusto, having more peacocks killed for the feast than had ever graced a single table before, and more musicians, jugglers, acrobats, candles, and jewels gathered together too. Catherine counted as an adult now; her mother had had new dresses sewn for her. She was allowed to attend; to fan herself behind her feathers; to try her hand at worldly whispering with dance partners.

The first person she spoke to was her cousin Charles, the

younger Duke of Orléans; a fair-haired, weak-mouthed, charming young man with a gift for poetry. "You look beautiful . . . very elegant . . . but thin," he said solicitously as they left the dance floor together. He looked much older than he had before the summer's fighting, too, she thought; but she was wiser now, so she kept her peace.

"You must have been worried for months," he went on. He fixed kindly eyes on her. He was trying to reassure her, she saw. He said: "The English marriage will never happen, you know."

"I do know," she replied wearily, and then she suddenly felt so soiled, so humiliated by remembering her moments of past excitement at the prospect of that marriage, and everything that went with the memory of it—the other, forbidden memories, of the beauty of Owain's face swimming down from above, and the heat of his skin on hers, and the touch of mouths and tongues—that she blushed a fierce, hot red, and burst into tears.

Charles of Orléans patted worriedly at her, dreadfully embarrassed, turning her toward a shadowy corner of the hall so no one could see her loss of control, not knowing what else to do. She took a corner of her skirts and dried her own eyes. Then she managed a watery smile, and the determinedly brave words that were what her cousin wanted to hear.

"I never wanted it anyway," she said.

PART TWO

The Book of Deeds of Arms and Chivalry

EIGHT

It was raining: a thin, hard drizzle that drilled into your skin and hurt your eyes. Owain, wet to the bones, was blinking it away. His legs, exhausted from the long day of riding, were still mechanically clamped to his horse's sides; but the English advance had slowed to a painful walk and he didn't think he could have stirred the horse, or himself, to do more, even if he'd heard the trumpets order a charge. His body was so tired he was in danger of letting the desolation of this autumn evening enter his heart. The other horsemen riding uncomplainingly beside and behind and ahead of him were dark shadows, slumped into their saddles, as overwhelmed as he was by the shadowy flatness all around and the impossibility of their mission. There was no talk, just endurance. There was nowhere to pitch camp. There had been French fires burning across the river at the Blanchetache ford. The plan to cross there had had to be dropped. His aching hands were slipping on his reins.

From somewhere up ahead, in a gap in the wind, he heard, with dread, a burst of music. The horns. It took him a moment to understand that they weren't signaling an advance. There were drumbeats too; and a thin wail of fifes. With relief, and astonishment, he thought: it's music. He stretched in the saddle, peered through the gathering dark; willed his eyes and ears to make sense of it. But even before he did he found his horse stepping forward with new vigor in its stride, as hundreds of others all around speeded up their pace too and squared their shoulders. He heard marching songs; and a drift of suddenly cheerful deep voices, and the quicker, louder tempo of the archers' heavy footsteps, coming back to the riders over the insistent drumbeats. The wet no longer seemed so daunting. Owain even found himself whistling. The music would be an order from the King himself, he knew, and he found himself lost in admiration, as he'd so often been during the three months of this campaign, at the King's instinct for drooping spirits; the deft ways he knew to raise morale.

When Owain recognized the leader of the group of horsemen he now made out trotting back down the English line, against the flow of soldiery, his heart filled with a joy as intense as that of a child seeing its father. Henry, the King, his master, was coming, with his body as jaunty in the saddle as if he hadn't been riding for ten hours. His face was glistening with water under his raised visor, but he had fire still in his eyes and a face full of smiling understanding as he stopped here and there to clap one soldier on the back or shout a word of encouragement to another.

The King reined in his shining black palfrey as Owain, tall and proud in the saddle, trotted past, feeling the energy of those big, intelligent royal eyes like heat. "Tudor!" he heard; and he bobbed his head manfully, trying to restrain the beaming smile he wanted to give at being singled out. "Good man; we'll be pitching camp just up ahead," the King said briskly. His voice was deep and confident. "There's a wood. You'll see. Get a dozen of your men into it for kindling. The rest can do tents for everyone. We need good big fires. Get everyone dry. Cheer us all up."

"Sir!" Owain said, and, as the horsemen spurred on back down the line, he let the smile out onto his face, and set himself to imagining the big blaze of a fire he was going to organize.

He'd been called back from the studies the King had permitted him to begin at Oxford, to join the King's French campaign, setting off from Southampton in the summer in the fleet of ships that had assembled to fight at an undisclosed location across the Channel. He hadn't wanted to come; hadn't wanted to fight; above all, hadn't wanted to fight Catherine's father's forces. But there was no disobeying orders. When John of Bedford had said his brother the King wanted Owain on hand, in case the need arose during the campaign for negotiations with the French King (since his previous trip to Paris, Owain was deemed to know the French court), he'd dared to ask, with a hint of sullenness: "But can I come back afterward and continue my studies?" Now, three months on, he could hardly remember the boy who could have felt aggrieved at commonsense Duke John's mild answer: "It all depends on the King. Duty comes first. You know that." He did, now. He knew about combat: the fear, the euphoria, and the need to obey orders. He'd been put to fight in the siege of Harfleur; he'd thought it would be a life of sneers at the Welshman, and he'd hate it. But he'd quickly found he was considered as much a part of the force as any real Englishman as long as he did his best; and by the time the dignitaries of Harfleur came out through the shattered walls to surrender to the King, he'd been cheering as loud and as joyfully as any of Henry's English knights. These days, he never even thought about following orders, or about whether he felt it morally justified to make war in France. He'd been swept away by the logic of where he was and who he was with. He'd stopped caring about anything else. What drove him to ride until his limbs felt they might fall off his body was no longer obedience, or thought, or principle. He just wanted Henry's eyes approvingly on his. He craved that lopsided, energetic grin; the clap on the back. Like every other soldier in the force, he took orders now out of sheer love.

The French army was waiting for them beyond the woods where they camped. In the last of the luminous gray light, Owain could see the rooftops and drifting smoke of the villages of Rousseauville and Azincourt. "They're behind there," his subaltern said, careful to keep fear out of his voice. "And over there. And there."

No one knew how they knew it; no one would say such a thing to his fellows; but it didn't take long for the knowledge to spread that there were at least three times as many French soldiers over there as there were English over here. And horsemen; hundreds upon hundreds of powerful horsemen; while this little

English force was mostly made up of yeomen archers in ordinary leather jerkins, who, apart from their bows, had only the most basic of equipment—axes at their girdles and pikes to force their way into the thickest fighting.

But as the darkness hemmed in the English troops, in the exposed, perilous fields and copses that God and the King had chosen for them, Owain and dozens of other English knights—and Owain Dwn, another Welshman of his own age, the sparkling-eyed grandson of Henry Dwn, a fighter who'd taken Henry of England's peace—brought forth fire from great steaming bonfires. Owain leaned as close as he dared to the flames, watching the merry orange crackle and spit of them, observing his men stretch arms and rub feeling back into their legs; feeling the despair lift from his own flesh like the damp evaporating from his skin. The earth smelled fresh and full of life underfoot. His subaltern was already supervising the first batch of men who were cleaning and greasing and sharpening blades for the morning. There would be time for everything: time to prepare; to rest; to eat; and to pray, just as there always was with Henry. The smell of sizzling rabbits and game birds rose through the smoke. Priests were passing from encampment to encampment, blessing men in batches. The air was alive with expectant talk and the neighing of horses scenting battle; and everywhere you looked men were singing and stamping their feet to the music. There was no reason to lose hope.

Owain reached into his bag for his box—with pens and ink inside; with pieces of parchment cut small for this life on the move. His other love. The finished poems lay under a cloth; the untouched sheets lay above. He couldn't write here. It was too muddy, too uncertain. But he'd be comforted, at least, by reading some of the thousands of words he'd penned, in quieter times, about the Rose. He leafed through the sheets. *"The Lover rides through the darkness,"* he read, *"in wind, and rain, and pain. But wherever he goes he carries the memory of the Rose in his heart."*

"We beat them at Crécy, we beat them at Poitiers," his subaltern was caroling from the weapons tent; and the men greasing his saddle bawled back, "We'll beat them *todaaaay!*"

Owain crossed himself at that. But there was a smile on his face. Even that brief glimpse of the inexpert words he'd struggled so hard to compose—and so often got into trouble for wasting his time on—reminded him of the true purpose of his life, even beyond this. "Amen," he murmured, and, putting the box away, strode into the tent to join in the singing.

Charles, Duke of Orléans, walking into the blackness outside the French commander's tent to consider the order he'd just been given, wondered how the English managed to make so much noise. They were thundering away over there, singing, eating, drinking, belching, farting, shouting. As far as his eye could guess at shapes, there were French horses tethered by French tents stretched out all the way to the horizon. He knew there must be many, many more French soldiers in these fields than the English could possibly have mustered. But the men he could make out closest at hand—silhouettes gathered round their smoking mounds of embers—were hunched and miserable. There were no musical instruments playing here. (Perhaps the Constable should have let the six thousand men offered by the burghers of Paris come; they might not have known how to fight but they'd probably have been a dab hand at picking out a tune on a pipe. Then again, you couldn't have city people in a battle; what did commoners know of war?) The French cavalry horses were all but silent. So were the men; though in two or three groups he passed as he wondered what to do he heard gruff voices muttering, "bygones be bygones" and "water under the bridge," and saw stiff, awkward embraces, and understood that old enemies, right across this black field, must be making peace among themselves, before facing death together at daylight.

Although he knew with utter certainty that the flower of French chivalry, assembled here, must beat the English, the Duke of Orléans was surprised, when he looked at his own long, thin fingers—a poet's hands, his wife called them; war wasn't his calling—to see they were trembling.

Right is on our side, he reminded himself, reaching for the rosary around his neck. Right is on our side. The flower of French chivalry has assembled to do God's will.

113

The Duke of Orléans was a man of simple, straightforward beliefs, or he wanted to be, if his treacherous hands would not betray him. A usurper had come to French shores with a wrongful claim to French lands. God, and the French nobility, under the Oriflamme, would smite him down.

But as his fingers touched the beads, and his lips danced through Ave Marias and Pater Nosters, he found himself trying not to remember all those long-ago battles when the French nobility had been destroyed by a cruel God's favor for the English armies of earlier kings.

And when he thought of his order for tomorrow—the order just given him by the Constable of Albret, who was to be commander for the day, because the King himself couldn't be on this battlefield—he couldn't help the prickling of his scalp that he couldn't believe was fear.

He wasn't going to obey that order, of course. No one but a king had the right to order a prince of the blood royal to do anything less than heroic in battle.

He wasn't going to stay at the back with his men.

He was going to join the charge.

Charles of Orléans had allowed two grooms into his tent at dawn to put on his armor. Once mounted, he'd cantered down from the royal enclosure to the encampment where his own troop had spent the night. No fires; it was too far from the woods; the men's faces were as gray as the skies. Their leather sallets were soaking and looked as heavy as his glittering breastplate. He thought: The subaltern's not up to it. He should have found them better shelter. But he contained his irritation and politely told the subaltern to take charge of the men on his behalf during the battle. "I will be in the charge," he said impassively; choosing not to see the man's look of fear.

Now, with a gauntleted hand over his eyes to keep the day's early drizzle out, he was standing in the shelter of an outcrop of trees on a slight swell of land, watching the other army rouse itself below. His spirits were higher than they'd been all night. The English force moving around like ants in the mud was much smaller than all that noise in the night had suggested. He could hardly see any horses. The English were encircled; in visible danger; they must be discouraged at the sea of French soldiery facing them. And their tents were gray and brown with mud; none of the magnificence there of the French equipment. He doubted their weapons and their tired campaign horses were much good either.

Owain was part of the group of knights called to the King's tent at break of day to hear Mass. Owain had dozed a little by the dying fire—he half remembered being happy in the dream, and feeling the butterfly kiss of eyelashes on his skin and yielding female flesh in his arms—but the damp streaks of colorless light that he'd seen on the horizon as he startled back into wakefulness, signaling time running out before it all began, filled him with dread. He was grateful for the armor that hid his pale face and racing heart. But, standing in front of the King's stained tent, he was heartened by the sight of Henry, looking far younger than his twenty-eight years, with every sinew of him hard and ready, pulling on his metal plates, cursing ruefully—"bloody hands shaking; it's the excitement, always like this"—then devoutly bowing his head in prayer and taking the sacrament in his mouth.

We're all afraid, Owain thought, reassured. He knows that. Even he is. Fear is natural. Nothing to reproach myself with.

Yet Henry showed no more signs of fear. He got up calmly on his gray charger and gave orders to each of the knights. Owain's troop was to be in the rear of the charge. Infantry to take the lead; follow up the arrows. Archers in flanks to left and right.

Then the King rode off among the men saddling horses or strapping quivers and axes on themselves, stretching bowstrings taut, restringing them, testing the blades of weapons wrapped in old rags to keep out the damp, binding up their feet. Every few minutes he stopped to talk, leaning down over his horse's great thick powerful neck, and what he said, in that brisk, no-nonsense, calm voice, with a hint of a laugh in it, was the same for every group of soldiers he addressed. *You can see the danger we're in; the only way out is to win.* Owain, back with his own men, making sure they were properly armed and ready before mounting his own dappled horse, strained to hear that beloved voice as hard as every other knight and foot soldier. And, in his heart, he joined their nervous cheers at that first mention of victory. The cheers got louder and more confident when Henry said, in a rhythmic, swinging echo of the song they'd been singing in the night: "Don't forget—we beat them at Crécy! We beat them at Poitiers!" Every now and again, some bright spark would yell back, "We'll beat them *todaaaay*!" And the King would clap him appreciatively on the back, and move on.

But Owain's heart, like that of every other English soldier, almost burst with devotion and breathless pride when Henry, having reached the front of the camp, first pointed out the jostling mass of French horsemen, ready to be off over there, yelled a few more words of encouragement to the entire English force, then swung off his horse.

On foot, with his sword held high in front of him, he roared to the joyful infantrymen crowding behind him, "Henry! Henry!" and, without Owain quite having understood that the battle was beginning, led them in a surging charge over the soggy ground toward the French.

It was still raining. Water dripped into Charles, Duke of Orléans' eyes from his helmet. He was running through the October woods, panting like an animal, as wet under his armor as everything in the watery gloom outside. He was running through branches looming out of the fog like outstretched arms, hooking at him, hooking at his sword.

He couldn't breathe. He stumbled; stopped; crawled into the doubtful safety of a leafless bush; and lay there, shutting out the world with arms over his head, sobbing in air, feeling the boom of his heart against his breastplate, not listening to the noises behind him.

He knew what he'd see if he looked back again. A gray-brown writhing hell of dying men, with Englishmen crawling all over them. He knew what he'd feel, too: a gray-brown horror of shame.

His men would be back there somewhere, still.

He should have stayed with them.

All the princes of the blood should have stayed with their men.

But none of them had. They'd all ignored the Constable's orders. They'd all left their men. They'd all jostled to the front line in their heavy armor, kicking and whacking and hacking at each other to get a place. They all wanted the glory.

He'd felt the glory, all right: when the horn had sounded and his horse had surged forward at a furious gallop, thundering over the mud, with its red and gold caparison flying, while he crouched over the pommel, jaw clenched, eyes narrowed, ready for combat, ready for death. There'd been glory surging through his veins like alcohol; a red haze in front of his eyes.

But only for a moment.

Then his horse had sunk into the mud under him.

He'd managed to roll free. But it was a long, dazed moment before he'd got shaking to his feet, leaning on his lance. His knee hurt.

It was only then that he saw the charge was over. All the other horses were down in the mud, too, wherever he looked, hundreds of them, squealing and screaming and flailing their damaged legs. And some of the screams were human.

With all the mud and drizzle and confusion, and everything so gray and brown, Charles of Orléans hadn't understood straightaway what was happening. Then he'd seen an arrow shaft land squarely in his horse's chest. Its feathered tip quivered. Pegasus rolled his head and rolled his eyes and died.

The English weren't charging. There was death in the air. The death of common men. The sky was full of yeomen's arrows.

He'd sheltered behind Pegasus' warm body disbelievingly, waiting for the danger to pass. Still calm; able, for a moment, to despise the enemy's failure to engage as the laws of chivalry demanded. It was only when he'd seen the gray and brown ants crawling out of the distant fields and tents and swarming toward him at such speed that, before he knew it, they became thickset English rustics wielding axes and pikes, led by a terrifying glinting war god in glittering armor, and heard the bloodcurdling yells of "Henry!" and "Saint George for merry England!" that Charles, Duke of Orléans, grandson and great-grandson of kings of France, whose veins coursed with the noble blood of Charlemagne and Brutus, panicked and ran for his life.

The news of Azincourt spread through France like the bitter autumn wind; the rains battering the windows felt like tears. Ten thousand Frenchmen had died and fifteen hundred been taken prisoner. Among the dead were the King's commander for the day, the Constable of Albret, and his two brothers, the Duke of Bar and the Duke of Alençon. The young Duke of Orléans, who'd written such lovely poetry in the style of Madame de Pizan, was a prisoner. So was the Duke of Bourbon, the Count of Richemont, the Count of Eu, and Marshal Boucicault. The sound of weeping drifted out of every open window. In just three hours, Paris had become a city of widows. There wasn't a noble house in France left untouched by the tragedy.

Even the Duke of Burgundy—who had not volunteered for the King's army, and who had locked his fifteen-year-old son up to stop him running away to fight—had lost two brothers.

The city whispered. The people of Paris could sense weakness in their rulers. Even in their grief, the mourners sensed trouble would be coming their way soon.

NINE

Catherine was at Mass with her parents when the messenger came.

There was a scuffle at the door. Then a dozen heads were pushed inside. "Sire," the voices said. The priest looked up through the incense at the expectant eyes. The King looked away. Catherine could feel how much her father, who was still frail and slow-moving as he convalesced from his bout of illness, didn't want to be interrupted. "Sire," the voices said, insistently.

It was clear to all of them that it must be bad news. Catherine could feel her heart quicken. Catherine's mother wheezed and heaved herself up. She put a hand out to the King, who was staring at his hands. "Afterward? Surely?" he said piteously, indicating the priest and the chalice; but she only said impatiently, "Come," and began tugging at his arm.

When they told him, he did nothing. It was the Queen who rushed out of the room, with big tears pouring down her face, yelling, "Call the council!" and "Send word to Prince Louis to come!" and "Why weren't we informed earlier?" and "Condolences to the widows! A list of ransoms! Mass at Notre Dame! Full mourning for the court!" The messenger and the courtiers rushed after her, remonstrating or agreeing or making busy suggestions; a wind of noise and importance. But King Charles just sat, with empty eyes, on his bench.

Timidly, Catherine reached out her hand and put it on his trembling liver-splotched one. Her head was spinning. She'd danced with Charles of Orléans only last week. He'd told her about his war horse. Pegasus, he'd said easily: the closest thing to a winged horse on this earth. He'd smite the King of England to the ground with his hooves alone. "It's my dream to bring him down myself in the thick of battle, with a single blow of my sword." Catherine had admired the ambition. Charles of Orléans had been wearing blue velvet sewn with pearls. Now she was trying to imagine him in chains, being marched through the mud to Calais and roughly embarked on an English ship, but found that her imagination failed her. This couldn't be real. There must be a mistake.

Her father twitched his head and said nothing.

"It's hard to believe," Catherine murmured; stroking his papery skin; remembering how just a few years ago her father had lifted her into the tree she could see through the window, roaring with laughter. How strong he'd been then. How young. He seemed like an old man today. He didn't seem to be listening.

"It will be all right, Father; you mustn't worry . . ." she ventured. He was shocked, she thought. How hard it must be to bear the burden of all this on your own shoulders; how heartbreaking to be a king in times of trouble. "We'll raise the ransoms. We'll get everyone back. Henry of England isn't a bad man. He knows the law of war. Even if it takes time . . ."

Quietly, her father said: "Not Henry of England." But it wasn't really an answer. She had a feeling he was thinking of something quite different. He gave her a knowing look. He grinned. "George."

"George?"

He grinned again. "Me."

She stared. Had she misheard? He burst out laughing. Then he looked cunning. Then surprised. "Don't tell me you didn't know," he said, and winked at her. "I am Saint George of England."

She didn't know what to do.

She didn't understand what he was saying.

She just knew she needed help. Father needed help. He wasn't himself.

She edged back, looking for a man-at-arms to signal to.

But before she could catch any eyes of the men in the doorways, her father looked down at the doublet he was wearing, which was decorated with woven fleurs-de-lys.

She saw the look of terror on his face; a terror so intense she nearly screamed with it. His face contorted. His eyes popped. "Spiders! Spiders!" he yelled, beginning to scrabble at them, getting a grip on one flap of the cloth and ripping it away from his body with hands that weren't, after all, so frail and old.

Now men-at-arms did start to appear, clustering near him, looking alarmed. "Spiders! Get them off me!" he was squealing in horror.

"They're not spiders, Father," she said faintly, but he was down on the ground now, snarling and grabbing the material with his teeth, saliva pouring from his mouth, worrying at the cloth like a dog chasing its tail. "They're French lilies. Your emblem."

What she was most aware of, apart from the strange, unreal quality of everything that was happening this morning, was that although the men-at-arms were frightened, they weren't surprised at the way her father was behaving.

They were grouping themselves around him; ready to pick him up. They didn't, though. No one dared touch the King's person. They were waiting for an order. With a slow buildup of horror, she realized they were waiting for an order from her.

"Filthy French spider lilies!" she heard as she turned away. She could feel tears welling up inside her. She couldn't cry. She swallowed. Seeing the captain of the guard's eyes on her, she nodded. There was nothing else to be done.

"Tell my mother," she said, covering her eyes with her hand as if shielding them from the wind. Guardsmen shouldn't see a princess of the blood royal lose her dignity.

She must have known, in a part of herself. But understanding it now was like feeling her own fabric being ripped agonizingly apart. No one was surprised except her, because they'd all seen it before. This was what her father's illness was. He was mad.

Catherine was still sitting in her mother's private chapel, what might have been hours or moments later, when Christine found her. Christine had decided to come to her as soon as she'd heard the news of Azincourt. This was no time to remember past bitterness, Christine thought determinedly, rushing to the Hôtel Saint-Paul; it was a time for old friends to come together. She'd been missing her visits for months. Catherine would need her.

The brazier seemed to give no warmth. There was a threat of early snow in the air. Christine was shivering under her furs with the shock of the news from the front; and even from here she could see Catherine shaking.

"My charge needs me," she said to the guard who automatically stepped forward to block the way of anyone trying to disturb the Princess's privacy. She turned tragic eyes on him.

"Seeing as it's you . . ." the guard said, perhaps seeing the red rims of those eyes. He let her through.

Catherine was on her knees, alone. She was looking at her hands. They were a bloodless, whitish blue. Christine didn't think she'd been praying.

She slipped down to her own knees beside the Princess.

When Christine opened her arms, Catherine let herself sink into them.

"I saw Father . . ." Catherine muttered, ". . . start . . . you know . . ."

Christine held her tighter. She hadn't known that. It took her breath away. She hadn't thought anything worse could happen today.

"He said he was Saint George of England. He tore the fleurs-de-lys off his own back. Called them spiders."

Christine smelled the Queen's overblown rose oil on the girl's hair; but she smelled the freshness of youth there too. Catherine should have had so much to hope for. But there was so much to fear as well. How sorry Christine felt for this girl, facing a hardship she couldn't yet begin to understand. The first of many, maybe.

"They should have told you before," she said, and by "they" she meant "the Queen." "You're not a child anymore."

"He's . . . mad," Catherine said, raising her eyes to Christine; and in those unfocused pupils Christine saw bottomless depths of horror; demons and crawling spiders. "Possessed. We're cursed. All of us. France is cursed."

It was so close to what Christine was thinking that she drew in breath. Catherine was being braver than she'd expected—naming her fears. Still, she shook her head.

Catherine said harshly: "But it was you who taught us. The King is the head of the body politic. The nobles its arms and hands. The peasants its legs and feet. You remember?"

Reluctantly, Christine nodded.

"Well, doesn't that mean that, if the head goes mad, the country goes mad with him?"

A pause.

"That's what's been happening all this time, isn't it?" Catherine said.

Christine couldn't bear to agree.

"They've always just shut him away," Christine said in the end, changing the subject, aware she sounded disjointed but unable to compose herself fully. "Whenever this happens. Everyone's scared to admit he's gone mad. He used to get violent. He's not violent anymore. I go to him sometimes. There are servants. We know. But he's afraid; always afraid. He never has anyone he loves with him."

"What about my mother?"

Christine shook her head. She knew it was disingenuous not to tell Catherine that whenever the King, in his madness, saw his wife, he attacked her. But years of dislike of everything about the Queen—a dislike she couldn't discuss with Catherine—stilled her tongue. She let the accusing silence deepen.

"But he loves *you*," she said quietly. "If *you* went to him . . . if you weren't afraid . . . if you listened to the things he's afraid of . . . who knows what good that might do? It might help make him whole . . . it might even help heal him . . ."

Catherine drew in breath. She could hear that even Christine, who was suggesting it, thought it a faint hope. She bit her lip. She said, with dread: "You mean . . . me . . . *go to him?*"

Christine nodded.

"*When he's* . . ." Catherine muttered, looking down. Flexing her fingers.

Christine drew her closer; put her own hands over those fingers; let Catherine bury her head in her breast. The girl needed comfort; it would help her make her decision. Then, through their shared heartbeats, Christine murmured, with utter certainty, "Yes. Now."

He was in a white shift. He was in a white room she'd never seen before, with guards outside. Christine stayed behind with them; squeezed Catherine's arm as they opened the door.

He was up on the window ledge, with his feet drawn up from the floor, staring out at the white sky.

"I'm parched," he said, not looking at her, in a little-boy voice. But when Catherine poured him water from the jug on the table, he ignored it.

She waited. The voice began again; cunning this time. "You won't fool me. You're pretending to be my little Catherine. But I know who you really are and what you want. You want to steal my soul. And you're cruel, cruel . . . you know how thirsty I am . . . the thirst of the damned . . . my soul's so parched and desperate . . . you're just trying to trick me with your water . . . you know I can't drink."

Catherine sat very still, feeling the stool beneath her. She thought: I have to say something. She said: "Why?"

There was a strange cackle of laughter. "Because you'll steal my soul if I do, of course. Don't think I don't know. Let you in once and you'll take everything; leave me nothing. It's what you always do. You stole my sword, didn't you? You, or her, you're all the same . . . And now the sun's gone black and the world is ending you're going to steal my soul too." He stopped. Hummed to himself. Picked with one gnarly hand at his gnarly foot, keeping his head averted from Catherine all the time.

After a while, she heard his voice again; softer this time; pleading. "Don't look at me, though, will you?" it said. "It's dangerous to look at someone who's made of glass. One look goes straight through, you know. Pierces me to the heart. One look and I'll splinter. You'd smash me to bits if you looked. And you don't want that, do you?"

She shook her head, feeling tears on her hand. Then she remembered he wouldn't see her movement. He wasn't looking. "No," she snuffled, wishing, impossibly, that he'd hear her distress and come to; come running over to comfort his little girl; that she'd be lost in his big embrace, smell the warmth of him, and forget all this. "No, Papa, I don't want that."

It felt an eternity before Catherine heard sounds at the door. Christine slipped in; looked alertly round at Catherine, giving her a look glowing with warmth and admiration and compassion. At last, Catherine thought, so wrung out with relief that she loved Christine unconditionally and forgot their past coldness in the warmth of this moment.

She noticed that Christine didn't even look at the King of France, clawing up there against the bars of his window with his feet off the ground. But she said "Good morning" to him, over her shoulder, in a brisk voice.

Christine sat with Catherine at the table and put a hand on hers. It was warm. It was blessedly normal. Catherine clung to it. But she kept her face brave.

"Have you been talking?" Christine said, raising her voice for the silent third person in the room. "You two?"

The voice began. Whining; singsong; tale-bearing; treacherous. Things Catherine's father would never be. She listened, hating it. "Oh, it's cunning," her non-father said to Christine (and Catherine thought suddenly: Perhaps he had a voice like that, long ago, when he and Louis and Christine were just three children playing together in the gardens?). "It's cunning all right. It's come here to the ghost of the weed garden . . . to the windy desert . . . so it can steal my soul. It says it doesn't want it but I know."

Christine tightened her grip on Catherine's hand, as if sensing her distress. "But you're here with us," she said matter-of-factly to the voice. "You're still here."

"No I'm not," it said quickly. "I'm not here. I've hidden

125

myself. There are wild beasts in the woods. I'm staying still. So still. They won't see me. I can be nothing. Quiet, quiet. Stop breathing. Nothing moves. Nothing is alive. Everything's outside. They can't see me here. I'm nothing. Nothing."

Despite herself, Catherine felt her face pucker. She concentrated on Christine's hand, feeling its strength.

But she couldn't bear it. A voice as strange to her as her father's singsong broke out of her own mouth: an angry, excruciating wail: "You're not! You're the King of France! You're my father!"

The voice stopped. Christine was shaking her head. It was clear Christine thought she'd done the wrong thing. But she could feel the man in the window thinking.

"No . . . that's what they say, but it's not me," it said in the end, very reasonably. "What's a king? It's a crown. A horn. A flag. That's what they want. A symbol. But that's not me. I'm not made of gold or scarlet, am I? I'm not made of metal. I'm not made of anything. I'm a ghost. I don't deserve to be anything else. Golden feet . . . it would be scary to have a golden belly."

Christine's tense hand relaxed. But then the voice screamed and the man in the window covered his head with his hands.

"I'm a good boy! I do what I'm told!" the voice said, then dropped to a whisper. "Look after him when I'm gone; he's my hope of eternity; and he's so young. Flighty. Make him serious and as wise as Solomon. Read him philosophy." Then it said brightly: "Make him strong and brave and bold." Shouted: "A soldier-king! Fight off the English! Give him armor! A sword! Let's go hunting! Let's fight! Let's love each other! No, let's fight! Save the blood royal! Shed the blood royal! Make love, not war! Love your wife! Have children! Perpetuate the blood royal! Have mistresses! Don't cry when the children die! The blood royal knows no grief! Don't cry, dance! Let's have a ball! The biggest you've ever seen! Fountains running with wine! Show them what you're made of! Cure the sick! Kings cure disease . . . Kings, and Jesus . . . Kings are God's anointed. Cure! Marry! Spend! Save! Fight! Love! Hate! Dance! Kill! Forgive!" Her father stopped screaming. He had tears running down his cheeks. He sniveled, "He's gone to the bad, of course; doesn't think of anything except hunting and dancing all night. She doesn't love him. She loves his brother. He's not the man his father was, this one. No hope against the English. Not with this one." Plaintively, "I love my brother."

His energy was spent. He curled up into a ball, muttering words Catherine couldn't hear.

Regretfully but calmly, Christine was shaking her head.

Catherine was shaking. But she'd found pity somewhere deep inside herself. She shouldn't have said he was the King. That was what had started it. She could see that now.

"I'm sorry," she said, without looking at Christine for guidance. "I've upset you. And I only meant to say, I love you."

Christine patted her hand, then said: "She didn't understand. But she doesn't mean to hurt you. You know you can trust me, don't you? You can trust her too."

The muttering went on.

"I won't look. I won't steal your soul," Catherine said. She suddenly, desperately, wanted to do something to ease the desolation in the sick man's soul. She wanted to quench his thirst.

She got up and took the cup to him on the windowsill.

She kept her head turned away.

She put the cup down and walked away, with her head down.

Only when she'd sat down did she take courage to glance up at Christine's face. The older woman's eyes were alive with hope. She raised her eyebrows, nodded, and mouthed: *He drank it.*

Catherine began to go to the white room every day.

It was the place where secrets were unraveled. Everything she hadn't understood became clear. What she didn't understand for herself, Christine explained. Christine was showing her the adult world—at last, the truth she'd only ever half seen. By turns, Catherine was horrified and grateful.

Christine said she believed that the King of France had taken refuge in madness because he was mortally afraid of facing the realities of his life.

He had been a child king—an orphan, with no one to guide him. His own father had wanted him to be brought up as a wise philosopher like himself. But, as it turned out, Charles' childhood passed very differently—being squabbled over by noblemen who all wanted to steal the absolute power that was his destiny, and then in a fast-moving, free-spending blur of entertainments and escapades with his wild, witty younger brother Louis of Orléans.

Then he'd married: and he'd thought for a while he'd found salvation in his wife's love. But that had been as much of an illusion as his father's love. Queen Isabeau had been a beauty, in her youth. King Charles fell completely under her spell as soon as he saw her. He did whatever she wanted. She was charismatic; loved parties; loved jewels; loved fun. And a girl who'd grown up quietly in Bavaria, never expecting to be Queen of the greatest court of Europe, couldn't believe her luck at being the most important woman in glorious France. It had gone to her head. The balls she'd held . . . the entertainments . . . the lovers she'd taken . . . the *havoc* she'd caused. The King had never questioned anything. He was her slave. She'd driven him wild.

"Lovers?" Catherine had questioned. Christine only raised her eyebrows and let the accusing silence thicken again. There was a lot of silent accusation in this account, Catherine was beginning to see. She sensed that the duty of explaining the Queen's shortcomings wasn't one Christine found altogether unpleasant.

Queen Isabeau's most scandalous affair had been with her husband's brother, Louis of Orléans, Christine said.

The brothers had gone to Provence together. For a bet, they'd raced each other back to Paris—on boats, horses, whatever they could find. Louis got there first—after five days. While Charles was still on the road home, his brother went straight to Isabeau.

That affair was what had finally done for King Charles' sanity, Christine believed. The King's madness began as soon as he'd found out. He'd lost himself in his wife; and now she was destroying him.

Charles and Louis had gone hunting a few days later. It was hot; Charles was sweating in black velvet. But no one expected

him to start screaming that there were eyes behind the trees . . .
enemies . . . and to start running his own pages through with a
lance. He'd killed four by the time they managed to get him
down and restrain him.

His madness had only driven the Queen back into the arms
of her lover. And her favoritism had offended the Duke of Burgundy, Louis of Orléans' rival for power. So Burgundy had
killed Orléans, and the vicious spiral of aristocratic feuding
had begun. Isabeau's troublemaking had eventually called into
existence two armies of warring Frenchmen, destroying their
own country.

Now a predator from England was prowling in the darkness
too, and France was being dismembered.

But the Queen was too lazy to try and put right the wrong
she'd done. The Queen's only solution had been to provide her
husband with a bourgeois girl called Odette de Champdivers—
half nursemaid, half mistress—and, whenever his madness came
on him, lock the pair of them away together and titter that she'd
found him a "Little Queen" to look after him.

The Queen, Christine told Catherine, as she caught the girl
up with the history of her own family, had also found it conve-
nient to blame the King for this infidelity, whenever she was
angry or it suited her to feel oppressed. But as soon as Catherine knew, and started visiting her father, Christine had Odette
quietly sent away; and she stopped locking the white room too.
"We won't need *her,*" she said, of Odette, with grim satisfaction. "Or"—jangling the keys—"*these.*" The Queen wouldn't
know of these changes unless someone told her, for Isabeau
certainly wouldn't come and check for herself during one of
her husband's bouts of madness.

But, even with Christine and Catherine in the room with
him, the King didn't take advantage of the unlocked door and
come out. He was too scared. No wonder, Catherine thought,
as she began to understand. Catherine's cousins and uncles
were building battlements around their houses wherever you
looked, even in Paris. The country roads swarmed with hungry
men and highwaymen; and the green of the farmlands had
gone wild with weeds. No wonder everyone was so frightened.

No wonder her father escaped into his dark nothingness of terror and fantasy. "We call it madness, but the darkness he loses himself in isn't far from reality," Christine said sadly. "We're all in that place . . . a France full of fear and ghosts . . . we just don't see it so clearly as he does."

"Why are you torturing the poor girl?" Jean de Castel asked Christine. "She can't help her father."

It was late. They were watching the embers of the fire. Christine was looking stubborn.

"Why not just try to encourage the Queen to marry her off and get her away from it all?" Jean persisted. "What's the point of keeping her there, rubbing her nose in the madness?"

Christine's eyes glittered.

"This is no time for marriages," she said tartly. "You know that. The young princes she might marry are all prisoners of the English, or away fighting."

She got up, straightening her skirts, trying to look strict, though Jean noticed she was actually looking secretly pleased with herself. She added: "But, when the time does come for Catherine to marry, it won't do any harm at all if she's known to be especially close to her father."

"Why?" Jean asked.

"In case of wagging tongues," Christine answered, with a speed that betrayed how much she'd thought about the question. "In case anyone remembers how her mother's affair with Louis of Orléans ended with his death—but started the year before Catherine was born. It wouldn't take much to make people think about how the Bavarian woman wouldn't think twice before putting cuckoos in the nest."

Jean shook his head. "You worry too much," he said, relaxing. "No one does say anything like that."

"Gossip comes from nowhere," Christine replied. "When you've spent as much time at court as I have, you'll understand that. Catherine and Charles both . . . brought up in corners as they've been . . . it would be an easy conclusion to draw. I wouldn't want Catherine's chances of a good marriage spoiled by . . . doubts."

She looked defiantly at her son. "It doesn't matter about Charles. He's married already—and he has two older brothers. No one is going to worry too much whose blood runs in *his* veins when he's only third in line to the throne. But Catherine has everything still ahead. Her husband will need to feel sure of her line. It matters for her. So—let her tend her father. Let the world see their bond of familial love. Father and daughter together. Blood tells."

"What if," Jean asked, playing devil's advocate, "she actually *is* a bastard? What if, by building up that relationship, you are conniving at passing off a cuckoo child as the King's own—and maybe perpetrating a fraudulent royal marriage? Wouldn't you feel that was a sin?"

But Christine only shook her head. She enjoyed these little jousts with her son. "No," she said, grinning too. "*That* knowledge is for God, not me. I can't know His mind; I'm only mortal. I can only concern myself with how things might appear to other people like myself. Those two children have had a hard enough start in life. They don't need any more trouble. I want that girl to have the happy marriage, the children, and the love she deserves. This is a way of helping that to happen."

Jean de Castel shrugged, accepting his defeat. "You're much too devious," he said, as she kissed his forehead and moved toward the door. It was only when Christine was already in the doorway that he remembered the obvious point, and called: "But—does your Catherine even want to marry? Are there princes she talks about? Friendships? Affinities?" He couldn't remember hearing of any.

Christine turned. For a moment he saw doubt in her eyes. She shook her head. "She says there's enough to worry about with the King as it is," she replied. She looked down. Jean could have sworn his mother felt guilty about something, though he couldn't imagine what. "She won't talk about it."

The Queen didn't know Catherine had found her way to the white room. Although Christine insisted she go on attending her mother every day, Catherine couldn't find words to tell her mother she knew about her father's madness.

Her head was full of questions. Her mind was full of pictures of her mother—or a younger version of her mother, still slim, in the enormous veils she used to favor, cackling wickedly over a racy joke, pertly sticking her breasts out—kissing the uncle Catherine only vaguely remembered: tall, blond Louis of Orléans, with his floppy hair and mischievous eyes.

Could her mother really have . . . with her own husband's brother? Catherine found the idea almost too shocking to believe. She wanted to ask her mother, but fear stopped her tongue. She couldn't imagine her mother's face if she dared to ask. The thought of trying made her blood run cold. She kept her peace; the questions stayed in her head.

So Queen Isabeau was mildly puzzled by her daughter's accusing looks in the hot boudoir, between the *calorifères* that poured out heat and rose oil fumes from the burning coals in their bellies, and the elaborate frescoes of woodland scenes and happy children eating fruit among the flowers.

The Queen dipped her fingers into the bowls, sampling the flavors, as the two dwarfs unwrapped the sweets and laid them out. Twenty pounds of dragées. Twenty pounds of coriander balls. Twenty pounds of paste du roy. Twenty pounds each of sweetmeats flavored with cinnamon and rose sugar. Forty pounds of sugared nuts. She licked the sugar off her sticky hands. There could be no dances this winter, of course. But there was nothing wrong with a little something sweet.

"Good," she said thickly. "The rose sugar—try."

The dwarfs both grinned eagerly and began stuffing their faces. But Catherine just shook her head and went on looking glum and sulky.

Queen Isabeau didn't know what was the matter with Catherine. Girls were mystifying. It wasn't as if she was one of those poor duchesses, running round pawning their valuables to raise a ransom for their husbands.

Isabeau munched on, looking at her daughter with a sudden speculative interest. Unless . . . She couldn't, by any chance, be in love with one of the young chevaliers imprisoned at Azincourt?

She shook her head. She could see Catherine wouldn't tell

her. Too cross. Well, it was her loss. The sweets were delicious. She reached out two pink fingers and helped herself to more.

The next day, when Catherine went to her mother's rooms they were empty. The tapestries had gone off the walls; the furniture had gone off the floor. But there was a letter for Catherine; a guard gave it to her. It said Isabeau and her household had left Paris for the castle of Melun. The Queen explained casually that she'd decided to spend Christmas there. Paris—full of noblewomen in widows' weeds, selling art objects to each other and to the Italians to raise ransom money for their husbands in England—was too depressing. She'd move on to Vincennes after Christmas.

"The selfishness of it. She should have stayed," Christine said angrily; "at least in the same city as her husband. The last thing we need now is rumors that the King's marriage is over."

But Catherine was quietly relieved at Queen Isabeau's thoughtless departure. At least, she thought, she needn't worry about confronting her mother and discussing the past for a while longer.

Outside, there was only bad news. All the strongmen kept advancing across the spectral landscape of France, threatening to converge bloodily on Paris. An English army advanced across northern France. The Duke of Burgundy's separate army advanced across eastern France. In Paris, the widows and the surviving princes of the other French side—the Orléanist princes fighting with the Count of Armagnac—trembled. There were comets in the night sky; plagues in Paris; freak storms in the vineyards.

Inside, silence descended on the palace. War, Catherine found herself thinking, seemed to be about silence; about no longer having words or a common language that you could share with other people. Now the Queen was gone, and there were just servants, a princess, and a mad king, there were no guests at the Hôtel Saint-Paul. The only person who came to talk to Catherine and her father anymore was Christine. Sometimes Catherine's father was silent for days on end. Sometimes he made his own entertainment. Sometimes he shouted. Sometimes he stank. Once he defecated in front of her, and sang mockingly, "There! Golden crown shit! What d'you think of *that*?"

But Catherine sensed she was being tested; and any display of life was better than the dead silence. So she kept her face calm and cleaned up the mess on the floor herself; with rags and the bucket by the door. "There," she said brightly to the wet floor when she was done, "that's better. Nothing to worry about now." And, in the window, her father started humming.

She'd started by being always afraid he'd turn violent; always aware of how many steps there were from where she was to the door. But he never did. She stopped needing Christine's hand to hold (though she was always overjoyed to see Christine; to talk; it was exhausting being alone with her father's desolation). He wasn't angry with her. There was nothing for her to fear from him.

Soon the King began to come to her at the table in the white room. He'd sit down cautiously beside her, still averting his eyes. He'd drink water with her. Once he ate with her. He held her hand. He let her order a bath. He let her change his stinking shirt. And he didn't seem to mind that she was there when he put his head on the table and wept, inconsolably, for the losses they were getting used to accepting.

"There's no comfort, no comfort," he'd whimper. "Everyone's dying; because I'm dead."

The next day she began to feel he had been right. The messenger who came said her eldest brother, Louis—heir to the throne—had died. Suddenly, of a fever. There was an epidemic in Paris.

She and Christine went out to hear the man's news. Visitors from the outside world sent the King into such terror that all newcomers had to be screened. Catherine had never really known her brother; the prince with the white face and black eyes and sneering ways with his wife was years older, and had never had much time for her. She'd heard enough from her mother, about Louis' bad character and cruelty, not to feel much love for him. But he was her blood, as well as the figurehead of all the French princes standing against the armies of her cousin of Burgundy; and she'd never see him again. Tears came stinging to her eyes. She nodded; thanked the man; sent him away; blinked her moment of grief away too. Christine's face was ashen as they walked back in to her father.

Christine broke the news gently, saying "We must be strong" and ". . . a great sorrow." But it did no good. A moment before, her father had been sitting with them at the table, and saying, earnestly, sadly, but almost sanely, "You're the only people I can talk to; you're the only ones who understand; I'm in a nightmare I can't wake up from, and I can't get help; but you're here with me . . . and that's a comfort . . ." Now, suddenly, he drew himself out of Christine's embrace and flew across the room, back to the safety of his window perch, from where he stared out of the window. "The ravens are there," he said conversationally. "Look. Pecking out our eyes."

It was April when the next royal brother to have been heir to the throne died. Jean. He'd been a creature of the Duke of Burgundy, whose niece he'd married. He hadn't come back to Paris since becoming Crown Prince. He'd been kept away by Burgundy. He'd been Catherine's blood; but again she hadn't known him. Catherine let the rumors—a fever? poisoned by her mother, or by the southern Armagnac princes who knew poisons?—wash over her. She felt remote. Her tears wouldn't come.

The thought that came into her head this time was a flash of sunlight. Jean's death meant that Charles—her little brother, who'd once been her dearest friend—would be Crown Prince and would soon come back to Paris. Charles was anything but the creature of the terrifying Duke of Burgundy. He hated Burgundy as utterly as Catherine did—beyond reason, beyond logic—the older cousin, as thin as death, whose hooded eyes and paper-thin skin and cold, cold voice had haunted their every childhood nightmare. Charles had been growing up as far from Burgundy as possible, in the heart of the Armagnac south: he was a model prince for a France that might finally shake off the Duke's stranglehold. Charles' closeness to the Armagnac faction was reassuring, but it wasn't what made Catherine happiest when she thought of the brother whom fate was bringing back to her. The older, quieter, more capable young woman who came out of the white room nowadays wanted nothing more than her childhood friend; a chance to be a girl again, and to be reunited with the brother she'd always been able to talk with.

"Don't cry; don't cry," Catherine muttered at her father's hunched shoulders, wondering where her own tears had gone. "Charles will come home now to be Crown Prince. Little Charlot."

And somehow she made her voice so encouraging, so loving, so full of hope, that her father, who was himself that day—not made of glass, or blighted by a black sun, just sobbing in anguish at the death of his sons—looked up and gave her a watery smile.

TEN

Charles wriggled in his splendid black velvet, and turned to his mother-in-law, Yolande of Aragon, for reassurance. The new Crown Prince of France—the Dauphin, who also bore the title of Duke of Aquitaine, for those vast tracts of southern France that Henry of England wanted for himself—had grown used to the sophistication of southern clothes in his time away; the elegant ways of troubadour castles. He was missing the lovely safety of the scent of wild garlic and rosemary in his nostrils. It was making him deeply uneasy to be back here, at the château of Vincennes, outside Paris, where his mother had established her court, about to meet his real parents again. It was raining. The peasant cottages outside had soaking straw roofs. He smelled mud and fear wherever he turned. His stomach churned darkly; feeling full of ground glass.

Yolande screwed up her pretty dark monkey-face into a comforting grimace. It almost made him laugh. You'd never guess from that wry expression that she'd had the strength of purpose to write energetically back, as soon as she'd got the order from the Queen to release Charles to the court, and Paris, saying she had no intention of letting a youth who'd become her son go back to the hell of the north for good. "What, let you be poisoned, or die of plague, or neglect?" she'd said, with her lisping Spanish intonation, half indignant, half laughing. "Let you fall into that woman's clutches? Thertainly not!"

So she'd come north too, even before her year's mourning for her husband, the Duke of Anjou, was up, bringing the powerful, pug-faced Count Bernard of Armagnac, her closest ally, to accompany Charles and Marie, his wife. They'd agreed among themselves that Charles would go back to the south, or at the very least to Angers, Yolande's home in the Loire Valley, as soon as was feasible.

Charles had discovered a great many things since he'd got away. He knew now that his father was mad. How that felt or looked or sounded or smelled he couldn't imagine; all he remembered of his father were rare, happy walks in the garden with a big, laughing, easygoing man who flung Charles in the air and carved him little flutes out of twigs. When he imagined his father mad, it was, nowadays, with the big fleshy drunk face of the Count of Armagnac. It was Armagnac's pleasure to stretch his eyes wide, so they looked crazy, and pull them down at the corners, so the red rims showed. He'd let his mouth flap foolishly underneath, make his hair and clothes rumpled and wild, and complete his impersonation by howling, "Woo—wooo—WOOOH!" and running round the room. Charles would cringe with embarrassed horror at the thought of his father losing his royal dignity and turning into that wild animal. If Charles couldn't understand what his father must be like mad, he did understand it was bad for France, and that only a new king—the man he was now destined to become— could save the land from the English and from his uncle of Burgundy. When news of his brother's death had reached him, on a visit to Yolande at Angers, Armagnac had been breathless with excitement—even during the solemn Mass said for Jean— and, afterward, downing his favourite Gascon wine, had clapped him on the back, over and over again, saying, "We're all in your hands now, my boy; all in your hands."

Charles had also discovered, and also mostly from Bernard of Armagnac, that his mother was evil. That, he had no trouble putting mental pictures to. He had so many painful memories from his early life: of going hungry when Odette the cook walked out tearfully because she hadn't been given any wages for the three months since the King had been ill, and had eventually run out of savings. He remembered being told he must have stolen all the sweets, when he'd been nowhere near; when it must have been his mother who'd eaten them. He remembered not having clothes to put on his back, and not having anyone to dress him. He remembered knocking on his mother's door, and being turned away. "Go and play in the gardens," he remembered the Saracen saying; "your mother's busy," and no one noticing he had only a ragged shirt on his back, and it was raining.

With the hindsight offered by his new fifteen-year-old life, these memories had come to the fore. They'd got mixed up with the whispers and snickers of the southern courtiers; the vicious stories Bernard of Armagnac told in his cups about the Queen's sluts of ladies-in-waiting, getting drunk at dinner and stripping for the guard commanders, while their fat old mistress cackled and cheered them on. They were stories he was too embarrassed, still, to repeat himself, but couldn't entirely doubt. Not to mention the angrier talk about the thousands and thousands of livres she'd spent on her pleasures; the muttered judgments that she, single-handedly, had all but destroyed France; that she was even more dangerous than Burgundy. Charles had almost forgotten the other nightmares, the dreams that had so troubled him while he was still a child in Paris, in which wild-eyed butchers with axes chased him up and down the palace corridors; or in which the hard, cold eyes and eagle nose of his uncle of Burgundy stared at him in wordless fury as a flash of steel hissed down at him. They had receded, and blended themselves into the all-encompassing fury he felt toward his mother.

When he thought of before, what he remembered best was always feeling guilty. It came back to him now, with a surge of seething, hateful resentment: back then, he'd always thought it must be his fault; that he and Catherine must somehow have done something naughty; that they were being punished. He remembered his mother's voice: "No, it was the *green* one you were given," when he knew there'd never been a green one, only the blue one, and that was in her hand, and she wasn't going to give it to him. Her voice, accusing: "You had the *green* one, and you've deliberately hidden it." Or lost it, or broken it.

The beatings, for the made-up wrongs he hadn't done. He knew better now, though, than to still feel guilty. He knew, with a fierce, implacable rage, which had been stoked by every bitter flash of memory that he'd ever had, in the sunny, luxuriously feather-bedded existence he'd been delivered to, that all those childish guilts had been mistaken; that he'd never done anything wrong. That it was his mother, with her angry rolls of fat and the dark whiskers quivering on her chin and the malevolent eyes, who was to blame for everything.

He knew he had to make an appearance here; for form's sake. But he didn't want to see his pathetic, mad, broken father, who they said had been locked away, raving, practically since he'd left; and he certainly didn't want to see *her*.

"Your father's already arrived from Paris, with your sister Catherine," Yolande whispered, and her eyes flashed encouragement. "They say he's in good health; and you'll be happy to see her again."

Dutifully, Charles nodded; but he wasn't even sure of that. There'd been a time when Catherine had been his only protector; of course there had; he'd relied on her utterly. They'd spied on council meetings from behind the arras; they'd foraged for food in their mother's kitchens; they'd begged Christine to bring them picnics. But now—when he'd found so much rocksolid love in his new world—he could hardly remember his sister. She'd just been another ragged child with her eyes full of anxieties and guilt and fears. He didn't want to feel those things again. He wanted to get away.

Catherine looked calmly down at her mother—who hadn't got up; who never got up if she could avoid it. The Queen was as magnificently dressed and jewel-studded as ever, and, as ever, had a light dusting of sugar down her front. Catherine wasn't entirely surprised to feel a reluctant stirring of love for her. She knew it would only be a moment before her mother would be digging fingers into a bowl again; mumbling, "dragées; very good; try," and twinkling conspiratorially at her. She found herself even looking forward to the predictability of it. She might forget you if you were out of sight; she might accuse you of stealing things she'd lost, or of knowing about things she'd never told you, or of plotting to keep her from things you'd never thought of for yourself, but you could rely on Isabeau to be sweet with you if you were in the room with her when she was in a good mood. You might share a pleasure, or have a mischievous laugh together. God knew there were few enough pleasures these days. No wonder the Queen sat here all day, eating and dreaming.

Catherine's peace of mind today came from the knowledge that enough time had gone by to make a difficult conversation about the past unnecessary. They both knew now that Catherine looked after the King; they both knew she must know everything. But caring for her father had changed Catherine. She had decided, when broaching a meeting of the family at Vincennes, that she didn't want to risk making her mother angry, or open more Pandora's boxes and let more demons out. There were enough in the air as it was. She'd let the past be. She needed to concentrate on today—to scotch the talk that had taken hold that the King and Queen lived irreconcilably apart; that the King's madness was permanent; that a weak fifth son was coming into a divided, ruined kingdom.

It hadn't been easy to persuade Isabeau to let the rest of the family join her here at first.

"Charles coming back north is an opportunity for all of us," Catherine told her mother, when she rode to Vincennes to discuss it. "We can show that our family is strong and united . . . make Papa feel secure . . . give Charles a good enough welcome to encourage him to stay permanently in Paris."

Her mother pursed up her lips and looked skeptical. Her fingers were feeling along the tabletop. Catherine pushed the sweet bowl closer.

"We need Charles here," Catherine said. "We need a good king-in-waiting. Papa will never be strong enough. You and Papa need to greet Charles together. You and Papa need to live in the same place."

She didn't try to explain. She shouldn't have to. Isabeau must see that it was her duty to be near her husband. But the Queen just gazed expressionlessly at her daughter.

"Huh," Isabeau grunted in the end. "I suppose you know he attacks me . . . whenever he's *like that*. Tried to strangle me once. Not safe for me to go near. Hasn't been for years."

She didn't sound upset, or frightened; she sounded glib, as though she was making an excuse to get out of an unwanted social engagement.

Catherine pushed every angry response out of her head.

"Papa's not mad now," she said firmly. "He's fragile; but he's sane. He talks about you. Misses you."

Whenever Catherine felt angry with her mother, which was often, she tried to call to mind the explanation she'd come up with over the past year or so for all Isabeau's excesses. It was too simple, Catherine had decided, to believe the Queen had deliberately brought darkness on the royal house of France—although most people did say something of the sort. Catherine's own, kinder conclusion was that almost everything about her mother could be explained by her terror of poverty. She knew Isabeau of Bavaria had come to France with none of the financial provision for her old age that usually formed part of a royal marriage contract; her family had been too delighted to get the glittering marriage to the French King to make too many conditions. So Isabeau had suddenly become queen of what she liked to wave her hand and call "all this"—but "all this" would be snatched away without warning if the King died. And King Charles' illness must have been a perpetual reminder that she might at any moment end up a widow, and a penniless one too. That explained why Isabeau couldn't look at the poor—why she turned away from beggars in disgust; hid behind her fan or shawl; wouldn't give alms. It explained why she'd always squirreled away the little gold treasures she liked to be given, and stole, magpie-fashion, when she wasn't given them, getting baubles sewn into curtains, or packed into false linings in trunks, or bagged up in cubbyholes in stables, ready for escape.

Once the King and Queen were back together, Catherine thought, she'd ask her father to settle a proper dower on her mother. That might be enough to keep the Queen out of politics; stop her trying to fight Charles over money and influence as she had Louis. For now, Catherine reminded herself, if her mother couldn't resist helping herself to things, perhaps it wasn't entirely her fault. For all the vast bulk of her, the wrinkles, the whiskers, her mother was, in some ways, still a child in the grip of a nightmare. If she couldn't deny her appetites, it was because they were signs of her fears. The important thing was to calm her mother's fears; then she would, possibly, behave with the public-spiritedness expected of a queen.

"Papa was saying only the other day that it was time he settled a proper dower on you," she murmured.

Isabeau sat quietly, sucking on a sweet, nodding her head. She didn't acknowledge the comment, but Catherine could tell she'd heard.

"You're the key to everything," Catherine said. "Please, Maman—say you'll try; make this meeting a success."

Isabeau's answer, when it came, was casual. "Ach, you know I'll do whatever I can," she said, swallowing her morsel. "Anything, if it brings us all together again—and banishes that scum John of Burgundy back to where he belongs. If ever I saw true evil, it's in that man. Those eyes, full of darkness. The Destroyer, that's what he is. We all know where he should be. In Hell."

She snapped her lips shut; but her eyes went on flashing with the memory of her enemy.

However, once she'd helped herself to another sweet, Isabeau turned affectionate. "And of course I'm delighted we're all to be reunited—me, you, Papa, and dear, pudgy little Charlot, with his fingers always in the sweet bowl . . ."

For an exasperated second, Catherine wondered if her mother remembered, or had ever even realized, that she and her brother had spent most of their childhood stealing food because Isabeau hadn't bothered to make sure they were properly looked after. She took a deep breath in, determined not to let herself feel any irritation. There was too much at stake today.

Isabeau sighed sentimentally, and caught Catherine's eye. Catherine made a point of smiling. "You know, of all my children, I think you two were always my favorites . . . So pretty . . . so adorable . . . and so happy together . . . What a joy that those days are coming back."

Catherine's father, blinking in his old mild astonishment and looking round in the sunlight, had not left her mother's side since they'd met in the gallery. Isabeau had heaved herself to her feet and put her arm affectionately around the husband she hadn't seen for a year. Now she was whispering into his ear and twinkling. Catherine could hardly believe how overjoyed the old man was looking; how well her mother was behaving; how her own heart was bursting with hope.

"Let's go for a walk," she said gently to her father. She'd arranged for Charles and his followers to meet them in the gardens; she thought birdsong and green leaf-light would lighten everyone's mood.

She wanted everything to be as relaxed as possible for the meeting with Charles. She'd heard about the hostile letter his mother-in-law had written to Isabeau; she knew his southern family were suspicious. He must be frightened; he must have spent the two years since he'd left Paris expecting a peaceful future in the south, not to be forced to lead France out of its wars. Charles was timid by nature; she remembered his nightmares. And he was just fifteen. She wanted to reassure him.

There was so much to hope for; but what was making her heart beat fastest, as they stepped out through the flowers, was simply the prospect of seeing his face again.

There they were—a dozen of them, walking under the lime alley, led by a tall young man with the tiny, spry, black-eyed Yolande of Aragon on his arm. Catherine recognized the big thickset man just behind, the one with the broken nose, as Count Bernard of Armagnac. They were all wearing respectful black; all elegant with an undefinable foreign grace. She just couldn't see Charles.

She shaded her eyes and kept walking, expecting the features of one of the indeterminate figures moving toward her under the trees to resolve itself into Charles' fragile little face, with its freckles and baby skin and blue eyes. When she finally realized he must be the tall young man with Yolande of Aragon—thin as a rake, with big ankles and knees and wrists, and his skin browner and harder than she remembered, with his facial features altered and lengthened and roughened by manhood and a giant Adam's apple bobbing in his throat, though still with the solemn blue eyes she remembered—she nearly laughed with the sheer relief of it.

"Look," she said excitedly to her father and mother, "that's Charles—and look how he's grown!"

And she flitted off ahead, kicking up her heels, feeling everything coming right at last, with the sun on her back, laughing out loud as she ran toward him.

She could see them lift their heads to watch her.

She thought Charles might see her and come running to meet her. But he didn't. He stood stock-still, staring.

Still flying over the flagstones, her face full of delight, Catherine felt a prickle of apprehension, as if by showing her pleasure at seeing her brother she'd broken some unknown rule of etiquette.

Was she . . . should she have . . . ?

It was too late to change anything. She reached the Provençal group; rushed past them with little nods and bows; and came to a breathless halt in front of Charles.

She'd meant to hug him and whirl him round until he squealed with laughter. She was longing to hear his laughter. But the cautious look she caught in those owlish eyes made her realize she shouldn't do anything to dent his new adult dignity. He hadn't let go of Yolande of Aragon's arm; he clearly didn't want any whirling. So instead she put her hands on his shoulders, smiled as joyously as she dared, given the frigid correctness of this group of strangers, and bent decorously forward to kiss him on each cheek.

"Sister," he said, and bowed, and smiled. But she didn't detect any real pleasure in his face.

She thought: He's feeling shy.

Then she thought: He looks almost—*angry.*

The walk helped dissipate some of the tensions. After Charles had bowed frigidly to his parents, who hung back looking wary, he paired off with Catherine. Yolande of Aragon moved graciously back to take Count Bernard's arm. The King and Queen, both clearly relieved that Catherine was going first with her brother, who'd become so tall and such a stranger, walked with them. The retinue streamed behind.

Catherine slipped her arm into that of this new, near-adult Charles; felt the awkward stiffness of his muscles under the thick doublet. She was trying not to be disappointed. A voice in her head was telling her: It will all take time; it's been two years; we all have to get used to each other again.

And it felt for a while as though it was happening. As Catherine peppered the stranger Charles with questions about his journey, his answers gradually grew from monosyllables to, at least, polite chitchat. In a pause between questions, he even glanced sideways at her, and volunteered, in his new, deep, unnatural-seeming man's voice: "I wouldn't have recognized you, you know . . ."

That startled her. "I haven't changed, have I?" she said, a little uncertainly. She hadn't had much time these last months to think about her appearance; but she was pleased, at least, that he was taking this personal tone.

He nodded. "You look so serious. Your face is thinner." He laughed, but not the laugh she'd dreamed of; instead a distant, short bark. "You seem older."

She didn't know how to take that as a compliment; but she nodded her head, a little sadly, accepting it was probably true. "It's been a difficult time," she said. "It hasn't been easy with Papa . . ."

He nodded, and looked properly at her; and she saw a spark of life, maybe even of understanding, in his face. But she didn't want to talk to him yet about their father, so she added, more brightly: "I've been so looking forward to seeing you again," and squeezed his arm. She was encouraged to see a reluctant smile turn the corners of his mouth up.

Trying once again to reawaken the natural, free-talking, hushed conspiracy of children, she whispered: "So, tell me, what's it like to be married? Is Marie of Anjou still so grand?"

For a second, he almost relaxed; almost giggled. They'd

laughed so much together at Marie of Anjou's haughtily turned-up nose before; how could he not? But she felt him stop himself. "She's a good wife," he said stiffly. "I'm blessed in my new life."

Abruptly, he turned his head back to add a word or two to the conversation between Bernard of Armagnac and his mother-in-law. Catherine saw light come to his face as he turned their way; an impish grin flickered on his lips. He looks so happy with them, she thought; not owlish at all. I don't remember him looking like that.

Unexpectedly, she found herself full of a childish emotion far from the carefree mood she'd been trying to foster. She felt left out. Charles had found a new family; he loved them most now. He knew marriage; whereas perhaps she never would. Disconsolately, she thought: No one even thinks of marrying me to anyone anymore; and I couldn't go away and leave Papa even if they did . . .

Knowing this feeling to be illogical, Catherine put it aside. She was the one who refused to discuss marriage, after all; who'd pursed her lips and hurried about her business whenever Christine had begun musing, apparently innocently, on the charms and talents of one young prince or another, trying to draw her out. Christine's inability to stop harping on about marriageable young men and the virtues of the married state, however often Catherine discouraged her, whether gently ("There'll be time enough after the war") or, occasionally, brusquely ("Haven't we got enough on our hands already with Papa?") was the real reason Catherine had not asked her to come to Vincennes for this family meeting. She knew Christine must have been quietly disappointed to be left behind in Paris. She guessed Christine would have loved to be one of the first to see Charles. And she respected Christine for being too proud to try and invite herself. Christine had self-control when it mattered.

In Christine's honor, she touched Charles' arm and murmured: "Christine sends you her love . . ."

But she could tell, from the second too long that he took to turn back to her, that when he did his face would again be set in its polite, tense, reluctant expression; and that it would take much more than a walk under the trees to make the distance between her brother and herself disappear.

Catherine didn't know if there was any truth in the rumors that the three commanders of the Queen's honor guard at Vincennes passed their nights gambling away what were supposed to be vast fortunes and behaving improperly with her mother's ladies-in-waiting, while Isabeau egged them all on to misbehave with her winks and cackles. There was no point in asking her mother. But she didn't want to leave it to chance, either, with these set-faced, disapproving visitors.

So, before dinner, she called in Louis de Bosredon, a lounging, handsome, black-haired, big-boned creature, and told him, as authoritatively as she could, that the guard was to spend tonight outside the hall, and the officers were to eat at a separate table from the ladies-in-waiting.

The young commander wasn't used to sternness. He gave her a long, lascivious look; let his eyelashes insolently caress his cheek in a blink that was nearly a wink. Finally, just when she thought she should punish him in some way for insubordination, he drawled out the polite phrase, "Yes, my lady," and swaggered off, so slowly she could see each big, bulging muscle in thigh and buttock swell and flex, to pass on her order.

The men in her party were out hunting for the afternoon. Even her father—who didn't seem to be suffering from the nerves afflicting her; who'd been looking happier than she remembered for years, clinging to his wife—had gone. She counted anxiously on her fingers: dinner would be roast boar; four kinds of fowl; white almond soup; a dish of sorrel; brandy cream. All Charles' favorite foods.

She went to her rooms. She wanted to look pretty; she needed to keep her spirits up. As the women dressed her hair, she was remembering the picnic she'd once had with Charles, out there under the white towers. She'd made daisy chains. She'd take him back there tomorrow. It would all begin then.

When she suggested the picnic, over dinner, Charles only said: "I don't really remember—daisy chains?—it was all a long time ago." But he seemed to have mellowed: he poured wine for their father; talked politely with him about the hunting. When he saw the hopeful look Catherine gave him, he agreed, equally politely, that she should take him to the picnic spot again in the morning.

So they stood, arm in arm, soon after sunrise, watching the others skitter round on horseback. There was more hunting planned for Charles' entourage and the King. The Queen wouldn't go out. Catherine knew it was because she could hardly bear to look at the big square red face of Bernard of Armagnac, with the tufts of ginger hair sprouting aggressively out of nose and ears. ("So *ugly*!" Isabeau had whispered, piercingly, of the crown's closest ally last night. "He always was, even as a young man; and *so* uncouth.") Catherine was relieved that the Queen had more tactfully explained this morning that her gout was troubling her, and that she was going to rest her legs. Isabeau was sitting on a bench, seeing off the hunting party, wrapped up in rugs despite the hot weather and not taking much notice of the southerners but at least smiling at her husband. Perhaps it was best her mother kept herself apart. Catherine was cheered to see this meeting doing her father good. Up on his horse, with roses in his cheeks and the wind ruffling his hair, he looked almost the big blond laughing giant she remembered. The guardsmen riding with Yolande of Aragon and Bernard of Armagnac were treating him with extreme respect. He was smiling. She waved at him.

There was a clatter of other hooves at the gate. She looked up. So did Charles.

Three horsemen spurred their horses back into a gallop as they rushed in through the gate tower and toward the castle. The horses were sweating and rolling-eyed from hard exercise. With a prickle of dislike, she recognized the rider in front as the muscle-bound young commander of the Queen's troop who'd flickered his eyelashes so impertinently at her yesterday.

Louis de Bosredon, she remembered.

He was clearly in a hurry to get to the castle first; they must have been racing through the woods. They were whooping and whipping on their horses. Bosredon was sweating and grinning.

The trio of flicking, wild-eyed, noisy, laughing young men

came right up to the little cavalcade preparing to go hunting and galloped past. Unsettled, the hunting party's horses began to lunge and snort. Catherine didn't think the riders, now disappearing toward the stables, had even been aware of whom they'd passed. Guard commanders should dismount whenever they saw the King. But these hadn't even taken off their hats.

Catherine pursed her lips, feeling vaguely shocked. But her father didn't seem to have noticed the disrespect; he was leaning over his horse's neck, murmuring something calming in its ear. He was still smiling. And the Queen, who didn't give a hoot for discipline as long as people were having fun, couldn't care less, Catherine saw, letting herself feel relieved. Isabeau was grinning fondly after them. She'd probably shrug and grunt, "Ah, those *rrrap*-scallions," in a moment, and the incident would be forgotten.

But then Catherine looked round and saw the faces of the rest of the party, and went cold.

Charles was standing very still, but she could see he was bursting with anger. White-faced; thin-lipped; with bluish flecks down the side of his nose. He stepped away from her. When she looked down, she saw he was clenching and unclenching his fists.

Catherine had never seen this anger in him.

Yolande of Aragon was also staring after the vanished riders. Her little face, usually merry with court politeness and elegant jokes, was wiped of expression. She seemed deeply shocked. She sidled her obedient horse over to Bernard of Armagnac, whose always red face had gone almost purple under his orange hair, and whose eyes were bulging out of his head. She whispered. Then he kicked his horse and skittered over to Charles. He leaned down and whispered in Charles' ear.

Charles nodded. He turned to Catherine. She quailed at the look in his eye.

"What is that man's name?" he said; and there was ice in his voice.

She muttered: "Bosredon." Then, putting a hand pleadingly on his arm, "But, Charles, he meant no harm . . ." Then, when

Charles looked at her with the full bleakness of midwinter in his gaze, "... it was wrong ... I know ... I'll make sure he's disciplined."

Charles wasn't listening. He moved a step away, turning his shoulder to her, so her hand fell off his arm. He beckoned to Armagnac's guards. Four of them trotted up, bareheaded, blank-faced, bowing.

"Arrest those men," he said.

There was a terrible inevitability about everything that followed. The initial exchange between Charles and his mother had Isabeau, from her nest of blankets, fixing her son with her most baleful, terrifying look, and hissing, "You impudent boy—you haven't changed a bit—call them off *at once—how dare you* lay a finger on my guard!" Charles had looked a scared boy again for a moment. But then he'd glanced at the immobile figures of Yolande and Bernard. Seeming to draw comfort from them, he'd advanced on her, taut as a whiplash, until he was standing right over her, leaning on the back of her bench, with his eyes glaring so wide that the rims stood out pink and hateful all around, his voice grinding out:

"It's all true, isn't it? You vile, vicious old whore. You ..."

He stopped himself. Shaking his head, he turned his back on all of them and walked after his guardsmen into the castle.

Catherine could see his head, going on shaking until he was far away; as if he were continuing a furious row with his mother in his mind.

Nestling into her blankets, Isabeau was shaking her head too, but enjoyably, with the gloating look on her face that Catherine remembered of old. It was a look that suggested that, now she'd goaded one of her children into behaving badly, she would take pleasure in dissecting his misbehavior and bad character with her friends, and soliciting the sympathetic remarks about how much she'd suffered bringing up the ungrateful wretch, which she would then, later, repeat to the misbehaving child in question, as part of his punishment.

Catherine closed her eyes, feeling the old dread seep through her, and a new dread too.

Her mother didn't even seem to have noticed the closed faces and stillness of the southerners watching her, as she opened her mouth and began, in significant, sepulchral tones, "*Well* . . . nothing changes, does it . . . the same old evil temper as ever . . . the troubles we've had with that boy—"

"Madame," Bernard of Armagnac interrupted brusquely. Catherine opened her eyes again. The Count was all puffed up and ginger and angry himself. For the first time she saw the brute as well as the buffoon in him, the strength and pent-up rage in those bulging limbs; and she was frightened.

But all Armagnac said was: "We'll hunt later; we must attend our master now. Sire . . ."

And, bowing to the King, he turned his horse and walked it, with dignity, back to the stables, with Yolande of Aragon picking her way behind him, and the remainder of the guard following in pairs.

Catherine didn't know what to do. For a long moment she did nothing—just felt the sun on her back, and thought of the daisy chains she'd been going to make, and felt paralyzed.

But then she caught sight of her father's bewildered face. She pulled herself together. She smiled, too big and false a smile; the kind that would make your face ache if you kept it up for too long. "Don't worry, Papa," she said, too brightly; "you go inside with Maman; she's got a new card game she wants to teach you. You can hunt in the afternoon. I'll go and find Charles now." And, giving her mother a fierce warning look—mouthing, *Don't upset him*, when she thought her father wouldn't see, and trying not to be alarmed by the truculence in her mother's answering glance—she followed the southerners, on foot, over the grass and flags to the stables.

His face was all crusting blood and puff and angry blue-red swellings. One eye was closed. There was fresh blood trickling out of his mouth. Even when Catherine's eyes had adjusted to the hay-barn dusk, it took her a moment to understand what she was seeing.

They'd put a leather strap round Bosredon's neck and half

hung him from a hook on the wall. He could hardly stand, in the state he was in, but a precarious foothold on a broken cartwheel was all that was keeping him from strangling. Strange gurgling noises were coming from him.

There was no sign of Yolande of Aragon. But Bernard of Armagnac was striding up and down, up and down, very fast, very angry, in front of the four motionless men-at-arms. He was disheveled; so were they; but they were still correct.

It was Charles, with the wooden stick in his hand, who wasn't. Charles, in a rage she'd never seen, with flared nostrils and narrowed eyes and the white of hate burning in him like pale fire. Charles had blood and snot all down him. Charles had his doublet off and was stripped down to his linen shirt. Charles was administering the blows; vicious, regular blows to elbow and knee and foot, at the end of every question; as if the questions themselves weren't an assault.

"They take off their clothes . . ." *whack*—arm—silence.

"They get on the tabletops . . ." *whack*—leg—silence.

"They dance for you . . ." *whack*—ankle—groan.

"Wiggle their tits . . ." *whack*—other ankle—howl.

"Undress you . . ." *whack*—leg—groan.

"Suck you . . ." *whack*—right between the legs—screams; so bloodcurdling a scream that everything stopped for a few minutes, except the frantic scrabbling of the feet, trying to maintain their place on the wheel. Then Charles took up his stick again; thrusting his face right up against the bloody hanging mask.

"My mother's there, watching . . ." *whack*—left foot— shriek; scrabble; sob.

"Isn't she?"

Blessedly, no whack. Silence.

"Isn't she?"

A blubbering cry came out of the face: "Ye—"

"Grinning away . . ." *prod*—belly—silence.

"Cheering them on . . ." *prod*—side—silence.

Bernard of Armagnac stopped his furious pacing, as if he'd been distracted by the diminishing pain of the torture being administered by his young master. He turned and gave the poor vain guard's ruined beauty a look of indescribable malevolence.

"Come on, admit it," he grated, hands on hips; all bulk and threat; a voice like rust on iron, taunting. "She's doing it too, the old slut. We all know. Those black teeth and gums; disgusting; you should be ashamed. A special pleasure, is it? Mmmmmmm . . . Queue up for it, do you?"

His voice brought a frenzy on Charles. He groaned; then he rushed forward again, whacking and flailing at Bosredon like a madman. As Catherine closed her eyes in terror and moved silently out of the doorway, back into the safety of the morning, she heard a new set of sounds—the gasps and snuffles of strangulation that meant Bosredon had slipped off the wheel at last.

She sat for a while in the picnic spot under the east tower; listening to the birds, feeling the warmth on her hands as her fingers pierced each daisy's stalk and linked them together, but feeling as dead inside as her father always said he felt on his worst days.

She wasn't going to be joyfully reunited with her brother, and make her family into a source of strength and love. It wasn't going to happen, after all. Charles had been suppressing the fury she'd just seen ever since he'd got here. She realized that now. He couldn't bear the fate that had brought him back north. He couldn't bear his mother. Perhaps he couldn't bear his father or his sister either.

Her fingers shredded the next daisy. She'd never be able to look at Charles again and not see him attacking that poor trussed-up prisoner; never be able to shut out Armagnac's repulsive gloating. They made her soul shrink. How could they say—think—such things, of the woman who was Charles' and Catherine's mother? Charles' new family were supposed to be the King's closest allies. But it must be their fault. What had they done to Charles to fill him with so much rage?

She'd have to go back inside in a minute.

Her parents were playing cards in her mother's parlor; her

mother giggling and offering her father violet sweets and patting his hand. There was a little pile of coins on her side of the table. She was in good spirits. She'd taken off her headdress and left it carelessly on the floor. Catherine saw her hair had got thin and wiry and gray, with patches of skin showing. They didn't notice Catherine, pausing in the doorway, gathering her thoughts, drinking in the sight of them.

All at once, Catherine wanted nothing more than to protect these two aging, fragile people from the cruelty of the world; to make it possible for them to go on sitting like this, away from pain, eating sweets and laughing together like young lovers.

But, at the same time, she knew they would have to be moved. Now. Charles was too angry. The grotesque things he'd been saying . . . He'd been turned against all of them. It was dangerous to stay, when he was here, in that mood, with that man and that woman at his side. She should hurry them both back to Paris. She paused, trying to focus her mind on the detail of horses and carriages; on how to overcome her parents' dithery slowness; feeling dizzy with the urgency of it all.

If she told them they were just going out for a ride . . . in the woods . . . it was less than an hour to Paris; they'd be all right without refreshments . . . they didn't really need a guard . . . the road was so well-traveled . . . they'd be unlikely to meet footpads . . . they could send for their households later . . .

She stepped forward. They turned soft eyes on her. "Dear little girl," her father said fondly. He didn't ask whether she'd made peace with Charles. Catherine had the impression he'd forgotten the row.

They didn't protest when she told them they were going out. She thanked God quietly for their obedience, as they got up and shuffled along behind her. She almost laughed when, out of the corner of her eye, she noticed her mother furtively sweep her winnings into her purse.

But Charles found them.

She was just getting them into the hay cart—"A picnic vehicle! A rustic adventure!" she was exclaiming brightly, aware of the songbirds chirruping drunkenly in the summer air, and rejoicing as her father nodded with apparent pleasure—when she heard the footsteps.

Charles had put his doublet back on. He'd splashed water on his face. There was no blood. But he still looked wild with barely controlled anger.

He had all his guard with him; all on foot; but now she could hear their horses milling about by the trough round the corner. Bernard of Armagnac was big and grim at his side; and her mother's secretary, Laurent du Puy, an obsequious little stick insect of a man with hunched shoulders who was, as ever, wringing his hands, but who was also looking unpleasantly excited.

Charles strode up to his mother. He ignored Catherine. He ignored their father.

He grinned spitefully at Isabeau. He said: "No picnics for you, Madame. You're going away."

Catherine could see that the Queen, canny old animal that she usually was, was too startled to understand this at once as a threat. Isabeau had got so firmly into her head that everyone was to be gentle; that peacemaking was in the air; that despite her little boy's outburst earlier that morning no one was going to allow themselves to fight, that she just fluttered her pudgy hands until the emeralds on them glittered, and said gaily, "We're going on a rustic adventure!"

Catherine could hardly breathe. Thoughts were flashing through her head: random, terrified, guilty thoughts. She thought: I should have told her what they were doing to her guardsman. I should have prepared her. She'd have known what to say if I had. Then, with pity tingeing her fear: She's got too old to fight fast enough. And then: She might have been warier if I hadn't made so much of today as our chance for the future . . . if I hadn't put so much faith in Charles . . .

Charles ground out: "No. You're going to Tours."

"Tours?" the Queen said, with a first doubt creeping into her voice. "But . . ." She turned to Catherine. So did the King. Their faces were full of disappointment and puzzlement. "What about our picnic?" the Queen finished lamely; but by then she'd read and understood Catherine's face.

Charles turned to Catherine. "Don't interfere," he told her, as if he feared she might somehow undermine his authority; then blushed when, for a terrible moment, his newly deep voice disobeyed him and squeaked into treble. He coughed; and looked, if possible, angrier than before.

Catherine nodded submissively. There was nothing she could do.

"There's a carriage waiting for you," Charles said, turning back to his mother. He pointed a contemptuous thumb at Laurent du Puy. "He's going too. I've told him he's in charge of you. He'll make sure you don't get up to any more mischief."

"What? What?" Isabeau spluttered; and Catherine was almost relieved to see the venom spark from her mother's eyes as Isabeau woke up, finally, fully, to the presence of danger. But there was no time for her to start spitting and shouting at her son. He must have realized that would come, as soon as she understood. He signaled to his guard. They lined up round Isabeau, with their lances gleaming, and, slowly, painfully, shuffled with her across the yard.

The Queen didn't protest. She allowed herself to be walked away. But, before she turned the corner that would take her and the men guarding her away into the unknown, she stopped and turned back to fix terrible eyes on her son. All she said, very quietly, was: "You—will—regret—this." But the cold fury in her voice and face sent shivers down Catherine's spine.

Into the awful silence that followed, broken, for a long few moments, only by birdsong and the audible breathing of Bernard of Armagnac, Charles finally said truculently to his sister: "You go back to Paris."

"Charles . . ." Catherine murmured pleadingly, stepping toward him, wondering if she dared take his hand; hoping even now that she could say something to turn back time. "Maman . . . Please . . ."

Brusquely, coldly, Charles crossed his arms over his chest. He said: "Take *him*. He's in no fit state to be out." And he jerked his thumb again, toward their father.

Horrified, Catherine realized she'd been so paralyzed with shock that she hadn't even looked at her father, standing quietly by her side, to see how he was taking the arrest of his wife by his son.

Now she saw. The King of France was weeping; silent floods of tears pouring down his cheeks, soaking into his doublet. His eyes were vacant. It was as if he didn't know he was crying.

But perhaps, after all, he was aware that he'd finally become the center of everyone's attention. As they all turned to stare at him, King Charles VI of France began to hum; a strange, tuneless dirge, in a high-pitched, quavering voice. He pointed upward with a trembling finger, into the cloudless blue sky where the birds were still shouting out their joy at being alive. "A black sun . . . and ghosts . . . and clouds of ravens, coming to peck out our eyes," he sang; then, looking around, with a busy, cunning expression; "but they'll see right through me . . . I'm made of glass."

He laughed; laughed, and laughed, and laughed.

Charles quivered in what looked like disgust. Catherine saw him turn to Bernard of Armagnac, and saw Bernard of Armagnac quietly shake his head and wrinkle his nose and shrug.

"Go," Charles said, turning his back. He wouldn't meet his sister's eyes. He started to walk away. He tossed back his last words over his shoulder. "Take a carriage. Go now."

It was only once the carriage was jolting out of the gates, with her father hunched up in his corner, still singing to himself, with his disregarded tears still pouring down his cheeks, that Catherine gave in to the great, bitter, disappointed, frightened torrent of tears pent up inside her too—ugly tears that shook her body and forced snuffles of air and quick, sharp animal howls of pain out of her; that turned her face wet and red and blubbery and trembling with despair. Once they were safe.

It had all gone wrong. There was no hope.

Even the princes who were supposed to be allies were riven by hatred of each other. Even the one person whose love she'd been sure of all her life had turned against her. If they were made of glass, the glass was shattering now. They were all living under the same black sun as the King, and there would be no end to it; no end . . . She couldn't even stop when she felt the timid, trembling hand of her father, still humming his song, still hunched up in his own hell, stroking her hair as if to comfort her in the awful darkness they'd both found themselves in.

"He sent your mother to prison . . ." Christine murmured the next day, shaking her head, stroking Catherine's.

Catherine tried to stop herself from weeping again, and, except for a slight tremble about the lips, succeeded. But she couldn't bring herself to tell Christine about Bosredon's face as he balanced on that wheel rim. She couldn't bring herself to say what Charles and his bully friend the Count of Armagnac had been doing. She recoiled utterly from that memory. She didn't want it in her head.

"That's bad," Christine was saying, gently and sadly. "Very bad. He shouldn't have done that."

Catherine was comforted to know that Christine, who was so honest as well as learned that you could always respect her judgment, believed Charles had done wrong.

But when Christine got up to go, still shaking her head, she was muttering, "That poor fool of a boy . . ." And when she kissed Catherine goodbye, she whispered, ". . . horrible . . . but try to forgive him."

Catherine bit her lip and didn't answer. She wouldn't forgive Charles. There was no point in trying.

ELEVEN

"You'll go incognito . . ." Henry, King of England, said. "You're the right man for the job. You know their faces, where to find them; they'll remember you. And you're a bit of a man of letters, too." Behind him, Duke John of Bedford nodded—another royal brother with pop eyes; the spitting image of the King, and his closest friend. Owain didn't know him but he'd heard Duke John was a good master. He was known for never panicking under fire. Owain felt calmed in his presence, just as he did in the King's. The Duke had a steady voice and strong hands.

"The King's at Paris, with his daughter. The Prince is there; but separately. At the Louvre. They say the King's mad most of the time these days. So you'll need to talk to Prince Charles. And the Count of Armagnac. He's the one who pulls the Prince's strings."

"And the Queen?" Owain ventured. "Is she with them?"

Duke John laughed shortly. "No. She's in prison. They say Charles didn't like the rumors about her. He's had her shut up. They say she's hopping mad; doesn't know who to hate most, Armagnac or her own son. But she won't get out. The boy's got a nasty temper. And he hates her. A rum lot, the Valois. Especially when you think they're all supposed to be on the same side!"

Owain's eyes widened. That helpless-looking little boy had dared do that to his bully of a mother?

"What do the letters say?" he said, tapping the bundle he'd been given.

Duke John shrugged. "They reiterate the marriage proposal."

Owain said nothing. But his frown must have spoken his thought: But . . . they rejected it. Years ago.

Duke John patted his back, as if he was being naive. "Never say never," he replied briskly. "They may find it easier to say yes now. They must be scared. They're stuck in a city with no firewood, no grain. No river access. With us down the road one way, and Burgundy's army down the road the other. There's no way out for them. They may well feel it's time they talked. We've made it easy for you with the letters—there's one to her; and copies of another to the King; to the Queen; and to the Prince—so you'll be able to use your head on the spot to find the best way to proceed."

Owain nodded miserably.

"What does she look like?" King Henry asked suddenly; as if the idea had never struck him before.

"Freckles." It was all Owain could think of in reply. He cursed his clumsy tongue. But his face must be showing his admiration.

"Pretty girl, eh?" the King said, not unkindly. "So much the better."

Owain had been high in the King's favor since he'd found Charles of Orléans, facedown in the mud at Azincourt, white with fear and exhaustion, and marched him back to the English camp. No one had even asked what he, Owain, had been doing in those scrubby bushes next to Charles of Orléans. Everyone knew how few real heroes there were in battles; some questions were best left unasked. But Owain remembered. When the sounds were so loud he hadn't been able to make out any single sound in the roar, he remembered seeing a face in the scrum of French knights all around: a man lifting his visor to look down at the wound in his leg. A hard, thin, dark face, gray with pain, but stoical; the face of someone who had borne pain before. In a flash, Owain had recognized that face: it was Henry Gwyn, who should have been lord of Llansteffan; who, he remembered, had run from Henry V's order to join his enemies in France. He'd known Henry Gwyn once: had been a child, laughing and climbing up those muscular legs and being swung round somersaulting in those wiry arms. It was only a glimpse. The next time he looked up, he was yards past Gwyn; the face was lost in the flailing of arms. But somehow Owain had become more terrifyingly aware than ever, in the middle of that charge, of his body being soft and fragile and breakable inside its casing of heavy clothing; of the impermanence of everything; of impossible worlds colliding. He remembered the uncanny way everything had seemed to slow down around him, until even the sparks from the swords and axes seemed to be moving through the air as gently as feathers. He remembered the bursting of his heart when, after his horse fell, he staggered clumsily for shelter. However much he loved his King, he'd known since then that he wasn't made for war. He'd been lucky in the more than three years since; he'd managed to avoid battles; to stay back from the fighting; to make himself useful with negotiations and letters.

But he didn't want this job. Going to Paris would mean the end of this strange, busy, traveling escape from the feelings he refused to let into his heart: the comfort and camouflage of war. Going to Paris to try and negotiate the marriage of Catherine to his master would force him to think. He didn't want to think.

"Be careful on the roads," Duke John finished calmly, passing him a bag of money. "No one knows who owns what in France anymore. It's all abandoned farms; burned-out towns. Checkpoints. Private armies. Highwaymen. Bandit country. So—watch yourself."

He should have gone straight to the Louvre. But what he wanted to do instead was go to the modest stone house on Old Temple Street. He'd been fighting the thought all the way there; trying not to imagine he was going to be able to walk back into his past. He hardly knew what he was doing when he first felt his hands turn his reins so his horse ambled east off Saint-Denis Street, when he should have kept on right to the heart of the town. He was heading through the narrow lanes that led to Christine's house.

It was as close as he knew how to get to Catherine, whose memory was now only a lovely confusion of rose oil and glimpses of eyelashes, lips, breast, neck, freckles, and joyful silences. Catherine: the essence of beauty, and still the meaning of his life, but someone whose reality he could hardly recall. But standing outside Christine's house made him feel Catherine might, at last, be close again.

Yet he couldn't go to Christine. He stopped a little way down Old Temple Street from her door and stared, half hoping someone would come out or go in: Anastaise with a bunch of flowers, or Jean de Castel. Yet he knew, really, that there was no point in being here, feeling nostalgic for the easier times of the past; for that first starburst of light and music inside the cathedral; for the tiny squares of light and color and beauty on parchment; or for the other thing—the feel of Catherine's body against his, the thing he tried to forget.

The past was past. He was the enemy now; that's how Christine would see it. He shouldn't be here.

But he was tired. He couldn't go to the Louvre and announce himself without resting. So he walked his mount down by the river and over to the Island, from where he could see the twin towers of the cathedral; telling himself he'd find a bed for the night at an inn somewhere on the Left Bank, among the students.

Paris didn't look as miraculously beautiful as it had before. He found himself noticing the boarded-up shopfronts; the piles of stinking rubbish in the streets; the beggars; the shabbiness everywhere. Had it been like this before? he wondered. Or was it just his own darkness of heart now coloring the way he saw the town around him?

He didn't go into the cathedral. He was too troubled; he didn't feel he deserved the blissful serenity that looking up into that heavenly light promised. But he did walk down New Notre Dame Street, dawdling past the workshops, letting the horse come almost to a halt, hoping to meet a familiar face who would welcome him; unable to stop himself from hoping it might be Christine.

There was a lot of bustle at the workshop: bags being piled

up just inside the open courtyard door; people rushing in and out with cheerful looks on their faces. Owain looked more carefully, trying to work out what was going on. When he saw that one of the busy pilers-up of luggage was a bald, nearly hunchbacked man with a freckled head and pale eyes—Jean Malouel, who'd shown him the first illuminated manuscripts he'd ever seen—he nudged his reluctant mount forward and bowed.

Malouel looked brightly up at him. "Christine's boy," he said, putting his head on one side. "I remember you." But he was too excited to ask why Owain had come back to Paris. It was perfectly possible he didn't know Owain had ever left. "I'm just off," he went on, gesturing at the piles, taken up with his own drama. "See? They're bringing the horses in a minute."

Owain was cheered by the little man's happiness. He grinned down at him. "Where are you off to?" he asked politely.

Jean Malouel snorted like a horse ready for the road. "Troyes," he said; then, giving Owain a slightly scornful look, as if not understanding why anyone need ask such an obvious question, "of course."

Owain couldn't see any reason why he should know what was taking the illuminator to Troyes. He smiled to himself at the man's self-absorption and, humoring him, asked: "What's there?"

Malouel gave him a distinctly fishy look this time.

"Have you been away, or what?" he said suspiciously, as if everyone must know what was at Troyes.

Owain nodded.

And what the old man told him next changed all his plans. French politics had been turned on its head again.

After Owain had set out for Paris, the Queen had found a way to escape from her son's prison. She'd managed to get a letter to her old enemy the Duke of Burgundy, asking him to rescue her. Burgundy had been besieging the town of Corbeil; but he'd dropped the siege and had come straightaway with his army. ("But why?" Owain stammered. "They're sworn enemies." And the old man chortled knowingly as he replied, "Not anymore, they're not; they're the best of friends now. She's for-given him everything; well, she would, wouldn't she? And it's good for him to have the Queen under his control.") The Queen and Burgundy had ridden off into the forests together and fetched up at Troyes. Yesterday, the Queen had proclaimed her-self Regent; and now she and the Duke of Burgundy were call-ing out artisans and bureaucrats from Paris to work for the rival government and Parliament they were setting up there. There was hardly a man in Paris who wasn't willing.

Owain's head was spinning. He needed to work out what to do; who controlled whom; who it would be best to see; where to go. He tried to pull himself together. If this was true, Paris might no longer be the place in which to negotiate a marriage between the King of England and Princess Catherine. He might be better off heading for Troyes himself; delivering his letters to the Queen and the Duke of Burgundy. Burgundy was negotiating with the English; Burgundy was almost on the English side.

"Where's the King? And the Princess?" he asked faintly.

"Right here," Malouel said readily; "in the palace; not that that makes much difference to anything. He's . . ." He shook his head and pulled a lunatic face. "You know."

It was only when Owain went on, "And what about Prince Charles?" that a hostile look came into the old man's eyes. He spat, and jerked his head back toward the Louvre. "What, him?" he said, without love. "He's here too, of course; in the Louvre, with his pack of greedy scavengers. They say he's as nasty a piece of work as the rest of them: vicious temper; never lifts a finger. I've had it with the lot of them. Why go on sitting in this bloody rabbit warren, grubbing for work from these princes who never pay, worrying about how to feed myself, when I could be His Grace's chief painter again? I only wish we could get shot of *him*"—he jerked his head toward Prince Charles and the Count of Armagnac in the Louvre—"and I could serve my Duke here, in Paris, without having to trail out to the sticks and start over. Still, who cares? It's not so bad, is it? I can't wait to be off." The illuminator's eyes were sparkling. Owain bowed his farewells. "Who knows?" Owain said, introducing the idea on his mind as casually as he could, and turning his horse to go. "Perhaps the next time we meet will be in Troyes."

Owain sat up late in a tavern on the University side of the river, half listening to the slurred talk of the students, a familiar mixture of song and threat and gossip and complaints; with one especially boisterous group pledging drunkenly to rush out and join the Duke of Burgundy's assault on Paris, whenever it came. (Was that why so many shopwindows were boarded up? Was half of Paris waiting for the Duke of Burgundy?) Owain shut out the noises around him, and went back to wondering uneasily whether he shouldn't join Jean Malouel at first light and set off for Troyes.

Even after he went into the back room with the straw pallet where he was to spend the night, sleep didn't come easily. He took out his box and wrote for a while: about a sliver of moon rising over a palace wall, about the sounds of the city all around, about the Lover, outside, pacing up and down, longing for a glimpse of the Rose within; but seeing only bricks and darkness. But it didn't help. Even he could see it was partly about Catherine. But it was all convention. It wasn't truly what he felt. He didn't know what that was. He tore up the page.

Even when the singing died away, Owain lay awake, listening to the small sounds of the night. Jean Malouel's news must have unsettled him more than he'd realized. He woke at every distant bang after the curfew bells faded; he told himself it must be a loose shutter, or a horse kicking its stall.

It was absolutely dark when he next sat up; wide awake and terrified. He could have sworn he heard feet creeping by outside the window. He couldn't see the hands in front of his face. The window was shuttered. But even now he was awake, his body racing with the energy of fear, those sounds outside still sounded like feet. Not just a footpad breaking the curfew, either. That was the quiet, measured tramp of soldiers' feet.

He didn't dare open the window. It gave directly onto the street. Someone might see. But he tiptoed out into the corridor; looking for a stairway so he could peep out more safely from an upstairs window.

He wasn't the only one to be unsettled. Two other people—an old woman and a young man with a taper, whom he thought he recognized as the innkeeper's son—were also padding up the corridor, looking scared.

The youth with the taper raised eyebrows at him. Shadows leapt satanically up from them. "You heard it?" he whispered. "Me too." He turned his ear toward the noises. "Sounds like they're coming from the Saint-Germain gate. Heading for the river. The city."

The old woman's eyes were round and terrified. "Ghosts," she quavered, in a high, thin voice; she had no teeth; "a ghostly army; headless soldiers, come to punish us for our sins . . ."

"Hush, Grandma," the young man muttered. "Don't you worry; it's not ghosts." But Owain thought he looked even more anxious than before as he pushed her back into her room.

By the time they found an upstairs window, and agonized over the squeak it made as the shutter came back, most of the quiet men outside had gone past. But they could still see their backs, streaming quietly along in the moonlight, toward the riverfront bishops' palaces and the Saint Michael Bridge. Hundreds of them; with streaks and flashes of silver at their sides.

He didn't expect terror at the sight of those flashes of silver. But he remembered this, or something like it. For a moment he was in another time, another place: burrowing into female arms, hiding from the men outside. His mother, perhaps. He could see the fine green stuff of her shawl, the weave up close next to his eyes. He could almost still hear the wild beat of her heart; the soundless *sh-sh*. They'd been near Glyndwfrdwy, on the sharp wooded hillside, on a quiet evening. There was a luminous sunset; he remembered that. Stars through the young leaves. She'd turned at the first hoofbeats. Quietly, without frightening him, she'd taken him into the shepherd's hut off the track and, tying up their horse inside with them, where the strangers wouldn't see it, squatted down in a corner with him in her arms. The men had ridden purposefully past. Peeping over her shoulder, Owain had counted dozens of them, all with swords or axes. He remembered the long quiet after: the distant whoops and screeches; the flickering lights. She'd put him down, gone to the doorway. "Can we go on now?" he'd whispered pitifully. He was hungry. There'd be supper at Glyndwfrdwy. She was in the doorway. She'd shaken her head without turning, gazing out, he thought, at the evening star, bright in the darkening sky. "We can't go on," she whispered. "We'll stay here, nice and quiet, then go home in the morning." It was only when she came back, and picked him up, and began rocking him and whispering a song about the evening star, that he saw she was crying.

That must have been when Glyndwfrdwy had been burned. They said his mother had died of grief after Glyndwfrdwy.

He wished he could remember her face.

"Not ghosts," he whispered, to reassure this other frightened woman in Paris, tonight, years later; trying to count the bodies, back here in the present. At the speed those men were going, if no one stopped them at the bridge, they'd be on the Island within minutes. They were heading toward the palace. The King was there. Catherine. There were other windows being cautiously opened now, all along the street; other tousled heads and stares following the backs.

"Burgundy," the innkeeper's son breathed; and Owain could see his eyes were shining. He grinned at Owain through his gap teeth. He added, quite a lot louder: "Come on!"

"My apologies for waking you," the young stranger said. "I hope His Majesty wasn't too startled."

He'd been announced as the Lord of l'Isle Adam. Catherine didn't know him. There was a whole Burgundian France she didn't know—the shadow side; the courtiers whose loyalties were to Dijon, not Paris. But she knew this youth's appearance now meant Burgundy was coming. His voice was smooth but the eyes in his blacked-up face flickered with battle fever. His hand was on his sword.

Catherine, in her nightgown and a shawl, standing protectively next to her blinking, bewildered father, inclined her head. Thank God they'd been staying at the well-fortified palace, on the Island, and not at the exposed, innocent Hôtel Saint-Paul.

She'd ordered the leader of the soldiers outside to be admitted; they hadn't been overrun.

She'd chosen the palace, when they returned to Paris, to protect herself and her father from Charles, who'd likewise chosen the elaborate fortifications of the Louvre for his home. Catherine had done nothing more to try to contact her brother. With a heavy heart, she even kept out of the way now on the rare occasions there were council meetings at the Palace. There was nothing she felt able to do to stop them all living these separate, fortified, lonely lives, building the walls higher and higher around their hearts. She could do no more to reach out to Charles. Even Christine, who had gone to Charles when he arrived in Paris, had not been received. Charles had cut himself off—had chosen to be another enemy.

There had been no hope in Catherine's life since her meeting with Charles. She spent her days with her father. She looked after him. Household money still came from the council, but, now that it was clear that royal father and son were not on good terms and the Armagnac faction was more active and powerful than the King supposedly supported, the money came only fitfully. It didn't matter; there were no visitors. Courtiers could always sense where power lay; and it wasn't here now. So Catherine made do with the reduced number of servants; the limited budget for food. It felt strangely familiar, patching and making do on the edge of the luxury of the palace. She and her father walked or sat in the gardens together every day, feeling the summer on their backs, fretting. King Charles was sane, but could think of nothing but his fears about his wife. When he was sane, there was no one he loved or depended on more than Isabeau.

"Is she all right?" he'd say anxiously. "Can I write to her? Where is she?"

Catherine told him, over and over again: "We'd hear if anything was wrong," and, "Please, Papa, don't worry." There was no point in worrying. Still, she felt as though she and her father were, like Isabeau, in a prison, and one from which she couldn't imagine escape.

When, a couple of days ago, Christine had rushed into her

rooms with the extraordinary rumor (which her son Jean de Castel had heard from the de Marles, his employers) that the Queen had got away from her prison with the help of the Duke of Burgundy, Catherine had, for a moment, been too astonished to speak. It must be a joke, she thought. But Christine never teased; there was no laughter in her round eyes now. "No," Catherine had breathed eventually. Burgundy: Isabeau's bitterest enemy. What could those two possibly have found in common?

"I swear by God and all the saints," Christine had said. "I couldn't believe it either."

For a moment, Catherine had looked suspiciously at Christine—all she felt, herself, at the idea of the Duke of Burgundy coming back into her life was utter, childish dread, and now it crossed her mind that Christine might be suppressing excitement. Christine had prospered under Burgundy before; she must have good memories of him, and perhaps she'd be pleased if his luck was changing for the better. But any positive feelings Christine might have had at the bizarre change in the Queen's and Burgundy's fortunes were well suppressed. If anything, Christine had looked worried too: after all, her son worked in the Armagnac administration now. "I was going to go to Poissy to see Marie," was all Christine had said; "but now perhaps I should wait till next year; be here in case of trouble . . ." Her voice trailed off.

"No," Catherine replied, gaining strength from the other woman's hesitancy, rising to the occasion for both of them. "Go. Take the children; take the women. It's the last year they'll let your grandson into Poissy, isn't it? They'll count him as a man next year. So, let him say his goodbyes to Marie. Don't let the war disrupt that. Go."

It was only after Christine, looking grateful, if still tormented, had bowed out of the room, that Catherine had let her mind away from Christine's family's problems and back to the news about Burgundy and the Queen. Her heart was pounding. Somewhere in the whirlpool of feelings was a grudging admiration for her mother's spirit—Isabeau would never let herself be locked up for the rest of her days without fighting back. Perhaps she, Catherine, should have shown more spirit herself, and somehow improved her own lot here in Paris in the same way. But Catherine had also felt the prickling awareness of danger close at hand. Her mother and Burgundy wouldn't just stay at Troyes. They'd move, soon.

And now here they were, or their men. Late in the night, with weapons and blacked-up faces. She hadn't thought her mother would put her and her father in such direct danger. She could hear what must be going on out there now, on the Right Bank: riots; a massacre; the mob. She could see the sky all lit up and hear the shouts. But it was important not to show fear. She raised an eyebrow.

"I have a letter for His Majesty from his wife, the Queen," the Lord of l'Isle Adam went on, with the same impeccable politeness. But Catherine could hear the slight trembling of his voice now; she could almost feel the tension vibrating through his body. It made her feel stronger to know this tall young man was also nervous. "May I deliver it?"

L'Isle Adam didn't comment when Catherine, rather than her father, opened and read the letter.

"Papa," she said gently, kneeling down before her father so she could see into his cloudy eyes, and showing him the letter. "Maman is asking us to go to her. She's the guest of my uncle of Burgundy now; and this gentleman will escort us to them. There's nothing to worry about; we'll just go to Maman at Troyes and be together again. She needs us."

She was nodding her head; smiling; persuading him to accept the inevitable.

Her father didn't look anywhere except back at her. Weakly, trustingly, he acquiesced. "Dear girl . . . if you say so . . ." Then he began to look at his hands, flexing them to and fro.

"I won't be a minute, Papa; I'll see our escort out, then we'll pack you up," she said sweetly.

Outside, she said coldly to l'Isle Adam: "I don't know what's going on out there, but whatever it is he mustn't see it. If you truly mean us no harm, you must understand how important that is. I don't want him distressed. We'll need a closed cart to the gate. And quiet streets. And a proper escort."

He nodded seriously. She thought he was relieved that they'd accepted his polite order so sanely.

"We'll go back by the Left Bank," he agreed; "through the University quarter. To the Saint-Germain gate. There's nothing planned there."

Briefly, Catherine was stricken at the thought of everyone on the Right Bank. Christine perhaps; her brother Charles and his wife; all the cousins and friends and servants in houses in the town, around the pleasure gardens of the Hôtel Saint-Paul, all along the river. They'd be right in the thick of it.

She pursed her lips. Closed her eyes. Felt dizzy. For a terrifying second, she imagined men—not individual men, but a looming mass of leather jerkins and muscly thighs, and bold, sneering eyes and glittering blades—coming for her. Breath on her face; tearing at her.

But she couldn't think of that now. She had to stay calm. With Christine gone, it was more important than ever for her to be the capable one. She opened her eyes.

Perhaps sensing how close she'd come to panic, l'Isle Adam added, with something like threat in his elegant voice: "But I can't guarantee that the students won't wake up and want to come and join in too. So please hurry."

Owain had put on his clothes and sword and followed the innkeeper's son and all the other curious, wary, excited men— with sticks and poles and bits of wood and daggers out in their hands, and poachers' bags on their shoulders—to the Island; to the palace; and on. The bridges seemed to be unguarded. There were men pouring out of everywhere in the moonlight, and shutters opening on all sides so scared-looking women could peer out after them. To Owain's relief, they went right past the palace. At least, he thought, Catherine was safe inside. But where were they going?

It was only after they'd started streaming over the Exchange Bridge to the town on the Right Bank, behind the quiet soldiers, that the noise started. Owain strained his eyes ahead to see. Outside the Châtelet there were hundreds and hundreds of soldiers already waiting; one force meeting another on the

Square. And, as soon as they'd met, the air was rent with yells and curses, and the ghostly reds of fire and blood began to twitch Paris into murderous life.

Owain was swept along with the baying crowd, east toward the Hôtel Saint-Paul and the Bastille Saint Anthony. But he was relieved to be out, in the madness, treading lightly, breathing shallowly, with his sword in his hand. The shouts were all about Armagnac and Burgundy, but he could see it was really a night for looters and private revenges. There were already men breaking into wine shops and taverns, under an unearthly flowering of flags bearing the red X of Saint Andrew's cross— Burgundy's emblem.

Grève Square was packed with men writhing against each other, gray and seething, like carp in a barrel. Glassmaking Street was full of broken glass and fighting. He had nowhere special to go; nowhere was particularly safe; he just needed to keep on his feet and watch his back. He kept his distance from the break-ins and gangs of thugs closing in on one victim or another with leering, drunken, sneering cries and eyes full of death. He let his feet guide him toward Old Temple Street. It was somewhere to head for.

It was heaving, even there. Someone had got a bonfire going on the burned-out site where a house had once stood. Owain could see silhouettes dancing around on either side of it, waving another red flag crossed with an X. The smoke caught his eyes.

Over the road, Christine's door was hanging from one hinge.

Owain edged closer, through the jostle of men; alarmed enough, suddenly, to have his hand on his sword, ready to draw.

He saw a rush of big thick men coming out through the broken door, roaring taunts. They were hustling three prisoners in nightclothes whose gray faces were full of dread. Owain didn't recognize the oldest of the men being manhandled; but a younger blond one seemed somehow familiar, though Owain couldn't remember from where. However, the dark one in his thirties, with the long Italian nose and the rumpled black hair, was definitely Jean de Castel, Christine's son.

He pushed and shoved with all his might, and managed to

get himself close enough that he was walking along in step with the men holding Jean de Castel. "What's going on here?" he yelled—you had to yell to be heard by now—and the nearest man, a thug with a butcher's apron and a broken nose, turned round and gave him a joyous, deranged look as he screeched back, "Bloody Armagnacs! Big cheeses too! This here"—and he jerked his head toward the oldest man—"is only the bloody Chancellor, isn't it!"

Owain felt sick as the dark tide of memory rushed through him. Jean de Castel's friend Jean de Marle, the handsome blond man who'd taken Christine's son off to work for his father, the Chancellor. That must be him. They'd been hiding at the de Pizan house. They'd been caught.

He had to do something.

He stopped as the next thought struck him. What if Christine was here too? And the young wife, Jehanette? The children? Servants? What would this mob do to them? Hardly knowing what he was saying, he yelled, "Any women in there?" and twisted his face into a leer. The thug grinned knowingly back at him. "Nah, mate. Not that we didn't look. This is it."

One less thing to worry about, then. Owain kept pace as the knot of men stumbled over the road toward the bonfire; but there were so many of them. They were closing in on the older de Marle now; but he was big and strong, despite his gray hair, and when the first one stepped inside the circle of legs and chests and landed a punch on his mouth he swayed but stayed upright, close to the leaping flames, with his lip coming up blue under the red and a mixture of shock and fury in his eyes. Then, with a howl, he flung himself at his attacker.

All hell broke loose. Suddenly there were men everywhere, fighting, rolling, snorting, grunting; teeth and eyes and snot and blood and sound; men on the ground; one screaming when he got too close to the fire and his sleeve caught alight. Owain couldn't even see either of the de Marles, the press was so thick; but all at once, as he was pushed out of one fight, then another, he found himself close enough to Jean de Castel to grab him by the arm, shout, "This one's mine," and pull him away.

He saw the other man's eyes fix on him; measuring the best

way to knock him down. *Don't fight me,* he mouthed; and Jean de Castel looked again, in a lightning flash of astonishment and recognition; and all at once they were out of it, and running as fast as their legs would take them, away from the bonfire, away from Old Temple Street, down the back alley Jean de Castel had dived into that, a moment later, brought them out into the narrow confines of Monkey Street, and quiet.

"Where . . . are . . . the . . . women?" Owain panted, as soon as he had enough breath back.

". . . Poissy . . . safe . . ." Jean de Marle panted back, with shoulders and head heavy on the alleyway wall. "Seeing . . . Marie . . . Thank . . . God." He raised his head; grinned. Blew out breath. Added: "Thank *you.*"

They let themselves be carried along by the tide for the rest of the night. They didn't think of heroics. Whenever they saw a knot of people moving in on a victim, they slipped backward into the shadows and danced nervously on. As day broke, Owain and Jean de Castel made their exhausted way back south over the bridges, through the debris of the city, over the glass and charred wood and bodies and looted houses and strewn gold coins and trinkets and household goods and prone bodies, either dead or drunk, to the inn inside the Saint-Germain gate.

Now the danger that had kept them light on their toes and light-headed with sheer relief at being alive was passing, Jean had fallen grimly quiet. Owain knew Jean would be reproaching himself for leaving his friends to a lynch mob. It was very likely that the de Marles would both be dead. "There was nothing you could have done," he said sympathetically. Jean nodded. But if that thought brought him comfort, it didn't show on his ravaged face.

The inn was untouched except for a couple of broken shutters on the ground floor. The innkeeper's son had a stab wound to the arm, and was sprawled on a bench, being bandaged up by the old woman. But although he was pale with sleeplessness and blood loss, he looked happy.

He winked when he saw Owain. "Do all right, did you, mate?" he asked cheerfully. Owain nodded without speaking.

"Yeah," the youth went on, as if Owain had answered; "me too. We were in the goldsmiths' "—over the other side—went straight there—best place to be, my mate said—and you wouldn't believe what they've got in there, some of them . . ." He patted his pockets. They chinked. "Rich bastards," he said contemplatively. Then, as if remembering what the point of the night's violence was supposed to have been, he added, more fiercely: "Armagnacs, the bloody lot of them. Been stealing our money for years."

Owain was aware of Jean de Castel's quiet rage, and of the effort he was making not to take on exactly the kind of looter who might so easily have killed him in the night. Owain patted the wounded looter's good shoulder, turned away from his truculent, guilty eyes, and took his friend off to sit down.

Neither of them had much to say. They swapped stories in half-hearted whispers: brief accounts of their lives in the four years since they'd last met. Owain was relieved to realize that it didn't seem to give offense that he'd been a soldier in Henry of England's army; you had to do as you were ordered, after all; and he'd become Jean de Castel's comrade too during this last night. But their talk kept petering out. Jean de Castel clearly didn't want to talk about the de Marles—who'd genuinely been Armagnac supporters—and all his days had been spent with them recently. The Frenchman was embarrassed, too; his life had been saved by this semi-stranger, but he had no way of thanking him; not even the price of a glass of wine in his pockets. He was in Owain's charge, for the moment. Besides, they were too tired to talk much; too low in spirits. Still, the inn was a good place to gather news. They ate. And, as the crowds of pink-eyed rioters came in for a bite and a cup of red, they listened.

They heard that the Count of Armagnac was in prison—he'd thought he was being hidden from the mob, but he'd been betrayed. They heard that most of the Armagnac nobility were dead or on the run. They heard that the Provost of Paris, Tanneguy du Chastel, had whisked Prince Charles and his wife away to the Bastille; they were out now, and heading for Corbeil, or Melun, and safety. "Saved his own skin, that one," sneered one battered student. Everyone else laughed. The King and his daughter had been seized and taken to the other side— to the Duke of Burgundy at Troyes.

More and more often, as the morning yawned and stretched into day, they heard that the Duke of Burgundy and his royal pawns—the King, the Queen, and Princess Catherine—would almost certainly now make a triumphant re-entry into Paris. And every time the rumor was repeated, the rowdy cheers grew louder.

The civil war was taking an ominous new turn for the Armagnacs, now Burgundy held so many of the royals. Without Armagnac himself, the feeble, untested, near-child Charles, with his southern in-laws, wasn't up to much, every drinker in the tavern agreed. "Long live the Duke of Burgundy!" the old crone Owain had seen creeping the corridor at night, worrying about ghost armies, kept crowing now. There was a gloating smile on her face.

"What will you do now?" Owain asked Jean de Castel quietly, noticing that the Frenchman's hair, which he remembered as a luxuriant southern black, was silvered now; that there were lines round his eyes and mouth; that the other man no longer felt young, or lucky.

"I don't know," de Castel said in the end. "It wouldn't be wise to go back to the house. This isn't over yet. I need to find my family; I need to get them to safety. But where that is . . ." He paused.

Owain could see him run through the possibilities. Jean de Castel knew now that he was an Armagnac in the eyes of a mob turned Burgundian. His family was safely out of town, at least; but they'd be on the road home today, or tomorrow. And how would he find them? The rioting would start again as soon as the men thronging the taverns, shouting and laughing and yawning, got the energy back to go burgling again. No wonder Jean de Castel looked gray.

Someone needed to take control. "If I may make a suggestion," Owain said, feeling the benefit of his time in the army, dealing with apparently impossible situations every day, "you should take my horse, now. Ride toward Poissy and find your family—they'll be somewhere on the road back. Take them to Anastaise's convent, not to your house. The beguines are safe enough; no one will give you away there. Once you're back in Paris, with them, we'll work out the next step."

Jean de Castel nodded.

"But your choices are limited. The mob has decided you're an Armagnac. So you count as one. You're going to need to take your family to wherever Prince Charles goes—leave Paris and start again."

De Castel nodded again. "We have some money with Anastaise's nuns," he said, turning to practicalities. "Enough to start again, maybe; if we're modest." But then he froze, as if the awfulness of what he was beginning had only just struck him. He said: "I can't just take your horse." And he hunched in on himself, looking ever more dazed. "I can't repay you. I can't . . ."

Owain stifled impatience. This wasn't the time for false pride or false starts. Surely Jean could see that. He pulled the older man's tense body up from the bench and began walking him to the back of the hall. "Look, I'm here on my King's business," Owain said, as they came out into the sharp daylight. "I'm well supplied. I won't need a horse for a couple of days. I was supposed to take letters to the King. But I need to see where he is; and whether he comes to Paris. So . . . take the horse, and this," he dug in his purse and found ten Tours livres, a substantial amount. Jean de Castel looked at the coins and shook his head. But he did transfer them to his purse.

There were no grooms today. Owain brought the horse out himself: found the saddle and bridle and packs and water bottles. Called for bread and cheese for the traveler. Jean stood, blinking, staring at something near, not at Owain.

When the horse was ready, Owain led the other man over with an arm round his shoulder. He had to nudge him up the mounting block; there was no question of Jean putting his own feet in his own stirrups. Jean stared down at him with a dull question in his eyes. Owain settled the reins in his unresponsive hands.

"I stayed with you for weeks," Owain said, addressing the

question Jean wasn't asking; "you felt like a family to me. You were kinder than you needed to be." He laughed; a short man-laugh, consigning the treasured memory that followed to history. "You even nearly sent me to the University of Paris, you and your mother, do you remember?" He didn't want to remember how angry he'd felt with Christine when he'd left. She'd been right, after all; he'd known it really. He couldn't aspire to love a Princess of France; that wasn't for the landless, status-less creature he'd become. That was the stuff of dreams. He'd have to make a real future for himself before even thinking again about love. He'd tried war, but fighting wasn't for him; he might have better fortune as a negotiator. Come what may, he had to stay in the realm of the practical; to keep his feelings for his poems. He led the horse out to the street, and whacked it firmly on the flank to set it walking. This was practical enough. "I owe you gratitude," he said firmly. "I want you to find your family."

Finally, feeling himself on the road, on the move, Jean seemed to come back to life. He looked back; blew out a whoosh of air that made the hair on his forehead rise and dance. He took the reins. Nodded back at Owain. "We'll be at the beguine convent by noon tomorrow," Jean said, and, pressing his knees and heels into the horse's sides, rushed off.

It was only when Owain was alone in the street again that he realized how much he'd been relying on the man he'd been helping to keep his spirits up. He didn't know what to do with himself now.

Where to go to deliver his letters to the King? Owain didn't know. He stayed on at the inn, half listening to the gossip, drinking to mask his loneliness, with time hanging heavily on his hands, waiting for everything to become clearer. No one was in charge in Paris anymore. The Prince's administration had fled. The Duke's wasn't yet here, despite the red Burgundian crosses hanging from every window. But, even if Owain had had his horse, there would have been no point in rushing off to Troyes, where the King had been taken, if Burgundy and his royal "guests" were just about to re-enter the city.

There was so much time, and only so much ale and wine you could put inside yourself without feeling sick or sleepy with it. Sooner or later, as morning turned into a tired, scratchy-eyed afternoon, all Owain's strictures about sticking to practicalities foundered. He found himself unable not to start wondering what it had been like for Catherine, whatever she must now be like, four years on, and her father, the mad King, to be taken off to Troyes, almost as prisoners, under armed escort. Had she wept? He couldn't imagine that: she had too much dignity. He could imagine the way her green eyes would have hooded and her face become neutral; her back straightened. But she must have been afraid, and not just of the sounds of fighting and madness in the streets.

He remembered the way she and her brother had talked about the Duke of Burgundy, back then, in the gardens. They'd both feared him like fire; beyond all reason. She couldn't be happy at the prospect of living under Burgundy's control now. He took another swig from his cup, reproaching himself as he did so for letting his mind wander off like this. What did he know, after all? How could he possibly guess? Everything had obviously changed since then; the reality was that he knew nothing about her and could know nothing. Catherine and Charles had been close back then; but now they were on opposite sides. He couldn't imagine how that had happened; though he'd hazard a guess it must be something to do with that vicious stinging beetle of a mother. Perhaps things had changed so much that Catherine was looking forward to being with the Queen and with Burgundy. Burgundy might even strike her as a safer pair of hands than Charles. Owain shook himself. Stop, he told himself. All you should be thinking about is how to marry her to Henry of England; this is foolishness. He finished the cup and, dragging tired feet on the stairs, collapsed onto his pallet and fell asleep.

Owain's head pounded and ached the next morning—he wasn't usually a drinker—but he was up early, and at the gate of the beguine convent at noon. Anastaise, as red-faced and barrel-bodied and hearty as ever, hugged him warmly, muttered, "My, how big and handsome you've got!" and hurried him into the whitewashed room where pallets and travel bags were piled up against the walls, and where de Castel's family were sitting quietly, waiting, the two children with their mother's arms around them.

Christine—a small, tired Christine—was on a stool by the window, staring at something very far away. But she got up and smiled with real warmth when she became aware of Owain. Going to him, she kissed him on both cheeks, and, looking straight at him with her fine eyes filling with tears, she said: "Thank you for saving my son."

Owain muttered something self-deprecating, then hurriedly moved on to business. He wasn't sure whether, in the muddle of feelings he had for Christine, there was still any of the resentment he'd felt back there; but he knew he wanted her to see him doing good effectively now. "They say the Prince and the Armagnacs are heading for Bourges," he said. "They'll be setting up a court of their own there. So that's where you need to go, too."

He didn't tell them what this morning's revelers at the inn had been gloating over: that the Count of Armagnac himself wouldn't be heading for Bourges, since more mobs had broken into the prisons of Paris overnight, and Bernard of Armagnac had been torn to pieces. Charles had been lucky to escape; he'd have met the same fate if they'd caught him. The puny, nervy little boy that Owain remembered couldn't have changed out of all recognition—he must have been terrified. For a moment, Owain felt sorry for Charles; then he wondered what Charles might do, now he was safe, to get his revenge on the Duke of Burgundy. Then he stopped himself. All Christine and the de Castels needed to know now was where to go to reach safety.

Jean nodded. Owain could see he'd already got the little bag of money that the family would need from the convent storehouse. Jean had it strapped to his belt. He'd got his resolve back now, with his family. "We've got horses arranged," he said briskly; "and I'm sure to find colleagues there. So we can set off as soon as we're ready."

Jean put Owain's ten Tours livres back in his hand—a gesture of finality. "Thank you for this," he said. "Your horse is stabled here; they know to return it to you."

Owain could see he couldn't wait to be off. It would be a relief once all his family were on the road to safety.

So when Christine said, very quietly, from her window seat, "I'm not coming," they all turned to her with big shocked eyes.

"Don't be difficult, Maman," Jean said, too sharply. "Please. We need to get the children away."

"I know," Christine said calmly, as if, after long doubt, she'd made up her mind. "You have to go. I'll see you off. But I'll stay here."

"The danger," Jean said.

"There'll be no danger. Not for an old woman like me," she replied firmly. "I'll stay here, with the beguines, till things calm down. Then we'll see."

She looked up at Owain. "And Owain can help me get to you if I need to, later . . ."

"Why?" Jean de Castel said. He wasn't arguing. He knew it was a waste of time to try and make his mother change her mind. But he didn't understand.

Owain thought he did. If Christine went south to Bourges with her son, to follow the Prince in setting up a court to rival the King's, she'd have definitively taken sides. She'd have cut herself off, perhaps forever, from her daughter at Poissy, in the hinterland of Paris. That wasn't a choice she wanted to make now. If she stayed here, even at worst, as things were now, she still had that choice ahead.

Perhaps Christine was embarrassed to explain her softer maternal feelings. All she said was, "It's not right for us all to go haring off. I know you have to go, Jean; and you have to take the children. But someone needs to be here, near the house. Things might change . . . The Prince might come home, make his peace with his parents, as he should. And my Princess will be back here soon; and she's going to need me."

She sounded more decided with every word. "But give my regards to Prince Charles," she said. She'd taken to calling Charles "Prince" since he'd arrested the Queen; since she'd

182

stopped being able to think of him as a nervous child to be cosseted. "My warmest regards." She couldn't quite say "love." She knew the difference. Love was what she felt for the family she was perhaps losing.

Jean sighed. There was no arguing with Christine's sense of honor and duty. Jehanette lifted her eyes to him and did a tiny shrug with arms still spread about her cowed children, signaling, Accept what she says; we have to go.

Two weeks later, when the Duke of Burgundy and his royals finally entered Paris—a city hastily sluiced down and tidied up, with the blood all scrubbed away and the bodies hastily buried on the edges of graveyards and the only touches of red the rose petals scattered through the streets and the Saint Andrew's flags—Owain was part of the cheerful crowd at Notre Dame, waiting for the two royal litters to wobble into sight, followed by the rest of the Duke of Burgundy's triumphal parade. Standing beside him, composed in her neat blue and white, was Christine.

From her horse, moving at a stately walk, Catherine watched her father and mother, lying in litters side by side, holding hands. The King of France was laughing a little at something his wife was whispering to him. Catherine could hardly believe how calmly he'd taken all the hurried moving around in the past few days. He was happy whenever the Queen was kind with him, and she, triumphant at her escape and the defeat of her son, couldn't have been kinder. Papa hardly even seemed to notice the cheers of the crowds lining the Paris streets. Catherine crossed herself.

Perhaps she'd been too frightened, when it had happened. Perhaps her father was right to take it more calmly. The narrow streets stretching back from Notre Dame that she could see now were just as she remembered them: no blood; nothing out of place; just flowers and sunshine and smiles everywhere. Perhaps Charles had been the one who'd been mistaken to take fright, and take flight . . .

No . . . And, despite herself, Catherine almost laughed.

Charles hadn't been wrong to run away, now their mother was out of the jail in which he'd put her. She called to mind her mother's snuffling fury at the very thought of him. "Ashamed to have brought that one into the world," Isabeau had taken to ranting, whenever Charles' name was mentioned. "Should have strangled him at birth. I do not consider him my son." The servants' indrawn breaths; Burgundy's thin-lipped disapproval; her father's mild, worried-looking expostulations, "Come, come, my dear." None of it had cowed Isabeau. She'd just fixed them all with her most frightening look, making sure everyone was listening before she told her husband, as loudly and provocatively as she could, "Well, *I* don't consider him *mine; and he's certainly not yours.* He should think twice before he runs away with the idea that the throne is his birthright."

It would have rung far truer if Isabeau hadn't spent all Louis' youth telling him, every time they quarreled, that she could unmake him, too, as the future King of France. As it was, even Catherine's father only tutted sadly at his wife's unthinking temper tantrum and looked out of the window, giving her time to recover her poise. Yet, even after Burgundy had said, in thin, reproving tones, "Madam, enough," Isabeau went on looking truculently round, as if seeking approval for her claim that she'd foisted bastards on the royal house of France.

Catherine fixed her eyes on the Duke of Burgundy, just up ahead in the street with his son Philip, both bowing and waving to the people. The Duke was the real ruler of Paris today. He was wearing velvet robes embroidered with the diagonal red cross of Saint Andrew that the six hundred burghers of Paris who'd met them at the gate had brought him for this march into the city center. The robes hung loose off his long, lean, busy, jerky frame. But his face—long, bony, with hooded, burning eyes above his great eagle's beak of a nose—was almost relaxed, for once; he was almost smiling.

Catherine couldn't help herself. Despite the apparent warmth of the day, she shivered. She was still just as frightened of the Duke of Burgundy as she'd ever been. Every time Burgundy looked at her, from under those heavy eyelids, her heart almost stopped. She'd been brought up with the fear of him; she and

Charles both. Even if her mother, who'd whispered the stories in the first place, now seemed half in love with him, her cousin made her flesh crawl. Controlling it was beyond her, even if the stories were nonsense, which she knew they might be.

Being in Burgundy's control now felt worse, Catherine thought, than almost anything else that had happened to her; however polite he was; however correct. She didn't want to be here, with him. But there was no way out—except through Charles, and that way was closed forever too. Charles was dead to her. She was more of a prisoner than ever.

More to distract herself from her dread of her uncle of Burgundy than for any real reason, she glanced down at the people cheering behind the line of guardsmen.

She looked again. Her heart leapt. She rubbed her eyes. Smiled.

It was a wish granted. Christine was there, just as usual, in a blue dress and modest white headdress. Alive. She was waving and smiling straight back at Catherine, with her familiar piercing gaze.

Catherine nodded; breathed out; nudged her horse closer. Christine was safe, and here. She had a friend in the crowd. Suddenly even Christine's less engaging habits—her probings about marriageable princes; her awkward, prickly awareness of duty, whether her own duty or that of other people—seemed endearing; felt like home and family saved. There was nothing Catherine wanted more than to have Christine with her: to be talking over the events of the past weeks and getting back to normal. Catherine held Christine's gaze, and mouthed at her over the din: *Come to me! Please! Soon!*

It was only when she'd pushed her horse's head right through the line of guards, so she could have touched Christine's head if she'd leaned forward—and was stretching out her hand, hoping their palms would briefly brush before she had to move on with the procession—that she saw Christine wasn't alone.

Standing beside her was a tall, well-built, strikingly handsome young gentleman, also staring intently at her. He had blue eyes, and black hair.

She could hardly believe it. But it was Owain Tudor.

She felt no shame at the sight of him. Not anymore. Too much had happened; she wasn't the same person as the child who had once kissed him in the woods. Nor was he, probably: he was bigger, and more solid. He'd probably forgotten . . .

But he was here. And she was so ravenously hungry for happiness that she let the banned memories flood joyfully back: the shout of songbirds and the heat of that other morning's sun on her back; the rumble of his voice and the rasp of his cheek; the recollection of all the hopes she'd once had, long ago.

She'd let her mouth fall open, she realized. She put her hand over her open mouth. But she couldn't stop staring. Owain Tudor was staring back, and his expression was as gentle as ever, and the corners of his mouth were turning up.

PART THREE

Lamentations on the Troubles of France

TWELVE

The battered, bloodied city of Paris lurched into a future controlled by the Duke of Burgundy. This was what the rioters had wanted. But, now they had it, no one seemed happy. In sweltering July heat, the markets began to reopen, though many cautious stallholders stayed at home and the goods on sale were the cheapest and most disposable—just in case. Boatmen took to the river again. Houses that still had inhabitants had clusters of workmen outside, repairing the broken windows and bashed-down doors. But many more houses and taverns stayed boarded up. The goldsmiths' streets and those of the book trade operated only from behind bars, and most of the elegant homes in which members of the Parliament had lived were closed. The University stopped working. A lot of people seemed to have left town. The streets, with their patches of new paint and wood and stone, their scrubbed-away blood and their burnt-out plots, looked shabbier than before. They felt uncannily quiet. Anyone you did see out seemed to be flinching fearfully over his shoulder at imaginary sounds behind. There were more dogs and abandoned livestock than usual, howling in the alleyways. The churches echoed. There were rumors of plague.

When the heralds announced that the Duke of Burgundy was making a formal peace alliance with the English against Prince Charles and the Armagnac princes of the south, the remaining people of Paris only sighed and shook their heads. If that was what the Duke wanted, they muttered doubtfully; the

English were wolves, but the Armagnacs were dogs. Perhaps it would be all right.

All Owain's hard-won poise had vanished as soon as he had seen Catherine again.

He spent the night of the royal return to Paris alone in his room at the inn, transfixed by the memory of her. He couldn't sleep, couldn't eat, couldn't think of anything else. She'd looked perhaps a little thinner, taller, and more watchful than he remembered. But he'd have known that neck, those shoulders, anywhere. And when she'd actually turned, and looked right into his eyes . . . he shivered at the thought of it. Grabbed his hair in his hands. Almost howled with the pain of it.

He was ashamed—worse than ashamed—to feel a lovesick boy again. This was much worse than before; more knowing, and, at the same time, more hopeless. He'd promised himself not to do this, or feel this. There was no future in letting his heart run away with him a second time. He knew his place in life, now; he'd accepted it. He was his English master's servant, here to set in motion arrangements for a royal marriage. This woman, whom he'd once known, a little, was perhaps to be Henry's bride. He didn't want to be filled with this madness. He had to rip it out of himself.

But he couldn't. He couldn't help it. Couldn't help himself. Couldn't do it.

Owain knew he could see Catherine again. He had the letters from Henry, and he had instructions to deliver them personally to the King (or Queen, or Prince, or Count of Armagnac, depending on the circumstances)—and to Catherine herself.

He didn't know whether it was his mad or his sane self hugging that knowledge to his heart and laughing.

Owain looked at the Duke of Burgundy's bowed head and thought, in surprise: But he's an old man.

The Duke, in black velvet, was cadaverous and beaky. Owain had seen him once before—during a battlefield meeting with Henry, when Henry had tried (unsuccessfully, back then) to persuade him to join forces with England against the other

French princes. Owain had had no trouble today recognizing that great grim scarecrow of a man, with his spare movements and cold lizard eyes. But the Duke seemed to have shrunk. His skin was leathery and desiccated. His stillness no longer made you think of a snake about to strike; just of the cautious movements of the elderly.

But the Duke still had power. It did no good Owain protesting, "But, but, one of these letters is addressed to His Majesty the King, and the other is for Princess Catherine. I was told to deliver them into their own hands, personally . . ." The Duke took no notice. He just held out his jeweled hand and fixed Owain with his unblinking gaze and waited for the envoy to stop talking.

Owain had entered the room hardly able to breathe for the beating of his heart. He'd expected Catherine to be at the audience, but she was nowhere to be seen. And the Duke had said nothing that suggested she would be called in. While the Duke read, Owain breathed in and out, slowly, rhythmically, trying to get control over himself.

He couldn't read the Duke's face as the Duke read the letter. But Owain felt almost certain that the Duke couldn't accept the marriage proposal he was carrying, even though he'd just made an alliance with the English against Prince Charles. (How Burgundy and Charles must hate each other, Owain thought, looking curiously at the older man's impassive face; he couldn't imagine any of the tight-knit circle of English royal brothers and cousins ever betraying each other in that way.) The English terms for the marriage were even greedier than before; Owain was old enough now to recognize that. He'd told himself he would count his mission an unexpected success if he even managed to deliver the letters. He'd take the chilly refusal of Henry's marriage proposal, which he knew Burgundy would get round to in a minute, with fortitude. But, if he could only see Catherine, for even a moment, before he left. Just one glance, as he put her letter into her own hands.

The Duke gave Owain a bleak smile. Here it came.

"You may or may not know," the Duke said, and Owain wondered at how that thin, nasal, slightly stuttering voice had the power to make his heart quail and droop, "that I've just concluded a military alliance with Henry of England against Prince Charles. That's a separate question, of course. But you should know that I would look favorably on a marriage; and of course on a peace agreement between France and England. If the t-t-t-terms were right."

Burgundy waited for Owain to smile, look overjoyed, bow his gratitude. Owain duly did what was expected of him, and dropped his head and back. He was glad, at least, that this hid his eyes.

He should have been pleased. If he'd been a good diplomat, he would have been pleased. This unlikely soft answer made it just possible that he might, after all, return to Henry with the promise of a wife.

But looking overjoyed now was almost beyond Owain, who felt instead as anguished as though his stomach were full of ground glass. As though he'd been hit in the face; or had his legs chopped off.

There was no one in the world he admired . . . revered . . . adored . . . more than his master. But he didn't want to think of Catherine marrying Henry of England. Even the idea of anyone else laying a finger on her, let alone owning her in the eyes of God, filled him with a resentful, seething, jealous rage. There was nothing in what he felt now of the poetry he'd wrung out of his boy's love before—all those wistful lines about the moon, and roses, and a timid kind of longing. All that was left was this white-hot fury of frustration. He'd never write another line of poetry. He wanted to take her in his arms and to hell with the pale, pining lovers of chivalry.

He kept his eyes down as he rose from his bow. He didn't want the Duke to see any of his thoughts.

"There's n-n-no need for you to meet the King or Queen of France at this stage," he heard Burgundy saying, still with that cold smile playing on his face, still with an unearthly light in his wolf-colored eyes. The thin voice seemed very far away. "Or the Princess. I will discuss the terms with them. Perhaps you will ask your master to reconsider his. I am sure we will find a way to agree."

He nodded dismissal. Owain bowed again, and left. He couldn't bring himself to speak.

Catherine saw him already out in the courtyard, foot in stirrup, swinging up onto his horse. She ran down the stairs, two or three at a time, her skirts held up round her knees: a girl again.

He saw her race across the courtyard. The sun was in his eyes. He put a hand over against his forehead and stared.

She grabbed his bridle. There was a big smile nearly splitting his face. She grinned back.

"I nearly missed you," she said, suddenly shy, looking down, breathless from her undignified sprint down corridors and stairs and over cobbles. The horse snorted in her ear, unsettled by the speed of her. She patted its neck and danced from foot to uneasy foot with it.

After what seemed a long silence, she heard a whisper. "Catherine . . ."

Then the shape on horseback slithered down, so hastily that he stumbled as he touched the ground. He put a hand on her shoulder; then, righting himself, snatched it away as quickly as if it were burning.

But now he was down on the ground, and she could see him, away from the dazzle of the sun—his eyes were gentle.

They stood very still, looking at each other. She didn't even know why she'd run so fast to find him. Bashfully, uncertainly, she smiled.

"I'm so happy you're safe," he said at last. "I was in Paris that first night. I was worried for you."

She was surprised at the soft glow of gratitude spreading through her. No one else had said that.

"Christine says you rescued her family," she breathed, suddenly wondering what it must have been like to be out in the streets, in all that . . . She shuddered at the memory of the flickering torches, the shouting, the bitter smoke. "She's so grateful," she hurried on, wanting to ask more—had Owain been scared? had he been in danger?—but suddenly, deliciously tongue-tied. The irony of it was that she remembered herself and Owain talking together so confidently that she had never even worried about whether words would come to her tongue. Still, it didn't matter; even in this awkward silence she was happier than she remembered being for a long time. She looked at the horse; surprised to find she was still holding the dancing creature's bridle.

He smiled; something like his old carefree grin. "I thought I'd have to leave without seeing you," he said, and she was drawn into the grin again now, happy just to be standing there, shifting from foot to foot in the midday sun. "I've been in with the Duke," Owain was saying, looking so searchingly at her that her eyes were forced modestly down. "I thought—hoped— he'd send for you. But he didn't."

She mouthed, *Why?* She meant, Why would he send for me? He understood at once.

"The marriage," he said, and his face clouded. "My master's raising the marriage question again."

She wasn't supposed to want that marriage. But she felt a prickle of something: the beginning of a new possibility.

"Part of a new peace . . ." she said; a kind of question. He could see that, to her, the notion of marriage was an abstract proposition, something that must mean statecraft and sums about dowries and dowers. She added, with the beginning of disappointment, as she searched for the meaning of Owain's suddenly gloomy expression: ". . . but he said no?"

Owain appeared worried, then looked around. There was no one in earshot. The grooms and guards were busy. She understood that look; it meant, I shouldn't say anything, but why not tell you? Quietly, he went on: "Burgundy's not against the marriage, in principle. In fact, it looks more positive than it did before."

That surprised her. She asked, "Why?"

She knew the English had long ago stopped muttering about Henry of England's dubious right to his throne. As far as the English were concerned, Henry's years of victory in France were proof God was with him; no one had even whispered, for years, since Azincourt, that he was the son of a usurper. But Henry's battlefield success against the French was no sort of proof for the French that he was the God-given King of England and France. Was it?

Owain shifted awkwardly. She realized she was being stupid. He said: "I don't think His Grace of Burgundy worries anymore about my King's legitimacy. They are allies, after all . . ."

She nodded hastily, and felt embarrassed that she'd been so slow-witted. She still found that change strange. Both Burgundy and the English had been the enemy for so long, in the minds of those around her, and she'd always been told Henry's blood was not a king's. Now it was only Charles who disbelieved in Henry's right to his throne, and Charles had become the enemy. Charles, whose armies had marched north, whose men kept taking towns such as Melun where she, Catherine, or her mother, had recently been or might have been; places frighteningly near to home.

Did Owain realize she felt a fool not to have mastered the new upside-down logic of the latest stage of the war? If he did, the confidential tone he adopted next was a kindness that restored her self-respect. "My personal opinion, for what it's worth, is that my lord of Burgundy will probably hold out for big territorial gains in northern France, both for himself and my King. But, once he's got those, I sense that he'll be willing to recommend that France and England move toward a full peace agreement. And everything that goes with it, of course—including the marriage."

He stopped. His face had twisted again at the word "marriage."

But Catherine was feeling dizzy at the rest of what he'd been saying. She felt as if the cobbles were shifting underfoot as she glimpsed just how much plotting and scheming was going on around her. She thought: Here I am, thinking we're all just being swept along by the tide, but really everyone except me is planning how to get the best out of their situation for themselves. I should be doing that too; not just waiting. I should be thinking about what I want, and how to get it, now.

But what did she want? For a moment, looking at Owain, she didn't want anything more than to go on being here, talking quietly in the courtyard. Then, knotting her fingers, and pushing herself on to be more ambitious in her imaginings, she thought: What I want is to get away from all *this*.

She didn't know whether the "this" she wanted to get away from meant the Duke of Burgundy, or the war, or her father's madness, or her mother politicking, or her brother's enmity, or France itself. But she thought there was a little of all those things in it. She knew that the only escape she was permitted by her royal blood was one to another country, through a royal marriage. She'd always remembered that Owain had once told her England was orderly and dignified, decorous and calm; that the King of England and his brothers and uncles ruled together, wisely and in perfect unison, and that their people loved them all. Back in the days when Henry's blood had been in doubt, that hadn't been enough to secure a marriage with France for him; but now? If Burgundy believed him to be a legitimate king? Catherine could imagine nothing lovelier than that harmony. She wanted not to live on the edge of fear, with everything so sad and out of control.

If those were the things she wanted, she reasoned . . . perhaps she should be doing everything she could to encourage the marriage with Henry of England. That would be the way to get away from everything she was afraid of here; and it would bring peace to France, too. There'd be nothing to reproach myself with, she thought. If I'd helped to make peace with England . . . that's the most realistic good I could do in my life . . . who could quarrel with peace?

She felt her face clear. It seemed suddenly simple. She looked up at Owain Tudor. A little hesitantly, she said: "Well, peace is a good aim."

He looked doubtfully back.

But the quickening beat of her heart, the strange flicker of a feeling that it took her a while to recognize as hope, wasn't really about marriage, or peace. She was just remembering, and the thought made the corners of her lips turn up a fraction, that she'd once kissed Owain Tudor, once been a child with her head turned, and he a handsome boy, and the air had been full of songbirds.

She shook her head at her own foolishness. She wasn't a

lovestruck innocent anymore. It was just a memory, that day; a moment's madness. Something to laugh over by the fire with your children and grandchildren a lifetime later.

"I'm glad it's you they sent, anyway," she said daringly. "I've often wondered. How you were. What became of you. After . . ." But that was too brave. She couldn't go on.

He shook his head. "What children we were," he muttered.

But he was looking at her, as steadily as she was looking at him. She moved closer, so close she could almost feel the breath rising in his chest. No one was looking. The horse's big chestnut neck and powerful shoulders were between them and the gatemen. A black cloud was beginning to cross the sun, heavy with the threat of rain, and the grooms in the courtyard were looking up, and dragging the hay bags they'd been filling into the shelter of the stables before it started.

She looked up at where the cloud was glinting darkly against the sun, then nodded at the horse, indicating Owain should mount. Still looking at her, Owain got back up on the block and swung his leg over the horse.

She stepped up onto it too, as, once mounted, he leaned forward to gather the loosely knotted reins. She meant to kiss his cheek in brotherly farewell.

He turned round as she landed lightly behind him. There was utter disbelief in his eyes.

"Take me out of here," she breathed. "Just for a while."

She was behind him on the horse, riding pillion, with the bag that had been on the pillion pad now jigging and bumping across her knees. She had her hands on his hips. His back rose straight in front of her; he was so close she had to look up to see the back of his head. The golden horse under them both was ambling toward the river; toward the Saint Michael bridge and the Left Bank and the University. The street was half full of tradesmen and animals, shouting and grunting, loaded down with bundles: Parisians going about their daily business. Neither rider had any idea where they were going; only the horse knew it was going home.

When the rain began—big, thick, heavy, warm drops of it,

with thunder growling and banging and rattling the shutters—it sent everyone else scurrying for shelter. Not Owain's horse. Owain kept the animal at his stately gait as the street emptied; as the water bucketing noisily from the sky drenched him and the passenger behind him, whom he couldn't see, whose hands he could feel on his hips, whom he could hear, whenever the thunder let up, breathlessly laughing.

"It's good to be out," she said in his ear. The wind snatched away her words. She might have been shouting against the drumming of the rain, but he could only just hear. She leaned closer. She said, tickling the side of his face with her hair, which had come loose: "Show me where you're staying."

Owain was too astounded to answer. He felt as though, in a moment, he and Catherine had ridden right out of reality into a dreamlike other world; a place as perfect and highly colored as one of Anastaise's miniatures. The blood was drumming through his body louder than the rain on the streets. The hands on his hip bones were warm and small and surprisingly strong. He kept his back straight. He nodded. He clicked the horse on. He was drenched; with hair flattened against his eyes, warm rivulets running down his neck. He didn't care. Not about the wet; not about anything. He wasn't going to ask questions. He was going to stretch this moment out for as long as she wanted.

He heard a snatch of that exhilarated voice again: ". . . soaking!" He heard her laugh. This time he laughed too: letting himself follow her into the unknown.

All the way to Owain's rooms in Saint-Germain, Catherine was looking around at the mess of backstreet Paris: staring at boarded-up windows and abandoned spots where there used to be street markets. But it wasn't them she noticed. She was too aware of the golden smoothness of the horse under her, the rain on its shoulders, its long neck stretching out away from Owain's tall back, and his breath, and the way her hands were trembling on his body, and the way she couldn't stop laughing. Free. Just like that: just by riding away, as if she'd never go back.

She'd always known she could trust Owain. He was her friend. She'd known he'd take her; give her a taste of the freedom she craved; and ask no foolish questions.

She looked curiously around as they entered the little mews alley. Owain dismounted, then handed her down, with a face that was alive with excitement at this adventure as much as hers must have been, even if his sodden hat and clothes were plastered down on his body and rainwater was running off his cheeks. Owain put the horse in its stall and slipped off the saddle and harness and called for the stable boy. As soon as he heard the rush of footsteps, he inclined his head merrily at Catherine and, with a hand that didn't quite touch her elbow, showed her the door to inside.

Suddenly they were out of the rain, in half-darkness. It was hot inside; the fire was always burning at the inn, the pot was always on, and the smell of boiling vegetables and herbs, with a hint of chicken, was wafting as savory as ever through the hall. There were two elderly men nodding at a table in a remote corner. Through a door, Owain could hear the old crone shouting at her grandson.

Owain and Catherine stood on the threshold, getting used to the sudden quiet.

". . . Buy you a meal, lady?" Owain whispered joyfully. "While we sit out the storm? Chicken stew?"

Their eyes danced and laughed together for a moment. Catherine looked down. Her sodden clothes were dripping. There was a puddle gathering where her tan silk gown touched the floor. She shivered and put her arms caressingly about her own shoulders.

"Yes," she breathed back, dimpling up at Owain, with her chin nestled against the hand hugging one shoulder, "please . . . and do you think I could dry off this gown, too, while we eat?"

Catherine ate wrapped in the rough blankets Owain had brought down from his tiny room, with her gown spread over a stool by the fire, steaming, beside them. The crone hovered delightedly and patted Catherine's arm in its damp linen when she brought the bread and broth and wine. "A lovely girl like you," she kept muttering through puckered old lips; "just what he needs. He's a good boy."

Owain, who'd changed into his dry doublet and hosen and

tousled most of the wet out of his hair, was now standing up, hovering around Catherine, making sure she was comfortable. He gave the embarrassing old thing a gentle nudge on the shoulders to send her on her way. But Catherine only grinned back at the crone, her eyes sparkling.

When Owain sat down on the other side of the little table, Catherine said, "I don't know why I've only done this twice in my life," and, grinning even wider, with that daredevil gleam in her eyes, "just gone, I mean, got on a horse and gone away—because it's wonderful to get away when you dare."

Owain was tongue-tied. He gazed dumbly, adoringly at her. She gazed back at him and crumbled a little hard bread between her fingers. They both splashed spoons in their broth. Afterward, remembering the rapt silence that came over them at the table, Owain had no idea whether either diner had actually raised a spoon to their mouths.

The robe steamed. They drank the wine. They moved away from the table and sat down on a bench at the side of the fireplace, looking into the glowing depths, not at each other, listening to the crackling and bubbling, with their hands on the rough wood of the bench, not quite touching.

"I should take you back," Owain said, perhaps much later. "The rain's stopped."

She stretched a little. "So warm here . . . sleepy," she murmured. But she stood up. "May I use your room?" she asked, picking up the damp robe. "It will take a few minutes to put this back on . . ."

He took her up the stairs. It crossed his mind to say, I'll send the old woman up to help.

He didn't know how it happened that he never got the words out. That, as soon as they'd reached the top of the stairs, as he reached for his own door, she was in his arms, and they were kissing.

"You have to stop," she whispered, but dreamily, only half opening her eyes: and she was laughing and moving under him.

"I can't," he said helplessly, laughing too. "You know I can't."

He woke up. He wasn't alone. It wasn't a dream. Catherine was curled up with him, in his room at the inn with the bucket for the dripping roof, and she was whispering and rhythmically stroking his hair. She sounded happy. Excited, even. "You knew. You came back. I always knew you would. You took me away. It was easy. And we could just go on. Take money. Ride. We'd find a way, wouldn't we? The Holy Land. Venice. Wales even," he heard.

He groaned. He sat up. He put his head in his hands.

Her sleepy, contented voice stopped.

There was a silence broken only by a drip of water into the bucket.

He rocked his head back and forth; screwed up his eyes; clutched at himself. He couldn't bear to think of what they'd—he'd—done. He couldn't bear to look at her.

". . . or just here somewhere . . . a quiet estate in Guyenne . . . something . . . love always finds a way," he heard her clinging to her dream, going back to stroking him along with the rhythm of her words, although only his calf was within easy reach now, but with her voice beginning to falter. "We'd find a way."

He moved his hands back over his pounding head so he could see her; so she could see his torment.

There was a defiant half-smile on her face, and it was the loveliest face in the world, even when he pulled her up, almost roughly, to sit beside him, and put one arm around her shoulders, and looked sideways at her, knowing what he would have to say to stop her saying what she was saying.

Because of course he loved her, but where? The reality was that it was impossible to love her. She was the greatest unmarried lady in Europe. And he was who he was: no one much anymore, but a minor English gentleman and Welshman born, who'd betrayed a master who had been good to him; a master he also loved. He shouldn't be here; he shouldn't have thought whatever sinful thoughts had led him here. Even the stories about love ended tragically if the lover ever dared take his lady to his bed. Guinevere's faithful knight, Sir Lancelot, cuckolded King Arthur; that forbidden love ended by destroying Camelot. In real life, nothing like that happened; it couldn't.

It never would again.

"What are you saying?" he said.

She gave him that half-defiant, half-yielding smile again. "We could," she said. Then, falteringly, as if reality was just beginning to touch her: "Couldn't we?"

He shook his head. Made his heart harden, even when she quailed and looked at him with heartrending love and fear.

"How could we?" he said despairingly. "It doesn't make sense. There'd be half of Christendom out looking for you before sundown . . . There *is* no way."

She said nothing. But tears formed in her eyes.

He looked away. How could he comfort her?

"I can't help you; you can't help me," he said, and the harshness of his own voice surprised him. "Our destinies are different. We can't escape them. You're supposed to marry my master, not me. You don't need me to tell you that. You know it too."

Then he stood up.

He wanted to say he was sorry; but he wasn't. He wanted to tell her that he'd remember all his life how they'd lain together here; and he'd never forget the pain of driving her away now. But he couldn't tell her any of that, any more than he could tell her how much he loved her. "You have to go," he said roughly, suddenly desperate to force her to accept the finality of this parting without arguing. He'd be lost if they talked. He could see her recoil at the coldness in his voice. He closed his eyes. "Please. Dress."

He waited for her outside the door, still shaking his head, still overwhelmed by the madness that had come over them. When she came out, her face was lowered. The light had gone from it. She slunk by, not meeting his eyes.

He put her up on the horse. He took the bridle and led it, on foot, back through the puddles and afternoon sunshine. He couldn't ride. He couldn't bear for them to touch. He couldn't bear to think of what would become of him after he'd taken her back to the palace.

She slid off the horse herself, without waiting for a hand or a block, when they came in view of the palace gate. She brushed down her robe, looking uncertain. He could feel her seeking out his eyes.

"We mustn't meet again," he said, staring at his feet. He spoke sternly, to hide his anguish; to stop himself throwing his arms around her again and pouring kisses on her head.

A thought had been slowly taking shape in his head as he walked. If he went back to England, if he went back to his studies, he could go further than completing his degree at the University with the monks. He could become a monk himself. He could swear lifelong celibacy; devote himself to the reading and writing of books, and to the peaceable, humble, innocent harvesting of fruits and grains and honey; give himself to prayer. But, he wondered, refusing to turn as her footsteps receded, would even that cure him of this love?

He did turn round to catch a last glimpse of her, though. Of course he did. And he did stare hungrily after her until her very straight back and head, held nobly high, disappeared through the gateway. He stayed like that for a long time, staring at where she'd been, lost in thought, until the horse began to whinny and snicker at him, and nudge his arm.

Then he mounted. He couldn't stay in Paris anymore. He couldn't say goodbye to Christine. There would be guilt too clearly on his face. It was time to rejoin Henry to report on his mission. But then he should give up this career as a diplomat; he should go back to Oxford and pray for deliverance.

Catherine went to her rooms. She could smell him on her. She ordered water heated for a bath.

She stopped them scenting the water with rose petals and rose oil. "I don't like the smell anymore," she said. "Throw it out."

She put her damp linen aside. "Burn this," she told the water carrier.

The tan robe had a tide line from the rain, above the ankle. She gave it to her attendant. "Have this," she said; "see if you can repair it, get the stain out. But keep it for yourself."

Then she asked to be left alone in the tub, by the summer fire. She didn't want to have to talk.

She felt sick inside, but she kept her face cold and hard to stop the nausea as she stepped into the water. She would never think of Owain Tudor again. She'd thought he was the one person she could always talk freely with; the one relationship in her life not muffled and silenced and deadened by the war. She'd given him her heart; her body; her hope. She couldn't stop the hot blush or the waves of humiliation at the memory of what he'd done back.

So she scrubbed every inch of her skin, hard, angrily, till it was raw and painful, as if she were scrubbing away the shame of the day—scrubbing away her own stupidity, scrubbing away Owain, and scrubbing away everyone else in whom she'd ever placed a misguided hope of salvation.

No one else was going to help her. She got up and wrapped the linen sheet around herself. She could feel the set line of her jaw. It was time she started looking out for herself.

"You're supposed to marry my master, not me," he'd said, as he pushed her away.

Well then, she replied now, inside her mind. I will. I'll marry your master.

THIRTEEN

"What exactly did the English messenger want?" Catherine murmured that evening, massaging the thin gray hairs clinging to her mother's scalp; wishing the braziers weren't burning in this heat.

Isabeau shivered sensuously; she loved being caressed. "H-h-hr . . ." she grunted; "they're offering the English marriage again . . ." she purred, without hesitating over whether that was supposed to be a secret.

Catherine went on rubbing the old, balding head. "And what does my cousin of Burgundy think?" she asked, after a pause.

Isabeau's voice came wafting up like a drift of rose oil: "Well . . . dear John is so cautious, of course . . . he says they're being greedy . . . they want too much, of course, but that's the English for you . . ."

Catherine stopped massaging and clasped her hands together. She took a deep breath. Then she moved round her mother's bulk and sat on the floor in front of her, at Isabeau's feet. She took her mother's hands in her own, and looked into Isabeau's eyes. Her heart was racing.

"I want that marriage," she said. The words hung on the air, and as she heard her voice saying them she realized how changed she was. She'd never articulated a wish of her own to her mother before.

Her mother's eyes were gleaming. There was nothing Isabeau liked more than a good intrigue. With relief, Catherine could see her mother was already excited at the idea of a bit of marriage mischief now—a plot in which the whispering, fun-minded girls outsmarted the dull soldier men; the triumph of love. This was going to be easy, after all.

Isabeau nodded, several times. Her smile grew so wide it practically split her face in two. "Hm," she muttered excitedly; "we'll have to see about that, then. You know it was always what I wanted for you." Then the Queen murmured wheedlingly, "Now where were those aniseed drops they brought this morning?" And she glittered at her daughter, pushed the bowl at her, and added, "Try," and then, more plaintively, "Weren't you doing my hair just now?"

It was a winter of waiting.

For the Duke of Burgundy, it was a winter of disappointment. Even though he'd declared himself the friend of the English, his supposed ally Henry of England continued to advance, until Paris itself—battered, hungry, shabby Paris, no longer the greatest city in the world, but still the greatest prize in the civil war—was within the English armies' grasp. The Duke did nothing; just looked pained, and thinned his already thin lips, and steepled his fingers. Catherine almost felt sorry for him as she watched him suffer, so tight and dry and wrapped up in his frustration, imagining how baffled and angry he must be feeling. She knew Burgundy's reputation had always been that he was able successfully to orchestrate fights and feuds among everyone around him, nudging others into folly, so he could step quietly in and profit from their disarray. But now he seemed as paralyzed as anyone else: trapped between the stubbornness of Prince Charles—who was still at Bourges, with his rival court and his Armagnac war against Burgundy's armies, and who wouldn't come to terms with him on a French peace—and the power of the English.

Looking at the leathery wrinkles on Burgundy's bleak face and hands, feeling the irrational tinge to her fear of him fade, Catherine thought maybe age was wearing away at his immense ambition. Perhaps he was just too tired, too weary in the bones, to fight on. But her uncle's nature was too forbidding for a flicker of warmth to develop. It still felt uncomfortable to be near him.

Inside the walls of Paris there was plague again: shutters, and prayers, and the stink of fear. Inside the palace, Catherine spent her days with her parents, listening to her mother chatter about the past, or watching the two old people, one bent and skinny, one bent and blubbery, murmur together over their cards.

Once or twice a week, Christine came from the beguine convent to the palace and tried to interest Catherine in reading with her. With a book open, Christine would then, every time, try subtly to introduce the subject of Charles and his life in his southern realm, the need to let bygones be bygones and to make peace within the royal family. And Catherine would nod, and obstinately not reply; and turn the page. Catherine didn't want books, any more than she wanted lectures about forgiving Charles. If she got a chance to take the initiative, she made Christine walk in the gardens, if there was a little sun; or she sat with her by the fire, if it was wet, and she asked after Christine's children. Christine sighed and shrank into herself. Catherine knew that was the reason for Christine's dogged hopes of peace between Bourges and Paris. There was so little news, though she never gave up hope. Catherine could see Christine wanted Jean and Jehanette, Perrette and Jacquot, and she could see there was no point in talking about the English marriage when things were like this.

Even if no one else had the heart to do anything but wait, Catherine began quietly to act to help herself.

One December morning, she asked Christine whether Anastaise might come to the palace to paint her portrait in miniature. Christine agreed enthusiastically. The de Pizan workshop in Christine's old home had never reopened after the riots; Christine didn't like to admit it, but she was frightened to move back alone. She was talking about renting out the house, but the times weren't right; she didn't have the energy to make it ready or find a tenant. Making the house ready would mean admitting to herself that her family had gone, and her business too; and she couldn't quite bear that. Christine didn't even like to admit that she'd stopped writing. What was there to write about in these unhappy times? She had nothing to say. Meanwhile, Anastaise's talents were going to waste.

Christine brought Anastaise to the palace every day from then on, with her bags and baskets and boxes and bottles of paints and gold leaf, and Anastaise's cheerful coarseness warmed the room they sat in better than any fire. She taught Catherine a lewd student drinking song. She showed her how to work gold leaf. She brought her an early spring flower. She left mess everywhere she went; making Christine breathe tight through her nose and call Anastaise a lamia, one of the fairy women who were said to come into houses at night to empty the barrels, peer into pots, throw infant children out of their cradles, light snuffed-out lamps, and pester sleepers. Catherine liked the fairy stories; they made her feel a happy child, playing at a peasant hearth. She sensed they comforted Christine, too (and she wanted Christine comforted, because she could see her old friend shrinking into herself, getting scrawny and threadbare in her blue and white dress, looking elderly and frail in a way she never had while she'd had her family with her). In Anastaise's folksy otherworld, there were always happy endings.

Anastaise had so many stories. She'd be fiddling with her little pots or grinding up her colors or applying new layers to the sketch she'd made or getting Catherine to help—she was no great believer in the dignity of kings—and her voice would just keep coming. "Now, as for sprites," she'd say, and Catherine would be soothed again by the lullaby in that rough voice, "everyone knows that they can take human form and show up in public places, without being recognized by anyone. They actually live in the depths of rivers—pass me that brush, there's a dear—and they catch people, especially women and children, swimming at the edge of their rivers by taking on the appearance of golden rings or goblets floating in the water. One grab and whoever's spotted the lovely glittery thing is done for. Usually it's nursing mothers they carry off, to act as wet nurses to the sprites' babies—stay still now, do—but after seven years the nurses are sometimes allowed back into our world, and they've always been well rewarded, and oh! The stories they tell, about the sprites' palaces, great beauties of palaces, right under the banks of the rivers!"

The last coat on the little picture was dry by the end of March. It showed Catherine looking wistful, pretty, and sweet, with a rose in her fingers and a fine tracery of gold in her hair and on her robe.

It was the only good that had happened all winter. All attempts to have talks between England and France had got nowhere. The English wouldn't agree to anything. Everyone was sour.

When Isabeau heard the suggestion her daughter whispered into her ear as she presented her with the picture, the old Queen nodded several times. "You're a clever girl as well as a beauty," she wheezed thoughtfully. "Oh, I'm blessed in my daughters . . ." and her eyes flashed angrily for a moment; perhaps she was thinking of her many errant sons, all but one now dead. Then she twinkled at Catherine. "Call in the man, will you, my darling? The scrivener?"

So, at the beginning of April 1419, the portrait was sent, with a formal letter of greeting from the Queen of France to the King of England.

Catherine felt a little guilty that she hadn't told Christine or Anastaise what she had wanted the portrait for. But, she reasoned, knowing would only have made Christine angry. Unlike the Queen and the Duke of Burgundy, Christine still hated the English, and still didn't accept Henry V as a true king. She wouldn't have wanted any part in sending him gifts showing her princess wistful, pretty, sweet, and marriageable. It had probably been best to say nothing, just act, Catherine thought.

The King of England must have appreciated Catherine's likeness. At any rate, a meeting of monarchs was arranged within days.

FOURTEEN

Isabeau looked disgruntled with the arrangements as soon as she saw the field at Meulan. She whisked with surprising speed round the conference tent in the middle of the field, with its twin gold thrones for her and the King of England, and its tapestries, prodding at things and frowning. She walked across the boards the full hundred paces to the French encampment at one side of the field. Shading her eyes in the May sunshine, and staring at the other side's encampment, she said grumpily, "It's just as far to the English tents, the other way. Impossible. Quite impossible."

The Duke of Burgundy had done all he could to ensure that quarrels couldn't arise between the negotiators, or fights between men-at-arms. Nothing was to poison the atmosphere. The English party was lodged overnight at Mantes; the French and Burgundians nearby at Pontoise. Each delegation was to arrive at first light, at its end of the field at Meulan, to the sound of music; then, at an agreed time, to the tooting of horns, they'd enter the conference tent in the center of the field.

But Catherine could see that all this caution and display didn't please her mother.

Hesitantly, she said: "Maman, what's the matter?" Her mother had been so excited when the Duke had told them the talks would take place that she'd packed Catherine off for a long series of fittings with vestment-makers and embroiderers and jewelers. Where the money for it all had come from so suddenly Catherine couldn't imagine. Christine, who'd understood at once that all this display and finery was intended to trap Henry of England into a marriage that would cement a peace agreement and alliance with the House of Lancaster, had been tight-lipped and disapproving through the entire fitting process. Catherine had been glad to leave her behind in Paris. At least Christine believed Catherine was being bullied into a match she didn't want; at least she didn't realize the extent to which Catherine herself was nudging her mother forward with this plan. Christine's parting words had been, "Be careful," and then, with an anxious look Catherine had been obscurely grateful for, despite her irritation, "Don't let them push you into anything you aren't sure is right."

Catherine, meanwhile, had been more flustered every day with her own quiet mixture of excitement and fear—with the knowledge that she had to use these talks herself, and make the King of England fall in love with her, if she was to break the deadlock and move the marriage and peace negotiations forward. She knew so little about what made life a delight. She didn't know what would please him.

She'd become so anxious about the problem of how best to charm the King she hadn't met—which soft looks or breathy laughs or clouds of satin and sparkles of diamonds or flashes of wit she should employ—that she couldn't imagine what might trouble anyone else on the eve of these talks. She certainly couldn't understand what it was about a gold throne draped in cloth of gold, here, at this luxuriously kitted-out meeting site, that would make her mother look so annoyed. Isabeau didn't even seem to like the special little tent for the Queen, over on the French encampment side, flanked by a smaller tent for the Princess, flanked by a still smaller tent for a lady-in-waiting.

Isabeau, not her husband, would sit in the throne at the talks. The King had reacted badly to the traveling. In his rooms, over Catherine's at Pontoise, he was hovering between weak sanity and one of his mad times; and no one wanted him to suddenly start screeching like an eagle or running around the room tearing off his clothes in the presence of Henry of England. So Burgundy had ruled that it would be better if he and the Queen represented France in the King's place. But Burgundy had done as much as was possible to make sure the Queen's taste for luxury was respected; to lavish visible honors on her. "It's all just right, isn't it?" Catherine went nervously on. "Don't you like it?"

Isabeau only squinted malevolently at her, as if she'd said something very stupid, and grunted.

Henry of England looked round the room. There were half a dozen secretaries to hand, but no one he trusted like Tudor. He beckoned. He pulled a ring off his finger and held it out to the young Welshman: the rubies set in it glittered.

So did Owain Tudor's eyes. "I've got a job for you and your cloak of invisibility, Tudor," Henry said easily. "Take this to the Princess at Pontoise, and tell her thank you for the pretty portrait, and, mm, anything else that strikes you as right . . . love talk. Only don't tell the whole world, all right?"

The Welshman nodded. But he didn't enter into the spirit of the thing. His face was set.

Henry went on whistling under his breath as he watched Tudor go out to his horse. But he didn't altogether like that look. He liked his men to be enthusiastic.

Tudor hadn't wanted to come to these talks, he recalled. He'd been asking all winter to go back to England. Perhaps that was what the smoldering look was about. He'd been useful in France; and he'd done too well with that first negotiation with Burgundy to be sent away yet. But it would be time, soon, to let him go. He wasn't a boy anymore. He was big and strapping; old enough for a wife and children.

Henry of England turned back to the portrait, forgot Owain Tudor, and grinned. The French Princess with the pushy mother really was a very pretty girl. He couldn't believe his luck.

Owain rode as far as the inn, got down from his horse with a face like thunder, went in, and wrote a brief note from Henry to go with the ring. He'd asked the King seriously enough and often enough for permission to go home. It hadn't been granted. Loyalty and obedience were one thing; but he couldn't run lover's errands to Catherine.

He put everything back in his saddlebag. He looked around. He breathed relief. There was his old comrade Owain Dwn, drinking in a corner. Thank God for Welshmen, he thought.

"Dwn," he said. "Do me a favor. Take this to the Princess at Pontoise for me, and I'll buy you all the drink you can swallow for the rest of the talks."

Dwn gave him a skeptical look. "Why?" he said.

"*Cer i'r diawl*, man, don't ask stupid questions. I don't have to explain a favor. Just take the bag."

Dwn shrugged. "More fool you," he said cheerfully. "We could be here for weeks. Do you know how much I can drink in weeks, if someone else is paying?"

Owain passed him the saddlebag. "There's a ring in there, and a letter," he said shortly. He didn't want drinkers' camaraderie. "From the King. Give them to her, personally."

It was only when Dwn had already cantered off down the Pontoise road that Owain realized he'd been so eager to get shot of the ring that he'd handed over the whole saddlebag, containing most of his own possessions too—his knife and spoon, his little box of poems, and a change of linen. He hoped Dwn wouldn't get drunk over there and forget it somewhere.

Catherine stared. The King of England was slightly built and not very tall, with rat-colored hair, a long, thin, pale face and pop eyes set very wide, like his brothers'. He had gray at his temples. He had lines running from nose to mouth, where his too-red, too-full lips were fixed in a determinedly cheerful grin. She rather liked the grin. But he was nothing like the prince she'd been expecting.

She had to call consciously to mind that this man represented England, and England represented everything she should want for herself—calm and order, dignity and decorum, in a place where she'd never need to be frightened—and very likely also peace for France.

She tried to make her eyes lose their focus and swim and be

dazzled in the sunlight and glitter of cloth of gold outside the tent. She wanted to feel that her heart was stopping and her breath was coming fast and shallow. She'd felt that before; once. But now she felt nothing. He was here, the man she was going to try and marry, and all she felt was desperately uncomfortable in her gold and red gown, with the ruby ring he'd sent her scratching away at her finger, and awkward at the knowledge that, by her side, her uncle of Burgundy's grim face would be split apart by the rictus he wore for a smile.

In her mind, she was reviewing all the scenes she'd ever imagined with her future husband as Queen of England—redrawing the wedding scene, which still took place in a Westminster Abbey that looked exactly like Notre Dame Cathedral—so that the groom at her side no longer had the black hair and height and grace she couldn't quite scrub out of her heart, but was this odd-looking rat of a man with the awkward eyes. Redrawing what followed. The dinner. The disrobing. She was a fool to feel so disappointed. What had she expected?

At some point in the morning's negotiations—long speeches of formal praise which Catherine couldn't pay proper attention to—Catherine became aware of her mother. Isabeau was busy. She'd called a lady-in-waiting to her other side and was whispering instructions. Catherine felt uneasy when the woman left the tent a few minutes later and headed for the French side of the field. Her mother sat on, looking smug.

Isabeau had musicians playing in her tent after the single combat that ended the morning's events.

Catherine didn't know whether it was a put-up job that the King of England had won his sword fight with his brother, the grizzled Duke of Bedford, in the open center of the field, but she certainly admired his skill. He fought with concentration. He was utterly still; then struck like a snake when he saw his opportunity. He was far more impressive when he was with men than Catherine had found him in conversation.

When it was over, and the King and his brother were sweating and laughing and putting away their swords and clapping each other on the back, Catherine walked toward them to try her luck at flirting. She let her eyes go wide and her voice husky with appreciation, and told him, "I've never seen such skill as yours." She was pleased to see his already glistening skin go a touch pinker with pleasure.

It was Isabeau who slyly invited the King and his brother to her tent for refreshments, going against Burgundy's strict rule that no one, under any circumstances, was to cross the field. The Duke of Bedford looked dubious and excused himself, heading off with the tight-lipped Duke of Burgundy to the table on which a restrained meal for the negotiators had been set out. But Henry, flushed and victorious, bowed with more confidence than before and replied, too loudly, "With great pleasure!"

Isabeau's tent contained a great many cushions and embroideries, as well as a small table on which wines and meats and, of course, many bowls of sweets were set out. She made a point of showing the King of England the embroideries and plying him with wine and food, cackling cheerfully, and explaining that the finest cushions of all were in her daughter's tent.

With a blush so hot she thought it might take her face off, Catherine realized what the lady-in-waiting had been ordered to do that morning—take cushions and rugs out of the main tent, which still seemed overstuffed and wadded to anyone not used to the preferences of the Queen, but which an expert in the ways of Isabeau might guess had been denuded of several hundredweight of luxury goods. The cushions must have gone to Catherine's tent.

"Stay, listen to the music," Isabeau ordered Henry breezily. "You will be tired. So much talking. Have a rest. Sleep if you like. The tent flaps shut. My daughter will attend to you personally."

It was too late to protest. Blowing her daughter a merry kiss, Isabeau was already wafting fatly away with her servants, over the walkway boards set across the field, back to the conference tent. She and the King of England were alone, in the Queen's tent, with its flaps up; looking out at the musicians.

Henry stayed a few feet away, staring at Catherine with a mixture of intense delight and alarm. He couldn't have expected this any more than she had. But she'd been willing enough to go up and shamelessly flatter him after he'd displayed his fencing skills; and this was just one step further down the same road; and she probably should have expected it of her mother.

Henry of England grinned again. There was panic rising inside her, but it was hard to be afraid of that grin. "Well," he said awkwardly, "aren't you tired after all that talk?"

She smiled and moved closer, thinking, very coolly, This is one way forward, I suppose, with one part of her head, while, in another part of it, all she could hear was the whoosh and rush of blood and breath.

He patted the nearest cushions. "Let's sit down here," he said, and she could hear he was trying to seductively soften his tone. Perhaps he was feeling as scared as she was. "Get to know each other a bit better."

The smaller tent was a love nest. They'd thought it all out. It wasn't just cushions and strategically placed wine behind the closed flaps. There was a basin of water, too, and towels; and someone had set out a table with pins and brushes to repair her hair and torn linen with.

He kissed her before he went, an hour or so later. Held her close—quietly, with none of the wild urgency that had been in him before, but very tight—so tight she could hardly breathe. The musicians were still playing outside.

All he said was one awkward phrase: "I had no idea you'd be such a pretty girl."

Yet she liked the soft look she surprised in his eyes as he said those uninspiring words: the kind of look that made her think that she might, when she stopped hurting, and dripping, and discovering new bruises and bite marks every time she moved a muscle, want to come back into his arms. She'd had to shut her eyes at first and imagine him looking different; she'd been surprised and disappointed every time she'd touched that stringy hair; but now, afterward, when she'd learned what it felt like to be in this man's embrace, she didn't like to remember any-more that she'd started by wanting to imagine black hair and blue eyes and youth.

There'd been a fierceness in her own body's response to this stranger that she hadn't expected. There was a slack, unques-tioning wonder in her now at the fact that she knew where the veins rose in his flesh; how his muscles felt under her hands; how his hairs curled on his skin; what made him sigh and tense and cry out. He had a mole on his left shoulder. She'd kissed it. She glowed at the memory of his skin. She was too confused to be sure, but she thought she felt proud. She'd done it. She'd tasted sin, and power. She'd become one flesh with Henry of England. She was beginning to see that that would change everything. Her mother had been right to push her into this. The Queen was no fool. There was no way back now. There'd have to be a deal . . . a marriage and a peace. All of France would be grateful when the marriage ended the war, Catherine told herself, wondering why she had to persuade herself of this. She was doing something better than just helping herself.

There was a messenger waiting for him outside the tent.

Henry looked irritably away as the man stared at his feet and muttered, "Sire, my lord of Bedford wanted to know . . ."

No wonder the man sounded miserable. There was no sub-stance in the message he'd been sent with. Henry knew his brother John of Bedford just wanted to show he knew what had been happening in the tent.

Still, it wasn't the messenger's fault.

"Thank you, Tudor," Henry said, with his usual punctil-iousness. He strode off to the main tent.

He was thinking, as he went, how sickly that pale Celtic skin under black hair could sometimes seem.

"*Wellll?*" her mother whispered from her golden throne, with an expectant grin; her whole face was jigging and moving. "*Telll . . .*"

The two entourages were filing into the tent. There was a

buzz of quiet talk; flurries of movement at the tent flaps; people finding chairs. Catherine was torn between embarrassment and exasperation and laughter: how could her mother expect to have the gossipy, racy, confiding talk she clearly wanted now—*now, here*?

But she opened her eyes as wide as she could and flashed Isabeau the briefest of smiles as she sat carefully down—a return signal of sorts. There'd be time later for the whispers; the bashful lowered eyes; the dazed nodding of her head; the shy smiles and sighs and blushes. Her mother would get it all out of her, she knew.

Meanwhile, she didn't mind in the least when Isabeau's hand crept out from the side of the throne, and, through the afternoon's dull exchanges of compliments in French and Latin, stroked her arm.

On the second morning, Catherine saw Owain Tudor. She'd dreaded this moment coming. But now it was here it wasn't so bad.

He was looking frantic with worry, being turned away from the tent. "I have no orders to let you in," the commander was saying mechanically, without really looking at him. "You're not on my list for today."

"But I'm needed! You must have me there! Let me see!" Owain was stuttering back.

He was very pale. He'd lost weight. There were unhealthy dark smudges under his eyes. She could see how threadbare his doublet was, how worn his boots.

Coldly, Catherine looked him over. How young he is, she thought. She felt confident in a way she never had before, with the memory of her whiskery, wiry royal lover's embraces so recent in her mind. She didn't need to care.

Without greeting Owain Tudor, or helping to get him access to the tent, she moved serenely inside, turning her back on the hapless Welshman and his problems.

A routine was established as the week wore on. Every morning there was the ride from Pontoise to the field, with Catherine's mother winking and glittering at her from her litter. There was the awkward jostling as the two entourages assembled, with men guarding the two entrances and commanders snapping at anyone who tried to get in through the wrong set of tent flaps and resigned faces on all sides as weapons were removed and identities checked.

Once everyone who was anyone was inside, there were the speeches—sometimes barbed, sometimes tense, though with their intent so veiled in diplomatic words that Catherine was only vaguely aware of why the French negotiators at her uncle of Burgundy's tent were whispering. She felt, blithely, that it didn't much matter anyway, since the outcome of the talks was now a foregone conclusion; and it was only natural that men who'd fought each other for so long would feel suspicious of each other when they began to talk again. Her mind was elsewhere. At midday there'd be the walk across the boards to her mother's little encampment; and, waiting inside, Henry.

No one seemed to see him come or go. No one mentioned the arrangement; no one indicated, by the merest gesture or eye movement, that they were aware of it. Her mother's servants would quickly serve Catherine and Henry food, then vanish. After that, there'd just be the music playing outside, behind the tent flaps, and the two of them, alone with each other. They'd laugh breathlessly as Henry pulled the cloth down and opened his arms to her; they'd melt together, leaving the food untouched on the platters, and all the responsibilities that had been loaded on her shoulders for so long would slip off, like a shiver of silk.

She couldn't believe the freedom of it. She'd thought she would need to run away somewhere to know freedom, but it had been here all along, waiting for her to find the right goal, something that would make every door open effortlessly, as they were all opening now . . . She'd never been so happy. She'd never felt so needed. His eyes never left her. She'd find him gazing at her with pleasure in his wide-set eyes, as she stretched languorously out on the cushions or shivered with pleasure at his touch, or eased herself up his body, kissing his chest. Just looking. He didn't talk much, and she was happy with that, too; it was part of the joy of being with him that the careful, watchful weighing of words didn't matter.

Once or twice she folded her hands on his chest, feeling safe with the steady rhythm of his heartbeat below her, and, looking up, asked him, "Will I like England, do you think?"

He only laughed. "Like a kitten," he replied softly; and, the next time, "Do that again; with your hands under your chin . . . you look adorable." And he'd kiss away her words as if they were nothing; a kitten's mewing.

She'd forgotten already that she'd once imagined him otherwise; that she'd been disappointed at the sight of him. She couldn't think of anything else anymore but being with him.

There was only one moment when she'd felt uneasy with Henry. It was on the day when, lying on the cushions, he had wanted to talk to her. When he'd asked, with a curious look, "They say your brother Charles is at Melun—just nearby— asking for talks with your cousin of Burgundy; doesn't anyone on your side think to say yes to him?"

She'd known Charles' army had seized Melun. ("Spite," Maman had said crossly, when she heard her favorite castle was in enemy hands; "he did that out of spite.") But there hadn't been any request for talks that Catherine knew of. Burgundy hadn't said a word about Charles wanting talks.

"Are you sure? What would those two have to talk about?" she said blankly. "They hate each other."

She didn't like the look Henry was giving her: calm, carefully assessing, and mildly amused, as you might be watching a cockfight or a peasant behaving uncouthly.

"They're cousins; they're both of France. So they might have many things to talk about, no? They might want to join forces to stop me marrying you, for instance . . ." he said, raising an eyebrow.

Alarmed, she breathed, "No!" and "They couldn't do that, could they?" She so wanted the future she saw opening up for herself now. She was already enjoying the first feelings of safety and companionship that this new relationship with Henry would bring her more of. She wanted to get away into the warmth of a life where she and this man would know each other well enough to tell each other all their secrets, all their innermost thoughts; a life full of children talking and laughing; a future in which the walls wouldn't look mockingly back at her in silence. She didn't even want to hear the possibility that Charles—the hateful, violent person Charles had become—could cheat her of that future.

Henry only laughed. "One never knows," he replied lightly. "Does one?"

She could imagine—vaguely—what was worrying Henry. They always said he and his brothers and uncles, the Beauforts, ruled and conducted their war together, in perfect unison. He must find it almost impossible to understand the hatred between the French royals; in particular, the one he'd be most aware of, between her brother Charles and her cousin Burgundy.

She couldn't begin to explain the ambivalence and suspicion that tainted every relationship in her own family, to someone who didn't understand families being that way. She didn't understand herself where all the complex feelings came from. She just knew they had always been there, and always would be; and, in her turn, she didn't really believe the English royal family could be so perfectly united. Deep down, she thought, surely those English brothers and uncles must all harbor quiet hatreds for each other, too.

Henry's face turned up in an inquiring, unemotional smile. "But don't *you* worry about what Charles wants?" he asked, quite kindly. "After all . . . he's your brother. You grew up with him. And he'll be King of France one day. If there's to be a good, lasting peace between France and England, wouldn't you say he should be part of making it?"

She shook her head fiercely. "Why should there be peace talks with Charles?" she asked. She was reasoning with herself as her words rushed out. Of course she wanted a good, lasting peace between France and England; that was what she told herself every day. Seeking the blessing of peace for her country was the reason for seeking out this marriage. But why should Charles—the hateful, violent person her brother had become—get a chance to spoil everything now? "Charles isn't the King—just a son. My father's the only king you need to talk to," she went on hotly, ignoring what they both knew to be true—that the negotiations were being led, for the French, by the Queen and Burgundy, not the sick French King, who wasn't, in reality, in any sort of state to conduct peace talks. "All Charles should do is come back to my father and ask his forgiveness for leading an army against his King. He should ask my mother's forgiveness, too. For putting her in prison."

Catherine paused. Assessing how she must look to her lover, she became aware that her face was flaming and her teeth had clamped tightly together. She must seem much too angry, she thought, making a conscious effort to smile and shrug and move her body languidly closer to Henry's.

Then, letting herself trust that everyone, deep down, understood the quiet rivalries and hostilities that must seethe away at the heart of every family, she laughed a little and looked into Henry's eyes. "Though my mother might not forgive Charles so easily," she added, with an attempt at merriment. "Naturally . . . after all those months in prison . . . he's caused so much harm; though she too . . . it's hard to explain. But she's still so angry that she's spent weeks saying that Charles is no son of hers, for doing what he did, and no son of our father's either."

She laughed again at her last line. She knew she meant partly to signify her own exasperation at the hugely exaggerated spite that was so typical of her mother. She waited for Henry to understand that and laugh too. But his eyes were gleaming. She'd got his serious attention now. He didn't offer any comment on the motivation of a mother who would, out of sheer malice, question the legitimacy of her own son's birth—and, by doing so, admit she must have been an adulteress. Henry was much too interested in what Isabeau had said to worry overmuch about why.

"Is she saying that? Really?" he asked intently. "The Queen of France, saying Charles is a bastard?"

Suddenly Catherine saw that statement through his eyes. If the only male heir to the French throne was a bastard, and his father's royal blood didn't run in his veins, there was no male heir to France. That left the way open to . . . anyone, really . . . to seize the French throne. No wonder the King of England, here to negotiate a peace settlement after winning most of northern France on the battlefield, had eyes that had started to gleam.

Her laugh faded a little. There'd never been any real talk about Charles being a bastard; that wasn't the impression she'd given, was it? It had all just been Isabeau's hyperbole, hadn't it? "It's just her way," she added faintly, feeling suddenly unpleasantly compromised; associated with her mother's jibe and trying to shrug it off. Perhaps he *really* didn't understand how unhappy families fought among themselves? Perhaps things really were different among the Lancasters? "We don't pay any attention, really . . . She often says things like that . . ."

Henry began to nod. He began to dress, too. "Quite, quite," he said, nodding a little too fast, looking both disappointed and, at the same time, slightly amused. "Just her little joke . . . I understand." Still, he went on grinning while he dressed.

He bowed as he prepared to leave the tent. "But still," he said, almost to himself, from by the flaps, "if only she'd meant what she'd said. About Charles. It would have made everything so much simpler." The grin—almost a smirk—that he couldn't quite keep off his face broke out again. "Till tomorrow," he said, through lips trying hard not to open into a laugh, and was gone.

Catherine had spent her mornings in the tent dreaming of the meeting to come. She'd spent her afternoons in a new dream of sticky honey kisses and whispers.

And so, on the last afternoon of the week, she was surprised to find her mother, turning around at the talks to touch her arm and whisper a comment, not giving her the usual pleased, mischievous look Catherine had come to expect—the look of a sensualist who'd successfully introduced her child to the pleasures of the flesh—but muttering, with narrowed eyes and an angry quiver to her jowls, "What is the man thinking? Did you hear? They have to offer *something*. We can't just . . ."

But Catherine hadn't been paying attention. "What's the matter?" she whispered.

But her mother shrugged her off. She was staring balefully at the English speaker: Henry's brother, John of Bedford. She was listening hard, and breathing hard. She didn't want to be interrupted. After a few more bass phrases in Latin, which Catherine, despite Christine's best attempts, wasn't expert enough in to follow properly, Isabeau raised her hand.

The English delegation, sitting fanned out around Henry at the other end of the table, went quiet. Heads went forward; a couple of men leaned around Henry's throne and whispered.

Miserably, Catherine realized something was going wrong.

"My lords," Isabeau said, in formal, clipped, furious French, "I beg your forgiveness. But the Princess my daughter is indisposed and wishes to be excused. Perhaps, while she makes her departure, the rest of us might benefit from a short pause in which to gather our thoughts?" She prodded Catherine, who, startled to be dismissed, but obedient, rose from her chair and eyed the French tent's entrance. Isabeau fixed Henry with a steely gaze. He stared coolly back down the table at her. She snapped out her final words: "An opportunity to meditate on the virtues of compromise?"

Henry nodded, but not in a way that suggested he was about to discover the virtues of compromise. He was drumming his fingers on the table. He didn't look at Catherine as she began, very slowly, to make her way toward the daylight.

She was almost out when the Duke of Burgundy stood up. Under his hooded eyelids, her uncle's eyes were the color of flints. He stood very tall and straight. He, too, stared at Henry.

"We can't agree to what you w-w-want," he said, with ice in his voice. But he'd started stammering. "There's no point in being here unless you agree to l-l-look for other ways. We can't dismember France to satisfy y-y-you."

There was an ominous silence. Catherine stopped in the doorway and looked back. She saw Henry sit up straighter too, and, very slightly, shake his head. But the men-at-arms, so close now that she could smell the wine and greasy meat on them, were already moving aside to let her out. She could do nothing but step, blinking, into the daylight.

She was already outside when she heard her uncle's next words: still quiet, but trembling with pent-up anger. She could imagine his eyes now.

"Change your demands, or there'll be no point discussing a . . . m-m-marriage either," he grated.

And then there was chaos.

She heard a chair overturn, and a furious shout from the other end of the room—in French, not Latin, but she knew it was Henry's voice. "Don't try to dictate terms to me!" it yelled, and she heard a fist bang on the table and the shuffle of paper falling. "You have no choice! You'll do what I say, you bloody fool, or I'll chase you out of France, and your King with you— and have the girl anyway!" And now there were chairs bashing down on the carpets everywhere, and everyone was on their feet, shouting and jostling and pushing at the enemy, wherever they saw the enemy in the uproar, and Isabeau was struggling up from her throne, with a dreadful look on her face, and yelling, "Quiet! Quiet!" but no one was listening.

The men-at-arms at the tent flap weren't standing to attention anymore; they were staring in with terror on their faces. Catherine stood behind them, thanking God her uncle of Burgundy had had the sense to make sure everyone was disarmed before they entered the conference tent.

Inside the tent, Henry of England was advancing on Burgundy down the side of the table, so fast and dangerous that he seemed to be about to hit him. Then, as if remembering himself, he raised his arms high in the air instead and walked on past. He stopped at Isabeau's throne and bowed.

"Madam," he said, through gritted teeth, before walking out through the French entrance, straight past Catherine, so close he could have touched her, so close she could almost feel the dark wind in his wake. He didn't see her; or if he did, it didn't make him stop.

The uproar went on for a second more. Then the rest of the English delegation walked out too, through their own door, led by John of Bedford.

Burgundy closed his eyes and stood very still at his place,

absorbing the humiliation. The rest of the French negotiators waited, hardly breathing. Isabeau sank back down onto her throne. Her face was red. She lifted a hand to fan herself. She rolled her eyes. "*Well . . .*" she said. "After all that . . ."

Burgundy opened his eyes. "Have all this cleared up," he said. His voice was clipped, his stutter gone. "The talks are over." He didn't look round as he walked out, past the men-at-arms, past Catherine. No one seemed to be seeing her anymore today. But she could see him. His face was dead white.

Catherine sat in her litter, bolt upright. Every jolt, every stumble, made her wince.

It had ended so abruptly. It had been going well until today. What had gone wrong? This couldn't really be the end of everything. Could it?

He'd said: "I'll have the girl anyway!" She clung to that. She repeated it to herself; her rosary. *He'll have me anyway; he'll have me anyway.* He'd made love to her. He couldn't just walk away from the bed of a Princess of France. Could he?

But he'd pushed out past her without a word. Without a look. As if he hadn't noticed her.

As if he wasn't coming back.

"He'll be back," Isabeau said stoutly, as they began the miserable, bewildered trip back to Paris. "He's just negotiating. Pushing for more. Nothing really changed—that's the mystery of it—he just started demanding more, all of a sudden. But he's a greedy man. Always has been. So don't worry."

Then the French Queen said, "He *has* to come back. He . . . you . . . after all . . ."

It was unheard of. By making love to Catherine, Henry had signified that he intended to marry her. It was against every rule of honor for him to walk away.

Catherine nodded. Her lips were tight. She hadn't cried. She felt cold; chilled to the bone. She didn't want to think that her lover might just be using the fact of having deflowered her, dishonored her blood, as part of some cynical campaign to get

226

more for himself out of the French peace talks. But there was nothing else she could think.

Even if he did come back, Catherine would never feel safe with him in the way she'd hoped might be possible.

She lay quietly back in her litter, jiggling along beside her mother's, marshaling her thoughts. She needed to marry Henry. So she needed to work out how she could bring him back. What extra reward might Henry be after, if he'd only stormed out as a way of negotiating for more?

Suddenly, she knew. "Maman," she muttered. "I told Henry what you said about Charles—that you didn't consider him your son; and that he was certainly no son of Papa's . . ." She gulped. "And Henry was all ears. And when I said you didn't really mean it . . . it was just a figure of speech, because Charles had been so cruel to you . . . he said"—she paused—"that that was a pity."

She kept her eyes down. She stared at her hands. More than anything, she wanted to glance up at her mother's face and assess whether Isabeau's wish to make a success of the talks, make peace with Henry and marry her daughter to England, would be enough to persuade her to denounce her son and dishonor the royal house of France. But she didn't dare.

After what seemed an endless pause, she heard a grunt from the other litter. Isabeau was shifting a little uncomfortably around, turning her back.

Gruffly, coldly, from over her shoulder, the Queen of France told her daughter: "I never said that. I never said anything of the kind. Charles a bastard—I don't know what you're talking about."

Catherine sighed. She knew there would be no point in reminding her mother that both the King of France and the Duke of Burgundy, along with dozens of servants, had heard the remarks, made in a piercing voice in the great hall at dinner. It was always like this: if Isabeau chose to forget something she'd done that subsequently embarrassed her, the memory had to be unmade—ripped from the minds of every witness. It was a shame, in a way, Catherine thought, knowing she was being cold-blooded but not caring: a public announcement that Charles was a bastard would certainly have brought Henry rushing back. But she could see why her mother wouldn't want to make that announcement. Doing so would have shamed Isabeau in the eyes of the world, forever.

Isabeau lowered her head. "I'm exhausted," she said. "I'm going to try to sleep." And she shut the curtains of her litter, to keep her daughter's assessing eyes out.

FIFTEEN

The bag came to light when the servants were unpacking Catherine's boxes and trunks.

Catherine nodded listlessly from her bed. "Leave it," she said. "I'll look later."

When she opened it up, she thought at first it had probably been packed in error. It must belong to the Pontois merchant whose house they'd taken. It was a dirty leather pouch, the kind a man might put on a horse. There was nothing much in it—just a patched shirt, a spoon and knife, and a box.

There was nothing remarkable about the box either, when she got that out. She opened it. A bottle of ink. A few scratchy old quill pens. Some sheets of parchment, cut into small enough squares to fit inside.

Halfheartedly, she pulled the top few out. No clue. Blank pages. But there were more pages underneath, hundreds of them, and they were covered with writing. She picked one up. Scanned it. It wasn't good writing. It was tiny and scratchy. She could hardly read it. She went to the window, in her nightgown. "*The Lover . . .*" she made out. Then, "*The Rose . . .*"

She held it up against the light, briefly interested despite herself. It was a poem.

It was many poems, she realized a few moments later, when she'd picked up a few more. Poems written at different times, over months or maybe years, but all with the same theme of loss. A lover, forced to go on existing alone, while the object of his devotion, a Rose, was locked away, behind the high walls of the Palace, behind the glitter and bustle of the River, under the light of the Moon . . .

It was like the *Romance of the Rose*. A memory of reading that, long ago, with Owain Tudor came into her head; the giggles they'd suppressed as Christine came back into the library. She banished the thought.

It was the mention of lions that caught her attention . . . lions in cages, regretting their lost glory. Then a reference to the Rose, blushing outside the nunnery wall. She caught her breath. She knew this story. Any poet might write about lovers and roses, but only Owain Tudor would mention lions and nunneries too. If he was the languishing Lover of all those poems, then the unattainable Rose, she realized, with a sweet rush of astonished gratitude, must be herself.

She read them all, concentrating intently. She didn't have the literary skills to know whether Christine might find these good poems. But the very fact that they'd been written to her kept her attention fixed on the words on the page—the fact that someone—that he—had been thinking of her, every time he sat down alone, so many times, for so many years.

Even if Owain had ended up . . . She couldn't finish the thought; couldn't conjure up his face; the memory of their last meeting made her feel sick. But at least he'd loved her, or thought he'd loved her, while he wrote these.

She let her fingers shuffle through the little pile of parchments, and her heart was soft with a feeling she couldn't name. The poems were balm for the pride wounded by Henry's departure.

When the soft tears came, the first since the abrupt end of the peace talks, she let herself sink into her cushions and weep, and told herself it was for Henry. But she wasn't sure that was true.

She knew she'd keep the box forever.

Christine came to the palace to see Catherine as soon as she heard the royal family was back in Paris, but she couldn't help going first to visit the King to pay her respects to her childhood friend.

Christine hadn't been able to sleep for weeks for worrying about the way the war was going. She wanted to get Jean back to Paris. She wanted to go home to Old Temple Street. If only the King would agree to a different peace—a peace between the French, and not that wrongful peace with the English enemy that had been the aim until now—then she, Christine, could perhaps get her children and grandchildren back. If Charles and Burgundy were allies, there would be nothing to stop Jean and his children from coming home to Paris with the rest of the court at Bourges. If only the King would try to make that French peace, his own family would be better off too. There would be no need to consider marrying poor, brave, long-suffering Catherine to the Lancastrian usurper and condemning her to a dreary lifetime among the English—for, however bravely Catherine was taking it, that was no future for a girl raised gently in France. If only King Charles understood what he was asking of his stoical, uncomplaining daughter. If only he understood how eager his son was for peace. Jean had even written to Christine from the south that Prince Charles had asked for talks with Burgundy, but Burgundy had ignored the request. But now, with the English initiative in ruins, surely it was time?

So she told herself it was a God-given coincidence when, as she hurried through the palace gate, ready to welcome Catherine back to Paris and comfort her on the failure of the English peace talks, she saw the King, alone at a table, just nearby. He was sitting in the middle of the walled gardens, with a game of cards set out in front of him. But he wasn't really looking at it. He couldn't keep card games in his head unless Isabeau was there to remind him of the rules. She must have been there just now; would be on her way back. Meanwhile, the King was looking very worriedly at the changing of the guard; listening to the troop commanders' barked commands as if they were a declaration of war on him.

"Charles," she said softly, changing direction and moving in on him with her usual neat speed. She sat down in the Queen's place.

He nodded and smiled at her, with dawning relief. "My dear friend," he said back. He almost always knew her, and he was always happy when he did. Childhood memories were the strongest by far.

"I'm sorry the English talks went so badly," she said. Immediately he looked worried again.

She looked round. It would only be a moment before the Queen came back and the game of cards resumed.

"But my dear," she went on, caressingly, reassuringly, seizing her moment, "perhaps it was a sign. Perhaps God wants you to make a different kind of peace? . . . A French peace? With your son?"

Owain Tudor had been laid low. He'd spent days lying down in the dark—since, oh, early on in those damn-fool pointless talks. Not that there seemed much wrong with him: no fever, no sores, no purging—nothing you could get hold of. But he wasn't eating. Now he'd finally staggered down, Henry of England could see he was as gaunt as a scarecrow. There was something up, all right.

Henry looked thoughtfully at him.

"Feeling better?" he asked, not unkindly.

Tudor nodded. He was a good boy; he was trying, at least. But you could see it wasn't true.

"I've been thinking about sending you home," the King of England went on. "Time, isn't it?"

He saw hope flicker; a bit of blood come into Tudor's gray-white face.

"But I can't. Not yet. This"—Henry waved magnificently around at the miserable, smoke-blackened inside of the fleapit inn at Mantes, where the English leadership was still crammed, days after the talks had broken down, with a couple of hundred soldiers outside in tents. They all hated Mantes by now. Everyone wanted to be off. But Henry had kept them here. "This bloody awful mess has changed all our plans. So I need you to do one more thing for me here. Will you?"

Tudor nodded again. Henry could see him swallowing his disappointment.

"You went to Pontoise, didn't you?" Henry went on. "When the French lot were there?"

"Yes," Tudor said. His voice was muffled; Henry noticed his face drain of expression. Odd. But not important now. Briskly, he said: "You'll remember the road, then. I want you to take a troop back this afternoon. Advance party. With scaling ladders. The rest of us will join you at dawn for the attack."

That got the boy's attention all right. He jolted upright. Pontoise was rich. It was the grain store for the whole area—and the gateway to Paris. Henry grinned. Henry had thought of this plan as soon as he'd heard Burgundy had torn up their deal and gone running off to the little Prince Charles of Bourges. He was pleased with it. If they wanted a fight, he'd give them a good one.

Henry was still irked by the way they'd tried to buy him off with their Princess. Not that she wasn't a pretty enough girl: freckles, soft breasts, big eyes. He couldn't believe they'd offered her up, just like that. Still, she wasn't a fair exchange for Normandy and Aquitaine. Did they take him for a fool?

"Isn't there a truce . . . ?" Tudor began, breaking through his list of detailed commands: some men in the vineyards for the night; some in the dry ditches round the walls; put the ladders up when the night watch goes to bed before dawn. Then let Huntingdon's men in as soon as you get over the walls and get control of the gate.

"No truce," Henry said, with cheerful ruthlessness. "Not anymore. We're back at war. I've written, saying the truce is off if the talks are off. No point in one without the other, obviously. True, they won't have got the letter; I only sent it this morning. But that's not my fault."

Tudor's mouth opened. Henry grinned wider.

"Anyway," he said kindly, "your kind of thing, I thought. Stealth mission. Then—if you want—back to Oxford." He was keeping a careful eye on the boy's face; he could see Tudor wanted it. "But the important thing now is, are you up to it?"

The boy was transformed: standing twice the height, suddenly. "Good man," Henry finished, clapping him on the back. "Now, go and get yourself fed before you start preparing."

"The English are at Pontoise," Christine said in tragic tones, coming into Catherine's bedchamber. "No one can believe they took it so easily. From there, they could attack Paris *at any time.*" She opened her eyes very wide and took a deep, alarmed breath. "The *treachery* . . . " she added, letting her voice trail away. "Surely, at last, it's time for a different kind of peace?"

Catherine waited. She'd heard Christine talk in this vein a lot in the past few days.

". . . a peace between the French?" Christine went on. Catherine knew Christine believed she was being subtle. Christine had, often enough, looked innocent and begun to reminisce about one moment or another, in the gardens, long ago, with Charles. Catherine knew Christine longed to move on to making Catherine forgive her brother; she just didn't quite know how to begin.

"Thank God," Christine continued, and Catherine sighed quietly, "that Charles and His Grace of Burgundy have at least agreed to meet and talk. I've been offering up prayers, every hour of every day," and at this she crossed herself busily, three or four times, "that their meeting bears fruit."

Catherine's eyes were veiled. She didn't cross herself in response. She thought: Christine thinks if she tells me often enough that this meeting is good, I'll agree.

Defiantly, Catherine finished the thought: But I won't. I don't want Charles back. I don't want Burgundy either. I want to marry Henry of England, and get away from the lot of them.

SIXTEEN

On a gray September afternoon, under a sky of circling crows, the Duke of Burgundy dismounted at the approach to the stone bridge at Montereau. His troop of guard made to follow suit. He stopped them with a silently raised hand. He was here to pay homage to his future king. They waited quietly on horseback; watching.

There were barriers at either end of the bridge—stout wooden gates that locked.

The agreement was that Charles and Burgundy would meet at the middle of the bridge. Their men would wait behind the barriers.

But Charles, who had got to the meeting place early, had three or four of his young companions inside the pen in the middle of the bridge with him.

Burgundy, who was a man of his word, and had been fighting wars long before any of the young men waiting were born, didn't let that worry him. He strode toward the barriers. He looked perfectly calm. His eyes seemed nearly closed; his leathery skin drawn tight over his hook of a nose. He was gaunter and more brooding than ever.

Charles watched him approach. He was trying to stay calm. He didn't want to look at Burgundy and think. This is the man who chased me and Tanneguy here out of Paris that night—Tanneguy de Chastel, who'd been Provost of Paris, back then, in charge of law and order. Charles didn't want to remember his terror on that night.

Charles had spent the morning alone, in prayer, seeking God's guidance. He knew he needed to keep calm. He knew he needed to be reunited with his family. He knew that everything that had divided them had opened the way into France for the English. He'd made public proclamations to the effect that there was nothing he wanted more than to lead a great, united French army into battle to destroy the English invader. But that wasn't the only reason he'd agreed to be here. There were private reasons too; bursts of realization he'd come to in one muddy, miserable battlefield or another, or in the quiet of the night; thoughts that had become easier to admit to since Bernard of Armagnac's death and the end of all Bernard's talk about Charles' kin. He wanted to see Catherine. He missed his father. Sometimes he even wanted to see his mother. He wanted to live at peace.

But now the sight of his uncle—as terrifying and unyielding as he remembered him from childhood—unnerved him. He felt a child again. It was brave of Burgundy to walk onto the bridge alone to face Charles and his friends; but even that display of courage was a slight. Perhaps Burgundy simply didn't see Charles as a threat. I'm seventeen, and I've seen my share of fighting, he reminded himself stoutly, as the measured footsteps came closer, pace by rangy pace; there's no reason to be rattled. But that didn't stop him from being aware that his skin, under its leather jerkin and the velvet doublet covering, was soft and pink and unlined and suddenly crawling with baby fears.

By his side, Tanneguy de Chastel was twitching his own big red barrel of a body, so the ax at his belt thudded against his leg, demanding permission to break the silence. Tanneguy was a brave man and a good fighter. He took wise precautions before taking risks; today, for instance, he'd insisted they come an hour early to the meeting. But Tanneguy had to take those wise precautions, because he was so prone to exploding with uncontrollable rage. I shouldn't have brought him here, Charles thought with sudden foreboding; and that thought made him move his eyes sideways, to see that Tanneguy was, indeed, on the brink of a towering fury, and inadvertently gave his aide a chance to talk.

"He's late," Tanneguy said—a mutter, but full of blazing intensity.

But we were early, Charles thought. He's on time.

He looked away; muttered back: "Calm yourself."

"The murdering bastard came late," Tanneguy repeated, a little louder; as if he hadn't heard Charles' command. Charles knew Tanneguy was doing what he was trying not to do himself: conjuring up the terror of their nighttime escape from the streets of a Paris packed with howling Burgundian killers.

"Be quiet," Charles said.

Tanneguy's voice dropped. But he didn't shut up at once. He said, in a monotone: "No—bloody—respect." Then he stared down, over the side of the bridge at the choppy white water below. Tanneguy went so quiet that all you could hear were the birds cawing and Burgundy's footsteps coming closer; but Charles could almost feel him seething.

Tanneguy didn't speak through the opening formalities. Nor did he look up when Burgundy, bowing his bare head as soon as he got within speaking distance, said, with his eyes unmovingly on Charles, "My lord; I am grateful that you offer me this chance to combine with you against our ancient enemies, the English." His voice had always been that hard monotone, Charles remembered, but the sound of it now grated infuriatingly on Charles' ears.

Charles had Tanneguy at his side, and three men behind.

He couldn't stop himself. Bitterly, he cried out: "Ancient enemies? The English? They haven't been *your* ancient enemies for long, have they?" But when Burgundy just went on looking at him with that calm snake gaze, he realized his outburst had sounded petulant. Childish. The very things he hadn't wanted to be. He bit his lip, saw Tanneguy look up and catch the hot blush on his face; and hated Burgundy, and the correctness in which his ambitions were cloaked, more than ever before.

The snake eyes blinked. With spare, economical grace, the Duke of Burgundy went down on his knees, and as he went he tucked his sword out of the way behind him.

What Charles always remembered afterward was how, at that moment, he was watching that elegant gesture with almost unbearable loathing and resentment, and thinking that here was a man who would never put a foot wrong.

He remembered it because, at that moment, Burgundy did, at last, put a foot wrong.

The Duke, not young anymore, wobbled on his bony knees.

Burgundy wasn't a man to make himself ridiculous by falling over in front of these young fighters. With dignity, he moved to steady himself. He reached out his right hand for support. He put it on the hilt of his sword.

Charles had been wrong to think Tanneguy would start the trouble. It was Robert de Loir who drew in breath so fast and loud they all startled—their nerves were jangling anyway—then screeched: "What! Get your sword out in the presence of the Prince?"

But it was Tanneguy who rushed into the quiet space of everyone's indrawn breath after that screech, pulling his ax from his belt and whirling it above his head, and yelling: "It's time!"

The ax fell. Very slowly, Burgundy staggered and began to collapse. Everything went red. Charles could see Burgundy, down on one buttock, pulling at his sword, trying to get it out. But it was too late. He was slipping in the blood pouring out of the wound in his head; and they were on him, all the strong young men Charles had brought to the bridge. He was old, Charles saw, with bright adult understanding, too old to move as fast as his enemies; and, under the flash of steel, Robert de Loir was hissing, "Kill!"

Charles was frozen a few feet from the fight, watching, surprised at the coherent thoughts still coming through his head. Charles thought judiciously: He must have known this would happen one day. Ever since he killed my uncle of Orléans and got off unpunished, he must have been waiting for someone to take vengeance. There've been too many crimes.

It felt a long time after that that Charles realized, I don't want this to be happening. He looked round, half hoping for help. Burgundy's men were rushing to the barrier on their side of the bridge. But it was locked, and their master was already still and heavy under his attackers' legs.

Burgundy's men came back without even the body. L'Isle Adam didn't exactly tell Catherine that his troop had panicked and fled. But it was obvious.

Perhaps that was why the King didn't understand. The King only rolled his eyes at Burgundy's dusty, stuttering lieutenant, and said cunningly, "Ah, the darkness got him. It's waiting for us all." Then he added, with sudden alarm in his voice, "Don't look at me. I'm not here. I'm in the darkness too."

And Charles VI was off: tearing his hair; tearing his clothes; running to the corners of the room; hiding behind tapestries.

Catherine watched him run. For what felt like a long time, she didn't move. She felt remote from the scene in this room too: from the soldiers and the bleak faces and the panic and the lengthening shadows. There'd been a lifetime of madness: not just her father's, but the madness that was on all of them; each of them surprising the others by the new depths to which they might stoop; and all always doomed to failure.

She'd hoped, herself, for these talks to fail. But she hadn't expected even Charles to murder their cousin, a man so advanced in years, a man who'd come in peace. How could she have foreseen that baseness?

"Was it actually my brother?" she asked l'Isle Adam, who was beyond diplomatic tact, who was staring in open, horrified fascination at the King's caperings. "My brother who . . . killed?"

It took an effort for l'Isle Adam to bring his eyes back to hers. He stared at her so blankly that she didn't know whether he had even understood. But when he spoke he sounded very certain. "Yes," he said. "I saw. The Dauphin Charles said, 'Kill.' He stabbed my Duke through the heart. There was nothing we could do."

Catherine turned away, remembering Charles torturing Bosredon; the fury in him.

"Thank you," she said. Quickly, l'Isle Adam left.

Catherine felt sick. There wasn't an honorable man in all of

France. Wearily, she nodded to the soldiers waiting for her signal to remove the King. She couldn't charm her father into coming voluntarily to his white shelter today. She was too tired. Whatever Papa thought, he wasn't made of black glass; the reality was that they wouldn't break him, however much they touched him. He'd just have to live with his fears. They all would. There was no escape for any of them. She let them close in and drag him off screaming.

There were riots in the town as night fell. The people had wanted peace among the French; their disappointment was taking violent form. Soldiers were sent out to calm them down. But the yells and flames and clash of weapons continued through the night; the windows never quite got dark.

Burgundy's closest family (except his son Philip, who would be here tomorrow) sat all night in the chapel, letting their eyes lose their focus in the candle flames; listening to the unearthly purity of the singing; thinking their private thoughts as they stared toward where the dead Duke's still, beaky nose should have lain, in a more orderly world, under a neat white shroud.

Catherine's muddle of thoughts flashed between her agonizing mental picture of Charles hitting the guardsman to Charles making daisy chains by the lion's cage with pudgy child's fingers. She saw Burgundy's cold eyes on her brother Louis while the butchers of Paris broke screaming onto the dance floor; Charles waking up whimpering from a nightmare; her father screaming at his window. There was no hope of happiness for any of them. No Roses, no Moons, no Lovers: their destiny was different. The foreign King she'd thought would save her had instead just taken her virtue, or what was left of it, and walked away without a backward glance. This was the destiny her royal blood brought, perhaps forever: the sounds of mutiny at the window; the endless treachery of her kin; death at every turn; smoke on the air. She couldn't imagine anymore that there would be a way out.

She was aware of Isabeau watching her, from behind a separate candle, in her own pale nimbus. Isabeau wasn't praying, or even pretending to. The Queen was nodding grimly, as if she'd made her mind up about something, and she was muttering words under her breath that definitely had nothing to do with God.

"No son of mine," Isabeau was muttering venomously when Catherine caught up with her in the corridor after Mass, as dawn broke and they headed toward their rooms. "That murderer is no son of mine."

Catherine looked challengingly at her. ". . . And certainly no son of Papa's," she said, experimentally, capping her mother's phrase, realizing that now was the time to see if she couldn't, after all, draw Isabeau into a definitely held position that Charles was no part of their family. "I know. You've said that before."

Catherine's voice was quiet but determined. She'd been thinking. She had to ask for what she wanted. And this was the time.

She had Isabeau's attention. She couldn't afford to be squeamish, she thought.

"Maman," she said, "I've been thinking. You can't love Charles . . . after all he's done to you, and now . . ." She winced, but forced herself on. No time to be squeamish. ". . . to our poor dear cousin John. And to France."

Isabeau's little eyes glittered. She shook her head.

"You'll have to respond now to what he's done," Catherine said. "To his crime . . . to his shedding of royal blood. You heard the riots last night . . . and there'll be many people elsewhere who will also think that what Charles has done is an act of blasphemy, of sacrilege . . . that by committing murder he's lost God's grace and the right to rule France. They'll look to you. So what happens next is really all in *your* hands."

Isabeau drew in a breath so deep that all her green iridescence—flab, silk, jewels, eyelids—wobbled.

"If you and Papa were to repudiate Charles now . . ." Catherine breathed. "If you told the world what you've told me . . ."

She waited. After a long pause, Isabeau nodded again, looking harsher and more vengeful now.

". . . then Charles would never be King of France," Catherine said, in the voice of temptation: naming Isabeau's dearest wish, speaking it out loud, conjuring it into existence. "You could stop him."

There was a pause.

"We'd need to send armies south and clear up his rebellion," Catherine said, adding with contempt, "what's left of it. So there wouldn't be peace straightaway. But that would be easy enough. Because once you'd repudiated Charles, Henry of England would be back to talk peace with you straightaway. And if you had *his* armies at your disposal, it would take no time to deal with Charles."

She smiled. She knew it was a hard smile. She sensed she was winning.

"And if we had an agreement with Henry of England, there'd be a marriage. I would be his Queen . . ." Catherine said: her clinching argument. "And your grandson would be King of England."

Isabeau still said nothing. The Queen was still nodding. But, suddenly, Catherine wasn't completely sure anymore that her mother was agreeing; she might just be weighing up her options.

Catherine knew what the catch must be. However much her mother wanted to prevent Charles from taking the throne, she would be reluctant to pay the necessary price: admitting to the world that she had been an adulteress, a sinner who'd broken her marriage vows, who had taken a lover . . .

Well, she thought brutally, Isabeau couldn't afford squeamishness either. The Queen would have to pay the price if she wanted the reward.

"You know I want that marriage," Catherine finished, wondering how she was managing to be so brave, and where her old fear of her mother had gone. "Anything else would mean dishonor. I already am Henry's. You know that too. So when I think about it, what I ask myself is, what do you want most—Charles' happiness, or mine?"

Isabeau's lips were crimped together. She'd gone opaque.

Catherine couldn't tell at all what she was thinking.

When her mother's lips did, finally, open, Catherine leaned breathlessly forward to catch the words.

"Don't you worry," the Queen told her daughter. "I know exactly what to do."

Then Isabeau disappeared, and all that was left of her were the wheezing noises going down the spiral staircase.

Owain's horse was already saddled for the return to England when they called him to the King's tent. They were bringing his bundles out of the tent. They'd be loading them up in a minute.

He went at once, picking his way through the mud, not even seeing the encampments and cooking fires and saddles being greased on all sides anymore; already, in his mind, on the quiet road home. He didn't worry about the summons. They knew he was off. Henry had only laughed when he'd turned down the King's offer of a knighthood after Pontoise. "I'm not a soldier," he'd told the King; "and you're already giving me the best reward I could hope for—letting me go." He was ready now to make his farewells.

But they hadn't called him to make any farewells. The King was sitting on a rough stool, laughing with his brother John of Bedford: two big pairs of hands slapping at themselves, as if there were flies on their thighs; two sets of pop eyes popping out more than ever with merry disbelief.

"You'll never credit this, Tudor," Bedford said. Then he stopped and hiccuped and began helplessly laughing again.

Owain stared.

"The Prince has murdered Burgundy!" Bedford got out, with his eyes almost out of his head. "Actually during their talks! Unbelievable! So much for peace between the French!"

Owain thought: It must be relief that's making them laugh. They must have been scared. Henry was roaring and snuffling.

"And now the Queen and the new Burgundy—Burgundy's son—have sent proclamations to every town in France—denouncing Charles! The Queen's own son! Saying this proves he's unfit to rule!" the King of England somehow got out.

Bedford hugged himself. "Oh, these people!" he sighed. "If they didn't exist, we'd have to make them up!"

Henry finished: "And there's better! We've just received a messenger who says the Queen's even starting telling all and sundry that Charles can't rule France—because"—he stopped; tried to overcome a snicker; gave way to it; went on: "because . . . she says . . . her son's a bastard!"

Bedford snorted again. He spluttered: "She doesn't seem to care . . . if the whole world wonders . . . if Charles is a bastard . . . who's the father . . . and what does that make her?"

"They don't need us here at all, do they?" Henry said to his brother in a moment's calm; as if he didn't mind the bewildered Owain being here, or had forgotten him altogether. "They could destroy France all by themselves, even if we weren't here . . . they've got a genius for self-destruction . . ."

"Genius!" Bedford agreed, and the two brothers started rocking and guffawing again.

Owain waited until their helpless laughter had subsided a little. Even with his mind already fixed on home, even with all his defenses up against beginning to imagine the distress Catherine might feel about the latest chaotic turn of events, he could see what good news this was for the English war effort. Of course they'd be pleased. They were right to be. Then, clearing his throat to draw attention to himself, he stepped forward and said, "Your Graces will remember that I'm leaving today; I've come to ask Your Majesty's permission to set off . . ."

Henry stopped laughing. But there was still a smile on his face as he got up, walked to Owain's side, put an arm round his man's shoulder, and said, with his lips twitching, "Refused, Tudor. Refused."

Owain tried not to let himself flinch visibly. But he felt as though the ground were opening up beneath his feet.

"Can't possibly let you go now," Bedford was saying from somewhere beside him. "This is the moment we've been waiting for. Our big opportunity: take France through the hole in the Duke of Burgundy's skull. They're in chaos. Can't let the Prince be King now. No one else in the picture. King's as mad as a hatter. They'll say yes to anything. We'll say: Henry marries the daughter; Henry becomes King of France. And they'll say yes, no question. We've won the war; we're about to win the peace!"

Henry added: "We've just had word from the Queen ourselves. The French are asking us for more talks. So we're off to meet her at Troyes. And so are you, Tudor. You do talks. Your kind of thing. We'll need you."

He nodded determinedly. But he was a good enough master to remember what he was depriving Owain of. He added: "Your books will still be there in a few months. Oxford's not going anywhere . . ."

He looked at his brother, and, as if they were aware of some secret signal Owain couldn't see, they both began to shake with laughter again.

PART FOUR

The Vision of Christine

SEVENTEEN

There were birds singing all around. Catherine was sitting on a chamomile bench, enjoying the scent of the crushed leaves and the little star-faced daisy flowers, as she absorbed the news.

The English had agreed to talk again within two days of Burgundy's assassination, and within a day of Isabeau's announcements that Charles was unfit to rule and was illegitimate. They would all meet at Troyes within three days—as soon as possible.

"No corridor-creeping now," Isabeau had grunted playfully. "I know you girls."

Catherine had begun to say something indignant, then subsided. It would have been ungracious to remind Isabeau that she'd been the one who'd pushed her daughter into bed with the King of England. Isabeau had got the English back now, and Catherine should be showing gratitude. Isabeau had added, with triumphant cynicism: "Better he's hungry. We'll keep you in your rooms this time. Make him wait."

This time, with her mother's help, it would surely all come right. In a moment Catherine would go inside and begin to pack. For now, with the sun on her back, she was happy to lose herself in reverie.

"... I knew you'd come back," she'd whisper to Henry when she saw him next, in a swooning, shimmering, scented bower of dewy roses. "... I knew you'd rescue me." And he would smile very tenderly, and take her in his arms, and kiss her . . .

"You must wonder, whatever can have possessed your mother?" Christine said, letting her eyes rise to Catherine's face with the new near-timidity that age and hard times had brought her. Christine wondered about it all the time. She still couldn't believe what the Queen had said, and in public too, any more than she could believe in the murder of Burgundy. The Bavarian woman wasn't a disgrace, Christine thought helplessly to herself; she was worse: an, an . . . *outrage*. An *abomination*.

Catherine shrugged, and put another robe on the pile of garments to be ironed and hung up. She wished Christine would stop nagging away at this difficult question. She wished, too, that Christine didn't look so frail and old and helpless as she did so. It made her feel—almost—guilty.

Catherine knew perfectly well why Isabeau had finally made up her mind to repudiate Charles and say he was a bastard: because she'd been asked to by her daughter. That in itself didn't especially trouble Catherine's conscience. She was grateful to her mother for taking the step she had. Reasonably grateful, at least: though she also knew her mother had wanted revenge on Charles at least as much as she'd wanted to save her daughter. Still, the results were more important than the reasons, Catherine thought. Isabeau had chosen her daughter's future over that of her son, and she'd been right to. Charles had done his best to destroy his mother, and had spent years demonstrating the contempt in which he held his sister. He shouldn't expect either of them to care overmuch what became of him now.

She didn't feel sorry for Charles. He deserved his fate. The more Catherine thought about it, the more she'd come to believe that Charles' viciousness and disloyalty to his blood relatives alone was enough to disqualify him from taking the throne. She'd been raised in the belief that God chose only the wisest and most virtuous to be anointed kings of France; her ancestors numbered saints and emperors. She'd grown up with the certainty that she must therefore act with virtue and nobility; do everything in her power to be worthy of her royal blood. Surely God would not allow a murderer—someone who had ignored that sacred duty and chosen sin—to be anointed His chosen vessel. That would be a mockery of kingship itself. And Charles was a murderer, there was no doubt about that. She'd seen him kill once. Now she also knew he'd murdered his cousin, with his own hands. It was possible, she thought, that her brother shed blood because his own blood was literally impure—because he actually was the fruit of some liaison between her mother and one of her lovers, rather than the legitimate son of the King of France. But she didn't care whether that was why. The facts she knew were enough.

"Oh, who can ever tell what Maman is up to?" Catherine said lightly. "She says so many things . . ."

"Well, you mustn't believe it," Christine replied, very gently, as if Catherine were a child with a hurt knee. "Not for a moment. And try not to be shocked that she said it. I think . . . perhaps . . . she did it out of love for you . . . she means well . . . she just doesn't understand how wrong it is . . . to say such things . . ."

Without meaning to, Catherine let irritation harden her voice. What made Christine so certain? How could Christine possibly think she always knew the answers?

"But what if it's true?" she said. "What if he *is* a bastard?"

She knew at once that this had been the wrong thing to say. Even without looking up, she was aware of a change in Christine. The old woman was puffing up like an enraged turkey cock.

"You can't think it's true," Christine said angrily, and the forlorn air was gone; she was suddenly as formidable again as the powerhouse of a woman Catherine remembered from childhood. "You can't think that a Queen of France would allow a lover to father her child?"

Catherine raised her hands, as if to hold off the tide of angry words she sensed coming.

But, privately, rebelliously, she was thinking: Well, why wouldn't it be true? If they all accepted that the Queen had had many lovers, including the King's brother, why should

Christine be so angry at the possibility that a child might have been conceived by accident? However careful you were, however many sponges soaked in vinegar and pig's-bladder hoods and consultations with the stars, mistakes happened. Everyone said so. There would have been no reason to think, back then, that the boy who might have been the mistake of an illicit liaison might ever be called on to rule France. Charles was Isabeau's fifth son, and her eleventh child; back then he'd been very far from the throne.

Christine was still talking, furiously and very fast. "Because if you *did* allow yourself to believe that of your mother, you'd be admitting the possibility that she might have done the same with you—that you might be a cuckoo too. If I were you, I'd think very carefully indeed about that before you—"

"Please," Catherine said impatiently. "Of course I'm not a bastard."

Christine stopped and looked shocked. At herself, Catherine thought; as well she might, after the absurd suggestion she'd just made.

On the night before the talks began, the two sides were to sit down together at a dinner. "You can go to dinner, at least," Isabeau said with an excited grin. "Flirt a little with your Henry. Then leave."

The thought of seeing Henry again—after last time—both excited and alarmed Catherine. She sent Christine away and spent all afternoon with her ladies, bathing and choosing her clothes and dressing her hair and trying to calm her nerves.

But when she entered the hall and went to her place on the dais, she saw that the English guest of honor was not Henry but John of Bedford, his brother. She didn't like to ask where Henry was. Keep him hungry, her mother had said. But perhaps he was not dining here tonight because he was thinking the same thing? Her mother, four seats away, was too far off to consult.

Her unease was compounded when she looked down the table and saw Owain Tudor among the English guests. He looked older, thinner, and harder than before, with his face drawn tight. Stopping herself on the thought that the change suited him, she forced her eyes to slide past.

She had to concentrate—make the most of her one public appearance here. She had to think how best to charm the Duke of Bedford tonight, so he went to bed thinking her the mistress of the situation. She wanted to feel mistress of the situation herself. And suddenly she knew how.

As soon as Catherine had sent the page to her rooms for the box she would need, she turned, with teeth flashing in her most flirtatious smile, to Bedford. He just looked uneasy. None of the English royal brothers were good with women. He flopped into his seat, hiding beside Isabeau, then looking alarmed at whatever scurrilous story the Queen whispered into his ear and began cackling over.

Catherine let him be. But, in the noisy confusion of clearing away the second course, and laying out the sweet and savory dishes of the third course, Catherine raised her voice to call across the top table to her possible future brother-in-law.

"Sir," she piped sweetly.

Bedford looked cautiously back.

"You will of course know our French court's long-established fame as the Court of Love?" Catherine sang on. "And our tradition of writing poems about courtly love . . . ? Tales of the faithfulness of a knight to an exalted lady he can never possess . . . ?"

Bedford harrumphed uncomfortably. She could see he wasn't a man for poetry.

Catherine didn't care. She let a pretty tinkle of laughter escape from her lips.

"I thought you might like a small entertainment now," she went on. "In the French courtly style. To celebrate the start of your talks about making a marriage in the Court of Love . . ."

She pulled out the box, and, with flamboyant gestures, opened it up.

There was a murmur at the prospect of entertainment, a shuffling of knives and cups, then an expectant hush as she looked round at the bobbing crowd of faces down the hall.

Catherine was aware, too, of her mother's delighted smile. Isabeau hadn't realized this was coming.

She projected her voice to the back of the hall. She wanted everyone to hear.

"I would read them myself . . . but of course these poems are written by a knight to his lady . . . so we will need a gentleman," she called.

The Duke looked suddenly, deeply anxious, as if suspecting she was about to ask *him* to make a fool of himself reading out a Frenchified love poem.

She nodded reassurance at him. "So may I trouble you," she asked the Duke, aware of all the eyes on her, "to name one of your number to read this modest poem?"

The Duke stumbled. He had no social graces. He clearly couldn't think of an Englishman who'd be willing to read any such soft, foolish thing.

She looked around the hall again, as if trying to help him out. "Perhaps," she finished, beaming at the crowd, before supplying the name herself, "Owain Tudor?"

There was a moment's silence. She kept her eyes on the Duke. He stared back at her, with his pop eyes bulging and his mouth opening and shutting like a carp's.

Then he burst out laughing; a big, rough, relieved guffaw of military mirth.

"Tudor!" he snorted noisily, and everyone joined in; a wave of laughs and swaying cups. "Good idea! Get the Welshman on the job! They're all poets, the Welsh!"

She let go of the little sheet of parchment. It was passed down the table, from hand to hand. There were feet drumming to the chant of "Bard! Bard! Bard!" She didn't need to look through the dancing shadows at Owain to see his face, going white, then red, then white again as he recognized his own outpourings coming back to him. She could picture it all in her mind's eye.

But, as she heard the shuffle of him rising, all that way down the murmuring table, she looked anyway—stared him straight in the eye with a hard smile, flashing her teeth.

He was standing up. He was holding the poem. He was

looking back at her with shocked eyes: willing her not to have those poems; willing her not to be doing this.

She just went on flashing her smile at him. So Owain read. From the top of the table, his low, agonized voice could hardly be heard for the cheerful English drummings of feet and catcalls—they were no respecters of artistry, these English—just the occasional disjointed word: "Lover" or "Castle" or "Moon" or "Rose." Catherine hardened her heart as she listened. He stopped at the end of the page, bowed his bloodless face, and sat quietly down. For a few more moments, the English went on howling: "Come on!" and "Get on with it, man!" and "Let's hear the bit when he gets the girl!" But he had nothing more to say.

As the catcalls died away, Catherine turned her bold smile on the Duke of Bedford, and bowed her own head.

"I hope you enjoyed that glimpse of our French tradition," she said, still in her sweetest, loudest, most carrying voice. "And I hope you will also believe my assurance that—however much I love the land of my birth and all the splendors of its civilization—there is nothing I long for more, today, than to relinquish my place as Princess of our court of impossible love. To be your Queen—the wife of your King. In a happier land, where dreams can come true. And. Lovers. Live. Happily. Ever. After."

The French and Burgundians at the table were applauding. The English were appreciatively drumming their feet again. Catherine's mother was chortling with joy, and nodding her head eagerly at the sentiment her daughter had expressed so prettily. Bedford was nodding his head and grinning, looking amazed that a mere slip of a girl could manage such a long and flowery speech.

She stood, and held up her cup. "To the success of your talks!" she toasted merrily, and the cheers grew louder.

She told herself that the hard, tinny taste of blood in her mouth was the taste of success. She was cutting all ties with the past.

When she put down her cup and looked along the table one last time, she saw that Owain had gone.

EIGHTEEN

The Troyes autumn came and went. On that December night when they finally announced that a peace agreement had been made between France and England, Christine made her way to the stables to ask for her horse to be saddled and ready at first light.

"Where are you going, lady?" the stable boy asked politely.

"Poissy," she said. And she sighed.

"Don't you want to stay for the celebrations?" the boy asked. "They say there'll be fireworks tomorrow, and wine in the fountains . . ."

She snapped her jaws shut over the word: "No."

Isabeau had a jeweled cup of wine in her hand. She was waving it about and laughing at the look of incredulous pleasure on her daughter's face.

"I told you I knew exactly what to do," she said smugly. "Right from the start. Didn't I?"

Catherine—who'd run straight to her mother's chambers when she heard the talks were over; when she'd heard the first whispers of what had been agreed—couldn't find her tongue. She nodded.

"England is all very well," Isabeau added. "The Queen of England . . . a worthy enough title. But—not as good as France. I've always expected my grandson to be King of France. So I thought—if my son isn't going to be King of France"—a fat

256

smirk lit her face at those words—"why shouldn't my daughter be Queen of France instead, and her son the next King?"

Catherine tried to stop the picture forming in her mind of Charles, pink-eyed and trembling as he heard out the messenger bringing this news. It made her feel uncomfortable. She'd rather not think of him at all. So she fixed her eyes on her mother instead, who was shaking her head now, remembering the months of arguments that were over at last.

"Still—he drives a hard bargain, your Henry," Isabeau finished ruefully. It was true enough. Henry of England hadn't let up until he'd pretty much forced the French to give him France. The Treaty of Troyes' stipulation that Henry would keep all the French lands he'd conquered in the past five years was only the start. He'd get much more, too. When King Charles died, a single dynasty—Henry's—was to rule both France and England. King Charles would be allowed to remain formally in control of France during his lifetime, but Henry was recognized as his heir, and Prince Charles, in Bourges, was to be deprived of all his rights of inheritance. The deal gave Henry free rein to take his war south, to the territories still loyal to Prince Charles, and conquer the whole of southern France if need be. Meanwhile, any French religious bodies and universities which wouldn't swear loyalty to Henry of England would have their funds and official licenses removed. Henry was to be Regent of France during King Charles' illnesses. And Princess Catherine would marry Henry as soon as the peace agreement was formalized. She would be Queen of England at once, and Queen of France later.

Isabeau drained her wine. She was nodding busily and all her rings and silks were glinting. "So, go to your room, my darling . . . you may have a visitor this evening . . ." she whispered, tapping her finger against the side of her nose in her usual vaguely lewd gesture of secrecy. "And please . . . do send that difficult Madame de Pizan away before the celebrations begin . . ."

Catherine smiled, a little sadly. Maman had been saying for months that Christine's face was so sour it could curdle the cream. She'd been right. Catherine had taken to going out for long walks alone to avoid poor Christine—Christine couldn't walk well anymore; she had pain in her knees and hips. Day after day, Catherine had brought Christine back little bunches of autumn leaves, or late berries, by way of apology for hurting Christine's feelings by withdrawing her affection. "Oh," Catherine replied now, "I think you've seen the last of Christine. She was the one who told me the talks were finished. She said she was packing her trunk. I think she wants to be off pretty much at once."

Coming back from the stables, Christine was nearly knocked off her feet by a large dark shape rushing across the icy unlit courtyard in the opposite direction.

She'd spent so much time up in Catherine's rooms, sewing, reading, praying, thinking, sitting with Catherine (though not nearly as often as she'd have liked), and working up her courage to admit to herself that if these talks succeeded, as there was every indication they would, she'd never see her son and his children again, that she didn't even know most of the English negotiators' faces.

But this shadowy face she knew.

"Owain Tudor?" she said disbelievingly. She hadn't even realized he was still here. She'd heard he'd been here one night at the beginning, reading love poems at dinner and being heckled. But she hadn't seen or heard of him since. And she'd been lonely. "If only I'd known . . . Have you been here all the time?"

He shrugged. "Intermittently," he said. She wished the light was better. He sounded so grim, but she couldn't see his face. "I have to be off in the morning to take news to the Duke of Bedford." He added: "I won't be back."

"Nor me," Christine said, equally somberly. "I'm going tomorrow to my daughter, at Poissy. I don't have a place here anymore . . . all these Burgundians . . . and Englishmen. Not for me. High time I left."

Owain was looking carefully in her direction. She didn't want him to pity her. To stave off any possible questions about her son, or her financial situation, or the painful months she'd spent here being avoided by Catherine, she added, with a threadbare boastfulness that embarrassed her even as she affected it: "Poor little Catherine. I feel so badly for her. I've been here with her, trying to prepare her . . . she's the sacrifice, of course . . . the reward, poor lamb . . . but she's become so withdrawn . . ."

Owain didn't respond. But after a pause he said, "I can't help remembering that boy—your little Charles. He was so small and so scared when we knew him. I feel sorry for him sometimes."

She nodded, warmed by that humanity.

She touched his arm, realizing that this was farewell. "Where will you go after this?" she asked in a small voice. For a moment she half hoped he'd brighten and tell her some story of everyday happiness, a reminder it still existed, for other people, in other places, somewhere: some pretty bride waiting at home; a manor house waiting for the lord to come back and put the neglected fields in order. Then she realized what sentimental folly that was; remembered he was Welsh, and had lost his family lands, and depended entirely on his King's favor to survive; and that he, too, had been kept by the war all these years from any hope of a normal life.

"You should marry," she said; "have sons and daughters. Be happy with a wife. That's what life's for; not war."

But he shook his head, and winced as if that thought pained him. "Not made for that," he muttered; "not what God intended."

He gave her another anguished look. "All these years," he said unexpectedly; "haunted by Catherine . . . haunted."

She didn't know what to say to that; she just stared at him. Could a single kiss—what, six, seven years ago?—really have meant so much? She could hardly credit the devotion; the constancy of Owain Tudor's heart. The irony of it seemed painful now—that she'd saved Catherine from this good young man only so the girl could be sacrificed for a disgraceful peace with the wolf of England.

"That was my poem she had me read, in the hall that night. Mine, to her. I wrote hundreds of them. The Lover, the Rose. She found them."

259

Christine went on staring, hardly able to bear the dawning knowledge of his humiliation, or Catherine's cruelty—Catherine couldn't have known, surely, she couldn't have understood?—finding a place, even in her own darkness, for a stab of pity for his. There was so much she didn't know. She tightened her grip on his arm. He nodded fiercely, condemning himself for something she'd entirely forgotten she must once have said: "You were quite right. I should never have read that nonsense. Roses and Lovers. If I'd only kept away from it all," he shrugged miserably, "who knows?"

He took a deep breath. "So, no—back to my studies," he went on, giving her a watery smile and sketching a small bow of recognition; striving for normality. "Oxford. The monks. I'm going to become one myself, if they'll have me." Echoing her determined voice a moment before, he stood up straighter and said: "It's time I kept my promise and became a real man of learning, isn't it?"

After Christine had gone, Owain carried on standing in the darkness. He could see his breath, white and sharp. He could see squares of light in the walls. He could hear cheers and whoops from inside.

He wouldn't go and join in. There wouldn't be any real happiness at those celebrations—just the counterfeit that passed for it in wartime. And he'd had enough of all that.

He tried to remember the last time he'd seen generosity, or hope, or good wishes, in anyone's eyes. But he couldn't. The war, which had gone on for almost all the years since a younger Catherine had kissed him at Poissy, had eaten away at the souls of everyone it touched, like rust on metal. It was worse than just one wicked old Queen, sniggering as she gave away her kingdom and destroyed her family to spite her son. Something more insidious had happened, all over France; some devilish alchemy had darkened every soul. It was every man for himself now, with friendships faded and old loyalties crumbled to dust and secretive new silences on all sides. All you saw in every pair of wild-beast eyes that fixed on you was fear, or calculation, or mistrust. You couldn't expect grandeur of spirit from people who had reason to fear they'd be forced apart from the families they loved, or who'd buried their children before their time, or been betrayed by people they'd trusted, or casually robbed of what they'd thought would be theirs forever. All those survivors had been separated from each other by their sufferings, until each of them felt he was alone in the darkness with his fears. People who'd had to live with hate had forgotten how to love. They couldn't even talk to each other. The war had taken their innocence. Perhaps none of them would ever get it back.

He thought of the hollows under Christine's eyes and cheekbones; the defeat in her eyes tonight. He was overwhelmed with pity for the one woman he could think of who hadn't lost the capacity to love. Christine had a vision of a future in which hope and honor and generosity were still possible. But she'd lost the people she loved and the life she'd treasured anyway. She knew she'd have no place in the peace that would come tomorrow. She was taking her losses with courage. It was too late to tell her how he admired her. He wouldn't see her again.

He bashed his hands down in impotent fury at the futility of all that effort; all that bloodshed; all those years wasted. Trying to calm himself, he drew in great gulps of homely stable stink. He told himself that his blackness of spirit was because he'd never been a soldier at heart; nor a negotiator. This was reality: he'd wake up in the hay bale outside the stables when dawn broke, pick the stalks out of his clothes and hair, and begin his journey back to England, to his books, to try and recover his peace of mind; to find his own life at last.

He didn't know why that thought wasn't a comfort; why he couldn't stop tears coming to his eyes.

In the mirror, Catherine's eyes sparkled. They'd lit dozens of candles in her rooms.

When she heard the door, she ran lightly toward it, with her lustrous ringlets of hair streaming back from the filmy lace and fine linen, to welcome the lover she'd been waiting for all these months.

But it was Christine.

"I've come . . ." Christine began, a little nervously. She'd been going to say goodbye; to pray a little with Catherine; to commend her bravery; to wish her the strength to bear all the trials life still had in store for her.

But once her eyes took in the scene—the rose oil, the ribbons, the finery, and the flushed, radiant young face—she stopped. She understood at once. The girl was waiting for a lover.

She'd had no idea. There was a black pit yawning inside her. It must be shock. She'd been so blind. There was so much, everywhere, so much she didn't know.

It must be Henry of England. She didn't know why it had never occurred to her that Catherine might *want* to marry Henry.

She looked harder at the bride-to-be; the future Queen of England and France. The radiance had ebbed out of Catherine's face. She'd hung her head. The flush had become guilty. Her poise had gone.

"Give me your blessing," Catherine mumbled, but she didn't dare look up. "Please. Wish me well."

Very tenderly, Christine took the Princess's hands, feeling as she did how they'd been softened and artificially scented for the tryst to come.

"My dearest girl," she whispered, "I wish you the best of everything, always . . . of course I do . . . I always will . . . but I can't bless your marriage."

She felt, rather than saw, the glance Catherine stole.

Remembering Owain Tudor's wintry voice by the stables, Christine added wistfully: "I'd rather you'd married away from royalty altogether than this. I'd have been happier seeing you with the Welshman. At least that would have been honest."

She drew the unresisting Catherine to her, praying for the girl to be protected from whatever demons her mother—it must be her mother—had set loose around her. "We won't meet again," she muttered, memorizing the warmth of that beloved young body against hers. "I'll pray for you."

NINETEEN

In brilliant June sunshine, in cloth of gold, Catherine dismounted from her horse in an explosion of light and glory. She entered the gloom of the church, closing her eyes and drawing in the rich scent of incense, then letting her eyes take in the candlelight everywhere, as if surrendering herself to the lifetime of ecstasy that was to follow this ceremony. As she processed toward the altar—not a long procession; Saint John was only a tiny church, more suitable for merchants' weddings than the alliances of kings—she kept her eyes lowered. But she was aware, all the same, all the time, of the profile of her husband keeping pace beside her, another shimmering column of gold and jewels; the straight nose; the big eyes. She was overwhelmed with love and success; drunk with happiness.

This was the hour of her greatest triumph.

She looked around. She hardly knew any of these English and Burgundian faces. A flash of memory briefly troubled her: her younger self, lying in the grass on a hot happy day before the war, with Christine and Charles and Owain, talking lazily about the day she'd be married in gold, and they'd all be there to cheer her on. But there were no friends here.

It didn't matter. She nodded at her mother and father, sitting by the altar, frail and old on their thrones, but her father in his right mind again at last, and giving her a long, soft look, and those two old hands on each other's, together. She flashed loving, hopeful glances at her English ladies-in-waiting, the beautiful strangers who'd made the journey to France to attend her on this day; who would become her friends and confidantes in the peaceable future she was going to; who would perhaps be the great ladies of the glittering English court she was going to establish with Henry.

At her side, Henry stifled a yawn.

Henry of England was dog-tired. One last tedious ceremony, he told himself, trying not to let his eyes close as the Bishop intoned the solemn vows of marriage; one last dull feast; then a good night's sleep.

He and his sixteen thousand·Englishmen had set off from Rouen a full month ago, at the beginning of May. He'd judged it important to give the French a fearsome display of English military might. He'd marched his men into a glittering semicircle around Paris while he went to pray, as the Kings of France always had, at the royal abbey, Saint-Denis. A good symbolic touch, that; and it had the extra benefit of allowing the skinny, ragged people of Paris to climb their city walls and gawp at the spikes and helmets of the soldiers they'd surrendered to. After Saint-Denis, the English army had marched across the plains of Brie, past Prince Charles' various enemy strongholds, leaving permanent encampments of soldiers at strategic bridges. They'd been met at Champagne, and Troyes, by the young Duke of Burgundy and as many Burgundian and French dignitaries as he could muster.

There had been more work to do at Troyes to make sure there was no possibility of treachery. Young Burgundy had assigned Henry's men the lower part of town. But there was no room in those twisty cobbled streets for anything like sixteen thousand men. Most of them would have to camp outside the city walls. Henry didn't want his men separated. So he'd had the city walls taken down.

Only when he was satisfied that the English were not vulnerable had he agreed to get down to the real business: the peace agreement.

Two weeks ago now, they'd given the formal declaration of the treaty the full trumpets-and-triumph treatment. A glittering ceremony in the Cathedral of Saint Peter in the center of Troyes; Henry with his sister-in-law of Clarence on his arm; and the place stuffed with forty English lords and knights, the Queen of France, the Duke of Burgundy, and forty of his councilors.

His bride-to-be had been there too, of course. After they'd heard the recital of the articles of peace, they'd tagged a betrothal ceremony onto the end of that day.

Then there'd been two weeks of celebrations. Two weeks in which, while his lords made fools of themselves swigging and toasting and capering about in their finery, the important business of proclaiming the peace went on, both in French and English, throughout the city; throughout the English army; throughout the land. At the same time, Henry completed the equally important business of accepting vows of allegiance from the Burgundians and French who'd come over to him.

And when he was done, at the end of each day, there was little Catherine. She'd got prettier and more clingingly sensual than ever. No more skulking in the Queen's tent or other people's rooms with her anymore, either. Proper long nights, in his own rooms, in his own bed. No interruptions.

They'd been married, to all intents and purposes, in body at least, for getting on for a year now. She was a good girl. It was a stroke of luck. Still, it was time to wind the whole business up. A quick churching next door to his rooms. Tie up the loose ends. Get back to normality.

Henry had never had much time for courtliness; for dances and dressing-up, those distractions from reality of life in the field. As the Bishop droned on, Henry let his mind wander eighteen miles away, to where he knew the Earl of Huntingdon was besieging Prince Charles' men at Sens. Huntingdon would need reinforcements soon. The King of England was aching to get back under canvas; to his men; to the straightforwardness of the war.

In a dream, in the dusk, Catherine let her beautiful new sisters, the English ladies with their long, dignified faces, flit solicitously around her. Gradually they removed each item of her jewelry and clothing with their lovely fingers and passed it out, in the candlelight, to lesser ladies, who would fold and care for her treasures with all the ceremony due in a court at peace; ladies who would, in their turn, pass on to yet lesser women those items that might need cleaning, or polishing, or repair. This was how things should always have been, she thought dreamily, as her hair was brushed out and her face and body smoothed with creams and scents. Murmuring melodiously to each other in English, a language she didn't understand, though she was beginning to try, now she would have to master the language of her future home—stammering new words every day—the ladies slithered the fine white nightgown over her shoulders and led her into the bridal chamber, hung with a king's cloth of gold, scented with rose petals and lavender.

They turned back the bed. They helped her in. They arranged her hair on the pillows. Then, gravely, they bowed and withdrew as Henry appeared in his doorway, also neat and spruce in night linens, with his retinue of advisers. Her husband. Her King.

"You can go," he said gravely to his men. They too shuffled away in silence. He shut the door and came to the edge of the bed. He stood looking down at her, without expression. She hoped he would tell her how beautiful she looked; more beautiful than ever before on the day she'd become his Queen; that she was the jewel in his crown; that he would always love her. But what he did was scratch his head. Then he smiled at her, a little absentmindedly, and she melted at the sight of those good-natured wrinkles in the corners of his eyes.

"Well, thank God all that's over," he said, puffing out his cheeks as he sighed. "I've had enough larks' tongues in honey to last me a lifetime, haven't you?" Without waiting for an answer, he climbed into the bed and pulled the covers up. She didn't wait for him to pull her to himself. She poured herself onto his body; let her hair hang heavy over his face and shoulders as she leaned down and kissed him. It was their wedding night. She didn't think twice; she knew his body would respond.

But it didn't. He shut his eyes; grinned, kindly enough, but without interest; lay inert under her; pushed a little at her shoulder as if to dislodge her, and mumbled, in French, as always, even though she was now supposed to speak English with her ladies, "Tired . . ." Then, with a sleepy echo of what must be a crude English soldiers' joke, "Can't conquer France tonight . . ."

He didn't even notice her flinch. He was already asleep.

Isabeau gave Henry a look in which natural suspicion tussled with the conscious determination to love. She leaned forward, scattering bonbons over her cards, wishing her son-in-law wasn't lounging so insolently against the fireplace, yawning; wishing she still had the power to intimidate at a glance.

She hoped he wasn't going to be as difficult about the wedding celebrations that Isabeau had planned for the next few days as he had been about negotiating in these last, extra six months, when every hour had seemed to bring some new, unreasonable additional demand, until the Queen of France, who'd never been a patient woman, had been ready to scream and slap his long, smug face.

In a minute, Catherine would be here, with Charles, and she'd have to stop hissing instructions at her new son-in-law. Best, she thought, to get it all worked out properly beforehand.

"Now. The tournament this afternoon. You will carry dear Catherine's colors, of course . . . and you will win," she said, in firm, chivvying tones, adding, as an afterthought, "my dearest son."

Catherine sat with her father for an hour every morning, and walked with him in the gardens. Today was no exception. Why would it be? It wouldn't be long before she set off for her new life in England. She wouldn't have much longer with her father. She didn't want to miss any of the precious moments she still had left. This morning, they were walking down a stone path; in dappled shade; between clouds of blue and yellow flowers. She was holding his arm, and she was talking in her quietest, softest voice, as if she were gentling a horse. This was what they did now. They remembered things together.

Sometimes, if lucid, he told her things he had done when he was a child. Once he'd told her how his own father had offered him the choice of a book or a tiny suit of armor, made in his own five-year-old size; and he'd asked for the suit of armor, and everyone in the ballroom had cheered. She'd laughed. He'd said, with regret: "I always wanted to be a hero. But I should have had the book."

But today he didn't want to remember happy moments.

"Where's Christine?" he said mournfully. He hadn't forgotten her.

Catherine said brightly: "She's gone to Poissy, Papa—to the nunnery; to see her Marie; and our Marie."

But her father ignored the brightness of her tone, and just echoed, "Gone . . . gone . . ." and shook his head sadly with every melancholy word.

The little sprig of forget-me-nots Catherine had picked for him fell out of his collar. He didn't notice.

"You're going too," he said, and there was nothing unclear in the heartbroken look he gave his daughter. "Aren't you? You all go . . ."

She put her arms around him; stood there, feeling him tremble.

"Papa, I'm going to be happy," she said, with all the courage she could muster; "and you'll have a grandson who'll be King of England one day, and of France too . . . and he'll have a suit of armor when he's five, just like you, and be a hero . . . and we're all going to be a loving family forever."

He nodded. She stared at the blinding freshness of the buttercups, wishing away his pain; wishing away his affliction; wishing him peace.

But there were tears on his cheeks. "They're taking you away too," he whimpered.

"Oh Papa, don't," she begged. "Don't cry."

He bent his head to her shoulder and sobbed.

She whispered: "I'll come back, I promise. You won't lose me." Mostly she wanted to comfort him; but she thought it was true, too. Henry would often want to be in France.

"They're taking everything away . . ." He broke through her

thoughts, his voice a miserable, quavering treble. "And what about Charles? Where's my little Charlot?"

She held him tighter. She couldn't think about Charles. "Don't think about Charles, Papa. Charles has been a bad boy," she murmured, stroking his shoulders; but that only made the King cry in earnest.

"Poor Charles," he snuffled. "Poor Charles . . ."

Catherine didn't know whether he was weeping for his son, or himself.

The King cheered up, or seemed to, when Catherine made him a chain of buttercups and hung them round his neck, and made one for her own wrist, too, and kissed his tears away. Then she led him in to Henry and her mother, and the knights' dinner in the open air, which was to lead on to the jousting in the court-yard, where a platform had been erected for the ladies and hung with flags and draperies and flowers, and scattered with cushions.

"Ach, what's this nonsense?" Isabeau said, but kindly, when she saw the buttercups as they sat down to table, taking away the hand she'd clamped to her own two-horned headdress to protect it against the breeze ruffling through every gauzy veil. She had a soft look about her today, too, Catherine saw. To marry your last child was, in itself, a milestone. Catherine realized that her mother would be sympathetic to her father's wistfulness because she felt it too. The Queen of France fussed around her husband, tidying up his clothes; but she left the buttercup chain where it was.

The two kings sat on either side of Isabeau. Catherine was still astonished and grateful that she was allowed to sit at Henry's left, in full view of everyone; that the lords who approached her bowed and called her the Queen of England, that there was sunlight and music playing.

Too dazed with heat and happiness to remember to eat the food being put on her platter, she sat, sipping from her jeweled goblet, watching the courtly smiles. Suddenly she remembered. Her mother had given her a little yellow silk ribbon that she was to give Henry to wear at the joust. "He'll want to carry his wife's token," Isabeau had muttered persuasively; "he'll be grateful."

She wrapped the ribbon round the wilting buttercup bracelet at her wrist, and, touching her husband on his strong, lean arm, passed it to him with an expectant look.

He looked blankly at the little yellow scrap.

"My token," she murmured—wondering, for a moment, whether she wasn't saying the right thing—"for the jousting. For you to wear . . ."

He nodded, took the token, and put it in his purse. Then he cocked his head a little mischievously in Isabeau's direction, on his other side, and said, under his breath: "Aha, I see . . . she's been talking to you about the tournament, has she?"

And he patted her hand. Gently enough; but it was the dismissive kind of gentleness you might show a dog or a child. He wasn't overwhelmed at all, as she'd hoped he might be; and there'd been no gallant lover's words about how he would fight to the death for her honor, either. He just stretched out the same hand immediately afterward, and touched a passing page's arm to remind him that the King's goblet needed filling. She fell silent—trying not to look wounded.

As soon as Henry's cup was full, he stood up. For a second there was a little buzz of talk, then silence. The English lords and knights all looked at him with utter devotion; ready to do whatever he commanded. The sight of their adoring eyes filled Catherine with pride on her husband's behalf. She thought, with relief: So he's going to make a speech . . . and I interrupted him . . . it never occurred to me to think . . . He had something more important on his mind . . .

The memory of the wilting buttercups and the yellow ribbon made her blush; her girlish nonsense.

Henry cleared his throat.

"We are summoned here to celebrate the union of our two countries with a joust," he cried, loud enough for everyone to hear, bowing formally to Queen Isabeau and her husband as he spoke.

His face darkened. "But while we're all here, enjoying ourselves, the enemy is massing more troops," he went on somberly. "The siege at Sens is reaching a decisive stage."

Sens, Catherine thought, confused—the town where Charles' troops were walled in, surrounded by Henry's men, hoping for reinforcements. Sens was just under forty miles away; but it was a million miles from her marriage celebrations. What did Sens have to do with today?

"We, and our knights and soldiers, could make or break that siege," Henry's voice continued. "If we were there."

There was a ragged cheer from some of the Englishmen on the other side of the courtyard, preparing for the joust. Henry raised a calming hand. It wasn't their time yet. He had formalities to get through first. They fell silent again, but Catherine realized every pair of English eyes was shining with hope and excitement.

"With the permission of Their Majesties of France," the King of England went on magnificently, sweeping another bow at Isabeau and Charles (and now, peeping sideways, Catherine could see her mother's face contorted with a look of such utter, vindictive Gorgon fury that it made her wince and turn her own eyes hastily back down toward her plate), ". . . I would like to command my men, and beg those of the King of France, to make ready at once, to join the siege of Sens."

There was a new quality to the silence now. Every French and Burgundian lord was visibly stunned. Some things were sacred. No one interrupted royal wedding feasts. No one changed the plans of the King of France. Not like this. Not for this. But the English didn't know that. Every English lord was turning, shifting, drawing in breath, catching someone else's eye and grinning; enjoying the change of pace; ready to be off as soon as they heard the word of command.

"Better a real-life victory in the field than an idle demonstration of our skills in the courtyard!" Henry almost shouted, firing them up so that the flickers of applause and roared approval began, again, to eddy through the crowd of men drawing closer to the banqueting table. "There we may tilt and joust and prove our courage and daring! For there is no finer act of courage in the world than to punish evildoers—so that poor people can live!"

And now there was no holding them back, the English. In open defiance of every possible rule of French etiquette, they were standing up, raising goblets, banging on tables and trestles, laughing out loud and yelling, "Sens! Sens!" and "Henry!"

"Well then. No time to waste. Let's prepare ourselves," Henry finished very simply, sweeping the hundreds of men in the courtyard with an approving smile of his own.

Catherine felt his kiss, bewilderingly, on the top of her head. Then he was gone, walking very fast and determinedly back into the palace, and there was chaos everywhere. The English all began milling around the most senior commanders they could find, asking enthusiastically for instructions, or galumphing off toward stables and back quarters to pass on orders and prepare weapons and packs and food. The table was half empty already. Within a few minutes the unruly crowd had moved off. There were just the French left at the table: still sitting in their finery, with long, appalled, desperately correct faces, not knowing what to do.

"My lord?" the young Duke of Burgundy said to the King of France.

But the King's face was streaming with quiet tears again. He was murmuring, "Poor Charles, poor Charles," and, once again, Catherine didn't know whether he was weeping for his son or himself.

It was Isabeau who took charge. Rising to her feet, all her bulk swollen and dark with frustrated anger, the Queen reluctantly grated out the command the French lords needed to hear. "The joust is canceled. Follow the King of England."

The afternoon sky was so low and threatening it looked as though you could touch its big gray wallows. There was mud everywhere: on every bedraggled soldier scurrying past, caked to every horse's legs and belly, in the tents, in her boots, smeared on her skirts up to the knee. She was alone, in the little house Henry had had built for her, on their third battlefield together: a miserable dwelling of mud and thatch that rattled and clanked with the noise of war.

"Of course you'll come—I want my bride with me," Henry had said simply. It was a declaration of love, as her husband understood it. He made love to her every night now. He'd lost his fatigue. But now she saw it was the battlefield that exhilarated him, not her. She understood, too late, that what she'd chosen, when she chose to become English, was to be a part of the King of War's war machine.

Catherine had had no idea war was like this, when you were so close up.

Even when two kings, two queens, four dukes, and thousands of lesser men had set impetuously off for Sens, immediately after her wedding, there'd been something dashing and ceremonious about it, something close to the nobility of the jousting she'd grown up with. There'd been pennants and banners and the gleam of silver and iron. Sens had surrendered in a day or two, in sunlight. Living in tents had seemed an adventure; and even the sight of the prisoners trooping out in their chains, with their glum faces, hadn't frightened her.

But then the English army had marched on to Montereau, leaving Isabeau and the French army behind. The English ladies had been sent back to Calais—but not Catherine. And the terrible punishments had begun. Henry had a gibbet built under the walls. He had the townspeople dragged, one by one, to beg the lord of Guitry on their knees to give in, open the castle gate, and save their lives. Catherine would never forget the impassive look on Henry's face when, after each silence from behind the walls, he'd raise his hand again and watch one gray-faced prisoner after another shiver in terror as the rope was put round his neck. She'd never forget the noises; the wriggling; the feet.

And now they were at Melun, where, despite the never-ending rain, the English soldiers were digging mines and trenches around the town. They were fighting in the trenches. Fighting in the mines. In the dark. And they were all mud. Everything was mud. Seas of it. Hells of it.

"Once Melun is ours, we can go to Paris," Henry kept saying. "The hinterlands will be safe then. Paris will be safe."

She nodded unhappily. She had to nod. But she didn't believe he'd stop.

She could sense that, after Melun, after Paris, Henry would want to go on fighting; to move, town by town, village by village, fortress by fortress, south across France, until he'd driven Charles out of the south. He lived for this. He didn't really want to go home to England. So she couldn't meet his eyes, even when he came to her at night. She knew already that the next morning she'd wake up to find him gone—he always left before first light—and herself huddling under the covers, alone, with just the panicky voices outside, and the wind banging at the windows, and the boom and roar of cannon.

PART FIVE

The Prison of Human Life

TWENTY

It took months more before Henry could be dragged away from the war for long enough to take his wife back to England. The subject of return wasn't even raised until after their muted English military Christmas—in a Paris that was, although now a poor and ragged city, at least safe (or almost safe) from attack by the Armagnacs.

Her first queenly Christmas didn't match up to Catherine's expectations of her return to civilization, although it was a pleasure of sorts to be able to walk along stone-walled corridors again, see tapestries on walls, and not touch mud from one entire day to the next. Yet there were none of the Christmastide rituals she'd grown up with: none of the dances, or songs, or Masses, or seasonal foods, or meetings with the people of Paris that she'd expected. English Christmas was functional: a table groaning with food; a few dances; a lot of ale; some inexpensive gifts at New Year. Her parents were holed up at the Hôtel Saint-Paul, which, on the one occasion she went to see them there, seemed strangely quiet too. There were no courtiers, no balls, and Anastaise, who had accepted Catherine's request to tend to the King's daily needs, was as worried as Catherine's mother about where the next bit of money was to come from. Although Catherine savored—or at least noticed and found odd—being called "Majesty" by the servants at the Louvre, where the English party was staying, she also saw it didn't seem to be the English way to bow and scrape and treat their Queen with the exaggerated respect that had always been accorded her mother. She accepted their quiet nods and minimal bows with something like bafflement. She did her best to take pleasure in the new order. And she smiled—only a little wanly—over Henry's first gift to her, stingy though it seemed: the plainest gold bracelet with just one decoration, the entwined letters *H* and *C*.

Even after making Paris secure against the Armagnacs, Henry didn't really want to leave France. Catherine's English was worse than hesitant—she couldn't really imagine forming words in any language but French, even now—but even she was able to follow the slow, emphatic shouts of her husband's brothers when they'd had too much to drink in the evenings and took, peasant style, to thumping their fists on the table and roaring at each other. She sat up in bed one night when the noises got especially loud, listening.

"You have to go home. You're out of money. You can't afford another siege," she heard Thomas of Clarence bawl. They were always talking about money, these English dukes: as if they were clerks trying to balance their books. They had none of the magnificence, the *gloire,* she'd grown up expecting royalty to possess. She wrinkled her nose in distaste.

"How, then?" Henry, this time; sounding just as blurred as his brother after a pitcher or two of Île-de-France red. "Because we have the advantage. Madness not to press on."

"I keep telling you how. Obvious. Take the girl home and put a crown on her head," Thomas shouted. "Then you'll get the dowry. You have to make the time for that. It needn't take long. That money would keep us going. I've told you a thousand times."

Eagerly, she strained her ears to hear Henry's reply. If only he would agree they could go to England . . . But the voices dropped to an inaudible murmur, and she felt her eyes closing.

When Henry came to bed, a good hour later, the heavy fall of his fully clothed body beside her woke her again. Her husband saw her open eyes and kissed her. He smelled of wine. He was drunkenly contrite.

"I've kept you here too long," he muttered. "Haven't I? Thomas been telling me off. Quite right. Neglected my duty . . .

sorry. But it's time you saw your new home . . . time we got you crowned . . . so . . . home to Westminster . . . soon."

She didn't mind knowing that Henry mostly wanted to take her to England only to get her dowry money for the war. She longed to go; to start her new life, not this garrison imitation of it. Her husband was doing the right thing by taking her to England at last, even if his reasons were not the ideal ones; he would always do the right thing in the end. Joyfully she put her arms around him and tried to marshal appropriately gracious words of gratitude. At least with Henry and his brothers, who'd been brought up speaking French with their own French mother, she didn't have to struggle (at least while they were all still in France) to find the gracious words in a foreign language.

But there was no time. A gentle snore told her that Henry had fallen asleep in her arms.

England came swiftly on her, even before she'd forgotten the tears of her parting with her parents, even before she could quite smell the sea that would take her away forever.

The gateway to England came as you picked your way through the empty marshland outside Calais. Inside the town's towering fortifications, Calais looked like any other settlement along the northern coast: wattle and daub, muddy inhabitants, the glint of salt water in the reeds. But the sounds were foreign. There wasn't a French or a Flemish voice left. All the staring shopkeepers, wool merchants, innkeepers, and market women were settlers, speaking English. The last English king to make war on the French, Edward III, had thrown out all the locals and colonized Calais with his own sort. She could hear a babble of foreign voices, whispering.

Catherine stared back down from her horse at them. She hardly listened to the military tattoo as their cavalcade made its way to the castle. She was straining to hear those voices beyond the fifes and drums—proof she was on the move at last: overseas, before she felt she'd really even left France. How strange it all was.

"So—England at last!" Henry said lightly, when the obligatory dinner with the Castle Keeper was over, and the King and

Queen of England had retired. "Saw you take it all in as we came in—what do you think?"

Privately, she thought: Thank God it isn't all going to be like this: sea air, garrison food, and mud. She felt honored to be asked. She said, "It's a joy to be here," and the sincerity in her voice must have been audible. There was a cheerful light in his eyes as he pulled her close.

But there was a lot more mud. Her new home at Westminster Palace backed onto the Thames, a great swamp of a reed-fringed river, which they said would be alive with ducks and insects and fumes and agues and fevers when the heat began. The views across to the dubious pleasure places of Southwark to the east, and west to the more innocent Surrey woods, were pleasant enough. But in winter, under the jetties and ropes and boats used by the brown and gray local people to go after salmon and carp and perch, the nearside riverbank was all fierce-looking swans, with nicks on their beaks signifying who owned them, and rats scuttling through the brown rushes, and mist.

She couldn't believe how small and provincial London was— a quarter the size of Paris: a walled market town a couple of miles upriver, dominated by the Tower, with a single bridge over to the wilderness of dock and hovel and wood and those prostitute-infested riverside walkways in the south. There was no great charm in the squat churches and religious establishments of the city itself, and certainly nowhere remotely like the colleges and spires of the Paris University. The bishops' and noblemen's palaces that lined the Strand connecting the City and Westminster were great hulking castles, gazing out over the water, built for defense, not beauty. One, known as the Savoy, was a blackened ruin, with trees growing between the stones. They said rioters had burned it down long ago, and it had been left like that: a warning of the mutability of fortune, the fragility of wealth. The thought of rioters made her shiver. So did the mud and mist.

The mist got everywhere; the biting winds too. She couldn't get away from the smell of damp. The palace was a great drafty barracks with only the bare minimum of tapestries and screens to keep out the chill, set against walls that seemed to have soaked up centuries of coldness like frozen sponges. Catherine set herself and her ladies to sewing several new tapestries, to elaborate French designs of hunting scenes, which the English ladies professed, in their solemn way, to admire, but she shivered at the thought of how long it would take before they were completed. Meanwhile, however, many candles and tapers and torches bravely burned. However many fires were lit, it seemed impossible to get warm.

Catherine didn't want to complain about anything, of course. Nor could she, even at the times when she felt most ill at ease and alone among strangers. A tacit rule seemed to have come into force, which no one had told her about, in which she was no longer supposed to speak French even with those she'd always spoken to in her own language. It was English only from now on; if she tried French on anyone from Henry down, they looked patient and answered in English. She wished she'd tried harder while still in France. Her English was still so bad, and she didn't like to make a fool of herself by opening her mouth only to fail to make herself understood, so she felt herself shrink into a smiling, nodding, perpetually concentrating, perpetually surprised, perpetually overpolite simulacrum of herself. She'd seen her mother's enjoyment of running things in France. But a foreign queen, who couldn't properly make herself understood, didn't seem to have much chance of any kind of power in England.

It wasn't just queens, either. All Englishwomen seemed quieter and dowdier than their French counterparts, and certainly less powerful, both at home and at court. Love of women was not considered the high art it was in courtly France, or celebrated in poetry and song, arts that, as far as she could see, scarcely existed in English. This was a place where courtly festivities seemed to consist of little more than eating and drinking in silence for several hours at a stretch, dressed in simple fashions that followed the colors of the English riverbanks—dank greens and drab browns and muddy mists—followed by the dancing of outlandish rustic dances to outlandish rustic music with men whose voices had gone slurred with ale or wine, and whose bodies lurched to and fro almost independently of the primitive banging of the rhythms.

But at least she had Henry often at her side now, organizing their time in England as if it were another military campaign, and everyone obeyed Henry, so everyone she met was very respectful to her, and no one seemed to mind if she just nodded dumbly back, and bobbed her head, and felt a fool to be the one foreigner sticking out like a sore thumb in their dun-colored English uniformity.

And Henry was a man of his word. He set his men immediately to preparing the coronation. It would take place before Lent was over, because they'd have to be quick. Once she was crowned, he wanted to take her around England to show her to his people, before getting back to Westminster for a Parliament in May.

She stifled questions as to what she would wear for all these ceremonial occasions. No one suggested she would have new English robes made. She felt she would probably be expected to use the French robes she had brought with her. She didn't mind: the jewel-bright French robes, in velvet and silk, were more beautiful than anything she saw around her. But didn't they prefer their English fashions? Didn't they care if she wasn't dressed in their style?

Apparently not. Perhaps the English dukes didn't want to lay out more money on making their Queen's clothes as English as her language was supposed to become. Perhaps they just hadn't thought ahead to the traveling. The only discussion was about the coronation itself.

And even with the coronation, Catherine realized, there was a great deal she was failing to understand.

It was only at the end of a Council meeting, in which Henry had carefully explained to her the finalized timetable of the entire two-day crowning ceremony for her, starting from the overnight stay at the royal apartments at the Tower, to the barge ride downriver, and the serenades, and the cloth of gold, and the fireworks, right through to the ceremony and the feast at Westminster Palace, that she thought to ask (and found the hesitant English words for her question):

"Where will *you* be?"

Henry looked at her in surprise, then laughed as he realized what she meant. "Not with you," he said, not unkindly. "This is your coronation. You'll be on your own."

"But . . ." she stammered, not knowing how to express her fear. She widened her eyes; drew in breath.

There was no point.

Henry patted her hand. "That's our custom," he said easily. There was nothing more to say.

In the event, she rather enjoyed the ceremony. There was nothing to worry about, after all. At every stage there was someone to nudge her, politely if firmly, into doing the next right thing. They'd thought it all out for her. They'd left nothing to chance. By the time she sat down to the Lenten feast, back at Westminster Palace, and watched her husband's subjects—*her own, too, now,* she admonished herself, catching herself on that thought—tucking into the salmon, sole, sturgeon, crayfish, porpoises, whelks, lampreys, and tench on offer, she was tremulous with relief.

Between each course there was a pastry-cook subtlety, a sculpture whisked up out of hardened sugar strands. They were brought out into the hall to cheers and wolf whistles. The best was a magnificent tiger, striped in yellow and black sugar stripes, led by Saint George. The entire hall went wild at the sight of it, yelling and drumming their feet under the table.

Usually she found the English drumming-feet habit strange and slightly threatening. But now the euphoria was catching. Catherine opened her mouth to laugh. Then, looking round, she realized there was no one willing to catch her eye and share her merriment. Everyone was enjoying the moment of appreciation with someone else. Uncertainly, glancing from side to side before turning her gaze back toward the tiger, she fixed a determined smile on her face. It was either a queenly smile, or the smile of an outsider with no friends. Or perhaps those two things were the same.

"You did well," Henry said that night. His voice was warm. Catherine glowed.

She wanted so much to do well for him now. She was lonely; but with her husband, at least, she had enough of a connection to be sure that, if he met her eye, he would then talk to her, make sure she understood what was happening around her, and reward her with appreciation if she managed to join in. Perhaps this warmth that Henry inspired, whenever he singled someone out for a glowing moment of appreciation, was what made his soldiers and servants so devoted, she thought; so ready to conquer their fears for him. She shared their devotion now. There was no one else to attach herself to. She lived for his smiles of approval; wilted when he forgot her.

"Tomorrow," he whispered in her ear, wrapping himself around her, half dancing, half marching her to the bed, "St. Albans." He nudged her down onto the quilts. She laughed up at him, relieved to see her emotion reflected back on his smiling face. He added: "And soon, an heir."

St. Albans was followed by many other English towns and residences in the next eight weeks. They went west to Bristol and Shrewsbury and Kenilworth Castle. They went north to Coventry and Leicester, Nottingham and Pontefract, York and Bridlington. They went south and east to Lincoln and Lynn, the holy shrine of Walsingham and Norwich, before the procession turned back toward London, in time for Parliament at Westminster.

Catherine had never ridden so much. She wore the same three French gowns at every stop. No one ever even commented on what she wore. There was no time for frivolity.

"Tell me if it's too much for you," Henry said, kindly and seriously, at every stop. "We don't want to do anything to damage your health." And he'd give her that questioning look— had she conceived yet?—but without asking directly or making her feel a failure for not yet being with child. She was so grateful to Henry for his tact; so full of admiration for him. His polite consideration made her pray, each day more humbly than the last, for the baby boy they needed.

All the same, she was increasingly ill at ease. It was the public conversation at every stop that worried her. At every banqueting hall, at every discussion with every mayor and lord, Henry had just one topic: raising more money for the war. And the King of England's desire to return to the war overseas became more visible after York, where news came to them that Henry's brother Thomas, Duke of Clarence, had been killed in France, near Anjou. Not that Henry wept for his brother in front of Catherine or anyone else, but he shut himself away for a day, and delayed their departure for two, and ordered a solemn Mass said at York Minster. After that he couldn't stop himself talking, passionately, everywhere, about the war Clarence had died at.

"We've achieved a lot, of course," he'd say, looking modestly at his hands as his fingers ticked off victory after victory, from Azincourt onward. "We've secured Paris, at least for now." Then his face would tighten, and whoever was watching him would lean forward, already eager to help.

"But we haven't permanently secured Paris," Henry would continue. "Dauphin Charles can still move forces in a big theater around the city. We have to close all of northern France off to him before we can pursue him south and finish him off."

By now, whichever local baron or duke it was would be nodding and working out how many men, or how much money, the lands under his control could spare to help complete the conquest of France.

Henry didn't leave a single town without a pledge.

They were back in London just in time to see the maypoles, with their ribbons forlornly loose, being taken down ("Next year," Henry said, following her gaze, "we'll see the dancing next year; you'll like it")—the night before Parliament convened. They entered the great hall at the palace hand in hand, to be greeted with cheers by a great crowd of men in dark clothes. Catherine smiled and bobbed, half hiding behind Henry. She was allowed to leave shortly after.

She needed to get away from the ceremonies and the men's speeches. She was exhausted. And she was full of secret hope. Her monthly bleeding was a day late. She wanted to go to the abbey, if her English ladies would let her while Parliament was on, and pray for a son.

It took only ten days for Parliament to ratify the Treaty of

Troyes, confirming Henry's victories in France thus far, and formalizing their acceptance of his marriage to Catherine, and to grant him more money. He'd get one-tenth of the clergy's income, and one-tenth of the lay lords'. With the £38,000 in loans he could also count on—half of which had come from the King and Queen's royal progress round England, he told her—he had enough for another season's campaigning, without touching Catherine's dowry, which might take more time to secure.

"Where did the other half of the loans come from?" Catherine asked faintly. She hadn't realized how quickly money might be raised; how quickly Henry might be drawn back to the war.

"Oh," Henry replied, and briefly there was a glint of amusement in his eye. "My best fund-raiser. My uncle, Bishop Beaufort." Catherine had met Beaufort, but not fully distinguished him from the blur of other royal relatives. "Sly as boots. Not to be trusted. Wanted to be a cardinal. I put a stop to that; so now he's trying to get into my good graces again by raising fortunes for me. And I'm grateful . . . I'm grateful all right," he twinkled. "But he's still not getting his cardinal's hat."

Henry was intensely excited by the discussions at Parliament. He could hardly sit still. He paced around, thinking, in the evenings when the sessions were over; calling servants to send messages to people Catherine didn't know, even after dinner; even at dawn.

Keeping her secret was easy enough. Henry was too busy with the Parliament to do more than tumble into bed at night, make perfunctory love, and fall asleep with scarcely a word exchanged. She had an unpleasant suspicion that even this lovemaking might, in his mind, now be a duty.

Catherine sat very quietly all day, sewing her corner of her tapestry, not talking to her ladies, who would only speak English, and praying that she might be able to tell Henry she was pregnant before he left.

She watched her husband's growing inattention to her with a sinking heart. In spirit, she could see he was already on the road to France. She didn't want to go back to battle herself. He hadn't asked; and if she were pregnant she couldn't. But she didn't want to be left alone here, either.

So she was surprised and honored when, on the sunny morning before the Parliament was due to break up, Henry sent for her to join him outside the palace, to watch a team of palace servants take on the townsfolk of Westminster at quintain.

There were big crowds at the green. The knot of people around Henry came at once to her and her ladies. Henry bowed to her, then took her arm and led her forward through the crowd, with their retinue blending and following along behind. Catherine felt the brilliant sunshine on her back, and in her heart, too, at being so generously acknowledged by her master. The most forthcoming of her ladies, Elizabeth Ryman, had already explained the rules of quintain: a game in which players took turns to run at a dummy, dressed as a turbaned Saracen, and whack it on the shield attached to its left arm. Catherine had stifled her private worry that she must have misunderstood, as the game sounded too primitive and crude to be worthy of a royal audience. Now, as the first member of the palace team began running toward it, Henry laughingly pointed out to her the dummy in the middle of the green: an eight-foot-high monster in brightly painted turban, standing on a pivot. As well as the shield on its left arm, it had a mock sword attached to its wooden right hand.

"You have to watch out as you aim your lance," he began, but his explanation was forestalled by events. The servingman's lance went wide of the target marked on the shield, and unbalanced the dummy. It swung sharply round on its pivot, so fast and hard that when the sword in its right arm whacked the unfortunate servingman it knocked him right off his feet.

Henry roared with laughter, just like everyone else, as the man got blearily to his feet with mud all over his face. Hesitantly, not really understanding why she should be amused, but, all the same, wanting to fit in, Catherine tittered too.

The palace servants lost the game. The townsfolk got the prize: a peacock, with its blue and green tail plumage still hanging gloriously, if incongruously, down from its pink, plucked corpse. Henry presented it, to jeers and cheers from the two teams.

How crude this is, Catherine thought, trying not to purse her lips. Why does he bother?

But she began to think she might understand why, when, after the prizegiving, and after the palace team had withdrawn inside the gates, Henry gathered all his own men round himself, and gave each of them a coin from the bag at his belt, and grinned his thanks to each grateful individual, and pressed their hands with his.

It was only a single coin each. But the joy was so intense. Suddenly Catherine realized she couldn't ever remember seeing her parents paying anyone in person; she didn't know whether the simple act of payment, among Frenchmen, would put the same radiant smiles on every face. In France, she thought, there was a lot more talk about the King's body being a miracle, and the King being able to perform miracles and cure the sick with his healing hands, and generally about royalty being sacred. But there was seldom anything so simple as paying the wages, even through intermediaries—and never, ever directly. Perhaps the loyalty Henry inspired could always be this easy to achieve. Perhaps you didn't need to trail clouds of sacred glory to rule well. Perhaps all a king needed was to be reliable.

This was how England was, a lot of the time, she realized, feeling suddenly pleased to be here. Not as beautiful or as decorous or as grand as she'd have liked; duller and uglier and more provincial than France in almost every way, in fact; but not so bad when you got used to it. Perhaps peace was always dull. The important thing was that Henry worked hard at keeping the peace, and looked after people, making them happy. That was impressive, in its own quiet way.

Henry would process to Canterbury directly from the closing of Parliament, with his representatives, ready to embark for France in a few days. The troops and supplies were waiting for him there.

Catherine and her ladies would travel separately an hour later, to join him and see him off.

That was the plan, anyway. Catherine watched the trunks and bags being assembled for her afternoon ride as she heard the men's procession move along the street under her window.

But the next thing she knew she was on the floor, with her head being cradled by Mistress Ryman, wondering why she felt so dizzy.

"You passed out," Mistress Ryman said, her face moving alarmingly to and fro above her. The other ladies' heads were craning down toward her too, all with the same hungry hope in their eyes. But it was only Mistress Ryman who dared voice it. She said: "Are you with child?"

Mistress Ryman said Catherine was in no state to ride to Canterbury, even in a litter.

"But—I want to tell my husband . . ." Catherine said. "That I am . . ." She didn't know the English for "pregnant." The pause while she thought of how to express her thought more forcefully lost her the argument.

"You can write to him," Mistress Ryman said. "That will be safer."

Mistress Ryman took Catherine's brief letter to her husband, breaking the news. Catherine thought Henry might delay his departure; ride back to London; share the joy of the news and say goodbye. But he didn't. He did no more than the right thing. He gave Mistress Ryman a big reward—a manor somewhere. And he sent words to order Masses for the child's safe delivery.

It would only have been a day's ride, Catherine thought disconsolately.

But there was no point in complaining. She knew Henry's priority was the war; the return to France. She knew her ladies would think her grossly self-indulgent if she complained. So she ordered the Masses said, and kept her hurt feelings to herself.

TWENTY-ONE

Catherine had been lying there all day, for hours, just like this: utterly spent, but utterly at peace too, gazing at her baby.

She didn't mind the aches, the rips, the soft sag of belly that still hung from her bones, or even the strangely ugly reflection of a much older woman with dark patches round the eyes and a shapelessness to the jaw that had stared back from the mirror they'd brought her. She'd shooed them away when they'd tried to comb her hair and make her beautiful after her bath. She didn't need anyone weaving flowers into her head. She was clean and warm and free of fever; her milk was coming; that was all that mattered. That, and the little creature staring back at her.

She'd done her duty. She deserved her English crown. She had a son: a King for England.

But the truth was that she didn't care about her son's royal blood. She was too full of awe at his very existence. Her baby had big, blue, wondering eyes, and perfect miniature fingers that curled pinkly around hers and held on tight whenever she put her giant's thumb into his hand. His tiny body startled out into a star of alarmed arms and legs if she moved it too fast. When he slept, he whiffled and sniffled, screwed up his eyes or opened his mouth or muttered, as if he were dreaming; but what could a person so fresh and new, who knew nothing of anything yet, possibly have to dream about? He was full of mystery. He was so small, so helpless; he couldn't move by himself. Yet, if she put him on the bed away from her, it seemed no time before she'd feel his little body relax luxuriantly against hers again; he'd somehow have dragged himself to her, without muscles, without understanding, just full of a child's natural urge for warmth and love. He had his father's wide-set eyes in a red, wrinkled little face. The top of his head smelled milky—of happiness, she thought, drawing him to herself to kiss again, knowing that she would give him all the warmth and love a child could want, for every day of the seven years he would be in his mother's care, and for the rest of his life, too, even once they took him away to teach him to begin to be a man. She couldn't imagine that future; but, for the first time in her life, she was completely confident that it would be full of happiness. She'd make it be. How beautiful he was.

She didn't bother to turn her head when people came in to tend to her. She didn't know the midwives' and nurses' names. She didn't need to. She had enough, right here in this room. There was nothing she wanted to do except be left with her baby for the rest of the forty days of her lying-in, until she had to go out and be churched, and rejoin the rest of the world. She just wanted to get to know him, undisturbed.

The first disturbance came well before the forty days were up.

One morning, Catherine raised her eyes to discover Mistress Ryman, standing determinedly in the doorway, muttering, "If you please . . ." and "If your Grace would be good enough . . ." until, in the end, Catherine had, reluctantly, to acknowledge the extraneous presence.

She looked up. Mistress Ryman was one of those common-sense Englishwomen with a big pink wrinkled-apple face. At Catherine's glance, she colored up and bobbed, with an awkward grin that only half masked the pugnacious bossiness of her nature. In the past nine months, since Henry had gone, Catherine had come to detest Mistress Ryman. But Mistress Ryman knew how to get the better of her mistress every time—knew Catherine didn't like having to try and speak English, even after all these months, how she hated to be betrayed, every time she opened her mouth, by the words coming out deformed and hesitant, so that she felt she'd been made a fool of by her tongue.

Mistress Ryman just waited for Catherine to make a mistake with a word. Then, while Catherine cringed, she'd tell Catherine, with puddingy English solemnity, what to do—over and over again, if necessary, though always politely—until Catherine did it.

"There's a messenger, Your Majesty," the woman said now, making a point of speaking slowly, grimacing as if she were addressing an idiot. "With word from the King's Grace in France."

Catherine smiled. So Henry had heard he had a son. This was the moment she'd been waiting for. She held out her hand for the letter.

The woman shook her head. "He wants to give it to you himself," she said doubtfully. "Says it's the King's own will."

Impossible. Men weren't allowed here, to the birth chamber, were they? Not until after she'd been churched. Catherine's brow furrowed. She said, in her fractured English: "But . . . I . . . can . . . not . . . receive . . . him." She let the hint of a question enter her voice. The English had their ways; they didn't like anyone to step out of line. And she was always doing the wrong thing, she knew; always embarrassing Mistress Ryman.

No, she realized, while her words were still hanging on the air: they'd have thought of that. No one disobeyed the King's orders; so they'd find a way to make it proper in their minds for Catherine to receive this guest; of course they would. The woman had a robe hanging ready over her arm: an embroidered wrap. It must be to dress Catherine to receive the guest. She stood up obediently and let herself be eased into it, suddenly remembering the pale round face that had stared back from her mirror, almost wishing she'd let them braid and beautify her hair after all.

"We'll come out here, Your Majesty—to your parlor. Much nicer for you to meet your guest out here," the woman was saying, still overenunciating every painfully slow word. She moved to the bed to scoop up the little Prince, who'd wriggled out of his blanket and was lying naked but for a twisted napkin, entranced by a sunbeam.

However obedient she'd been till now, Catherine wasn't going to allow that. She stepped adroitly past the woman and picked up her son herself first; wrapping the blanket tenderly round his limbs; letting her hand and arm support his neck and head. She'd carry him herself.

The woman bit her lip, but said nothing. I've probably committed another offense against English etiquette, Catherine thought, rocking the baby against herself, rejoicing privately at the warmth of this new life that had come so mysteriously from within her own body. But she didn't care. He was her baby. The messenger would want to see him. She would carry him.

The woman led her out. Catherine had both hands around her child, whose body fitted so naturally against hers. She was still looking at little Harry, memorizing the expression in his eyes, when the messenger at the back of the parlor began his deep bow.

She went on rocking the baby, and waiting, without particularly resenting the interruption. It was easy enough to do whatever was expected of her here, at least. Everything worked, if you just always did what they told you.

She thought nothing had the power to disturb the peace that had come upon her.

But she was surprised when she recognized the man, rising to his full height again and squaring his broad shoulders, and stepping forward through the half-darkness, with a sealed document that must be Henry's letter in his hand, and saying, "A healthy, beautiful boy."

He spoke the words correctly and calmly, but with none of the warm tenderness she'd heard from every woman who'd said the same sort of thing in the past couple of weeks. He kept his eyes on the waving arms and the tiny fingers curling and uncurling near his nose, not on the baby's mother. His lips were tight, as if he didn't want to be here, saying these words. But he was speaking French, at least. That was a joy. She hadn't heard French for months.

"Owain Tudor," she said, and smiled.

Perhaps it was the sound of her native tongue that touched her, or the confidence that came from achieving her life's goal—this child she was holding in her arms. Or perhaps it was just the loneliness she was suddenly also painfully aware of: the prickle down her spine that told her Mistress Ryman's hostile eyes were on her, as usual, and that the lady-in-waiting was tut-tutting behind her back at the messenger's murmured French.

At any rate, she found herself looking at Owain with all the warmth of a long-lost friend. With her body still so battered from childbirth, she couldn't remember, or even imagine, physical desire, even for this man, who had once, briefly, been her lover; but Owain was someone she'd been close to, who reminded her, in a rush, of summer, and the scent of rose oil, and youth, and the sounds of Paris. And there were so few friends here in England, in the darkness of December.

He didn't smile back.

He just held out the letter.

It seemed a long while before she remembered the last time they'd seen each other: her cruel, childish, public humiliation of him; that evening of forcing him to read his own poems out loud. A foolish revenge, she could see now, since all she'd been angry with him about was that he'd understood her destiny and delivered her back to it. She should have been grateful. Now that she understood she was happy with her destiny, she should be grateful. And ashamed.

He was still holding out the scroll.

"Would you like to read the letter from your husband, Your Majesty?" Owain Tudor said patiently, when she did nothing to break the silence.

She nodded, keeping her eyes owlishly on him, hoping she would get a chance to apologize; hoping he would accept. For, after all, all those upheavals seemed a lifetime ago to her.

She took the letter. With a shock, she saw he was wearing black clerical robes; a hood. The robes of an Augustinian—a lay brother, she guessed, since he was out in the world, walking about, not shut up in a cloister somewhere. A humble Austin Friar.

Why? she found herself thinking, dully. Surely he's not a clerk? Does he beg for a living; tend bees? Why is he dressed like that?

Her imagination failed her. It couldn't, surely, be anything to do with . . . the poems? Her?

She broke the seal.

When she showed no signs of starting to read, Owain Tudor added: "He wishes you to know that he received the news of his son's birth with humble rejoicing and devout exultation, his joy being shared by the English army . . . and he wishes you to hear devoutly a Mass of the Blessed Trinity, as soon as you can, and dedicate the Prince to Almighty God, humbly praying that his ways and actions should be directed in happy succession to the honor and glory of God."

She nodded. Suddenly the impatience she'd tried to suppress ever since Henry vanished to France, sending back no letters, no gifts, no word, nothing but military dispatches and impersonal instructions to do the right thing, came rushing back. Suddenly she was overwhelmed with resentment of Elizabeth Ryman, sitting so infuriatingly out of sight behind her. Elizabeth Ryman, who'd been in charge, during the birth, of the casket containing the silver jewel, Our Lord's foreskin. It was renowned in France for its help to women in labor. Henry had made sure to have it brought over in good time for her confinement. That was just the kind of detail her husband would make sure to organize: the kind of proof of his thoughtfulness that would win popular approval on both sides of the Channel. She hadn't actually wanted the relic in the room when her time came, all the twists and prongs of its great silver casing glittering and winking in the firelight, reeking of incense and rotten wood; but Elizabeth Ryman had insisted. She was as stubborn as a mule. What the King said went. Catherine's personal wishes didn't matter to her. It was best to give in.

Now Henry was writing to tell her to have Harry churched, and Owain Tudor, who'd been her friend, was reading back the King's orders in that official, pompous voice they all used here.

Of course she'd had the baby baptized and confirmed within hours of his birth. All kinds of solemn Masses had been said. She knew the right thing to do. She didn't need these detailed instructions from her husband. What kind of fool must he think her, to believe she'd need reminding to protect her infant son from the risk of eternal damnation?

"Please tell His Majesty," she replied very formally, glancing round at the wretched Mistress Ryman, who'd sat herself down on a stool by the doorway, in accordance with some English notion of propriety, and was showing no sign of going away, "that his wishes have been carried out. And that all the bells in London were rung on the day of the birth, and *Te Deums* sung in every church."

Owain answered, just as solemnly, as if they were two mummers in a play: "His Majesty also wishes you to know that his siege at Meaux is going well."

She inclined her head, with all the stiff English pride she was now learning.

"God willing," Catherine replied formally, "Meaux will soon surrender to my lord."

"So, are you campaigning in France again, Owain?" she then asked, in a more human voice, raising her eyes to his averted ones, wishing the conversation weren't so stilted, trying to draw him out a little without allowing Elizabeth Ryman to feel an impropriety was taking place.

He shook his head. "No. Now I've left Oxford, Bishop Beaufort has taken me into his household while I think about whether to take holy vows."

So he wasn't a clerk—not yet, at least. For reasons she didn't understand, she was relieved to know that. Still, getting conversation out of him was like wringing blood from a stone. He didn't want to talk. He was angry with her, all right. She gestured for him to sit. He stayed standing.

She said: "But you were in France?"

Shortly, he replied: "My master sent me to Meaux with messages for His Majesty. I was fortunate enough to be the bearer of the news of his son's birth."

He bowed. He looked ready to go.

She turned to Elizabeth Ryman, and nodded down at the baby in her arms. The woman came bustling up, eager to end the conversation. "Please," Catherine said, trying to get the balance of haughtiness and politeness right, without compromising on her pronunciation, "take him; he needs changing . . ." and, with a last brush of the lips on her son's soft head, she handed him over.

Then, to Owain, she said hurriedly, "I'm sorry . . . so sorry . . . for everything I did . . . I've been meaning to say, ever since you came in . . . I was so unkind . . . I didn't realize what I was doing. I was a child. Please forgive me."

His face closed. He shut his eyes. Tightly, he nodded. She understood: she hadn't made it better. But she didn't want to let him go. Without him, there'd be just the Mistress Rymans.

They stood for a few minutes in silence. Every time Catherine dared glance up at him, he was looking away. She tried to think of new questions. She couldn't. But he didn't retire, either.

There was a sound from the doorway. Elizabeth Ryman was standing with the baby wrapped in fresh linen, a watchful look on her rosy-cheeked face.

"I don't suppose," Catherine said carefully, and ignored Mistress Ryman's shake of the head at her use of French, "that there's any talk of His Majesty coming back to England?"

She'd known the answer without having to ask. That wouldn't be Henry's way. He was a king with a vision, and it wasn't a vision in which his wife had much of a place.

Owain was moving toward the door now. Catherine followed him, after taking Harry from the lady-in-waiting, relieved to have him back in her arms.

"I'd love my husband to see him," she said, bending her head to Harry's scalp, reassured by the milky smell of him; "and my parents if it comes to that."

She added sadly, looking at Mistress Ryman, as if expecting to be countermanded, "Though I know I can't. Go. Of course."

He'd started fiddling with his belt; checking he had his belongings with him. She could see he was about to leave; go back to his life; leave her alone with the dour women.

But he looked up at that. Perhaps, she thought, he'd heard the desperation.

"You could," he said, considering, though still without warmth. Out of politeness to Mistress Ryman, to whom he was bowing a courteous farewell, he switched into English. "Go to France. Why not? Once your lying-in is over, there's nothing at all to stop you."

She stared. Could she? Wasn't there?

"You're the Queen of England. Future Queen of France. Your husband is in France. Your parents. Take your son to them. Who could blame you? They are your family."

There was a glitter in his eye and a bitterness in his tone that Catherine couldn't miss. And then he was gone.

"But a newborn," said Humphrey, Duke of Gloucester, another pop-eyed, ponderous brother-in-law with no time for women. He shook his head. He wouldn't meet Catherine's eyes. He looked out of the window, as if wishing she would go away. "You couldn't travel with a newborn."

"My son is three months old now," Catherine protested faintly. "He's got a tooth."

"Never been done," Humphrey of Gloucester added more firmly. "Heir to the throne. Risk."

"Heir to the throne of France as well as England . . ." Catherine prompted. She couldn't give up. "That's new too . . . he'll need to learn French ways if his French subjects are to love him . . ."

She smiled winsomely up at her brother-in-law. But Humphrey of Gloucester just shook his head again, so the cloud of gingery curls above his eyes quivered.

Catherine felt tears of disappointment prickle behind her eyelids. It had taken her so long to pluck up the courage to ask; to master the words. He'd turned her down without even thinking. He wasn't an unkind man, though, she thought. Just stubborn and domineering. He was even twinkling at her in his awkward, bear-like way, as if he had suddenly thought of good news.

"Not to say *you* can't go," he added suddenly. "Show us all that France is English now. Not just Calais. A lesson for every-one. Quite right. Get a bit of an entourage together. Leave the boy here. Mistress Ryman—good woman—capable hands.

Meanwhile, you: a month or two with your parents. See your husband. Though . . . battlefield . . . not your style, eh?"

He chuckled and ruffled her hair. He hurried away. He looked relieved to have finished the interview.

She didn't want to leave Harry. But now she'd sensed the opportunity she wanted to be home so badly, just for a while. "I'll miss you," she muttered to her baby son, hugging him so tightly to herself that he wriggled and squealed, and the fierce red patches on his cheeks grew redder; "it will be as if half of me is missing. But you'll be safe with Mistress Ryman." She laughed at herself for wanting this so much; she, who had tried so hard to get to safety in England, and now felt so stifled by it. She was already imagining the garden at the Hôtel Saint-Paul. She was imagining her mother's grin; the hand sneaking out to the bowl of sweetmeats, the dirty laughter over the filthy jokes. She was imagining her father's handsome profile, and his question-mark back, and his lost eyes.

She wanted to see her husband. She wanted to share the joy of parenthood with him. That was why she was going. He would come to Paris to see her when the war allowed. Soon.

But sometimes she also found herself imagining the journey: being led under the green sunlight of trees by Owain Tudor, whose eyes would sparkle again with the friendly warmth of long ago.

She was trying not to think about that. That wasn't why she wanted to go. Owain Tudor had given her the idea. But he was no part of this plan.

Bishop Beaufort, splendid in his purple, was easy to persuade.

"Of course, my dear, of course," he said urbanely. "Whoever Humphrey recommends. It's peaceful enough between Calais and Paris; for security purposes I doubt you'd need more than a small company of knights. And, as you say, my man Tudor is fresh back from France and knows the northern roads like the back of his hand. A familiar face to you, too. He'll be a good guide."

Catherine felt a little uneasy that she'd gone so out of her way to bring Owain Tudor with her to France, when he so clearly hadn't wanted to renew their acquaintance. But seeing him here in England had been a kind of trigger to her memories. Owain seemed to have found a way toward the next part of his life—those monkish robes. Surely he wouldn't hold a grudge forever? She remembered feeling so close to Owain. She wanted to make amends; to show him the past was past; win him back as a friend, at least. She needed friends. If she, as Queen of England, chose to ask a soldier of her acquaintance to lead her entourage on their trip from Calais to Paris, what was wrong with that?

Was there something quizzical in her new uncle's glance? Was he wondering why she was so interested in borrowing this particular guide, when the English court was full of other young men who also knew northern France like the back of their hands?

No, she thought, banishing the flicker of embarrassment. Bishop Beaufort—lettered, civilized, and a beautiful singer—was more like a French nobleman than anyone she'd encountered at this court. She felt she understood him. He was probably only hoping that, by helping his new niece so promptly, he'd encourage her royal husband to forgive him the crime that had brought five years of King Henry's brooding resentment—being offered the cardinal's hat that he'd been forced by his nephew and monarch to reject. There was no place in Henry's scheme of things for anything he deemed to smack of disloyalty. All must serve one cause.

"I will tell my husband," Catherine said gratefully, "how quick you were to help me. I'm certain he will be grateful to you for reuniting us." She squeezed his strong, clean hand, which glittered with rubies. She knew she was right when she saw the matching glitter of gratitude in his eyes.

The France party grew. By the time Catherine set off it was late spring and Duke John of Bedford, the King's next oldest brother, was her highest-ranking companion on the journey.

She traveled with little Henry and her own household as far

as Dover. He'd walked his first steps the day before they set out. She'd never seen joy so intense. Now, cooped up in a jolting litter with his mother, he cried inconsolably.

"I wish you could come, I wish you could come," she muttered, but he only cried louder. She cursed Duke Humphrey's stubbornness. "Next time . . . next time we'll go together," she added, hoping she might make him understand her meaning and be consoled.

She believed all of her attention, all her mind, all her heart, was taken up with sorrow at the parting to come with her son. The gulpy panic that filled her was real enough; the anxiety gripping her heart whenever little Henry cried was more intense than ever. But there was a fizz of excitement bubbling quietly up in her too. Perhaps it was the prospect of seeing the land of her birth again that had made her put on midnight-blue velvet skirts with a scattering of silver stars. In a day or two, God willing, she'd be riding through the quiet green swell of Normandy, with French wind in her hair.

When Mistress Ryman took Henry away, what seemed hours later, he was still crying—thin, fretful wails that rent the air and set Catherine's teeth on edge. All Catherine wanted to do was sit in silence and recover. But there was no time. The traveling party was already on board ship, waiting. She'd seen Mistress Ryman's censorious look at her rich velvets and knew what she thought: Too grand for travel. But she didn't care what Mistress Ryman thought. She discarded the tearstained, crumpled linen she'd prudently put between herself and Harry. There was no time to call any of the ladies to help repair the travel damage. She'd just look over herself. She took out the comb and glass she'd been farsighted enough to bring, and began setting her horned hennin headdress straight, pinching pink back into her tired cheeks. She had to look her best.

She only realized that she must have imagined she'd be on board beside Owain—feeling the exhilarating chop and tug of the tides, watching the gulls swoop in the ship's wake, looking over the side, throwing crusts, laughing, with the painful awkwardness between them vanished—when, instead, John of Bedford offered her his big hand up the gangplank. She was aware of

Owain, bowing his head from a distance with the other knights and ladies. His eyes were fixed on her. She'd thought he'd be looking happy to see her, but his expression was pinched. He didn't acknowledge her private glance. He didn't want to be here. She could see he had no intention of coming near.

"Welcome on board, my dear," boomed Duke John cheerfully.

She inclined her head and smiled, trying not to feel crestfallen. She should be pleased to be traveling with Duke John. He was the brother-in-law she minded least: the one with the most wit and consideration mixed in with the charmless warrior virtues of the English royal brothers. He was speaking French. So it was probably just the uncertain movement of the floor under her feet that was clawing at her insides, like disappointment, and bringing a prickle to her eyes.

"English," she heard, as they passed through villages and towns. "English," from mouths hidden by drooping heads; all eyes carefully averted.

No one else seemed to notice how disliked they were. Perhaps her English companions didn't hear. Perhaps they didn't care.

None of these peasants seemed aware that she, the Queen of England, was as French as they were. Perhaps in their minds she wasn't anymore. She was as English as the rest.

Catherine hung her head.

But she was proud of her new identity when, with the four-man escort Duke John had given her, she set out at a smart trot from the Louvre across Paris, through the familiar smells, past the familiar sights, to her parents' home at the Hôtel Saint-Paul. The Parisians who saw her nudged each other and said loudly, "the Queen of England!" and knew her for a French-woman. They grinned at her, and raised their hats and fists, and sometimes, raggedly, cheered.

She was prouder still when they announced her at the Hôtel Saint-Paul, with bugles and great bass cries of "Her Majesty the Queen of England!" As she walked into the great hall, she saw, in the middle of the huddle of elderly palace folk gathered to look at their Princess coming back as a grown-up married woman and a mother, her own father's and mother's eyes: their two faces fixed on hers as yearningly as if she were an impossible, beautiful vision, an angel come to earth.

"Cobwebs everywhere," she said. She ran her finger through the dust, drawing patterns like embroidery in it, making the air dance with motes. When she touched a hanging, the silk splintered and fragmented in her hand into tiny rectangles like torn-up scraps of parchment.

"Well, everything's old," Anastaise said resignedly back, and Catherine saw the gray threads in the beguine's dark hair too. "The things; the people too . . . no energy. I do what I can."

Catherine was glad she'd asked Anastaise to move into the Hôtel Saint-Paul and look after the King. Anastaise was a good substitute for Christine: with her heart in the right place. But even Anastaise wasn't the plump, powerful animal she'd been. She'd got spindly-shanked and weak.

No one much came to the King of France at the Hôtel Saint-Paul anymore. The courtiers of France didn't bother. The English King had taken all Paris' four strongholds for himself: the Louvre on the Right Bank, the Hôtel de Nesle on the Left Bank, the Bastille Saint Anthony, inside the Saint Anthony gate, to the east, and the Castle of Vincennes out of the Saint Anthony gate and out of town. Anyone with business to transact went there, to the foreigners who walked as tall and haughty as stags while the French around them starved. "There's not an Englishman anywhere who'll pay to build a wall, or paint a piece of wood, or grow a line of wheat," Anastaise said sadly. There were no tradesmen. There was no need for them. The luxury trades that had once served France were shutting down or moving—to Burgundy or beyond. For all her excitement as she'd ridden through Paris, Catherine had seen that for herself: whole streets of goldsmiths and illuminators and embroiderers and bookmakers, empty, boarded up, finished. Rubbish blowing over the cobbles. Packs of dogs. Loose boards flapping where hopeful burglars or tramps had got in. There was no work here. There were only the beginnings of crops in the fields. It was May now, but the hard winter had gone on late. Only a few weeks ago, Anastaise said, the hungry had been grateful for what the pigs left. It had become commonplace by now for wolves to be hungry and dangerous enough to have lost their fear of the city, swimming across the Seine by night to dig up and worry newly buried bodies in the graveyards. When she could, Anastaise pawned the little treasures still lying round the Hôtel Saint-Paul to buy Isabeau her sugared almonds and rose jellies. Even the Saint-Paul gardens were running wild. Threatening foliage pushed in at the windows, stealing the light.

There was no hum and buzz of servants; no sweat and tinkle of harness and neighing horses. You couldn't even hear the lions roaring.

"They died," Anastaise said carelessly when asked. "Lions get old too."

Isabeau was shrunken: her fat had turned to soft, trembling, chicken-neck folds, powdered pink. She didn't get up when she saw her daughter, even the first time, but she held her arms wide, and clucked as Catherine came to her embrace, and, although her laughter was as rudely cheery as ever, there was a softness in her eyes. King Charles trembled too. He sat hunched in his cushions, skeletally thin, with his skin hanging off him. Catherine put her hands very gently on his shoulders, then eased herself into an embrace, feeling his brittle ribs and shoulder blades and the knobs of his spine under her hands. He didn't respond; just looked worried and shook, and wept, she realized as she drew gently back to see his wet cheeks. "It's me, Papa," she whispered. He nodded. She didn't think he understood.

Isabeau dismissed the decay around her with a grand queenly gesture, saying splendidly: "You look beautiful. More beautiful than ever. Now tell me, at *once*, all about my darling grandson . . ."

At once, Catherine put everything out of her mind except Harry. When she'd finished describing him, sometime later, she tried to make her account of her English life sound what her mother would have expected. She made the earthy dances into something more glittering; the thud and coarseness of the singing into English poetry; the dreary cold and damp-colored clothes into a sparkling ice kingdom. But as she talked and smiled, overjoyed to have her family with her again, she couldn't quite keep at bay the various painful small humiliations of the past few days.

One had come when the English arrived at the Louvre yesterday. There was no personal message for Catherine from her husband, still at Meaux. Just word via Duke John, after the Duke had finished a muttered conversation with a waiting military messenger. Henry would come to Paris only when Meaux had fallen, Duke John said; meanwhile, he sent his respects. Catherine knew no humiliation was intended. This was just how the English were.

The other burden she tried to bear quietly was her memory of Owain's eyes. Hard on her when he thought she wasn't looking, on board ship—unmoving stares full of blackness—but sliding away whenever she came near; retreating into bowed-head, veiled politeness. The eyes of an enemy. There'd been nothing she could do but sit on her cushions, watching the gulls circle and cry; feeling the anticipation with which she'd begun the journey sour and seep away; watching his back. She'd found a way to spend time with him, in her new English life; but she couldn't force him to want to renew an old friendship. She couldn't chase him round the ship. She'd briefly been hopeful again when Duke John invited Owain, her only acquaintance on board except her ladies, to dine with them. But Owain answered her questions at table as minimally as he politely could. Yes, he'd slept. No, he seldom suffered from seasickness. Had he been to Paris on his previous French voyage? Alas, no. But he'd turned willingly enough to Duke John to discuss the siege at Meaux. He'd told Duke John, with considerably more passion than had gone into any of his replies to Catherine, that it could only be a question of time before Meaux fell to a soldier of King Henry's caliber. He'd gone into details of men and machines deployed a month earlier; strategies and tactics.

"You remember it very well . . ." Duke John had said appreciatively.

"Of course," Owain had replied, sounding every inch the military-minded Englishman he'd become; "because I love my King; and there's nothing about him I admire more than his fighting skills," and he'd nodded coldly at Catherine. It had been the only time in the whole three-day journey that he had willingly met her eye.

TWENTY-TWO

Meaux had surrendered, but the town was still smoking. English soldiers were repairing the great holes they'd made in the walls.

"No executions," Duke John was saying into the shimmer of heat. "They've suffered enough."

Duke John was visiting from Paris with Owain and a troop at his side, ready to escort the King back to greet his wife now this long and exhausting siege was over. Duke John was eager to be off. He felt sorry for the young Queen, waiting so disconsolately in Paris for her husband, asking so politely if she could help plan the reunion ceremony. As a newcomer to the fighting, the Duke didn't have the bitterness of battle in him; the desire to punish the losers that came on you after months of siege and risk and fatigue and smoke in your hair.

But Henry did. He'd spent all these months here; he'd missed seeing his newborn son for this victory. If they'd surrendered months ago, this could all have been avoided. He wanted the survivors from Meaux to remember him with dread.

"Well . . . if we can't execute them," he said brightly, brutally, "how about we dig up their saint, at least?"

He looked inquiringly round the circle of gaunt, tough, tired faces, as if ready to laugh.

"Take him to England?" he added.

No one laughed back. Owain thought he saw fear flickering on the other men's faces.

The patron saint of the people of Meaux was Saint Fiacre. He was said to have been an Irishman who'd come to Gaul hundreds of years ago and set up a hermitage near the town. A village had grown up beside the hermitage. Saint Fiacre protected gardeners and the sick, especially those with hemorrhoids. In life, he was reputed to have been extremely bad-tempered. The locals said he would heap misfortune on anyone who profaned his sanctuary by moving his relics.

Even joking about digging up Saint Fiacre seemed foolhardy. The worst kind of dysentery was called Saint Fiacre's flux— what if the peppery saint cursed you with a dose of that? Or any of the humiliating piles and pains and afflictions in his arsenal? Owain also thought this aggression was out of character for Henry. The English King's most appealing characteristic had always been his moderation. There was no need to look for exotic ways to humiliate the people of Meaux. It was Henry's moderation that had ended the Welsh troubles, after all, bringing even the most hardened rebels out of the hills in the end to ask for a royal pardon and permission to live at peace with the English. And it was Henry's moderation that had persuaded Owain to start thinking of himself as—almost—English; or, at any rate, as someone who could find a future for himself among the English. Owain didn't want to hear Henry sounding so harsh.

The King must be exhausted to be talking this way, Owain thought, pardoning his beloved master. It's a good thing he's got to take a break now; go to Paris. He's overwrought. He'll calm down once he's rested.

Then, with disappointment, he also thought: Or perhaps everyone just gets crueler with age.

Very faintly, Duke John shook his head at his brother. But Henry seemed not to notice or be much discouraged by his brother's distaste. He just grinned and swayed slightly. He was thinner than Owain had seen him. Stringier, too.

"Well, perhaps you're right. We won't decide for now. Let's see what we think when we meet again," he said, as if reluctant to let go of his wish to dig up the saint and bring more sorrow on the people of Meaux. "We'll talk again after Paris."

It was the first time Catherine understood that, as Queen of England—even the quiet, awkward, tongue-tied, beginner Queen she felt herself to be—she did have some power.

When she returned to the Louvre after seeing her parents, she asked the Duke of Exeter if her parents could be supplied with new curtains. The old ones had fallen to pieces, she said. The Duke of Exeter—who was one of Henry's uncles, and the brother of the sly, clever Bishop Beaufort—was too intelligent not to respond quickly. Men were at the Hôtel Saint-Paul the next day, measuring the windows.

Catherine mentioned at the Louvre that her parents' kitchen supplies were low. Hampers of chickens, hams, eggs, cream, flour, honey, jams, and an entire wheel of cheese followed her back.

Anastaise supervised the unpacking. Her eyes were open wide. "I'd forgotten there could be so much . . . so much," she said incoherently. She snatched at another jar, undid the top, and stuck a finger in. Licking it, she said happily: "We need never have gone hungry . . ." and "Have they been eating like this all winter?"

Then she gathered Catherine impulsively in her arms, squeezing her so hard it hurt, and added: "You're a good girl . . . even if you've turned English. Looking after us like this. Whatever . . . well, never mind whatever. You really are a good girl."

Catherine wriggled out of the other woman's embrace, laughing. But she wondered what Anastaise had meant to say, before changing her mind. "Whatever Christine said?" Part of her wished she'd had the courage to ask after Christine. But, she told herself, what would be the point? Anastaise was unlikely to know. And it might only make awkwardness if Anastaise did know anything of the coldness that had crept into Catherine's relationship with Christine at the end. Anastaise had already let one monumentally tactless remark slip in front of Catherine: overhearing some passing servant's muttered comment that

Charles' army would have to surrender at Meaux if they were commanded by a bastard, Anastaise had practically shouted back, "Ah, don't call the boy a bastard until you know! Good blood tells; it will show itself; give him time!" It had only been when she'd seen Catherine's appalled eyes fix on her that she'd colored up and said, with shame in her voice, and no trace of bluster for once, "Beg pardon, Madam."

It wasn't that Anastaise didn't love Catherine. It wasn't personal. But Catherine could see Anastaise wanted Charles to be the next King of France.

She tried not to think about it. Anastaise was old, and perhaps a bit wandering, and unimportant; and she did an excellent job of looking after the old King and Queen. And at least they had food now. Catherine thought with relief that she'd personally managed to make at least one thing better. If I stay for a month or two, she told herself, I can make sure they're all right. If there was no other reason to come, it will have been worth it just to have done this.

When Catherine returned to the Louvre that evening, there was no more discussion of her parents' plight. There was no time. The Duke of Exeter, Henry's uncle, doffing his hat, smiling splendidly and smoothing back his mane of gray hair, told her that Henry was on his way to Paris with Duke John. She was to meet her husband at the castle of Vincennes and process into Paris with him. There would be more pomp and magnificence than for their Christmas here together, the Duke said. Henry wanted to make the meeting one that all of Paris would remember. Pentecost would be celebrated in style. They hoped Catherine would help them design festivities suitable for France.

She could hardly believe it. They were going to meet at last; and, if the smooth Duke was to be believed, in a way that suggested her husband had been thinking how to please her, too.

She didn't mind if there was no personal word for her from Henry. There'd be time soon enough; they'd make up for everything they'd missed during this long year.

She gasped, "Thank you . . . and I don't have any appetite for dinner," and rushed to her room to begin choosing what she would wear for the reunion, and thinking of what to say.

It would be Pentecost. She would wear green and gold. She'd learned last year that the English celebrated Pentecost, as they celebrated so much else, by drinking ale and racing their horses and performing mystery plays. This would be her chance to show Henry the beauty of the Pentecostal traditions of France. She'd take him to churches scented with the green boughs and fresh garlands of early summer. She'd show him how, during Divine service in France, the faithful were reminded of the mighty rushing wind—the spirit of God which filled Christ's disciples—by the joyful blowing of trumpets. She hoped that by gently showing Henry some of the beauties of France, she might encourage him to cultivate and preserve the civilization she'd grown up believing to be the greatest in the world, but which she now saw vanishing before her eyes. She knew she might not have another chance. This might be her last visit to her homeland.

Then she threw herself on her bed, put her chin in her hands, and rocked from side to side, feeling love and excitement fill her, as ecstatic as the Holy Spirit.

She didn't care about showing him things. She just wanted to see Henry. She'd been so lonely.

All the way to Vincennes, in the sunlight she let her mettlesome horse prance and kick up its heels. She and the Duke of Exeter, whose horse's stride remained utterly precise, utterly rhythmic throughout the journey, rode in the middle of a hundred knights. She'd been busy. There hadn't been time for all the ceremony she'd wanted, but green was the dominant color: green belts; flowers woven into the horses' manes and tails. And she, in gold and green, a vision.

She thought her heart would burst with joy when she saw the white towers and ramparts at Vincennes. They looked even lovelier than she remembered them. She could see the other column of horsemen, and hear them: another gay blast of color and trumpets coming out of the castle to meet them and escort them inside.

It felt strange to be part of a procession of people who still felt like strangers. There were so few familiar faces among the English: just the sleek Thomas of Exeter, another Beaufort uncle, at her side, and, somewhere in the middle of the throng in the packed courtyard ahead, John of Bedford and her other traveling companions. Owain Tudor, perhaps; she hadn't asked what had become of him. And, waiting under the canopy that she made out as soon as they got through the gate, Henry.

Her heart beat louder than the drums and trumpets. Her eyes were seeking him out from the first moment she saw the canopy. She was smiling wider than ever before, so wide it hurt her face.

But when she finally saw him in the crowd and fixed her eyes on him, trying to stare him into finding her face too, his distant features seemed smaller and less imposing than she remembered.

There was a mighty drumroll as she stepped under the canopy. Henry, close now, stepped forward from a phalanx of Englishmen and bowed. She raised him to his feet, laughing out loud from relief at being next to him, and with delight at seeing those familiar wide-set, prominent eyes, that long, thin face, and those slightly overfull red lips—no one could hear a thing for the noise of the drums, so it didn't matter how loudly she laughed. Then she stepped forward to give him the ceremonial public kiss and embrace expected of them both.

Henry's face came up toward her, past her; he leaned down into the kiss. He smelled the same, and she recognized her husband's light, detached smile. But the face behind it was fleshless as a skull and the skin an unhealthy white. Why was he so thin?

The drumroll held and held. The knights cheered and rattled their swords in their scabbards.

How white he was. And he was swaying.

"Henry," she shouted anxiously, though her shout passed for a whisper under the fifes and drums. "Are you well?"

Never better, her husband mouthed back, with wild, gay eyes. A lie, she could see almost at once, when his face suddenly contorted. He buried his head in her shoulder so no one could see. He leaned heavily on her. She could hear his hissing intakes of breath. Sensing he didn't want to display weakness, she put her arms round him, and the knights cheered and rattled louder than ever.

She bowed and smiled to them, so wide she bared her teeth and gums, then withdrew behind the hangings, half carrying him inside.

"What's wrong?" she asked as soon as they were alone. "You're frightening me."

But he pulled away, and began urgently feeling his way along the wall to the broad staircase that would take him to his rooms. "Nothing," he said, hurrying unsteadily toward the stairs, concentrating. There was sweat on his greenish skin. "Touch of the sun . . . something I ate . . . fine in a few minutes."

He only came back a few minutes before the cavalcade was due to leave. He looked drained but less green. A purging sickness, Catherine could see. But all he said was, "Nasty," and then, after another deep breath, "Over now." He was trying to be normal.

"Thank you for covering up for me out there," he said more coherently. He even managed a faint grin. He added: "You won't get rid of me that easily."

"Well, thank God for that," Catherine said. Then, softening over the familiar clipped way he talked, she added with a burst of affection, "I've missed you."

And when he crinkled up his eyes and said, "Missed you too," her heart swelled so she thought it might burst. She thought he meant it.

There was so much to tell. About Harry: the little boy's wide blue eyes, the way he smiled, the way he crawled, the look on his face when he'd first tasted egg, the shape of his fingers (Catherine's) and legs (Henry's). There was so much to ask. It had been more than a year.

And he was still so pale.

"You're still not well," she said. "I can see. You can't ride to Paris. Let's ask for two litters."

But he wouldn't. He only laughed; and she laughed along at the revulsion in his eyes. "Me, in a litter," he said in a stronger voice, shrugging the absurd idea off. She could see he didn't think it at all a suitable vehicle for a warrior. So she let him ride, and took the Queen's litter herself.

Sitting back in it, letting the curtains be hooked up around her, she chuckled with relief at the memory of his laugh, and relaxed back against the silks. Henry was back—her protector; her friend—and all was well with the world. Henry's qualities now seemed familiar: his straightforwardness, low-key humor, underlying ambition, and his love of war. Looking at her husband just now, she'd felt she'd come to know him through and through since marrying him. His qualities were all the best possible ones for Harry's father to have—little Harry, the center of her world now, whom she missed so much at every moment of every day, who was so young and so vulnerable and so beautiful—and who, for many years to come, would need a strong man's protection. Even Henry's stubbornness would help protect their son. Although Catherine was aware that she could look at her husband, touch him, kiss him, without her heart doing any of the melting, swooning things dwelt on by love poetry, it didn't seem to matter anymore. Romantic love was for overwrought children, maidens, and striplings, the young, under a full moon. She was a matron of twenty, and a mother; she was beyond all that. She liked Henry and admired him more than anyone she could think of. That was grown-up love. In the privacy of her litter, lying back and smiling over the knowledge that she had both husband and son in her life, both Henry and Harry, Catherine felt more contented than ever before—blessed.

There were frequent stops on the way to Paris. From inside her litter Catherine didn't always know why. It was only once they had processed back to the Louvre that she saw Henry was still unwell.

He retired with his wife to the royal rooms. "It's been too long," he said, putting his hands round her waist and laughing down at her. Catherine laughed, happy enough at the thought of making love to her husband; happy that God had been good to her in her life.

He was pulling her clothes off her as soon as they got

through the door; hurrying; muttering hasty endearments in her ear. Flattered, she thought it was the intensity of his desire pushing him on. It was only after they'd separated and she'd sprawled languorously across the bed, ready to talk, that she saw there might be another reason for the rush. His face had got that deathly pallor again. He didn't want to lie and chat with her—or couldn't. He kept interrupting her stories of Harry and vanishing to the privy. And he was still stubbornly pretending nothing was wrong.

"Call a doctor," she said.

He flapped a dismissive hand, and replied too casually: "Oh, doctors . . . Quacks, all of them. Bunch of old women."

That, she realized, meant no: meant that real men got better by themselves. She suppressed her impatience.

"How long have you been like this?" she asked an hour later when he hadn't improved.

He tried to laugh. "It's bloody Saint Fiacre," he said. "Getting his revenge. That's what they'll say. Isn't it?" He caught her eye as if inviting her to echo his mocking laugh. But his mirth cut off before she could join in, and he clutched at his gut and curled in on himself, going pale again.

"What do you mean?" she asked.

"All my generals said we shouldn't have executions after taking Meaux. But we were there for months . . . lost a lot of men, wasted a lot of time," Henry muttered between spasms of pain. "Had to do something to show my displeasure. Didn't want to let the French think I'm soft. So I'm having Saint Fiacre dug up. Going to take him back to England."

Catherine crossed herself and winced. She didn't know whether she truly believed a saint would take revenge for the indignity of being disinterred; but all the stories about Saint Fiacre suggested he'd been a curmudgeonly, vindictive sort of holy man in life. He was the patron saint of piles. Why run the risk?

"What—Duke John, and your other generals, they agreed that it was a good idea to dig up a saint's relics?" she asked, unable to believe they could all be such reckless fools.

Henry shook his head. "None of them," he mumbled. "So I

said I'd leave it till after this break in Paris. Then thought . . .
this morning . . . why waste time? . . . Gave the order after all."

He laughed again at the look on Catherine's face. It seemed
to make him feel better. He sat up.

"Well, send word back now," Catherine said. Henry's stubbornness was not a good quality; not in this situation. "Tell
them to stop."

"Ahh . . . you don't believe it too, do you?" he said. He
leaned forward, chucked her under the chin. Smiled defiantly
back. "With all your book learning, as superstitious as . . . ?"

She never learned what superstitious being he'd been going
to compare her with. He stopped; clutched at his gut; choked;
and ran for the door.

Henry's disappearances went on all through the banquet at the
Louvre that night. The pains let up a little, allowing him to
sleep, but he refused to share a bed with Catherine all the same.
He had a pallet made up next to the privy. The pain came back
before the Mass at Notre Dame at dawn. The King of England
was in no fit state to notice the cathedral interior, decked with
greenery and ribbons in the fresh colors of early summer—his
Queen's design.

There was a further delay at midday, before the procession
of the English lords of Paris, waiting in the courtyard of the
Louvre, could set off with their King in pride of place. They
crossed the city to the Hôtel de Nesle on the Left Bank, where
a group of hopeful, opportunistic Parisian mummers had mastered the unfamiliar mystery play of Saint George for their foreign audience.

Henry left before the performance was over. "I'll come too,"
Catherine muttered as he got up. He shook his head. He was
sweating again.

She sat in the gardens under a lime tree the next day, half sleeping, feeling dazedly sorry for her husband. Henry had sat up all
night in his privy, trying to be quiet, trying not to groan. She'd
followed him there. She'd sent away the servants. She'd put water and rags outside, where he could get them. But whenever

she'd said, "Henry, can I help?" through the door, he'd just tried to sound normal and said, "Go to sleep . . ." and "It's nothing serious . . ." and ". . . almost over."

He wasn't grateful. He wanted his servants back. He couldn't let her see weakness.

Sighing, wishing he'd heeded her advice about Saint Fiacre, she had called his men back.

He had left at dawn. They all had. They were on their way to a new siege against Charles at Cosne-sur-Loire. He had whispered to her, as he came to kiss her goodbye, that it didn't matter if his gut was still churning. It happened to everyone on battlefields. It would pass.

"Stay a couple more days," she had pleaded. "Rest. Let your body recover."

But he had only laughed that dismissive laugh again: the laugh of a man with work to do. "You'll be sending me off to battle in a litter if I'm not careful."

After he'd gone, when she could still see the evidence of his having been there—crumpled sheets, a forgotten nightgown, the smell of man's sweat, and a privy she'd prefer not to enter—Catherine had gone on lying on the bed, looking at the bright stripes of light that seemed to burn round the edge of the shutter, feeling disappointed and alone and unimportant.

She'd thought of the unnoticed green branches at the cathedral; the charms of her green and gold dress, which he hadn't mentioned; the unheeded elegance of the flowers woven into all those horses' manes and tails. She'd thought of her unheeded advice about doctors and Meaux. She shook her head. He'd been ill; but he hadn't had time for her either. He never had. How had she convinced herself that everything was so perfect? If only her husband would pay attention to what she said and thought. If only . . .

Lying there, not wanting to get up and think of things to do to fill the day, and the next day, and more days—the weight of all those pointless days looming emptily ahead—just so she could justify being here without Henry, and without Harry. Perhaps she should have stayed with her child all along and left her husband and parents to fend for themselves. Catherine found herself feeling as invisible and ghostly and lonely as in those long-ago days at the palace, when she'd been her father's nurse. Only it was worse now—more invisible and ghostly and lonely—because there was no one here to talk to anymore; no confidante; no Christine.

At least her parents still needed her. At least she could go to the Hôtel Saint-Paul. She could stay a few days there, now there was nothing else to do.

But even that didn't seem as much consolation now as it might have done before.

She was sitting alone under the lime trees in the Saint-Paul gardens that evening, watching the sun set, when the King's messenger came.

She knew it must be Owain Tudor. Who else would have known to look for her here, in the depths of these gardens?

He was out of breath; the horse behind him jangled. The heat of the perfect day lingered. He wiped his brow before bowing; took his hat down into his hands. He looked careful, as if telling himself not to let his guard down, she thought.

Stung, she barely greeted him. Just lowered her head and raised one eyebrow.

When he told her the King had stopped at Corbeil to regain his strength, she only nodded.

"He's sent the rest of the party on," Owain continued. He had a few freckles on his cheekbones. His bare head was sweaty and rumpled. She loved the way the black hair fell on his neck. With *him* there'd been poetry and moonlight all right; there'd been a time when she'd invested the fall of that hair on that neck with a significance that, even now, tied her tongue and put heat in her cheeks. She never should have . . . if only she could wipe the memory out forever . . .

She inclined her head again. She wanted him to go. But he stayed, shifting from foot to foot as if he had more to say.

She looked up.

"You mustn't worry," he said, and for a flash she could see the old tenderness in his eyes; hear softness in his voice. Even though she knew Owain would only say something like that if

318

he was worried himself about the King's illness, the very fact of his wanting to reassure her was reassuring.

Like a flower turning its face toward the sun, she leaned gratefully forward, sighed, smiled. But even that tiny shift of atmosphere was too much for him. He flinched and remounted.

"I'll leave tomorrow, early," he said through his teeth. "If you'd like me to take a letter back . . ."

She said, bewildered: "Where will I find you? Do you need rooms?"

"No. The Louvre," he said shortly, letting his horse frisk— an excuse to be excused. He didn't want to take letters for her, she could see. She couldn't write a letter and get it to him at the Louvre by dawn, anyway; he'd have to volunteer to stop here on his way back out of Paris.

She said sadly, "Then . . . no letter."

The June heat didn't let up. The crops were burning up in the fields. There was smallpox. Anastaise said it was commonest among the English, but Catherine thought that was just her wishful thinking. There was a lot of dysentery: the worst kind, Saint Fiacre's. The kind Henry had. There were doctors attending to him now, Catherine heard from Paris. She sent daily to the Louvre, or visited in person so she could have news as soon as it came. That was an admission of her own lowly status among the English; they all knew that word about the King's health never first came to the King's wife.

In July, the churches of Paris started praying for his health. There were many messengers. But the next time Owain came back, it was from Vincennes, in the middle of August. He looked as though he hated the task he'd set himself, but Catherine was grateful that he, at least, made a point of seeking her out after reporting to the dukes, to bring her up to date on her husband's health.

The King was no better, Owain said, so he'd left Corbeil and gone by barge to the comfort of Vincennes castle. He'd tried to ride the last leg of the journey, but failed. He was weak: almost at the end of his strength.

"They put him in a litter," Owain said.

Catherine bit her lip. It must be serious.

After a moment, Owain added: "The Duke of Bedford and the Duke of Exeter are called to Vincennes."

Vincennes was only an hour's ride away. Humbly, Catherine said: "And me, should I go too?"

Distantly, Owain replied: "I have no instructions."

"Owain . . ." she pleaded. "Tell me . . . please. He's my husband. Is he dying?"

Owain looked startled at that. Perhaps he hadn't had time, with all the riding to and fro, to imagine the end of Henry. He looked back at Catherine with dawning horror in his eyes.

Very slowly, he nodded. "I think . . . yes." There was none of the old guardedness in his voice now, just shocked honesty.

"Will you take me back with you?" she asked. "To Vincennes?" She was thinking only of Henry. She was thinking: Has he no time for me, even now, even when his death might be upon him?

Owain had lost the distance and the quiet hostility that he'd come with. But he shook his head nevertheless. "He's only called for the others to help him draw up documents," he explained, every inch the Englishman; every inch the devoted disciple of Henry of England. "A will, a war plan, plans for who should govern England and France if he dies before your son grows up. It's a business meeting . . . he didn't send for you . . . he's not ready for farewells . . ."

He looked agonized. She could see that he was imagining the torment she must be in; that there must be pity for her mixed up in his hero-worship of her husband. Then he said in a rush: "He doesn't like to feel vulnerable. It would unman him if you were there. He might get well anytime. I can't take you now. But I'll come back for you . . . if"—he lifted apologetic shoulders—"if it's the last minute." He put a hand on her arm. "I promise."

Catherine was ashamed that even at that moment she could be so aware of Owain's touch.

She was glad that night to be at the Hôtel Saint-Paul. She wanted to feel at home; to have people who loved her close by.

Before dawn she went to the chapel and lit twelve candles, spiking a couple of them sideways so she could enjoy the wax pouring in a sweet rush down their sides.

She'd come downstairs when she heard the monks finishing their singing of Matins. The air was hot and scented with incense.

She couldn't sleep.

If Henry died, if England were to be ruled by a baby, she'd been thinking, how long would it take before that united phalanx of English royal brothers and uncles divided, just as the greatest families in France had a generation ago? John of Bedford, Humphrey of Gloucester, the Beaufort uncles . . . soon enough they'd all be grabbing for their share of her baby's inheritance. The Kingdom of England would destroy itself with greed; would turn into the same hell France had become. And in France there'd be Charles, waiting to grab back her Harry's title and future . . .

They'd all be swept away.

Harry was only nine months old. The thought of his pudgy cheeks and feet, of his trusting eyes, made her sick with longing for him, sick with the need to protect him.

But how? Catherine had none of the influence her mother had once had as Queen. The English had no time for women. Or for the French. England was full of French prisoners. Her uncle of Bourbon, who couldn't raise his ransom. Her cousin Charles of Orléans, another prisoner, who spent his days writing love poetry to no one. Her husband's stepmother, Queen Jeanne of Navarre, who had had her lands and rents confiscated shortly after Henry and Catherine married (officially, the suspicion was that Queen Jeanne had tried to kill Henry by witchcraft; unofficially, everyone knew the King had just desperately needed every penny he could get his hands on).

She could never hope to win any battles fought in England. Still, if Henry did die, if the need really arose, she'd have to find a way through her powerlessness. She'd have to fight for her son.

She was itching and creeping with fear. She gathered up her skirts so she could kneel down. If only she wasn't so alone.

It took a moment to realize that she wasn't quite alone, at least now, here, in this chapel. Her mother and father were already kneeling, crossing themselves, mouths moving. Anastaise behind them. Her mother looking up already, waving glittering fingers at her.

There was a ghost of her mother's old mischief in that smile. "We don't sleep much," she explained in a piercing, cheerful whisper. "We're old. We are praying for your Henry."

The sky was going from pallid to bright blue by the time Catherine went to her chamber, a little comforted by her family's presence around her. The first thing she heard was something loud banging against her window. A branch. A pebble.

She went to it. Owain was standing below, shading his eyes and looking up. Catherine's first thought was a joyous rush of recognition: How did he know this was my room? Her second only came after she'd taken in his bleak, exhausted face. Like her, he was still in yesterday's clothes. He must have been riding all night—there, then back. He had bad news.

"Should I come now?" she called quietly. "I'm dressed. It won't take long to get new horses."

He shook his head. "I'm sorry," he said, and the red-rimmed eyes turned up to hers reflected her terror of the future. "It's too late."

For a moment she thought, in a flash of panic, of her son, so young, and all alone at the mercy of his English relatives. Then, in another flash of panic, she thought Owain would ride off. She could hear a horse somewhere behind, with its head down in the grasses, jingling. He must be in a hurry.

She called down, "Wait!" She remembered the rush of silk against her thighs, the muscle and dash of her panic as she ran down the stairs. They were cast adrift on this new storm, all of them. And no one knew yet. No one but her and this man.

She burst outside, sobbing with breathlessness, into the gentle cool of the morning. There was a bird singing overhead.

"Wait!" she cried again; but now she saw her voice was far too loud. He was right there.

She whispered: "Tell me what happened." Her head was drumming with thoughts, each one banging for attention, a disbelief she thought would turn to grief for her husband, and pulses of *I must get home* and *Harry* . . . but the one that came to the fore was this. Owain Tudor had brought his news to her first. He'd known she was here, at the Hôtel Saint-Paul. He'd stopped to tell her. He'd done her that courtesy. It was on his way west across the city to the Louvre. It was only a few moments' detour. And she was Henry's wife . . . Queen . . . widow. She deserved no less. But no one else would have bothered. None of the English would even have remembered her.

He was stammering something out, but she couldn't make sense of the words. What could you say to explain death?

He was weeping. She could see wet on his cheeks too, tears falling unheeded and soaking into the dark wool of that incongruous Augustinian habit. "Gone," Owain was saying, with the bleakness of a child losing a beloved father. "Just like that."

And then she was in his arms, holding him, comforting him. And then they were two bodies, pressed together, young and alive in the shadow of death, twining closer in the dew of a late summer's morning, ignoring the tang of turning leaves. And then they were kissing.

There was a rhythm and a timetable to death. Henry's entrails would already be being removed. Soon they'd boil his body to separate flesh and bones for the long journey to England. A King of England must be buried at Westminster. She would follow the procession to her adopted home. There was no escaping that reality. Owain needed to carry word of the King's death to the English administration at the Louvre. They'd have to start the mourning. Ring the bells.

Let them wait, she thought, wrapping herself closer to Owain's height, holding the back of his head with one hand, running the other hand down his back. Let reality wait.

She whispered. She only meant to mutter, Thank you. She was so grateful.

She shouldn't have spoken. Shouldn't have reminded him of

this grab at life's fleeting beauty that they were both making, while pretending not to notice what their bodies were doing.

He stepped back; removed his hands from her back; turned his body away and put his head in his hands. "Oh God," she heard him groan, "what have I done?" Then, so quickly and quietly she could hardly make out the words, squeezing out between clenched teeth, "My vows. Betrayed." He pulled his hands away from his eyes and the gaze that fixed on hers was both horrified and accusing. As if the next thought that struck him was even worse than betraying the vows he planned to make, he added: "Betrayed my lord."

"He's gone," she said tenderly, reassuring him as though he were a child. "You haven't betrayed him. Henry's dead . . ."

Was that the first time either of them had admitted that out loud? As the meaning of those words sank in, Catherine's calm faded. She added, more hastily: "You haven't betrayed anything. We shouldn't have . . ." Shrugging off their kiss as if it hadn't meant anything to her; as if she'd hardly been aware of his desire, or hers. "A kiss. A mistake. We didn't know what we were doing." But then she clutched at his arm. If he went, she'd be alone. Holding on tight, she finished in a small voice: ". . . I'm so frightened."

She must have sounded scared enough. Owain took her back in an awkward, rough embrace—a brother's embrace, this time, or pretending to be. "Of course," he said, in a muffled, penitent voice from somewhere above, rocking her, yet holding her at a more modest distance. "You must be."

A reprieve. She buried her head in his shoulder, breathing in his smell. Stealing a memory of his essence, a part of his soul, in case there was nothing else.

"My father was a child king," she said, losing herself in the rocking motion. "They say all the wars here started after he went mad—because the uncles and cousins and brothers knew there'd be no one to stop them grabbing a bit more power here, and a bit more land there. But that's not true. The wars started long before he went mad. The uncles and cousins and brothers were already used to grabbing whatever they wanted by then. They'd been doing it ever since he was a child. Poor

Papa . . . he grew up watching them doing it, brazenly, right under his nose. What could a child do to rein in the most powerful men in the land? He never learned to use his authority to stop them. They just laughed at him: sent the boy off to joust a bit more, climb more mountains, get drunk at another masked ball—throw himself about more. And he rushed about like a lunatic, eager to please, like any child, doing their bidding. That's what did it. The rushing about; a child helpless before adults but supposed to rule them. The helplessness. That's what sent him mad."

Owain rocked her.

"You're thinking . . . you'll have to stop anything like that happening to your son," he muttered, after a while. After another pause, he said: "You're wondering how."

She nodded. She was so grateful to him for trying to imagine her dilemma. She didn't want this gentle moment to end. She couldn't bear for him to go again.

"I know so little about England," she said pitifully. "I can't even make my ladies do what I want. I wish I had someone to guide me."

Perhaps Owain was beginning to be aware of the gossamer threads she was casting around him. At any rate, he stopped rocking her and stepped back—not in a jolting, angry panic this time, but quietly, as if he sensed it was time to leave.

"You'll find a way," he said. "You found a way to bring your father back from utter insanity . . . you found a way to bring your mother back to him . . . you found a way"—and here his voice hardened a little—"to the marriage you wanted. You're capable."

He clicked to his horse, and, when it refused to pay attention but went on placidly eating the patch of greenery it had established itself in, stretched out a hand and took its bridle.

"I'm a widow now," she pleaded. "Henry's widow. And you know what it means to be a widow. Do you remember Christine complaining that everyone ignores widows, or cheats them, or steals from them—or all three at once. We both know that. I can't look after Harry—can't even look after myself—without help."

She was about to say, I need you. But even as the words formed on her lips she could see him shake his head.

She'd lost him.

Owain said: "I have to go." He wriggled his foot into the stirrup; mounted. He went on, looking down, as if he felt safer talking to her from up there, "We're in grief. Both of us, in our different ways. We've lost our lord." She could see from his face that he wasn't, after all, going to take the comfort she'd offered of pretending that kiss hadn't happened. His anger was back. He added, with a tinge of bitterness: "I wish we hadn't . . . I hadn't . . . dishonored him while he's still warm."

She thought he might leave without another glance, but he stopped in the doorway. There was something almost like regret in his voice when he said, "I can't help you with what lies ahead. You're a queen. All I could be is your creature. And I can't be your creature."

She said, "Please." She could think of nothing better to say.

Owain replied, with a finality that proved he'd thought about this before: "It would destroy me. I've chosen a life I can live."

That dingy habit. He couldn't mean to be a friar. Not really. And it couldn't be because of her . . .

She opened her lips to say "Please" again, but he'd gone.

Duke John guessed at Catherine's sense of abandonment and tried to comfort her a little.

"He would have sent for you," the Duke said. "Once he was through with the papers." He patted her hand ineffectually. "But there was so much business to do first. He'd never thought he might die so young, and with his son so young. He had to think it all out . . . there and then . . ."

He shook his head. He didn't like to remember the horror of those fetid rooms at Vincennes: the purgings; the buckets; the cloths; the stink. Henry's eyes burning in that shrunken head as he tried to frame each clause of the will carefully enough so that his baby son's inheritance couldn't be whittled away. His bones sticking out. Calculation and legal jargon, broken by vomiting and death on the breath. The care; the clerks; the scratching of quills on parchment. The prayers. Duke John would have given a lot to have been spared the sight of his brother's miserable, unsoldierly end. He thought the girl was lucky not to know how ugly it had been.

"But didn't he ask for me?" Catherine couldn't help asking. "Wasn't there anything personal?"

Duke John patted at her hand again. "It was all done for you," he said sincerely; "for your boy."

He couldn't see the difference. But he could see the hurt in her eyes.

"He's made good arrangements," he added, not knowing what else might comfort her. "You can rest assured of that."

She nodded, feeling defeated. Duke John had already detailed the arrangements that concerned Catherine and Harry. Duke John was to be Regent of France and stay in Paris to run the war, while his brother Duke Humphrey would be Protector of England with responsibility for Catherine and Harry. Mother and son, with overlapping households, would live together in the royal castles of the Thames Valley during Harry's infancy. Once the King turned seven and his infancy was over, Catherine's influence would diminish. Male tutors and guardians would be appointed, and Harry would be taught the ways of men and warfare, and be crowned. Catherine hadn't asked, and he hadn't spelled out, what her role as Queen Mother would be after Harry's seventh birthday, when her household would be unlinked from her son's. She assumed she might have remarried by then. Otherwise, nothing seemed to be suggested. It didn't matter. It was over six years away. It seemed too remote to imagine.

She dug her fingernails into her palms until they nearly drew blood. Petulantly, she thought: I don't want good arrangements. She was grateful, more than grateful, of course she was, because she was terrified of the chaos that might so easily come upon them all at any time; and this hasty last-minute ordering of Henry's effects, while imperfect, at least left her in a better position than the cruel tumble into widowhood and financial ruin and legal chaos, all at once, that so many others had experienced and Christine had written about. But she so wanted her husband to have left her something else, too—a final prayer, or word, or note, or kiss, or instruction—something, anything, to show he'd had her on his mind, and not just his duty.

It was too late for any of that now; too late for anything except a future without Henry's protection.

Masses were sung all over Paris while the arrangements were made to send Henry's body home.

Catherine, the Duke her brother-in-law, and the Duke her uncle-in-law, in the plainest of black, attended the cathedral of Notre Dame, followed by a cortege of Englishmen.

Catherine and her mother and father and Anastaise prayed together in the quiet of the Hôtel Saint-Paul's chapel for her husband's soul.

Catherine thought they might be the only French people to do so, for all the ringing of bells in Paris that the dukes had ordered. And even Anastaise only prayed for the English King out of a servant's loyalty to the whims of her masters.

The King of England's cortege set off from Paris two weeks later, on a gray, gusting morning. The summer was over. The weather had turned. Men in white, carrying torches, surrounded the bier. The household servants streamed behind in black, with the great procession of lords behind them, including the King of Scotland, who had been in France attending on the King of England. At the very back of the procession, a mile or two away from the bier, sat Queen Catherine in her black, in her litter.

Above the coffin, visible to all the crowds lining the roads and filling the churches at every one of the hundreds of Masses sung along the way, lay a figure of boiled leather made in Henry's likeness, complete even to the hair. It was wrapped in purple bordered with ermine. Its feet wore golden sandals. There was a diadem of gold and jewels on its head, a scepter in its right hand, and in the left a golden cross and ball. Catherine shuddered at the sight of it—a nightmare version of Henry, the kind of image you could imagine squelching out of a night bog on a moonless night. It had been Duke John's commission: designed to terrify the French into submission. He was a good man, Duke John, but with no taste. She kept her eyes down.

She was glad to be far from the horrible image. When they stopped for the night, she kept her face veiled.

It would take till November to get to London. There would be an important stop at Saint-Denis, the holy abbey dedicated to the patron saint of French royalty, where all the kings of France since the dawn of time had been buried. Catherine's duties at Saint-Denis had been much discussed among English brothers and uncles. She was to intercede for Henry with the Abbé. She was to ask for a blessing for her husband, who, while not a King of France himself, was the father of the next King of France, and had for many years ruled a significant part of the Most Christian Kingdom with the blessing of the current King Charles VI. Once that had been obtained (and it would be obtained, of course, since the holy abbey of Saint-Denis was in English hands now), the English procession would move on, through Rouen, Abbeville and Hesdin, making many stops between each town for prayers, then to Calais and England.

Catherine had submitted quietly to the frenzy of planning and ritual from the start. She'd moved, as she was required to, from her family at the Hôtel Saint-Paul, looking glassy-eyed at her mother and father, her father lost in his own confusion, her mother seeming shrunken too, patting helplessly at her. "I didn't know you would take it so badly," Isabeau said, strangely hushed, so understanding that Catherine felt her red-eyed, silent composure would crack. "But you have a son; you'll find your strength in him, believe me. Whatever else happens, our children are our great joy, our consolation . . ."

Her father was unwell on the day Catherine left. She went up to his chamber to kiss him goodbye, and found him sitting on his bed, with white stubble on his trembling chin, staring at the great billows of gray cloud folding up in the sky outside. "They all go," he said anxiously, as if Henry's spirit was about to come at him from the clouds.

But she didn't want to have a nonsense conversation with him; not now, when she was leaving. She cut through his words. "Pray for me, Papa," she whispered, embracing him. "I will for you."

He only looked back at her, then smiled a pleading smile. "You'll bring the boy next time?" he asked.

"Of course I will," she promised, softening, lingering in his arms, touched by the idea that he was longing to meet little Harry and hold his grandson in his arms.

She had to go. But she stole a last look at her father from the doorway. He was staring at the clouds again, and his lips were moving. "Poor Charles," he was saying. "Poor Charles."

Isabeau came out, with Anastaise attending her, to settle her in the litter and bless her for the journey. Catherine watched them fuss around, tucking in her robes. They all knew it was unlikely she would be back—unlikely they'd meet again on this earth. "I will come back," she said anyway. "God willing. I will bring Harry."

She had to lie. They all did. She couldn't cry for this farewell. There were so many other tears to be shed; and once she started, would she stop? Catherine turned away from her mother's eyes, which weren't tearful either but haunted, as soon as her litter started shuddering off down Saint Anthony's Road to the Louvre. She felt frozen; hardly able to move, weighed down with a fear that went beyond tears.

No one seemed to mind if she did very little or excused herself very early or appeared at dinner—at every improvised banquet of kings and dukes—without a word, without eating. She was supposed to be heartbroken. It was in the order of things. The great machine of statehood was built to cope with her grief and move on.

She didn't know what had become of Owain. She didn't dare ask where he had been sent; whether he was in the cortege somewhere, avoiding her, or at the front, or back in England. There was no point in thinking about Owain, who didn't want to know her, when everything was lost. She tried to make her thoughts of the husband she'd lost. She tried to pray.

Owain would have done anything to get away from Paris after letting his body betray him into that mortifying kiss. He'd done everything since that other return from France, two years earlier, to make sure he would never get caught in this trap again. At least he thought he had. But here he was.

Back then, his plan had seemed so clear: forget poetry, a young man's rash self-indulgence, and follow Christine's ascetic example instead, devoting himself to learning; taking himself, step by step, through the great classics of history, philosophy, science, and devotion, so that sooner or later the furious anguish in his heart would fade, and he would gain wisdom and peace of mind. Then, when he fully knew himself, he would take his eternal vows.

But now? Every one of those hundreds of days at Saint Mary's—in the honey-stone cell, in the library, in the chapel—wasted. All those resolutions made after all those endless hours on his knees, staring into candle flames—broken.

She'd seen him, and thought, like a cat noticing a mouse, that she'd like to call him back to play with. She'd broken his composure. He'd let her. What a fool he was. And she: so cruel, so cruel.

He'd been so sure he'd mastered himself.

He crossed the Channel in a wool packboat, sitting in the hold on stinking, greasy bales of wool, muttering rosary after rosary in a frenzy of self-reproach that seemed to get worse, not better, with every exhausting hour. He hated himself, and her, even, for the way this turmoil was getting in the way of what should be all he could think about—his grief for his lost master.

Even when he fell asleep, it was not to memories of Henry but to wild dreams of galloping all the way to Jerusalem, in a pilgrimage that would at last rip the sin from out of his heart.

If not Jerusalem, he thought, waking up under gray skies to see white cliffs looming up ahead—the southern English chalk faces that now signified home—he would lock himself away in some great act of penance, a mortification of the flesh. A hair shirt; lashings; forty days of hunger. He'd ask the Bishop to set him the penance, he thought heatedly.

Then he imagined the Bishop's clever, worldly face with its wide mouth—a mouth that often quivered on the brink of unkind laughter—looking back at him as he made that request.

Unlike the other royal brothers and uncles, who'd been irritated by Owain's wish to leave the war and return to Oxford, the more sophisticated Bishop had been interested in the young Welshman's self-questioning, his yearning to find the most honorable way to live his life (or perhaps the Bishop had just wanted to further irritate his kinsmen by taking Owain up). Yet Owain could suddenly imagine the Bishop's amused, nasal reply if he now requested that dreadful penances be imposed on him: "Too much mortification, surely . . . what can you possibly have done that is bad enough to justify all this punishment . . . are you by any chance taking yourself too seriously . . . indulging in the sin of pride, dear boy?"

Cringing at the thought of the humiliation he would bring on himself, he shook his head. He'd have to think of another way. He'd have to wait till he'd delivered his message to Westminster, and prayed, and rewarded himself with a full night's blessed sleep. There must be a way out of this pain; a way forward. Perhaps once his head had stopped whirling with sleeplessness and sorrow at the loss of his master, and shock at the memory of *her,* the one he refused to call up but couldn't let go of either, it would be easier to see where that path lay.

TWENTY-THREE

The bells were already clanging at Saint-Denis long before the procession reached the abbey gates. Catherine, whose head ached from the stuffiness of the closed litter, opened the curtains and felt she could almost see the deafening waves of gloom buckling and bending the trees. But it was only the wind.

There was a knot of peasants standing at the roadside. Weeping. There were more coming from the muddy fields, with hay in their hair and their pitchforks still in their hands. They weren't coming to stare at the King of England's image, a mile ahead. They were staring straight at her: and those who weren't sobbing and keening had haunted eyes.

Catherine sat up straighter. "God rest his soul," she heard one female voice sniffle.

God rest his soul.

There'd been no tears till now. Who in France would truly mourn the passing of the King of England? There'd been just awe at the passing of life, the stillness of death. She'd seen fear of change in some of the faces that had passed before her, anxious eyes, but no grief. She began to listen properly. The litter-bearers too. The litter bucked and heaved as they craned their necks.

The main cortege was already at the abbey gate. Far ahead, she could see Duke John riding back down the road toward her from the center of that procession, at a stately canter, followed by three knights. She stared dully at them, in case one might be . . . But none of them was Owain.

She watched Duke John's face coming up, turning from a blur to a gooseberry-eyed whole. He looked worried; worse. She leaned forward, pushing the curtains away. He swept his hat off.

"Your Highness's father, His Majesty of France," Duke John said without preamble. But she knew by then that her father was dead. She knew because she'd opened the curtains so wide she could see three of the litter-bearers, and they all had silent tears streaming down their cheeks.

No one could have expected two kings to die.

Duke John spent less than an hour at Saint-Denis before riding off to supervise the other funeral preparations now starting in Paris. He and Catherine's mother would be the chief mourners at the King of France's funeral.

Catherine said: "May I come? May I attend to my father? Mourn with my mother?"

But he shook his head. There was no time for girlish feelings in all this. "Your place is here with your husband. You were his Queen. Take him home. Your son needs you."

She began, "But—"

Duke John said warningly: "Your son, Harry, King of England, is now King of France too."

Titles no man had held together before, she realized: the most powerful titles in the world. Held by a child of nine months old, she thought, dazed. No wonder the peasants had frightened eyes.

"But you won't know how to bury my father," she insisted. She was surprised to hear her voice trembling. All her childish fear of the English, with their casual, improvised beliefs, was rushing back. The English here had no possibility of understanding how sacred were the rituals the French lived and died by. She could guess why Duke John might not want her to stay. He wouldn't want much made of the King of France's death. There would be no coronations in either country until after Henry had survived infancy. Meanwhile, Duke John would almost certainly want to stress the continuity in power, rather than any unsettling change. But, however important he said it was for her to take Henry's body home, however important it was to go home to Harry, she couldn't leave Papa's mortal remains in this man's amateurish charge.

"Papa was old," she quavered. "And he was King from the cradle. And so many of the—of *our*—great French nobility have died. There may not be anyone left who remembers how to bury a king . . . in the proper way . . ."

Duke John shrugged, at first with infuriating English carelessness, as if that sort of thing didn't matter in the least; as if you could just make up some sort of solemnity and it would be all right, more or less, and God would excuse it, and no one would much care. But he stopped when he saw her face crumple. He was a kind man, deep down, even if he didn't understand how a ritual could be so important. He put an awkward arm around her as her body curled up on herself—as her eyes at last filled with tears; as her chest heaved and jerked and hiccuped with misery. He wasn't altogether without imagination, Duke John. He had an idea of how to comfort her, at least.

He walked her through the crowd in the courtyard. It was like a beehive with a stick in it out there. The Duke of Exeter was shouting for calm; rushing the lords to their quarters to stop the hum and buzz of panicky talk. But the English earls, all the same, were eluding him, pacing up and down in twos and threes, muttering. Half the earls and dukes of England were here, and all of them were on high alert, nostrils flared like warhorses, sniffing danger in the air.

Now Catherine had started crying, it was just as she'd feared: she couldn't stop. She couldn't look up. She couldn't open her eyes. She was choking; she couldn't get it out fast enough.

"Losing a parent . . . nothing quite like it. Especially when you've just lost a husband," she heard Duke John's voice say with rough embarrassment from somewhere far above. "Here we are . . . you'll feel at home here. Go into the abbey, say a prayer for your father. It'll calm you down."

"I should stay and bury him," she said again, but so tearfully now that it no longer counted as an argument. "My own father."

"No," Duke John said back, kindly but very firmly. "Your place is with the next generation. You can come back to France when it's time to crown the child; not before. So say your prayers for the old man now; this is your chance. It'll be my job after that to clear up the past."

Catherine shrank into the familiar dusk of the abbey, away from the sounds of English, into the scented air of a place that represented everything sacred about France and its royalty. She sank into a corner, far from any of the chapels, and sobbed her heart out.

She was safe here, at least, among her own. There were no hostile eyes; no don't-give-a-damn shrugs; no need to explain. Gradually the awe that always filled her here stopped her tears. She bent her head in prayer.

Three of her brothers were buried in these walls, and all her kingly ancestors. The same family had always been kings of France, and always would be. God had blessed the dynasty for all eternity. The sacred blood of Charlemagne and his descendants ran in her veins and Harry's: *purus* and *clarissimus,* they said, a darker, richer, purpler color than ordinary people's blood. And all future kings for the rest of time would come here, just as she was doing now, to seek protection from Saint Denis, who interceded for the princes of that sacred bloodline with God.

"God preserve them all," she muttered. He would. She knew that He would.

Saint Denis—converted to Christianity long ago by Saint Paul himself, later Bishop of Athens, who'd evangelized the French, and became in his saintly afterlife the patron saint and guardian of the kings of France—was the most powerful saint in the French canon. He protected France's kings bodily from wounds and sickness. He shielded every king's soul from evil and ministered to him at the hour of his death. With Denis' help, the kings of France escaped Hell and Purgatory at death, and were guaranteed entry into Heaven.

Every sacred French symbol was here at the abbey. The abbey's banner, the Oriflamme—scarlet silk on a cedarwood pole—was the flag the French had always carried into important battles, to ensure they were blessed with God's grace. The holy crown of Saint Louis was preserved here—a tall circlet of a single piece of gold, with a large central stone and deeply cut metallic foliage containing thorns and hair from Christ's Holy Crown of Thorns. So was the crown of Charlemagne, with its four hinged sections and its lilies. So was the emperor's great jeweled sword, *Joyeuse*. This was where the heart of France beat strongest; this was its home, with Saint Denis.

Humbly, she asked Saint Denis to save the soul of her father, and to protect her poor mother, left alone in Paris, and to intercede for her own soul, when her time came, and, most important of all, to protect her son, whose future, since he was now King of France, also depended on the saint's goodwill. Only after that, with a slight sense of shame, did Catherine offer a mumbled prayer for the saint to bless the soul of her departed husband. She wasn't sure in her heart of hearts that, even now the abbey was in English hands, Saint Denis would take kindly to Henry—not just because Henry had invaded France, the Most Christian Kingdom, but generally because he'd been the ruler of an irreverent nation whose people had a habit of sloughing off inconvenient kings whenever it suited them and ignoring the sacred pact made between God and King. The English, coarse and cold-blooded, only snickered at the most glorious traditions and holy beliefs. They didn't understand or respect the Word of God, or the sacredness of the blood of kings.

It was different if you were French. The gist of every sermon she'd heard here was that royal blood was blessed. "The lords of the blood are members of and belong to your body," every abbé had told the King her father at every ceremony she'd attended here throughout her childhood. "The lords of the blood are the eyes of the body of the state, watching over it continually. They have a singular affection for it, and a nobility, and a special perfection."

How she'd revered that belief as a child . . . how awed she'd been, gazing up at the blue and gold-starred vaults, at the idea of being the eyes and the limbs of the body of the state. She'd loved the idea that the sanctity of the blood royal and the sanctity of France itself were intermingled. The kings of France ruled the Most Christian Kingdom by virtue of their pure, purple, sacred blood—a land where faith was illuminated; where, as Saint Jérôme said, no snakes or Jews or pagans lived; a place where royal blood was only ever spilled in defense of France and its faith.

But then everything changed—in her lifetime—when the lords of the blood royal of France had started to destroy each other, shedding each other's blood for no purpose.

Perhaps it was those two royal murders in her lifetime—both the terrible acts of *lèse-majesté* and high sacrilege—which had made Saint Denis' power start to fade. The saint had not cured her father's madness. The Oriflamme had not protected the French army at Azincourt. Her brothers Louis and Jean were not buried in these walls, not protected by Denis; France had been too troubled by the time of their deaths to bring them here.

Her living brother Charles would not be buried at Saint-Denis either, Catherine thought. He had shed royal blood. He no longer belonged to this sacred land.

She crossed herself one final time and got to her feet. Even remembering those disconcerting years when Saint Denis' protection had seemed to stop working, she felt calmed by being in this ancient refuge where it was known that her existence was part of the great sacred order of things; where saints and archangels would protect her and her kind.

She thought: Charles' impure blood . . . Charles' unroyal brutality . . . there had been good reason for him to be cast out. But Saint Denis would protect her, Catherine, and those she cherished. Saint Denis would surely protect her father in death; help him to Heaven.

Even if Duke John didn't know anything else about how to bury a King of France with proper honors, she thought, composing herself and moving back to the shouting crowd of Englishmen outside, she could at least make sure that he brought Papa's body to its eternal rest here.

With his duty done, Owain took a boat back from Westminster to Bishop Beaufort's house at Southwark, where his two modest rooms had been kept during his absence. It counted as home.

Fatigue had stopped his mind racing at last. He was so dirty, and every muscle ached. He had no energy left for thinking. In a daze he watched the river water flow by. The clangor of mourning was already beginning: church bells booming out their one harsh note of grief. He could see wherrymen and their passengers, on his craft and all the others jostling down the waterway, turning, listening, and starting to talk, very fast and anxiously. You couldn't hear much of what they were saying for the bells, but you could guess, or read their lips. The words "dead" and "King" and "infant" and "What will become of us?" and "God help us all" were easy enough to make out. He shut his mind to them. Even at high summer, and it was a hot afternoon, the river water was gray. It stank. He needed to sleep.

Perhaps, he thought—and in his tired daze the thought no longer had the power to cause pain—Catherine hadn't meant to be cruel. Perhaps she had just been scared: clutching at a familiar face, a familiar pair of arms, because, unlike these worried-looking Londoners, trying to guess at their future, Catherine knew exactly what lay ahead for herself now she was a widow.

Owain knew as precisely as Catherine. There was no need for either of them to guess. Christine had spelled out the misery of widowhood so precisely that nothing was left to the imagination: how from the moment you became a widow you also became suddenly invisible to all your former friends . . . and the only people who still seemed able to see you were those taking advantage of your defenselessness by making up claims that you owed them something. "*Problems sprang at me from everywhere; lawsuits and trials surrounded me as if this were the natural fate of widows,*" Christine had written. "*The leech of Fortune did not stop sucking my blood for fourteen years, so that if one misfortune ceased, another ordeal happened, in so many different ways that it would be too long to tell even half of it. And the leech did not stop sucking my blood until I had nothing left.*"

Catherine, who knew so little about England, and who was so accustomed to the respect and deference of everyone she encountered, probably had no idea yet how pliable and willing to adapt she'd have to become to survive and prosper. Owain, who knew all about adapting and bending, masking his Welsh-ness or brazening it out, could be sure of that . . . She'd be help-less, all right, without her husband's protection. There'd be no one to knock all those headstrong dukes' heads together for years.

Without intending it at all, Owain felt the pity seep into him, and with it he began to sense a new possibility. His desire might be a sin, a crime that needed to be punished, but his anger, his repentance, should be directed at himself, not at Catherine. She would have enough to contend with already.

He should direct his efforts at helping the needy. His punish-ment should fit his crime.

Owain would never have recognized his cousin. They were about the same age, which must mean that he'd last have seen Glyndŵr's one surviving son, oh, fifteen years ago, maybe; back in that time of smoke in the eyes and loyalty and hope and ex-hausting night rides, when everything still seemed real in a way it never had since. They'd been half children still, somewhere be-tween five and ten, Owain thought vaguely—messengers at best, running or riding occasionally between men, then boasting about their errand to the other children for months afterward, but usu-ally only frightened observers of the fighting around them. There was nothing left now of the bright, brave boy Owain remem-bered his cousin having been in the grown-up Maredudd ap Owain Glyndŵr he saw here at this Southwark inn, nursing his tankard of ale and his grudge. This grown-up man who'd come slipping into the Bishop's house on a tired old nag this afternoon, asking for Owain Tudor—and lucky to have found him just hours after he got back from France—was small and rat-like, with none of his father's lordly charisma. Maredudd had watch-ful eyes and resentful lines branding his forehead and face, which were half hidden by an enormous, misshapen, provincial hat. He looked far older than twenty-two.

"But why are you here?" Owain asked again, trying not to let his disappointment show.

Maredudd and his father had vanished into the hills thirteen years before, after the fall of Harlech. The English had never caught them, although there was always an enormous bounty on Owain Glyndŵr's head. What had become of Glyndŵr had, formally, remained a mystery. Owain chose to believe the story that most often circulated—that father and son had taken shelter with Maredudd's sister Alys, over the border in English Herefordshire, and that she and her English husband had sheltered the rebels from her family with the connivance of almost everyone else in the border region. The story had it that Owain Glyndŵr had "become" the confessor of Alys' family by marriage, the Scudamores of Monnington Stradel—pretended to be a Franciscan called Siôn Cent, who'd become known far and wide as a trickster as wily as any in the old Welsh tales. Owain Glyndŵr's son was always said to be masquerading as a lesser friar. The great charm of the story was that Alys Scudamore's husband John was the Sheriff of Herefordshire, appointed by Henry of England himself. For Owain, a still greater charm was that Henry himself knew the story that his old enemy might have gone on living right under the nose of the English crown's man on the Welsh Marches, and had been confident enough of his generous handling of Wales never to have tested the truth of it with searches and arrests.

Who could say? It could be true. Owain Tudor, who hadn't quite managed to rip every shred of secret sympathy for his Welsh brethren out of his heart, had always quietly hoped it might be true. That story was the last flicker of hope for a Welshman, after all. All those other relatives imprisoned in the Tower—the Mortimer womenfolk and Maredudd's elder brother Gruffydd ap Owain Glyndŵr—they were all dead now, long before their time. And Owain's own direct family, all the children of his grandfather Tudur, were as doomed as the Owain Glyndŵrs; with the children and the children's children of that part of the clan also paying the price of their forebears' rebellion against the English crown. Even though they were still alive, and living in what was left of their lands, it was clear that Owain's immediate family would never have their old powers again. And he, Owain, wouldn't be seeing those faces again, or those lands either. He was banned for all eternity from Wales. He was banned from owning land in England too, or claiming rents from Englishmen. He lived modestly on the grant of twenty pounds a year that the young King Henry V had made him when he was still a boy: enough to keep a squire in horses and armor and gentleman's clothes, just. Anything above that he had to earn. And, as a Welshman, it would always be almost impossible for him to do that. That was his poisonous legacy; that was what his blood had brought him. Since he was cut off from his homeland by the King's orders, and cut off from making his fortune at war by his own choice, and cut off from marriage by the English government's stipulation that he seek official permission before taking a wife, as well as by the cruel disobedience of his own heart, he'd realized that if he wanted to avoid the poison of resentment—which he did—he could only thank God that he had an aptitude for learning that would eventually help him flourish in the Church. He'd found a path.

Still, anyone would dream sometimes; it would be too hard not to allow yourself a daydream from time to time. So Owain had spent years thinking—idly, mostly—that one day the Glyndŵr family might come marching out of the hills again: that there would be another time of riding like the wind for freedom and a future. But for that to be possible, Glyndŵr himself would have to have survived, or cousin Maredudd be as much a hero as his father, able to lead his people through their wilderness to their Israel. But this little man—short, dark, and wiry, in shoddy, old-fashioned clothes, with that bitter yet calculating look—seemed anything but a hero. There was nothing to hope for from Maredudd.

"He died," Maredudd said. "Father. We buried him." There was a little glint of truculence in his grin; a "and-don't-ask-me-where," "you-didn't-suffer-with-us-so-you-can't-know-our-secrets" sort of look. He added, "And then I thought, what now for me?"

Maredudd was muttering, looking down, throwing him those bright little birdlike glances only every now and then, when he raised his nose from his pitcher. But Owain was very aware of people around them listening, of heads turning furtively toward them, then turning away. This was Southwark, after all. These rough South London tradesmen might think nothing of a burst of Sicilian or Flemish or French—but Welsh? It was still banned; still the language of danger.

"God rest his soul," Owain said in English, a bit louder to appease the silent listeners; feeling to his horror almost sympathetic to them. His cousin seemed so . . . foreign.

Maredudd, with the recklessness born of not knowing what it was to be a Welshman in London, repeated a little louder in Welsh: "And then I thought, what now for me?"

Sighing, Owain inclined his head. If Maredudd would only go back to muttering.

"So I've decided: I'm going to take the pardon."

Owain stared. Years before, King Henry had offered Maredudd a pardon, hoping to tempt the Glyndŵr son out into the open and separate him from his father. There'd never been anything but silence in reply. But now—surely Maredudd hadn't rushed straight to London from his father's grave to take up that ancient offer?

"What?" he said dully, shaking his head. "Is that why . . . ? But . . ."

Maredudd was ready to argue. He was boiling over with guilty resentment; seething with it. His words came rushing and hissing out. "Don't look at me like that. Don't. Do you think it's easy being the son of a rebel?" he said, very fast, very angrily. "No way forward, no way out—do you think I've enjoyed hiding out in *robes* pretending to be something I'm not, and afraid all the time?" In his agitation he'd knocked the strange hat off his head. Owain saw (with secret satisfaction) that a tonsure was growing out. So, he thought, it was true: you *were* dressing up as a pair of Franciscans. But there was no point asking Maredudd, who was whining in a thin, hungry voice: "I want to be a man again. Hold my head up. A wife, children; some land. To go out on my horse without fearing they'll be along any second to hunt me down. I want a normal life."

Gently, wonderingly, Owain shook his head. Maredudd clearly had no idea about the anti-Welsh laws in force here if he thought it could be that easy to remake himself. He didn't yet know that his blood was tainted; his family ruined and himself doomed, whatever he did. Owain could already begin to see how this evening would develop. He'd buy his cousin many tankards of ale, and listen as Maredudd sank further into self-pity, then carry the Welshman home. He'd promise to put his cousin up for a few days and arrange him an audience with the Bishop. It would only be later, after that, and after the excitement of the pardon, that the miserable truth would begin to sink in for Maredudd. Owain thought: I could have done without this, after all that's happened.

Maredudd had hardly mentioned the passing of the King. He didn't even seem to be worried that Henry's death might affect the old offer of a pardon. He certainly didn't ask whether Owain was saddened to lose his master. He didn't seem to be aware of Owain's fatigue.

"It's not much to ask, is it?" Maredudd was saying. "A marriage and a bit of land? Of course I accept that I'll never get a title, because of being Welsh. Nothing we can do about that. Look at you—plaything of the English half your life." Owain winced, but his cousin only shook his head and slurred, "Don't take offense now. Figure of speech. Though it's true enough. Still, I've been following what's happened to you since you've been in England. You were good in the war. In France. They say you captured the Duke of Orléans at Azincourt, with your own hands?"

Embarrassed, Owain nodded. He didn't tell anyone that story; he knew there'd been no great bravery in what he'd done. But Maredudd shook his head with grim pleasure; his prejudice confirmed. "And you weren't even knighted. Even for that. You see, as a Welshman you haven't got a hope. Even if you're the best, transcendently much better than the rest, you still haven't got a hope. They'll pass you over all your life."

So Maredudd did have some idea of a few of the problems of being Welsh then, Owain thought, feeling suddenly sorry for him, knowing how many more unpleasant discoveries there would be for him in the weeks and months to come.

Maredudd leaned forward, grinning as if the thought of being cut off from the normal life of a man of honor gave him a perverse kind of pleasure, and clapping Owain on the shoulder.

"So what you and I need, cousin, are good marriages. No

hope for us as things are. They'll trip us up at every turn. 'Bloody Welsh savages.' All that. But a good English wife each . . . eh? A girl with a family to look up to, and a dowry. That's what will set us straight. Put a generation between my father and a decent future. Give us children who can hope."

He didn't even seem to have looked at his London cousin carefully enough to see that under his black cloak Owain was wearing friar's black. The realization irritated Owain. Had Maredudd spent so long assuming robes were something you dressed up in for pretense that he didn't notice them at all anymore, or at least couldn't see them as a sign of a genuine wish to be considered a man of God? Was the man utterly self-absorbed?

Worse still, Maredudd had started talking loudly. Too loudly. He looked triumphantly around, then he did a tipsy double-take. The Southwark tavern folk had given up turning away their eyes. A dozen faces were turned toward him, giving him assessing stares that seemed to mean trouble.

"Welsh, eh?" the tavern keeper said.

There was a murmur from his mates; an edging and a tightening of bodies. They didn't like Welsh, their bodies were saying.

Maredudd's eyes rolled. He eyed them, seeming to be wondering whether he could take on this whole crowd and quite relishing the prospect. But you couldn't spend your life brawling in taverns for the honor of a Wales that no longer existed. Peaceably, Owain replied, "No, no. Brittany. Saint Malo. Breton." Breton sounded just like Welsh; he'd made himself understood, more or less, in Brittany. They'd have to believe him. He looked the tavern keeper straight in the eye, baring his teeth in a determinedly naive smile that he felt probably looked foolish, but did the trick of easing the man's anger, then passed him a coin. "Here," he added, knowing this would calm any last suspicions the mini-mob were being made fools of. "Let us buy our friends from London a drink."

The men turned away, thronging round the tavern keeper with a quiet hubbub in which Owain sensed embarrassment, watchfulness, and excitement at getting something for nothing.

It wearied him, the whole shameful business of living in the world he found himself in. There was so much of this: of small lies and evasions in the inglorious name of peace and quiet.

"Come on," he muttered, and Maredudd, looking shocked, followed him out. They didn't talk as they hurried back to the Bishop of Winchester's palace. Owain could sense Maredudd weighing up a future in which you often had to pretend to be Breton to avoid being roughed up by a Southwark ruffian.

Suddenly, in the darkness, with the whiff of whale tallow coming from the barrel down the street, the pity Owain felt for Maredudd overwhelmed him, and he put an arm out and laid it over his cousin's shoulder. Poor Maredudd, who was probably doing the right thing by making his peace with the English lords, but who would hate so much of the adjustments that would be forced on him along the way. Maredudd, who still didn't understand that he would never have the life of an English lord that he hoped for. Maredudd, who might just about manage to wangle a marriage of sorts, but certainly not the glorious sort he wanted. Maredudd, who hadn't understood yet that if you truly wanted to find peace, as a son of defeat, you had to step back altogether from the world and give up the notion of fathering children who'd only have to go on paying the price of their fathers' and grandfathers' crimes against England.

Owain could feel the uncertainty, the hurt, and the awareness of worse to come in the other man's tense shoulders. But, for the first time, he also felt peace in his own heart at the knowledge that he'd accepted that his blood was tainted; that now all he had to do was live, and trust in God.

"I've chosen my way, and it isn't marriage," he muttered. They were safe enough talking Welsh in the quiet of the night street, going at this pace. The chastened Maredudd nodded him on, listening properly for the first time. Owain nodded down at his robes and saw his cousin take in the cut of them and their meaning. "I'm choosing the world of beauty and meditation; not this. In due course, I'll join the Augustinians at Saint Mary's in Oxford," he went on. "There's a place for me; it's all arranged. But I have to wait seven years. I'd do it before then, to get away from all this faster, if there weren't one last task tying me to this world."

Maredudd turned to give him a closer look.

"I promised to look after the son of my King while he's an infant," Owain said, still walking but uncomfortably aware of that turned head beside him, the slow eyes. He pushed himself on to add, in the most neutral voice possible, ". . . and the widow. I'm going to work in her household."

Maredudd didn't look away. It was Owain's turn to feel uneasy. He didn't know why he felt rattled enough that he added: "It was the King who wanted me to. His last wish." He knew he was telling a lie.

"Why not go to Oxford now? What is the King of England's last wish to you?" Maredudd said, and there was no offense in the hard words, just a kind of astonishment—as if Maredudd was wondering what had happened to the brave young Welsh cousin he remembered.

Owain shook his head, thinking of Henry; lost in admiration he couldn't put into words. The rage of the road slipped away, leaving only the fatigue. He felt his eyes soften and moisten. "He was . . ."

His voice cracked. They both stopped walking.

"A kindness. Seven years," Owain said when his voice came back. "It will slip past in no time."

TWENTY-FOUR

Two months later, with the first snow in the iron air of November, Catherine sat before Duke Humphrey and listened warily to the statement he'd prepared about her future life.

It didn't matter what the ginger Duke said really, she told herself, keeping her breathing steady and the polite little smile on her face. Nothing mattered now she had Harry back; a Harry who, at eleven months old, could walk properly and cheerfully yell "No!" at anyone who crossed him. And a Harry who'd remembered his mother. As soon as he'd seen her for the first time since the summer, he had said "Mama" with such treble reverence that it had wrung her heart and brought tears to her eyes, even before they'd run into each other's arms and she'd swung him round and round until they were both dizzy and laughing and crying and chattering at once.

For the past two weeks, between solemn Masses and funeral rites, Catherine and her son had been inseparable—however much Mistress Ryman still clung on, hissing and clicking her teeth, and muttering disapprovingly that the King had been used to doing this or that or the other thing at this hour, and that the routines she'd established were important for the child's well-being, and upsetting them would only be damaging.

It was strange to be back in England—not as Queen, with at least the possibility of winning the respect of her new subjects (though she'd never felt that was a very likely prospect), but as Queen Mother—an old woman's position, she thought bewil-

348

deredly, whose importance would dwindle with every passing year; an acknowledgment that, at twenty-one, the best days of her life were over. True, it didn't feel very different from being Queen yet—she'd been ignored or bossed around before Henry died, too. The only difference now was that there was a little more edge to both being ignored and bossed around, though it was all still very polite; and she knew she'd have no one to complain to if it did stop being polite.

Yet, strangely enough, being reunited with Harry after the strange emptiness of those months of separation seemed reward enough. They'd have nearly seven years together, she and her son, just as they were, living together, each with their little household. Each day would be a blessing. Her thoughts wouldn't move beyond that time, not yet. It was long enough. There was too much to get used to as things were. If she were really honest, she couldn't make herself imagine any time period beyond the next few weeks or months; beyond the small hope in a corner of her heart that somehow she'd find a way to get rid of the obnoxious Mistress Ryman. (Mistress Ryman was full of unpleasant ideas and harsh notions: she liked to swaddle Harry so tight in the evenings that he could scarcely move, to keep him docile; and she insisted that it was undignified and unqueenly for Catherine to sit on the floor and play with her son.)

Still, Catherine knew she'd have to be strong and watchful of events outside the nursery. The tussles of the dukes that she'd suspected would come had started already. The Council of England had taken one look at Henry's will and decided that it would be asking for trouble to let Duke Humphrey, the harsher, more capricious, younger royal brother, have the complete control over little Harry's person and over England that the dead King had stipulated. So they'd overridden Henry's will. This was largely because Duke John, writing from France, had made plain that he didn't want his little brother to be given too much power back in England, and no one else wanted to annoy the older royal Duke. It was Bishop Beaufort who'd masterminded the change and got the Council to limit Duke Humphrey's power. Under the new rules set out by the Bishop and Council, no single person—by which they meant Duke Humphrey—could substitute for the King until Harry was old enough to exercise royal power for himself. Instead of Duke Humphrey being considered the Protector, the Council and Parliament were to reign collectively. Duke Humphrey would open and close the Parliament next month that would formalize little Harry's inheritance of the crown, but only because the older Duke John was away and the Council had given Humphrey permission to act on his infant nephew's behalf.

That wasn't what Duke Humphrey wanted. Catherine had observed him hurting at being deprived of absolute power. She could see it in the twitch of his bulging eyelids; in the extra effort he made to bow and hand her into her seat, and ask after her health, consciously and a little pompously, projecting power and affability though such courtesies came unnaturally to him. He was a stocky, bluff man with weather-beaten cheeks, a booming voice, and a habit of breaking into conversations with an opinion that would always be forcefully expressed, but might not always be wise. He was uncomfortably aware that his appearance struck some people as funny: his great lion's head and deep voice; his short stumpy legs. There was nothing he hated more than being ridiculed.

Still, he was the man she had to obey, and she needed to look gracious about it. Not that there was anything very hard to stomach in the orders she was hearing now. She'd already settled in at Windsor with Harry and begun the job of displacing Mistress Ryman. All he was telling her now was that she'd have to pay for that privilege out of her widow's dower.

It was only when he got to how much she'd have to pay that she began to feel shocked. "My brother's will leaves you well provided for," Duke Humphrey was saying. "You will keep your own suite of retainers, separate from His Majesty's household but attendant on His Majesty at all times until his seventh birthday. Since you will be sharing living quarters you will be expected to contribute seven pounds a day to the shared household expenses."

Catherine was glad of the seat's hard back propping her up. Seven pounds a day. That would come to more than £2,500 a year—or more than a third of the total income from the various estates in England and Wales and France that had been settled on her. It would be enough to pay for both households. She'd probably be paying, out of her own purse, for the entire running expenses of the King's household, saving the treasury the cost of an expense that England should rightfully have paid.

She had no idea whether this was genuinely Henry's wish, or just Duke Humphrey driving a hard and rather dishonest bargain of his own. She hadn't been shown Henry's will, so there was no way of judging. She had no choice. Submissively, she nodded.

Mopping his brow, and grinning for the first time—he couldn't control himself enough to hide his relief that she'd knuckled under, she thought, with quiet resentment—Duke Humphrey went on, "Now, as I'm sure you're aware, your principal duty will be to bring up His Majesty to understand his French kingdom as fully as his English one . . . speak French with him . . . tell him"—he paused, flummoxed—"well, French stories. Sing him French songs. That sort of thing."

She lowered her head. Her lips were twitching. She wondered whether Humphrey had any idea how many French songs and stories and histories were about the English, or how unflattering they were. But she didn't think it would be politic to explain that. So she just nodded again. She was aware of his relief at the ease with which she took orders.

Perhaps as a reward for her obedience, he went on, "I've—we've—drawn up lists of household members for both of you. If there are names you want included or left out, please make your preferences known."

He held out a sheaf of papers. Glancing at the top sheet, she saw columns of names and wages for Harry's personal women servants—ungenerous wages, too, for tending the King. After Mistress Ryman, she read: *"Joan Astley, nurse, £20 a year. Matilda Fosbroke, £10 . . ."* "Mistress Ryman," she began hesitantly, testing his offer. Perhaps, after all, she could begin to exercise a little control over her life. "She was very useful while I was away. But, with all these others coming now, is there any need for Mistress Ryman anymore? I'm back, after all."

But Duke Humphrey only tut-tutted and looked vaguely irritated. "Done an excellent job for the past six months. Good housekeeper. You'll need her," he said briskly, remembering to smile mid-sentence.

There was no room for maneuver then. Catherine suppressed the sigh she'd have given if on her own, and approved the rest of the appointments, clearly designed to fill the household with Duke Humphrey's men, doing no more than to run her eye down each of the sheets and nod, even though she knew Sir Robert Babthorpe, named here as steward, would have a hard time doing the job, since he was actually in France as the English army's paymaster, and Lord Fitzhugh, the former treasurer of England, named on the list as Harry's chamberlain, was far too old for the work. It was true what people said about Duke Humphrey, then: he liked to control things, but he wasn't very good at working out how.

It was only when she got to the less political list, of staff who would work in her own household, that she noticed one name that startled her. There, below the familiar Walter Beauchamp, her chief steward from before, and George Arthurton, the clerk of her closet, and various others she knew or at least half remembered, was an insertion. It had been made late, by a different hand from the one that had written most of the list.

"Ahh . . . someone new?" she said carefully, holding out the document but making sure not to startle Duke Humphrey, or let him think his authority was being questioned in any way.

Duke Humphrey took the parchment and paused while he deciphered the name. "Oh! Yes . . . Tudor," he vouchsafed, and the too-wide smile seemed to be held on artificially. "My uncle of Beaufort's man. Bishop Beaufort, that is. My uncles were keen to help staff your household; put a few of their own men in. Keep everyone happy. Balance of power. Tudor volunteered." Humphrey harrumphed out something that was half-sigh, half-laugh. "Not really a soldier, Owain Tudor. We thought he would be early on; he bagged a big fish at Azincourt." Humphrey stopped, perhaps remembering that the prisoner he was talking of with such disrespect would be Catherine's blood, some close cousin, someone she might conceivably love. Collecting himself, he went on: "But after that—nothing. Now he's thinking about the Church, but can't bring himself to take the plunge. A lightweight." Duke Humphrey's next thought amused him hugely. He spluttered: "A poet, too!" and caught Catherine's eye as he rocked with laughter over his final joke: "And a Welshman to boot!" He sobered himself, though he couldn't resist adding mockingly: "Well, what can you say? A Welshman, but he's taken my uncle's fancy."

She smiled back. "I know him," she said gently; "a little."

"Good with paperwork, though; might be a decent administrator," Duke Humphrey finished benignly. "Got him down as keeper of your household. Only if you want him, of course."

Catherine's head was full of the words *he volunteered*. They rang like bells. She couldn't understand how she could be still standing there, talking courteously with this threatening buffoon as if the sun and moon hadn't shifted on their course; as if, in her lonely, shadowed universe, a little more light hadn't suddenly started to glimmer. *He volunteered.*

At her noncommittal nod, Duke Humphrey came round from behind his side of the enormous table, which was scattered with papers. He was still beaming, but more naturally now.

"Well, that's it then," he observed with satisfaction. "All sorted out." He moved closer, offering her an arm to help her rise from her seat. "For now, anyway." She was on her feet now, but he didn't move away. She was uncomfortably aware of the big pores on his face; the slight odor of onions and beef fat. He lowered his face closer, still grinning. She was glad of the two clerks writing away at the end of the table. "Though all too soon we'll have to start thinking about the Queen Mother's marriage, eh?" he said, chuckling again until the whiskers on his chin were almost touching her cheek.

Catherine stopped herself from stepping back until she'd flattered him by saying neutrally, "I will be advised by Your Grace. Naturally. When the time comes. When I am no longer in grief for my lord."

It was the best she could do. As she sank her head, gathered her skirts, and prepared to leave the room, he tightened his arm on her waist, patted her hand awkwardly, and said, with the roughness of a man not used to flirting, ". . . a shame for such a pretty face to be hidden away behind veils for too long."

She hardly took the words in. She was floating. My old friend, she was thinking, almost singing with relief and something else she found it easier not to name or think about. *He volunteered.*

They walked in the rose garden, between the gnarled skeletons of bushes, ignoring the snow. Owain was in black. The pointed hood of his scapular stretched down his back. His head was shaved. She could see the roughness of the linen on his sleeve. He'd been wearing those robes ever since she'd come across him again in England, she knew. But she was more aware of them now. Something in him had changed, become more unyielding, and the monk's habit seemed to symbolize the distance he was putting between them.

Timidly, she glanced sideways and upward at his face, tight-boned now, stripped of its youthful softness and optimism. She could hardly believe how light-headed with relief even the sight of him made her.

"I've thought about you a great deal," he said, and although those were gentle words there was nothing especially gentle about his delivery of them. "You're a widow in an unfamiliar place, in unstable times. We both know why that is frightening. You told me how vulnerable you feel; you asked for my help. If you still want that help, I've made it available. If you so wish, my Bishop is quite happy for my secondment to your household to last the full seven years you share living quarters with Harry—that is, six years from now."

She bowed her head, so nervous of saying the wrong thing that she found her voice dropping almost to a whisper. She replied: "Yes . . . Duke Humphrey said . . . I've accepted, with pleasure . . ."

She smiled at him. He didn't smile back. He looked away.

"The post suits me," he added, by way of explanation. "I owed everything to . . ." Owain's voice tailed off. Bleakly, he crossed himself. ". . . King Henry," he finished. "He helped me through my time of troubles; he showed me the way to a new life. It seems fitting to me that I should serve his son and his widow now."

She was chilled and a little surprised by his tough, businesslike demeanor. He was making plain that he'd made a man's decision. He was telling her he was here not because he loved her, but because he'd loved Henry.

She still felt lucky he was here. Protected. He would advise her; they would talk; for years and years to come she would have him to confide in. Perhaps they might become friends.

She nodded gratefully, not daring to speak.

"I'll do everything I can to serve you and your son in that time," he went on. "The Bishop's delayed my going to the Augustinians until after I leave you, even though I'm still to prepare myself . . . spend time at my devotions . . . wear the habit. God will wait seven years for me."

He smiled his hard new smile. Breathlessly, eager to find her way to obeying the new rules he was setting out, she began to try to laugh with him.

"Then," Owain's voice ground on, "you'll marry. They'll find you someone of your own rank."

There was no chivalry in his voice, no yearning. All that was gone. If anything he sounded irritated. Perhaps he'd thought her breathy giggle flirtatious and out of place. He added baldly: "So there are no misunderstandings"—he looked away before he finished—"we won't be lovers."

The word "lovers" felt like a slap in the face. But she hid her shock; lowered her eyes. For a moment the beginnings of indignation pulsed through her. She'd surely done nothing to deserve . . . suggest . . . she hadn't meant . . . how dare he . . . Then she sighed. She did deserve it. There was the past, what could she call it, indiscretion . . . She felt her mind avoid calling it up. And, if she were really honest with herself, she might even have wondered whether in the future, too . . . It would always be hard to talk to this man without a thought, a memory at least, of bodily attraction. But, if she were to keep him and his goodwill—and she needed to, for there'd be no one who didn't want to use her now she was so weak—she would have to try to put all that aside. She needed all the friends she could get.

She muttered: "Of course." She shivered. She sensed he wasn't even planning to become a friend; just a dutiful servant, waiting quietly for the day he could leave. But even that would be better than nothing. It was a time for making do with what there was.

PART SIX

The Book of the Body Politic

TWENTY-FIVE

Both Catherine and Owain knew the household of the new Queen Mother of England would be no place for lovers.

For the first few months that the infant King and his mother and their new entourages lived at Windsor, and Wallingford, and the other castles of the Thames Valley, in their tightly swaddled child-world of milk and napkins and isolation from whatever passed for entertainment for adults of the court elsewhere in England, it seemed it might scarcely even be a place for friends.

Catherine still barely knew most of her servants, and was kept at a distance by her slowness to master their customs and language. The only person she did know, Owain, kept at his own formal distance. Catherine busied herself with her son, spending most of her waking hours with Harry in the nursery, evading Mistress Ryman when she could. Outside his working hours, Owain kept himself occupied with his studies or his prayers. At least, Catherine had to assume that, since Owain shut himself up in his rooms or somewhere else out of her sight, and never came out.

Yet Catherine didn't let her courage altogether fail her. She told herself that this more austere Owain was helping shape Harry's life, just as she'd asked. She should be grateful for what she'd been given. If he'd found something else to make the center of his life—the wish to serve God, not her—she had to respect his wishes. Catherine knew now, had known all along really, that

Owain had been right from the start about the shaming proposition she'd once made to him. Her royal blood would always have stood between them; she could no more have loved him than a dog could love a cat. She'd been a child. She'd hated him for shutting her out, and taken a cruel revenge, but he'd been right to know his place, and remind her of it.

She tried to remember that, and be contented with her lot.

Her intuition—that having Owain Tudor near was better than not having him at all, and that there was at least the possibility that they would draw comfort from each other's presence eventually, if their shared embarrassment about some of the moments they must both remember from the past could be overcome—seemed, as the first year wore on, to be being borne out by reality. Catherine was impressed to see that, as Duke Humphrey had so condescendingly remarked, Owain was a good administrator. For someone so modest and without pretensions, he kept order extraordinarily well. He never raised his voice or looked out of sorts, but Catherine's household ran smoothly. The accounts were done, the cupboards full of food and linen, the furniture repaired, the servants paid, the gardens planted, the pottagers harvested, and Catherine's every material need or wish anticipated and satisfied, as if by magic, down to the gorgeously scented rose petals and lavender scattered in her bath, under translucent muslin.

There was more. Even if he was no more than correct in his rare conversations with Catherine, Owain was so affectionate with little Harry—playing jumping and singing games with him, carving and weaving him tiny toys—that it wrung his mother's heart. Gradually, as Harry turned one, then two, a new atmosphere came into existence between his mother and the master of her household. Not a loving one, exactly; not a friendship, quite. Nothing that would have offered true emotional satisfaction, if Catherine hadn't been so absorbed already with raising a child. But at least a businesslike warmth.

As Harry learned to talk, Catherine and Owain learned the ways of comradeship too: smiling stops on stairs and in corridors, careful, not unfriendly conversations, exchanges of commonplaces, asking after each other's health, sleep, or observations about the child's behavior. Living in the same household, they could talk together many times a day, even if each conversation was brief.

Every week he brought her the household accounts. Increasingly, he encouraged her to speak English, until at last she stopped being scared to open her mouth for fear her tongue would betray her. Occasionally, when Owain's duties permitted it, they might read together. Once Owain read her the teaching of his order's master, Saint Augustine of Hippo, that it was always right to pursue, intelligently, what you loved: " '. . . *nothing conquers except truth, and the victory of truth is love,*' " he quoted, "that's why the Augustinians pursue knowledge through their books." And then, so coolly that she could do nothing but swallow and look away with a brittle smile, he added, "That's what I have come to see that love most genuinely is."

They sometimes prayed together, if she managed to find herself in the chapel when he was there. They walked together to the great hall for meals, when there were no guests to escort her. Owain personally served her food there, twice a day. Owain's robes, as well as the chilly formality of his manner, protected them from evil tongues.

Quietly, scarcely knowing she was doing it, Catherine treasured these moments. They were the closest she had to friendship. She knew, if she thought about it, that she'd started to wake up every morning calculating how long it would be till they met that day, and to go to sleep every night treasuring each of the day's small memories, not just of the hours spent with her son, but also of the time with her master of the household. But she would try not to think about it; try not to admit such things to herself.

When they put the little boy up on a horse for the first time, and he waved his fat little arms in a comical mixture of delight and terror, Catherine looked at the answering delight and amusement on Owain's face and, taking her courage in her hands, risked more: a confidence.

"You don't think," she ventured, "that riding will overexcite him?"

Owain looked round, composing his face as he let his eyes rest lightly on her so that every trace of softness and joy disappeared, to be replaced with politeness.

"Overexcite him?" Owain repeated.

"I worry . . ." she hesitated. "They said my father went mad because he was always being overexcited when he was too small . . . and I don't want Harry to . . ."

Owain looked back at Harry, who sat high enough for their eyes to be at the same height. The little boy was tentatively stroking his mount's mane and rich bay shoulders with one hand while gripping for dear life with the other. He was concentrating completely on the animal, with his lips drawn over his baby teeth and his outstretched arm moving very slowly. His legs flopped uselessly on the dark barrel of the horse's back.

Owain laughed and put a fond arm around the child. He lifted one of the King's fat little legs up—it came too easily—and said, "You need to hold on a bit tighter than that, or you'll come off!"

Then, turning back to Catherine, he added in a calm adult voice: "Surely learning to ride can only be good for him."

She knew that was true really. How strange it would be not to know how. But Harry was only two . . .

Still, she tried to calm her fears. At least, she did until a couple of minutes later, when Owain picked up a whip and put it into the little boy's hand.

"Here," he added, patting Harry as the child took the whip. "This can be your sword."

"Oh no!" she cried, and snatched the whip away. Harry looked balefully at her and began to howl. She kissed him, put her arms around him; but she went on shaking her head. "Oh sweetheart," she said regretfully, "you're much too small to be thinking of swords."

Over the wailing back, feeling Harry's hot tears of rage wetting her gown, she looked reproachfully at Owain. "I want to keep him as quiet as possible," she said, in almost a whisper, still patting at Harry. "I thought you understood. I don't want swords. I'm not even sure about horses yet. He's so small."

She could see Owain turning the question over in his mind. "The dukes are going to turn your son into a warrior king as soon as ever they can," he said after a moment. "Don't shut your eyes to reality."

"Well," she said mutinously, feeling foolish; but at the same time utterly determined not to let Harry's mind be fuddled into the madness that had afflicted her father, if all he needed to do to avoid that was avoid doing too much, too young, "they haven't got him yet. He's mine till he's seven. And he's going to have peace and quiet till then."

Owain nodded. "Peace and quiet it is," he said, without protest. "No swords till he's older." He put a hand on Harry's hair. He let the ghost of his Harry smile come back onto his face. "But," he added, challenging Catherine to be braver, "he does like horses."

She laughed out loud, and Harry looked up from his wailing to see what there might be to laugh about. "Yes," she said, with relief like sunlight in her veins. "It's time for him to learn to ride."

She sensed, in that conversation, the beginning of the small daily negotiations of friendship; the dawn of trust. While she was still shakily mastering English and learning her way around her household and country, a few moments like this—of shallows and sunlight—would be enough.

Even with the quiet help Owain was offering in interpreting this new world; even as Catherine's knowledge of English improved, and with it her ability to distinguish between the pale faces and strapping limbs of the English courtiers, and her understanding of their customs, dances, foods, and feuds, she still couldn't operate politically on her own. However proficient she became at mimicking Englishness, she continued to feel as visible and vulnerable as an exotic beast—a lion, say, or a tiger, hiding in gray-green English bracken. That feeling of eyes on her made her circumspect. She couldn't summon up the courage even to try and exert any influence on public life, except through a protector.

But there were protectors available now. And within a few months of her return to England, the most powerful agent for change in Catherine's life became Owain's master, Bishop Beaufort.

There was nothing especially saintly about Bishop Beaufort, the dead King's uncle. He was a courtier through and through, in the worldly French mold. Tall and bowed and very thin, he had sunken cheeks below the characteristic bulging eyes of the Lancasters, and a big, ugly mouth, always twisted up at the corner, ready to smile. Yet the impression he gave was not of ugliness. For all the sardonic good humor of his expression, the knowing quips that fell from his tongue and the flashes of cunning she could see, every now and then, in his eyes there was a nobility about him that she appreciated. He was learned, subtle, and polished. The Bishop always showed respectful courtesy to Owain, despite his own incomparably higher rank; Catherine even thought he might be privately grateful to Owain for bringing him into the orbit of the Queen Mother. In her turn, she was equally grateful to Owain for bringing her into close contact with the cleric whose smooth poise would help her through Harry's childhood. No wonder the Pope had wanted to steal Bishop Beaufort to Rome to wear a cardinal's hat, Catherine thought. Like Owain, she felt safe in his presence.

The Bishop made a point of coming to stay wherever Queen Mother and King had established themselves, and celebrating Mass in her chapel. He'd eat—he might be a churchman but he didn't stint himself—and laugh, though only a little, about Duke Humphrey's frank greed for wine and women. Catherine laughed, too, because his mocking stories made her remember Duke Humphrey's body, far too close, and how uncomfortable it had made her feel. Bishop Beaufort would watch little Harry totter around floors and swing screaming with joy from his embroidered sleeves. He patted the child's head. He turned him upside down and swung him by his heels until Harry, exhausted by his own giggles, squealed, "Stop, Unca Bobo!" and

Catherine sighed with laughter. He played Harry the rough little flute that Owain had carved him: lilting tunes that made the child's eyes go bright with wonder and brought silence to the room. He brought Harry jumbles and a silver ship that ran on wheels across the floor.

When Catherine plucked up courage to complain that Duke Humphrey had chosen the royal household badly, and was paying her few loyal servants inadequately, Bishop Beaufort listened carefully. Then he nodded. "Who would you actually like around you?" he asked. Catherine stopped. She hadn't thought that out. But she shouldn't be so helpless. There had been good people around her before . . . she searched for names.

After a moment she said, "I would like Sir Walter Hungerford, who used to be the King's steward, and Alice Butler, from my household before Henry's death, and Sir Lewis Robessart . . . And Lord Bourgchier, who used to be Henry's standard-bearer, who's a Hainaulter, who'll speak French."

Bishop Beaufort was nodding. Taking courage, she added, speaking faster now as more names came back: "And I'd like George Arthurton, who used to be the clerk of my closet, to be Harry's confessor; he's a good, honest man. And I'd like Sir Walter Beauchamp, my chief steward . . ."

The Bishop was laughing and putting up his hand. "Enough!" he said gently. "Rome wasn't built in a day. Let's see what we can do."

Catherine didn't know how he did it. But within a month or so the servants she'd wanted were in place, and Henry's women had all had their pay doubled. Best of all, Mistress Ryman was gone for good. Had the Bishop guessed? Could Owain have told him? She hadn't even asked.

As she watched Owain's hands, putting down the paper at which the details of the newcomers' pay and terms were set out, she thought how tentatively he was holding the document—at a distance; as if he felt cautious about accepting the reality his Bishop had created for her.

Owain wasn't as contented as she was. "Be careful," he was saying somberly, waving the paylist. "The Bishop is being mischievous—he's using you to goad Duke Humphrey. They don't like each other, you know. Never have. But they're trying hard to keep the peace. So don't let Duke Humphrey think you've taken sides against him. Don't let yourself be drawn into their quarrel."

She looked at him in quick surprise, then laughed. A carefree laugh. She'd had all these needless worries herself earlier on. But now that she could see how things were really working out, she was beginning to think she'd been wrong. England wouldn't, after all, collapse into bloodshed as soon as there was no one strong man to keep men from each other's throats. Things were different here: saner, more disciplined, safer. There was something to be said for England. And she was fond of Bishop Beaufort. She said: "Oh, let's not worry too much. Bishop Beaufort's a man of the world. He's got us what we want. He likes to tease, that's all."

Yet Owain was subtler than she realized. For all his caution about trusting Bishop Beaufort, it was Owain who kept the Bishop close when Catherine unwisely came close to alienating him.

At Christmas, Catherine returned the tiny jeweled sword the Bishop tried to give the little King. She said: "There'll be enough time for fighting. Let him have a bit of peace now."

The Bishop raised an eyebrow. Catherine felt tears come to her eyes. "Dear girl," he said, a little reprovingly, "your son will one day be the supreme authority on earth for his subjects."

"I know," she said.

"He'll have to be seen by them. Talk to them. He's the one who will decide their disputes—be their personal champion in war as well as in peace. His personality, more than any councils and parliaments, will be what determines the whole nation's quality of life."

"I know," she repeated, and she was aware of the stubborn cast of her lips.

"If he's to do all that, the English will have to respect him. And the English are used to being ruled by heroes. Prayers are only going to be so much use. Shrewdness and a quick mind will help, but they will not be enough. He'll need muscle and sinew . . . a presence majestic enough to inspire loyalty . . . the respect born of his mastery of the arts of war. He'll need to learn to carry a sword."

The Bishop was nodding his head persuasively. She was shaking hers. Obstinately, with a tremble in her voice, she said again, "Still. I want him to be brought up to peace."

It was Owain who interjected.

"The sword would really come into its own," he said, ranging himself beside and slightly behind the Bishop—his usual stance—"if His Majesty had other children of his rank to play with—children whose respect for him would shape his own royal behavior. Don't you think, my lord, that an excellent first step in training His Majesty for kingship would be to make that possible?"

Catherine bit her lip. Briefly, she felt betrayed that Owain was arguing for the sword. But then she remembered the wish she'd expressed to Owain, a day or so earlier, that Harry could have some playmates. She was being petulant; he was just using that thought to solve this problem.

The Bishop was listening to his man. Catherine could see from his gleaming eyes that the idea of a school of the nobility, invited by the Bishop himself, had caught his fancy. "Who?" he said.

Owain had thought out his answer. "The wards," he replied. "Every orphan of noble blood who is the King's ward. I can think of a good half-dozen. James Butler, heir of the Earl of Ormond—he's five. John de Vere, the Earl of Oxford—fifteen. Thomas, Lord Roos—sixteen. The little Duke of York, Richard—he's about thirteen." He turned to Catherine. "The royal household should offer to pay for them to live here; each with his own master paid for by the King."

The Bishop was nodding, a great smile spreading across his face.

Owain picked up the child's sword and tested it in his hand. "A beautiful thing," he said appreciatively, before putting it gently aside on a chest. "In due course—once the school is in residence—I know my lady will agree that His Majesty will be very grateful for it."

The Bishop nodded absentmindedly; the small sword almost forgotten in the new idea. Catherine nodded, grateful too. Those great youths, all so much older than Harry, wouldn't want to cross swords with an infant. It would be years, after all, just as she wanted. Harry could have his peaceful childhood and no one would be offended. Owain's quick wits had kept the peace.

TWENTY-SIX

There wasn't much feasting in England. But Duke Humphrey held a banquet on the anniversary of King Henry's death, in August, after the royal party had returned by barge from a Mass for Londoners at St. Paul's Cathedral, and a further Mass at Westminster Abbey.

Catherine, out of her black and russet weeds for the first time in a year, was wearing rich red silk robes and a tall double-horned hennin headdress, with a gossamer silk veil glowing and dancing in the river breeze. She'd arrived at Westminster with Harry and their households two or three days before, riding up from Waltham Abbey in Essex, where they'd been staying, to make ready. In the normal run of things, occupied as she was in the nursery, and with only mourning clothes to worry about, Catherine didn't have much need for ladies anymore. Once she'd got rid of the unlovable Mistress Ryman, she'd got by, for much of the year, with the quiet help of Dame Alice Butler, who made it part of her house duties to help the Queen Mother dress and undress. But Catherine was eager to make a special effort for this dinner—the obit in Henry's memory, after which her time of deep mourning would be formally set aside, and something new might begin. So she had requested that Duke Henry find suitable ladies to attend her while at Westminster, and she'd had Owain have the Bishop send down vestment-makers to fit her out beforehand for a new gown. It was an enormous, gathered French-style houppelande, trimmed with dark fur, which didn't count as a French style anymore as some English ladies had also taken to wearing it, rather than the old-fashioned cotehardies or fur-trimmed jackets that reminded Catherine of Christine's clothing. That was enough of a concession to English taste, she decided, surprised to realize how much she was enjoying planning this. She wasn't going to spend money on cloth in some shade of English winter sky—gray or sludge. She'd keep to her own taste in colors: a glorious jewel shade. And she'd wear the ruby jewel that had been Henry's first gift to her long ago: a fitting tribute. It would set the robe off perfectly.

It was only when she'd reached the royal rooms at Westminster, settled Harry and the servants in and ordered the trunks unpacked (and found the suite, even in August, even with sweet clean rushes on the floor and a new tapestry on the wall, as dank and gloomy as ever), that she was introduced to her ladies for the stay. Immediately she saw that Duke Humphrey, who, as the host and the leading bachelor of the court was to be the Queen Mother's partner for the evening, had arranged an extremely odd pair of companions to prepare her for the soiree.

Both ladies were wearing brightly colored clothing for England, and the lustrous fabrics were embroidered in gold, just as her robe was—one a cotehardie in luscious golden silk trimmed with fur, and the other a still lovelier figured silk in the softest green, patterned with Eastern flowers. Yet one lady was old and wrinkled, with bright but confused blue eyes in grayish skin, food marks on her clothing and masculine-looking iron-gray hairs sticking out wildly, like straws, under her gauzy headdress and on her chin. The other was younger than Catherine—only just a woman. She was unnaturally tall—at least as tall as most men—and though she was slender, fair-haired, and beautiful, her looks were of that frightening, haughty, unsmiling, iron-gray-eyed variety that reminded Catherine of stories of witches and ice queens.

Yet both came forward as soon as they saw the Queen Mother and bowed over Catherine's hand with surprising grace and fluency. Surprising for Englishwomen at any rate; but, Catherine realized, as soon as they opened their mouths and began murmuring their introductory speeches, larded with compliments, they were both native French speakers.

Bowing back, smiling, murmuring, "The honor, the joy" and "I never expected," Catherine found herself thinking very kindly indeed of her brother-in-law Duke Humphrey, who must have intuited how badly she still missed hearing her own language around her, even now her English was getting better; and who had gone to the trouble of searching his dominions for French ladies to send to her for this visit.

The older lady, it transpired, was Queen Jeanne of Navarre—Henry's stepmother, whom he'd once accused of being a witch so he could get his hands on her dower income. Catherine knew of her but had never met her. She knew Henry must have felt guilty about his behavior, because he'd never allowed the two Frenchwomen, his wife and his stepmother, to compare notes. But she also knew Henry had found time, on his deathbed, to give Queen Jeanne back at least enough money to live on—his conscience must have troubled him badly at the last. Getting that money hadn't much improved matters for the old Queen, though; the taint of unpopularity and the sulfur of the witchcraft accusation lingered on. No one wanted to know her. There was always an excuse. People said she'd got stranger with age; she never wanted to leave her home at Langley Manor in Essex, where she spent almost all her time alone in one room with a pet parrot, staring out of the window. But Catherine could see the old lady was seldom invited anywhere. She could feel it in the wonder of that pale-eyed stare as Queen Jeanne greedily drank in her surroundings, and in the vague, astonished way the old lady shook her head, as if she couldn't believe she was out.

As for the younger, more terrifying lady, who was she? "Jacqueline of Hainault, Holland, and Zeeland," the Ice Queen murmured languidly, rising, heavy-lidded and slightly sullen, from her graceful if careless obeisance. Astounded, Catherine recognized Jacqueline as the grown-up version of the tall tomboy girl-child, Henry's protégée, whom she'd met a couple of times before. The previous times, Jacqueline had been a child countess who, she vaguely remembered, had been brought up in England (she had been Henry's ward) and been supposed to marry Henry's brother, John of Bedford—until the girl's own overlord, the Duke of Burgundy, had decided he didn't want that much English influence in his Low Countries, and had married her off to his own cousin the Duke of Brabant instead. Catherine remembered Jacqueline being sent off overseas to her marriage . . . oh, not long ago—soon after Harry's birth, it must have been, because as far as she could recall, Jacqueline had been one of the small army of godparents. A year, or a few months more . . . so shouldn't the girl be at Brabant with her husband? Why was she back in England?

"Why, how beautiful you've become," Catherine said hesitantly, hoping they would become friends and the ice in the other young woman's eyes would melt. "Now that you've grown up I hardly recognized you . . . now you are the Duchess of Brabant . . . ?"

Even as she was saying it, she realized she was being unwise.

Sure enough, Jacqueline sucked air into her lungs and her eyelids lowered still further, until only an angry slit was open on each side of her elegant nose. Holding her height perfectly still, she gazed back at Catherine with what could only be called contempt.

"I regret," the tall girl drawled witheringly, "that marriage was not for me. Nor was Brabant. I am petitioning the Pope for an annulment. I remain the Countess of Hainault, Holland, and Zeeland."

Not knowing whether to feel shocked at the snub, or just to smile to herself at the baleful childishness that Jacqueline couldn't quite strip out of her proud answer, Catherine bit her lip and looked down, murmuring something soft. How ignorant she was of court stories, shut away in her traveling nursery, she thought. She should be better informed; she should follow the dramas of the English court. She should have known Jacqueline would come rushing back to London, where she felt at home, to get away from her own people. When Harry was older she'd have more energy; when it was time to think of remarriage . . .

But she could already see one thing. The thought made her smile wryly to herself. Between the fumbling fingers of confused old Jeanne de Navarre, and the sneering hostility of Jacqueline de Hainault, she'd be better off dressing herself for the feast, or calling in Dame Alice Butler.

Dinner was over. Duke Humphrey was sweating slightly as he rose and handed Catherine up to her feet too. Catherine had lost count of the number of small birds he'd crunched through. No wonder he was getting a little portly. But he was going out of his way to make himself agreeable, and the evening had been a glittering success. Catherine was enjoying herself.

There were tapers and torches everywhere, and flashes of light, like fish in a river, glinting off jewels and the pewter, gold, and silver of the tableware. There were more than two hundred people present.

In her best English, Catherine thanked Humphrey again, as prettily as she knew how, for his thoughtfulness in providing her with French ladies. As she did so, she noticed Jacqueline of Hainault a few places away, between the Bishop and another lord whom Catherine didn't know. The girl was more beautiful than ever. She was wearing blue and gold tonight, and she'd had plenty of time for her own toilette: she'd sent word to Catherine that she was unwell and wouldn't be able to help the Queen Mother dress. Perhaps that was why she was staring at Catherine now; perhaps she was feeling guilty? Catherine didn't think so. The look coming from Jacqueline's eyes had nothing of guilt in it. It was black, concentrated, and full of hate.

Shivering a little, Catherine looked away. Jacqueline de Hainault must be a little mad, she thought. That was a rival's look.

"The first dance," Duke Humphrey said lightly, not noticing, "in a moment. Once I've gone and had a word about the musicians. Shall we?"

Catherine nodded, looking forward to dancing, even English dances. But she was aware, from across the table, of Jacqueline de Hainault's eyelids drooping and her lips tightening, as if even that polite moment of acquiescence was a crime.

Left to herself for a few moments while Duke Humphrey organized his evening, she bowed and smiled and accepted the obeisances of the formal, awkward English lords and ladies who wafted past. Some of them seemed rather elegant tonight, in their dark clothes. She was beginning to know a few faces. Perhaps soon it would be time to learn more.

As soon as the tables had been cleared and pushed back against the walls, the dancing would begin.

She'd caught a glimpse of Owain while they were eating, far down the table in the gloom, separated from her by the bustle of pages and servants. As the guests milled and talked, walking through the halls to the dinner, she stayed aware of where he was, drawing comfort from his distant presence: a head in a black hood.

"My dear," a voice said, very close. A cultured man's voice. She turned, startled. The Bishop was standing behind her shoulder—as if he'd materialized there, without moving toward her; as if he'd sensed that his irritating nephew Humphrey would be gone for a few minutes and they could talk. He had his dinner partner with him: not, thank God, the prickly Jacqueline of Hainault, but a tall, rather beautiful lady in her middle years, with dark curly hair, a straight nose, and a generous laughing mouth, and what must have been perfect skin, now just beginning to dry into parchmenty folds. Her mischievous eyes glinted at Catherine in friendly fashion as she dropped into a deep, impeccable curtsey. Catherine liked her at once. "Margaret, now the Duchess of Clarence," the Bishop said by way of introduction, putting a hand on Catherine's shoulder and another on Margaret's, and drawing them into a walk, three abreast, down the side of the hall, alongside the tables with their swarms of pageboys, ". . . though previously she was married to my dear brother John Beaufort, the Earl of Somerset, God rest his soul." They all crossed themselves in memory of the dead Beaufort earl. "We still consider ourselves brother and sister, Margaret and I," the Bishop continued, not sounding particularly grief-stricken; but then again, Catherine remembered, his brother had died a good twelve years earlier, and Margaret's six Beaufort children were now grown up. Margaret flashed another friendly look at Catherine. "An honor—a joy—the two most charming ladies in England," the Bishop finished. "I hope we'll all see more of each other now the deep mourning is over . . . now that there might be a little more merriment at court . . ."

Catherine knew her cheeks were flushed and her heart was beating faster than usual. To her surprise, she found herself looking forward to that too: to hunts and tournaments and dances and ceremonies, where she could be at home among adults of her own kind, who'd look on her with the understanding eyes of this lady; people she might perhaps laugh with.

The Bishop and Margaret of Clarence moved off, bowing, to begin the stately basse danse. Humphrey was still out of sight. Catherine stood back against the tables, in the shadows, as the last of the pages, busy as ants, carried off the last of the dishes of meat, and watched the couples begin to advance down the room.

She was hardly aware of another tall man until he'd tapped her on the shoulder, and then, as she turned warily round, swept a deep bow full of French elegance. "Sister," he said, in a French voice that had lost its confidence, but with his thin, handsome face lit up with pleasure. "You've become lovelier than ever, I see, in spite of all your sorrows."

She stared, so full of joy that she could hardly speak. It was her cousin Charles of Orléans, whom Henry had refused to free on ransom after he'd been captured at Azincourt. She'd always been so fond of Charles. He was the son of her murdered uncle Louis of Orléans; but he called her "sister" because, long ago, he'd briefly been married to Catherine's elder sister Isabelle, who was dead now, as was his second wife. Catherine hadn't met him since coming to England, though she'd always known he was here somewhere. He'd been locked away in a country castle while she'd been briefly in England as Queen, and she hadn't thought of him once in this last year of mourning, alone with her child and her household, turning Windsor and Wallingford into nurseries. Would they really allow him to take part in court banquets, like any free nobleman? Could this really be him . . . ?

"Charles . . . ?" she stammered, before forgetting her dignity and throwing her arms around his neck.

Long ago, when she'd first known him, when she'd been a little girl and he a radiant golden youth married to Isabelle of Valois, Catherine had hero-worshiped him enough to listen carefully to all the stories about Charles of Orléans' troubled past. How well he's recovered, the servants would whisper; and how handsome he's become, considering what a miserable little shadow he was when his father was killed. By hiding under tables or behind tapestries, and shamelessly eavesdropping whenever no one noticed her there, Catherine had learned that Charles of Orléans had, as a suddenly fatherless child, had to swear the traditional vow of revenge against the Duke of Burgundy for killing his father, then, confusingly, promise the King of France not to take the revenge; and after that he'd had to watch his mother fade away and die of grief and shame. When, a few years later, Charles had found new happiness with Isabelle, everyone had rejoiced with him. The whole French court had grieved with him when his bride had died in child-birth; Catherine couldn't imagine what pain he must have suffered when, soon after, he was taken prisoner, and his second wife, Bonne, the Count of Armagnac's daughter, had died too. But he was born with sunlight in him. Nothing could destroy his optimism. He must be nearing thirty now, and his fair hair had thinned. He looked almost translucent. But he still had that endearing capacity to appear transformed by joy.

Arms tightly linked, they moved toward the table. Catherine forgot everything else—forgot Duke Humphrey, forgot to stay aware of where Owain was—as she questioned her cousin and rejoiced in his laughing, effortlessly charming replies. He still wrote poems. He'd written beautiful verse before, she remembered. "There's precious little else to do, after all," he said ruefully. "A little hunting; there's good hunting at Wallingford, don't you find? I spent time there a couple of years ago. And thank God I like hunting and poetry—because I think I'll be spending the rest of my days like this. Your husband, God rest his soul, always refused to let me be ransomed, in case I went over to your brother . . . to Bourges . . . as if I would . . . and who will reconsider my case now, until your son grows up?

Which means I'm here forever, I think . . . but at least I love filling my days with writing."

"But," she said, shocked that his existence could be so utterly without hope, or that he could take his punishment so lightly, "isn't there anything . . . ?" She stopped. She was a prisoner of fate, too, she thought. Everyone was. What power did she have to change the terms of his imprisonment?

He shrugged, and smiled with only a hint of wistfulness. "I don't want to complain," he said lightly. "Not on a night that has brought me a reunion with you. I want to give thanks!"

He bowed again, murmured, "We'll talk again, I dearly hope; perhaps we will dance, later"—but without trying to pin her down to a promise she might be embarrassed to keep, she realized, touched by his delicacy—and vanished to the place assigned for him. In spite of his glorious rank, she saw with chagrin that it was below the seats of princes of the English blood.

She'd been so absorbed in these last conversations that she'd lost sight of Owain, she realized, once she was left to herself again. The thought surprised her. Even if she didn't spend much of her day talking to Owain, she was almost always aware of where she could find him if she needed him; as if he were the north on her compass. Not knowing where he was now disoriented her. She peered down the table at the shadowy heads sitting out the dance, rather than at the dancers, hoping to see him. She wasn't altogether surprised when, a moment later, another hand touched her shoulder.

She turned round to greet him with a warm smile.

The smile stayed uncertainly on her lips as she saw it wasn't Owain.

How could she not have realized? The hand on her shoulder was big and meaty—with nothing like Owain's careful touch—and it had grabbed her shoulder as if grabbing its prey. It was Humphrey of Gloucester standing above her, with a hand still clamped onto her bare shoulder.

There was something proprietorial and vaguely threatening about his smile. For the first time, too, she could see he was tipsy, or worse—which hadn't been obvious during the meal—and looking lecherous. The heavy-handed courtesies of dinnertime, the awkward pauses, had passed. The wine had made him over-confident. Now, she could see, he seemed to think he could just come and claim her as his, with no more fuss and bother.

It was the last thing she wanted. Turning up the corners of her mouth in an imitation of a smile, she quickly looked down, but there was no escape in modesty. Her downcast eyes could see nothing but the close-up swell and bulge of tree-trunk legs and privates. Hot-faced, she looked up again.

"Rediscovering old friends, eh?" her brother-in-law said, nodding toward Charles of Orléans. Heavily, he propped him-self against the table beside her. There was no need, Catherine thought with another hot burst of shame, for Duke Humphrey to press himself quite so close.

It was only after several minutes of whiskery, difficult, onion-breathed conversation, as Duke Humphrey leaned practically into her face to question her about her household, which he'd omitted to do earlier, and rumble disapprovingly that it had been a mistake to let Mistress Ryman go, and what was the point of the Butler woman, and was the Welshman utterly in-competent, and, patting her repeatedly on hand and arm, com-plimenting her on the red velvet robe, that Catherine became aware, with relief, of Bishop Beaufort moving elegantly by in the dance, glimmering at her with quiet, mocking laughter that he was inviting her to share. She dimpled at him and watched the corners of his mouth go up. Suddenly, it didn't seem quite so bad. A little later still, after Duke Humphrey abruptly got up to rush off to the shadows and relieve himself, half tripping over a dog on the way, Catherine managed to locate Owain's still, dark, watchful presence. He was halfway down the table, perched on a bench, looking at the dancers. He must have felt her eyes on him. He nodded just once in her direction. He wasn't smiling.

Duke Humphrey didn't let her out of his sight or stop paw-ing at her all evening. But it was only when he'd managed to get her to dance with him, and, sweating heavily, was leading her around the floor, that he breathed noisily into her ear, "Time you thought about marrying again, now you're out of your weeds, don't you think?" and edged the hand sweating on her back round her rib cage toward her breasts.

She winced and, pretending to be adjusting her neckline, dislodged his hand. "Oh," he muttered, with the beginning of a dirty guffaw, "no need for that; the view is lovely as it is."

Ignoring that disrespectful last remark, she said with no great warmth, "It's too soon to think of marriage. The memory of my husband is still as dear to me as that of my cousin's wife, long dead in France, is to him." She nodded in the direction of Charles of Orléans, moving by in the dance with Jacqueline of Hainault.

"Lovely girl, that," Humphrey said inconsequentially, and to Catherine's amazement he seemed to be literally licking his lips as his eyes followed Jacqueline of Hainault. "One of the finest. I hope that Frenchman isn't thinking . . ." and he glowered at Charles of Orléans.

Was there no difference between the way the English treated princes of the noblest blood in Christendom and the contemptuous way they might behave to slaves and whores? She shook her head brightly, as if Humphrey's idea was absurd but charming, but inside she couldn't help the stirring of anger at his disrespect.

Then, gently disentangling herself, she added, "If my lord will excuse me . . . so much excitement after a year of solitude . . . I'm worn out." And she left him standing in the middle of the dance floor, mouth open.

Not that Duke Humphrey was disconcerted for long. By the time she'd pushed between the dancers to the edge of the crowded hall, the dance had come to an end. Charles of Orléans was nowhere to be seen. Catherine was amused, when she looked back, to see Duke Humphrey already had his hand on Countess Jacqueline's arm, and he was leaning in toward her, eyes fixed on her breasts, grinning.

Quietly, with an economy of movement that, even under his dark robes, suggested his athleticism, Owain followed her out. They walked up the stone stairs, away from the din and echo. Owain and half a dozen lesser servants were to sleep near her rooms. Catherine was laughing rather hysterically at her escape from the Duke. She started to giggle her story out: ". . . you wouldn't believe the look on his face . . . staring at me . . . staring at Jacqueline of Hainault too . . . the *crassness* of it."

If she expected an answering laugh, she was disappointed. Owain's face stayed somber. "It would be a mistake to make an enemy of Duke Humphrey," was all he said. "Even if you don't want to marry him . . . treat him with respect. Don't go too far."

Bowing from a safe six feet away as he took his leave of the Queen Mother and tried not to be moved by the trust in her long, lovely eyes, Owain clenched his hands into fists inside his robes and prayed for fortitude. There'd been peace, of a sort, in the certainties that had taken shape in the royal household. Whichever castle it moved to, the routines, always exactly the same, were comforting. He knew he had a place. He felt he understood his life. Catherine, so helpless, so absorbed in her role as a mother, needed him. The little boy too. Those facts were simple enough for him to believe that the needs of the flesh could be overcome; the yearnings of the heart ignored. But here, in the grandeur of Westminster, people and events were buffeting painfully into him, and he felt helpless—as bitter as poor Maredudd, and as invisible.

Now—now she'd gone and he was alone—Owain recognized the agonizing writhe and flex of jealousy in his gut. It was so obvious that this entire festivity had been arranged to allow Duke Humphrey to press his suit for Catherine's hand as soon as decently possible. Far too soon for real decency, in Owain's view; it was his own dead brother's wife the shameless goat was lusting after, after all. Had the man no respect?

Yet she'd been so excited about coming to Westminster—calling in tailors, insisting most of the household trail off to the dance in her wake. Like a child with a glittery toy.

Had she no idea?

No wonder Humphrey had got so drunk and started groping at her with his butcher's hands. Humphrey had understood her dressing herself in bright sinful scarlet and decking herself out in her wedding jewels just as everyone else in the hall had—as a signal she'd accept his advances, when they came.

But then she hadn't accepted his advances. She'd kept him dancing attendance all evening, then taken offense at some trifle and humiliated him by walking away in full view of the entire court. He could see now that she wasn't the strumpet they'd all taken her for. But was she an utter fool?

Owain was walking so fast he felt he was on air. When he reached the spiral stairs up to his own rooms, he took them four at a time.

Worse yet, she'd practically fallen round the neck of the Frenchman. Owain had never been proud of having taken Charles of Orléans prisoner all those years ago. He'd liked the Frenchman's thin, sensitive face, and he'd felt the same fear of battle that the Frenchman had. It was just dumb luck that had allowed him to come second to that God-forsaken copse, when the Frenchman was already caught in mud and undergrowth, and play the captor while the other man stumbled before him, tied with a rope. Once back in England, Owain had read the French Duke's wistful verse and found it elegant. He'd always kept back from Charles of Orléans in any situation in England where their paths might have crossed, fearing the other man might be humiliated by meeting him again, or even by having been captured by a man of lesser status. Still, he'd sometimes wished that things were different, and that somehow, one day, he and this man of graceful words might have a conversation. The fact that they couldn't he put down to the ugliness of war.

But tonight, when he'd seen how Catherine had devoured Charles of Orléans with hungry eyes, gobbling up the faded blondness of him, nuzzling up close . . .

Owain banged his door behind him. He was trembling with fury. He wished now that he'd had the sense, back at Azincourt, to take his sword and run the thing through the bloody man's heart.

Even Bishop Beaufort, who usually so enjoyed a cruel little laugh at Humphrey's expense, wasn't as lighthearted the next day as Catherine had expected.

"You do have to remarry," he said seriously, coming to her rooms in the hot midmorning, as she watched the packing of chests and trunks begin. They'd set off for Windsor soon after midday. "You're a *parti*. There will be suitors. And Humphrey wants you for his wife. True, that's partly so he can score off Duke John, but he might take tremendous offense if you turn him down too harshly. So tread carefully."

A little startled, Catherine nodded. She hadn't considered the risk.

"You need to give this real thought," the Bishop emphasized, looking at her with none of his usual sardonic humor. "Your remarriage is probably the most important decision you'll ever have to make. If there's someone you want to choose, you should put the idea firmly into your mind now. Choose your own candidate, if there is one. Don't be girlish; forget modesty. Don't run the risk of finding yourself married off to someone you don't want."

He leaned forward. "Think," he pressed, without a smile. "Is there someone you would choose?"

She was acutely aware of Owain in the shadows behind the Bishop, sitting with one leg laid over the other knee, arms concertinaed over each other, closed in on himself, scowling. All blacks and blues and angles. He looked like an angry god. She didn't know why he looked so angry.

"If there's no one," the Bishop went on, "but you'd still rather not marry Humphrey, we should find another candidate . . . it's always better to choose for yourself . . ."

Catherine continued trying not to look at Owain, tight-lipped and unspeaking, behind the Bishop. She didn't know why she felt so guilty.

Or did she? She'd received a message from Charles of Orléans at first light, by manservant. It was a poem called "The Return of Spring." The lovely gay words were still dancing in her head.

> *Now Time throws off his cloak again,*
> *Of ermined frost, and wind, and rain,*
> *And clothes him in the embroidery,*
> *Of glittering sun and clear blue sky . . .*
> *River, and fount, and tinkling brook,*

Wear in their dainty livery,
Drops of silver jewelry;
In new-made suit they merry look . . .

The Bishop was raising his eyebrows at her, looking for her attention.

"Otherwise . . ." he said.

She didn't answer directly. But, with a little smile on her lips, still reluctant to leave the pretty shallows where her mind wanted to dwell, she said, "Did you see my cousin last night? Charles of Orléans? It was the first time I'd seen him since . . . long ago . . . in France."

She paused. She'd thought she wanted to ask the Bishop if there was really nothing they could do to help poor Charles of Orléans return to France. But now she saw that by mentioning him here, in this conversation, she'd somehow seemed to suggest him as a marriage candidate.

Perhaps that hadn't been entirely unintentional, she thought a split second later. Perhaps . . .

"Suicide," Bishop Beaufort replied swiftly, answering both her questions. "Madness. Don't think of it. Don't even correspond with him. You may only mean to help him, but you would be wasting the goodwill you've begun to build up here if you started fretting about marrying a French prisoner. Don't get caught up in . . . Frenchness. Don't throw yourself away. It means nothing, the old familiarity you feel for your cousin; though it's all too easy to mistake the shared memories of youth for love." He twinkled kindly at her, but she saw it as a warning. "That isn't the kind of association you need."

"But," Catherine stammered, "Charles of Orléans is my blood. My cousin. He was my brother."

"Trust me," the Bishop said. He didn't even want to discuss it anymore.

"Trust him," Owain confirmed, and his face was as sharp and cold as steel. "He is the guardian of your honor."

Catherine bowed her head. There was a muted kind of pleasure in self-denial. She could see the force of their argument. She would not pursue a friendship with her sad, lovely, long-suffering cousin, she thought; just in case. She could see it would be mis-construed as not wanting to become part of England. And she would not harbor thoughts of marrying Charles of Orléans just to feel more at home. She should probably not even seek him out to thank him for the poem.

The next day, as she checked the corners of the Westminster Palace apartment before mounting her horse for Windsor, in case there was any last little thing that had been forgotten, she found a new scrunch of parchment tossed into a corner.

She unraveled it. It was another poem to her, from Charles of Orléans.

"Strengthen, my Love, this castle of my heart, and with some store of pleasure give me aid, for Jealousy, with all them of his part, Strong siege about the weary tower has laid," Charles of Orléans had written—no letter, no words of everyday affection, just a plea. He was jealous. He wanted her. He was asking for patience and perseverance to help him to get her.

Catherine's heart bled for her poor, gallant cousin and the hopelessness of his situation. She didn't know how this message had missed its destination, but she could imagine the Bishop tak-ing it from a messenger yesterday, reading it himself, and seeing it represented a danger that he, the Bishop, thought she shouldn't take, throwing it into a corner.

Or . . . For a moment she wondered: Could it have been Owain?

All the way to Windsor, Catherine thought, a little apprehen-sively, but not without pleasure too, about the possibility of a new marriage. Her thoughts were in the abstract. She couldn't really imagine the intimacy of any real-life man's form or face turning toward her, or smiling, or whispering (except Owain's—she could always imagine Owain; but then Owain was always there in front of her; all men, in her mind, had something of Owain's dark, quiet, height, and poise). When Catherine thought of marriage, she thought primarily that she might enjoy a more public life, attending dances and dinners such as the one Humphrey had organized, where she'd been surprised to have so enjoyed the sight and sound of so many adults of her own rank gathered together, talking and laughing. She might enjoy having a new title—becoming, if not a queen again, for she couldn't leave England and Harry, then maybe a princess or duchess to an English duke—and having guests to invite, or alliances to nurture for her husband.

As long as the husband wasn't Duke Humphrey, she thought. A lifetime of beef breath and hair bursting ginger from nostrils and ears, and coarseness of speech: worth planning to avoid.

As it turned out, however, there was no need for Catherine to rush into a defensive marriage plan to ward off the Duke's amorous attentions. Duke Humphrey had abruptly married someone else. His bride was Jacqueline of Hainault. The lovers had papal permission to marry—but not from Pope Martin of Rome. They'd decided the dubious dispensation of the rival Benedict XIII of Avignon, whose rulings were not accepted in England, would be enough. As soon as they were churched, furtively, in Essex, the Duke and his new Duchess had rushed off to the Continent together. Duke Humphrey was apparently planning to fight her battles for her, and force the Duke of Burgundy to accept that Jacqueline's pre-existing marriage to the Duke of Brabant was null and void.

Catherine stared at the Bishop, who'd been delighted to be the bearer of this news, and was looking cheerfully back at her, smiling with tremendous, visible satisfaction.

"What . . . gone?" she stammered. "For good? Just like that?"

The Bishop's smile grew broader still. "Just like that," he agreed. Catherine could see him thinking of all the Council meetings that would become easier now Duke Humphrey wasn't there to throw his weight around and nag for a larger share of power than the Council wanted to give him—which would leave the Bishop to organize things in his own subtle way. Duke Humphrey had, in effect, impulsively left England to be ruled by the Bishop. No wonder the Bishop looked glad.

But the Bishop didn't say any of that. He just said kindly: "We'll have more time now, to find you a good marriage," as if he had nothing on his mind but Catherine's well-being, and pressed her hand. "You'll be happy about that."

Catherine stole a glance at Owain, standing behind the

Bishop. She was learning to trust Owain's reactions; to see England through his eyes and rely on his cooperation. It was one of the few things she was certain of in her life here, she thought, gratefully; that she and Owain Tudor had moved beyond the impetuousness of their long-ago feelings for each other to the graver, more restrained, more enduring affection that prevailed now. She counted him a friend. She wanted to see how he'd taken the news that Humphrey had gone, and her remarriage was in the hands of Bishop Beaufort. But he had his eyes fixed on his former master, and his features were expressionless. Try as she might, she couldn't read the studied neutrality in that dark face.

Months passed before the Bishop brought up the question of Catherine's marriage again—happy, quiet months, in which, with the Bishop's gentle guidance, the affairs of England seemed to run smoothly enough, far away from Catherine's and Harry's tranquil child-world, and Catherine forgot the brief flicker of interest she'd felt at hurrying back to the company of adults.

The next mention of marriage came only after Harry had made his first bone-jolting four-day trip to London, stopping at Staines, Kingston, and Kennington, before riding on his mother's lap through the City of London to Westminster, to be introduced to a cheering Parliament. It happened only after Christmas, at Hertford Castle, with the entire school of royal wards now in residence. The entertainments had been organized by Owain, from Jack Travaill's London players and the Jews of Abingdon, with New Year gifts to the King of coral beads, a gold brooch, and, from Duke John in France, a gold ring set with a ruby.

Harry was nearly three, in fact, when Bishop Beaufort came to chapel with them and raised the matter again. Watching the little boy's head, folded in prayer, in the chapel (to Catherine's relief, the child loved the solemnity of candles and stained glass and chanting, and spent willing hours on his knees—better, she thought, time spent quietly in prayer than rushing about fighting), he said, "If you were still minded to marry again . . . I have given the matter long thought . . . and there is a possible match . . ."

He gave her a sideways look.

Catherine wished Owain were with them. But he was busy with household duties. Feeling a little alone, she composed her face and hands; made a point of looking up at the Bishop with willing alertness, as if about to acquiesce. She didn't need Owain, she told herself. She was close to the Bishop. She could trust the Bishop to have found the best candidate for her, couldn't she?

"Edmund Beaufort," the Bishop murmured, watching her face.

Catherine's head swam. She hadn't met Edmund Beaufort—he was a prisoner in France—but she knew of him. She'd met his mother, she recalled—the charming, elegant, dark-haired Margaret of Clarence whom the Bishop had introduced her to last year, at the feast at Westminster. She remembered liking Margaret of Clarence at once. She remembered the Duchess's lovely profile too, and the willowy grace of her movements. A son who took after that mother would be unlikely to be ugly, she thought with relief.

Beyond that guess, she realized, she knew only the sketchiest of facts about Edmund Beaufort. He was younger by five years or so: maybe nineteen now. And he was a prisoner of war—like Charles of Orléans in reverse. The fourth son of one Earl of Somerset, and the brother of another, he'd been one of the English lords captured a few years back at the battle of Baugé. He'd been held at Bourges by Catherine's brother Charles ever since, though in his case a ransom had been agreed and he would shortly be released and allowed to return to England.

She knew the Bishop and Duchess Margaret had been drawing up plans for a celebration of Edmund Beaufort's return. Was a marriage to Catherine to be part of the celebrations?

"What do you think?" the Bishop whispered.

"Your nephew," she replied slowly. "You're suggesting I should marry your nephew?"

As those words crossed her lips, it occurred to Catherine that, if she accepted this marriage, organized by one member of the Beaufort clan, to another member of the Beaufort clan, she would be demonstrating to all England that both she and her son the King were utterly at one with the Beauforts. It wasn't at all the neutral marriage proposition she'd expected the Bishop would come up with, after all his talk about how she must find a husband to avoid angering Duke Humphrey. It would infuriate Duke Humphrey, and Duke John over in France, too, if she married a Beaufort. Of course it would—it would elbow both the royal brothers further away from the King, and replace their influence definitively with Bishop Beaufort's. It would be a brilliant marriage—for the Beauforts. But would it be so brilliant for Catherine of Valois, Queen Mother of England?

Then again . . . perhaps it was necessary to choose one set of allies. Perhaps she couldn't spend her whole life sitting on the fence. Perhaps the Beauforts were better for her than the brothers.

If only Owain were here, she thought, panicking inside, but smiling back at the Bishop to hide her turmoil of conflicting thoughts with what she hoped was an appearance of interest that was warm enough to be courteous but not so warm that it signaled instant acceptance.

With a flash of relief, she realized that she knew where Owain had been planning to be this afternoon: supervising the harvest of the last roses of summer from the walled garden, to be made into potpourri and oil, and the cutting back of the remaining foliage for winter.

Rising from her knees, and raising a startled-looking Harry from his prayer, thinking to herself that there was no point their being in chapel if they were only going to talk among themselves, and that they might as well take the last of the summer sunshine while it was there, she said, a little louder: "An interesting idea . . . I'd like to know more . . . shall we go and walk in the gardens?"

Catherine felt relieved once she'd managed to bump into Owain and the servants in the gardens, and the Bishop had rumbled, in his urbane way, "What a pleasure . . . join us for a stroll, if you can spare five minutes." In the sunlight, Owain had eased himself into the position he'd grown comfortable in during his time of service to the cleric, walking just behind the older man's shoulder, looking thoughtful. But when Owain heard the subject under discussion he had no guidance to offer. His face closed up. After one brief turn around the paths, he excused himself and returned to his work.

Catherine was quietly panicked again to see him go. The Bishop took no notice. He continued to talk, gently, insistently: describing Edmund Beaufort's charm as a child—"my favorite nephew," he said with a reminiscent smile—his physical beauty, and, of course, the extraordinary bravery Edmund Beaufort had shown as little more than a boy, at the battle of Baugé.

"His courage deserves reward. I've raised the question at Council, and I think I can safely say the councilors may decide to give him—oh, an earldom at least—"

Catherine widened her eyes, hoping she looked appreciative enough. Even without Owain's guidance, she could smell a rat now. So, she thought, Edmund Beaufort has no title.

"And appropriate estates for an earl . . . or a duke," the Bishop added beguilingly. "Revenues."

Catherine smiled and nodded. But she was thinking: So Edmund Beaufort has no money either.

She knew of one more problem with Edmund Beaufort, which the Bishop hadn't mentioned. Like all his powerful Beaufort relatives—even the Bishop—Edmund wasn't quite royal. He was the product of Prince John of Gaunt's relationship, a generation or two back, with his mistress Katherine Swynford. This union had become marriage after twenty years. The children of the union were now considered legitimate, as far as that went, but they were barred in perpetuity from holding the throne of England. A royal marriage to Catherine, a genuine princess, would be a clever alliance for Edmund Beaufort. It would raise his status, possibly enough to allow the Beauforts, at some future stage, to bypass that irksome barrier to their highest ambitions.

"It's got cold," Catherine said, looking up as if the sky had filled with clouds, feeling less sure than usual that she liked the Bishop, who was looking at her with such determinedly agreeable eyes, and who wanted her to advance him and his kin with this marriage. "Let's go inside." Yet by the time, much later, that the persuasive Bishop had left, Catherine had let herself be half convinced that Edmund Beaufort was tomorrow's man, one of the great warriors of the English aristocracy, and therefore a potentially worthy match.

She'd asked for a picture. She'd agreed to consider receiving a letter. She'd even dared ask, "How do you think Humphrey would feel about a Beaufort marriage?"

And she'd heard the Bishop's wry reply, pronounced over a shrug, "Ahh, Humphrey—a spent force now, wouldn't you say . . . I doubt we'll see him again for many a long year."

"Well . . . what about Duke John?" she'd persisted.

But the Bishop had only shrugged again. "As for John, I'd say *he* has his hands full with running the war effort in France. It's not going as well as it was. He should have cleaned up every last soldier from Bourges long ago, but he doesn't seem to be able to get near the south." Then he grinned, with friendly malice. "What's more, he has Humphrey to deal with now too, charging around the Low Countries making a fool of himself. Can you imagine—they say Humphrey's challenged the Duke of Burgundy to a duel to settle the question of Jacqueline's marriage! So . . . poor John . . . a lot to contend with. He won't worry overmuch if you marry young Edmund."

He tittered. Reassured, Catherine tittered too. She was letting the picture into her mind of a future of amusing, gossipy fireside evenings with a younger, handsomer version of the Bishop: talking French with an Englishman who'd spent half his life at her brother's rebel court; a man who, once he was made a duke by Harry, would achieve greatness. A man Harry would love.

Owain excused himself from service for the next two days. A fever, he said. A lesser servant set out Catherine's food at table in his absence.

But she found him on the third day, in the chapel, on his knees. He was very pale. There were shadows under his eyes. He looked angry and set-faced.

She knelt beside him, trying to catch his eye. She saw his nostrils flare and white dents appear. He kept his head averted.

She didn't care. For once she wouldn't respect the privacy of his prayers. She needed his advice.

He closed his eyes. Then he opened them and turned to her with visible self-control. "If you would like to talk to me," he said, "shall we leave the chapel?"

She could scarcely keep up with him outside in the long echoing corridor, as the arches flashed past. His legs were doing seven-league strides.

Breathlessly, she said, "What do you think?"

Owain carried on walking; his expression frightened her.

"About what?" he said, though it was clear he knew what she was talking about.

"The Bishop's choice of husband for me," she said patiently, or as patiently as she could, considering the speed at which she was having to trot to keep up with Owain. Then, "They say he's a brave soldier?"

Owain stopped, so suddenly she almost cannoned into him. His face was black with fury.

"Edmund Beaufort. A reckless fool of a boy whose only act of valor was to get himself taken prisoner. What do you want me to say in his favor?"

She gaped at him.

Eyes blazing, Owain held up one finger after another, and rattled off, with insistent logic: "No title. No hope of one. A fourth son. Blood not quite royal enough. And no money. He'd live off you. Of course Beaufort wants you to marry his family. But Edmund?" Owain's lip curled. "You'd be a fool. You'd be no better off with him than you would with me."

They stared at each other. She'd never seen such hostility in his eyes. She was aware of their breath rising and falling in their chests.

She thought childishly: This isn't fair. I don't deserve this. I wasn't the one who thought of this . . .

Taking a deep breath, trying to keep her voice peaceable, trying to stick to the narrow question of Edmund Beaufort's prospects, she persisted: "But he'll earn rewards at the war. The Bishop's already working on a title for him . . . for his service so far . . . an earldom or a dukedom . . ."

For reasons Catherine didn't understand, that only made Owain seem angrier. He raised his hands in a gesture that was supposed to look resigned, but didn't. "Well . . . you've made your decision, then," he said coldly. He turned as if to stalk off.

Catherine shook her head. "No; no, I haven't," she answered, and there was anger creeping into her voice too now. She was surprised at how loud it was. "I only want advice. I need your help." She stared back at Owain, right in the eyes. He had no right, she thought, no *right* to rage like this; she'd done nothing to offend.

"He's playing you, can't you see?" Owain said tightly. "Thinking you're so bored with your life in the nursery that you'll jump at the chance of a husband. That you'll want this one enough that you'll raise him to your own level so you can marry him. That you'll be the making of all the Beauforts. Don't be a *bloody fool*."

His voice was still quiet, but ringing with anger. He turned away, but she wasn't going to let him go. Quickly she put her hand out and held on to his arm.

If she'd thought that touch would keep him, or even calm him, she was wrong. He jolted back round at the touch of her flesh as fast and painfully as if he'd been burned. He flung his arm up in the air to shake off her hand, and spun his body out of her reach. There was a look of horror or near panic on his face.

"Get off me!" he cried loudly. Too loudly.

Then there was a long silence. They could both still hear the memory of his voice echoing through their heads.

Finally, Owain shook his head and let out a big pent-up breath. He was still standing too straight and drawing breath up through flared nostrils. He didn't apologize for yelling that she shouldn't touch him. But he made his voice sound calm again.

"This is my advice," he said. "Since you ask. I don't see the need for you to think of marrying again so soon. Let Harry turn seven. Why hurry? You have four more years with him. Enjoy the time."

Their eyes met again. Catherine didn't know what she'd expected him to say but, after that anguished howl, she'd thought it must be worse. So that was all Owain wanted—for things to stay just as they were, for as long as possible, for the full four years that were left. She could understand that.

She thought she understood something else, too. If it was only Harry he wanted to see grow up a little more in that time, Owain wouldn't care one way or the other whether the household had a new master. Owain would only care if he were mostly there because of her. She took a deep breath, then sighed out the sweet air. For all his calm and control, perhaps Owain was jealous.

Before she'd even begun the smile that was coming next, he'd bowed and was gone.

TWENTY-SEVEN

The Bishop, scenting a major victory through this marriage, became more confident, smoother than ever, and impossible to avoid.

Catherine didn't try very hard to avoid him. He was always so charming; and the prospect of becoming part of a powerful family cast in his mold was not unattractive. She found herself thinking of the objections to the marriage as Owain's objections, not her own; and dithering over whether to reject or press ahead with a marriage with Bishop Beaufort's nephew.

In any case, it would have been hard to stop the Bishop. Even as she fretted about how most delicately to handle the question of his candidate, Bishop Beaufort came back with a page of a letter from Bourges, bearing a miniature likeness of Edmund Beaufort.

He must have had it before the question of asking Edmund Beaufort to get a likeness made had even arisen. That had been less than a week ago. He couldn't possibly have sent to France for it in that time. Catherine realized uneasily that he really was playing her like a fish on a line.

He pulled the picture out for her to see during another visit to chapel, when Owain was absent. Resisting the temptation to glance furtively around—what did she have to feel guilty about, after all, even if Owain were to see?—Catherine looked. The man in the picture was tall, dark, and slim. As far as you could tell from a picture of that sort, he was handsome. He was in battle dress, wielding a sword. Behind him was a bright castle. Bourges? She'd never been to Bourges. Beside him was a pink-eyed young man in a turban.

"Why," Catherine said, surprised, looking closely at the miniature but with her eye turning straight to the pink-eyed man, "that's my brother . . . Charles . . ."

She fell silent. She didn't usually like to think of Charles, but she hadn't expected him to be there. Before she stopped herself, she'd been going to say: ". . . and how sad he looks."

Had Charles always seemed so unhappy? Or was it just the troubles of his adult years that had given him that miserable air?

She glanced up at the Bishop. He was smiling patiently; and he'd lifted a finger to the page, to guide her eye to the right figure. "Yes, your brother," he said, "and *this* is my nephew."

Obediently, Catherine looked. But the unknown figure meant nothing to her and stayed flat on the page. It could have been Owain, or any other tall, dark-haired man. It was her brother's image which stayed in her mind, with its pink eyes.

Nothing, it seemed, could dent Bishop Beaufort's overweening confidence—not even Duke Humphrey's angry return to London.

Duke John had sent his brother home after stopping him fighting his duel with the Duke of Burgundy. They said Duke Humphrey's wife had given birth to a stillborn child. They said Duke Humphrey had deserted her and, now he was back, was taking up again with his old mistress Eleanor Cobden. At any rate, Countess Jacqueline was nowhere to be seen, and Duke Humphrey was in a mean mood—out for a fight.

The news that Humphrey was back was, in one sense, a relief for Catherine. It meant the Bishop stopped riding down quite so often to Eltham, where her royal household was, whenever he felt like reminding her of a few more of Edmund Beaufort's impressive characteristics. It was fun, in a way, to have a suitor dangled temptingly in front of her eyes. These had been more lighthearted weeks than she remembered in a long time. But she was beginning to feel a little hunted. She was aware, too, of Owain's suspicious eyes on her every time the Bishop arrived. She wanted time to make up her mind for herself.

None of them realized early enough that Humphrey's return meant trouble. Bishop Beaufort, perhaps feeling he'd already got the upper hand over his nephew, abandoned all his usual subtlety and went out of his way to humiliate Humphrey. When Humphrey and the three hundred armed men he was traveling with first marched into London, Bishop Beaufort refused to let them lodge in the state apartments at the Tower. The Bishop said he was acting in the name of the Council of England, and Humphrey represented a security risk.

The next messenger who galloped through the gates at Eltham, where Catherine's household were waiting helplessly for news, brought worse tidings. Duke Humphrey's men, coming from the City, and Bishop Beaufort's army, advancing from his luxurious inn at Southwark, were fighting a pitched battle at London Bridge. The merchants of London were supporting the Duke with their pikes and longbows and halberds. Houses were burning on the bridge. There was wildfire in the air.

Catherine went quietly to Harry's chamber and stood, with her taper in hand, watching him sleep—pink in his cheeks, a smile chasing across his face as he dreamed, a fat little hand sticking out over the quilt. This was the trouble she'd dreaded for so long; how had she failed to see it when it came? Please, she begged—and she didn't know herself whether it was a prayer to God or to the Duke and the Bishop—don't let him be dragged into this. Let it stop.

It did stop. The Archbishop of Canterbury walked out, through the arrows and smoke, the charred, battered bridge-top homes and the groaning bodies, and negotiated a cease-fire.

"It's not over," Owain said bleakly when Catherine told him.

She could see he was right. She set her jaw and waited fearfully for more news.

The next messenger was Duke Humphrey himself, muddy and truculent, bursting into the great hall at Eltham at the dinner hour at the head of a troop of knights, demanding that the King go to London to ride through the City—a sign of peace.

Catherine had hurriedly risen to her feet at the clangor in the corridor. Trying to ignore the frantic beating of her heart, she bowed a welcome and said: "We will come together."

But Duke Humphrey gave her a look in which she saw only dislike and boredom. The old flirtatiousness had gone for good. "No need for that," he said roughly. "He's a big boy." He turned away and barked out, at no one in particular, "Bring His Majesty down."

Catherine bit her lip. Owain, standing tall and still before her with a dish of rabbit in his hands, nodded almost imperceptibly. There was no point in trying to argue.

They could hear Harry protesting long before he became visible in the doorway. "Don't want to go if I can't take my ship!" he was wailing, dragging his heels and catching at chests and stools and tapestries with flailing hands as Dame Butler, white-faced and worried, pulled him forward. "Want to play with my boatie!"

Duke Humphrey marched up to him. Towered above him. "Be quiet," he said ominously.

Harry gave his uncle a look of horror, then burst into tears. No one had ever spoken so roughly to him before.

Duke Humphrey leaned down, grabbed both the child's shoulders, and gave him a hard shake. Beside herself, Catherine began to rush forward to stop him. But Owain and the dish of rabbit were in her way.

Harry gulped away his tears. He fastened big, terrified eyes fearfully on Duke Humphrey.

"Now, behave," Duke Humphrey admonished, still severely. "Crying like a girl. Disgraceful. You'll be back tomorrow. You'll get your ship back then."

Still saucer-eyed and silent, Harry nodded again.

Duke Humphrey barked at the assembled servantry: "Sword. Breastplate. Horse."

There was a scattering, a rush of obedient feet. Catherine said, steeling herself, "He has no breastplate."

Humphrey gave her an unpleasant look. "Mollycoddled. No

wonder he's so namby-pamby. You've been neglecting your duties, Madam." Viciously, he added: "Spending too much time planning your marriage, no doubt."

Catherine gasped. What could Humphrey know about any marriage plans? There were no real marriage plans. The whole idea had been nothing more than a twinkle in the Bishop's eye. She didn't like the harsh look in Humphrey's eye. She wished he hadn't said that.

Owain had put down the dish. He stepped forward. "I will fetch his sword, my lady," he said loudly to Catherine. And, calmly, to Duke Humphrey, "He's outgrown the breastplate, Your Grace."

None of the schoolboys or tutors or servants had ever even seen Bishop Beaufort's gift of a small sword. It had gone straight into a chest. No one had anything to say. Everyone listened, dazed, to Owain's steady footsteps recede, then return, as if by a miracle, with the tiny chased weapon in his hand.

Kneeling before the little King, Owain fastened the sword belt round his waist. Catherine could see the encouraging pat he gave the child; the tiny affirmative nod. She could see Harry, taking courage, nod back.

Humphrey snorted, but he was slightly mollified by the sight of the sword. He's not a bad man, Catherine told herself, trying to make herself believe it; it's not as if any real harm will come to Harry. She tried to imagine Duke Humphrey and Bishop Beaufort riding side by side through the streets of London, flanking the Archbishop, getting over their quarrel, learning to talk to each other again. Tried to see merit in Harry's being there too, learning the importance of peace.

Still, she didn't like the way that, as the knights trooped out behind Duke Humphrey, Harry failed to meet her eye, or the gaze of any of his other agonized, helpless well-wishers in the hall. He was staring blankly into the middle distance, letting the sword bump uselessly at his side, and, in a low, loud, tuneless voice, he was humming.

When the knights, without Duke Humphrey this time, delivered Harry back to her the next evening, the little boy waited, slack-jawed and vacant-eyed, till they'd gone, then threw himself into her arms and clung so tightly to her that she could hardly breathe.

"It's all right, all right . . ." she soothed anxiously, walking him to and fro, rocking away his hurt. She put him to bed herself, dispensing with the services of Dame Butler.

He didn't want to play with his ship. He didn't say a word as she undressed and washed him, just whimpered and hummed, in that loud, strange, repetitive way. It was only when his eyes were heavy with sleep and the humming had finally stopped that she dared ask, "Was it nice to see Uncle Beaufort?"

He loved the Bishop. She'd thought that would be the part of his trip he'd be least unhappy about remembering. She hadn't expected his face to crumple and tears to come to his eyes at her question. He turned and buried his face in the cushion, sobbing.

"Unca Bobo wasn't there," she made out. "They said he'd run away. They said he was a coward."

"Uncle Humphrey said that?" Catherine questioned, with her heart turning to iron against the Duke.

"No . . . everyone," the little voice sniveled on. "When we went past the big wharf in the Vintry . . . all the men coming out of the inn to look at us . . . they were all shouting . . . saying rude things . . . they were going to throw Unca Bobo in the river . . . teach him to swim with wings."

Bishop Beaufort didn't appear anymore at Eltham, or Wallingford, or Windsor. They said he was in hiding at Southwark, in fear of his life. Later Duke Humphrey had him put on trial in a parliament held in Leicester. The Bishop was stripped of the Chancellor's great seal, and encouraged to go overseas on an extended pilgrimage. Once he'd left England, Duke John made a gesture of peace by allowing him to take the cardinal's hat that Henry had always refused him. But Cardinal Beaufort wasn't expected home anytime soon.

Catherine didn't expect to meet Edmund Beaufort now. But, by a quirk of fate, she was, after all, introduced to him by his mother at the end of the stormy parliament at Leicester. Catherine had traveled there with Harry, so the child could appear at

the opening and closing sessions. Beaufort was as tall and handsome and dark as the picture had suggested; lightly muscled and
elegantly dressed; with his uncle's wit and humor. He bowed
low over Catherine's hand and gave her soft looks from under
perfectly respectable yet mischievous greenish eyes. "Ah, if
only," he said, with a mixture of charm and apparent sincerity,
"our marriage had been arranged in time . . ." Then, since they
both knew that, at that very moment, at the other end of Leicester, Bishop Beaufort was being hustled out of his rooms to begin
his long journey overseas, and the whole project was dead, he
shrugged lightly. "How happy I would have been."

He spoke impeccable French, she noticed. His mother clung
to her son, bursting with pride. "I can't believe he's back," she
kept saying. "I can't believe our good fortune." Catherine kept
watching the perfect young man, long after the two of them
had moved on through the hall. The Bishop had been right, she
could see: Edmund Beaufort was full of promise, and would
certainly rise to be something grand. But he wasn't for her. She
was surprised to find she didn't mind at all. She remained oddly
contented with her lot, husband or no husband.

But Catherine missed the Bishop. She missed the delight
she'd sensed about him when he'd thought she might marry his
nephew. She missed the elegance and wit he'd brought to life.

There was no more wit, or fun, or lightness of heart, now
that Duke Humphrey was back in charge.

Duke Humphrey's New Year's gift to Catherine was a law. It
stated that the Queen Mother was forbidden to marry without
the express permission of the Council of England.

Now that Humphrey controlled everything, it meant that
Catherine wouldn't be allowed to marry without the express
permission of Humphrey. She'd have to beg. He'd almost certainly turn her down. It was punishment. It was vindictive. It
was revenge.

"Are you sure?" Catherine asked when Owain first brought
her the news. "Is this law real?" She couldn't believe it.
Humphrey wouldn't be so contemptuous as to remove her one

real liberty—to choose a new husband—without even bothering to tell her. Or would he?

"Real enough. The scrivener who's just come back from London heard the proclamation there. He said everyone was talking about it," Owain said baldly back. He added: "He must have heard about the Edmund Beaufort plan." His voice was stripped bare of the accusation she felt might have been there.

Humphrey must have seen the miniature, Catherine thought, her mind racing to grasp what this might mean. Or someone must have told him something. If only she'd been clearer with the Bishop from the start. If only she'd said she didn't want that handsome boy for her husband.

She'd been a fool. She'd been too weak; too eager to please. Why hadn't she thought?

Too late for regrets now; too late for everything. She shook her head.

"I wish I'd encouraged you to marry the Beaufort boy quickly," Owain said into the silence. "While there was still time. I gave you bad advice, maybe. I'm sorry if I did."

She was so moved by that that she almost reached out and squeezed his arm in gratitude. But the memory of how he'd reacted the only other time she'd tried to touch him came to her just in time. She made her hand drop back to her side.

They walked on, side by side.

"Humphrey will never agree to any marriage that I want," she said bleakly. "He'll cut off all my paths to the future."

Owain shrugged. When he spoke, his voice was studiedly neutral. "There will be reasons of state for marrying you off sooner or later. You're too valuable to be ignored. He'll have to relent."

Catherine shook her head. "Why?" she said. "He hates me."

She waited for Owain to protest again that, no, it wasn't so bad. But he kept his silence. There was just the sound of their feet, matching pace for pace on the iron-hard January earth.

It wasn't just Catherine who came in for punishment at the hands of Duke Humphrey. It was Harry too. The Duke sent word that Harry was to have more male discipline, and less mollycoddling.

The gentlewomen Catherine had surrounded Harry with were removed. Featherbedding, Duke Humphrey barked, and he sent Richard Beauchamp, the Earl of Warwick, a stick-thin, stringy, mean-faced man, whom Catherine disliked on sight, to take charge of the King's upbringing instead, as guardian and tutor.

"He has my personal authority to beat the boy if he misbehaves," Duke Humphrey told Catherine at the ceremony, just before Harry's fifth birthday, at which he knighted Harry, and Harry, in his turn, waveringly touched his miniature sword to the shoulders of thirty-eight other young noblemen. Catherine made to protest, but Duke Humphrey overrode her voice. Raising his, he added, "And we'll have no more of this nonsense about no fighting. The boy's a king. It's time he learned to behave like one."

Catherine said mutinously: "But he's just turning five. He's in my care until he turns seven. Until the protectorate ends. That's what was agreed."

Duke Humphrey gave her a withering look. Ignoring that (the rules of the protectorate had been made up on the spot, and could be changed by the Council, and Duke Humphrey was, now he'd got rid of Bishop Beaufort, the leader of the Council), he finished: "I've told Warwick he can remove anyone he chooses from the household, too. So—no obstructive behavior from anyone, do you understand? Make sure my orders are obeyed." With a brief, hostile bow, he moved away.

Catherine stared resentfully after her brother-in-law, letting her thoughts chase through her head. This disrespect would never have happened in France, she thought, proudly remembering the Court of Love, and the exquisite charm of the princes, and trying not to remember the wars that had arisen out of that same French pride.

The hot, reckless response that came first to her mind was that she wouldn't ever let Warwick lay a finger on her son, and he'd better not dare try to.

But Owain advised her to put aside all thoughts of resisting

Humphrey's changes. Owain went very quiet at first, when he heard that the Earl of Warwick would run the King's household. But when, after a pause, he recovered his words, he quickly counseled Catherine: "Harry might thrive. He might be at just the age to enjoy having more men in his life. There might be more good in it than you realize. Warwick's a hard man; a soldier. You don't want to make an enemy of him needlessly. So, keep a close eye on things; but try and make the best of it, if you can."

Catherine wasn't sure she trusted Owain's usually astute judgment on this point. There seemed to be something too quick about the way he was rushing out this appeaser's opinion. But in the end, with no one to support her if she tried to rebel, she found herself agreeing that caution was probably the most prudent course. Her only patron in England had been swept away, leaving her surrounded by powerful enemies; her own freedom had been limited; and she was still a foreigner who didn't understand these people's ways. She'd have to treat Warwick with care. She couldn't fight by herself. Warwick wasn't quite of her rank—not quite a royal duke—but Humphrey stood too close behind him to take him on.

So the stern new order took shape. Instead of nursemaids, Harry was given four knights and four esquires of the body, all Beauchamps or other connections of the Earl of Warwick. He was also given his own doctor, the learned Master John Somerset, a wrinkled man of middle years, always cold, always wrapped in his furred robes, shivering.

"You'll like Master Somerset," Owain said quietly, catching her wrinkled nose when she first caught sight of him at the other end of the great hall at Windsor. (The royal household was confined now to four castles; her favorite, Eltham, was off limits.) "He's a learned man. I met him at Oxford; he's studied at Cambridge too. Give him a chance. He'll be good for Harry."

So, for all her suspicion of the newcomers, Catherine tried to follow Owain's guidance and make the best of things. Somerset and Owain began to spend time together in the evenings, in Somerset's quarters (Owain's, which she had never seen, she knew to be cell-like, too bare for receiving guests). She learned to feel affection for the old doctor, someone she could consult about Harry's education and preferences and skills and trust to give her an honest answer. And although she didn't warm instinctively to the Earl of Warwick's hatchet face and thin, hard voice; although she was horrified when she saw the miniature suit of armor he'd had made for Harry being assembled around her son's soft little body; she found, if she made an effort that she could, at least appreciate his loyalty to the English crown, his generous patronage of the poet John Lydgate, and, above all, his excellent French.

But she could no longer slip into Harry's chamber at night and sit quietly watching over him, praying for a future of peace and calm for him. She didn't dare venture through the antechambers, with their charge of young men snoring and groaning and sweating and belching and thrashing their naked young limbs out of their blankets and curtains. So she couldn't know for sure whether her child still slept soundly and quietly through the night. She just had to hope for the best, and shut her mind to the rest of her thoughts.

"He's a good little boy," Master Somerset told her reassuringly every time she asked. "Very obedient. Very eager to please."

But obedience wasn't the quality the Earl of Warwick was supposed to instill in King Henry VI of England. Sometimes, on her anxious travels up and down stairwells, where the stone muffled and distorted sounds, she could swear she heard Harry's voice screaming in fear. She saw so little of Harry now—glimpses, between bouts of riding and swordplay and archery, at meals or chapel—that she couldn't check his little body for bruises and whip marks. No one ever admitted chastising him. There was nothing she could do.

Once or twice she caught him hurrying somewhere, on mysterious errands of his own, set by his masters in the new world of men, with a busy, worried look on his face. She'd stop, leaning down, hugging him very tenderly, close enough at last to smell the innocence of him, and drawing him hastily aside into whatever the nearest quiet place was. "My darling," she tried,

"I've seen so little of you lately; tell me what you're doing today . . ."

But he'd just submit to her embraces without enthusiasm. Look vacantly past her. Say, "My lord of Warwick will be angry if I'm late." And wriggle away. Perhaps, she thought disconsolately, trying to comfort herself, all boys distanced themselves from their mothers in this way sooner or later—he was five now, not a baby anymore—and perhaps all mothers felt the same distress.

It was only at the next Christmas festivities that her vague fears were given definite shape. When, after the New Year gift-giving, with the minstrels wailing away in the gallery and the hall full of young men, Harry gave the gawky young Earl of Oxford a hard, suspicious look as he fastened the present that had been selected for him—a gold collar—round the youth's Adam's apple, with sudden suspicion, Catherine thought, He doesn't like John de Vere. I can see it.

She gave Oxford a hard look herself. She caught herself midway through it and shook her head. No, there was no harm in Oxford. He was a sweet boy; awkward but kind. He'd caught and set free the pigeon that had come fluttering into the hall last week. He'd never have done Harry any harm. She must have been imagining that look.

She turned away and began chatting to Master Somerset, who was red-cheeked and talkative after too much claret. So she didn't quite see the action that hushed everyone in the hall. By the time she whipped round, following the other staring eyes, Harry was standing with the gold collar in his hand again. Its clasp was broken. Oxford, who she now realized she'd heard yelp with surprise and pain, was rubbing his neck and looking bewildered. She realized Harry must have ripped the chain off the older boy's neck. Defiantly, Harry turned away from Oxford and walked off to another young man she hadn't yet spoken to—a Polish knight visiting the court, a tall young man with pale blue eyes and a snub nose. There'd been no gift for him. Harry must be troubled by what he saw as an injustice, Catherine thought. He was only a little boy, after all.

"Sigmund," Harry piped self-importantly, holding up the collar to the newcomer, who, mortally embarrassed, blushed to the roots of his white-blond hair and looked around in agony for guidance from other eyes as to whether to accept this stolen present. Harry looked at the foreigner with adoration. "A gift from the King."

The Earl of Warwick wasn't in the room, Catherine saw with relief. It was Master Somerset who caught the Polish youth's eye and nodded that he should take the gift.

The crowd settled and moved, with backs turned to the scene, as the onlookers pretended they weren't aware of the King's odd behavior. Catherine saw Master Somerset quietly approach Sigmund, beckoning. He clearly planned to wait until Harry's attention was elsewhere, then reclaim the collar. But little Harry had trustingly stretched his hand up to the young knight's and was walking him away to a window seat, chatting to him in his high child's voice. Blushing deeper than ever, Sigmund made helpless eye and shoulder signals to the doctor. They could all see there was nothing he could do.

Catherine hadn't seen Owain. But he was there, moving with the swirling crowd. "The gold ring," he said quietly as he passed. "You could give it to Oxford. Amends."

She looked down at her hand. She was wearing the gold ring John of Bedford had sent Harry for Christmas three years ago—a foolish present for a child—which Harry, on Dame Butler's advice, had given her last year. She nodded. Owain had an instinct for these things. That was the right course of action.

Oxford was standing alone, still rubbing his neck with one hand. No one wanted to go up to him. No one wanted to be involved. Coming close, Catherine said quietly, "He's very young," and shook her head, "but I am sorry for the pain he caused you." She slipped the ring into John de Vere's huge, raw-boned, skinny hand. "It was my fault; a mistake with the presents. He knew this was the one meant for you, not the collar. But of course he shouldn't have made the exchange like that . . . are you all right?"

The young earl flushed up; his eyes went bright and soft at the gentleness of her voice. He mumbled his thanks—"a beautiful gift"—bowed politely, and, with dignity, retreated to the shadows at the edge of the hall.

There was an angry bruise on Harry's face that evening when Catherine came across him on the stairs. "Who did that to you?" she asked indignantly. He didn't answer. He just came into her arms, keening. She sat with him in the nearest alcove, feeling the stone cold against her skin, cradling him as he sobbed himself to exhaustion, then began rocking against her, to and fro, humming and droning, staring at the sky. Rocking him in her turn, trying to restore a rhythm to his jerky movements that might calm him into sleep, she was suddenly, terrifyingly transported in her mind back to the white room where her father had once felt safe. To that other beloved figure, rocking and murmuring and staring at the birds wheeling free in the sky.

"Rock-a-bye," she crooned under her breath, as sweetly as she could, trying to sing this child's sadness away. It wasn't the same, she told her fearful heart as she sang. It wasn't the same.

Owain had told Harry to watch himself around the Earl of Warwick more times than he could recall. He'd squat down by the child and put his arm round Harry's shoulder and say, man to man: "Your master likes discipline. He always has. So— don't forget. Be as good as you can for him."

Once Harry had looked seriously back at him and asked: "How do you know? Did you know him when you were a boy, too?"

Owain nodded. "Yes," he said briskly. "I did. He ran your father's household when your father was Prince of Wales. And he was strict then."

TWENTY-EIGHT

Catherine did her best to keep her fears about Harry's treatment and his behavior to herself, and in proportion. If she could do nothing else, she could keep her dignity.

At least she still had Owain. She needed her walks with him and their quiet talks a little more every day. She'd come to rely so completely on his advice and his company. However much he'd hated the way he'd grown up, his hard start in life had taught him how to survive; and she was grateful to him for sharing his expertise. With him at her side she could find a careful way through any storm.

It was the realization that Owain would be leaving her—even sooner than Harry—that weighed most heavily on her spirits as her son turned seven. After Harry's birthday the household would have less than another year in its present shape, with Catherine, at least in theory, still running things. After that, when the seventh year was up, Harry would assume the crown in his own right and the Council's protectorate, theoretically at an end, would be transformed, in practice, into direct control of Harry by Duke Humphrey. She couldn't bear to think of that moment; for the past seven years she had avoided letting it into her mind at all. Now it was almost upon them.

Echoing her thought, kicking snow away from his robes as they paced around the inside of the walls at Windsor, on the December day after Harry's birthday, Owain said: "Less than a year left." His breath was a white cloud in sharp sunlight; his

408

expression was unreadable; but the words made her catch her breath. Until now, no one had said them out loud. Now they were down to months, and to daily dread: of the humiliations to be expected at every stage of the way, and partings, coming soon.

"It will be my time soon too," Owain went on, with his gaze lowered as if he were watching his feet kicking rhythmically out from under his robes. "They're expecting me back at Saint Mary's at Michaelmas next year."

September, she thought: nine months away. The cold fingers of fear were clutching at her heart.

"What will I do when both of you have gone?" she asked desolately, thinking of all the other French prisoners of one sort or another, walled up in England, gasping for air. Her mother-in-law, Jeanne of Navarre, old and mad in her castle, with no one left for company but a few old maids and a parrot in a cage. Charles of Orléans, still holed up in one country residence or another, hunting, writing his melancholy poetry. Jacqueline of Hainault had been lucky to get away. No one in England liked the French. There would be no pity for Catherine either once she'd lost the protection that being her son's custodian had so far afforded her. Humphrey would treat her no better than he had the other French prisoners. She'd be walled up too, and left to die alone.

Owain stopped walking. Catherine stopped too. Glancing sideways at him—they were so used to this, pacing side by side around the inside of castle walls, voicing their thoughts carefully, not looking at each other—that she was surprised to find a boyishly irresolute look on his face. He'd become so composed in all this time. She'd forgotten that look.

He stood looking at her, not seeming to notice the bitter wind flapping his hood back from his face. He was biting his lower lip as he thought.

"What will you do? I don't know," he said at last, and his voice was as uncertain as his eyes. "I think about it often."

The wind, all mixed-up brilliant sunlight and knives of frost, was coaxing tears from his eyes, she saw. Not real tears; just trails of wet that froze on his skin. He blinked.

"I worry about it," he added after a while. "And about you, much more than Harry. I don't want to leave you on your own like this."

Then, as if making up his mind, he added, "But there's one thing I've thought of . . ." Then, "Wait." He strode off with tremendous, long-legged strides.

Anyone who had looked out of their window to see the single figure waiting in the bright dusting of snow, gazing at nothing much as she walked up and down, with the beginning of a smile on her lips and her arms wrapped around herself, stroking gently at her furry cloak, would not have imagined the Queen Mother was thinking of anything special. But Catherine was going over Owain's last words, as rapt if they were the miracle she'd waited all her life for. Everything was so bad, and getting worse. But he'd said, with the tender look of the boy she remembered, *I worry . . . about you, much more than Harry.*

As soon as she heard those words she had stopped feeling a careworn mother walking through a December snowfall without a soul to turn to. The years fell away. She became instead a radiant young girl, waiting in the springtime for her lover to lean down and take her in his arms.

For all these years, for all these years, she'd hidden it from herself. But she'd known in her heart; she'd known all along that she loved Owain Tudor. She always had. Not just in a way that would make her want to touch his skin and hair, though now that she could feel the ice inside herself melt she was faint with desire for that too. This love went deeper than that; than anything. He was her other half. His existence gave hers meaning.

She'd borne every trouble in England so far with fortitude, because he'd been there with her. What would she have done without him if, in the past few years, she'd been fool enough to marry one of those other men? She'd never thought that far ahead: never to the point when, if she'd become another man's wife, Owain would actually have left her service. She'd never have imagined completing a marriage if she had thought it would mean not seeing Owain. Thank God none of those marriages came to anything, she thought, and for the first time she was almost grateful to Humphrey for his severity; for his return.

Owain was breathless as he entered the cell-like chamber where he slept, and reached for the plain calf-bound book he'd made, in his early evenings in this household, years before. He kept it by his truckle bed, on the plain wooden table that was the room's only furniture. The book contained copies, in his own hand, of a collection of his favorite of Christine de Pizan's many pieces of advice to widows, whether princesses or paupers, young or not so young, on dealing with a life of adversity with the greatest possible grace. He'd known from the start that, as well as being a gesture of affectionate remembrance, it might be an invaluable guide to him in helping to deal with Catherine's problems as a widow; for, beyond Christine's wisdom, what knowledge did he have of what a widow might expect from the world? He'd consulted the book throughout his time with Catherine, and added to it as the occasion demanded. He fingered it at night; planning her next moves; using it to keep her safe.

Making this book had been the biggest part of Owain's work in refashioning the unholy passion he believed he'd conquered into a more serviceable form of devotion to his lady. Making this book had helped him resist the power of illusions, the scent of rose oil, the wiles of the senses, and seek only the truth to be found in Catherine's situation, and in his. It had been a better way of achieving peace of mind than the scratching of the hair shirt and the ache of bodily deprivations he'd also imposed on himself. It had gone further toward reconciling him to his lot than anything else. His book was an imperfect summing-up of Christine's thought. He'd only taken from the author what he needed, but it had stood him in good stead and shown him the way forward many times. Now that so many of Catherine's choices for the future had been blocked off, he thought it might help her.

Owain had begun his book with some of the poems Christine had written early in her widowhood, describing the consuming, secret grief all widows carry in their hearts. Her saddest verse was here, a virelay. He'd taken it as his; he kept it in his heart too.

> *My eyes may overflow,*
> *But none shall guess the woe*
> *Which my poor heart conceals.*
> *For I must mask the pain,*
> *As nowhere is there pity . . .*

It wasn't what he'd come to find, but Owain let his fingers trail over the beloved words for a moment, thinking. Owain felt all Christine's depictions of grief rang utterly true. His own memories of his dead King were full of the same devotion as she'd expressed in these lines. It had never occurred to him to doubt that, for all Catherine's poise in widowhood, she was also privately tormented by lifelong sorrow at the loss of her husband. That unspoken love seemed entirely natural to him, as natural as his own silent devotion for Catherine. He pictured her praying for Henry's soul, by night and by day; feeling the loss of him as acutely as a soldier, waking in the night, racked with pain by a limb cut off long ago by an enemy sword.

Owain had long forgotten how angry he'd once been with Catherine for the madness of the kiss they'd snatched in the hour of Henry's death; how all those years ago he'd railed against the cruel loveliness of women, the snake of sin in their hearts. It hadn't been her fault; she'd been mad with grief, just as he had, grasping for animal comfort. He'd come to understand that in his time with her. She was an innocent. She wasn't to blame.

Owain had never seen Catherine tending to her father in the old days in France. But here in England, he'd observed Catherine's bravery for himself. He knew that she never gave up, however hard things got. He'd always loved her; he always would love her; but the love he thought he'd felt had changed and matured as he watched her face her problems, as the admiration and compassion he'd come to feel were fused into the heat of that earlier emotion.

He liked to tell himself that his devotion had, over the years he'd lived in her household, therefore become brotherly and innocent. But in his heart he knew that to be a pretense. He knew really that what he felt for Catherine was still as sinful as it ever had been. He wanted her so much that he'd yelled in physical pain, as if he'd been burned, when she'd once touched his arm.

It would have been easier, perhaps, if he'd gone on writing poetry; pouring his feelings out on paper. But he couldn't do that. Not anymore. Once, in one of the castles that had been their home, she'd asked him, "Don't you write anymore, Owain? Poetry, like Charles of Orléans? Anything?" He'd said, without sadness, "No; I am no longer searching for illusions . . . just the truth." He'd thought then that this was the truth. It was his resolve; had been for years. He'd already put aside love poems. And later, when he was through with Catherine, he believed that he would go back to the cloister and write—not about love, but about life; the life of the mind.

It was only now, stroking this page, losing himself in the beauty of the written sadness that Christine had conjured up— and with the words he'd spoken out there in the garden still echoing in his mind—"less than a year now"—that he realized how little he really wanted to do any of that. He'd never be able to discourse knowledgeably about the state of the world; would never want to either. He'd never be able to clear his mind of Catherine. All he wanted was to know he'd see her again: today, every day. Suddenly the thought of the cramped spaces of Saint Mary's in Oxford made him feel claustrophobic, and the dry little future he'd hoped to make for himself seemed nothing better than a cell door yawning open.

He wanted to stay with her. To touch her; to protect her. She needed protection. There were so few possibilities in the prison of human life. Doors that closed didn't open again.

He took a deep breath and turned the page. Firmly he told himself: The answer isn't in love poems. It only unsettles a man to sit mooning over love poems. You should know that by now. The answer never was in love poems.

He flicked through the pages till he found the text he'd intended to show Catherine. Then he closed the book with his finger at the page he'd chosen, and strode off back to the rose garden, to show her Christine de Pizan's suggestion for the rest of her life. A last hope of grace: a way they could, almost, share each other's fates.

Catherine stood out of the wind, hard against the brick of the garden wall, so intent on her reading that she didn't seem aware of the scrape and rattle of thorns on the dead branches behind her head.

Owain knew every word of the text by heart; he was reciting them in his head as he watched.

"Here is what you must do if you want to be saved," Christine had written long ago. *"The scriptures tell of the two ways that lead to Heaven: the contemplative life and the active life.*

"The contemplative life is a way and state of serving God wherein one loves Our Lord so deeply and so passionately that one completely forgets father, mother, children, and everybody, even oneself, on account of the all-consuming attention one unceasingly devotes to one's creator. A woman devoted to contemplation never thinks of anything else; nothing else is of any importance to her; no poverty, trouble, nor suffering preoccupies her heart, the heart of the true contemplative. Her lifestyle completely disregards everything in the world and all its transient pleasures.

"The perfect contemplative is often so ravished that she no longer seems to be herself, and the consolation, sweetness, and pleasure she experiences can scarcely be related, nor can they be compared with any earthly joy. She feels and tastes the glories and joys of Paradise. No other exultation compares to this, as those who have tried the contemplative way know.

"I am sorry that I cannot speak of that exultation any more than a blind man can describe colors. But, above all others, this is the way that is most pleasing to God . . ."

There was more, much more; right down to the conventional proof that God loved those who devoted their lives to contemplation—because Jesus had found Martha's busyness less virtuous than Mary's contemplation.

Catherine let her hands drop, with the book still carefully

cradled in them. She looked up at Owain. Her eyes were dull and dazed. "Why are you showing me this?" she asked, in a small, hurt voice.

"I thought," he began eagerly, "that since I know that after leaving this life in your household I will have a safe future in my cloister, the contemplative future that Christine chose in the end, that perhaps you too . . . that we could both . . ."

She was being slow to grasp his idea. She only looked horrified.

"You mean," she said, "that when Harry is gone from me . . . and you too . . . that you think I should . . . ?" Her voice trailed off.

Owain made his voice strong. "Enter a nunnery," he said. "Devote yourself to God."

But even as he said it, he realized the vanity in it, the pridefulness; saw that he'd only wanted to close her up in a nunnery to marry her fate to his in the last way he could imagine. It would be easier for him to leave the world behind and enter his own cloister if he knew that, somewhere else, she too was giving herself up to the embrace of Christ rather than that of another man.

Catherine had expected something else, he saw. Something better.

"Christine did it," he repeated, with less conviction.

She nodded a few times, as if about to accept resignedly, politely, that he'd at least had good intentions in putting forward this awkward idea. Then something changed in her. She took a deep breath and looked up, and met his eyes more candidly than usual, so he could see the fugitive sadness in them; the sadness he suspected she always carried within.

"I don't want to go to a nunnery," she said. "It's the last thing I want. I don't know why you want to shut yourself up either. Or why she did. She didn't want to. It took her years to decide to."

She looked down at the book. She said: "I want to *live*. Don't you? Not bury myself alive."

She flipped backward through the pages. Stopped at Christine's poems. There was another long silence as she made out the words of grief; with the only sound the whistle of the wind and the thorns tapping against the wall.

"Christine was so lucky in some ways . . ." Catherine said wistfully, raising her eyes again. "If only I'd felt so much for Henry, perhaps all this wouldn't seem such a waste."

She passed him the book. Her fingers brushed his. He'd learned his lesson, though; he couldn't help drawing in a little hiss of breath at her touch, but he kept his hands still and didn't respond. She added: "It would have been a kind of consolation, at least, to remember having loved a husband like that."

Silence. Owain felt the entire basis for his existence slipping away. He didn't know what to say. He had always believed that she *had* loved her husband like that. His certainty on that point had, in fact, been the foundation for the entire respectful, distant relationship he'd built up with Catherine. He didn't know what she could mean now, by just airily suggesting she'd never felt that love at all.

He stared at her, feeling like a fool, feeling she was expecting something of him that he didn't know how to give. The silence deepened. There was something hot and angry in her eyes now. He'd definitely done something wrong. He could see it. Something he didn't understand at all, and seemed powerless to put right.

As if trying to goad him into action, she added: "Sometimes I wonder what I can have done wrong in my life, to be so harshly punished." But she didn't explain. Perhaps she was shocked by the bitterness in her own voice. Those were tears in her eyes. She nodded toward the gate; and abruptly began to walk toward it.

There was no point, he thought, in following. He couldn't think what he could say to comfort her. So he watched her go, helplessly, feeling more wretched than he remembered ever feeling before, seeing that his clumsy attempt to find a way in which their two futures could be lived out, if not together, then at least in parallel, had only brought her closer to despair.

Catherine stopped at the gate, ten feet away. "Don't you have any idea, Owain Tudor?" she called from there, intently, almost angrily, he thought. "Don't you understand . . . *anything*?"

Owain was turned to stone. Roiling, churning anguish inside; stone outside. He couldn't move. He'd have given anything to know what to say.

She closed her eyes, shook her head very quickly, and ran off.

TWENTY-NINE

Catherine avoided Owain for weeks after that. She felt too humiliated by the way the conversation had ended to want to risk starting it again. She'd made herself utterly vulnerable, and had been answered with a blank stare. She would not beg for Owain Tudor's affection, she told herself stiffly. She was a queen.

She couldn't avoid letting him serve her food at table, in front of all the children and servants. There would have been too much explaining to do if she'd changed that ritual. But there were points of hot color in her cheeks and a tightness about her mouth that discouraged him from speaking. She let her eyes slide past him as if he wasn't there. There was no more table talk.

For days, he tried other strategies. He followed her down corridors. He followed her into chapel. He brought Harry to her. He pleaded, "Could we speak?" or, "Could we take a walk?" But she just smiled coldly and shook her head, and let her eyes slide past him again. She refused to take in the bewilderment in his eyes; the hurt. She knew herself to be alone now. The unity of spirit she'd imagined she felt with Owain had always been an illusion. He hadn't had any idea what she was trying to say. He couldn't have had, if all he'd been able to suggest was that she shut herself up in a nunnery for the rest of her days.

She told herself: You must get used to being without him

anyway, and without Harry too. They'll be gone soon enough. You must start to learn to live with solitude now.

Owain's little book had calendars at the back—calendars he ticked off, day by day, to show how much time he still had left in Catherine's household. He sat at his table by the light of the candle, looking at the diagonal ink lines advancing across the boxes of months. So little time left; yet it seemed so agonizingly long.

She couldn't have meant what she seemed to have meant. Could she?

Because Catherine had so much more time alone than before, she took to sitting in the rose garden as spring came, trying to feel hope as she watched life come back to the bony sprays of branches on the walls; seeing them turn green again. But there was no parallel renewal in her own affairs: only more disastrous news, this time coming out of France.

Humphrey and his brother had been quarreling for months over Duke John's failure to complete the English conquest of France. Duke John couldn't capture her brother Charles in Bourges. The cost of the French campaign was astronomical. The merchants of England were fed up with paying. Humphrey was demanding better results. He said Duke John had gone soft, and was only in France for the fleshpots.

Duke John had done his share of writing angry letters back to Parliament. He'd been so nettled by the things Duke Humphrey was saying about him that he'd gone to the lengths of spending an entire winter—seven months—besieging Orléans, the gateway to Charles' southern domains. But strength seemed to have deserted the English troops. They couldn't break the town.

Instead, in the spring of 1429, Dauphin Charles' French armies forced the English to retreat from Orléans. Flush with victory, the French then advanced north, deep into English territory. English-held Paris lay helpless before them, waiting to be attacked. But the French ignored it. They whisked south and east of the capital, through the Seine Valley, accepting the homage of French townsfolk everywhere they appeared—even in Troyes, where the English peace had been agreed by which Catherine's son was recognized as the King of France.

The French swept on to Reims, the ancient coronation place of the kings of France. There, Catherine's brother was crowned King Charles VII.

They said a peasant girl called Jehanne of Arc had led Charles' troops to victory. They said the Maid of Orléans was guided by the voice of God. It was Jehanne of Arc who'd placed the crown on Charles' head.

They said it was a miracle. And that was just what the English said, over here: people who didn't in the least want to believe that God would be performing miracles in favor of the French.

What the bemused people of France would be saying, after all these years of war, Catherine could only imagine. Blood tells, she thought they might be muttering. If God wants to give this man back the crown of France, he can't ever really have been a bastard.

What Catherine herself thought, she didn't know. Each new dispatch only left her quieter, more stunned, more fearful. There were all kinds of rumors. People said the English were finished in France. Duke Humphrey, in London, was fuming at Duke John in France; accusing him of carelessness in the prosecution of the war. From France, Duke John was writing equally furious letters back to the Council and Parliament, accusing his brother of undermining his authority, and of trying, still, to seize control of England for himself. People said that Cardinal Beaufort was on his way back to England.

There were only six months left till the end of the protectorate—till small, anxious Harry was to take control of two kingdoms in turmoil. This wasn't how she wanted her son to come to power.

She still couldn't bring herself to speak to Owain. But when, one spring day, she happened upon a dark robe crumpled over a clump of reeds, on one of her solitary walks along the riverbank, watching the dragonflies make their drunken, jeweled progress over the ripples, and recognized it as Owain's habit, which he must have thrown off to bathe, she wasn't able just to walk away. Instead, she slipped behind a tree. From the safety of its boughs and shadows she looked down at the glitter of the water. Owain's head was bobbing there. Birds were singing above her and there was a sleepy drone of insects all around. There was sunlight on his wet head.

She could hear him singing, even from here. Then he splashed noisily out and stood naked, staring innocently out over the river, like a picture of Adam in the Garden of Eden.

She kept very still. Defiantly, she thought: Everyone would say it was a sin, but loving that man has been the only act in my life that has made me happy, loving him and my son have been the only two pleasures that I don't believe I need ever regret. She knew she shouldn't, but she was committing Owain's beauty to memory. Even a memory might be a comfort of sorts, in whatever future Fate had in store for her.

A consignment of trapped game birds was waiting in cages in the courtyard, destined for the kitchen. Owain walked through the gate with his face still damp from the river. He looked, Catherine thought, as though the swim had washed him clean of worry. He saw her and the birds waiting for slaughter at the same time. She saw the weight of his thoughts settle on him again; the furrow reappear on his brow.

He came toward her. She didn't sweep off. She could see now that there'd been no point in her pride. It was souring what little time there still was. She missed him already, but he was still here, near her. She would have a lifetime more in which to miss him, when he was really gone.

She could feel Owain giving her a careful look from the side. She could feel the hope mounting in him that they could at least—at last—talk.

"I'm sorry," he said, cautiously feeling his way. "About the other time . . . If I said or did anything to offend . . . or failed to understand . . ."

She smiled sadly. "It doesn't matter," she replied, cutting through his stumblings. She was grateful for those words, inadequate though they were. At least if nothing else they had a few more months of this tantalizing bittersweetness, of whispers on the way somewhere, of stolen moments, of the sight of one another. But what he said next took her breath away.

"I can't stay till September," he added very quickly, looking down. "I've thought a lot about it. Give me permission to go away before Michaelmas. Please."

She turned sharply up toward him.

Warily, he stepped back. "It's unbearable," he said.

"What do you mean?" she asked, inching toward him. "Unbearable?"

He inched away. They were circling each other like hunter and prey. She didn't know who was which. There was an imploring look in his eyes.

"Being here with you. The hopelessness of it. Waiting for the end," he said too quickly. She sensed there was more. She held his gaze. After a pause, he added: "Loving you."

The words hung on the air.

Loving me, she repeated to herself wonderingly. He said *loving me.*

"Wanting you," he added. "A torment." He looked up. She thought: He really did say that.

"Always," she said quietly, not knowing whether she was talking about his feelings or hers.

He nodded. "Always," he confirmed in the same monotone, as if it didn't matter whose feelings; as if they'd both always known they felt the same need anyway.

They went on looking at each other. "You too," he said expressionlessly.

"I didn't realize you . . ." she answered.

They couldn't touch. Life had caught them in separate traps. There was her royal blood; there was his tainted Welsh blood. They'd both always known that, too. The only honorable thing to do, after this admission, was for her to let him go at once. It wouldn't be decent for him to stay in her household.

"Stay," she said very quietly, not caring. "Please."

He looked anguished. He shook his head. "It won't make it any easier to have said all this," he told her. "For either of us. It will be worse than before. You know that, don't you?"

"Don't think about that," she replied, wondering if he felt the same burning, unsteady heat she did, whether his yearning to touch her made him as faint as she was now, wondering what she'd do if he really did go. "So little time—six months. We need you. I need you. Don't leave."

They stood in silence, looking down at the birds in their cages, pecking disconsolately at bits of chaff, waiting for the knife.

"Stay," she persisted.

"What," he said, pointing at the doomed fowls, still shaking his head, "like them?"

She nodded impatiently. Those birds had a bit more life to enjoy, didn't they? He had to say yes.

She couldn't breathe. It seemed an eternity before Owain nodded too. "All right. I'll stay," he muttered. He looked miserable. But before he walked away, for the briefest of seconds, he reached out and blindly squeezed her hand.

PART SEVEN
The Song of Jehanne of Arc

THIRTY

Was it easier, this feverishness? This new daily agony of glancing toward and glancing away, this twitching and pacing, the heightened awareness of the other body's proximity and position, the new muteness and blushes and arranging of their own limbs, for modesty's sake, or beauty's, and the hands, always on the move, always beginning to move together, held apart only by acts of will or prayer?

Often, Catherine thought Owain had probably been right. Knowing they loved each other but would have to part made both their lives more of a torment. Yet she was still more grateful than she had words to explain that he was there.

She tried to tell herself that the tension she could see that both of them now felt—like the electric crackle in the air before a storm—had nothing to do with their new knowledge. Wasn't it, she suggested to herself, just that everything around them was really moving faster; events piling up on each other: the frenetic jingle of harnesses from the courtyard; a rush of consultations between the Earl of Warwick and the powers at Westminster; vestment-makers pinning coronation silks and fretting over the placing of lacings; the end rushing up?

Harry's coronation date had been set, long ago, for November 6, 1429, close to his eighth birthday. After that date Catherine would lose her right to run his household (though Humphrey, with his usual chaotic disregard for detail, hadn't actually set out for her what would become of her from November 7). But, after Charles of Bourges had had himself crowned in France, the English coronation plan acquired a new dimension. No wonder Humphrey was too preoccupied to talk to Catherine. The dukes decided they wanted their King to have not only an English coronation, but also a French one, as soon afterward as could be organized, and a better one than Charles of Bourges' at that.

The Earl of Warwick told Catherine that the word from Duke John in Paris was that a French coronation for Harry was considered vital for the war effort. It would impress the French enough to help the English forces seize back the military initiative from Charles and his peasant miracle-worker. Privately Catherine doubted that any awkward English-style ceremony, concocted by Duke John and wrong in every detail, would impress the French in the least. In France, which had been governed by one family for a thousand years, tradition and ancient ritual were woven too tightly into the fabric of life for a foreigner to hope to get it right. Especially an English foreigner, with Duke John's awkward, careless, sweaty way of improvising some sort of tawdry, second-rate mummery, shrugging away all doubts and hoping it would somehow do. It wouldn't do; not in France. In any case, she feared the English couldn't do anything to compete with the memory of Charles' near-miraculous coronation at Reims. She wished it wasn't so, but she feared that battle was lost already. There was scarcely any point in trying.

But Catherine kept quiet about her Frenchwoman's doubts. There'd be time to discuss them later. For now, there was only one question she needed answered.

"Who will take Harry to France?" she asked.

Warwick's eyes glittered. "I will, Madame," he replied officiously.

Catherine bowed her head over her food. But she'd decided, inside her head, that she was going too. Humphrey wouldn't like it, but she'd find a way. If she could get permission to accompany Harry to France, she could spin out her time with her son by months. Perhaps more. If they left after the November coronation, maybe only after the worst of the winter; if they made their way slowly through northern France, it might be as much as a year. There'd be delays everywhere; there was war everywhere; and how long would it take the English to plan a French coronation? There was no telling how long she might spin the trip out before she'd be forced to return to England and accept whatever new humiliations Duke Humphrey had devised for her after her job as the Queen Mother was done; whatever half-life in the shadows, waiting for death.

A return to France: it would be something to plan for, at least. Something to distract her from the knowledge that the feast of Saint Michael and all the Angels was only weeks away, on September 29, and Owain would have left before then.

Harry didn't admit to liking being cuddled, now he was tall enough to seem almost grown up at times, and would be eight before the end of the year. But when no one was looking he didn't mind snuggling back into Catherine's arms. And Warwick, mercifully, was away in London, conferring again with Duke Humphrey. So Catherine ordered a bath for the King in her chambers, and once he was clean, and in his nightrobe and cap, and had drunk his milk and honey and cinnamon, she and Harry lay side by side on cushions, with his head on her shoulder, looking into the dying fire.

Warwick couldn't complain if, for once, the child wasn't in that herd of boys, she thought defiantly. It was part of her duties to talk French to her son and prepare him to rule France. Humphrey had told her that himself. If they were going to crown him over there, she should begin to prepare him for that possibility too; tell him the right way it should be done; spread the knowledge she had.

"One day," she said dreamily, stroking Harry's soft hair, "you'll be crowned King of France, too, did you know that?"

He curled tighter into her.

"Do you know what happens when they crown you King of France?" she whispered in a singsong voice, enjoying the peace of this moment, the relaxation of his little body against hers.

She could feel his head shake.

She paused. She didn't really know herself the detail of what should happen at a French coronation. No one did. Her grandfather had died so long ago, and the war and upheavals since had killed so much of the nobility that there could hardly be a soul still living who'd remember actually seeing her father's crowning nearly fifty years ago. But she knew the general picture.

"Well," she said, stroking his head, "of course, it's not unlike what you will do for your English coronation at Westminster Abbey . . . there's an *ordo* of special words and prayers, promising God that you will do your duty to Him, and to the land He's sent you . . ."

Uneasily, she felt Harry squirming away. She added: ". . . though the French words are more beautiful, of course."

He liked that. He looked at her with delighted shock. No one was disrespectful of English ways. They giggled like conspirators.

"In fact, your French coronation will be the most solemn and beautiful moment you can imagine . . . the moment when you know you have the same clear lovely blood in your veins as ran in Saint Louis', and Charlemagne's, and Clovis'. The best blood in the world. When the spirit of God comes to you and transfigures you, so that you know you are the latest in an illustrious line stretching back to the dawn of time—the holiest and Most Christian King . . ."

He nodded, reassured by the familiarity of these words, and snuggled up to her again.

"It all starts when you enter Reims Cathedral, with all the nobility of France gathered to watch you . . ."

He piped, in his awkward not-quite-native French: "Why Reims? Why not Paris? Or Saint-Denis, or somewhere else? What's so special about Reims?"

"Well, you do process on from Reims to Saint-Denis, down the Saint Marcoul of Corbeny road, and after that on to Paris, with crowds cheering all the way—but only afterward, when you're already the King, because the abbey of Saint-Denis is the spiritual home of those who are already king," she replied patiently, wondering at how much he still didn't know about

France. She added: "Once you've been granted the divine royal power to cure sickness and work miracles," because as a child that's what she'd been told happened to a King of France after his coronation. She stifled the brief thought that came to her now: If only Papa had really been able to work miracles and cure sickness—even his own.

"Reims is the place where you're crowned King of France because that's where our ancestor Clovis became the first king of the French . . . and a Christian . . . and where a white dove flew to him with holy oil for his baptism . . . and for the thousand years since then, that ampulla and the chrism inside have stayed at Reims Cathedral . . . waiting to anoint new kings . . . waiting"—she turned to him and widened her eyes and touched her nose playfully against his—"for *you*!"

He squealed an answering squeal of delight.

She was enjoying losing herself in this recitation of how things should be, or might have been. So was her son. "You wear gold, and you carry the sword of Charlemagne," she intoned, and he looked at her with shining eyes. "And you can choose your crown. You can wear the Holy Crown, Saint Louis' crown, which has a true thorn from Jesus Christ's crown of spines embedded in it . . . or you can wear Charlemagne's imperial crown, covered in French lily flowers."

He nodded again, but sleepily now, with eyelids beginning to droop. "The holy one," he muttered importantly. "I'd like that one."

She stroked his drowsy, happy head again. She was imagining the soft trace of chrism on forehead and hands; the catch of myrrh in the nostrils, the fleeting knowledge of the holiness in majesty that a whiff of that bitterness would bring him . . .

"That's all you need . . . those are the symbols that are sacred to France," she murmured, almost singing. "When your people see you in that crown and with that sword, lit up in gold and sunshine, they'll know you as their true King for the rest of your life. You and no one else."

His head dropped. She kissed him. "You and no one else," she repeated, more to herself than him.

But he wasn't quite asleep. He stirred as she quietly rose. He said, with his eyes still shut: "But Maman, what about the other King of France?"

Catherine froze. "What other King of France?" she said.

He wouldn't open his eyes. He dug himself deeper into the cushion and it muffled his words. "The one who's just been crowned at Reims. The boys told me. There's another one."

"Oh, *him* . . . he's not the real king," she replied quickly, trying to sound casual, wishing that the little boy stretched out below her, hugging at the cushion, didn't look so like Charles had long ago. "He's just a bad man, pretending. We're trying to catch him and stop him."

Harry was quiet. Catherine snuffed out lights and tiptoed toward the door.

"But how do we know he's pretending?" Harry called insistently. "If he's already gone to Reims, and done those things, and said those prayers, and God did nothing to punish him? How do we know it isn't me who God will think is pretending?"

She laughed uneasily from the doorway. "We just know," she said, peering back into the darkness where he lay. "Trust me."

It wasn't enough. She could hear that in the expectant quality of his silence. Harry wanted more.

"God didn't recognize him, and nor did the people of France. They all knew he was cheating," she improvised.

"How?"

"Ah," she said. "Because he didn't have the crown or the sword; because he wasn't the King."

She heard the little sound from inside the door. A satisfied "Ohh." He believed her now. If only it had really been that simple, she thought as she hurried away.

She'd spoken the truth, in a sense. Charles *hadn't* worn the full regalia of kingship in the hasty trip to Reims. The crown jewels were stored at the abbey of Saint-Denis, which was in English hands. They had been unavailable to him. No one knew what crown had been used for Charles, though one had been found somewhere; but a copy of the coronation *ordo* had been released to him from the nearby abbey of Saint

Rémi. Having the sword and the crown that had always symbolized French belief in their King's sacred blood *would* help Harry when it was his turn to be anointed. But the very fact that Charles had managed to cross enemy territory to reach Reims had been enough to convince many Frenchmen of his royalty. It might take a lot to convince them now—perhaps more than a sword and a crown, however sacred—that a little boy from England, who knew nothing of France, was really their leader.

The Earl of Warwick was the one who broke the news to Harry, at the midday dinner right after his return to Wallingford. Loudly, so everyone in the hall could hear, he told the King he would be required to travel to France for a second coronation immediately after the English crowning.

There was a hush up and down the great hall at his announcement. Even the hungriest of the young noblemen, exhausted from a morning on horseback, stopped the cheerful spearing of bits of meat from the joints and put down their knives. They gazed up at the top of the table, with eyes as suddenly wide and watchful as deer in the woods. They all knew France was dangerous, if exciting. France was where you went to fight.

Catherine hadn't known Warwick would make a public announcement like this so soon. She had no idea they were in such a hurry. So she was staring too. But, sitting two places from the head of the table, with Warwick on her right, standing up, his arms and hips blocking off her view of her small son, she couldn't tell what impression the information had made on Harry. All she could see was Warwick's bony frame swelling with rage.

The Earl turned rudely away from her to face the invisible child. "You say, 'Yes, my lord,'" he grated, pushing too close to Harry; planting his wiry arms threateningly on the table. His voice was icy with dislike. "You say, 'I am grateful to Their Graces the dukes for their efforts on my behalf.'"

Catherine heard the little voice pipe up in reply; but, although she was craning round Warwick's back to try to catch Harry's eye, she still couldn't see his face.

Harry said, and his treble voice was full of alarm: "Will my mother be with me?"

Catherine closed her eyes. She felt sick with fear for him.

Warwick's voice—hollow, fiercely quiet—carried to the farthest reaches of the hall. "No," he said. "Learn to think like a man."

From behind the Earl, Catherine heard a muffled, defiant "I don't want to go to France."

There was an indrawn breath from all around the hall. Warwick said: "Go to your room. Now."

"You're not allowed to hit me!" Harry squealed, and she could hear panic now. The eyes all went down; fixed on their food boards; boys imagining themselves elsewhere. "I'm the King!"

Warwick said, still in the same grim monotone: "And I am your master."

"Stop," Catherine said faintly. Her hands, clenched under the table, parted to touch the Earl's shoulder and hold him back. But a tall form stepped between them, brushing her hand gently back, and stood between her and Warwick for what seemed an age, slowly and deliberately laying a small roast bird down on her platter. Owain turned and shook his head at her. Warwick was too angry. It would do no good to intervene.

So Warwick carried on. There was a scuffle; a flailing of arms and hair. Then Warwick was walking out of the hall, half pushing, half carrying the little boy, higher and higher, till Harry was hanging by the scruff of his neck like a kitten about to be drowned, his feet uselessly kicking at the air.

Through the open door, echoing down the corridor, Catherine heard the animal howling begin. Every instinct in her body was telling her to go and protect her child from the brute carrying him off. She was furious with the other body right in front of her; hot and light with her anger. But she couldn't start scuffling with the official who was serving her food in front of the entire hall.

With tears of helpless rage forming in her eyes, she stared down at her food. The other boys were still looking down at their platters too. She knew now. They'd seen this before.

Owain remembered the Earl of Warwick's eyes like that. Like fire. Or like charcoal: hard and dark gray, glowing with the pleasure of inflicting pain.

He remembered the Earl whispering in his ear, enjoying the fear he could see on Owain's face. "Do you know what they do in Muscovy with traitors' sons like you? They impale them on spikes and leave them to be eaten by wild dogs."

Warwick had got a reputation for chivalry after fighting in the Welsh campaign. He'd gone on a pilgrimage to the Holy Land but spent most of his three years away jousting in different parts of Europe. On the return journey he'd gone to Muscovy. The cruelty of the Russians had made a lasting impression on him.

Owain had had nightmares for years after his boyhood in Warwick's charge: dreams in which those eyes were burning in the darkness, and that hard voice was muttering in his ear; in which Owain forgot his pride and howled.

He tried not to think of the beatings. But it wasn't just the beatings. It was the very sight of Warwick's tight shoulders and that bleak, quiet face that had always made Owain shiver, long before the man's hand had been raised against him in something worse than anger. Owain had felt that instinctive, involuntary coldness—something walking on his grave, something deeper than fear—at ten or eleven, when he'd first been put in Warwick's charge. He'd felt it again when, as an adult, he saw Warwick again. He'd tried not to; he'd tried to leave it all behind and see Warwick with a grown-up's objective eyes. But he couldn't help it. He felt it still.

Warwick probably wasn't even aware that, in the confusion of the battle of Mynydd Cwmdu, when Owain had still been a very small child, when Warwick had rushed the English contingent forward, nearly caught Owain Glyndŵr, got his banner instead, and forced the Welsh to flee down the valley of the river Usk, he was said, among the Welsh survivors, to have been the

Englishman who'd delivered the sword blow that later—much later, after it had festered for weeks, stinking and driving its victim mad with pain and fear—had killed Owain's father, Maredudd ap Tudur. Owain had always hoped Warwick hadn't known that. If Warwick had known, Owain felt he might have wanted to use it to inflict more pain on his charge.

Owain hoped little Harry would have the sense to fold himself up small and submit.

Owain only moved away from the table, where he was blocking Catherine from rushing after the Earl of Warwick, once the noises had diminished. In the hall, the silence continued.

Several minutes later, Warwick returned to the table alone. He finished his meal without another word. Owain withdrew from the room.

Catherine—feeling guiltily appalled that she'd been unable to protect her son from this man's cruelty—was still too angry to speak. Warwick must have been beating Harry all these months; she'd suspected something but no one would tell her. Had everyone known all along? She tried to concentrate. It didn't matter. She'd recognized him now as the enemy, but she didn't know how to act. She couldn't just stalk out or shout at him; Owain's intervention, infuriating as it had seemed, had given her a moment or two to understand the hopelessness of that. It was all very well feeling angry, but if she didn't have a strategy, or a hope of achieving something with her anger, she knew it would be counterproductive to show it. One day there'd be a time when she could take on this bully and his paymaster, Humphrey, and beat him, she hoped—beat the pair of them. Until then, she'd just have to bide her time.

Warwick knew how helpless she felt. When he stood up to lead out the quiet boys for their afternoon's activities, he turned, just enough to show Catherine his grim, thin line of a mouth, and said: "His Majesty will not be riding with us today; he will spend the afternoon in quiet contemplation, alone. He asks to be excused from supper."

She nodded mutely at her plate. But as soon as she saw Warwick outside, on horseback in the courtyard, with boys whose breastplates gleamed in the sun as they mounted and fiddled with saddles on all sides, she ran straight to Harry's room.

Harry was sobbing, still; but quietly. It wasn't the lowing animal noises she so dreaded: the howls of a lost soul. He was lying on his bed, facedown, with his dark blond hair rough and tousled, and half a dozen angry red and blue stripes on his bare, quivering back.

Owain had got there first. He was sitting on the edge of the bed, gently rubbing the bruises with goose fat while talking even more gently: a nonstop stream of reassurance.

". . . Not too bad . . . you'll be fine by tomorrow . . . but it always hurts . . . I know . . . I used to be beaten all the time when I was a boy . . . your father was the first one to do it . . . can you imagine that? Said it was the only way he could think of to stop me singing in Welsh . . . he said he'd heard enough of it to last him a lifetime . . . language of traitors and slaves . . . took me years to stop . . . was in my blood . . . but I respected him for it in the end . . . he was so clear about what he wanted, and didn't want . . . and generous as anything once you grasped what he wanted and did it."

"Did *he* beat *you?* When he was *your* master?" Harry sniffled.

Owain saw Catherine motionless in the doorway. She drew closer. She couldn't stop herself.

Owain didn't answer the question. Even now, all these years later, he didn't like to remember fearing Warwick. Instead he turned his head down to Harry again: ". . . It won't be so bad, going to France . . . nothing to fear . . . you'll see . . . and you'll see Paris . . . I envy you that . . . the most beautiful city in the world . . . white turrets and cherry trees . . . Haven't I told you about my first time there? Couldn't stop staring . . . so beautiful . . . like falling in love . . . ."

The sniffles stopped. Harry was thinking.

"But I want my mother there," he said after a pause, with his head still buried in the pillow, his voice muffled and weak, but calm. "She's French. She'll want to see too. And she knows what to do in France. I don't. I'll be scared without her."

Catherine reached the bed, and, kneeling by Harry's head,

began stroking the rumpled hair. He showed no surprise that she'd come. He kept his head in the pillow, as if he were ashamed of his tearstained face. But he put out a hand and laid it trustingly on her arm.

The three of them stayed close there for a few more moments: Owain rubbing the child's back, Catherine stroking his head; Harry with a warm little hand on her arm. Catherine wanted that moment to go on forever, but then Owain got up, put the lid back on the jar of ointment, and quickly left the room.

"I want to come to France with you," Catherine murmured, kissing her son's head. "I'll try to. But we have to be careful about how we ask. Uncle Humphrey needs to think he's thought of it for himself. So I'm going to try to ask when the moment is right. Not yet: not till Earl Richard's forgotten being so cross today . . ."

Harry shifted his head. She could see half of one blotched, snot-smeared cheek now, and one swollen eye looking carefully at her. Overwhelmed by tenderness, she whispered: "It will be our secret . . . that we're trying for that . . . so do you think you can keep quiet about it for a while?"

The eye went on looking at her. Then, with a damp slither, Harry wriggled his arms around her. With his head buried in her bodice, he muttered: "Yes."

She found Owain again just before Vespers, in the chapel. She was so full of her fury with Warwick and her worry for Harry that she scarcely thought to keep a safe distance from Owain. Or perhaps, she thought with vague misgiving, even as she rushed to him, she was really just using that tumult of feelings as an excuse to come too close to Owain and whisper with him. She put that thought aside; it was too unsettling.

"That man is bad for Harry," she muttered tightly, kneeling beside him, so full of her feelings that she didn't even care about interrupting his prayers. "I don't want his peace of mind destroyed."

Owain shook his head. He kept his eyes closed; his hands reverently folded. "Nothing you can do about Warwick," he whispered, as if in prayer. "Just watch and wait."

438

Taking her cue from him, she put her own palms together and bowed her head. The door was propped open. The boys would be here in a minute. Owain was being discreet.

There was a joy even in this; in kneeling side by side like this.

"But it frightens me," she went on, still in a whisper, after making sure there was no one in the doorway yet. "That howling noise he makes."

She meant Harry. She couldn't stop herself shivering as she said it. She glanced round again.

"My father did it too," she went on, suddenly desperate to share this fear she'd been alone with for too long, "when he was . . ."

There was a rush of footsteps. Two youths hurried in, pushing, bright-eyed at each other and giggling under their breath: Oxford and Ormond. Shushing each other, bumping into things as they came, smelling of fresh greenery and rank horse sweat, they knelt behind Catherine.

She turned her eyes to her hands. But not before she'd noticed Owain's one quick, bright, curious glance her way.

He came up behind her afterward, in the throng jostling out toward supper. She could see the tight waves of Warwick's dirty-blond hair safely up ahead. They boys were rushing toward their food, chattering eagerly in the failing light. No one was taking any notice of her.

Quietly, he said: "You mustn't worry. Harry is not like your father."

For a moment she began to turn toward him, wanting to see him say that, not just hear it. But he took her elbow and spun her quietly back; kept her walking. She kept listening. Owain's reassuring voice was so low it was almost lost in the bright echo of boy talk. "He's a perfectly normal little boy . . . a lovely child . . . a sensitive soul, that's all." She glanced sideways. He sounded so certain. "Too sensitive to take naturally to Warwick's schooling, perhaps . . . but there's nothing mad about that." She nodded; beginning to feel relieved.

"Maybe he'll never be a great hero," Owain went on. "I've watched the boys train; I don't think he's got warrior instincts any more than half the others; any more than I ever did, come to that. So he'll probably never be the apple of Warwick's eye. But does that really matter?"

She began to smile. They turned the corner and watched the boys' heels up ahead, flicking toward the doorway of the great hall.

Owain went on: "England's had its share of heroes. It would be no bad thing to have a wise and peaceable king either—a Solomon—someone who could teach his people to live gently, in grace. Harry might be that. You've already given him a great love of God; he'll find solace in his faith all his life. When the time comes, he'll probably take just as much pleasure in his books. Your father isn't the only person whose blood runs in his veins, after all. Think of your grandfather: the wisest man in Christendom. No one ever criticized *him* for being a philosopher-king." He stopped. Sketched a bow. "You go on. I'm not coming into supper," he said, more prosaically. "I have letters to write. But I'll make sure Harry gets some food later. Don't worry."

Gratefully, she nodded back. It would be less embarrassing for Owain to go to Harry at night, through the throng of other boys, than it would be for her. And, even if she wasn't fully convinced about the rest of what he'd said, it was enough, at least, for the tight knot inside her to have loosened so she could breathe.

He looked at her. It was that slow, expressionless stare that turned her heart over; that might mean, Come to me and be damned with everything. But it didn't. As usual, it didn't. When he finally spoke, what he said was: "I'm going to try to think of a way to help you get to France with Harry."

Harry was up and in the chapel early, long before Lauds. He'd got over yesterday's distress. He was alone there, in a shaft of sunlight that gilded his hair and skin. He had a parchment in his hand. He was peering at it with tremendous concentration, with his lips moving. He was still an awkward reader.

"Mama," he said excitedly when he saw her. "Look. Owain's written me my own prayer."

Owain doesn't write anymore, she thought, wondering why she felt alarm mixed in with pleasure at Harry's happiness.

But she stepped into the light, kissed Harry's head, and looked. There were only a few lines on the page; simple Latin words, elegantly penned in strong, clear letters without flourishes. *"Domine, Jesu Christe, qui me creasti, redemisti, et preordinasti ad hoc quod sum, tu scis quid de me facere vis; fac de me secundum voluntatem tuam cum misericordia. Amen."*

She smiled despite herself. It must be Owain's response to their conversation after chapel yesterday, she saw. It must be what he'd done last night, instead of supper or writing letters.

"Do you understand it?" she asked.

"Most of it," Harry said cautiously; then, darting a look at her that apparently convinced him she wouldn't mind if he didn't, ". . . but maybe you could help me with the words I don't know?"

She pointed out each word in turn, nodding appreciatively as he got the first *"Jesus Christ, Lord Almighty,"* prompting him when he struggled over *". . . who didst create me and redeem me and preordain me to that which I am . . . ,"* and, when Harry fell silent, gently supplying the last few phrases herself: *"Thou knowest what Thou wilt have me to be; deal with me according to Thy loving-kindness, and show me Thy mercy. Amen."*

How compassionate Owain is, how full of love, to have thought of giving Harry the words to accept whatever fate God has in store for him, she thought. She wished she didn't feel so sad.

Harry said, looking anxiously up at her: "Do you like it, Mama?"

She said, "It's lovely," and, "He used to be a poet, you know; you can still tell, can't you?" And Harry's face shone again.

Holding her hand, he led her up to the altar. "Let's pray together," he said, and made sure they were both kneeling to his satisfaction before folding his hands and, sneaking frequent looks at the parchment on the floor in front of him, slowly and proudly repeating the words of Owain's prayer.

He'll be a poet again soon enough, Catherine thought desolately. She'd let herself forget how little time they had left; how Harry's coronation robes were already being sewn, a little large.

He's waking up to it already. Beginning to write. Remembering his future. Getting ready to go.

A horseman came from London the next morning. He had a parcel for Owain: a square package in a brown leather pouch. Catherine saw Owain bow, take it, glance at it, look more closely, raise an eyebrow, and then, with a busy air, leave the hall where the clerks were going over the accounts, to deal with the package in private. She passed by the window several times on her solitary walk, so she knew he was gone with it for more than an hour. At dinner she noticed Owain's preoccupied look as he leaned over her, serving sorrel and salads. He was clearly thinking about something that was taking most of his attention and was clearly not unpleasant. He was humming under his breath. She wished he would look sadder; as churned-up as she felt. She wished he looked as though he were afraid of the unknown looming up ahead.

Owain's parcel was a thin book, bound carelessly in anonymous calfskin, with stitching that was already coming undone. It was the hand on the letter tucked inside that tattered cover that caught his attention: a sloping script, scribe-like in its neat elegance. He recognized it at once. Bishop Beaufort's writing—or Cardinal Beaufort, as he was now.

"You've ridden from overseas?" he asked the messenger in surprise. He'd lost track of where Cardinal Beaufort was on his foreign travels. But this man looked as fresh as a daisy.

"No," the man replied, sounding equally surprised. "Only Southwark."

The letter confirmed it. The Cardinal was back in England. Various matters here required his attention, he wrote vaguely. He'd decided to attend the coronation. He wanted to meet Owain. Of course, Owain thought, enjoying the idea of this wily old schemer's return to politics: the Cardinal will need all the information he can get, about every flicker of everything that's gone on anywhere, if he's to take on Humphrey again now he's back. He'll be out talking, walking in gardens, chatting, glad-handing . . .

That mental picture made Owain smile. And then it made him thoughtful. Tapping his fingers on the table, he read on.

The Cardinal had a small gift for his former secretary: the book he'd sent. *"Perhaps you have already seen this curiosity,"* the letter finished. *"New verses by your old friend Madame de Pizan. I picked up a copy on the road to Calais. You can buy it everywhere. It's being copied at lightning speed, and recited in taverns, even in areas under English rule. I thought the sentiments expressed in it might interest you. You might also judge it appropriate to show this book to the Queen Mother. I doubt my dear nephew John will be fully aware of the antagonism his armies have aroused among the French; so I doubt any proper briefing will be available to His Majesty if there is to be a second coronation in France. But it is my view that it would be realistic to prepare His Majesty for some of the challenges he is likely to face on the ground. It might be foolhardy not to."*

Owain put down the letter and picked up the little book. There was nothing much to it, it seemed: ten pages or so of hastily transcribed verse. But the title was arresting. He whistled when he saw that.

Christine's poem—written, what, a decade after she'd left the world of wars and politics for what was supposed to be the quiet routine of prayers and fasts of the nunnery—was called "The Song of Jehanne of Arc." You couldn't get much more political than that.

Abruptly, as if the force and muscle had gone out of his legs, he sat down on the bench and started to read. It wasn't more than ten minutes later that he put it down again, shaking his head. Oh, Christine, he was thinking ruefully, transported back in time by the familiar music of her turns of phrase, echoing in his ears again. Christine was still too frank and forthright, but she was so well known for her honesty and virtue that her opinions would carry weight all over France. And, if the Cardinal was right, a lot of people already believed the kind of thing she was writing here.

It was bad. It was worse than he'd expected. The poem was an open call to rebellion against the English, as much as it was a love poem to the Maid of Orléans—who, in Christine's view, had been sent by God to restore the French throne to Charles.

"A young girl of sixteen years to whom weapons seem weightless, she seems to have been raised for this, she is so strong and hardy. Enemies flee before her; not one can resist. Oh, what an honor to the female sex! That God loves her is clear, with all these wretches and traitors, who had laid waste the whole kingdom, now cast out, and the realm elevated and restored by a woman—something a hundred thousand men could not have done! Before this, who would have believed it possible? And so, you English, lower your horns . . . beat your drums elsewhere . . . or more of you will taste death like the companions you have left as corpses in the fields, waiting to be devoured by the wolves . . ."

He wouldn't show this to Catherine, he decided. It would only upset her. Not because of the praise for the peasant-girl warrior, but because too much of the poem was a wild, over-wrought outpouring of love for Charles himself.

Owain remembered only too well how Christine had re-fused to follow her son Jean to Charles' court at Bourges years ago, while the old King of France was still alive, because it would have been against her principles to support Charles' re-bellion against his father. She'd stuck to her principles even though she'd known that doing so meant she would never see her own son and his family again. Owain had admired her courage for that, and pitied her. But now, apparently, Chris-tine's hatred of the English had altered her views. She seemed to have come to think of Charles as the one true King of France, standing firm against the English wolves destroying the land. She called him the *". . . cast-out child of the legiti-mate King of France, who for so long has suffered such great troubles but who now approaches, risen up like a man going to Mass, coming as a crowned king, in wonderful and great power, wearing spurs of gold . . ."* She called him *"You, Charles, French King, seventh of that noble name."*

If everyone in France felt like that about the English, and about Charles, it would be more dangerous than he'd realized for Harry, and perhaps Catherine, to go to France.

Owain sat and hummed and drummed his fingers on the table, thinking. Finally, he pulled a box of writing materials toward himself. The first glimmer of an idea was forming in his mind, and he needed to consult the Cardinal.

Owain avoided Catherine until he had the Cardinal's reply. He couldn't talk to her unless he knew whether the idea might work. But there was no delay. The return message came the next day.

At dinner, leaning over her with the silver platter, noticing her pallor, her fingers fiddling with the keys at her belt, yet trying to avoid gazing so attentively into her eyes that he aroused suspicion, he said quietly, "Cardinal Beaufort is back in England."

Her eyes widened. *Humphrey?* she mouthed.

"Furious, I think," Owain said. He permitted himself a small smile. "But even Humphrey can't prevent his uncle from attending the coronation of the King of England."

"But it's still three months away?"

Owain shrugged. Whatever other trouble the Cardinal wanted to make while he was here was the Cardinal's business, not Owain Tudor's. He had something else to tell her. He raised a finger from the edge of the platter to draw her attention back to the here and now. He could hardly wipe the grin from his face at his next news. He had to struggle; draw in breath; keep his expression composed.

"He wants me to stay with you till after the coronation," Owain said. "Here. He's written to Saint Mary's in Oxford to delay my return."

He allowed himself just a split second of enjoying the relief in her eyes; the color coming back to her face and making it lovely. Suspended as he had always been between worlds, he'd never allowed himself ambitions, beyond the monastery or the King's service. But looking at her expression now made him feel he'd realized one ambition, at least. He hurried off.

The golden weather stretched on, past Michaelmas into October, as if God, like Catherine, was celebrating the borrowed

445

time she'd been given. But the future couldn't be kept at bay indefinitely. Henry's coronation robes were ready; the elaborate choreography of the spectacle at Westminster was being drawn up.

To Catherine's worsening frustration, even at this late stage there was no face-to-face contact with Humphrey. The Duke of Gloucester sent substitutes to rehearsals at the castle and stayed away. In his absence, Catherine didn't know how best to begin campaigning to be allowed to go to France. If the household was to remain as it was—just Warwick and boy warriors and tutors—she didn't see how she or Owain could exert the least influence. She could hardly bear Harry's trusting gaze on her whenever Warwick began lecturing him about his forthcoming expedition to France. If I don't think of something soon, she kept catching herself thinking, they'll all have gone and I'll be left behind here alone.

The leaves were turning. There were fogs in the morning and an urgent sharpness in the air. Owain kept himself to himself. He seemed to be always light of heart these days; always humming a bittersweet folk tune in his sweet, rich baritone. But he spent a lot of time alone in his room, and she saw with quiet dread that he'd found something new to interest him. Once, she caught up with him, overheard the murmured words *"pe cawn i hon"*—Welsh—and asked as boldly as she dared, "What are you singing?" But he just shrugged, without giving anything away. "My old bad habit," he said apologetically, "mumbling away in Welsh." He didn't seem to understand the misery enveloping her, as the stay of execution she'd hoped might be within her grasp through the French journey failed to materialize, and the days shortened. He didn't seem aware of time slipping through their fingers.

When, on All Hallows' Eve, a week before the coronation, he waited until she'd settled Harry in her rooms with her, playing chess, before unexpectedly asking permission from the King and the Queen Mother to leave for Southwark to pay his respects to Cardinal Beaufort, Catherine couldn't speak for shock.

Just like that? her eyes said. There was a pain in her gut.

"Will you come back tomorrow?" Harry asked.

Owain shook his head, softening the blow with a smile. "I expect he'll want me with him till after the coronation," he told the boy kindly. "A week. But you'll be too busy to notice. After that, we'll see."

Catherine just nodded with a choke in her throat. This was the end, or the beginning of the end, she thought despairingly. She couldn't believe he'd said nothing until there was Harry here to protect him from questions. He was trying to avoid the pain of farewells, perhaps. He wouldn't be back.

She didn't respond to the final pressure of his hand on her shoulder. She didn't understand when he met her last quiet, accusing look with a nod and a screwing-up of the eyes, which, to someone else, might have looked almost like a wink.

THIRTY-ONE

Catherine's companion at the coronation was Queen Jeanne of Navarre again—up from her ramshackle manor house, half of which they said had recently burned down without the old lady even noticing the smoke and screams. The old Queen was utterly confused this time, white-haired and babbling. Being paired with her by Humphrey for a public ceremony no longer seemed a compliment.

Nor did it seem a compliment that Warwick's tight-lipped daughter, Margaret Talbot, the Countess of Shrewsbury, was chosen as the shared chief lady-in-waiting for both former queens. Catherine had been told that Lady Shrewsbury was twenty-five—close in age to Catherine—and the mother of three children already. Beforehand, Catherine had let herself hope that they might at least talk about their children together and draw comfort from that. But when she actually reached Westminster and said her farewells for the night to a round-eyed, nervous Harry (he was to go to his own apartments at Westminster and pray through the night with the Archbishop of Canterbury, and, to both Harry's and Catherine's relief, also with Cardinal Beaufort), reality dawned. Catherine immediately recognized the features of the young matron sweeping toward her with an unwelcoming gleam in her eyes as she dropped exactly the regulation depth, and no more, of obeisance. The daughter was a vindictive-mouthed, pale-eyed, thin-lipped, raw-boned double of Warwick. Catherine's heart sank. But perhaps it was just the black misery that had filled her for all the past week that was making her gloomy and unforgiving now. The sleeplessness, the loss of appetite, the fears.

She couldn't get any conversation out the curt Countess. But she made a special effort, as she and the old Queen processed haltingly across the way to Westminster Abbey, in their matching gowns of red, gold, and black, to keep the hopelessness at bay; to smile and stand tall for the crowd, at least. Still, she couldn't help hearing the disappointed voice of one little street boy whose eye she'd caught, who was standing on someone's shoulders so he could peer between the soldiers' shoulders and report back to his comrades on who was passing and whether it was worth hopping up for a look too. "Only the old queens. The mad one and the mum. Give it another minute." Her English was good enough for that now.

The bells pealing overhead were so loud that they sucked the sound out of people's mouths; made their moving lips appear silent. The air of the abbey was thick and gloomy with incense and thousands of beeswax candles making rich pools of light, and the rare, expensive scents of the bodies of the great, and the stink of the common people. In her furs, in the swaying press of the nobility on the scaffold between the great altar and the choir, Catherine was stiflingly hot.

When the great doors opened, letting in the troubled gray light of morning, dancing uneasily with snowflakes and a blast of wind that made the candles shiver, she leaned gratefully forward, welcoming the cold. It was another moment before she made out the little silhouette in the distant doorway, huddled next to Warwick's great bony frame, blinking at the size of the crowd packed into the church. Harry. Mesmerized. Big-eyed and baby-faced, clutching at his scarlet cloak.

Her heart moved, and her lips too, in a prayer for him to perform his task with the dignity expected of him. The bells changed their tune; rang out a glorious peal of triumph. But Catherine's ears were ringing with the remembered sound of the formless groans and howls of anguish she most dreaded; like evil spirits, she thought, shaking her head as if to get the memory of them out. Her great fear was that Harry would panic and start that howling, and prove himself mad, here, in front of his people. She folded her hands tighter, muttering.

It seemed an eternity before Harry began to move forward. When he did, putting each foot down with great care so he didn't get tripped up by the great rich folds of fur-lined velvet; when, finally, he sat at his seat in the middle of the scaffold, looking solemnly round at his subjects as the unearthly beauty of the singing began, she felt her heart racing as if she'd been running for her life, and dampness at her temples.

But Harry was doing magnificently. He listened to the Archbishop's proclamation. He walked with great dignity to the altar, and lay down flat on his face on the inlaid marble floor, as he'd practiced, and didn't move while the bishops read their exorcisms and chanted their anthems, and stripped him of the cloak and down to his plain white shirt, until they raised him up and dressed him again in the glittering garments of a King of England, until every inch of him winked and shone in the candlelight. He didn't flinch when the crown of Saint Edward was set on his head, with bishops crowding him from every side, propping the great heavy thing up between their palms, sweating with the strain of making that act of levitation look easy as they walked him back to his seat.

It was only when Henry was sitting down again, still with the bishops hovering around and behind him like bees round a honeypot, and the bass drone of the solemn Mass had begun, that Catherine dared breathe easy and look around. Of all the other heads craning forward, of all the other eyes fixed hungrily on the little boy in gold and rubies and ermine, who was moving forward now to kneel at the altar, she only saw one.

Owain was standing beside the Cardinal; no longer in his black hood and habit but with a prickle of black hair growing back on his head, visible under a big square-brimmed hat of blue velvet. She thought she could just make out green shoulders. He was wearing real clothes again. He'd gone back to looking like a nobleman rather than a man of God. She was too dazed with the oils and the smells and the heat and her fears for Harry, and the glory of seeing her son anointed monarch with such great pomp, to be able to make sense of Owain's utterly unexpected change of identity. She just stared.

Perhaps he noticed her head facing the wrong way; felt her eyes on him. At any rate, he let his eyes shift toward her; held them for a brief, expressionless second. Then he nodded acknowledgment, and, suddenly, impishly, and even more inexplicably, grinned.

The bells broke out in a new peal of triumph. The doors groaned open, letting in more dancing flakes and more gray light, and more cheers from the crowds outside. Harry began to move carefully back toward the daylight, with the bishops of Durham and Bath and Wells, one on each side, still dancing absurdly along beside him, taking the weight of the crown in their plump arms, and Warwick, walking behind, holding the child's golden train.

Catherine caught her son's eye as he passed. He gave her just the hint of a smile. He looked amazed that he'd pulled it off. He looked exhausted, too. At least, she thought with relief for him, he'd be allowed to eat in his rooms, alone. Even Duke Humphrey had realized it would be too much for him to attend the banquet. He was, after all, still only seven.

As the rest of the nobles on the scaffold also began to stir and move, preparing to take their own places in the procession behind Harry to the banquet at Westminster Hall, Catherine looked round again for Owain in his strange new finery. But Owain was nowhere to be seen.

She hadn't been among members of the Council for so long. They moved along, important in their furred cloaks, murmuring among themselves. Catherine kept quiet and kept her ears open as she too shuffled into line, keeping Queen Jeanne gently in line beside her. The banquet to come would be her first and perhaps her only chance to win support for the idea that she should go to France with Harry. She had to keep alert. It could only be helpful to know what these men, so close to power, were talking about among themselves.

"Cardinal Beaufort should watch his back," she heard from behind her, as she stepped blinking out into the daylight. A knowing voice. A cautious snort of answering laughter. She trained her ears on that conversation.

"He can't just walk in like this and not expect consequences." Another snuffle. "It's obvious Duke Humphrey won't stand it for long."

Catherine carried on shuffling forward, inclining her head left and right to the crowd, smiling . . . eavesdropping. The quarrel between Humphrey and Beaufort was just as bitter as ever, then.

Humphrey was smarting, she heard: now the King was crowned, and, in principle, about to rule for himself, Humphrey's salary from the Council had been cut in half. So he wanted to share the pain. He wanted to strip his uncle, the Cardinal, of the lucrative English bishopric that Beaufort had managed to hang on to, even while abroad: half *his* income. Humphrey had been telling the Council that the Cardinal couldn't be a Cardinal and Bishop of Winchester at the same time. He'd planned to take away Beaufort's English post quietly at the next Council meeting, but now the Cardinal was back to fight his corner; and neither of the whisperers knew how it would turn out.

"This is for your ears only, of course," she heard; and a quick murmur of assent. "But Duke Humphrey asked me this morning, in strictest confidence, whether I'd agree to vote to exclude the Cardinal from Council altogether."

There was a rumble of recognition. The second voice murmured in knowing tones, "Ah . . . you too . . ."

The first voice went on, against the rising sound of the crowd, "Of course, my view was . . . hasty . . . disrespectful to the Pope. The man's a cardinal." Rumble. "But he's Humphrey . . . when has he ever heeded . . . caution? All we can know for certain . . . the next Council session . . . explosive."

The voices were too quiet to hear anymore. The crowd was

cheering as she moved inside the line of soldiers at the doors of Westminster Hall. Here, Queen Jeanne smiled, kissed her and a baffled-looking soldier, and said, with radiant gaiety, "Very tired; no appetite. I'll go up now, I think, and sleep," and danced away up the stairs alone, toward her chamber, still in her cloak, waving back down at Catherine. Relieved, Catherine decided there was no point in stopping the old lady. As she removed her own cloak, handed it to a servant, and moved toward the great table, Catherine pondered what she'd heard. It was dispiriting news. If Duke Humphrey and Cardinal Beaufort were going to focus only on feuding with each other, how would she ever be able to get anyone to pay attention to her own hopes of getting to France?

They'd put her at a new place, farther from the top of the table, reflecting her declining status. She was between two bishops she didn't know. They bowed very formally, clearly uncertain as to whether it would be to their advantage to be seen talking to her, then busied themselves chatting with the neighbors on their other sides.

Duke Humphrey and the Cardinal shared the place of honor at the top of the table. She got a glimpse of Owain as the first toast was poured. He was serving the Cardinal's wine. But then he retreated into the shadows and vanished. Much later, as the third course was set out—wobbling jellies and stiff custard tarts and giant pastries in the shape of peacocks and pyramids of late fruits—she caught sight of him rising from a place much further down the table, on the other side from her. His platter was scarcely touched. He couldn't have been eating. His neighbors didn't notice him go. He couldn't have been talking either. He didn't nod to her. He was watching the Cardinal.

She watched him go to the top of the table and murmur into the Cardinal's ear. The Cardinal narrowed his long, clever eyes, as if amused by something while half asleep, and nodded. But she never knew what they might have been saying because, at that moment, after a sideways look of deep irritation toward his uncle, Duke Humphrey clanged his goblet against the table to get the diners' attention, rose to his feet, and roared out, "A toast to His Majesty the King of France's forthcoming coronation in France! May it be as successful as the one we've just celebrated in England!"

There were answering roars of approval on all sides as the goblets went up to all the thirsty mouths again. The nobles had been eating and drinking for two solid hours by now. There were dark drips of grease on surcoats and trailing sleeves; smears on bristly cheeks; tongues were loosening. Catherine hadn't been drinking; just watching and listening. Waiting for this moment; not knowing if it would come. She leaned forward now, with all her nerves twitching.

Humphrey sat down again. There was a dull red flush on his cheeks. He turned to his uncle. Loudly, his tone somewhere between belligerence and gaiety, he said: "Uncle. You—with all your experience of overseas—with all your poise and knowledge of the world—surely *you* should be the one to have the honor of taking His Majesty to Paris."

Humphrey looked round at the lords on either side of him, as if seeking approval. His voice wasn't loud enough—quite— to carry all the way down the hall. But a dozen or more people, including Catherine, could hear this not-quite-private conversation. Still, if Humphrey was expecting a murmur of assent, he was disappointed. There was only a downward shift of eyes in response; an embarrassed hush.

Beaufort didn't seem in the least discomfited. He just smiled easily, lazily, with his eyelids coming so low over his bright, sly eyes that he looked like a snake basking in the candlelight, and replied, "Dear nephew . . . I've only just got home."

Duke Humphrey wasn't going to let go so easily. He gestured for the Cardinal's cup to be filled again. Silently, Owain stepped forward and poured wine. Then the Duke returned to the attack.

"Still, *dear uncle,*" he rumbled, "you are a man of duty, are you not?"

"Oh yes," the Cardinal said casually, picking up the goblet and sniffing the wine appreciatively.

"You'd always be willing to do your duty to your King, would you not?"

"Oh, certainly," the Cardinal went on, and now he seemed to be examining the large ruby glittering on his left hand. "By all means."

"And," Duke Humphrey finished triumphantly, "you do agree you are the best man for the job?"

Slowly, the Cardinal put down the goblet. Even more slowly, he wrinkled his face into an expression of regret. Opened his arms. Spread his hands, palm upward; shook his head.

He said: "I've been so looking forward to taking up the reins at Winchester again . . . putting my house in order."

The mention of Winchester clearly angered Duke Humphrey. "*That,* of course, will be a matter for discussion at Council," he said roughly.

". . . and supporting my candidate for the bishopric of Carlisle . . . and a Council seat . . ." the Cardinal went imperturbably on, and his eyelids swept lower still, and he put both elbows on the table, steepled his long, thin fingers in front of him, and smiled. "Marmaduke Lumley."

"That's for the Council to decide, too," snapped Duke Humphrey, even more roughly.

". . . and, of course, joining the discussion on Anglo-papal relations . . ." the Cardinal said, with even more exquisite politeness. His ruby was winking.

"Out of the question. You can't. Those are English deliberations. And you're in the Pope's pay," Humphrey snapped, his patience with his tricky relative visibly at an end.

The Cardinal bowed his head. It wasn't submission, Catherine could see. She could hardly breathe. The Cardinal was deliberately goading his nephew. There was a mocking smile playing on his lips as he fell again to watching the glow of his ruby.

After an agonizingly long pause, in which conversation all down the table died away until the only sound in the room was that of a dog worrying energetically at a bone somewhere in a corner, the Cardinal went on, still in the same tones of gentle reason, "To be honest, dear nephew, I'm not sure that we need even be thinking in terms of the best man for the job of taking the King to France . . ."

His voice trailed away. He raised an eyebrow, as if inviting Duke Humphrey to follow his thought and agree. Baffled as an angry, lumbering bear outsmarted by the dogs, Duke Humphrey stopped and stared at him from red-streaked, bulging eyes. He growled, "Meaning?"

". . . The best candidate in this case being, of course, not a man, but a woman . . ." the Cardinal pursued, and, to Catherine's astonishment, he turned his eyes toward her for the first time, and bowed, as if introducing her to strangers. "The Queen Mother."

The blood rushed to Catherine's head. Through the pounding in her temples she heard the murmur up and down the table.

"What, her?" Duke Humphrey almost howled. Catherine heard a titter from somewhere nearby. She turned her eyes down. "What's *she* got to do with it?"

"Why, everything, dear boy; everything," the Cardinal purred. "She's crucial to the whole enterprise, don't you agree? She's the living symbol of the Treaty of Troyes—the vital link connecting the past royalty of France—her father—and its future—her son. Nothing could be more important than for her to be seen by the people of France at her son's Paris coronation. In fact, her presence there is just about the only thing that might convince them to embrace the new order we've fought so hard to establish."

Catherine didn't dare look up. She didn't dare display the gratitude in her eyes; the sudden hope. But she could hear the wave of noises; flurries of "hear, hear" from one side, and an approving drumming on the table from the other.

"That's as may be," Duke Humphrey's voice echoed through her heartbeats; truculent; uncertain of his ground. "But she's a woman. You're not going to suggest a woman takes charge of the army going to France, are you?" His voice was getting stronger again. He growled with alcoholic laughter, looking round for allies who would see the absurdity of the thought: "Like Jehanne of Arc?"

Into the nervous titter that followed this sally, the Cardinal replied with a little shudder, "But, dear nephew, you're surely not suggesting either that *I* should take charge of the army . . . and knock generals' heads together when they quarrel . . . and"—he paused, and a look of distaste came across his face—"get the supplies in?" He shook his head. "I'm a man of the cloth, not a soldier. I can't think of anything I'd be less suited for."

Stalemate.

Catherine flexed her fingers under the table. Far away, someone caught the noisy dog and dragged it out of the hall, howling for its lost bone, its claws skittering forlornly on the flagstones.

She couldn't resist. She peeped. Duke Humphrey was staring furiously down at his fists, clenched in two great meaty lumps, breathing heavily. Cardinal Beaufort was looking along the table over his steepled fingertips, still with that inscrutable smile.

She didn't expect either of them to notice her cautious glance, but suddenly the Cardinal looked straight at her, and, for a second, raised his eyebrows and those hooded eyelids in a quick, startling private signal. His eyes were glittering with fierce amusement. He's doing it for me, she thought. And then: He knows he's going to win.

"However," the Cardinal said into the silence, and the relief everyone felt at the sound of a voice became audible in a quiet sigh echoing around the chamber, "if needs must, needs must." He lowered his fingertips, folding his hands together. "*If* I were to accompany the King—and the Queen Mother—to France," he went on, very deliberately—so no one could doubt he was setting his terms as publicly as possible—"I would need assurances."

Duke Humphrey was leaning forward now, his fists turned into meat hooks dug into the tabletop; taking in the offer. He knew the rules of negotiation as well as his uncle did. He nodded.

Catherine let the pent-up breath begin to sigh out of her body. The nod must mean Duke Humphrey had agreed she should go. She knew for certain that was what it meant when the bishops at either side of her suddenly and simultaneously remembered her existence; when both started tapping at her shoulders so she didn't know which way to turn first. They were each bobbing silent congratulations, wiggling sycophantic eyebrows and grinning, as if they'd been campaigning for her trip themselves; as if her winning it had been all thanks to them.

Biting back her smile, she nodded politely and turned again to the top of the table.

"First, no fighting among the generals," the Cardinal was saying. "No unpleasantness for me to sort out."

Duke Humphrey nodded eagerly. That was easy enough to promise. Warwick would be there to handle the army, after all.

"Next. No other candidate but Marmaduke Lumley to be put up for the bishopric of Carlisle . . . and the Council," the Cardinal added.

Duke Humphrey breathed in deeply; then nodded again.

"And, of course, no changes at the bishopric of Winchester— *my* bishopric—in my absence," the Cardinal finished.

Duke Humphrey glowered.

The Cardinal raised his eyebrows; waited. But it was clear that Duke Humphrey wanted his uncle out of the country so badly he'd agree to almost anything to get him to go. Reluctantly, he nodded a third time.

"You can't come to the discussion on Anglo-papal relations, though," Duke Humphrey said, quickly and fiercely, before the Cardinal could demand that too. He had to salvage his pride somehow.

The Cardinal's smile widened. The deal was done. He could afford a concession now. "Very well," he agreed smoothly. Catherine didn't think he cared.

Feeling the pleasurable ache in her shoulders as she let them drop—she must have had them up round her ears for the whole discussion—she watched the rest of the table begin to talk again.

"So, off to France with His Majesty!" one of her bishops was twittering in her ear, leaning forward, twinkling in avuncular fashion. Duke Humphrey was draining his wine, wiping his mouth on his sleeve; looking relieved; leaning back to say something to the Earl of Warwick, who was two seats down. The Cardinal was signaling for more wine. Catherine replied to the bishop with all the polite attention she could muster, but, out of the corner of her eye, she was watching the Cardinal; and watching Owain, so altered in his court clothes, step forward, check that the Cardinal's cup was still full, then listen as the Cardinal murmured something else in his ear with another of those sly, knowing smiles. Owain straightened up. He and the Cardinal both looked down the table, straight at Catherine, catching her eye. They were both laughing.

"I should have told you earlier that this was what I was planning," Duke Humphrey said, escorting her out but making sure his stiff, unyielding arm scarcely touched hers. "Obviously you have to be there. In France. Uncomfortable; but duty calls. A living symbol; all that."

She bowed her head.

"April departure," he went on. His eyes were fixed firmly ahead. "Campaign season. Calmer seas. So—no point in changing your household till then. We'll keep you as you are for the winter."

She bowed again.

"Warwick will be leading the army that's going out with you," he said. "Knocking the heads together." Truculently, he added: "But he'll go on being in charge of the boy as well."

"Of course," she murmured, despite the obvious impossibility of such a thing, and bowed her head again. She didn't want Humphrey to see the smile on her face.

Surrounded by the bustle of robing, lost in her blissful thoughts, she was being folded into her cloak. She'd wake

Harry up as soon as she reached her rooms; tell him everything.

"Happy now?" a familiar deep voice breathed in her ear.

She whirled round. Owain was laughing down at her.

"Thank you," she whispered, gazing back into eyes the color of the sky. She didn't just mean for fastening her into her cloak. She could see this was all his work.

But he only raised his shoulders in a modest shrug. He wasn't admitting anything: just smiling.

They stood for a moment more.

"Your habit's gone," she said at last, embarrassed by the intimacy of the moment in the middle of this elbowing, fiddling, mellow crowd. Sad too, so sad; even with him here. She didn't know what had happened to Owain, but everything had changed, she could see. His time with her was clearly over. He'd become someone else; hadn't even felt the need to explain who, or why.

But he still had that opaque look in his eyes when he smiled back down at her. He shrugged again, looking a little embarrassed. "Ahh . . . well, the Cardinal made me," he said wryly. In accurate imitation of the Cardinal's smooth, worldly, faintly mocking voice, he quoted: " 'Dear boy—it's absurd to wear a religious habit you have no right to. How many years have you been dressing up like that, making God a promise you haven't got near to keeping? My advice is: Don't tempt the Almighty without good reason; leave it off until you're actually in the cloister.' "

She laughed quietly with him, lulled back into trust by the familiarity of his voice. He didn't sound as if he'd changed; as if he'd gone from her. But there was still doubt in her smile.

"But we'll be off in April," she said. She could see him grasp her thought: That's just a few months away; why spend a fortune on secular clothes now, when you'll be back in your habit by spring?

He wasn't abashed. Not in the least. He just flashed her another grin: the carefree smile she remembered him having long ago; having lost long ago, too.

"Ah," he said easily, "you don't know this part yet, do you?

The Cardinal's extending my leave from the cloister for longer than you—or I—expected. He wants me with him in France, as his secretary, until after the Paris coronation. He's planning to ask your permission; I'm not supposed to tell you until he has. If you say yes, I won't be in your immediate household anymore—but I'll be on the ship to France with you in April."

PART EIGHT

The Mutability of Fortune

THIRTY-TWO

The sun was bright behind the fuzz of young green. There was a buzz of talk above the gentle clip-clop of hooves. She could see the walls of Southampton; rooftops behind them; a glitter of happiness on the sea beyond that.

"I can smell salt on the wind," Harry was saying beside her.

Catherine strained her eyes to the horizon, wondering whether, with the skies so clear, she might somehow already be able to make out France.

Their own group was big enough: Lord Tiptoft, the steward, Lord Bourgchier, the chamberlain, Lord Cromwell, and, keeping Harry's back straight on his little skewbald pony whenever he slumped, the Earl of Warwick. Harry's four knights, their esquires, and the rest of the Beauchamp friends and relatives who made up the body of the King's household. Harry hadn't been allowed his women servants back; but Thomas Asteley, his former nurse's kindly husband, was in the entourage. So was Master Somerset, jigging uncomfortably along at the back, just ahead of the lesser servants.

There were many more men waiting for them by the Watergate and around the crane on the Town Quay: a crowd of several hundred men-at-arms, going all the way back inside the gate to the Woolhouse, jostling and joking in the wind, looking up at the glowing clouds rushing busily across the sky: earls, dukes, bishops, and Owain. They were all standing around

Cardinal Beaufort in his scarlet robe, watching him talk to a plump, worried-looking man in splendid furred merchant robes, who kept pushing up his long sleeves as if he longed to get down to some more practical work than entertaining this throng of nobility.

Owain was unfamiliarly bulky in his quilted breastplate and somber velvets, standing a little back from the center of the throng, in the shelter of a large merchant house built into the city wall, with a gaggle of women sheltering behind him against the wind. She hugged to herself the quiet sense of home-coming that the sight of him gave her. It had been six months. Then she stared at the nearest of the women behind him. She knew her. It was Dame Butler, with her gray hair escaping from under her dancing headdress and the fine wrinkles under her eyes showing as she screwed her face up against the buffeting of the breeze.

"Dame Butler!" Harry squealed excitedly. "She's coming to France with us!"

"Hush now," Catherine murmured, leaning over to put a re-straining hand on the child's knee, wondering gratefully at the same time how Owain had managed to pull off even this feat: getting the little boy's favorite servant (and her own) into this group of travelers. Even as she hushed her son, she realized that it didn't matter today if Harry shouted or rushed around like a child. After brief acknowledgments to the Cardinal and the worried-looking man from Southampton, Earl Warwick had trotted straight off to make himself known to his men. He'd forgotten his charge. It was all going to be all right.

Everything about this voyage seemed well-starred, Catherine thought with satisfaction. She didn't just mean the strange voyagers' happiness of setting sail with Owain; of months, maybe years, before they would need to return to their real fu-tures. There was so much more to be pleased about.

Humphrey had done his usual trick: handing out jobs with-out thinking through what they involved. He'd overloaded War-wick. One man couldn't possibly be in charge of the English army heading for France and, at the same time, keep a stern eye on Harry. So Catherine thought she would have her son pretty much to herself for all the time they were abroad.

And Owain seemed to have used his time in his new position as the Cardinal's secretary to hire back Harry's favorite servants—those fired by Warwick. How had he done that? Harry would be so happy with Dame Butler near at hand again.

Finally, the Cardinal's return meant that there was someone in whom Catherine had felt able to confide her fears about the planned French coronation. They'd discussed it at length a few weeks ago, when the Cardinal had visited Windsor. The Cardinal had nodded and narrowed his eyes thoughtfully, not in the least offended by her halting suggestion that Duke John might fail to organize a ceremony that would satisfy a French audience. "Please," she'd said, relieved at the serious understanding look on his face, the way he was absorbing her words, "you must persuade Duke John that he has to do it properly, or not at all. He must find the right form of words for the ceremony; make sure the right crowns and swords and robes are available; prepare Reims Cathedral and the royal road on to Saint-Denis and Paris. Unless it's right, there's no point in bothering. For us . . . for the French, these things are sacred, truly sacred."

She'd found she was nodding her head emphatically forward, desperate to convey how important it was. "People will only believe Harry is the true King of France if they see him crowned more authentically than Charles was. Otherwise there'll be doubts . . . dangerous doubts . . . and they'll go on forever . . . everyone *knowing* it's not right. I don't think Duke John understands . . . because he's English."

She'd hesitated when she heard those hasty words tumble from her lips. But the Cardinal had a wry little smile about him. She could see he wouldn't take offense. So she plunged on: ". . . and you English have so much less ceremony, less ritual, less . . ." she searched for polite ways to phrase this, not wanting to call the English coarse or provincial or uncouth; but the Cardinal only nodded again and said, "I know just what you mean." Catherine didn't want to say, I know this because Duke John gave my father a burial that wasn't good enough for a King of France. Even though I wanted to stay and make sure it was all done properly, he wouldn't let me. Instead, in a rush, she finished her plea: "I don't know if he'll listen to me—I think he just thinks the French are too fussy about these things—but *you* can make him see sense."

Thank God for the Cardinal's even temper and subtlety. His eyes were warm as he clasped her hands and said, "My dear, I will be more than happy to do whatever you feel best to make the coronation a success. We'll do it together, you and I. We'll lick John into shape." Getting up, he clapped her on the back as familiarly as if they'd always been fellow conspirators, and said with enthusiasm, "Excellent, excellent!"

"How brave you're becoming," he added admiringly. "Just listen to you. When we first knew each other you'd never have said boo to a goose."

Catherine drew back a little. That surprised her. Had she changed? "Well, I speak English a little better now . . . but it's Harry," she mumbled, suddenly shy again, if proud too. "Protecting Harry."

"Of course," the Cardinal replied reassuringly. "A mother's feelings. Very natural and commendable."

He walked her to her escort, patting at her all the while. He was genuinely excited at the idea of helping her create the coronation ceremony she felt appropriate, she could see he was. He was rubbing his hands and glowing, and breathing a little faster at the idea of this new opportunity for shifting and shaping; at his chance to influence Duke John in a way that would, in turn, increase his influence with the King. He was the type to enjoy making elaborate plans.

How bored the Cardinal must have been in his years of exile overseas, far from his own court, Catherine thought. How much happier he'd be—they'd all be—together, on the road to France.

They weren't going to set sail for Calais till the early tide tomorrow. They'd have a night at the castle at Southampton. The Cardinal and the rest of the noble visitors were to make their way through Castle Watergate, rest, and eat. The Earl of Warwick had already marshaled his troops and was leading them off to inspect their preparations.

Owain was at the elbow of the Southampton dignitary as the man approached the royal party, still looking flustered. There was warmth in the brief, direct glance Owain gave Catherine as he bowed; affection in the gentle shoulder-pat he gave Harry as he straightened up from his bow. Smoothly, once the introductory bowings and formalities were over, it was Owain who asked the frisky, pink-cheeked Harry, "You could go straight to the castle . . . but wouldn't you like to look round the town . . . let Master Soper here show you the ships he built for your father?"

No one said no. Catherine couldn't believe the freedom on this fresh wind. Master Soper's cheeks went red with pleasure at the glow in Harry's eyes. They stayed red for the rest of the afternoon, as he proudly showed the little King Simnel Street and Butcher Row and Bugle Street, where the bakers made loaves to victual ships for France and the butchers prepared meat enough to feed hundreds and sometimes thousands of soldiers. He walked Harry on board the enormous Genoese carrack, the *Marie Hampton,* with its smooth carvel-built hull, one of the finest of the vessels captured a decade ago from the French that now graced the English fleet which would sail tomorrow, to show him the miracle of the compass needle that always pointed north, encased in its iron-free binnacle fixed before the helmsman's place on the castle. He demonstrated the use of lead and line, and of running glasses, whose steady stream of falling sand told a captain how long he'd kept a particular course, and of tide tables, and of the rutter, the manual containing information about every sandbank and sounding on the route to Calais. He described the excitement of sailing for Bordeaux, La Rochelle, or Bilbao, for wine, or to Compostela with a cargo of pilgrims. Master Soper, a capable Southampton merchant turned clerk of the King's fleet, had personally built the biggest English ship ever, the *Grâce Dieu,* and the *Valentine* and the *Falcon* that had accompanied it; he'd built the *Holighost de la Tour,* too, and the *Ane,* and remodeled the *Gabriel de la Tour.* But, as Owain murmured to Catherine, walking along behind the small, chattering King and the eager, sweating shipwright, stopping every now and then to admire the skillful sealing of the planking with pitch, resin, and old rope called oakum, all that work had been done in the days when French naval attacks were a constant fear. There was no French threat from the sea anymore; which was why King Henry's will had specified that most of these expensive royal ships be gradually sold off and the funds returned to the royal coffers. Master Soper, who had built up the English fleet and cherished it throughout his youth, now had the melancholy task of dismantling everything he had once created. "It must be hard for him," Owain said quietly and sympathetically in Catherine's ear. "But it'll be something he'll remember for the rest of his days, that the new King was so interested in his work today."

On another day, Catherine thought, if she'd been feeling as wretchedly trapped as she often did in the familiar castles of the Thames Valley, she might have been plagued by a kind of muddled nostalgia at the mention of those long-ago naval clashes: nostalgia for the days when, however insecure she might have felt, she still knew who she was; when, waiting in Paris for war news, she and everyone around her would have rejoiced wholeheartedly at reports of a French raid on the English coast. But not today; not with this wind in her nostrils. Not with her son dancing and prancing in front of her, asking a thousand questions without a trace of fear of the sea. Not with yet another example of Owain's kindly resourcefulness to wonder at—how had he had time to find out about this man's fate? And not with Owain walking so courteously beside her, not close enough to take her arm, but stooping slightly to murmur information into her ear, so she could feel the warmth of him along her left side. The past was past. There was only now, and the tang of salt in her mouth. It was enough.

"What about Dame Butler?" she asked, almost timidly. So many arrangements she didn't know about had been made while she and Harry wintered quietly at Windsor; she didn't want to make any assumptions that might seem foolish. "What will her position be in France?"

But she could see as soon as she had the courage to look into Owain's laughing eyes that she hadn't misunderstood. "For now, she's in charge of the Cardinal's household," he said. "A capable woman, Dame Butler. But once my lord Warwick realizes how busy he's going to be controlling his army, it may be a relief to him that she's here. He'll need to find someone to take charge of Harry; keep the royal household. I think he'll find the Cardinal willing to let her go."

She laughed out loud, letting the sharp air rush deep into her lungs. Harry would be so happy to escape the Earl.

"You do think of everything," she said warmly. A gust of wind blew through them, so hard it put slapping white crests on the water and puffed out her skirts behind, almost knocking her off balance. She turned round, leaning backward into it, grinning, stopping her ears against the startling crackle of canvas and the softer creak of wood. Owain stood before her, one hand on his hat to stop it blowing backward off his head, laughing helplessly at the stinging force of it beating against his face; then he turned round, like her, to get it behind him. They were side by side again; wrapped in a cocoon of wind. Before she was quite aware she'd done it, she found she'd slipped her arm through his.

The captain was Portuguese: little and wrinkled, with bright pale washed-out eyes looking calmly out over the sea while his hands moved their instruments and his mouth moved in a stream of reminiscence: "The sun so hot on your back all day . . . the earth still hot underfoot all day . . . the scent of the flowers in your nostrils . . . great big sweet flowers, full of the magic of the moon . . . you're drunk with it, in love from it . . ."

Harry had been entranced for hours, ever since they raised anchor; standing up on the castle, his cloak stiff with salt, licking it off his lips, his eyes wide.

The sea here was bracing and harsh, the wind wild with seagull cries; but it was an easy run for these treacherous waters. They could all imagine the kind of southern place the captain was telling them about; the sensuality of those spice smells; the wink of starlight.

". . . sea the color of sapphires and emeralds . . . then sunset, and the calm coming down . . . sailors singing . . . deep voices, so deep . . . the stars, so bright . . . and sometimes, out of the corner of your eye, a flash of light . . . dolphins and mermaids, playing together in the surf . . ." the man crooned.

Cardinal Beaufort lowered his eyelids in languid enjoyment. He caught Catherine's eye. They were sitting on barrels on the ship's castle, watching Harry watch the captain. There were half a dozen of them, old friends reunited by leaving England and Duke Humphrey behind, wrapped against the wind in great rough cloaks that Dame Butler and her son had brought up from the captain's cabin. Catherine grinned back, wrapping her cloak tighter about her. She didn't dare look at Owain. He was leaning back, behind Master Somerset, but so much taller that she could still be aware of his silhouette without having to look properly. His eyes were closed; there was a faint light on his face; she could see he was lost in the pleasure of wind and words.

The sun was low in the sky; a spare, brisk, reddish sunset stripped of the land's gentle golds. The wind was freshening. Rysbank Tower, on its island at the entrance to Calais harbor, was a dark finger pointing up from the dark stripe on the horizon, getting bigger. They'd be there in an hour, God willing, the captain said, through the splash and crackle of movement.

"You know your stars, my boy?" the captain was asking now. No respecter of royal formalities, he was chucking the delighted Harry under the chin. "Know the phases of the moon?"

Harry nodded. "A full moon tonight," he said importantly. "I know."

"O-pa!" the captain exclaimed, with a kindly pretense at astonished respect. "Well, you'll see it in a moment . . . it's rising over there . . . faint still . . . but it'll help guide us in . . . just wait . . ."

There was silence for a while; or what passed for silence: the rush and slap and heave of water; the sound of sails.

"And the evening star, you see the evening star?"

Lulled by the rough old voice, yet feeling at the same time more acutely alive than she remembered feeling for years, perhaps ever, Catherine looked up. Such a familiar movement. How often she'd looked through the failing light of the evening for that bittersweet point of brightness. How often she'd remembered the strained, desperate glance that a much younger Owain had once given her, bowed with shame and the hopelessness of reality, coming out of the woods from Poissy at the end of a day's silent riding, yet not quite giving up, muttering at the sight of it, *"Venus . . . your star . . ."* and, when Christine, a few paces behind, didn't immediately seem to notice or to intervene, rushing on, *"I don't know what I can promise . . . but I'll always . . ."* Catherine had been as aware as he had of Christine clicking on her mount behind; catching up to make sure there were no last rash words. He'd probably never thought of those few hurried phrases again; he couldn't have any idea how often she had. She took in another lungful of air, forgiving both their younger selves, strangely at peace. It didn't matter anymore. None of it did. All that mattered was that they were all here now, together.

Harry was gazing up. He looked worried. She could see he hadn't spotted the star yet.

There was a rumble of encouragement from behind in the half-dark: Owain. "This way, look," he said, holding Harry's gaze, pointing up. "There, you see?" Harry's teeth flashed; he'd found it. "The most important star," Owain's voice went quietly on, and Catherine wished they'd seen it a moment earlier, when the light had been brighter, when she might still have been able to make out the expression on his face. "Once you know it, you can steer your whole life by it."

Landfall brought a queasy rocking and tipping of the hard ground underfoot, the flicker of lanterns, the heat of the fire in the great hall at the castle, the rush of soldiers trooping off the ships and to their quarters, the fifes and drums that marked the start of the night shift for the three troops of the scruffy-looking permanent garrison at Calais, and, when Harry had begun to whine that he was hungry, and she was almost dizzy with lack of food herself, the simple traveler's supper of herrings and beef and Bordeaux claret and English wheaten bread, baked that morning at Southampton. As quickly as she could, Catherine retired to help Harry to bed. The Earl of Warwick had been quick to give permission for her to attend her son; he wanted his knights and the Governor to discuss troop movements and supplies as soon as the meal was finished, and the Governor was to brief him on the military situation.

Harry was asleep on his feet before he even reached his chamber. She eased his clothes off as he lolled against her on the side of the bed, thanking God for the warmth of the evening that would allow her to slip him naked between the sheets without worrying too much about lacing up nightshirts. Her own head was swimming with fatigue and sea air and what she told herself were too many new impressions to absorb so quickly; but she knew deep down that what she meant was the tremulous new shyness that had tied her tongue and made it all but impossible to talk to or even look at Owain, ever since he'd said what he'd said to Harry about the evening star. You're overwrought, she told herself, watching the little rumpled head on the pillow; listening to the innocence of her child's quick breathing; glad of the silence; glad to be away from other people's eyes. You need a good night's sleep as much as he does.

But she couldn't sleep. She was jangling with life and exhilaration; she needed to walk, to breathe this new air that was so nearly French. Not that she was homesick exactly, or nostalgic for her childhood. Her memories of her own past she simplified into just two emotions: boredom and fear. She could do without both. No, this excitement about getting into France was more about escaping from the next life she'd made for herself in England. The air she was breathing here, with its sea scents, seemed full of memories, but fuller still of tantalizing whiffs of the unknown future. Once they were out of Calais, completely away from the sounds and sights and smells of complacent Englishness, into the strange war-ravaged place that lay beyond, they'd be somewhere uncertain, undefined, where they would never quite know whether they'd be safe . . . but, when she got back to France, it just might feel like home.

The seagulls were circling outside. Their mewing made her restless. She just couldn't go back to the great hall. She hesitated on the stairs, then slipped past the cries and clinking of knives and cups, out into the courtyard to gaze up at the glittering sky, where the full moon was sailing serenely through the clouds. To look at Venus.

It was cold now, even in the shelter of the castle keep, where there was no wind. Catherine could hear the rough English voices of the soldiers scrambling along the top of the earthworks; calling to each other as they paced from one corner tower to the next; and the faint answering cries of others, southeast of the castle, patrolling the walls of the town, looking out to sea to make sure no enemy ships were sneaking unnoticed to shore, or across the marshes. Other towers and miserable forts were dotted in the watery gloom—by the dunes of Sangate, or by the bridges and roads to the Hammer River. Every landmark had its uncouth English name: Ballangers Bulwerk near Cowbridge; Boots' Bulwerk; Newenham Bridge, crossing the canal of ditchwater that ran out of the town's upper districts into the sea. Every landmark was patrolled to reassure the settlers that no enemies were somehow approaching by what passed, in this boggy wilderness, for land. It was all like this, right across the Calais Pale: Guisnes and Hammes and Marc and Terouanne: grim little towns cowering behind walls, towers, and earthworks, lines and squares set in water by the will of man. It was all the squelching of feet and endless damp, the cries of seabirds, and the quiet calling of scared men at night, waiting for the creep of boots.

The town of Calais' four gates were locked by sundown to keep its three thousand Englishmen—wool merchants and mint gatherers and herring fishermen and publicans—safe in their beds. Usually only Lantern Gate was ever open at all, even by day.

She knew what the soldiers of the guard would see from up there on their walls; she'd spent enough dreary days and nights here, on the way to somewhere else, to know everything Calais had to offer. They'd be looking down at Pillory Haven, the wool storage hall. They'd see the neglected hospitals of Saint Nicholas inside the walls and Saint James outside, where people said the poor, the sick, and the vagrants were routinely refused admittance and where everything that wasn't nailed down had long ago been stolen. Their eyes would move over the roofs of the half-forgotten churches of Notre Dame, Saint Nicholas, Saint Peter, Saint Mary, and Saint Clement, and the near-derelict Carmelite monastery, which all lived on the King's charity. None of the English locals would part with a penny of their tax-free Calais income for the upkeep of the monastery. Yet it was the thankless calling of the forlorn and penniless Carmelite monks to pray for the souls of the community—this godless, greedy, thrusting, perpetually discontented, perpetually drunk settlement of Englishmen on the make.

Henry's grandfather, Edward III of England, had captured Calais from Catherine's great-grandfather. He'd meant to kill the inhabitants, but in the end he'd let them escape to Saint-Omer instead. Their descendants were still out there, waiting. No wonder there were so many beerhouses at Calais. The English settlers, lured out here by the promise of easy money, on their long, dank holiday from reality, drank to stave off their homesickness. The five hundred soldiers of the garrison drank to forget that, in reality, their promised wages so seldom came. The few foreigners who came to Calais for the market or for the herring season, who were watched so carefully from the moment they passed through Lantern Gate in single file, drank to blot out the knowledge that the innkeepers were spying on them. And everyone drank to forget their fear.

Catherine remembered growing up with a kind of abstract horror of Calais: thinking of it as a shameful symbol of French defeat at upstart English hands. But when you got here you saw it wasn't really the terrifying military stronghold it was made out to be, however many weapons were crammed into the keep. It was too squalid for that; too makeshift and too tainted by greed. It stank of rancid mutton fat and wet wool. It was only when she'd actually seen it with her own eyes for the first time—still tearful and lost from her farewell with her parents, still tongue-tied among her new escorts—that she'd realized what English hands had made of their first little corner of France. It was so ugly.

Perhaps the English could never have made Calais lovely. Perhaps the French would never have made Calais lovely either. For all the towers now looming over her, this place had always been a hopeless, watery no-man's-land of salt marsh and flattened, windswept, acid grass. But the English hadn't done much better, later, with Paris. All the beauty there'd once been in Paris . . . She shook her head, wondering what strange magic this air was working on her, so that all these wisps of melancholy and rebellion, the thoughts that she normally kept out of her head, came crowding in. All the beauty of Paris was long gone. All that was left, now the English had stripped the city of its color and grace and luxury, were closed shops, tired churches, high walls, and battered paint and stone, with English earls strutting through the streets. She imagined them, proud and graceless and insulting, heads held as high as stags'.

Looking up, catching the guards' voices, shivering, Catherine couldn't help wondering whether she'd find the English ugliness had spread further once they got into real France this time. Still, she hadn't come out here to worry. Determinedly, she put out of her mind all thoughts of reality; and, at the same time, of this strange, in-between place where she found herself, neither fully on land nor on sea, neither truly in England nor in France, where no one felt they owed the next man anything, and which no one, anywhere, truly felt was home. She leaned her back against the rough stone of the wall and turned her eyes upward, beyond all this, to the moon, to the rush of clouds, to the evening star.

She knew they were his footsteps. She didn't straighten up as he approached; just turned her head a fraction, with a smile as faint as starlight.

He leaned against the wall next to her, looking up. She returned her own gaze to the prickling of the skies.

There was a silence.

"They're saying we'll have to stay a while," he said, so quietly she could hardly catch the words. She could sense the pace and panic of the discussion he must have witnessed in the great hall. "The war's too close . . . they can't be sure it would be safe to leave."

She took in a long breath. She didn't understand what the war risk could be so far north; but then the dukes of Burgundy had always been fickle allies. The news didn't make her unhappy. She was enjoying being out of reality; in between. She wouldn't mind staying here, like this.

She laughed a little, keeping her eyes fixed on the star. "Stay a while . . . in this miserable little place," she murmured. "Well, at least we're all friends together."

He laughed too. The darkness of that sound, so near, filled her with delight. "It's not so bad," she heard. "Did you know they call the harbor basin Paradise?"

She turned her head toward him. He was closer than she'd thought. There was still just enough moonlight to see the laughter fading from his face. She could feel the smile fading from hers.

She didn't know how they came together; how the kiss began. Except that everything had been leading to this, for hours, days . . . months. Except that she'd always known. Just as she knew the smell of him; and the contours of his body enveloping her in the shared warmth of his cloak; and the line of cheek and jaw and nose that her fingers and lips were now rediscovering.

His eyes were open, looking straight into hers. How blue they were. How tender.

There was no time anymore; just the night air, and the happiness, and the two of them.

"You won't mind . . . won't reproach yourself?" she murmured, maybe much later, pulling her head back a little to see his face better, though lacking the strength of purpose to edge her body away from his; suddenly remembering the pain and misery that had ended the other time.

He only smiled. He breathed: "Why?"

Hesitantly, she muttered, "Oh . . . the things you worried about then: reasons of state . . . the importance of my marriage . . . your loyalty to Henry . . ."

He pulled her closer so she couldn't see his eyes. Kissed her forehead. Let her bury her face fearfully against his neck. She couldn't bear to look, in any case. She shouldn't have said anything. She shouldn't have spoiled everything.

She was so close that when he laughed she could feel his chest vibrate with it. "Why?" he breathed again, and he was still laughing. He stopped. Putting a hand under her chin, he lifted her face toward his.

Seriously, he went on: "It's all gone, all that, hasn't it? Long gone. Who's watching now? Who's making you a new marriage? You've raised your son; done your duty. What you do with your life now is between you and your God. What I do is between me and mine. Nothing matters anymore; except us. We're old enough to know our minds."

She could hardly understand the ease; the vanishing of barriers. "Like the people of Calais," she whispered, trying unsuccessfully to make light of it. "A law unto ourselves." She giggled foolishly, then screwed up her eyes, wishing she hadn't said anything.

But her clumsiness didn't matter. Owain always made everything come right. He put his lips to hers again.

A little while later, it was Owain who drew back. "And you?" he whispered, looking as stricken as if the thought had only just occurred to him. "*You* won't reproach yourself? Have regrets?"

She shook her head. This wasn't forever, a pact in the sight of God. Here, now, they didn't have to worry about her blood; his blood; or the disapproval of others. This was just . . . a space. God looking away for a moment, a moment that no one could guess the end of . . . How could he ask?

"We've left reality behind here, haven't we? We're somewhere else . . ." she breathed. "Free."

He nodded, as if her nonsense words had reassured him. She sensed he understood.

"At the harbor of Paradise," he said, "under the evening star," and the corners of his lips turned up, and her heart turned over.

Her mind knew it couldn't last. But somehow this magic went on.

The first night was full of casual, thrilling deceits—the feigned yawns while dismissing the Governor of Calais' wife, who'd been courteously sitting up in Catherine's chamber, waiting to undress her and settle her in her bed; the polite order, through eyes half closed to mask their bright anticipation, that no one was to disturb her in the morning so she could sleep off the journey; her request to the guard a moment after the Governor's wife had left, that they let past any messenger from the Cardinal if he should choose to send word to her; Owain's careful timing, appearing just before the guard changed, so the next guard wouldn't know he was with her; the breathless, disbelieving grins at having managed to conjure up the hours that followed, alone together, behind curtains, behind a locked door, shut away entirely from the world.

But there was more. After that, Owain managed to rearrange the household so that things were easier. The Cardinal's rooms were changed, and Owain's antechamber with them. Owain suggested his master might prefer the sea view from the suite directly above Catherine's. The Cardinal had no reason to use the unguarded back staircase for servants, which linked the two floors.

Dame Butler was reassigned to attend the Queen Mother and run the King's little household. That was easy enough, too. The Earl of Warwick had been preparing, ever since that first dinner, to set off with the English army for the siege of Compiègne, where, it was rumored, Jehanne of Arc was planning to lead a French force to relieve the townspeople defending their homes. He wanted to be back in the world of men. He was relieved to have a plan put to him that would salve his conscience while keeping the King occupied.

Dame Butler was as delighted as Harry to get her little charge back. "I hoped this might happen," she confided, with her kindly gray eyes crinkling into a smile; "though I didn't think it would be so fast." There would be no more fencing and hunting marathons for Harry here, she added briskly. There was no point, and nowhere to ride without a military escort, and no one to practice with anyway now all the young knights had ridden off with Warwick. The child needed rest and thought to counteract all the overexcitements of travel.

She'd have Master Somerset show him around town, maybe; they'd start lessons in a day or so; but for now Harry should be catching up on his sleep. She didn't seem to suspect a thing when Catherine begged her not to trouble herself by waiting up to undress her last thing at night. "You'll have far too much else to do," Catherine heard herself say, and wondered at the smoothness of her deceit. "You'll be up at dawn every day with Harry as it is; and I like to sit up late. I don't want to keep you up till all hours . . . There aren't enough ladies here; but it doesn't matter in the least . . . I'm quite capable of taking my own clothes off at night; it's not as if any of us have to be especially beautiful here. We'll all just have to make do a little while we're on the road."

Catherine felt no guilt at any of the lies she told or heard drop from Owain's lips. In fact, she even enjoyed them: took pride in the quickness of wit she needed to remember each small untruth and fit them plausibly together; enjoyed the business of constructing a wall around her movements behind which she could be private.

They were all idle here; there was nothing to do but wait.

Any news that did come from outside was a tale of frustration. When Duke John wrote briefly to Catherine, a formal word of greeting, his letter referred in passing, equally briefly, to a coronation for Harry *in Paris*. She sighed over the word. Not Paris! Reims! He'd already started to imagine it all wrong.

She learned something similar from the Cardinal. He laughed a little as he told her; and he softened the blow further by starting, "Poor dear John; he always means well." But what he presented as a minor slip-up, Catherine felt to be a catastrophe. Duke John, it seemed, had mislaid Charlemagne's sword.

"Mislaid?" she said, openmouthed. "What do you mean, mislaid?" The Cardinal shrugged and tried to look serious, but he couldn't stop his lips twitching as he explained; he was clearly enjoying the idea of his nephew's discomfiture more than he was fretting over the loss of the sword. Seven years ago, after the burial of Catherine's father, Duke John had gone to Paris from the abbey of Saint-Denis with the sword. He'd had it carried before him without touching it himself: a sign he was Regent of France but not quite King. His idea had been sound forward planning, not self-aggrandizement, or at least that's what he said: he'd wanted to have the sword safely at hand for Harry's coronation. But there'd been so much moving about since then, so many campaigns and shifts and panics, so many retreats, advances, surges, pullings-up, that the Duke was shocked but not altogether surprised to find no one could turn it up in the armory.

"He's saying a replacement will have to be used," the Cardinal said.

Catherine looked at the Cardinal, wondering whether even he had the least understanding of what he was saying. The English couldn't have lost Joyeuse, as if it was some old piece of rubbish. Joyeuse was sacred—a miracle in itself. It had a piece of the Holy Lance that had drawn blood and water from Christ's side embedded in its pommel. Charlemagne used Joyeuse to behead the Saracen commander he had vanquished after creating the Empire of the Franks. *The Song of Roland* had boasted four hundred years earlier that Joyeuse was the mightiest sword in the world and changed color thirty times a day. It was the most potent symbol of French majesty you could imagine; proof you could hold in your hand that Harry's French family, stretching back through the generations, united by their blood, had been favored by God since the dawn of time. And this man in front of her was talking of replacements . . .

"It will turn up. The worry must be that a sympathizer of your brother's has stolen it to pass to him . . . But at least your brother doesn't have it either," the Cardinal said.

She shook her head.

"Don't lose hope yet," the Cardinal added.

But Catherine felt the hairs on the back of her neck rise. She said: "This is just the kind of thing I feared."

The waiting dragged on through April, through May, and into June. It was easy enough for Catherine to plead headaches; stomach upsets; mysterious pains. All to be alone and think of Owain while he was occupied with his daytime tasks; while he wrote letters with the Cardinal. No one noticed her distraction. Everyone else was fractious and bored. Only Harry was contented and cheerful to be with Master Somerset at his lessons, and following the guard to and from Lantern Gate four times a day, and, out of the demanding company of young men and the Earl of Warwick, playing on his own, finding hiding places behind curtains and under tables, making tunnels from cushions or just gazing out at the world going by in the courtyard. Catherine and Owain hardly spoke by day. She lived through the overcast daylight hours lying down: curling her feet up under her; listening to the sea; hugging her arms to herself; dreaming.

She slept late after Owain slipped away at dawn every day. She lay in bed, listening to the ragged fife-and-drum salute that marked the morning opening of Lantern Gate, peacefully watching Dame Butler move round her room, tidying away clothes, marking out items for the laundry and items for the menders; feeding Harry little morsels of sweets; letting herself be eased into her clothes; reveling in what they didn't know. It was as if everything outside her room—and everyone, even the old friends she was so happy to be with again—had become nothing more than shadows moving faintly on a cave wall. The light that illuminated her came from somewhere else; somewhere they couldn't see. And nothing mattered except her secret.

Catherine made a point of briefly leaving her own four walls each day. She walked and talked and helped Harry with his books, discussed meals with Dame Butler, prayed, and listened to Cardinal Beaufort's charmingly malicious accounts of the various mishaps that had befallen Duke John's forces in the field, or the Governor's more worried statements, that he was putting an extra guard on the walls by night, and hadn't heard back from the Earl of Warwick for a week, and then for two. But all she really saw every day was her own enchanting vision of what would happen later, when darkness fell. All that mattered was the joy of being alone in her room late at night, brushing out her hair, cleaning and scenting herself before the fire in a trance of anticipation, while waiting for the quiet knock at the servants' door. Waiting to see her lover's eyes on her and his arms opening.

He'd said playfully in the night, one night: "Do you know how you often sit, when you think no one's looking, with your hand over your mouth, as if you were forcing yourself to keep quiet?" She'd been amazed; had started, almost indignantly, to deny it. "No, really. You do. Like this," he'd said; and showed her: a mask of baffled silence with eloquent, anxious eyes over a mouth tightly bound by fingers. Hesitantly, she'd raised her own hand to her face, mirroring his action; felt the familiarity of the movement; the comfort of the fingers and thumb clenched to her jawbone, the pressure of her palm against her lips. She'd laughed uncomfortably and dropped the hand. "Do I really?" she'd asked. "You always have," he'd said. "As if you were afraid to speak. Less, these days. But you shouldn't ever be afraid to speak; not here, with me."

It was the gray of dawn; darker than the gray of midmorning at midsummer in Calais, though not by much. Catherine didn't care. It was warm where she lay. She stretched luxuriantly. She could hear Owain feeling about on the floor beyond the bed, stepping lightly so as not to disturb her. He must be looking for his shirt. He was humming under his breath.

She felt her cheeks redden with quiet delight as she remembered how he'd lost his shirt last night. She opened the bed curtains. He looked back at her, smiling. He was holding up the shirt. He was shaking his head in wonderment. She could see he was remembering the same slow, intent passage from door to bed; every breath of it.

"Welsh," she whispered, in mock reproof. "You're singing that Welsh song again."

"*Pe cawn i hon,*" he whispered back. Still smiling; still gazing at her as if he were memorizing every inch of her nakedness.

"I have to go," he said. But he came back to the bed. She sighed as his arms enfolded her.

"You have to go," she whispered in his ear. Then, "But what does it mean?"

He didn't answer. She pushed the hair out of his eyes. He was biting his lip. He was blushing.

"Please," she insisted, laughing again.

Looking carefully down at her with that bashful smile, he shrugged, then, trying to look casual, murmured, "It means, *'if she were mine.'*"

She felt herself blush with her own embarrassed pleasure.

"And the rest of the words?" she prompted, encouraged to press him further; and when he didn't answer she sang as much of the rest of the lilting melody as she could remember. Her own singing voice was small and breathy; just enough to catch the notes. It didn't matter. "Your favorite song . . . see how well I know it . . . what does the rest of it mean?"

"You listen too well," he said reluctantly. He kissed her lips, silencing her.

"Tell me," she pleaded, running a hand up and down his back; reassuring herself, through the feel of skin and sinew, that he really was here with her. "Please."

He laughed. Sat up. Pulled the shirt over his head. Stood up to hunt for the tunic that had been left somewhere further off. She was watching his legs move across the floor when he went on ". . . the song, then . . . *'If she were mine, and loved me well . . .'*"

She sat up. "Go on," she said.

He eased himself into his leggings. "*'Life would be only pleasure,'*" he continued more fluently after another pause, yet still pretending to be too busy dressing to look back at her. "*'I would not care for sacks of gold, nor other earthly treasure. Her winning ways, her wistful eyes, throw such a charm about her. She must be mine, yes, mine alone; I cannot live without her.'*"

He shrugged and bowed, perhaps embarrassed only to be caught out in the small vanity of having clearly thought out this translation in case, one day, someone asked. In case she asked. Or perhaps for some other reason. He bent down to push his foot into a pointy-toed boot.

Then she realized something. The soft glow that began to spread through her at this thought stopped her tongue again.

Owain had been humming that song for years. Everywhere she'd seen him. Everywhere they'd lived. Even in the years when he'd hardly spoken a word to her beyond what was strictly necessary; when she'd thought he must hate her. It was proof.

Finally she said, almost in a whisper: "Did you always know? Really? Did you always feel . . . this?"

He was at the door now, struggling with the second boot. He didn't answer till he stood up again. His face mirrored the radiant softness in her heart.

"Always," he said.

The Cardinal was sitting at the Governor's desk, going through the dispatches. He didn't look embarrassed when Catherine walked in, thinking she might be alone here to watch the rain and think of Owain humming his song. She'd settled herself in the window and was humming it under her breath before she noticed the figure at the desk. He just nodded, as if spying on official correspondence from London was the most natural thing in the world for a cardinal to do, and said, in his honeyed voice, "It seems my troublesome nephew Humphrey is storing up more trouble for me back home."

She looked up at that. She still had the private smile of a moment before on her lips.

"Dear Uncle," she said. The Cardinal never looked worried, so she wasn't unduly concerned.

"Something to do with jewels," the Cardinal went on in mild, world-weary tones. "The jewels Henry gave me as a pledge against my loans to the crown. To finance the war. Years ago now; perhaps too long ago for anyone to remember things straight."

She raised her eyebrows. Tried, she thought successfully, to banish the memory behind her smile, in order to concentrate on the Cardinal's story.

"He seems to have got it into his head that I've stolen them," the Cardinal said gently. "He's being very pompous about it, in fact." He tapped the offending letter and shook his head in regret. "Stolen the crown jewels of England, he's saying. I don't know where he gets these ideas." He gave her a faintly quizzical look.

"Oh no; but why?" Catherine said faintly. He had her attention now. She'd been so happy that the Cardinal had come back to court; she didn't want any more open conflict between him and Duke Humphrey.

"The truth?" the Cardinal said. "I think it's really about politics . . . He thinks the Pope is about to recognize your brother Charles as rightful King of France—to go against the English war effort, in other words, and displace little Harry. And I'm the Pope's man. He doesn't know which way I'll jump. He thinks he needs to disgrace me in case I go against him."

It made her head spin. "Oh, but I know you'd never . . ." she said. "You'd always be loyal to Harry." As she said the words, however, she wondered: charming though he'd always been with her, he was a manipulator of men. She had no illusions about that. How far could you ever really be sure that he'd always be loyal?

That thought made her uncomfortable; made *her* feel disloyal. The Cardinal was her friend. Still, the Cardinal didn't seem to notice her sudden thoughtfulness or indeed seem unduly worried by what he'd dug up about Humphrey. He just shook his head as if it wasn't worth going into. "Well, I expect it will all blow over in its own time," he said. "And it's no bad thing to be away while he's in one of his tempests. No bad thing, either, to know what's being said."

Sympathetically—extra sympathetically to make up for her moment of doubt just now, she said: "But of course it must worry you terribly . . ."

He waved a hand at the papers he was putting down. "Humphrey was always headstrong; even as a boy," he said. "What a time he's given us over the years. You as much as me."

She sensed he might be offering her a kind of pact with those words: an alliance of victims. Realizing suddenly that she had her hand clamped over her mouth, just as Owain had said, she lowered it a little uncertainly to hover at her throat;

and continued to look, also uncertainly, at the tall, stooped figure in red. She wasn't versed in the ways of courtly scheming.

But the Cardinal left it there. With tremendous charm, he came over to the window and sat down beside Catherine. Fixed her with a kindly eye.

"You've been very patient with all these delays, dear girl," he added. "It must be trying."

Catherine lifted helpless shoulders and smiled her prettiest smile. "All you can do is wait."

The Cardinal patted her knee. "And you've been unwell, I know," he went on. "Headaches . . . indispositions."

She didn't altogether like the searching look he was giving her. She found herself wishing she hadn't been humming Owain's song as she came in; hadn't given her thoughts away, however slightly.

"Oh," she said hastily; "yes, aches and pains . . . nothing serious."

"But if you'll forgive an old man of the cloth a compliment," the Cardinal swept on, "you're looking more beautiful than ever. Radiant. Sea air and boredom must agree with you."

Catherine felt herself blushing. She didn't think it mattered if the Cardinal guessed the reason for her shining eyes, not really. No more than it would matter if it were Dame Butler who'd tidily arranged the coins and purse Owain must have left behind one morning on the chest in her room. She thought both of them would turn a blind eye. She was safe, or relatively safe, among friends. Still, she'd rather they didn't know.

She nodded awkwardly, acknowledging the compliment. "I'll be fine to travel," she muttered, "there's nothing the matter." Then, to change the subject, she added: "Is there any news from the war?"

"As a matter of fact there is," the Cardinal replied readily enough. "Good news, too, for once. A man came from Warwick at Compiègne this morning. The French have surrendered at last."

Catherine's heart lurched. Change, she thought; and her mind was suddenly full of the memory of Owain moving against her in the night; the words he'd said. She didn't want change.

But the Cardinal was too relieved at the news to notice how still she'd gone. He grinned; not afraid to show her his sly side. "So it's good you're feeling better. We'll be on the move again soon," he added. "Off English territory; into France. To Rouen, I think; that's where our old friend Warwick is making for now." And he grinned mischievously at her, inviting her to dimple back at him. "From the look of those letters, it can't be soon enough for me."

THIRTY-THREE

How grand Warwick had become since going back to the war, Catherine thought with a hint of amusement, watching the Earl ride out through the gates at Rouen to meet the approaching royal party. The Earl's horse was far more impressively caparisoned than his monarch's little pony—all gold thread worked into the red cloth. Unlike his troop of tired soldiers, who looked as though they'd need the chance to recuperate here on the banks of the Seine after their long and grueling siege, Warwick held his head very high and his back was straight.

He'd got more gnarled . . . stringy, Catherine thought with dislike. He wasn't young; many other men his age would have retired peaceably to their estates. But he was in his element here—among men; close to death—a place where he could take wild chances. Warwick had war in his nature. This was as close as he could come to being happy.

He'd grown very formal and courteous with Harry, too, Catherine noticed (even if his eyes still had that cold boiled-gooseberry look as they slipped past Catherine herself). He called the little boy "Sire" and "Majesty," and bowed very deeply whenever he could. Was this one of the sacred mysteries of the crowning ceremony Harry had undergone at Westminster? she wondered. Or just a sign of Warwick's new, soldierly mood?

The Earl dismounted from his horse and knelt on the ground,

bare head bowed, to greet his King. His men stumbled obedi-ently to their knees behind him. Now he was pointing out the sights, riding around the walls, so the people of Rouen could see their King and so Harry could see the castle, the Seine River packed with boats, the town, and the towers. Thank God, Catherine thought, that Harry's natural politeness had been re-inforced by the terror that Warwick inspired in him; thank God he was behaving so formally back, bowing solemnly and listen-ing. (His mother's guess was that the child was just baffled by this new behavior from his old tormentor.) Catherine didn't want any conflict between her son and Warwick. They'd all do their best to keep Warwick happy until they could leave Rouen.

She hoped Warwick would stay at Rouen. He cast such a chill. Even Owain, usually so resourceful at finding his way round problems, had never done anything but bow and cave in to this man.

There were soldiers all around the gray tower at the castle with its witch's-hat turret. They were whistling disrespectfully and calling up English words Catherine didn't understand and didn't want to.

"We have our most important prisoner up there . . . tried to jump out more than once . . . strength of the devil . . . need a good strong guard," the Earl of Warwick told Harry, and his horse skittered back on its hind legs, as if the very idea of the prisoner was jolting it into celebratory action. The midsummer sun flashed and glinted on Warwick's breastplate.

Obediently, Harry squinted up. They'd dressed him up in armor for this introductory parade of the castle and town. It was so heavy; and he looked so hot and uncomfortable, slumped on his pony. The sight of his little head turning on his neck wrung Catherine's heart. She feared it would be all pa-rades and sword practice again, now they were back with Warwick. The calm of Calais, where Harry had been happy, was already only a memory. That was almost as bad as the thought of the prisoner inside, in chains on the straw, head drooping, listening to the catcalls.

Catherine already knew who the prisoner was. The Cardinal

had told her last night at supper at the roadside inn. The big prize of Compiègne had been Jehanne of Arc.

Catherine could see the tower from her window. She couldn't stop looking, even after darkness fell, when the only light apart from the stars was the bonfire in the courtyard; when the guards were only shadows on the wall.

It was right that the girl in there should have been captured; that Charles' advance should have been stopped. Catherine knew she should have been pleased; pleased for Harry, pleased for England. She should have turned her eyes away from the tower and left the girl to her fate. But she couldn't. Perhaps it was the mutter of French she'd at last started hearing, on the edge of her English-language surroundings, now they were away from Calais. She was aware of it everywhere here, the language she didn't have to make the least effort to catch. It was like suddenly being able to understand the birds and the beasts; as if her hearing had sharpened tenfold. So she could hear the whispers between servant boys clearing fires and bringing in logs and mucking out stables, and the peasants and townspeople muttering at the roadside as she passed; people wearing shirts she could see faintly embroidered with the little upright crosses of Saint Michael. White on white. French crosses. Charles' crosses. Each cross a quiet act of rebellion against English rule, sewn by one of the hundreds of women at their firesides, dreaming of escape. She'd found her ears pricking up eagerly for days at these quiet rustlings of French; her heart warming at the sight of that mute white reproach to the invaders. Then she'd realized—remembered—that the "they" she meant must be "we"; that she was part of the invading force.

The girl in the tower was the one who'd awakened all those people's hopes. A peasant in boy's clothes; a girl who talked of having had visions of Saint Michael—who'd destroyed dragons—and of Saint Catherine, the holy virgin who couldn't be dissuaded from her faith even by fifty philosophers, who'd only been silenced by being broken on a wheel of knives. The girl in the tower had wept at the beauty of what the saints told her. She had a tongue so golden that she'd raised France for

Charles, put a crown on his head at Reims, nearly breached the walls of Paris, and, according to Owain, impressed Christine de Pizan out of a decade of silence. Miracle after miracle after miracle.

Jehanne must be a lunatic. Or a fraud. Or a fool. She must have been a fool to trust her fate to Charles, who'd done nothing to ransom her; who'd passively let her be turned over to the English. But she was gallant, all right. You couldn't fault her there. She'd been captured because she'd taken the place of honor at the back of the field after ordering a retreat. The Cardinal had said so. She'd been easy pickings for the Burgundians cleaning up the rear guard.

Catherine tried to imagine what that must have been like: tried to picture dressing as a short-haired boy, or holding up a sword, or yelling a command to a sea of men, or charging. The surge of muscle and intent; the heat and dash of it. But her imagination failed her. It was too far from herself: from all the anxious retreats and defeats and defenses and worrying that had made up Catherine's life. Try as she might, she couldn't see how an illiterate peasant girl, even one armed with a sword that she had miraculously found behind the altar at the shrine of Saint Catherine at Fierbois, a sword the rust had dropped from as she lifted it, could have found the courage to do all the things she was said to have done. She'd persuaded her family to take her to the garrison commander at Vaucouleurs. She'd persuaded that skeptical count out of his sarcasm and into letting her visit Charles' court, far away in the south, through hostile Burgundian territory, putting on her boy disguise to escape detection on the road. Once there, she'd somehow persuaded the brisk, snappy, hard little Yolande of Aragon, Charles' mother-in-law, to let her travel with Charles' army to Orléans. And how could she possibly have convinced enough supporters that she had the ear of the saints that they would give her armor, white armor, and a horse, and a banner and an entourage; that they would let her lead an army?

Catherine, aware of how her own courage had so often failed her at the prospect of looking Warwick or Duke Humphrey, or even her mother, in the eye and insisting on what she wanted, couldn't begin to fathom it. Comparing her own frozen immobility with these stories of wild, unhesitating, uncompromising courage, she thought: if Jehanne's a fox, then I'm a rabbit. For a moment she was ashamed that she had never done what the peasant girl had done; never found the strength to have gone out and spoken her mind and led adoring armies inspired by her golden words and the bright steel of her sword. If the stories weren't exaggerated to the point of complete falsehood—if the girl really had done all that—well, she thought, it did seem a miracle.

All she could really imagine, as she shook her own long hair out till it hung down her back, was taking the knife and chopping it away to boy-length: the sound of the blade sawing; the soft swoosh of the locks dropping to the floor; the freedom of wind on the neck. Experimentally she held her hair away from her own neck; put a finger to it in place of a knife; felt the night air on her nape. Would you be changed by that act of severance? Could you be changed enough?

She was so absorbed that she didn't even hear Owain come in. She'd only glimpsed him on the road here; only had the memory of his last quiet words back in Calais, with his arms encircling her: "I'll find you there; don't worry." But she hadn't known whether he'd manage to make his way to her room tonight, now they were all so packed in; in a castle so full of noisy soldiery.

She only became aware of him when she felt other hands take her hair; another finger held to it like a knife. With his arms on her again, she knew she was safe; the fears that always tied her gut in knots eased away at once. But now she couldn't help wondering what it must be like to live without fear altogether; to have the certainty that, even quite alone, you would find a way to do what you knew was needed.

Owain was smiling rather sadly as he leaned forward to kiss her ear, holding her close. "Cutting off your hair . . ." he said, knowing at once; nodding at the tower. "I know . . . I've been thinking about her too. You can't help wondering what set her off, can you?"

"How she had the courage . . ." Catherine sighed. "I can't help admiring her for that."

Then, feeling so terrified saying it, even in a whisper, even in the safety of here, with him, that her heart started to race before she spoke, she gulped out: "I hope she gets away."

She waited, frozen, for Owain to respond. Jehanne was, after all, the enemy. But he didn't condemn her for the thought; he only shook his head regretfully, as if he half agreed but thought it unlikely. "Look at that guard," he muttered. "She jumped seventy feet at Vaucouleurs—twice. They're not taking any chances here."

Even in her relief, Catherine's heart was still thudding as if she'd been running. But Owain only went on: "They'll have to put her on trial—some sort of full public trial. They can't just kill her quietly. She's too popular. They'll need a process of law. They'll need to call killing her an execution. But they do need her to die."

She chafed at the quiet remorselessness of Owain's voice. He liked the drama of Jehanne, the flashing sword. She could see that. But he clearly didn't feel the same empathy Catherine did with that girl, trapped in the tower, with only cruelty and death ahead.

"They—or, rather, we," Owain corrected himself, "—the English army, that is—have to prove she's flesh and blood, not a miracle-worker—not protected by God. Because she nearly won France for your brother. She crowned your brother King of France. And too many people have started to believe that's who he is—you've seen the white crosses, haven't you? Warwick has to get her executed to prove to the doubters that your son is King of France."

Catherine sighed. She could see the force of the argument, in principle, though now Jehanne was captured and Charles' army contained again, what difference need it make to Harry whether the girl were alive or dead? Still, obviously that wasn't what Warwick would say. So there was no hope. Just a stay of execution for the peasant girl, as, she supposed, was the case for everyone really; a lingering of days before an unthinkable end.

Owain smiled at her. He was putting Jehanne from his mind; he wanted to celebrate their reunion. But her mind shied away from that, and from thinking of Charles. She went quiet and still in his arms. She couldn't make love. She couldn't get that girl in the other tower out of her mind, and couldn't stop the pity and the anger filling her at the thought of Jehanne. At least she, Catherine, was only being shut away from a full life by those men; but Jehanne would be killed.

For a moment, Owain sighed too. She could feel his cheek-bone against hers; he was looking out at the tower and there was pain in his eyes. For a moment she loved him utterly for sharing her feelings so completely; but then she realized he wasn't sighing for Jehanne at all. After a while, he said pensively: "Poor Christine. How sad she'll be . . . I wonder if she knows."

The Cardinal's rooms were, as usual, the best in Rouen Castle, and he'd made them better still with the luxurious hangings and furs and furnishings he always traveled with. Owain didn't know quite how his master managed to create this appearance of grandeur wherever he went, and with no apparent effort, but he admired the effect.

But today Beaufort's sunken cheeks were more sunken than usual; his prominent eyes bulging. He was stroking his chin. The Cardinal made a point of never looking anything but good-tempered and worldly-wise; but, Owain thought, this was as close as he'd seen the churchman come to looking worried.

"My boy, I've just had a very odd conversation with War-wick," he began. He raised an eyebrow.

Owain waited.

"He doesn't seem to have been able to persuade any French judges to frame a case against his prisoner," the Cardinal went on. "Whoever he tries, they all just say the same thing—that she hasn't committed a crime—she's just a prisoner of war."

Correct though it was that Jehanne had committed no crime but was a prisoner of war—who therefore shouldn't, accord-ing to the laws of honor, be executed—Owain turned up his hands to indicate bewilderment. He didn't like to pre-empt the Cardinal. He was the servant; it was his job to defer to his mas-ter. They were both happy with their familiar roles. The Car-dinal nodded, aware of this restraint, and went on: "So, as you can imagine, Warwick isn't happy at all."

"He needs to put Jehanne on trial," Owain agreed.

"And here's the rub," the Cardinal went on, putting a veiny white hand to his forehead so that Owain could see for sure he hadn't made a mistake earlier—the Cardinal really was worried—"Warwick's saying now that if he can't have a secular trial, he's going to have to go to the church courts instead. It seems he's got some tame bishop in hand, promising him a guilty verdict." He raised his eyes to Owain's face. They were bloodshot. "If there's a religious trial, it puts *me* in a very awkward position indeed, my boy. As you can imagine."

Owain raised his eyebrows. "Why?" he asked. That was his job: drawing the Cardinal's thoughts.

"Because there are no real religious grounds for a trial either," the Cardinal said. "So whatever laughably trumped-up case Warwick and his little bishop come up with, using whatever nasty little religious court with its nasty little bought opinion, right under my very nose—when half of Christendom is for Jehanne and Charles, and even the Pope is half convinced Jehanne is a saint . . . well, *I* shouldn't be involved. *I* should have nothing to do with any of that. You can see that, can't you? A Cardinal of Rome, apparently condoning whatever it is that Warwick's going to do. The Pope's not going to like it . . . not one little bit . . ."

The Cardinal wrung his hands under his chin. Owain could indeed see his dilemma. The Cardinal was making this trip in the hope of cementing his friendship with the little King of England and making his own future secure. The Cardinal needed to take steps to protect himself because his position was so precarious. He was already out of favor with Duke Humphrey in England. If he also fell out of favor with his foreign master, the Pope, he'd be in a very weak position indeed.

"So . . . should you leave?" Owain asked, cutting to what he felt was the central question: what action the Cardinal should take. "Now . . . before it goes any further . . . before you are implicated?" But Owain could see the problem with a principled walkout even before he said those words. If the Cardinal left, he'd cut his ties with Harry and Catherine. And those ties were exactly what he was trying to strengthen.

The Cardinal shook the head still cradled in his hands. "Can't do that," he said. No explanations. He never offered explanations if he could avoid it; he tried never to pin himself down too much.

With private surprise, Owain realized that Catherine and the Cardinal, for very different reasons, each seemed to be inclining toward support for Jehanne, meaning conflict with Warwick. Owain didn't share their complicated feelings. As far as he was concerned, there were no doubts and no shades of gray. Jehanne's actions in the past, and her existence in the present, were a threat to Harry and to the English rule in France that King Henry had instituted. Owain's loyalties lay with Henry's son, and always would, so any threat to the child had to be neutralized. It wasn't personal. It wasn't that Owain didn't thrill a little to the idea of that girl taking up a sword—the gallantry of it. But it didn't make any difference. Jehanne had to die, just as a wasp, a rat, or a spider that came too close to the little King's person would be exterminated. Henry would have wanted no less.

Owain thought it might be advisable to keep Catherine and the Cardinal apart while this question was discussed. He didn't like the image that flashed into his head: the pair of them stalking out of the great hall together, leaving behind a furious, white-faced Warwick. He didn't want trouble. He'd advise Catherine to eat in her rooms; he'd advise the Cardinal to stick to theology. They couldn't combine forces that way.

He told the Cardinal: "Talk to Warwick again. He won't want to look a fool any more than you. If there are no grounds for a religious trial, explain why. Dissuade him."

"You look so tired," Owain said, kissing Catherine's eyes shut. "Rest. I'll have food sent up to you for today. I don't want you to get ill."

"No," Catherine replied determinedly. She rose naked from the bed. "I'm not missing dinner. Not today. Dame Butler says that's when Warwick's going to make his announcement about Jehanne. Apparently he's going to put her before a religious court—for heresy."

Owain hadn't asked the Cardinal exactly what the charge

would be. "Heresy?" he queried faintly. It sounded a dubious sort of charge. The visions; the voices? Were they heretical?

"Because she wore men's clothes," Catherine said. "He's saying that was heresy."

With something like dread, Owain saw her chin jut into an unfamiliar stubbornness. She went on, with undisguised scorn for the clumsiness of the accusation—and, he felt, for Warwick's choice of it, as well as Warwick himself: "But of course you'd need to dress up as a man on the battlefield."

Thank God we will be leaving Rouen soon, Owain thought. But even he hadn't understood everything. It was only when he was sitting in the great hall, at his place halfway down the table among the knights, watching Warwick's thin lips move as he made his announcement, that Owain realized what was happening. Warwick declared that the King, the Queen Mother, the royal party, and the English army would all stay at Rouen for the duration of the heresy trial he was convening for Jehanne. It was vital, he said, that the greatest lords of France were seen to witness the heretic being destroyed.

The knights filed out.

"Why heresy, may I ask?" Cardinal Beaufort called as the Earl also rose, looking grimly satisfied.

Warwick stopped when he heard the loud question. He gave the Cardinal a look of disfavor. The Earl had his new favorite with him—a soft-jowled bishop, Pierre Cauchon of Beauvais, the man who'd led the negotiations through which the English had bought Jehanne from the Burgundians who'd captured her. Warwick gestured to the Bishop to answer.

"Deuteronomy, chapter twenty-two," the cleric answered readily enough, with a faint curve of the lips.

Catherine hung back nearby, listening. She took no notice of Owain, who for some reason had come up from his place at table to hers, at the top end of the table on the dais, to try and nudge her out—a very indiscreet lapse, she thought, and quite uncharacteristic of Owain. She wasn't going to take any notice anyway; she wanted to hear out this bishop. She could see the fat French cleric knew his texts, but she disliked the way his cheeks quivered as he quoted: " '*A woman shall not be clothed with man's apparel, neither shall a man use woman's apparel: for he that does these things is abominable before God.*' "

The Cardinal only waved his hand. He knew his theology too. "But that won't hold up for a moment, my dear Bishop," he replied swiftly. "What about Saint Thomas Aquinas? The *Summa Theologica.* " '*It is sinful for a woman to use male clothing or vice versa; nevertheless in some circumstances it may be done without sin if due to some necessity, whether for the purpose of concealing oneself from enemies, or due to a lack of other clothing, or due to some other matter of this type.*' "

The Bishop quivered again. "Ah, but she never lacked other clothing," he lisped, with another ingratiating little smile. "Clothing more proper to a woman than hosen and doublet."

The Cardinal smiled back. Both Catherine and Owain could see it wasn't his usual smile—more of a baring of teeth. "But she was on a battlefield, among hundreds of men, and a virgin," the Cardinal riposted, and Owain was unpleasantly aware of the admiring glance Catherine was sending his way. "She had to protect herself. Wearing men's clothes was a way to do that." The Cardinal added, with a hint of menace in the velvet of his voice: "I think you'll find that most of Christendom will take the view that it's perfectly normal for a virgin to fear rape more than she fears death. Mmm?" He leaned forward and continued: "Perhaps you have forgotten, *Monseigneur,* how many theologians have made precisely that point in their writings. Guido de Baysio, Archdeacon of Bologna, for instance. *Rosarium super Decreto.* " '*If a woman should have a proper purpose—in order to travel abroad safely, or to protect her chastity under other circumstances when there is fear of losing it—she is not committing a sin if she should then make use of male clothing to more easily evade danger.*' "

The unpleasant Bishop let a look of extreme pained astonishment come across his fat features. He spread his arms wide and turned his clean pink palms toward the heavens.

Catherine expected the bulging veins at Warwick's neck and

temples to signal the beginning of an outburst of rage. She'd seen him with Harry. But all he said, in a cold, warning voice, addressing the Cardinal, was, "Henry."

They all stopped then and looked cautiously round. But it was all right. The last of the knights was loping out of the door. The table was clear. The servants were gone. The participants in this conversation moved closer together. Their voices dropped.

"Look," the Cardinal said, ignoring the Bishop and addressing Warwick directly, "Richard, I don't care what charge you use against her as long as it works. I quite understand that you need her dead. But you need a charge—and a guilty verdict—that the world can take seriously. Not *this*."

Owain breathed out. Catherine looked so disappointed by that cynical new note in the Cardinal's voice.

The Cardinal said: "I don't know that a religious trial is at all what you need. I fear you've been very badly advised." He gave the Bishop a nasty look, then continued, "This 'wearing men's clothes' accusation is so weak, for one thing—and heresy a messy charge at the best of times. It's all going to go terribly wrong."

Warwick, stony-faced, said: "How?"

"First, because if you do stick to the particular charge you've chosen, there are so many loopholes; so many theological arguments that Jehanne could use to get off the hook. I just quoted a couple, but there are dozens more. Her representative will easily find them."

"Not if we don't allow anyone to represent her," Warwick said quickly.

"But you must," the Cardinal replied sternly. "That's vital. It was my second point. No one will accept this as a proper ecclesiastical court unless you give Jehanne all the protection that a real ecclesiastical court would. Of course she needs a defender. And you should have her guarded by nuns, too; that's what the Pope will expect. Not those thugs out there. It's not going to help your case—that she has nothing to fear from wearing women's clothes—if, while you're making that argument, she's having outrages perpetrated on her body by your soldiers."

Warwick went white with rage—though, Catherine noticed, he didn't actually do anything to shut the Cardinal up. He just sat very straight, pinching his lips together, cracking his knuckles.

Gently, triumphantly, the Cardinal finished: "But, Richard, the real problem with a heresy charge is that it's not a capital offense. Even if your court finds her guilty, as I'm sure they will"—he permitted one side of his mouth a small upward twitch—"you can't execute her for heresy."

"Henry," Warwick said again, just as quietly. This time, Catherine thought she heard the faintness of desperation in his thin voice. He doesn't know how to reply, she thought. He's stuck.

How clever the Cardinal was, Catherine thought. He was looking almost kindly at Warwick now. He said: "She'll just swear off and promise to dress like a woman in future. And what will you be left with? You'll have to go to the trouble and expense of keeping your enemy's most potent symbol in dresses, not to mention bread and onions, for the rest of her days."

Warwick chomped on his lip, giving the Cardinal a murderous stare. He was beyond words.

It was the French Bishop who replied. "But heresy *is* a capital offense . . ." he said. His voice had the slither of snakes or dead leaves. He didn't seem in the least disconcerted by the Cardinal's arguments. ". . . The second time . . . if you re-offend."

The Cardinal laughed in open disbelief.

"But, my dear man," he said, with rather less than his usual politeness, "you surely can't believe she'd be sitting in your prison in her skirts, all safe and sound, then suddenly take it into her head to call for men's clothes again, just like that, so you could be justified in burning her?"

The little Bishop just smiled. He said: "Yes. That is what will happen."

The Cardinal replied, "But—even if she managed to persuade Warwick here to give her more men's clothes—because she couldn't do it without some help from her jailer, could she now?—that would be suicide. And nothing I've heard about her suggests she's a fool. So why would she?"

The little Bishop smiled wider. "But she *will* commit heresy a second time," he said, with perfectly circular logic, "because she is a heretic." Then, ignoring the usual rules of etiquette, he took Warwick's arm and led the usually decisive Earl out of the hall without a backward glance. Catherine could hear him muttering as they left.

Owain, Catherine, and the Cardinal were left behind.

"You were magnificent," Catherine said warmly to the Cardinal. "You knew all the arguments."

"Sometimes," the Cardinal replied, trying to sound modest, though unable to stop looking pleased with himself, "the pen really is mightier than the sword." He smiled. "Bishop Beauvais seems to have quite forgotten his theology. A mistake for a man of the cloth. He'll get poor Warwick into trouble if they're not careful. Still," he added, "I imagine they'll rethink now."

Owain thought the trial would be recast too. If someone as powerful and as close to the Pope as Cardinal Beaufort had such serious misgivings, surely something would have to change?

But it wasn't to be. Warwick stayed away from the table that evening. The trial began the next day.

The servants were run off their feet, firstly because of Warwick not eating at the main table, and secondly because of the flood of incomers to feed, on top of the already packed castle. Then separate meals ordered for the Cardinal and Queen Catherine too. Everyone wanted to be separate, it seemed.

At least, Catherine thought, sending back her untouched meal, Warwick had no time to torment Harry. Catherine was able to sit with her son in his rooms, day in, day out, playing cards and singing and listening to him falter through his Latin with Master Somerset. She had him fitted for a new set of hose, now he'd outgrown the old ones, and encouraged his hesitant French to the Rouen seamstress, pretending not to notice the discreet white crosses on the quiet seamstress's sleeves, trying all the while to empty her mind of thoughts about Jehanne.

She needn't have worried about explaining away the trial to her son, either. Harry didn't ask. When she told him that the Earl would be busy for a few weeks with state business, Harry looked glassily away at his hands and didn't respond. Instead he began humming under his breath, as if to blank out her words. For a moment her heart stopped: was he going to start making those disturbed noises, like an animal in pain? Then, with a flood of relief, she recognized what he was actually singing. *Pe cawn i hon.* She kissed him. Let him be happy, she prayed. Let him dream of love. Let him stay innocent.

Downstairs, she couldn't help but know that the trial was progressing with great speed. The Earl of Warwick didn't admit issuing death threats to help persuade various French clerics to participate, including the reluctant inquisitor, but you could see from the glum faces trooping into the hall in the mornings that they weren't there by choice. The Bishop of Beauvais denied Jehanne the right to have pro-French bishops represent her; and he denied her the right to appeal to the Council of Basel and the Pope, who would have stopped the proceedings. But, even though he wouldn't allow her a legal adviser, he couldn't yet stop her answering all questions so cleverly that, somehow, she'd so far avoided a conviction for heresy.

The Cardinal gave out that he was unwell. He sat in his rooms, writing. Even up there, he hardly spoke. Owain felt the Cardinal was probably ashamed that he hadn't quite had the courage to leave Rouen and avoid the trial. The Cardinal avoided Catherine, though Catherine, in her rooms, talked with admiration of the Cardinal's principled stance. And both of them avoided Warwick.

Warwick didn't seek them out. He was busy with the trial. But when Catherine saw him in the chapel at Mass, Warwick had lost the uncertain look he'd had, briefly, when faced with the Cardinal's arguments. He was full of purpose now: intent, fast-moving, with the secretive look of a man determined to win the day.

"We'll break her," Warwick said with gleaming eyes, walking out of the chapel by Catherine's side. "Jehanne."

"How?" Catherine asked, shocked by the loudness of her voice.

Warwick only looked smug. "Don't worry your head about it," he said. "Justice will be done."

Even in the peace of Harry's rooms, with him inside his bed curtains making cheerful trumpeting noises as part of his favorite game of hunting elephants, Catherine couldn't help but become aware of the sudden change to the rhythm of the castle's morning. Looking out of the window, distracted from her sewing, she saw half a dozen youths in livery rushing from the hall across the courtyard, well before the court session was due to end in time for dinner at midday. They disappeared into distant entrances; then two horses clattered out of their stalls, hastily saddled, with grooms scurrying around them and two hurried young knights still hustling on their quilted jerkins, barking commands for more bags and more water bottles, before cantering off through the gate.

She stared. The churchmen were coming out now; busy as ants on the move down there, talking animatedly, waving their arms. The French clerics looked less glum than usual. The Bishop of Beauvais was looking on, hands on arms inside his sleeves, with a smile on his moon-like face.

There was no movement around the tower, apart from the guards going in and out, changing places, grinning and scratching at themselves; but then there never was. They took Jehanne in and out through the tunnel under the courtyard; through the cellars. They didn't want people to see her, Catherine thought. They didn't want people to pity her.

Behind Catherine, the door creaked open. She turned hastily round, away from it all, hoping, although she knew him to be too cautious to seek her out by daylight, that this might be Owain come to explain what was happening. But even as she turned she glimpsed him down there in the sunlight, in intent conversation with a cleric she didn't know. Composing her face into a smile to mask a disappointment she knew to be foolish, she got up to greet Dame Butler.

Dame Butler wasn't smiling. Her gray eyes were clouded. She was breathless and doubtful. She was pleating her skirts in her fingers.

"The trial . . . Jehanne . . . she's admitted heresy," Dame Butler muttered, looking carefully over at the closed bed-curtains behind which they could both hear Harry.

Catherine gasped. What now?

Harry yelled suddenly—an elephant charging. Both women's heads turned toward the noise. Catherine let her pent-up breath go and her face muscles relax. Harry was happy. She was blessed in her son, at least. She shook her head indulgently at his innocence.

It took a moment for her to see Dame Butler wasn't so charmed. "Nearly nine years old," Dame Butler said, though almost absentmindedly, so Catherine couldn't tell whether she was really thinking about what was happening outside more than she was about Harry. "Still acting like a baby . . ." Dame Butler's forehead was wrinkled. She didn't seem to notice that she'd trailed off. Then she collected her thoughts and brought her eyes back to Catherine's. Catherine could see her remembering the thousand things she had to do in the day, before the housekeeper added, in a more ordinary voice: "Well, I must get on . . . I knew you'd want to know."

She bobbed and slipped away as Harry made another whooshing from his hiding place. Catherine tried to find comfort in the sound of her son's pleasure, but this time it eluded her.

Everyone wanted to see what would happen next. Catherine and the Cardinal both attended dinner.

Catherine couldn't read Warwick's expression. He sat as tight-faced as ever, not speaking, picking over piles of bird parts with his knife. He hadn't even smiled when making the announcement of Jehanne's abjuration.

The Bishop of Beauvais was equally quiet, equally inscrutable. There was a cautious lull in the hall. No one looked at the extra tables at the far end of the room—where the court had been sitting and the clerics were now tucking into their meal.

No one knew how they should react, Catherine saw. On the one hand all the diners clearly felt they should be demonstrating happiness that the enemy had confessed her guilt by admitting she had committed heresy by wearing men's clothes. On the other hand, the trial was over now. Jehanne was condemned to jail in perpetuity. But there was nothing to celebrate in that. She was the enemy; they needed legal license to kill her. Yet she was still alive.

It was just as the Cardinal had said. If the aim of trying Jehanne on a heresy charge had been to find an excuse to put her to death, it had been badly thought out. So everyone was watching everyone else; and watching themselves.

Catherine sat quietly, unable to touch the slice of meat in front of her. For the first time she felt she could imagine what the prisoner must be feeling, back in her tower, after giving in. She'd given in herself with Maman long ago, more times than she could remember; and with Duke John—when she should have insisted on staying in France and burying Papa, but hadn't; and with Warwick—when she'd let him take her son off to beat him, knowing what he intended. Now Jehanne would also know that first swift surge of relief that comes when you run from your fear and think you've reached safety; and maybe also the great dirty wave of disappointment and contempt for yourself that follows when you realize that, even though you've lost your integrity, you're still just as afraid as before.

Poor Jehanne. She was only human after all, Catherine thought. Even she didn't always have the courage of the saints.

Now they'd make Jehanne stop wearing her men's fighting clothes and start dressing like a woman. Catherine could imagine that too—imagine the jeering men she'd seen yelling their obscenities at the base of the tower, allowed inside, finally, rushing up to grab the girl and undress her by force and humiliate her into submission to the court's ruling.

Where would they get female clothes from in this garrison?

She didn't know she was going to do what she did next. "Let me take her some female clothing," she heard herself say, leaning across toward the Earl of Warwick. The determined sound of her voice made her heart thump, but she was proud to have spoken. It was about time she did something brave. And she wanted to help Jehanne.

Warwick looked slowly back at her. Was he surprised at her unusual boldness? If so, he didn't show it. He hardly seemed to notice her request at all. His eyes were veiled, his expression blank. He seemed to be thinking of something else.

"What for?" he said. "She doesn't need a queen's robes."

But the Bishop, at Warwick's side, was putting his hand on his master's sleeve, and muttering in the Earl's ear and nodding.

"I'll find something simple," she pleaded. "A shift. Let me."

And she held Warwick's eye until he nodded yes.

The door clanged shut. The heavy tread behind it receded. Catherine stood just inside, letting her eyes adjust to the gloom. There was just one lacy square of sky, high up, crisscrossed with bars.

It stank in here: festering straw; rats; unwashed flesh; excrement. There were small scuttling noises everywhere. Then there was a bigger stirring from the pile of straw she was beginning to make out in the far corner.

Eyes. Watchful, careful eyes: as still as a creature in the forest. Catherine could just make out a figure crouched on its haunches.

"What do you want?" Catherine heard: rough country words; a small, tight, high voice. "Who are you?"

She remembered terror like that in her father's voice when he thought he was seeing demons. Or perhaps Jehanne just hadn't seen her properly as she came in; had thought she was a man. Both must be terrifying thoughts: in Jehanne's view, man and demon must amount to much the same thing. Catherine's heart swelled with compassion.

Quickly, she said, so Jehanne would hear her female, unthreatening French voice: "I am Catherine." At the same time she stepped cautiously forward through the unnamed shuffle of stuff underfoot, into the one dusty shaft of light, so Jehanne could see her.

She didn't want to go too close in case she frightened the crouching figure in front of her. But she held out her bundle—

a worn kirtle and gray gown, found for her by Dame Butler within an hour of dinner—and added, as gently as she knew how: "I've brought you these."

Painfully, the girl got up, shedding wisps of stuff; clanking. She couldn't move forward. She was shackled to the wall, Catherine could see now, by a short heavy chain attached to one wrist. It was fixed low to the wall, clearly designed to keep prisoners bent half over even when standing up. But it didn't stop Jehanne from standing straight because she was only a little scrap of a thing, as small and skinny as a young boy, with tousled dirty-brown hair standing up wildly all round her tiny, pointy face.

Catherine stared. She'd imagined Jehanne as tall and strapping and golden, but this forlorn wisp with the wounded eyes had no more muscle or dash than Catherine herself; and didn't come up further than her shoulder.

"Catherine," the rough little voice muttered wonderingly. "Catherine . . ."

And then she was back on the ground with a metallic rush, bowing her head, folding her hands as if in prayer, pouring out a rustling, throaty stream of words.

"My lady, my lady," she muttered urgently, ". . . showing me the way."

Catherine didn't understand. She could see tears on Jehanne's cheeks. Was it just relief that the newcomer wasn't going to attack her? Confused, she said: "A kirtle . . . a robe." She unrolled them and held them up. "For you."

Jehanne raised her wet cheeks and gazed at Catherine, but not with any of the emotions Catherine had expected. Catherine saw the boy-woman's face was now incomprehensibly transformed: radiant with humble, unquestioning acceptance.

"The ring . . . the sword . . . God's will . . . the time of glory. Now this." Jehanne looked at the garments. Took a deep breath. Tightened her mouth. Crossed herself. "For the time of defeat you're bringing me."

Catherine thought, with failing heart: Oh no—Jehanne's mad after all; or in a dream still. She's taken me for Saint Catherine—her saint. She thinks she's having a vision.

Catherine didn't know exactly what she'd expected of Jehanne, but it had been something inspiring. Not this. Not someone driven insane by fear. There'd been too much madness in Catherine's life. She didn't want to be mistaken for a saint.

"I'm not Saint Catherine," she whispered, trying to keep her voice gentle. "I'm not your saint." She was bitterly disappointed. It was clear now that, whatever she'd hoped for, she wasn't going to get it. Just delusions. Just prayers and rats. "I'm not a saint," she said, louder.

Jehanne took no notice, but carried on crossing herself and mumbling. Catherine closed her eyes for a moment, still holding out the garments, feeling her breath rise and fall inside her, trying to conquer the misery filling her, until, when she opened her eyes and looked down again at the trembling, muttering figure of Jehanne, she found the strength to see her own selfishness for what it was, and let it go, and found nothing left in her heart but a great pity and love for the lost girl kneeling before her.

"Take them," she said softly, stepping forward, raising Jehanne to her feet, putting the clothes in her hands. How frail Jehanne's arms were—like a child's—and how heavy the iron lay over that chafed, scabbed wrist.

But Jehanne just let the clothes she'd accepted hang from her hands. She shook her head, over and over, from side to side. "The wolves have got me," Jehanne said in a monotone, fixing Catherine with those anguished bruises of eyes. "The English wolves. They've got me after all."

"Yes . . . but you'll be safe if you wear these," Catherine said, softly but firmly. "They can't kill you if you're wearing women's clothing. It's what they promised you. You'll be safe now."

Once Jehanne was in women's clothing, she would no longer be committing heresy. And, if she removed the men's clothes and put the women's clothes on while Catherine was here in the cell with her, she'd have no need to fear exposing herself to the gaze of soldiers, or to rape.

Catherine put her hand on the girl's trembling shoulder and let her arm lie warm on Jehanne's back. Jehanne was a bag of sharp bones. She was still shaking her head. "They'll devour me," she was muttering. "Tear me limb from limb." But Catherine just made low, soothing noises and stroked those jutting protuberances with gentle, heavy hands until she felt the shaking stop.

"I'm lost," Jehanne whispered. Then she stood so motionless that there was no sound even from the chains; just the disgusting skittering and squeakings all around; the unclean things waiting.

"You're not lost," Catherine replied, almost as quietly, into the silence, hoping it was true. "But you have to submit. Put on the clothes. You'll be safe if you do."

Then, since she didn't seem to have managed to convince Jehanne she wasn't Saint Catherine, she embraced the saintly role she hadn't expected to play, and added with all the conviction she could muster: "It's the will of God. Put on the clothes."

At last there was an answering movement. A chink of metal. The eyes focused on her again, faintly puzzled. Jehanne was taking in what she said, now Catherine was talking more like a saint should. She flexed her hands, dropped the clothes Catherine had brought, and lifted her fingers to her waist.

Catherine hadn't been aware of what the girl was wearing until she saw the stiff fingers start fumbling to untie the first cords. Jehanne's doublet of sturdy leather was attached to the ragged brown hosen on her legs by strong leather laces. Catherine stared. So many laces. Dozens of them—many more than Catherine had ever seen on such a garment—and each one tied into two strong eyelets on the hosen, and another eyelet on the doublet. Jehanne's fingers knew how to untie them without her looking, but even with those practiced fingers going at speed it was a slow business. It seemed hours before there was a fringe of maybe twenty bent strips of leather hanging all around the peasant girl's middle, allowing her finally to step out of the hosen and then unlace the doublet's side laces so she could pull it away from around her tethered arm.

It would be almost impossible to rape someone tied up in all these laces. It must also have been almost impossible for Jehanne to undo herself even to relieve herself; even walking must have been uncomfortable with all those knots and strings chafing against her waist. Jehanne must be living in mortal terror of violation, Catherine thought.

That wasn't all Jehanne had on. Underneath that layer was another doublet, of wool this time; and more woollen hosen, again with the two legs sewn firmly together at the gusset. There were another twenty or thirty leather strips binding these inner layers together. Another agonizing eternity of fumbling fingers.

These rough, monstrously inconvenient garments touched Catherine to the quick, more than any words could have done. They could only have been made for one purpose: to keep Jehanne's virtue safe. Jehanne's incomprehensible bravery had seemed miracle enough, even before. But Catherine hadn't understood until now how frightened the girl must always have been of the men who surrounded her.

Jehanne wasn't frightened anymore, at least. She dropped the inner hosen down over the outer ones and stood naked, painfully thin and flat-chested, with her head bowed trustingly before Catherine, waiting for her saint to solve the next problem.

Looking at the chain, Catherine realized what the problem was. It was going to be impossible to dress Jehanne in the women's clothes she'd brought without unfastening her from the wall. But, she realized, it was equally impossible to call back the guard to fiddle with keys and manacles while Jehanne, who was so fearful of soldiers' violence, was naked.

She had to find the answer. Jehanne depended on her saint. Catherine had to be the saint. With a little prayer of her own to the real Saint Catherine, she picked up the kirtle. The answer came out of her hands rather than her mind. She ripped the shoulder seam open on one side, all the way along the top of the sleeve, and dropped the underdress on the floor by Jehanne. Jehanne, apparently understanding what she needed to do, stepped into it and pulled it up over her unchained arm. One side of her body was now adequately covered. The cloth on the other side still hung down, needing sewing up along the ripped sleeve. Catherine was thinking of taking a few of the leather cords from the discarded hosen, and tying the sleeve together with them, when, with a flash of gratitude and memory, she looked down at her own sleeve. Saint Catherine might have answered her prayers—the needle she'd been using that morning when she put down her sewing was still flashing on her forearm. Catherine tacked the sleeve together until the kirtle hung securely and modestly on the girl's emaciated frame.

There was nothing she could do about the gown. It was old, but the gray broadcloth stuff was too stout and well-made to rip without a knife. Still, she held it out for Jehanne, guided her free arm through the first sleeve, then wrapped the loose side round the girl's shoulders, over the chain. At least it would keep Jehanne warm until she was moved next, when the chain would be undone; when she'd be able to put her other arm in.

She was gathering up the boys' clothes, not dissatisfied with her handiwork, when, in that small, expressionless voice, Jehanne said: "I've always obeyed you. I always will. You'll keep me safe. I pray, dear Saint Catherine, that you'll always keep me safe."

Catherine had wanted to stay and talk to Jehanne, but not like this. It would have been so strange and false to accept Jehanne's prayers to Saint Catherine. So she straightened up, putting the stinking bundle under her arm, then she bent her head and kissed the top of Jehanne's head. She needed to think of something in farewell that sounded virtuous, but not as though she were actually imitating a saint. After a moment's thought, she said: "Let us never be afraid."

Then she went to the door without looking back, and banged loudly to be let out.

She felt relieved, almost shriven, until she gave the bundle of clothes to the head of the guard outside. The men snickered when they saw the white Saint Michael crosses sewn on the discarded inside shirt. As Catherine turned away, trying not to see the ugly grins, she heard one of them mutter, "So much for Saint Michael. *He* hasn't been helping her much lately, has he?"

There was a full moon, and the evening star, and a soft breeze. Owain was beside her in the window seat with his arm round her, whispering in her ear, "You comforted her . . . it doesn't matter how confused she was . . . you did a good deed. She's safe now."

None of it helped. Catherine couldn't take her eyes off the tower, or the restless men. "They were so—*smug,*" she whispered back, knowing she was repeating herself. "As if they meant mischief. As if they knew something."

Both of them were still watching when a new man came out of the keep and walked across the flickering courtyard to join the crowd outside the tower. Catherine could only see long bony legs under a flowing houppelande; a dark cap on the head. It could have been any of the dozens of lords at Rouen. It was only when he stopped at the brazier where the guards were warming themselves to talk to the head guard—when he rubbed his hands together at the fire and turned around to take the bundle the head guard was offering him—that Catherine saw his face.

Owain said, and there was foreboding in his voice: "That's my lord Warwick."

"What's he doing out there?" Catherine asked, feeling suddenly cold. A pointless question, she knew. There was no answer Owain could give. But by then one of the guards was already unlocking the door to the tower and letting Warwick in.

The men had got a flagon from somewhere. They started passing it around as soon as Warwick was inside the tower, swigging and swaggering. Within minutes they were capering around their fire, singing and whooping like lunatics. They'd never normally be allowed to carry on like that unpunished, especially with Warwick so close. But no one came to stop them.

Catherine tightened her hold on Owain's hand.

The moon had gone before Warwick came out. Instead of disciplining the unruly soldiers, he just went up and stood by the fire again, watching them; tapping his foot to their lewd songs. When one of the rowdies danced up to him and pushed the flagon in his face, he took it, clapped the man on the back, and swigged at it himself.

They could see his silhouette against the flames. He was dabbing at his face with a big piece of cloth that he was pulling out from under his arm.

"What's he got there?" Owain muttered, more to himself than to her.

Catherine wished she didn't know the answer. "The sleeve of the gray robe I took Jehanne," she said harshly. "He's taken it. He's gone in there and torn the woman's clothes off her back."

She shut her eyes. She didn't want to imagine that scene. She was sure Jehanne wouldn't have submitted without a struggle. But how could you struggle against a big man like Warwick, if you were chained up and a girl?

And Warwick had taken a bundle inside with him. She didn't want to imagine what it had contained, but the image of Jehanne's discarded men's clothes, the ones Catherine had taken out, came too readily to mind to avoid. Warwick would have brought back the men's clothes for Jehanne to put on again.

It was the only answer that made sense. Warwick needed to convict Jehanne of heresy. But for heresy to be a capital offense, it needed to be a repeat offense. If Jehanne's sin were to be punishable by death, he had to make her re-offend. He'd needed someone to bring her women's clothes after the trial ended, but only so he could strip them off her again later, then condemn her. Catherine, by volunteering clothing, had made herself the two men's unwitting accomplice. But anyone would have done for the women's clothes stage of the proceedings; if it hadn't been her, there'd have been some nun or housewife somewhere who'd have served for this stage, who'd have provided the same kind of garments Catherine had.

Warwick and Bishop Beauvais must have been planning this ending all along. With a wave of nauseous anger, she realized: Bishop Beauvais knew; of course he knew; he as good as announced in advance that this would happen.

There was no trial scheduled for the next day, but the clerics who'd been so reluctantly taking part before now began turning up in the courtyard anyway. A dozen extra guests trooped into the hall with the English household at midday. There were places set for them all.

Catherine had slept badly, slumping down on the bed when Owain persuaded her to, but curling up on herself once there, pulling at her crucifix, praying, startling awake, furious with

515

herself for her weakness of purpose, getting up and pacing up and down the floor, moving her lips.

"You need to sleep," Owain had said, watching her from the bed, lying fully clothed with his hands behind his head.

"I'm praying for Jehanne," she'd replied fiercely.

"You can't do anything," Owain had said softly, sadly. "It's too late." And, once or twice, with surprise in his eyes, "I've never seen you like this."

She kept feeling her eyes staring wildly from their sockets. She tried to unclench her jaw and her fists, but a moment later she'd find them like that again. "You didn't see how small she was . . . how pitiful . . . how scared," she said stubbornly. She didn't tell Owain how flimsy the dress had been compared with all those stout cords the girl had protected herself with until then; how hastily she'd sewn the kirtle into place over that frail little arm and shoulder; how the solid gray robe had just been wrapped over one shoulder; how easy it would have been to yank it away. She didn't say: "That girl thought her saint was telling her to submit. She was always strong; I made her weak." But the thought beat through her body like a heartbeat; a rhythmic strum of horror at the cruel, cosmic injustice of it: *I made her weak. And they've tricked her.*

In the small of the morning, when Owain's eyes had closed and even the capering men outside had slumped like corpses over their dying fire, she thought she heard the sound of sobbing. But she couldn't be sure. It might have been the wind, or a bird.

She'd woken in a chair, frowsty and aching, to find Owain gone from the bed and a new guard outside kicking the night men awake. It had taken a moment to remember why she was there; that the sinking blackness inside her wasn't just the memory of a nightmare.

She'd told Dame Butler to let her rest; to keep even Harry away from her room. But she'd dressed in fresh clothes and gone into dinner at midday. Of course she had. She couldn't believe it, even now. She needed to look Warwick in the eye.

Warwick's pale eyes glittered. Or one of them did. The other was swollen half shut; blue and tender. His face was a crisscross of violent red and yellow streaks: gouges and scratches. But she could feel his triumph.

"The prisoner has reverted to wearing men's clothes," he announced with grim satisfaction.

There was a murmur: "The prisoner has reverted to wearing men's clothes." The clerics further along the table kept their heads down.

From beside the Earl, the Bishop of Beauvais said loudly and piously, "An abomination. A heresy."

Viciously, the Earl of Stafford added: "She deserves to burn."

There was another murmur.

Catherine felt the shout well up inside her: "What did you do to her?" But her voice echoed round her head and didn't come out.

Jehanne had fought, at least. She could see that from Warwick's battered face. The thought of Jehanne fighting back was like a reproach. As Catherine left the hall, after the meal was over, she slipped up to Warwick.

"What did you say to her?" she said quietly. "To Jehanne. I saw you go to the tower in the night."

She'd got Warwick's full attention for once. His head turned toward her. His one good eye narrowed. He was trying to terrify her into dropping her gaze. She stared boldly back.

"I had to see for myself that she was truly committing heresy again," he said coldly after a long pause. "Justice must be done."

She stalked along the corridors in a blue crackle of energy. She rushed to the Cardinal's rooms to tell him that Jehanne had been condemned to burn at the stake. She was certain her old friend, who'd had doubts of his own about the legitimacy of the trial, would be as outraged as she was at this travesty of justice.

She burst in unannounced. The Cardinal was sitting in the window seat, looking out, with a fur over his knees and a wistful look on his face. He was lost in an old man's nostalgia. He looks tired, she thought.

"Ah, my dear girl," he said, gesturing at the light summery

sky; the wisps of cloud, "I was just thinking how very *English* that sky looks. It will be good to get home after all this."

She brushed that aside and started to talk. But the Cardinal wasn't as horrified as she'd hoped when he finally made sense of her breathless rush of words. He wasn't horrified at all. He just shook his head and stroked his chin. "So Warwick's found a way, then," was all he said. Catherine thought he almost looked relieved.

After a moment, he added: "Of course, now she's committed heresy for a second time, the Pope will have to agree that she's guilty . . ." He began nodding his head.

"Is that all you have to say?" Catherine asked indignantly. "When it's so obvious what he's up to . . . forcing her into this! He attacked her! He must have ripped those clothes off her and forced the other ones back on! She's done nothing to deserve this death . . . It's a wicked, cynical trick!"

The Cardinal laid a hand on her arm. She couldn't see any answering flicker of indignation in his eyes. "Dear girl," he said mildly but a little reprovingly, "you're not yourself. Don't take it so to heart. After all . . . she *does* have to die. This *is* just what we need."

"We?" she said blankly. The Cardinal wasn't the honest ally she'd taken him for, after all.

"England," he answered. "Harry."

She stared. Wasn't there a single Englishman anywhere with a shred of honor?

Gulping, she stammered: "I must tell Owain . . ." And she was off again, running.

She'd stopped caring about discretion. She asked Dame Butler, who said Owain was with Harry. But Harry wasn't in his room. He was out in a corner of the courtyard, in the sunlight, playing knucklebones with Owain. She could see Owain's black hair under the green cap.

Harry smiled up when he saw her coming. "I'm winning," he said.

She patted his head; ignored his words. "We must do something," she said to Owain. "About Jeh—" Remembering Harry, she stopped herself and nodded up at the tower. Before Owain had even begun shaking his head, she said, "*I* must do something."

"What?" Owain asked. He sounded strangely cold. He didn't seem to understand the wickedness that was going on under their noses either.

There was a silence. She didn't want to admit that there was nothing she could do, or believe it.

"Do you want to play?" Harry asked, tugging at her skirts.

She said distractedly, "In a minute," and brushed off his hand, and went on looking at Owain.

In the end, Owain scrambled up. He put an arm through hers, and—leaving Harry looking disconsolately after them, squatting there with the knucklebones still in his little hand—walked her a few steps away. Then he said warningly, in a voice pitched too low for Harry to hear: "Choose your battles."

"I have," she said.

"Well, choose again," he snapped. "This isn't the time or place to make an enemy of Warwick."

"That bully; that brute. He's committing murder. It's *wrong*, what he's doing."

Owain shrugged. He said: "So what if it is?"

They looked at each other in anger.

Owain continued: "Listen to me, Catherine. You can't save Jehanne. You shouldn't even want to. Your only concern should be your son. Jehanne is Harry's enemy as much as your brother Charles is." He put his hands on her shoulders. He looked down with hard eyes. "So let her burn," he said. "Play Warwick's game. He tricked her. He probably raped her. He's a cruel man. He enjoys fear. But he's ours. He's doing what we need doing— what Harry needs. And what's Jehanne to you?"

She stared back. "Play his game? You're as bad as the Cardinal. Worse. At least he just sounded relieved. But you actually want to *help* that man get away with it . . ." She stepped away, out of reach of his hands. "You're all the same, you English. Christine was right all along. You don't have any idea of honor or chivalry or virtue, do you? You just get rid of anyone who gets in your way."

Owain said, very quietly: "I'm not English." His eyes were burning. His cheeks were burning.

She shrugged and curled her lip. "Then don't behave as if you were."

She would have walked off, but a pair of hands suddenly grabbed at her waist from behind and she heard a giggle. It was Harry. She'd forgotten him, she realized guiltily. He'd crept up. After a moment, he became aware something was wrong. He peered up at her with sudden fear in his eyes. He took his hands off her waist. He put one tenderly on her arm. "Why are you crying? Mama?"

Through her fingers she could see his scared face, a short figured-velvet coat and a thin black leg sticking out below with a small stumpy patten under his pointed shoe.

"I don't know," she said.

But she did know. She knew again as she'd kissed Harry and set off back to the keep. She knew that Jehanne would die as a result of dishonorable English trickery. She knew there was nothing she could do. It was enough to make anyone weep.

Suddenly she knew, too, that she didn't have to ignore her conscience. She'd given in to the strong all her life, but nothing was making her now. She had her pride and her honor. Unlike Jehanne, she wasn't a helpless prisoner—and so she could leave. It would be better for Harry, too. A child shouldn't watch a burning.

She found Dame Butler. She told her to pack.

At supper, she didn't wait for Warwick to sit down and bang his knife for attention, or make the announcement about the success of the trial. She could see what he was going to tell the table without waiting for that. It was shining like death in his boiled-fish eyes.

She went to him as he entered the room; and put a hand on his arm to stop him in the doorway.

"My lord," she said formally, "we're leaving, the King and I. We've been here too long. We should have been in Paris weeks ago, beginning the preparations."

He didn't take it seriously. He didn't take her seriously. He never had. He just shook his head dismissively. She could feel his arm strain, as if he were about to shrug her off. She tightened her grip.

"We're all staying until the burning," he said curtly.

"You are," she replied, just as curtly. "If that's your duty. But it's mine to take Harry to Paris to be crowned."

He lifted his free hand; fingered the angry weals on his cheek. He gave her a slow, cold look. She could see a new enmity congealing in it, but he must have seen her determination. "We'll be done in days," he said, keeping his voice low, bargaining with her. "By Michaelmas."

She shook her head. "I'm not letting Harry watch a burning," she said. "He's a child." She dropped his arm. She didn't want to drag this out. She'd finished with Warwick.

Instead of going toward her place, she moved toward the door. She wasn't going to eat with this man. "We set off in the morning," she said over her shoulder.

Owain didn't come to her that night. In the morning she walked, with her head held high, onto the deck of the barge that was to carry her and Harry and their servants and guards to Paris. There were no ceremonial farewells; no quiet farewells among friends either, since, as she heatedly told herself, she didn't seem to have any friends here. The deck was piled high with trunks and colored cushions. Harry was entranced—peering over the edge, running below deck, laughing, with Dame Butler trotting behind.

But Catherine watched Rouen recede, and the golden leaves flutter down into the bright water, with a shimmering uncertainty in her eyes. She'd done what honor dictated. She'd refused to participate in a crime. She'd shaken off the craven self-interest of the English and been true instead to the demands of her French royal blood—the best blood in the world. It was the bravest she'd ever been.

She should be happy. But she'd left Owain behind. And it felt like the end of everything.

PART NINE

The Treasure of the City of Ladies

THIRTY-FOUR

It took a week and a half to push up the Seine. In those long, overcast, often rainy days, Catherine discovered that the great river connecting Paris to the Channel was a stripe of thick gray, thronged with glistening dark boats, surging through a great brown wasteland of farmland gone wild. There seemed to be nothing in France but troop movements and mud.

"It wasn't like this before," she told Harry, as he looked mournfully out at the rain drilling away the last of the dead leaves from spiky trees. "France was beautiful." But had it really been? She tried to recall her childhood trips along the Seine. She couldn't remember what the beauty had looked like.

In this watery gloom, Catherine couldn't eat, and, even with Harry snuggled up against her in her bed at night in a way the Earl of Warwick would have most strongly disapproved of, she couldn't sleep. The air was so damp; the blankets were cold. Wet ran off the table. The river gurgled outside the rotting planks of the walls. She couldn't stop shivering.

And the farther she got from Rouen, the more she found herself flaying herself alive with regrets over what she'd done. She'd left Owain behind; left the Cardinal. She had no idea when she'd find them again. She'd pushed away her friends, and she was rushing ahead a French coronation for Harry that would take her son away from her, too. And for what? All in a futile gesture of support for a peasant madwoman with visions; someone whose one claim to fame was that she'd led armies in support of

Catherine's brother—her enemy. All to prove to an Englishman whom she didn't need to prove anything to, and who wasn't even really English, that she was brave and principled.

She could only hope the Cardinal would come to Paris. Surely he would, she yearned; surely he would have to follow the King, his charge.

But what about Owain? He might all too easily go back to his church. Somewhere, anywhere. Away. There was nothing binding him to her anymore, if he wanted to be free. The seven years he'd promised her were up. There was only love, and if that went wrong . . .

She might not see him again.

When the barge finally docked by the Louvre and Duke John came out to greet them through the thin rain, Catherine felt years older. She knew that the secret tears she'd hidden, even from Harry, and shed only silently and motionless in the dark, were visible on her drawn face.

There was nothing to do but accept her fate. She stepped up onto the jetty in her crumpled tan robe. She could feel the dread clutching at her gut. Harry was at her side, relieved to be off the boat, looking round for fresh mischief.

Weary and sick though she felt, she could see at once that Duke John's years in Paris had changed him. He was still pop-eyed and drably dressed, but he bowed with ease, spoke passable French, and had acquired some of the formal courtesy of a Parisian.

Before the Duke had even straightened up from his bowing and greeting, Harry had darted off. She let him be. She was too tired to mind him all the time, and too sad. But she looked up when he squealed, in his excitable treble, "Uncle Bobo!"

She looked, trying not to believe it. It couldn't be true. It must be a cruel trick; a game.

Except it wasn't. The Cardinal was right behind Duke John, under the canopy, laughing down at Harry, who was already chattering away without pause about the wetness of his clothes and the number of barges he'd counted (two hundred and thirty-seven on the busiest day) and how much he would like some hot milk and a fire to warm himself beside.

She drew a step closer. She was peering forward. The rain was getting in her eyes.

Right behind the Cardinal, hanging back a little, was Owain.

Patting Harry on the head, the Cardinal turned his gaze to her. She could think of nothing but those two pairs of eyes on her, those two slightly nervous smiles, as if neither man knew exactly how she'd greet them. "My dear, you'll get wet. Come under the canopy, quick," the Cardinal said, stepping aside to make way, and murmuring, as she flew up the carpet toward them, that they'd ridden all the way and got here last night. "Had to come, of course; follow the King," he added quickly. She could see he wanted to reassure her that she had nothing to reproach herself with. "But—grateful too. Very. Felt uncomfortable with all *that* going on . . . Distasteful. To be honest, I think the Pope would prefer me away from there."

His generosity made her heart sing. She'd never felt relief like this. She didn't care about ceremony or correctness. Not now. Not after everything she'd thought and felt in all that time alone on the water. She rushed to them, ignoring the astonished looks of the servants all around, and of Duke John. She flung her arms out and swept the pair of them into a three-person embrace.

"Thank you," she muttered, not knowing what she meant, hardly knowing who she meant it for, too euphoric to care, but somehow finding Owain's ear closest. "You're here. Thank you."

The smiles on both their faces, with Harry jumping around below, were reward enough.

Duke John lived at the Hôtel Barbette now, he said, as they jigged up the little distance from the Louvre dock to the Louvre castle under the drizzle, at a leisurely processional pace. The Barbette was an appropriate-sized place for a bachelor. Duke John might look a little like Humphrey, but even the shortest conversation soon revealed how different they were. Catherine liked his self-deprecating smile. He'd like to have invited them all there, he went on, to stay with him, but it was so small. So he'd put the King and his party up at the Louvre, where there would be room for their retinues.

Catherine hardly knew the Louvre. She'd visited her brother

Louis there as a child, and stayed briefly with Henry in the state rooms, that was all. It was the part of Paris she knew least, outside the old city walls to the west; inside the new walls her grandfather had built, and as far as possible from the Hôtel Saint-Paul to the east. She knew her mother, still alive, was almost certainly still living at the Hôtel Saint-Paul; but she couldn't quite bring herself to ask Duke John. She'd think later, maybe, about going to visit Isabeau. It would be too much now. She liked the idea of being in an unfamiliar place now she was in Paris; somewhere she had few memories. There was so much that was different that the city, the whole country, hardly seemed like the place she'd once come from. She didn't want to be snarled up in old memories.

She certainly didn't mind not visiting the Hôtel Barbette, not in the least. It had been her mother's house once; the private play palace where Isabeau had, at one time, entertained Catherine's uncle, the Duke of Orléans. Catherine didn't think she'd ever been inside there as a child. Back then it had been strictly for grown-ups only. But, over the years, since Charles had been denounced as a bastard, she'd come to think of it as the place where her brother must have been conceived in sin. The last thing she wanted was to revisit that memory. She wouldn't have liked going up Old Temple Street to get to it, even—past the burned-out site on one side of the road where her uncle of Orléans had been murdered, and Christine de Pizan's former home on the other. She thought it would have been Christine's house, shut up and decaying, something she'd known herself in happier times, rather than all the ghost stories and legends, that she'd have felt most uncomfortable with. She was happy to avoid the whole street, with its unclean associations. She had no room in her heart for any of that.

She had her love back. She'd been granted a happiness she didn't deserve in the least. She'd got back something she had almost certainly deserved to lose. Everyone she loved in this life was here with her. She knew now. And she was so grateful, and so full of joy.

Nothing could go wrong now, while they were here, and they would be here for a long while. Duke John didn't seem to notice, and nor did the Cardinal, that as soon as he'd dismounted and helped Harry down, Owain was at her side, helping her gently down, touching her arm and waist, letting his hand linger on her back. No one seemed to notice the naked pleasure with which she looked back up at him, or what she whispered, or how he laughed quietly back.

She didn't care that the great echoing downstairs rooms at the Louvre were stripped bare of all the beautiful statues and goldsmiths' work that she remembered from long ago. She'd been saving up the pleasure of showing Harry the almost miraculously lovely yet tiny representation of the Adoration of the Virgin she remembered from her childhood, standing in a shaft of sunlight in one of these halls. She remembered it perfectly—all in enameled gold and silver, with the figures of Virgin and Child and worshipers human and angelic set in a bower of tiny flowers and buds of pearl, and a handsome horseman below, feeding his miniature mount, dapper in parti-colored hose and fleur-de-lys sleeves. That would be proof, she'd thought: something tangible to show him the loveliness that had been France. But the table she remembered it being on was broken and held together with a cord. All that was left of what had stood on it was a shadow on the sun-bleached wood.

She only shrugged. The art had gone, she could see. Sold for the war, and no goldsmiths left in the quiet ruins of Paris to make more, either. The Louvre was like every other garrison now: empty and cheerless. But none of that mattered. Harry wouldn't care that the statue wasn't there. It was only a thing. And things, even beautiful things, didn't matter if you were happy. Beauty wasn't as important as love.

She didn't care that the curtains in her room were disintegrating and the bed linen was patched. She didn't care about the drafts where tapestries had been eaten away so badly that they must finally have been rolled up and thrown away; or about the bare halls with birds flying through.

"Maman says France used to be the most beautiful country in the world, when she was a girl," Harry announced to Duke John. He looked round doubtfully. "A long time ago," he qualified.

Duke John looked worried at that, as if Catherine might start to complain that standards had slipped since her time. Vaguely, he scratched his temple. "The war," he said, rumpling Harry's head with his big hand, "you see, my boy . . ."

But Catherine only laughed. Duke John was such a good man, she thought, as the Englishman fussed around, showing her to her rooms and Harry's adjoining ones, and explaining where the Cardinal could be found, one flight up, with Owain in the adjoining rooms. He took great personal care to make sure she was content, asking if he could send for hot water for baths, inviting her to eat as soon as she was ready.

She touched his arm with her hand as she murmured, "Thank you, dear brother . . . from the bottom of my heart. You've thought of everything." It might have been only a pretty phrase in the mouths of many French noblewomen, but she could tell from the warmth of his awkward, touched, answering smile that he'd taken it as sincere. And she'd meant it. It didn't matter in the least that everything was so shabby when he was so kind, so courteous—almost a Frenchman—and when, inside these bare walls, she felt happier than ever before.

Owain ran a tentative finger down her face, tracing a line from forehead to nose to mouth, over her chin, down the soft skin of her throat. It was the first time they'd made love since arriving from Rouen; it felt like a homecoming.

"I'm sorry," she'd been saying. "I was such a fool. It seemed right to leave; but I can see now that I was wrong. And then I was so frightened you'd go . . . give up on me. I didn't realize how much . . ."

She couldn't finish.

"I'd never," he muttered. "You shouldn't have . . ." Then he laughed with relief. There was no bitterness in him, no leftover anger. "You should have seen me. I practically forced the Cardinal up on his horse. He didn't mind leaving Rouen—he was relieved to have an excuse, in fact—but he was all for a leisurely barge ride. Not the mad gallop I put him on, to get to Paris before you. I've never heard him complain so much."

He kissed her softly on the lips again. She could still feel the doubt in him. "So," he whispered, "my Catherine again?"

"Always," she muttered back, and there was no doubt in her.

He laughed, and there was more confidence in his body as he gathered her to him again.

Always. Even though there were maybe only months left, maybe weeks, even if the trees were bare and the wind howling and the palace they were embracing in was crumbling, she would still always have this moment to treasure in memory. Whatever she was granted would be enough, she thought, with a humility that felt new to her. She was blessed to have this much happiness.

It took another day or so—once enough private conversations had taken place, and baths been enjoyed, and fowls been consumed, and sleep caught up on—before Duke John even mentioned getting down to business. Then, rather hesitantly at supper, he asked his adult guests to meet the following morning to discuss plans for the coronation.

"He looks nervous," Owain murmured to the Cardinal.

The Cardinal nodded thoughtfully. "Mm," he said. "Poor John . . . positively sheepish." He put an arm through Owain's. "I'm pretty sure I know why, too," he confided. Then he sighed, and, with a tragicomic grimace, murmured, "Ah, the confusions of wartime."

Owain had thought it might be the Cardinal who'd be looking nervous. Catherine had told him, months ago at Calais, about the letters from Duke Humphrey with their wild-sounding accusation that the Cardinal had stolen the English crown jewels. The Cardinal had never mentioned any of this to him; and no subsequent part of the Cardinal's correspondence, at least the letters that Owain had had a part in composing, had referred to it. But Owain knew Catherine wouldn't have made it up; that the Cardinal must be hiding some important question from even his own secretary. Owain had wondered whether the Cardinal might be expecting to be sent back to England once he'd reached journey's end in Paris with the

King; might have expected to face hostile questioning from Duke Humphrey, who must have had some trouble in mind to have started such an inflammatory rumor. But Duke John hadn't seemed aware of any trouble; hadn't mentioned any story about crown jewels. Owain thought he might not know the answer till they all got back to England; and maybe not even then. The Cardinal was the type to brazen out trouble. Even if he were worried, he wouldn't let it show.

Duke John was an altogether more straightforward character. His worry always showed on his face. The problem, as the Cardinal saw it, was that Duke John didn't know how to break to the Queen Mother the news that the coronation they would have to organize for Harry would, as Catherine had feared, be very different from the French coronation of tradition. Harry couldn't be crowned in the traditional place, Reims, because Duke John's forces couldn't guarantee security; so it would have to be Paris. Harry wouldn't have the traditional regalia. Poor Duke John still couldn't find Charlemagne's sword, Joyeuse, which was usually carried by a new king. Nor could he find the emperor's crown, which was usually worn, or that of Saint Louis. He'd hunted high and low for nearly two years now, but they'd vanished from the armory and from every other possible place they could have been put. Catherine knew all that already. But what she didn't yet know was that even the *ordo*, the form of words usually used by French kings to swear themselves true to God, had become a mystery. No one knew the order of prayers and hymns and invocations. No one knew where they might be written down, either. Or no one admitted to knowing.

Tomorrow, Duke John would have to admit all this to Catherine. But, the Cardinal said, nodding his head gravely, the Queen Mother had made it clear from the start that she wanted no compromise. Only perfection would satisfy the French, she'd said. Otherwise there was no point.

"He's done his best," the Cardinal said. "I feel for him. It's not altogether his fault. There is a war on. But what's to be done? The Queen Mother has taken this rather . . . *purist* . . . stance. As you know." Delicately, he raised an eyebrow. "And although that didn't appear to matter too much at the start of the journey, when she seemed rather more biddable, of course now she's made her stand at Rouen . . . shown herself a woman of spirit! And we should all be pulling together . . . natural allies . . . no telling what might happen if quarrels were to begin . . . so naturally he's alarmed."

He gave Owain a half-humorous look. Owain nodded and said nothing. He could see that for as consummate a politician as the Cardinal to be making what amounted to an appeal for help, he must be very anxious indeed to make a success of organizing the coronation. Owain guessed that the Cardinal believed his own welcome on his return to England must depend on it. Owain was also disturbed to realize that, since the Cardinal was making this appeal, it was clear that the Cardinal must believe him to have significant influence over Catherine. He didn't like that. The Cardinal finished urbanely: "Well . . . we'll just have to see what transpires."

Owain wanted his master and kindly Duke John to reach the compromise they needed. In the back of his mind, a memory stirred. There was something he thought he could try.

The door to the Tower of Falconry, where the King's library had been, where Owain remembered a big book containing the coronation *ordo,* was chained and locked, but that didn't seem to matter. Half of the door itself had been bashed in. You could bend down and step through the hole, two planks wide.

Owain only realized how ruined it was once he'd done that. The air inside smelled mildewed and full of regrets. He could hear a dripping from somewhere on the wall. His torch reflected a shimmery glistening. There were birds or rats moving about somewhere above. There were puddles on the floor.

He shook his head, suddenly considerably less sympathetic to Duke John. War or no war, there was no reason, except catastrophically bad housekeeping and ignorance, to have let this treasure trove of books get so wet. He could only hope the water was getting in from below, and the illuminated manuscripts above were safe. But it seemed likelier that part of the roof had come off and no one had bothered to mend it.

He went to the stone stairs. He climbed up carefully, letting his arms slide up the walls on both sides in case he slipped on the moisture underfoot. In the lowest of the reading rooms he stopped inside the door, slipped his torch into the wall sconce, and looked around.

The smell was worse here. As his eyes got used to the gloom, he could see why. Entire shelves of toppled books were soaked and stuck together, sagging and sideways, in a chaos of animal skin and ink puddles and rot. Other books were on the floor where they'd fallen. The pages that survived were brittle and stiff. There was a squeaking all around. There must be mice nesting everywhere.

He stood, shaking his head, lost in the pity of it, appalled by the sheer ignorant carelessness that had done more damage than deliberate violence. He was thinking of the library at the Hôtel Saint-Paul; the libraries of the Dukes of Orléans and Berri. There had been libraries at the University and libraries in the monasteries. Nothing so fine as this, but all of them repositories of beauty and memory, representing the thousands upon thousands of hours of thought from the men and women with the finest minds in the world, all intent on creating and preserving loveliness for the enjoyment of others . . . for the future . . . for children and grandchildren they would bequeath their knowledge to . . . and now lost, perhaps all of them. Lost.

He picked up the nearest book that he thought wouldn't crumble in his hands. Half an illustrated page came soggily away. A knight; a lady. A blurry border that had once shown red and gold roses. Owain made out the knowing, mischievous words: *"After all these efforts, when I finally approached the rosebush, so close I could stretch out my hands as I'd yearned to for so long, and pluck the rosebud from the branches, Fair Welcome started praying to God that I would do the rosebud no outrage, and I promised him solemnly, because he begged me and insisted, that I wouldn't do anything now that wasn't both her will and mine . . ."*

It nearly made him laugh. It was the lascivious, nudging, winking last page of the *Romance of the Rose:* the book whose lewd suggestiveness had so alarmed Christine and set her off on her defense of women. He dropped it. But he thought even Christine might have felt regret to see a book—even this one, which she'd so hated—destroyed so carelessly.

He shivered. This place felt and smelled unclean. He wanted to grieve for the end of that dream of civilization and beauty that Paris had once been. He wanted to get away.

He took the torch down.

He'd reached the top of the stairs before he remembered to check for the big blue book of the coronation *ordo.* It was on the floor, under two other books, but they'd melted together: a thick wet heap of decay. The pages wouldn't separate, they just clumped together and tore. It was hopeless.

Owain went downstairs, tight-faced. Now he really knew that the Paris of his youth was dead.

He was surprised at Catherine's calm. Sleepily, peaceably, she muttered, "Well, now we know, we can tell Duke John to mend the roof. He didn't mean any harm. And it's a great pity about the *ordo.* But some of the other books will dry out."

"But," he said, and his body was still holding on to the tightness of the memory, "so much will still be lost." He hadn't expected this indifference from her. She'd been the one who'd wanted the coronation just right.

She put an arm heavy with sleep over his chest. She murmured: "We've spent so long away . . . we were so young when we were here. It's all golden in our minds . . . we only remember how lovely Paris was, how civilized . . . but, perhaps . . . it wasn't, not really, was it?"

He thought of walking down Saint Anthony Street with Christine on his first evening, and seeing a sunset and cherry blossoms over walls, and bright clean white turrets rising up to the sky, as fine as needles, as intricately worked as lace. Yes, he thought passionately, grieving for its passing, that was loveliness.

She kissed him. "I didn't have you then," she muttered

drowsily. He could hardly make out the last words she mumbled as she drifted back into sleep. He thought she said: So now is better.

Morning brought a biting wind that howled through the streets outside, blowing hats off and knocking at shutters and doors like the undead.

They gathered around the table again, with a couple of scriveners at a lower table to take notes of their plans. Duke John sat uncomfortably, scratching at himself, looking ashamed, and letting the Cardinal, sitting just in front of Owain, do all the talking.

Catherine listened quietly. Duke John kept stealing uncertain glances at her.

". . . so a traditional French ceremony is out of the question," Cardinal Beaufort said brightly at the end of the litany of misfortunes. He leaned forward and his eyes were alight with enthusiasm. If Owain hadn't known better he'd have said the Cardinal was bringing her good news, not bad. "However, that may be for the best," the Cardinal swept on. "Because, as we all know, this is no longer the France of tradition. So it might be more fruitful to think of devising a new form of ceremony—one that reflects the marriage of our two kingdoms—one that shows the people of France how things are now."

"Yes," Catherine said.

"It could take place in Paris, for instance," the Cardinal continued, so intent on the persuasive case he was making that he seemed not to have heard Catherine agree.

"Yes," Catherine said.

"With a revised form of words . . ."

"Yes," Catherine said.

". . . and, mm, *revised* regalia."

"Yes," Catherine said, and Owain could hear now that there was a trace of humor in her voice. "Dear Uncle"—then she turned to Duke John—"dear brother. Please. I agree. I was wrong. We must have been working for, hoping for, the wrong thing. An old-style French coronation would be wrong. Let's do something different, as you suggest." And she smiled rather dreamily at the astonishment and relief flooding their faces.

"Thank you," Duke John said, and tentatively bowed his head. They could all hear the depth of the gratitude in his voice.

Later, when they were alone, Owain said, "Everyone's a little scared of you now."

"Yes," she said, sounding surprised. "I saw that."

"You did the right thing today, by giving way so graciously," he went on.

She nodded again. She said, still in that dreamy, accepting voice: "I wanted to make them happy. I could see how much it mattered to them. And they've been kind to me." After a while, she added: "In any case, there was nothing else to do, was there? What I wanted, thought I wanted—before—wasn't meant to be; I see that now. Now I'm here I can see that France isn't what I remember anymore; this doesn't feel anything like where I spent my childhood. It's just a place I can be with you and Harry for a while longer. So . . . if the Charlemagne treasures have been stolen and we can't have a real French coronation . . . I suppose that must be God's will. We'll just have to make do."

She paused, then shook that melancholy thought away. She even laughed.

"Anyway," she added, sounding, Owain thought, extraordinarily unworried, "it will still take months before those two work out what kind of coronation we *can* have." And she snuggled tighter into his arms, clinging to him, perhaps imagining them having a crown made, or sending to England for one, or consulting bishops as to the right form of words for a French crowning. "We still have time."

He could see, for a moment, that she really did want time—all the time she could still borrow, or steal. He was relieved at that, at least. Sometimes this new passivity of hers seemed like indifference; as if she'd given up.

But even Catherine was surprised by Cardinal Beaufort's swift next move. She hadn't bargained for his chess player's mind.

He called another coronation planning meeting for the next

afternoon. He was already in the room, wearing a pleased, slightly furtive smile, when Catherine walked in. He had two men waiting to open a box on the table.

Catherine recognized the box as one of the ones the Cardinal had traveled with from England. She'd seen it unloaded at every dock and stable along the way: a big rough lump of a thing, made of cheap oak, studded with nails. As soon as Catherine was seated, Duke John gestured for the box to be opened. The men prised the lid away with a rough blade. There were grunts, and the creak of wood as it came up.

Once the lid was gone, Duke John stepped forward and looked. Inside were many layers of old gray woolen blankets. Placidly, Catherine waited. Duke John pulled out a smaller box; equally roughly made. He looked at the lock. "Henry," he said, and, with a look of intense concentration that Catherine didn't think the task merited, the Cardinal fiddled at his belt, found the key, stepped forward, and opened the lock.

Catherine's mouth fell open as Duke John lifted out first a book, then, with a grunt, a crown. She recognized the enormous sapphire in it at once. Saint Edward the Confessor's. Harry had worn it at Westminster Abbey.

She didn't know whether to laugh or cry at the deceit being uncovered. So the Cardinal really had gone off with the English crown jewels, after all. Duke Humphrey hadn't been making the story up. For all his air of bewildered innocence, the churchman had been carting the most sacred of jewels around France with him for all this time. In a cheap old box.

When she looked behind the Cardinal's chair at Owain, she could see he was as dumbfounded as she was. His eyes were huge, his mouth open like hers. But when she looked at Duke John, she could see only that he was completely still; waiting. He couldn't meet her eyes. He wasn't half as good a liar as the Cardinal. It was obvious he'd known about the box.

"But," she stammered, "why didn't you *say*?"

The Cardinal looked a little pained. "Well, my dear, if you recall, you were against the idea of anything but the proper jewels—the proper everything—until yesterday. I didn't like to upset you, when you still had your heart set on perfection. But

I thought we should perhaps have a little something in reserve, just in case."

He folded his hands together. He folded his lips together. He was trying to look modest, and almost succeeding.

"But, Uncle," Catherine said, feeling her heart melt, as it often did, when, after he'd pulled off a successful stratagem, the Cardinal got that smug look which he tried so hard to suppress, "I don't mean why didn't you tell *me*; I can see that. I mean Humphrey? He's furious with you . . . out for your blood . . . calling you a thief . . . All you had to do was tell him in advance, surely?"

Now it was Duke John's turn to hang his head. Catherine softened further when she saw the misery on those straightforward soldier features.

Gently, the Cardinal explained: "We didn't want Humphrey to know the French sword and crown had gone. He's been making enough trouble for John over his handling of the war as it is. I didn't want to give him any more ammunition. Much better for everyone—for England—if we can all struggle on as we are, at least trying to pull together. I thought: Least said, soonest mended."

Catherine's head was whirling with all the small deceits he'd perpetrated; layer upon layer of them. How could she ever fully trust him? For a moment she hovered on the edge of anger. But then she looked at Owain, and remembered all the ways in which she'd never taken the Cardinal fully into her trust either, and took pity on poor, honest, good-hearted Duke John, who was looking so agonized at her side, and let out her breath.

The Cardinal sensed she'd accepted his maneuver. He spread his arms and said, as engagingly as ever: "Humphrey will thank me for it when he understands—as long as everything has worked out well and the coronation been a success. His heart's in the right place, really."

She smiled back at him. He was so convincing. When he gazed at her so positively she almost believed that Humphrey would be grateful. It was even possible that the Cardinal could present the borrowing of the English crown in enough of a favorable light that he and Duke John would be thanked for it.

"Dear Uncle," she said affectionately, "I just don't want you to get into trouble—even for Harry's sake. That's all." But she could see, from the naked relief on both men's faces, that they were satisfied—more than satisfied; grateful beyond words—with what she was now agreeing to. She was saving the situation for both of them. A coronation could go ahead.

Duke John got out a cloth and mopped his forehead. To her astonishment she saw he'd been sweating. How frightened they must have been, she realized, of the kind of conflict among noblemen that had started the destruction of France long ago. If this coronation was only good enough to stop that, it was good enough. "Thank you, my dear," Duke John muttered, and she loved the softness in his tired eyes. "This makes things much easier. It does indeed."

There was a pause.

"So," Duke John said, breaking the silence, "can we set a date?"

Suddenly brisk, the Cardinal broke in: "Coronation on Harry's tenth birthday?"

The room suddenly felt cold. Catherine looked from one Englishman to the other, realizing she was trapped. She hadn't understood that they'd come so far, so fast. They'd agreed on everything. December was no time at all. But all she could say was yes. Blankly, she nodded.

THIRTY-FIVE

However happy Owain had been to be reunited with Catherine, he didn't understand, or sympathize with, the dreamy tranquillity that had come on her in Paris. He was reacting to the end coming in quite another way—with increased urgency and an ever worsening sense of foreboding. More and more, he sensed it must be obvious to those around them, especially his master, who had been so close to Catherine and Owain himself for well over a year now, that he was Catherine's lover. Even before the alarming hints that the Cardinal had started giving in conversation, there'd been the moment with the keys. The Cardinal had made a point of locking the door connecting his rooms at the Louvre to Owain's, and giving Owain the key. "Here, my boy, you're less likely to lose this than me." In response, Owain had felt his face grow hot.

But perhaps he'd only started feeling this discomfort because of the manner of their leaving Rouen. It was haunting him. The Earl of Warwick had done nothing worse than purse his lips and bow, while the Cardinal had been wringing his hands, and bowing, and murmuring, ". . . a woman's whim . . ." and ". . . nothing I can do but follow the King . . ." as he apologized for the hurried departure. Warwick clearly didn't dare vent his rage on the Cardinal himself, but Owain shivered as he remembered the look of pure, vengeful enmity Warwick had given him when, plucking bonily at his shoulder, the Earl had held the Welshman back for a moment at the end of the interview. "And you . . ."

he'd hissed, with a malice that was no less frightening for being unspecific, "watch yourself. I know all about you. Don't think servants don't have eyes. Don't think people don't talk."

He felt much safer here, far from Warwick's eyes. At least in Duke John's spartan man-world there would be no sheet-sniffing. But he was saddened, too; oppressed by the howling emptiness all around in the great wasteland that the war had made of Paris.

He felt time rushing forward. Soon it would all be over. He'd be alone, in the twilight, with a future he'd mapped out for himself long ago, before he could have imagined this year and near-freedom with Catherine—a monkish future he hadn't really wanted even back then, and certainly didn't want now. He hated the idea of shutting himself away in the dark with a passionate intensity he'd also have found hard to imagine before. "With the eunuchs," he kept finding himself muttering— "shutting myself up in the dark with the eunuchs; and hating the good friars and their books, lovely as they are, full of knowledge as they are."

Catherine didn't seem to understand how final their parting must be, or she was deliberately shutting her mind to it. When Harry gets a bit older, she kept starting to say, with a vague kind of hope . . . when Harry has a proper court . . . perhaps I will be called back . . . and perhaps *you* . . .

She hardly seemed to be aware that Owain ignored those tentative half-offers of futures she had no control over. He knew them to be fantasies, and fantasies that would be unbearably painful to entertain. France was one thing—this strange, alternate life, where everything was possible, at least for a little while. But he couldn't go back to a life in England as Catherine's creature, even if it were offered. Not to serving her at dinner, or catching the occasional glance, or sneaking off to talk in gardens or chapels every now and then. He knew the future, and how it had to be, even though it made him dark with fury against his fate. When he went, it would be forever.

Now it was so nearly upon him, he was wild with energy, with the need to fit as much in as possible before the day Catherine would go to her life and he to his. He found fleeting wisps of thought coming into his head. Alternatives to prayer; because even if he could bear the quiet of a life bent over books, he thought, he'd never be able to reconcile himself to accepting the fate God had given him, and even the idea of thanking Him for it made Owain want to scream with fury. He couldn't even bear the notion of a long inactive lifetime of remembering. So perhaps instead he should go and hire himself as a mercenary; or go on a Crusade—die fighting somewhere. But nothing seemed quite real. He couldn't yet bear to think seriously of any future without Catherine. Yet being with her, here, now, so close to the end, was a perpetual, tormenting reminder of what was to come; and the clinging, forgetful calm she'd found was, for him, a worse torment still.

So he was almost relieved at Catherine's sudden alarm after the coronation date was set—when, it seemed, she also began to realize how fragile and brief this bubble of happiness was. It will all be over so soon, she said under her breath, as he escorted her away from the meeting. She'd gone very pale.

He was especially gentle with her when, that night, they were finally alone again. She'd understood at last, he thought; and there was gratitude and compassion all mixed up with his own grief. They'd be close again for these last days; at least they'd have that.

But he'd reckoned without Jehanne. Jehanne, who was to be burned at Rouen two days after the coronation date was set. It seemed to be the thought of the execution that was troubling Catherine as much as her own future prospects. When, within seconds of making love, she started talking very anxiously about blood—about the importance of her royal blood—Owain found himself feeling more lost than before, and further from her than he wanted to be.

"Do you think I am damned because I've betrayed my blood?" she asked into his ear. "Sometimes I think all this— the war, the troubles—might be because of me."

"No," he said the first night, kissing away her muttered words. "Of course not. Don't even think that."

He said something similar the next night. But on the night after the burning, when she began the same conversation a third time, he didn't try to kiss away her words anymore. Instead, Owain recalled the way she'd knelt, with her eyes tight shut, alone in her private panic, all through the thanksgiving service for Jehanne's death that been held in the Louvre earlier that day (they'd decided against public thanksgivings in the churches of Paris; Duke John feared there might have been a hostile response from the citizens). When Harry had asked his mother, on the way out of the chapel, "So will she really burn in Hell forevermore?" Catherine had replied, tight and loud, "No," so that Owain, the Cardinal and Duke John, walking just behind, had had to cough and stare at their feet and pretend not to have heard.

"No," Owain said now, holding her away from him so he could see into her anxious eyes in the last glow of the fire. "But why would you even think your actions had damned you, or any of us? For a while, back in Rouen, you seemed to be supporting Jehanne more than your son. But now you're here and he's here and all's well, and she's dead. You may have made an enemy of Warwick by walking away from the execution he wanted to turn into a big political show. But nothing worse than that, surely?"

She turned a little away. He sensed disappointment in her that he hadn't guessed right. "No," she muttered. "I don't mean that . . . any of that." She ran her fingers through her long tawny hair. "I mean that I might have done wrong long ago—by turning on Charles as I did. As we all did. It strikes me now . . ." Her voice trailed away.

"Charles," Owain repeated blankly. "You mean your brother Charles?"

He still had no idea why she would be blaming herself for what had happened to Charles, and what Jehanne had to do with it, or her blood.

"Yes," she said, a touch impatiently. "Because I've gone on thinking about Jehanne, you know. She moved me. She still does. I don't know why. All the way to Paris, I so regretted walking out and leaving you behind. I couldn't think what had possessed me. I risked losing you for her; and nothing would have been worth that risk." She raised her eyes. "But still, I think about her. I've prayed for her these last few days. She was brave. She loved France. I'm French too. I can't see her as an enemy."

"It was your brother's France she loved," Owain said, feeling toward an understanding of whatever it was that was troubling Catherine, but still unable not to add harshly: "Not yours. Jehanne was fighting to destroy your son and drive his armies out of France."

"Yes," Catherine said. She was frowning. "And that's exactly what worries me. Because Jehanne was a good woman— I could see that—and yet she was fighting for Charles. If she was really touched by God, if she was really sent holy visions by the saints—then why did she go to him? Does it mean God is with Charles? And if He *is*, doesn't that mean that Charles isn't a bastard after all? Even if we said he was? Even if we said there was no royal blood in his veins? There must be, after all. That's what frightens me. That we chased him out; that we denied his blood; that we may have been wrong."

She'd talked before about French royal blood. It was the story she always told Harry: that the same family had ruled France for a thousand years and always would, because God had sanctioned them to; that their blood was protected by God and the saints; that in proof of this it even ran a special color in their veins, extra purple and extra clear and pure. Harry had once even come to Owain, saying, "My blood looks different from yours. It's purpler; it's—" he'd lisped, not knowing the Latin, *"clarissimus."* With mild exasperation at the naiveté the story encouraged, Owain had laughed and said: "Ahhh, that's just a story; a way of explaining who you are and where you come from. You mustn't take it too literally. You probably know that if you actually cut yourself and so did I, our blood would look pretty much the same. Don't forget that." Owain was glad he'd spoken his mind to the little boy. As someone cut off from his own blood kin, by both fate and choice, Owain had thought carefully about how to make a good life for himself; he'd decided he would not limit himself to being whatever was said to be in his blood, and what others decided he should be predisposed to; he would decide for himself what he loved and follow it to the end. Harry should feel some of that freedom, for even a child, even a king, could decide a lot for himself, he'd thought. Now, Owain realized uncomfortably that Catherine must still believe this child's fancy about her blood and her kin, as literally as Harry had. More literally, even; perhaps it was the French way to be fanciful about these things.

Catherine was twisting a long strand of hair between twitchy fingers. Her eyes were fixed down and sideways, watching the movement. In a chastened little-girl voice, like a child at confession, she said: "I took my mother's word for it, that Charles was illegitimate. I never asked more. We all assumed the father must have been my uncle of Orléans. It fitted with the rumors and what she was saying, but no one actually asked. We told ourselves we didn't want her to get angry, but really we just wanted it to be true. None of us wanted to go into the detail, because we didn't want her to change her mind. Me least of all. I wanted to get Henry back to the talks. And he wanted the French throne promised to him before he'd come back. So I needed Charles to be a bastard. And yet I knew all along that my mother tells lies and is a bully; and I knew she was angry with Charles and would want revenge. What if she only said what she said so that we'd do what we did, and push him off the throne, wrongly maybe . . . and what if everything that has followed is God's punishment?"

Her eyes were diamond-shaped; brimming. Her voice was frightened. Owain sighed. He could feel her fear. He just couldn't share it.

"Look," he said very patiently, and he folded her back into his arms and held her tight. "Charles did you wrong. He betrayed you. He murdered your mother's servant in front of you. He imprisoned your mother—his Queen. He rebelled against your father—his King—and put armies in the field against them. Nothing he did suggested he had any proper family feeling toward any of you. He's been punished, and rightly so; and he's still being punished. Jehanne came to him, that's true enough; but she's been caught now and burned at the stake. He's losing. So how can you think God favors Charles' cause?"

It seemed convincing, and obvious to him. But she went on lying stiff and unyielding in his embrace; lost in her own darkness. When she raised her voice again, he heard it was as chilled and fearful as before. "My brother Louis was just the same. At war with her. And my brother Jean wouldn't come near Paris when he became Dauphin, for fear of crossing her. We're not talking about what Charles has *done*. We're talking about what he *is*." She gulped; then added, uncertainly: "or who he might be."

Owain said: "Even kings have to justify their right to rule." There was contempt in his voice, though she knew it wasn't for her. "As for your other brothers, none of them lived to take the throne. I don't think they had God's blessing for their behavior either."

Catherine nodded, but she hadn't taken in, or agreed with, what he said, he realized with a sinking heart. She just went back to talking about Jehanne.

She said, stubbornly: "Well, we can't tell who God favors from Jehanne's death. All we can know is that Jehanne fell into Warwick's hands and Warwick had her killed. There's no reason to claim God wanted to damn Jehanne. It might just be Warwick who'll be damned for killing her, at the Final Judgment. How can we be sure? What we do know, whatever you say, is that Charles hasn't lost . . . He's still holding court at Bourges, ten years on . . . He hasn't lost any more than the English have won."

She pulled herself out of his arms. He felt her prop herself up on one elbow beside him. He sensed she was looking at him; searching for his eyes in the darkness. "If I'm damned for it, I'll take my punishment. But what if it's Harry who is punished? That's what torments me. What if Harry ends up taking the punishment for my crime of spreading my mother's lie? What if Harry ends up losing France to my brother?"

Owain couldn't see anything anymore. But he could imagine the look of horror on her face as vividly as if they were in broad daylight. "God forbid," he said, firmly yet kindly, putting a hand back on her tense shoulder. Then he added, "I don't think you're worrying about the right things." There was so much else to fear; so much else to mourn. Why was she chasing these shadows? "But if you're truly this worried about the purity of Charles' blood, or yours, you're in the right place to find the answer to your question," he added. He tried to keep his voice light and gentle; keep the scratchy beginnings of anger at bay. "The only person who'll know the answer is right here in Paris. Go and see your mother. Ask her."

They took Harry away from a coronation rehearsal to ride across Paris for the day and meet his grandmother. He hadn't seen the city, nor had he demonstrated any curiosity, any wish to see it. Catherine and Owain watched his head turn, furtively taking it in, as they rode east from the Louvre. Under leaden skies, they took Saint-Germain l'Auxerrois Street, parallel with the river, to the center of the city, past the towers of the Châtelet and the two bridges leading over to the Island and the palace, and on down the embankment ride itself, past Grève Square and the wine port and the corn port and the hay port and the fish port and the charcoal port and the Archbishops of Sens' palace, with its private port. Catherine began to feel an uneasy sense of homecoming as she saw the Barbeau tower, and the beguines' convent, and as they passed into the Hôtel Saint-Paul itself.

There were dead leaves blowing everywhere. Owain liked the freshness of the wind; the choppy white on the waters. But he could see from Harry's disappointed face that the city no longer made the glittering impression it had on Owain, long ago. Harry didn't like the Hôtel Saint-Paul, either. He shivered and hunched down on his pony when he saw the overgrown gardens, with litter in the bushes and broken colonnades, arches ending in piles of rubble and toppled statues, broken panes of glass in the windows, and old men with no teeth guarding the doors from cobwebby cubbyholes.

They stood in a deserted hall, stripped of all but the most broken of furniture, waiting for someone to come and fetch them up to the royal apartments. They could hear the whispering; the tap-tapping of sticks along the corridors. The appearance of visitors had caused something close to alarm. No one here was used to outsiders.

When a little old woman finally came out from behind a door, peering at them in the interior twilight, Harry looked at her in doubt. "Is that my grandmother?" he asked Catherine in a piercing whisper, tugging at his mother's arm, looking ready to burst into tears. The old woman was dirty and frowsty, with a woolen shawl wrapped around her sunken breasts.

"No," Catherine whispered back, putting her hand over his. But it took even the adults a moment longer before they recognized her.

"It's been too long," Owain said, suddenly cheerful, suddenly realizing who this was, and rushing forward to kiss her and put arms around her. "It's years since I heard one of your stories. How are you, dear Anastaise? I've missed you . . ."

She grinned and hugged him back; and the ghost of her old robustness was still there in that cracked old smile.

"She's upstairs," Anastaise said, without formality—she'd never done formality very well—gesturing up the unswept staircase. "Still in bed though." She looked doubtfully at Catherine, then at Harry's frightened little face. "You might want to go to her by yourself for a bit," Anastaise went on, addressing Catherine. "She's not fit for visitors . . . not little ones," she added, giving Harry a careful grin, "who don't know her ways. You might help her make herself presentable."

Owain nodded. "Go," he said, giving Catherine a little push. She seemed frozen to the spot. "Anastaise can show the King and me the gardens for half an hour."

Catherine, looking uncertain, headed slowly for the stairs. But she kept looking back. Harry, visibly fighting the panic of a much younger child at being parted from his mother, nearly followed her. Owain took his hand firmly. "Stay with me. We'll go up shortly. Your mother needs a few minutes to say hello to her mother."

He nodded, willing Harry to nod back. After a long pause, Harry, keeping his eyes averted from Anastaise, stopped resisting. He trotted out, holding tight on to Owain, into the gray of the morning.

But even the lion cage didn't seem to impress him. "It was this big, the lion," Owain told him, gesturing with his arms, showing him an imaginary creature bigger than a horse. "And golden. And when it roared, the whole palace . . ."

Harry looked away, letting his eyes follow a dancing leaf.

". . . trembled," Anastaise joined in, very forcefully. There were broken veins on her cheeks, purple on white. Owain vaguely remembered that her cheeks had once been apple-red and healthy.

Harry only looked alarmed at the loudness of her voice. He nodded and bit his lips.

"Perhaps you'll have lions in Paris again when you're King?" Anastaise said. Harry nodded fearfully. Owain thought: He doesn't look at all convinced that he'd like lions.

Harry looked happier when they went back inside, out of the wind, into a little downstairs parlor where a fire was burning and there were still a couple of cushions and a settle by the flames. Anastaise got down a book from a shelf and showed him a long-ago picture she'd painted, a finger long and a thumb wide, of a woman in blue giving a book to a stately queen. "*That's* your grandmother," she told the trembling child, with the rough kindness that, till now, hadn't reassured him in the least. But now Owain could see Harry's fear easing. He looked cautiously at her, then, plucking up his courage, took the book in his own hands, sat down, and began to stare at the picture.

Over the top of his head, Anastaise winked at Owain. She still had the same cheerful eyes Owain remembered.

"My mother always told me that Paris was the most beautiful place in the world," Harry piped up a few moments later. "It's not, though, is it? It's gray and poor, and it's not very comfortable in the palace where we're staying. I'm glad I'll be going home soon. But," he added kindly, "I like your picture. I can see now. It was beautiful then."

Harry went back to his book, turning the pages, looking at other pictures: of hunting and dancing, and at monsters peeping out of sprays of foliage. But all Owain could think of was the painted woman in blue giving the book to the Queen. Christine de Pizan.

Anastaise guessed. She muttered, low enough not to disturb

Harry: "Dead, poor lady. Though perhaps she was lucky. She'd have been so sad to see how things turned out."

Owain let out his breath. He'd expected this, in a way. But it was a sorrow to hear she'd gone.

"God rest her soul," Owain said, and, in the quiet companionship of grief, they both crossed themselves. Then he added: "We read her poem, about Jehanne . . . so we knew she was alive last year."

With a look of regret from those cloudy eyes, Anastaise said: "Yes, she was excited, so excited, for a while. I went to see her last year, at Saint John's Eve. I brought the poem out myself. She'd just written it. The dawn of hope, she kept saying. We all thought that, back then."

Owain found his eyes were checking Anastaise's dirty old linen shirt for white Saint Michael's crosses. He couldn't see any. Perhaps it was the muddy reddish light.

"It worried Catherine, all that . . ." he muttered cautiously. "Even she's been thinking perhaps Charles should have been King, after all, if Jehanne . . . because Jehanne," but he stopped. He probably shouldn't say this sort of thing, even to this old friend. Doubts were dangerous. Even whispers.

He needn't have worried. Anastaise puffed herself up as if she still had a big barrel chest, looking furious at the very mention of Charles of Bourges. "What, *him*?" she said, so loudly and indignantly that Harry looked up for a startled moment before hunching down again over his book, determined not to look scared. Anastaise made a visible effort to contain herself. She lowered her voice, but she couldn't stop the words bursting out of her, as if the stopper had come out of a bottle and what was inside had to spill over. "Him, King? When a miracle was sent to him and he trampled all over it? When he let that girl sacrifice herself for him and didn't lift a finger to save her? No ransom, no negotiations, no nothing? I should say not. Nor would Christine have, if she'd seen the shameful way he cut her off . . . left her to be shamed and burned. After all that girl did for Charles, and for France." She shook her head with her hands on her hips. "No. He deserves everything he gets, that one."

Owain nearly laughed; mostly out of sheer relief that not all the French stayed up at night fretting about the color of the blood royal.

Anastaise looked abashed when she saw his smile. Then she lowered her hands from her hips and nodded. "Mustn't get too cross about it," she muttered ruefully. "I know." Looking down at the little boy with his nose in the pages of the book, she shook her head. "Though what that one's got to do with France, either, only God knows. Still; not my place to know who's the one for us and who isn't. Leave it to God to work out, eh?"

They looked fondly at each other. Anastaise gestured around. "I just wish He'd hurry up and decide. The Almighty. Because . . . just look at all this. Everything in ruins." She let her eyes turn again to the child staring at her miniatures. "I miss all that," she said wistfully. "The pictures. I'd have enjoyed working on that poem." She looked at her work-roughened hands. The time of beauty had passed for her, all right. Owain could imagine what Anastaise's life had become, in this forgotten place of sick old people, nursing the Queen.

Sympathetically, he said: "Whatever God sends."

A bell rang. A distant contralto voice shouted, "Hall-o-o-o-o!"

Anastaise looked up. "That'll be them," she said. "Come on. Let's go up." Giving Harry her biggest gap-toothed grin, she gathered up the book and put it carefully back on its shelf.

"What's that girl doing worrying about old history anyway?" Anastaise muttered to Owain as they set off up the stairs. "She needs a bit of happiness in her life, that's what she needs. A husband; more children. That's what Christine would have told her, if she'd been alive. Christine was all for families. More children—that would keep her too busy for fretting about her brother. Isn't it time one of those Englishmen thought of that?" She shook her head, looking comically astonished by the short-sightedness of the English.

"Well, it's difficult," Owain muttered.

She shook her head again.

They reached the top of the stairs. They set out along the

top corridor. There was a door open up ahead. Catherine was looking out. Harry raced toward her.

"And you—you're not cut out for the Church, whatever you say," Anastaise added. She gave Owain a penetrating look with a hint of a smile. "Time you stopped all that nonsense and settled down too. Found yourself a good woman; if you haven't already."

He blushed. He said: "All that . . . not for me." But he could see she wasn't convinced.

"You always were a deep one," she said, and went on shaking her head.

Catherine had blurted it out almost as soon as she'd got into the hot dark fug of rose oil and old body; right after they'd hugged and told each other how little they'd changed, and Catherine had said she'd come with Harry and he'd be up shortly, and why didn't they tidy Isabeau up a bit first. Catherine had pulled her mother's inert, slack weight up into a sitting position, and found her a new, clean nightgown. She'd helped her into it and done up the buttons over the withered flesh, holding the arms of the silken gown. She'd patted her cushions into place and straightened up the covers on the bed. It was easier, in a way, to ask the question on her mind while her body was so busy.

She was sitting on the bed behind her mother, with an ivory comb in her hand, when she began. "I've been worrying," she rushed, "about something very old. I have to ask. Was it really true what you said back then? Was Charles really a bastard, or not?" She gulped. In great fear, she added: "And am I?"

Ever since she'd let the fear out into the open, by saying it aloud to Owain, it had grown, taking ever more monstrous shapes. If Charles were legitimate, Catherine must be a sinner who'd brought destruction on France. But it could be even worse. If her mother had had all the lovers people said, perhaps it was she, Catherine, who was the bastard, cut off from the whole great glorious stretch of history she'd grown up belonging to . . . ? Which would mean she'd tainted the blood line of England's kings, too, and that Harry . . . ?

She'd expected many answers. Rehearsed what she thought were all the possibilities. But she hadn't expected what happened next as she sat on the greasy quilt, hardly daring to breathe. She hadn't expected laughter.

A great snuffle of it came out of the hunched shape in front of her. After a while, her mother's billowing curves stopped heaving with it enough to say, through the wheezes of mirth: "Ach, don't make me laugh. Who knows? About you, me, anyone? None of us knows the half of what's gone on; who's been in whose beds, who's been up to what mischief. Wherever you look. What does it matter now?"

She hauled herself round so Catherine could see one of her mother's beady eyes fixed on her, over a quivering shoulder. Isabeau took in the intent quiet on her daughter's face, and made an effort at control. More seriously, she went on: "It's just a game, royalty. That's the truth. We brought you up to believe kings were blessed by God; could work miracles; cure people of illness—and all because of their purple blood. But look at your poor father. No one could cure him. He couldn't even cure himself. A good king is someone who can command and be obeyed. That's all. If you ask me, you could put a peasant child in a royal nursery and bring him up to be King, and if he's got the knack of command he might do as well as a real prince; certainly better than half the kings I've seen. Your Henry was a good King, true enough; we chose well for you. His father, too, but no one was ever very sure if *he* had any blood right to the throne. What's blood got to do with it, when it comes to it? Who really believes that royal blood is any different from the other kind? If you had any sense you'd be hoping you *were* a bastard. Who'd want your father's madness running in their family?"

Matter-of-factly, she added: "Move that cushion, there's a good girl," and, when Catherine failed to move, said, more sharply, "that one there; under your hand; put it behind me, here. I can hardly see you. You're giving me neck-ache."

Once she was settled so she could look straight into Catherine's eyes, she reached out an arm packed with sagging flesh and patted her daughter's cold, unresponsive hand. "Don't look so worried," she said. "Put it out of your mind; forget all the fairy tales. You're too old for fairy tales. But not for living. That's what matters. Get on with that."

Catherine's head was spinning. "I don't understand," she said.

Isabeau looked patiently at her. "It's simple enough," she replied. "All you need to do is make sure you bring that boy of yours up right—so he's happy and strong and right-minded and honest—and so he loves you as much as you love him—and you'll have nothing to reproach yourself with." She nodded, and the laughter went out of her. Her face settled into lines of sadness. "It's the greatest thing there is, love for your children," she added. "When it goes wrong, you never forgive yourself . . . it's an endless sorrow."

Catherine realized, with a jolt of emotion she couldn't name, that she'd never asked what her mother had felt about being imprisoned by Charles, or hated by Louis and Jean, come to that. She'd just assumed: angry, vengeful. But why had she never asked?

"When it's right, it's a joy," Isabeau's voice went on. "You'll do anything for your child, anything. The only time I ever really fought for what I loved was over you . . . when I said"—she twisted her lips—"*that* . . . put aside my son . . . destroyed my reputation . . . so we could get your Henry back to the table for you." She sighed. Then she brightened. She patted Catherine's hand again. She said, in a stronger voice: "It was worth it. Sacrifices don't matter for a child you love."

Catherine felt dizzy still. This was so different from what she'd expected and hoped for. And yet, she suddenly realized, it was enough. Very softly, she put both hands on her mother's shoulders, leaned forward, and kissed one crumpled cheek.

"Thank you," she whispered.

They stayed like that for a moment, one flesh again, with no more need for words. Then Isabeau said, "Which reminds me . . . where's my grandson? He's had long enough out looking for lions with that handsome tutor of his. I spotted you out of the window earlier on . . . sent Anastaise down. I wanted to see you first. But we're ready now, aren't we?" She patted her night-cap. There was a hungry look on her old face. "Bring him up."

"I didn't expect Harry to enjoy himself so much," Owain said.

"My mother loved him, didn't she?" Catherine agreed softly. The light was failing. The Louvre was coming up ahead. Harry was trotting in front of them. She'd been quiet all the way back, but Owain thought she looked happy.

Owain said: "He's so much better now Warwick's not here." He wanted to jolt her into conversation. She didn't respond. He pursued the subject. "Don't you think? He's confident. Interested in what's around him. You should tell Duke John. Or the Cardinal. He'll have noticed the change, all right. Have them ask Duke Humphrey to keep Warwick away. Keep him at the war, maybe. He'd be happy enough in France, fighting. And it would make your life easier once you get back to England. Both your lives. You'll need to protect yourself. Warwick will never be your friend. It would be easier for you both if Warwick wasn't there."

He could hear the anxious note in his voice; the tightness. But she didn't seem to respond to it. "Yes," she said absentmindedly. But he could see she wasn't really taking in what he said.

He thought: She's sinking into lethargy; it's as if nothing matters to her anymore. Tensely he added: "Fight; you'll have to fight for what you want, and it's a good moment. You just might be able to get him out of Harry's life if you try now . . ." But she only turned up the corners of her mouth and looked weary, as though she was done with fighting; as though it was too much effort.

For a moment, though, looking at Owain, she suddenly flickered into life. "Perhaps *you* could be appointed in his place . . ." she said, with a kind of weak hope.

Unable to keep the impatience out of his voice altogether at having to explain this again, he said: "No. That will never happen. I'm Welsh. I'm not important enough. And I'll be gone soon. You know that. Don't waste a thought on it."

Her mouth went slack again.

More gently, he added, "What did your mother say about what was troubling you—about Charles' blood and yours?"

She just shook her head. "The same as you did," she said. "That blood doesn't matter as much as love."

He waited. She was thinking; he could see she was troubled.

"I believed her," she said. But he could hear doubt coming back. Then her face puckered.

"If nothing matters, and royalty is only a game, it all seems so wasteful," she whispered, so he could hardly hear. "Why are we fighting at all? Why did Jehanne have to die? What is the point of any of the things we plan and hope for and fight for?"

Harry wasn't looking. He was a couple of lengths ahead, staring round at the city. Owain stretched out a hand, found hers; held it tight over the horses' ambling. "There's you and me in the darkness, at least," Owain said, and he felt a flicker of answering pressure in her hand. "You're everything—more important than blood or beauty. Isn't that enough?"

But whatever Owain said, he couldn't find the peace of mind he needed, to stop trying to fight for Catherine, in that future he would have no part in. Later he went to see Duke John and, explaining that he was there on behalf of the Queen Mother, requested that the Earl of Warwick be moved on from Harry's household.

"Why?" asked Duke John with interest.

Owain thought: It's better I ask him; he'll be able to be franker with me; he's better with men than with women. "Warwick was Duke Humphrey's appointment—and he's always been more interested in the war than in child-rearing," he replied promptly.

The Duke only looked skeptical, as though this wasn't enough reason to meddle with the order of things; as though it wasn't a worthy fight to choose against his brother.

What have I got to lose? Owain thought, and went on, ". . . and the child is terrified of the beatings."

He was pleased to see Duke John look thoughtful at that, and hear him say: "I've heard this before. About Warwick and beatings." He was also pleased that, when Warwick arrived in Paris for the coronation a couple of weeks later, Duke John didn't put him up at the Louvre with the other English guests. Tactfully, he drew Owain aside and said, "I thought Warwick—better at the palace, away from it all, until after the ceremony, eh? Wouldn't want to put the boy off his stride."

The Earl and his troop of a hundred men were given quarters at the palace with the French guests. They wouldn't even meet the King's party until after the ceremony.

THIRTY-SIX

The coronation—in the end an exact replica of the English one—took place on Harry's birthday in early December. There were gusts of snow outside on this day, too. Duke John and the Cardinal did their best to deliver loyal French lords from every corner of the land. The Frenchmen stood together, looking uncomfortable at the unfamiliar service. Being mostly from Burgundian France, they had had little to do with the court of Queen Isabeau in her heyday. Those who had been courtiers under her kept their distance too; perhaps they were embarrassed that they'd left her alone all these years in her crumbling house. The old lady, wrapped up in furs and allowed to sit through the ceremony due to her advanced age, didn't seem to care. She watched with gusto; sucking on sticky titbits she pulled up, from time to time, from the depths of her pockets.

The English group stood to one side. Warwick kept well away from Catherine. He stood somberly apart from the other English lords, too, throughout the hours of prayer and crowning, with his troop of knights behind him. He held a candle in the glittery gloom. Every now and then, Owain felt a prickling in his shoulder blades and glanced round, expecting to find the man's hard stare on him; but he never caught Warwick looking.

"This isn't traveling weather . . . shouldn't we stay in Paris until after Christmas?" Catherine had said the day before as she, Owain, the Cardinal, and Harry had shared a hurried last meal before going their separate ways.

The Cardinal had agreed. Catherine had thought he looked sorry for her. "No need to hurry home," he'd said kindly.

The departure date they'd set was January 7. Less than a month—weeks; days. She'd clung to Owain that night. He was visualizing the parting, ready to weep and rage at the frustration of it, but she refused to think beyond the night. She'd smiled too brightly and said, "Don't look ahead. Let's be happy now."

There was a dinner after the coronation. Harry and Catherine were permitted to leave after the lords of France and Burgundy and England had filed in for the first course, and Harry, in his hesitant Englishman's French, had blessed them all.

The child was stumbling and fatigued and shivering by the time he gave the blessing: a little boy again. But an hour later, after a bath and wrapped in a nest of blankets by the fire in his rooms upstairs at the palace, eating a bowl of junket, his cheeks were pink and flushed, and he was grinning in embarrassed delight as his grandmother, from her similar nest of furred blankets by the other side of the fire, told him in her thick Germanic accent, with her ugly old face all lit up with love, "So good! Remembered all the words! That heavy crown!" and leaned forward to pat his damp hair.

That was the scene Owain saw when he entered the little parlor. Seeing Isabeau, he bowed formally and said, "The Cardinal presents his best wishes to Your Majesties. He will be up shortly to offer his congratulations to the newly anointed King of France."

"The charming tutor," Isabeau said, inaccurately but with great warmth. She gave him an arch smile. "Ach, young man, no need for all the ceremony. We've had quite enough speeches today. Come on in, do, out of that draft. Put another log on the fire; it's cold in here. And tell us what we're missing down there at the dinner. I could see the Lord of Albret was desperate for a drink; he was twitching even back in the church . . . Has he disgraced himself yet? How fat he's got over the years . . . he was such a handsome young man once, with such an eye for the ladies. Hard to believe now . . . though I did hear . . . Well, I'll tell you about that later," she cackled. "Once these little ears are in bed."

Within moments she'd organized Owain into fetching a stool by the fire for himself, next to Catherine's, who emerged looking tired, having completed her own toilette, in a houppelande of green velvet that reminded him painfully of what she'd been wearing the very first time he'd set eyes on her.

Isabeau was patting Owain on the knee, Catherine saw. The old Queen was telling him, with ferocious flirtatiousness, "You must be a comfort to my daughter; a good, strong, kind young man like you."

Owain looked up at her, and, for all his sadness at what was to come, he had the beginning of a laugh on his lips at what Catherine's mother was saying; he couldn't help it. This was so exactly how Catherine had described her mother. He and Catherine exchanged a quiet look before she smiled too.

Isabeau broke in. "Now, young man," she said chidingly, and the pat to the knee turned into a prod, "hurry off and fetch me some of that monk liqueur, will you? The green one. They say it's good for the digestion."

Bowing, with his lips still twitching, Owain got up.

"Catherine, didn't I see you had some sweets?" the old Queen went on, looking around. "And what about some more junket for the boy . . . or one of these?"

Before they knew it they were rushing around serving the old woman; puffing up her cushions; fetching footstools. They were laughing at her stories as the air got hotter and hotter and more strongly scented of her thick rose oil; shushing her when she threatened to say something too risqué for the little boy's innocent ears.

It was only when the Cardinal appeared, and bowed, and settled to his own merrily malicious conversation with the old Queen—catching her up, for a start, with the antics of the Lord of Albret, who was, as she'd suspected, now very drunk and had insulted both his neighbors before falling asleep at the table—that Harry began to nod off.

"Shh," Catherine said softly, and put her finger to her lips.

For a moment they all gazed at the little boy's pink cheeks and peaceful face. Then, quietly, Owain scooped him up in his arms to carry him next door, where the bed was waiting with a warming pan in it.

Catherine followed on tiptoe with a light. Giving it to Owain, once he'd laid the sleeping child on the bed and put the warming pan on the floor, she carefully tucked her son in and kissed his forehead.

This was the end. She knew that. But she couldn't be as sad as she'd expected to be. Something about the lighthearted little gathering in the next room—something about her mother's mischievous old presence—had raised her spirits.

How happy the Cardinal looked now the coronation was over; how relieved. Whatever Duke Humphrey's accusations about the theft of the crown, they'd have to be put aside once it became clear what foresight the Cardinal had shown. It surely wouldn't count against him, at any rate. They'd deliver back a happy, healthy boy, successfully crowned King of two countries. The Cardinal could end his days at home, at the court of a monarch who loved him. Suddenly more optimistic than she'd felt in a long time, Catherine thought that she too might be somewhere not too far away; that even if Owain immured himself away from her, at least Harry would still want her nearby; not everything would be over. There would be time for sadness. For now she was just thankful that she hadn't been too stubborn over the shape of the coronation; glad she had the friends and allies she did.

She could hear the loud banquet downstairs in full swing. She could hear the quiet sound of more arrivals next door; mutterings. Someone else had arrived to pay respects; perhaps Duke John, but too late. Nothing would wake Harry.

She looked down at her son, so innocent and fresh-faced and babyish. She didn't want this moment to end. Owain stood beside her, looking too. Then his hand found hers. He drew her close.

"They're just next door," she muttered, raising her face to his. But she was smiling, at least. She seemed almost normal again, Owain thought, almost fully alive, ever since her mother had started gossiping and piling up the warmth in the other room. After all, what did anything else matter but the moments they still had together, now that they'd done what they'd set out to; now Harry was truly King of France as well as England; now their time was running out?

"Never mind them," Owain said recklessly, turning his back on the door and the people behind it. "There's just us." And then they kissed.

Until the door opened, very quietly, then, in a rush of thundering footsteps and dark air, hands seized Owain, twisted one arm behind his back, and dragged him out, blinking and bewildered, into the hot, light room beyond. Following, stumbling, heart racing, aware that her cap was askew and her hair tumbling down, Catherine looked over the top of Owain's head at the pale, triumphant eyes of the Earl of Warwick.

Warwick's face was full of gloating disgust. "*Lèse-majesté*," he snarled, staring round at his appalled audience, shaking his captive prey. Owain didn't lift his pale face. It had the utter misery of a person who sees the end approaching. "Debauchery. An outrage against the Queen Mother's person. Here, in the King's own chamber."

Catherine faltered. "You misunderstand. He was just helping me put Harry to bed." But she felt her weakness. Her cheeks were flaming, her hair everywhere. She knew she must look the picture of guilt.

She didn't know what the penalty might be for Owain if Warwick were to punish him for having or seeking carnal knowledge of the Queen Mother of England. But she could see in Warwick's eyes that Owain's life was in danger.

"Are you saying, Madam," Warwick asked, stepping up to her, his eyes devouring her, "that you were a willing partner in the obscene . . . *spectacle* . . . that I just saw?"

There was a still more profound silence. Catherine couldn't speak. She knew, with a terrible, cringing fear, a black weariness that went to the depths of her soul, that she was in mortal danger too.

"I knew he hadn't spent a night in his own bed at Rouen,"

the Earl shouted, and Catherine could hear the delight mixed up with his rage. "I knew he had the morals of an animal. But *this*. *This* I didn't imagine. Corruption, filth; and so close to the throne . . ."

The shout brought men to the door. They could hear the clatter and tramp of feet. The Earl had had his knights waiting outside. He must have come looking for trouble.

The Cardinal looked dumbfounded. He was staring from Warwick, to Owain, to Catherine. It was a scene of rapidly shifting eyes. Owain kept his white, appalled face down, while Catherine was too shamed to meet the Cardinal's gaze. But she let her eyes rest on her mother. The old Queen of France was staring up at Warwick, twice as lively as before, looking at the malice contorting this newcomer's face, assessing his stringy strength. Her mouth was still chomping consideringly on one of her sweets. Isabeau had seen nothing of him, knew nothing of him beyond a bow and a name announced to the blowing of horns. But she'd never been shy of a good row.

The Earl turned to Catherine. His face was blazing. Owain was just an entertainment—a nobody. It was the Queen Mother who was his real target—the woman who'd defied him at Rouen. "And you—Madam—must consider your position; entertaining lovers in your son's bed . . ." he said, drawling the words pleasurably out, permitting himself to sneer openly at her now she was brought so low.

But he had to finish with his first victim before he could really concentrate on her. Over his shoulder he snapped at the men: "Take him away. Deal with him."

He pushed Owain out into the doorway. Hands took him. Before the men could move off with their prisoner, however, there was a rustle at the other door. Harry's bedroom.

Everyone froze.

"What's happening?" said a voice: a sleepy, alarmed little treble voice, followed by a shock of very straight dark blond hair and round eyes peeping round the door. "Why are you all shouting?" He looked round. He stepped out. His nightshirt was striped. His thin legs stuck out underneath. Catherine ached with love for him; with fear for the vulnerability of him; with hopelessness.

Of all the people now crowding into the overheated little room, it was only Owain who found the presence of mind to speak. Raising his head, he summoned up the strength to banish the dread from his face. Looking very tenderly at the little King, whom he'd spent the last years helping to raise, whose father he'd loved, he said gently, "Go to sleep, Harry. It's all right. Go back to bed."

Catherine's heart overflowed. But Harry didn't move. And the men-at-arms, knowing themselves to be in the presence of the King of England and France, waited.

Warwick shifted. Scowled. "Take him away," he repeated.

Harry turned toward the sound of that voice. He looked horrified to see Warwick's face. "What are *you* doing here?" he said. Then, with rising panic: "What are you doing to Owain? Let go of Owain. Tell your men to let go."

The Earl signaled again for the men to go with their prisoner, but no one stirred. They were watching Harry as his face twisted; as the hot, angry tears came to his eyes.

"No!" he shouted. They'd all seen it forming on his lips, but the high-pitched yell still came as a surprise. They all watched, slack with shock, as Harry rushed out of his doorway to pummel the Earl. He only reached up to Warwick's midriff, but he still whacked the commander with all the viciousness and strength he could muster. "Let him go! Let him go!" he shouted, as Warwick took a half-step back, parrying the blows with his forearms. Even when the Earl had pinioned Harry's hands, they went on flailing uselessly, and the voice went on hysterically shrilling, "I command you! I am your King!"

The men looked at Harry's arms pinned in the Earl's big fists. It was the signal they needed. They knew who was in charge now. They rushed off, bundling Owain away, clattering down the stairs.

They'll kill him, Catherine thought. They'll kill him, or worse. And what will happen to me? Everything seemed to be happening so slowly that she had endless time to think those thoughts; to look round; to see the stares, and dropped jaws, and clenched fists. But suddenly there was no time for thinking. Suddenly there was only time for a new kind of panic, even worse than before.

Harry's head dropped in defeat. And Catherine heard the lowing, keening animal noises she dreaded most coming out of his chest: the howling. She was aware of Isabeau's head snapping round; of her mother's quick look at the child. Isabeau turned back toward her with a quick, quiet exchange of understanding. Catherine could see her mother recognized those noises, too, from old King Charles' time: the sounds of the beginning of madness.

Wheezing, with difficulty, Isabeau stood up. Agonizingly slowly, wielding her walking stick like a weapon, she stomped across the room to Warwick. "Young man, I don't know who you think you are, barging into the royal chambers like this, but you're making a mistake you will regret," she said, puffing herself up to her terrifying snake-self, the rage-filled monster Catherine had dreaded most when she was a child, and hissing at the intruder.

It must have been years since anyone had called Warwick a young man. The battle-hardened old warhorse flared his nostrils and narrowed his eyes. So did Catherine. She couldn't take her eyes off her mother.

"It will be the worse for you if you don't heed the command of your King," Isabeau grated, getting closer, with her deep-set dark eyes fixed on Warwick as if she were about to swallow her prey.

The Earl just sneered. His mouth curled up with it: a display of hostile indifference that he must have known would only infuriate her further. He didn't care if it did. He said: "The boy is in my charge. The Council of England has entrusted him to me. With the greatest of respect, Madame, it's a long time since you've known anything of affairs of state; and you never knew England. So don't meddle in what you don't understand."

But Isabeau was right up against Warwick now, with her chin jutting out and her eyes glowering at him, and the hand with no stick in it hovering protectively over the little boy he had hanging from his fists.

"The *boy*," she said, and she sneered in her turn at his disrespect, "is the King of France too now. I don't see what the Council of England has to do with commands that the crowned King of France makes to his subjects in France. The King of France gave you a command. To disobey him outright would be treason." She stuck her face right in his, so close that he stepped back looking startled. "I don't think you'll be safe on the streets for long if you try to commit treason in the capital of France."

It would have been the perfect signal for someone else born to browbeating and furious family rows to join the attack she was mounting. But Harry had been brought up to quietness; and he was too young and too distressed to take his cue from her. He just went on howling like a lunatic. And Catherine was struck as dumb as she ever had been in childhood by the sight of her mother's anger. She couldn't speak. She couldn't move.

Warwick stepped back another pace. Ignoring Isabeau, he shook the boy. "Be quiet," he said with quiet savagery. He shook him harder. "Stop that nonsense."

Undaunted, Isabeau joined in the shaking, only the shoulders she put her hands on and began shaking for all she was worth were Warwick's. "Stop . . . that . . . at . . . once," she grunted in rhythm, refusing to let him shake her off, hanging on for grim death. "Didn't . . . you . . . hear . . . me. I said . . . *stop*."

Warwick was so astonished at being so stubbornly assaulted by a fat old woman with a stick that he released Harry. Harry ran to his mother, still howling.

Isabeau stopped shaking her prey, but went on standing too close to Warwick, holding his shoulders in her hands, hypnotizing him with her basilisk eyes. When he took another step back, trying to shake her off, she lumbered heavily forward.

"Now," she said, with grim satisfaction. "Give the order. Release the other young man too. Or you'll be sorry. You'll see."

Silence from Warwick. The Cardinal, who was beginning to

come to from his amazement, was raising his arms in his corner, making calming noises. Little sounds, the beginnings of words of remonstration, began coming through his nose.

"Don't ignore me." Isabeau shook Warwick again, like a hound with a giant rat. Savagely, she added: "Have you no manners? I said, give the order—set free . . ." She turned to Catherine for guidance. "I'm not good with names," she added, with superb self-possession.

". . . Owain," Catherine stuttered back. "Tudor."

Warwick couldn't quite bring himself to strike this unexpected protagonist, however much the look on his face suggested he wanted to. But he was willing enough to go on offering verbal resistance. "I don't think so. What for?" he replied viciously, giving Isabeau a stare so full of violent hate that Catherine was terrified for her mother. "So the Queen Mother of England can debauch our court like her mother did the court of France?"

Isabeau slapped him. Loudly. The stinging sound echoed round the room.

Harry stopped howling and looked up with saucer eyes. The Earl put a hand to his cheek. It didn't cover the red handprint the old woman had left on it. It didn't cover the trickle of blood where her enormous ring had broken the skin.

The Cardinal stepped forward with his hands patting the air, as if he were about to intervene. But he seemed to be able to say nothing more coherent than "Nh . . . mnhhh." All the eyes in the room shifted briefly to look at him, but then shifted away again.

It was left to Isabeau to speak. "Why, you ask?" she said softly, cruelly; pursuing her advantage. "Why, because that young man and the Queen Mother of England are man and wife, of course."

There was a complete hush suddenly; even from the Cardinal. Those words were so startling that even Warwick stood utterly still, for a moment that lasted an eternity, pondering them. Then, with a hand still clamped to his cheek, he opened his mouth again, snarling like a wounded tiger.

"What do you mean, man and wife?" he growled uncertainly. He turned to Catherine. Catherine was aware that, below her, Harry was wriggling round to see her face; that he couldn't believe his ears either.

"You're not telling me that you . . ." Warwick said, taking a step away from the termagant Dowager Queen of France toward Catherine.

"Yes," Isabeau said, stepping deftly between him and Catherine and answering for her daughter with tremendous certainty. "And make no mistake about it, if your men lay a finger on the stepfather of your King, I expect you can imagine what will happen to you."

Catherine couldn't possibly have answered for herself. She had never been so astonished. Her heart was thudding through her body so she could scarcely hear.

For a long, long moment there was only shame: the abject shame of dishonor. She was the Queen Mother of England; a Princess of France; the blood of Charlemagne ran in her veins. How could her mother have so disgraced her as to suggest publicly to this man, her enemy—someone who wouldn't hesitate to bruit it around the world—that she might have run off and married away from her blood . . . ?

Then, thickly, through the pounding, she started to understand her mother's strategy. If Warwick believed she'd married Owain, he and the rest of the world might be able to despise her utterly forever, and without hope of redemption, for forgetting her pride and the glory of her birth, for contracting a *mésalliance* that shamed her blood and lowered her in the eyes of mankind—but Warwick wouldn't, at least, be able to find her or Owain, who was at more immediate risk, guilty of a sin against God that might justify him in taking either of their lives. She could save Owain. She could live to see her son grow up. But she'd have to sacrifice her reputation.

She rocked on her heels, holding on to Harry; hearing voices, ghostly voices in her head. Christine's: *The blessed sacrament of marriage . . . the highest form of love.* Owain's: *Fight for what you love.* Her mother's: *It didn't hurt to sacrifice my reputation for someone I loved.*

And now her mother's voice came again, but there was

nothing ghostly about that cracked Bavarian command. "Catherine. Tell the man. Come along."

Looking at Warwick's blazing eyes, she realized: You will destroy Owain, and try to destroy me, and damage Harry so badly you might as well destroy him, if I don't fight. "Yes," she said, and from somewhere she found the strength to draw herself up to her full height and stare defiantly back at the Earl. "I am Owain Tudor's wife."

But Warwick's lip curled. He wanted blood, not social embarrassment. He was already regrouping. "I don't believe you," he said. "I don't believe you'd be fool enough. And if you were, you couldn't get married all by yourself. Who'd have been fool enough to have married you to the . . . Welshman?"

There was another hush. Catherine felt the flash and brilliance of her fighting spirit fade. She could feel herself droop, and Warwick grow in height and menace.

But Isabeau didn't quail. Not for an instant. She was a fighting animal through and through, and she was fighting for her child. The old Queen of France turned and bent a fierce, expectant glare in the direction of the Cardinal. Cardinal Beaufort, in his corner, with his arms raised and his hands patting the air downward, as if calming gestures might be enough to take the heat and danger out of the room. Cardinal Beaufort, whose relief at the successful completion of the coronation had, just an hour before, made his thin, sallow, pop-eyed face appear sleek and relaxed. Who was already looking forward to the praise and recognition he expected to be his lot on his return to England; to the gratitude of the nation for pulling off this coronation and bringing the King back safe and whole, after a difficult voyage in which he'd managed to avoid all the fighting, mutinies, failures, recriminations, and scandals that might have been expected. Who wanted a peaceful, wealthy old age, at home. Who had never, in a lifetime of intriguing, admitted he'd done anything wrong. Who never, under any circumstances, did political favors.

Cardinal Beaufort was swaying on his heels, with his apologetic little smile glued to his mouth, still patting ineffectually at the air, thinking. Only the slight furrow between his eyebrows suggested the agony of indecision he was in; only the faint "Mnh-mnh" coming again from his throat as he cleared it.

He's about to say he had no idea about any of this, Catherine thought. He'll deny us. Of course he will. It's not in his nature to do anything else. Trying to save us would compromise his own future; why should he? Even that thought, as she watched him shake his head and open his mouth to destroy her, didn't kill her affection for him. She was floating. She was holding tight on to Harry, preparing herself to be dragged away, waiting . . .

"Me," the Cardinal said, and his voice was light, and his eyebrows were raised in their usual quizzical way, even though he was smiling a little sadly at Warwick as he spoke, and gave away the easy future he'd thought awaited him. "I married them, dear boy."

It was not clear from Warwick's red face, the eyes bulging from their sockets, the mouth open, the strangled gargle of astonishment, whether he'd have more questions. As it turned out there was no time for further questions; no time for anything. Catherine had been too intent on what was happening inside the room to notice the noises outside—until the door burst open and Duke John stormed in. Not the apologetic, awkward, shy brother-in-law Catherine had always known, either, but the powerful commander she'd thought he must probably always have been with his men—loud-voiced, stern-faced, and in a towering rage.

"What in the name of God is going on?" he yelled. He advanced on Warwick until he was towering over him, pinning him against the wall. "I've just caught a dozen of your men kicking the hell out of Tudor," he growled. "They said it was on your orders. And now I see you up here, shouting, threatening; could hear you all the way up the stairs. Ladies present, too. Royalty. This is a coronation feast, not a brawl. All the aristocracy of France we could muster are here, and we had the devil of a time getting them to come, too; the last thing I want is for them to leave saying we invite guests here only to beat them half to death. Whatever the man's done, it will wait. You must be drunk. Or out of your mind." He put a hand on Warwick's shoulder and walked him firmly to the door.

Warwick's eyes were darting around and his mouth was opening and shutting, but no words were coming out. It wasn't hard to see why Duke John might think he was drunk. Catherine thought he might still be trying to find words and arguments; but nothing remotely answering to the needs of the moment seemed to present itself to his brain. He did look out of his mind.

There were two stolid sentries waiting outside, clanking. "My men are going to take you to your quarters," Duke John finished sternly. "Sleep it off; and be grateful nothing worse has come of it. We'll talk tomorrow."

Warwick gargled again.

"Go," Duke John said.

It was only when the footsteps had got right to the bottom of the stairs that Duke John took a deep breath, and, looking around the rest of the room, at the frozen faces of Catherine and Harry and Isabeau and the Cardinal, said again, more calmly this time, "Now, what in the name of God *has* been going on?"

Owain was bandaged everywhere a bandage could be wound. But one eye had escaped the fists and feet and was looking at Catherine. And, even if he couldn't talk beyond grunts, he could raise a splinted arm a little to signal he understood.

"If only I could hold your hand," Catherine said, "or *something*." She patted gingerly at his quilt. He drew in a sharp breath. She stopped.

"We're all in terrible trouble," she said, but her eyes were merry. She'd had a week to get used to the dizzying feeling of freedom. It had been a while before Owain had got well enough to talk. "It gets worse with every messenger. Duke Humphrey couldn't be angrier. He's threatening to put the Cardinal on public trial for stealing the crown jewels as soon as we get back. We think it's really because he's so furious about . . . the other thing." She looked down. ". . . Us. Duke John is coming back to England with us to try and keep the peace between them."

She put out her hand again, then remembered just in time and drew it back.

"But it's not all bad. Warwick's *not* coming. Someone has to run the war in France, so he's staying here. He's written to Duke Humphrey asking to be released from his duties with Harry. He says he 'despairs of Harry's excessive simplicity, innocence, and inability to distinguish good and evil.'" She grinned. "I think he meant that Harry is so loving of his old sinner of a grandmother . . . and was so excited to hear his sinner of a mother had married you," she added.

The hand lifted a little. The watching eye drooped and opened again. There was a grunting from behind the bandages. Catherine leaned forward to try to make out the jumble of sounds.

"*Why?* Is that what you said? Why what?" she murmured. "Why did the Cardinal say he'd married us . . . ? *Ohh.* That." She looked down. The faintest blush tinged her cheeks. She twisted her fingers against each other. "Because I was with child, he said. It was the only excuse he thought Humphrey would have believed or forgiven. He said he'd been planning to tell the rest of them after the coronation; but he was worried for my immortal soul, and that of the child; and he'd seen it as his duty before God to perform the ceremony as soon as I confessed." She couldn't bring herself to look up. "And anyway, it's true," she added to her plaited fingers. "As it turns out, I am with child."

There was a sudden torrent of noises from behind the bandages. She smiled wider.

"Duke John's suggesting a deal," she said. "With the Council, for me. If I return to England, but agree to retire from the English court for the rest of my life and live in seclusion, he'll ask the Council to let me have Waltham Manor and Hertford Castle as my residences, and keep my incomes, and see Harry— often." She looked up into Owain's one open blue eye. "The deal is for me and my unborn child."

There was another rumble from under the bandages.

"You," she said. "Yes. There's provision for you, too. As my husband, he's going to ask for the full legal rights of an Englishman for you—no more problems with Welshness. And the right to live as my husband, with our child, sharing the seclusion of Waltham Manor and Hertford Castle."

There was a silence this time—a thoughtful pause. When the rumbling started again, Catherine interrupted it almost at once.

"Let's not talk about blood," she said, and she couldn't keep a slight mistiness from her eyes. "I've done what a royal princess is brought into the world to do. I don't mind if I'm not considered royal anymore. Our child won't be a king. Just a Tudor. And I don't mind—if you don't."

Rumble.

"Which only leaves one problem," she added hastily, "apart from that you might still want . . . Oxford . . . and the monks?"

Rumble. It sounded like laughter.

". . . and you know what it is. Whatever poor Warwick thinks, we're not really married. Yet."

With a tremendous effort, the bandaged hand began to move toward Catherine's. She watched. She was getting used to miracles wrought by love. You could achieve anything if you were only willing to fight.

The fingers crept agonizingly over hers. Looking at them, feeling them on her skin, Catherine suddenly felt utterly certain that she and this man whom she loved would spend the rest of their lives together—decades; another forty years, maybe—raising children who'd grow up happy and innocent, far from the throne, in the calm of the English countryside, belonging to a pragmatic place where blood didn't count for as much as love—never had, never would. That their monarch, her son Henry VI, would grow up to become a wise, peace-loving philosopher-king like his French grandfather; that her brother Charles would be driven out of Bourges; and that peace would come again to both Harry's kingdoms. She should never have doubted. Owain should never have doubted. It was all going to come out all right.

From somewhere inside the bandages, a voice that was a shadow of Owain's, but, for all the pain in it, strangely light of heart, said: "Married. Well . . . isn't . . . it . . . time . . . we . . . were?"

HISTORICAL POSTSCRIPT

Catherine de Valois lived only another six years, until the age of thirty-seven, after returning to England to live in seclusion in the land of her adoption. She continued to see her son, King Henry VI, from time to time, and remained close to Cardinal Beaufort.

Catherine's son King Henry VI of England was always mentally fragile, a condition that worsened with age and the onset of the Wars of the Roses. Modern doctors believe he may have suffered from bouts of catatonic schizophrenia. The head of the House of Lancaster, he died in suspicious circumstances in the Tower of London, many years later, after being removed from his throne twice by noblemen of the rival House of York. His teenage son had already been killed after a battle between Yorkists and Lancastrians. Under Henry VI's rule, England was finally defeated in its century-long attempt to conquer France, and all English landholdings in France except Calais were lost. France's King Charles VII, Catherine's brother, returned from the political dead after decades of fighting from his capital in exile, Bourges, to take back the throne of France and rule from Paris.

Catherine's second marriage to Owain Tudor, a Welsh gentleman known to have worked in her household after her first marriage to King Henry V, was never publicly announced or celebrated, but there were no contemporary doubts as to the legitimacy of the couple's five or six children: three boys and either two or three girls, among them Owen (who became a monk at Westminster), Edmund (who was later made the first Earl of Richmond by his half-brother, King Henry VI), and Jasper (later the first Duke of Bedford). Most historians suggest the marriage took place between 1427 and 1432. I have set it toward the end of this period.

After Queen Catherine's death, Owain Tudor was briefly imprisoned at Newgate Prison, but later released. He was beheaded many years later after fighting for the Lancastrian side in the Wars of the Roses.

Edmund Tudor, Catherine and Owain's son, married Lady Margaret Beaufort, a cousin of the Cardinal. At the end of the Wars of the Roses, this couple's only son, Henry, the last Lancastrian leader in the wars, became Henry VII, the first Tudor King of England.